WORDS HEARD IN SILENCE

REDMOND CIVIL WAR ROMANCE SERIES
BOOK ONE

T. NOVAN
TAYLOR RICKARD

AUSXIP PUBLISHING

DEDICATION

Dedicated to our grandmothers, who told us tales of times gone by and made them live in our hearts, minds, and memories.
—T. Novan and Taylor Rickard

Special thanks go to Dani, Katrina, Kay, Michelle, Pam, Verda and all the folks who helped bring this to completion; your patience, attention to detail, and willingness to watch us work out the details of a very complex story are deeply appreciated.
—T. Novan and Taylor Rickard

FOREWORD

This book started as a pair of short stories. But over time, it grew until it is now the tome you hold in your hand.

Recent historical research has shown that there were many women who served in active duty on both sides during the Civil War. By the end of the war, many were open about their gender; others assumed the identity of a man and chose to continue their lives after the war using their military identity. We know of those who were discovered after their deaths. How many more were never discovered, were shielded by their families, or simply melted into the general crush of humanity during the opening of the West?

Women held positions of authority in both armies, as well. The highest ranking female officer identified to date was a Major under Philip Sheridan's command. We also know that advancement was very rapid for qualified leaders in the Civil War; therefore it is not difficult to envision a career that advanced a qualified woman even higher in the chain of command.

There are a number of historical personages and events noted within these pages. General Philip Sheridan was in fact in command of the Shenandoah; the 13th Pennsylvania was a real regiment that served with distinction at the Battle of The Wilderness. After that battle, the historical 13th Pennsylvania was so badly injured and had so many casualties that many within the Union command thought they should be disbanded. However, after months of recovery and augmentation of the force by fragments from other experienced field regiments, they were reconstituted. The historical 13th Pennsylvania was, however, part of the southern arm of Grant's three-pronged attack on Richmond and Petersburg that led to the final confrontation at Appomattox Courthouse. The battles depicted through these pages did in fact occur, and were commanded by the historical individuals noted. Uniquely, the Battle of Appomattox Station was indeed commanded by General George A. Custer and is the only battle in history that was the confrontation of unsupported artillery against unsupported cavalry. Very little else is known about the details of the battle, but historians do agree that it was a critical factor in Lee's surrender, as it cut off any chance of Lee obtaining fresh supplies for his forces.

Several of our civilians are also either historical characters or are based on composites of historical personages. In particular, Walt Whitman did work as a volunteer medic during the last months of the war, after spending hours walking the fields around Fredericksburg looking for the body of his brother following the Battle of Seven Pines. Our lady physician is loosely based on two very famous women physicians, Dr. Elizabeth Blackwell, who was the first licensed female physician in the US, and Dr. Mary Walker, who was the only woman ever awarded the Medal of Honor for services she rendered during the Civil War. Dr. Walker's Medal was later rescinded because of the scandal she caused by wearing men's clothing during the very proper 1870's in Washington, D.C. The Medal was reinstated in recent years after heavy lobbying by various women's organizations.

We chose the town of Culpeper, Virginia because of its critical place in the war in Western Virginia, even though it never saw a major battle. During the course of the war, Culpeper had both armies marching through it time and again. It does, in fact, sit on one of the critical rail lines, and the comments made about the condition of the town by General Grant and others quoted in this work are accurate. For those of you who are interested, there is also a stream south of Culpeper named Gaines Run, which flows through some absolutely lovely horse country.

All in all, we have taken a few liberties with history in this work, primarily with the history of the 13th Pennsylvania Light Cavalry, but only those necessary to bring the time, and more importantly, the sentiments and attitudes of the period to life.

—Taylor Rickard
November, 2003

Note to the Second Edition. Twelve years after we first published Words Heard in Silence, TN and I decided to edit this book, correcting some minor errors, and providing some additional insight into the motivation of the characters. The story itself has not changed; we have simply made some refinements that we hope with add to the richness and texture of the Redmond Family Saga. We hope you continue to enjoy our stories of this strong, tenacious family of survivors.

—Taylor Rickard
November, 2015

DRAMATIS PERSONAE

(Historical characters are in italics)

Colonel Charles Redmond, Regimental Commander, 13th Pennsylvania Light Cavalry

Rebecca Gaines, widow, owner of Gaines Cove Farms, Culpeper County, Virginia

Sergeant John Xavier "Jocko" Jackson, Redmond's batman

Dr. Elizabeth Walker, physician attached to the 13th Pennsylvania

Walt Whitman, medic and poet

General Phillip Sheridan, Commander, Department of the Shenandoah

General Ulysses S. Grant, Commander, Army of the Potomac

Lt. General Jubal A. Early, Army of Virginia

Master Sergeant Jamison, mess chief.

Master Sergeant Tarent, head hostler

Master Sergeant MacFarlane, farrier

Lt. Colonel Richard Polk, Second-in-Command, 13th Pennsylvania

Albert Samuelson, regimental chief medic

Major Aaron Swallow, Company A commander

Lieutenant Joshua Swallow, Company C adjutant

Captain Francis Hoffstader, Company B commander
Major Winston Andrews, Company C commander
Major Harrison "Monty" Montgomery, Company D commander
Major George F. M'Cabe, Company E commander
Major Timothy A. Byrnes, Company F commander
Captain George R. Maguire, Company G commander
Captain Benjamin Braddock, Company H commander
Captain Merrick Avery, Company I commander
Corporal Duncan Nailer, the trooper assigned to assist Rebecca
Colonel Angus McCauley, aide-de-camp to General Sheridan
Reverend James Williams, Culpeper Episcopalian Minister
Mrs. Margaret Williams, wife of the Culpeper Episcopalian Minister
Mr. Edward Cooper, Culpeper businessman, owner of the Culpeper mercantile
Mrs. Grace Cooper, wife of Mr. Cooper
Mayor Horace Frazier, mayor of Culpeper
Sarah, the cook
Beulah, the housekeeper
Reg, the handyman
Lizbet, the lady's maid
Lizzie Armstrong, Washington lady of ill repute
Mark Russell Redmond, Charlie's father
Emilia Huger DuBosque, Charlie's mother
Madame Prevost, Charleston mantilla maker
Joshua, Mme. Prevost's runner
Mamie, the Redmond family cook
Miss Katherine Reynolds, lady of Culpeper
Miss Mary Simms, lady of Culpeper
Constance Adams, refugee, Southern widow
Emily Adams, toddler, child of Constance
Esther White, widow of Alanthus, a small town near Culpeper
Jeremiah Carter, a ten-year-old refugee staying at Gaines Cove
Samantha Carter, mother of Jeremiah, widow, and refugee
Captain Edwin Harriman, Polk's aide

Marko, small boy who is one of the refugees
Trooper Shamus Davison
Ex-trooper Otis Dumpire
Ex-trooper Edward Osborn
Colonel Joshua Howard
Brigadier General Merritt
Colonel James
Trooper Abel Franklin
General Montgomery C. Meigs, Quartermaster General of the Army
Tess, Beulah's younger sister and the nursery maid
Trooper Raiford, Company D
Captain Peter Dewees, Company D commander after Major Montgomery's death

CHAPTER 1

GAINES COVE FARM, CULPEPER COUNTY, VIRGINIA

Friday, October 28, 1864

Rebecca Gaines stopped washing the wall of the foyer when she heard a loud rumbling. Wiping her hands on her apron, she tucked a loose strand of blonde hair, which had fallen from the knot on the back of her head, behind her ear. She still had not managed to fix a small hole in the roof of her house that relentlessly leaked into the kitchen during a hard rain, and worried briefly if there might be a late autumn storm heading in her direction. Saying a quick prayer that it was not going to be a hard storm, she opened the heavy front door and stepped out on the porch to see if she could determine the source of the sound.

Surprised to see cloudless blue skies, Rebecca tilted her head just a bit, listening intently to the noise that seemed to be growing louder with each passing second. As the source of the noise came into view,

1

her eyes widened and her heart began pounding in her chest. Rebecca watched the Northern troops thundering down the road toward her home. Fear, anger, and dread welled up inside her, making her feel very ill.

For a brief moment she considered returning inside and fetching the rifle she kept handy, but quickly put that thought out of her head, knowing any attempt to stand off the Yankees would only result in her being injured, or worse. So far, she had done an adequate job of surviving in these very uncertain times, and she had no desire to commit suicide now. She watched as the men rode and marched onto her land. Straightening her shoulders, she took on a proud, almost arrogant stance as a Federal officer dismounted his horse and slowly made his way over to her, taking his time to survey her land.

"I am Major Montgomery of the 13th Pennsylvania, and our troops will be staying on your land to rest and regroup."

"Just like that?" she challenged, staring down the steps at the man, who removed heavy leather gloves and tapped them against his leg.

"Just like that. If you cooperate, we will leave your place in one piece. If you do not, it is hard telling what will happen." He took a step toward the woman, placing a booted foot on the first step. The look on his face told Rebecca it would be extremely unwise to argue with him.

A deep voice fired from behind him, "Major!"

The officer whirled around, then immediately snapped to attention as another man in a dusty but neatly kept uniform rode up to him. "Colonel." He snapped a salute, which was returned by the dark-haired man. "Sir, I did not expect you for another three days."

"Apparently not." The Colonel dismounted his horse. "Did I just hear you threaten this lady?" The senior officer turned to Rebecca, giving her a polite smile. He noticed her dark dress and realized he was standing before a Confederate widow. He was determined that she should not feel threatened.

The blonde returned the smile to the officer, spontaneously

responding to the genuine courtesy being offered. She felt a slight shock when she noticed his startling blue eyes and felt butterflies take flight in her stomach. Placing a slightly shaking hand on her midsection, she tried to calm them.

The Colonel dropped the reins of his horse, taking two long strides toward Rebecca. "Ma'am, did the Major threaten you?"

The fact that the man was speaking in a civil manner startled her. Then his voice caught her attention, and she realized he had a very soft Southern accent. She had never heard of a Southern gentleman serving in the Federal Army.

Not much of a gentleman if he is fighting for Yankee rabble.

The thought crossed her mind as she narrowed her eyes at him, but she had the good sense not to let it pass her lips. "No more than any other Northern officer has in the past, Colonel."

"Well now, Ma'am, I apologize for those others; and I assure you it shall not happen while I am here." Removing his hat and gloves, the tall man took a step closer. "Ma'am, I am Colonel Charles Redmond, Regimental Commander of the 13th Pennsylvania Cavalry. I would like to billet my troops on your land, Ma'am. They are in need of rest, fresh water, and baths. We have our own supplies, and we will not be taking anything you might have here."

"I have very little, Colonel. Federal and Confederate forces have already seen to that." She wanted to be difficult and bitter towards this man, but for some reason she could not bring herself to do it.

Rebecca noticed right away he was clean-shaven. In a time when most men wore facial hair, the blonde found it to be a refreshing difference. Not to mention extremely pleasing to the eye. This Northern officer was undeniably handsome—with his pale blue eyes, clean-shaven jaw, and formal demeanor. She found herself hard-pressed not to admire his unusual good looks. Silently, she scolded herself for even thinking such a thing. There was absolutely no reason on God's green earth that a Southern lady should find a Northern officer attractive. If anyone ever found out she had considered such a thing for even a moment, she would never be accepted in respectable circles again.

"Ma'am, if you tell me to take my men and leave, I will. No harm will come to you or your property, I promise you. But my men are tired, some are injured, and the horses need to rest and recover as well."

She watched him critically as he spoke. She wanted to do it. She wanted to order this man and his troops from her land, but something in his face and the look in his eyes would not let her. She knew she really had no power to force them to leave. Even though he was being polite and more than respectful to her, Rebecca could see it in those azure eyes: he was tired, and something in the depth of them told her it was far more than just physically tired.

"No, Colonel, you may stay. If you are on my land, I will not have to worry about something worse coming along. At least not for a while." She turned for the house, leaving the Yankee Colonel standing on the steps, holding his hat in his hands.

She watched from the rear parlor window as the soldiers took over most of the land in the pastures beyond the barns. This was one of the largest groups she had seen come through the area. That thought gave her a bad feeling in the pit of her stomach. Rebecca watched as the Colonel moved his men around, arranging the camp to his liking. She noticed he had his command tent set up so he could watch the house, while not being obviously intrusive. She was not sure if that made her feel safe or nervous.

Once again, she noted how attractive he was—close to six feet tall, with short dark hair that was clean and neatly cut. His skin was tanned, but did not seem to have the extremely harsh, weathered look that so many men in his position had after years of service in the military. He carried himself with a grace and bearing she had rarely seen in a man, not even the most refined Virginian gentleman. There was also a certain charm about him. Shaking her head at her reflections, Rebecca considered that maybe she had simply been without the company of a gentleman for far too long. All the men were gone now, of course. Every man from the age of sixteen to sixty had been called to fight in the war. Presidents Davis and Lincoln had certainly managed to make a mess of things.

He unquestionably treated his men well, this Colonel, a sharp contrast with the other officers that had passed through the area recently. He seemed to care genuinely about his men. Rebecca watched as he stopped by the tent that had been set up as a field hospital. As the sick and wounded were waiting for it to be completed, he stopped and talked to each and every one of the men resting outside the tent. Then he turned to talk to a man Rebecca reckoned must be a doctor. It was then she realized that the Colonel must truly be an important man in the Northern Army. Having a real doctor in the ranks was a privilege that most officers did not enjoy. Unfortunately, many men like her husband and brother died because of this lack of field physicians.

The Colonel glanced at the house, and raised his hand in a gesture of agreement with the doctor. Rebecca watched the Colonel turn and begin walking toward the house. She tried to busy herself with dusting the parlor so the Colonel would not divine that she had been watching from the window. It was not long before there was a knock at the back door. Taking a deep breath, she moved to the screen door.

Once again, she found herself captured by blue eyes and an enigmatic smile. "Yes, Colonel?"

"Ma'am." He nodded slightly. "I have a wounded man here who really needs to be taken out of the weather. Would you have any room for him in your home?"

She wanted to rebel and laugh in his face, but she could not. "Colonel, I am a single woman trying to survive. I would be insane to tell you no. You will just take what you want anyhow."

"No, Ma'am, I will not. If you say no..." He looked back to the doctor, giving a slight shake of his head. "I am sorry to have disturbed you."

He turned to walk away, but before he could take his first step, Rebecca heard words leave her mouth unbidden. "Will the cellar do?"

"Ma'am?"

"Are you deaf, Colonel? I asked if the cellar would do for your man."

"Why, yes, Ma'am, it would. It would be perfect. Thank you for your kindness."

"The cellar is empty. You may use it. The door is on the side of the house."

"Thank you again, Ma'am."

Rebecca bit her lip as she considered her next question. "Colonel?"

"Yes, Ma'am?"

"Would you, by any chance, have any bread you could spare? I am out of just about—"

"Of course. I will bring it up myself after we get my injured man settled. Is that all right?"

"Yes, Colonel. Thank you."

As the tall officer turned and left the porch, she found herself watching him. He returned to the doctor and, before long, she heard them preparing the cellar for the wounded man. She blew out a fretful breath, knowing that if anyone found out about this, she would be accused of giving aid and comfort to the enemy. If they found her guilty of that crime, she could be hanged. For the first time in a long time, Rebecca was glad she lived alone and a reasonable distance from town.

She went back inside and resumed work, cleaning the house. After a while, she took a moment to check the larder. She rearranged what few dry goods she did have left, and found herself hoping the Yankee Colonel would keep his word, and his men would leave her with what she had had when they had arrived.

A short time later, while preparing a bath to sluice away the dust from her cleaning chores, she heard yet another knock on the door. Abandoning what she was doing, she went to the kitchen door to find the Colonel with a cloth sack in his hands. "The bread you asked for, Ma'am," he offered, as he lifted the bag slightly.

Unlatching the door, Rebecca pushed it open. The man hesitated for just a moment before stepping inside and placing the bundle on a small table right inside the door.

"Thank you, Colonel."

"You are welcome, Ma'am. It is the least I could do. There is some fruit and cheese there as well."

Rebecca could not help but smile at the Colonel. He seemed so caring and gentle. He was the kind of man she wished her parents had arranged for her to marry. As it was, she had been all but sold to her husband like a common field hand. Mr. Gaines had been some fifteen years older than his captive bride, and only wanted a woman who would take care of his needs, both domestic and marital. Her husband also believed it was his God-given right, and her wifely duty, to give him a child every other year. Much to Rebecca's secret relief, that had not been the case. Fortunately, she was not burdened with children while trying to survive this nightmare of a war. Her stomach fluttered when her mind whispered that she certainly would not have minded if this gentleman had been the father of those longed for children. She felt the blush rise to her cheeks at the terribly naughty vision that flashed through her mind.

"Well, if you will excuse me, Ma'am, I have to attend to my duties."

"Of course, Colonel." She ran her hand over the cloth sack he had brought. Her mouth very nearly watered at the thought of fresh food. "Thank you again."

"If there is anything else you need, please let me know." The officer turned to leave, and Rebecca noticed a dark stain on his shoulder.

"Colonel?"

"Ma'am?"

"Are you hurt?"

"Ma'am?"

"I do believe you are deaf. I asked you a very simple question. Are you hurt?"

The Colonel glanced back over his shoulder, as if he were trying to see the wound. "It is nothing, Ma'am."

"Colonel, if it were nothing, you would not be bleeding through your coat. You should have your doctor look at it."

"My doctor is actually a medic. I am hoping our regular doctor will rejoin us soon. As it is, Samuelson is little more than a young man, fresh out of school, who should not be here to begin with; he should be studying at a teaching hospital somewhere. Instead, he has men out there with serious wounds and long-term illnesses. This really is no more than a scratch. It would be unfair of me to take time away from a soldier who really needs him. My batman will tend to it later."

"Come here and let me look at it."

"Ma'am?"

"I swear, you must have been stuffing good Southern cotton in your ears." She took him by the arm and pulled him back into the kitchen. He dragged his feet a little, pulling back and reminding Rebecca of a billy goat. "Colonel, I do not bite. Come here and sit down."

She led the reluctant officer to a chair next to the table. "Take off your coat." Rebecca turned away long enough to get a bowl for water and a pitcher. When she returned, he was still sitting, staring at his boots, and still wearing his jacket.

"Colonel. Please take off your uniform coat."

"Ma'am, I am fine, really I am."

He started to get to his feet, but Rebecca was there beside him with a gentle but firm hand on his good shoulder. "Sit, Colonel. You know as well as I do, men die because of small, untreated wounds that go bad. Now, would you want your men left in the hands of that Major of yours if something were to happen?"

"Um...I...well..."

"Take off your coat."

After a long, tense moment, he began unbuttoning his tunic. Pulling it off, he folded it over his arms and then crossed them over his chest before taking a seat in the chair. Rebecca watched his head droop even further as she walked around behind him. She grimaced and bit her lip as she got her first look at the wound he had called a "minor scratch." Old and infected, it had broken open and was oozing an ugly combination of pus and old blood.

"Colonel, this will hurt. I am sorry I have no whiskey to offer you."

"That is all right. I am not much of a whiskey drinker."

She tried to make small talk as she pulled the dirty material away from the gash, hoping it would distract this gentle man from the pain she knew she would cause. "I thought all Army officers were hard drinkers."

"Not all of us, Ma'am. I prefer brandy myself."

She smiled, remembering the last time she herself had indulged in a fine after dinner brandy. Everything she had known in her world then was now gone. Her parents, brother, and husband, all that Rebecca Gaines defined herself by, had been stripped away. If she did survive to the end of the war, she would have to redefine herself and what she wanted from her life in the future.

As the Colonel unbuttoned the shirt and eased it over his shoulder, Rebecca noticed what looked like bandages around his chest, bindings that were clearly not covering a wound. In a sudden, blinding flash of insight, it all came together for her. This was no man; it was one of the women she had heard of who assumed the aspect of a man to fight for one side or the other.

She took a deep breath, and stepped away for a moment, fussing with her medical kit to hide her confusion. *Why would a woman willingly expose herself to such horrors? What had happened to this woman that she hid herself under straps and wool and played the part of a man?* She shook herself, and selected a small, very sharp knife from her kit to trim away the dead skin. *Whatever it was, it is no concern of mine. She is still a soldier and an enemy; in a few days, I shall be rid of her and her troops.*

She turned back to the patiently waiting Colonel, still wondering a bit at the rank that such a person had achieved. She shrugged; everyone found some way to survive the war. Perhaps this woman had joined up to be with a beloved husband or brother, and had risen through the ranks. Certainly, women had done so in the Revolution. Absentmindedly, she started trimming at the dead skin.

The soft hiss from her patient brought her back to her task. "I am sorry, Colonel. It must feel like I have the finesse of a field hand."

"Nonsense, Ma'am. Your touch is as gentle as an angel's."

"How did you sustain this wound?" she asked, as she tried to remove more of the dirty cloth and dead, infected skin.

"It is war, Ma'am. You do not want to know."

"Colonel, if I did not want to know, I would not have asked."

"Last week we encountered a small band of renegade soldiers. I took a bayonet in the shoulder."

"A Southern soldier did this to you?"

"No, Ma'am. The renegades were Federal soldiers."

As gently as possible, Rebecca washed and cleaned the wound, stitching it very carefully with small sutures. She sprinkled it with a dusting of comfrey powder before applying a clean bandage. "There, you are done. Now that was not too bad, was it?"

"Thank you, Ma'am. It feels better already."

"Your shirt needs mending. Take it off. I will wash and mend it for you."

"Ma'am?"

The blonde moved around to face the Colonel. She reached for the buttons of his shirt. He moved from the chair so quickly that he nearly knocked it over. As he made the effort to keep it from clattering to the floor, Rebecca laid a hand on his arm.

"I know," she said quietly, giving the arm under her hand a gentle squeeze. "You do not have to be afraid."

The Colonel stopped, not quite believing what he was hearing.

"Come now, Colonel. Let me have your shirt." The blonde moved slowly, closing the back door. "Your secret is safe with me."

"How did you know?"

"I saw the bindings when I cleaned your wound."

His head dropped. "They...umm...they will either hang me or throw me in prison if you turn me in."

"I am not going to turn you in. I am going to wash and mend your shirt." Rebecca smiled gently. "You need the protection of the shirt so the bandage will not come loose. Besides, it is so warm out today you must be uncomfortable in your tunic. It will only take—"

"Why? Why are you not going to report me?"

"I have done what I had to do to survive this war, Colonel; I assume you have done the same. You are at least a genuine Colonel, are you not?"

He laughed a little, starting to relax. "Yes, Ma'am. I really am Colonel Charlie Redmond."

"Charlie is short for Charlotte, right?"

He nodded again. "But my enlistment papers do not say that."

"I am sure they do not." The woman gestured at the Colonel's shirt. "Take off that shirt. You are about my brother's size; I will get you one of his."

Rebecca turned to make her way upstairs. She now knew why the Colonel was being so kind. She entered one of the old bedrooms. Most of the furniture was gone now—either broken with no way to repair it, sold to try and hold things together, or destroyed for firewood over the course of the last few years. She retrieved a shirt from a trunk, taking a moment to make sure it was clean and in good repair. Looking into the trunk, she also fetched a pair of trousers.

Rebecca returned downstairs, but did not go back to the kitchen. Instead, she went into the washroom, where the bath she had been preparing for herself when the Colonel arrived was still waiting.

Rebecca placed the clothes and a towel on a bench next to the tub. She lifted the cover from the reservoir and dipped her fingers in the water to make sure it was still warm, added some more hot water from the boiler, then returned to the doorway.

"Colonel, could you please come here? It is the last door on the right."

She listened to the heavy footfalls on the wooden floorboards. *She certainly walks like a man, clomping through the house in heavy boots.* Rebecca turned when the steps stopped behind her. "I thought you might like a bath."

Charlie looked toward the tub. The vision of a real bath and steaming water nearly did him in, and he unconsciously licked his lips. His eyes traveled to his hostess. "That is very kind of you, Ma'am, but I could not impose."

"Colonel Redmond, I have taken the time to haul water and heat it. The least you can do is show me the simple courtesy of using it."

Charlie could not hold the smile back any longer as he moved into the room. The thought of a hot bath with real soap and the luxury of being able to relax just a little was far too temping an offer to pass up. "Yes, Ma'am, it is the least I can do."

"And stop calling me Ma'am. I have a name. It is Rebecca, Rebecca Gaines."

"Rebecca? I like it."

"Well, that is good, because I do not intend to change it any time soon, Colonel Redmond. Now get out of those dirty clothes and enjoy that water while it is still warm."

As the Colonel sat down to get ready for his bath, Rebecca pulled the shades to give him all the privacy he needed. Lighting a lantern, she placed it on a small stool next to the tub. She glanced up when she heard a groan. Moving across the room, she knelt in front of Charlie.

"You will rip those stitches. Let me."

"Thank you, Miss Rebecca."

As she removed Charlie's boots, she grimaced at the sight of the officer's feet. He was wearing torn socks that revealed several large, infected blisters on his feet and ankles. She grimaced as he offered quietly, "It is the lousy quality of the boots they are sending us and we have been moving so much recently I have not had time to properly tend them, one of the hazards of very wet weather. I do know better."

"Surely as an officer you have access to better boots?" She very carefully removed the ruined socks and tossed them aside.

"I gave my boots and last pair of good socks to one of my men. His feet were in worse shape than mine."

"After your bath, I will tend to those, too. Now enjoy that water. I will be back in a few minutes."

The Colonel watched as the young woman left the room. He sighed, and then began removing his clothes, a process that was a very private ritual for Charlie—the transformation from male to female. After everything, including the bindings he was forced to wear to make his masquerade convincing, had been removed, she settled down in the tub, moaning at the feeling of warm water covering her body. She knew she should be washing, but the urge to relax was far too great. She closed her eyes, sliding further under the water until her neck rested on the edge. As she relaxed in the tub, her mind wandered to her own sense of identity. She was not concerned that Rebecca had found her out, because she knew she was Colonel Charlie Redmond. She had been living this way for all of her adult life and, to her conscious mind, there was no doubt: Colonel Charlie Redmond was a man. However, there was always that annoying little inner voice, the voice of the woman she had been so many years ago.

You are a fraud, Charlie Redmond. A lie. You can never be the "man" you pretend to be. You can never have the things you dream of. You will never find someone who will love you despite your sinful ways. The only comfort you will find in your pathetic life will be in the bed of whores who will never care for you.

Charlie shut out the voice and relaxed again, sinking further into the warm water.

When Rebecca returned, she found Charlie sound asleep. Placing a pair of clean socks atop the clothes she had left previously, she looked at the woman in the tub, she realized how ragged and tired she looked. She felt great sympathy for this woman, even though she could not fathom what had brought her to this place. Rebecca could not imagine fighting and being at war. Certainly, she knew how to fire a rifle, but the thought of taking aim and killing another human being made her just a bit sick to her stomach. She set her mending kit on the pile of clothes and then moved to the tub, where she knelt down and wet a cloth, making sure to lather it liberally. "Colonel Redmond?" She whispered gently, to coax the sleeping officer awake.

"Hmm?"

"Wake up, Colonel."

Charlie's eyes opened slowly. Rebecca could see many years of sadness in them. "I am sorry, Miss Rebecca. The water just feels so good." The tall woman curled in on herself, trying to be modest in this most revealing of circumstances.

"I am sure it does. Lean forward; let me wash your back."

"Umm, I am not sure..."

Rebecca smiled at the shyness, but bit her lip in order to keep from laughing. "Nonsense, Colonel. Regardless of your position, you are still a woman; and I am sure that nothing I see will be a great surprise, unless the good Lord was making a different style when he made you. Besides, you need to keep that wound clean."

Charlie leaned forward, wrapping her arms around her knees, which she had pulled to her chest in a clumsy attempt at modesty. She was in a truly awkward position. She thought of herself as a man, who should preserve the modesty of this gentle woman. However, she was in actuality a woman, who hid her gender from the world for very practical reasons of survival. In this moment, she was neither man nor woman, and instead, was both. She drew a deep breath, for this was new territory and potentially, very dangerous. Only the gentleness of the woman behind her made the situation tolerable.

When Rebecca dropped her eyes to the expanse of skin before

her, she did indeed find a great surprise. The Colonel's back was covered with scars left by a sound thrashing with a whip. "What happened?" she asked as she ran her hand over the old scars.

"I took a beating many years ago."

"Why?"

"Someone was going to be beaten for something he did not do. They accused him of stealing food."

"And you said he did not do it?"

Charlie nodded.

"How did you know he did not?"

"Because I gave it to him. He was starving, and he just wanted a little food. He did not even ask for it. I gave it to him, and when he was accused of stealing it, I told them he had not. But my father said someone had to pay for it, either the slave or me."

"So you took the beating for him?"

"He was a hungry ten-year-old boy. Anyway, it was a long time ago." She laid her forehead on her knees. Clearly, the subject was closed.

The thought that Charlie's own father had inflicted these injuries on her body touched Rebecca deeply; she had never known anything but great love and tenderness from her own father. As she carefully washed the scarred back, tears stung Rebecca's eyes at the thought of such harshness. There was so much nobility in this person. As the lady watched the officer, she could see other small hints of the toll all that nobility had taken on Charlie's body and soul. She was lean, heavily muscled for a woman, and the whip scars were not the only ones that marred that lovely skin.

Rebecca rinsed Charlie's back, then pulled her gently backward so her neck was resting in Rebecca's hand. "I will wash your hair."

"I can do that, Miss Rebecca. You have been so kind. I do not want to be a further burden to you."

"Let me," she whispered, moving closer to the tub. "Let me take care of you, Colonel Redmond. You need it; and you deserve it."

"I do not deserve anything, Miss Rebecca. I am just a soldier doing my job."

"You can tell yourself that all you want. You believe what you want, and I will believe what I want. I believe you deserve it."

"Thank you."

"You are welcome. I brought you some clothes that belonged to my brother. They are clean and in good repair. You can put them on after your bath," Rebecca said quietly as she poured water over Charlie's head and lathered her scalp, giving it a good scrubbing. Rebecca was a little shocked at first when a single, deep moan escaped the Colonel's chest. She felt Charlie relax as she continued washing her hair. Soon she realized that Charlie was sound asleep once again. Carefully, Rebecca finished; gently she placed the woman's neck back on the rim of the tub, allowing Charlie to rest in safety for what Rebecca was sure was the first time in a long while.

Leaving the bathing room, she gathered up the dirty clothes and horrible boots. She took the Colonel's dirty clothes to the sink in the winter kitchen to give them a good scrubbing. Once that was done, she placed the trousers on the drying rack, and took the shirt and the mending kit to the parlor. The boots were tossed out on the porch.

Rebecca settled down in her last remaining easy chair. It was her favorite; and she had decided Lincoln himself would have to come get it before she would surrender it. Placing the kit on the table, she removed thimble, needle, and thread. She was amazed at how happy an act as simple as mending the Colonel's shirt made her feel. Certainly, she had been forced to tend her own clothes, but doing it for Charlie made her feel useful again. It was a very comfortable feeling.

The tear actually required a small patch, but it was fixed quickly. Just as Rebecca was bringing the thread to her teeth to nip it, she looked up to find the Colonel standing in the doorway. He was bathed and dressed in the white shirt and dark trousers Rebecca had left for him. Charlie gave a shy smile and tugged at the suspenders. "I look like a farmer." He grinned as he down looked to his socked feet. "These are very nice. Thank you."

"You are welcome. It is a look that suits you."

Charlie gave a little snort. "I do not know how to be anything but a soldier. It is a good thing I do not own a farm."

Rebecca placed the shirt in her lap and considered Charlie as he stood there. "You are absolutely right, Colonel. A farm would not be the proper place for you. Now, a fine plantation or an outstanding stud stable would do well to have someone like you taking care of it."

"You are very kind."

"No. You are very kind. Tell me, Colonel Redmond, what will you do after the war?"

He walked further into the room, taking a seat on the davenport. "I imagine I will be given a base command somewhere. They may ship me to a fort in the Western Territory."

"Is that what you want to do?"

Charlie stared at his hands as he considered the lady's question. "I really do not know anything else. I have been in the Army most of my life. It is my home. At least, the only home I know. I am sure it probably will be until the day I die."

For some reason, Rebecca had a vision of a casket being lowered into the ground with only a minister and the gravediggers there to pay their respects. The thought that this very kind person would have no one with her in her final days gave Rebecca an unpleasant feeling. "It sounds lonely."

"It is. But it is the life I chose. I can never have a normal life, Miss Rebecca. I will always be Charlie Redmond. It is who I am, for better or for worse." He drew a deep breath, and then stood up. "Well, Miss Rebecca, thank you for the lovely bath," he gestured to the shirt in the woman's lap, "and for fixing my shirt. I will go back out to camp now and get out of your way. However, I seem to have misplaced my boots."

"You are not in my way, Colonel. And you did not misplace them. I put them on the back porch." She rose from her seat and retrieved a fine pair of gentleman's boots from behind the chair. "These were my brother's as well, Colonel. Please see if they fit and if they do, take them. I cannot bear the thought of you trying to get those others back on." She shoved the boots into his hands.

"Please call me Charlie." He said quietly as his hands traveled over the fine leather. "Miss Rebecca I..."

A small laugh escaped as she quirked a brow. "It suits you. Please try them on."

He retook his seat on the sofa and slipped his left foot into the soft leather. "Yes, I know. Charlie always fit better than Charlotte."

"Maybe it is because you are so darn big."

"Could be," A small, quirky grin lit his face for a moment. "Thank you very much." He flexed his feet in the boots. "They fit very nicely."

"Colonel Redmond," Rebecca started in a most shy fashion. "I have been alone here a long time. It is nice to have someone to talk to. Would you stay for a bit? Maybe you could tell me some news of the world."

"I am not sure you would want the kind of news I have to offer. I have not had leave for some time. I am afraid the only thing I could tell you about would be the battles I have been in; and I would not dare offend your sensibilities by telling you such things."

Rebecca nodded. "Thank you, Colonel Redmond. Perhaps we could talk about other things. Where are you from?"

"Charleston."

"Charleston, South Carolina? How...?" She stopped, knowing that she had no right to ask how a Southern woman ended up in the Federal Army. "Me, I have never been out of Virginia."

"Virginia is a beautiful place."

"When we are not at war."

"Indeed."

Rebecca took a deep breath, looking as if she were remembering a time very long ago. "Everything has changed, has it not, Colonel?"

"I am afraid so, Miss Rebecca. Things will never be the same again. The world we knew is long gone, left to historians and philosophers."

The blonde smiled. "You read philosophy, Colonel?"

"When I can get my hands on books. They are rare, and very hard to come by when you are moving from one campaign to the next."

"When was the last time you had leave?"

"Two years ago."

"Why so long?"

"No sense in taking leave when you really have no place to go."

"What of your family? Your home in Charleston?"

"I have no family. Not any more."

Rebecca's heart knew the pain of losing everyone you loved: her parents were long dead; her brother had been killed soon after eagerly joining the Army of Virginia; and her husband had died almost exactly a year ago in yet another senseless battle. While she had never really loved the man she had been forced to marry, she did mourn for the useless loss of life. To her, it was all so senseless. "I am so sorry, Colonel Redmond."

Charlie shrugged. "I guess it is too late to be sorry. I made my choices a long time ago. I have learned to live with them." He sighed, and then looked at her. "Miss Rebecca, I think you should know. My men probably think I have been in here...umm...well..."

"Having your way with me?"

A slight blush crept up his neck, onto his face. "Yes."

"Will it keep them from trying the same thing?"

"More than likely."

"Then let them think it. Go back out and tell them it is so, if you want to."

"Now, why would I do that?" he asked indignantly.

"Would any of your men dare touch a woman you have claimed?"

"Probably not."

"That would be the reason, Colonel."

"I see."

"If it will keep them from my door, I will be happy to let you sleep inside."

Charlie's eyes dropped shut for just a moment, as a soft sigh left his lips.

"How long has it been since you slept in a real bed, Colonel?"

"Do they still make real beds?"

"I am not sure, but I have one here if you would like to use it."

"No, thank you, Miss Rebecca. That really is too much of an imposition."

"Why? You are going to be here for at least a little while. I can offer you simple comfort, and you can offer me protection. Actually, it sounds like the perfect arrangement to me."

"A soft bed?" Brows lifted momentarily as he considered the offer.

Rebecca rose from her chair, offering Charlie her hand. "Let me show you. Then you can decide."

He stood and took her hand, instantly enjoying its warmth. Rebecca's hands were not as soft as a lady's should be. Charlie knew it was because she had been forced to work her own land. He realized what a determined spirit this gentle lady must have. Most of the women the Colonel knew would simply have given up and fled to someplace far safer.

Rebecca lifted her skirts just slightly as they began climbing the stairs. She felt herself tightening her hold on Charlie's hand, amazed at how much larger it was than her own. The Colonel's hand was strong and rough from years of hard work, yet Rebecca could feel gentleness in it.

At the top of the stairs, they turned down the hall, with Rebecca leading the way. She opened a door in the middle of the hall, gesturing for Charlie to enter the room. It was a small sitting room, with another door that opened into the bedroom beyond. Although Charlie did not know it at the time, it was the only room in the house in which a complete bed remained.

Charlie entered the bedroom and looked at the large, inviting four-poster bed. The hand-made quilt covering the feather filled mattress made it look even more comfortable. Rebecca gave the reluctant officer a bit of a push. "Go on, Colonel. Try it out."

Taking a seat on the edge of the big bed, a look of pure pleasure swept across Charlie's face. Rebecca crossed the room. Standing before the officer, she gave him a little push at the shoulders. Charlie lay back on the bed, his booted feet still planted firmly on the floor. "Ahhh..." Any other comment he might have made, died on his lips as he sank into the thick, down filled mattress.

"Nice, is it not?"

"Oh, yes." He nodded, then sat up. "Are you sure?"

"Absolutely. Spend as much time as you like, Colonel Redmond. I will also enjoy having the company. I am afraid I have taken to talking to myself. Sometimes I fear for my sanity."

"Do not, Miss Rebecca. I also talk to myself. It becomes a habit after a while. I am sure some days my men think I am truly insane. How long have you been alone here?"

"Nearly three years now. My parents had both passed over before the war started. That left my younger brother, my husband, and me to tend to the place. We had a few servants of course, but they all either ran away or were taken to help with the war effort. A few stayed for a time, until my brother and then my husband were taken. After that, they fled as well."

Rebecca knew she sounded angry and bitter, but she could not help herself. Everything that had been her life was gone, everything but the land she fought so hard to keep. She knew that at the end of the war, she would no doubt lose the land as well.

"I really am sorry, Miss Rebecca."

"I just pray to God this horrible mess ends soon."

"I have a feeling it will be over soon." Charlie looked to Rebecca as his hands ran across the bedspread. "My men and I are eventually headed toward Charlottesville, and then, perhaps on toward Richmond. I have a bad feeling about it all. I am afraid it will be," he paused, refraining from using too descriptive a term to relate the horrors of the battle, "like The Wilderness was; but I do believe it will be over soon, Miss Rebecca. This area should remain fairly quiet for now."

"The South has lost this war?"

"Long ago. It is only a matter of time now."

Rebecca nodded. She had known in her heart that the end was near. "I will probably lose this house and the land when the dust settles."

"Why?"

"Taxes will be the most likely cause. I have no resources, and no hopes of funds to take care of these things when the time comes. Besides, what chance does a widowed woman stand against anyone who wants to...?" She stopped and shook her head, taking a deep breath. Charlie could tell she had no desire to consider such things.

Suddenly she smiled at the officer. "Colonel, could I possibly interest you in joining me for supper tonight? With the fresh bread and fruit you brought, I believe I could manage a filling meal that would suit you."

"Again, Miss Rebecca, you honor me with your kindness. I would be delighted to join you. I assure you anything you may offer would be better than field rations. My mess Sergeant is a very talented man, but when he has had no time to set up a proper kitchen, there are only so many ways he can prepare beans and rice before it grows very tiresome."

With a grateful smile and a few words about having to check on the troops, Charlie left the house, promising to return in time for dinner. Rebecca watched as Charlie donned the jacket she had loaned him along with the rest of the clothing. Suddenly, every trace of the woman was gone, and the diligent army officer had returned.

CHAPTER 2

FRIDAY, OCTOBER 28, 1864

Colonel Redmond returned to the temporary camp that stretched from the nearby railroad yards in Culpepper, across Gaines Cove Farm and almost to the house. As he began his inspection of the facilities his men had set up, his mind strayed to the lovely lady he had left back at the main house. Charlie had not been in the company of a woman for many months. And unlike the sweet Rebecca Gaines, Lizzie Armstrong could not be considered a lady. She was notorious among the officers and Washington political society, a little bit whore, a little bit mother confessor, and with a reputation of being totally, completely, utterly discreet. As far as anyone knew, she never spoke of the secrets she knew.

That was the main reason Charlie had visited her most recently. To relieve the stress and the tension that had settled deep in his body and soul after the horrors of Vicksburg. He was sure that his ability to feel had finally been ripped away by the nightmare of watching men and horses torn to shreds yet again, leaving the ground stained dark with blood. But Lizzie had proved to Charlie that he could feel, and for a few short hours, even feel alive again. The Colonel had not only been satisfied in matters of the flesh, but also in the matter of soothing a raging soul. The woman had passed no judgment; she had listened with an intent ear, even allowing concern for the officer to show through her normally cool demeanor. And in the morning, as Charlie dressed to leave, pulling several bills from his wallet, Lizzie had pressed them back into his hand, refusing the money she so readily took from the others who visited her. Although the good Colonel was unaware of it, one thing that could be said about him was that he inspired kindness and compassion in the most unlikely souls, including Lizzie's. But his last visit to the sanctuary that was Lizzie's arms and bed had been many months and many, many miles ago.

As he rode through the camp, he was pleased to see that the men had done their work well and efficiently; as he knew they would. When he had taken over command, there had been many changes in the way things were done. While the men had balked at first, it did not take them long to realize their new commander did indeed know the art of war: how to prepare, how to fight, and how to survive.

Initially, they did not understand why he ordered latrines dug as far away as possible from quarters, or that the bath had to be set up down stream from the mess. He also required that every man bathe as regularly as possible and wash his uniforms. No, they had not understood all the new rules when Colonel Redmond had taken over; but when it became apparent that the overall level of health had improved, they did the Colonel's bidding without question.

Charlie's final stop was to check on the horses. His command was light cavalry; their horses were their lives. Each man who rode was required to groom his beasts, carefully tending to their hooves, keeping them clean and trimmed, and making sure their shoes were in good shape and not loose. A bad shoe could make a horse lame in a matter of hours, especially if ridden hard.

The land on which they were currently camped was a horse's

version of heaven. Fenced pastures and a network of small creeks running with fresh water guaranteed each animal the freedom to roam, with plenty of clean water and fresh, sweet grass instead of being staked at picket lines eating rotting, moldy hay. Charlie knew that more thanks were due to Miss Rebecca.

Returning to his own tent, he changed into spare uniform breeches, clean shirt, and vest. He considered putting on his day coat, but even though it was October, it was still very warm. Back in uniform, Charlie stuck his head out of his tent, giving a whistle that was known to be the call for his batman.

"Aye, Colonel C?" Jackson slipped into his tent quietly and, as they had done for many years, dispensed with the formality of a salute. Other than Dr. Elizabeth Walker and her field assistants Mr. Albert Samuelson and Mr. Walt Whitman, Jackson was the only person in the entire army who knew Charlie's secret.

Jackson and Charlie had been together since Charlie's early days in the Army; since the gruesome battle of Buena Vista, which had put Charlie on the career track as an officer and saved him from being mere cannon fodder under the command of another. He had saved Jackson's life during that campaign, and Jackson had saved his numerous times since by safeguarding his secret.

"I borrowed our hostess's brother's clothing this morning, Jackson. I think I should return it without the smell of the stables. Would you handle it?"

Jackson smiled at his commander, giving a gentle sniff to the air. "Aye, Colonel C. Seems you "borrowed" more than the clothes. Is that perfumed soap I smell?"

Charlie sighed. He should have known his companion would torment him when he discovered what had transpired at the house.

While Jackson did not really know, he had a good idea. "Had yourself a nice bath in a real tub did ya?"

"I did." The Colonel hoped his short answer would suffice for the man.

"And would you be returning these duds to the lady yourself?"

"I would, my friend, and extending her my protection as well. Let the men know, if you would, that any insult to her will be an insult to me."

"You know, Colonel, the men will cheer you on. I think your tendency to stay to yourself worries them sometimes. You know—not manly enough. Though the good Lord knows, they have seen just what you can do on a battlefield."

Charlie laughed. Jackson regularly defended the Colonel's manhood. Generally, it was done with his very dry and droll wit, but occasionally, when someone had the bad sense to suggest that the Colonel preferred the company of men to the charms of the ladies, he had been known to bust the occasional head. Given Jackson's Irish temper, Charlie was surprised there were not more men on the injured list due to a solid thumping from his batman.

"Well, if things work out as I hope, I will probably be moving my command up to the main house."

"Oh my. That sounds serious." He grinned at his commander. "You had better be careful there Charlie boy."

"Yes. I know, but there is something about her Jocko. I trust her. I have to, she already knows."

"How?"

"I let her tend my wound. She noticed."

"Sweet Jesu, Charlie. What did you go and do that for? She could destroy you!"

"I know, Jocko, I know. But there is just something about her. I trust her."

"Dear Lord," the Irishman crossed himself, "Save me from gallant Southerners and frustrated women. I thought you had more sense than that." Jackson grabbed the clothing Charlie had left in a pile and started to stomp out of the tent. He turned back just at the entrance. "Well, for all of our sakes, I hope you are right, Charlie. I hope you are right."

Charlie appreciated Jocko's concern and was grateful for his friendship, even though it often led to suspension of the traditional relationship between commanding and non-commissioned officer. He took his seat at his desk to review the morning's dispatches and to write his own reports to General Sheridan. As he sifted through the various papers, his mind ran over the engagements that his men had been in since General Grant had ordered them east. They had joined Phil Sheridan's forces after the worst battles of the year—those campaigns that would be recorded in history as The Wilderness and the Battle of Spotsylvania Courthouse. Charlie had joined the regiment after those engagements, with his own experienced troops from Vicksburg being used to replenish the ranks of the tattered 13th Pennsylvania. Almost as a kindness, Charlie's regiment had been sent to their current location. It was a strip of counties just east of the misty Blue Ridge that had seen more traffic during the war than any other, as first one army then another moved through. His orders were to take control of the western supply lines and the critical rail bed that ran to Charlottesville and beyond.

Since their arrival, they had been fighting hit-and-run sorties against Jubal Early's forces. It was ugly—light cavalry against light cavalry, sweeping back and forth through the foothills of Page and Warren Counties, up and down through the rolling hills of Fauquier, Culpeper, Rappahannock, and Madison counties, always looking for a path south through Green and Orange Counties into Albemarle and the railhead in Charlottesville.

Occasionally, they were called to serve as a lightning strike force, as they had been the previous week. Sheridan directed them north, across the pass toward Winchester to face Early's forces at Cedar Creek. Fortunately, they were on the weak flank. Generals Sheridan and Wright took the brunt of Early's forces head on and won the day. The 13th Pennsylvania was then free to return to the rail patrol.

On the way back south, there was that ugly day in Brandy Station, where the skirmishing was not with Early's raiders but instead with their own men, troops in the uniform of one of the New York conscription brigades. Charlie turned his back on one of them and paid for it. His men did not leave even one of the turncoats unmarked before they were sent back to Sheridan's command post in Winchester for court martial.

Charlie was tired. He knew his troops were tired. He smiled as a thought suddenly took form. *Maybe… maybe we can winter here. If I promise to care for Miss Rebecca, to make sure she is not harmed by our presence, maybe she will let us remain. The land is good. We have plenty of supplies. The horses will be able to get healthy here. There are barns and stables that my boys could fix up with a little work.*

Then there was Miss Rebecca. She had asked about the scars on his back. He had not thought about them for years, but it had been a turning point in his life. He shrugged to shake off the old memories and the old pain. It was so many years ago—what seemed like a lifetime: the day Charlotte died and Charlie was born.

Enough. A beautiful lady awaits my company, and I will be the gentleman she thinks I am—if only for a few hours.

When Charlie returned for dinner, Rebecca noticed he had changed back into uniform trousers, a white shirt and vest, and his mess coat. His disguise was a good one. Even looking him right in the face, no one could tell. His voice was deep enough not to arouse suspicion. It was truly amazing.

He smiled as he came through the door with the clothes Rebecca had loaned him earlier. They were folded in a neat pile as he offered them to the blonde. "I had them washed," he offered with a quirk of his brow.

"You must have had them on for what, two hours?"

"More like three, but I had to inspect camp and they got a little dirty."

"So did you." She crinkled her nose just a bit to indicate the odor coming from the officer. "Good thing I happen to like the smell of horse. However, after supper you are getting another bath. In the meantime, at least wash your hands and arms."

"Yes, Ma'am. Should I eat on the porch?"

"No, just stay downwind. What did you do, Colonel, set up the stables?"

He laughed as he washed his hands at the pump at the sink. "No, I just lent a hand where it was needed. Lots of work to prepare a camp."

"I would imagine. You seem to do it very well."

"I have been doing it since I was fifteen. I am thirty-four now. I have lots of experience." He took a cloth from the sink and dried his hands. "I know all the little tricks."

Rebecca gestured to his uniform as she finished setting the table. "You know all kinds of tricks."

"Uh-huh."

"So you have been living life as a man for nineteen years?"

"Just about that, yes."

"And you have never been discovered?"

"Not yet." He sighed hard as he moved to the table to hold Rebecca's chair for her. "I am very convincing."

"Is that so?" Rebecca smiled as her chair moved toward the table. "You mean to tell me you can sit here through dinner and make me believe I am having supper with a gentleman?"

"Well now, you are a little different because you already know; but yes, I am confident I could make you believe it."

"Try."

"What?"

"Try, Colonel Redmond. Try to make me believe it."

"Miss Rebecca, this is silly."

"Play the game, Colonel Redmond."

"All right, Miss Rebecca, all right."

As he settled down across the table from Rebecca, the blonde smiled. She was not sure Charlie could do it. He could see it in her face, and he quirked a brow in challenge.

And so the evening began.

Their conversation ranged over many topics, from gracious

comments on the land, to authors they had both read and enjoyed. Rebecca stayed away from the obvious question of how did a Charlestonian end up in the Federal army, and the even more obvious one, how did a girl become a Colonel, a career officer.

Charlie skillfully created a mood of cultured peace, of two people enjoying a time of quiet, thoughtful companionship. It was a taste of the elegance and culture that Rebecca had once enjoyed in her parents' home, and lost with the advent of war.

Supper was a delightful experience. For one night, Rebecca forgot the nearly empty larder, the lost friends and family, the vacant stables of her family's once spectacular horse-breeding enterprise. By the time the simple dessert of fresh fruit and real coffee, brought as a house gift by this enigmatic guest, was over, she realized that Charlie was holding her hand, lightly brushing his...her thumb over the back of it.

"You win," Rebecca smiled from behind her coffee cup.

"Excuse me?"

"You win, you had me convinced. You win."

He smiled. "Years of practice."

Rebecca looked down and noticed Charlie had not released her hand and she had not moved her own.

Very gently, with a courtesy Rebecca thought had died on that terrible day when the Army of Virginia mobilized, Charlie bowed, and raising her hand, gently caressed it with his lips. "Thank you for an evening of civilization in a very uncivilized time."

After supper, Rebecca prepared another bath. This time she provided Charlie with a nightshirt and robe that belonged to her brother. While Charlie bathed, Rebecca turned down the bed and retrieved a spare blanket and pillow from the cabinet. She was just about to slip a nightgown over her head when she heard Charlie clear his throat. She let it drop over her head and shoulders, draping to the floor around her body before turning around. "Ready for a soft bed?"

"Ah, you have no idea."

Rebecca picked up the pillow and blanket, heading for the door. "Enjoy it, Colonel. You have earned it."

"Miss Rebecca, is this your bed?"

"Yes."

"Oh." Then, very gently, "I will not take you from your bed. Give me those. A davenport is far better than an army cot."

"No, Colonel, it is all right."

"No, it is not. Now come, Miss Rebecca, be reasonable."

"You do not know much about Southern women do you, Colonel Redmond? We have been called many things. Reasonable is not generally among them."

His laughter rang over Rebecca's head at that last comment. "Darlin' Miss Rebecca, I know quite a bit about Southern woman. And they are eminently reasonable when they want to be. Now, I will not take your bed."

"Well then, it will go unused this night!"

He growled a little as he tightened the belt of the robe and ran his hand through his hair. "Tell you what, it is a big bed. We can share it."

"Hmm...how do I know this is not a ploy on your part to get me in a position where you can take advantage of me, Colonel Redmond?" Rebecca said.

All the blood drained from his face as he took a step back. "Miss Rebecca, I...I...I would not...I..."

"Colonel, I was teasing. Of course, we can share the bed. You are right. It is a big bed. Now come on in here and get into it."

"Maybe I should take the davenport." His voice struggled a bit to get out of his throat with a barely vocal squeak instead of his normally rich, low voice. He seemed to sag against the doorjamb.

"Nonsense. Now come on," Rebecca gave his arm a little tug and pulled him inside the bedroom, closing the door behind him.

"Miss Rebecca, you do not understand." Charlie swallowed hard, afraid to make the admission. He released a deep breath, gathering his courage. The worst that would happen was that she would order him from her home. "One of the reasons I play the role so well is because...because..." He dropped his head, then lifted it again. "Because I prefer the company of women."

"Then come to bed, because I assure you, Colonel Redmond, I am the only woman within five hundred miles willing to share her bed with you."

Charlie's eyes grew wide. "Miss Rebecca? Surely you do not...you have not..."

Rebecca had never seen such a confused combination of emotions in one human being before. Hope, fear, longing, an aching loneliness, shame...all of them and much more crossed Charlie's face in that moment.

"Colonel Redmond, I offered to share my bed. I asked for your protection because I believe you are a person of unquestionable honor. Therefore, your preferences in companionship are your own business. Now, come to bed."

The blonde watched as the strange combination of man and woman before her removed the robe and climbed into the bed. "Umm, do you prefer the right or the left?" Charlie asked before settling in.

"Actually, I have been sleeping alone for so long I have pretty much taken to sleeping in the middle of the bed, so you pick a side and I will try to stay on my own." Charlie nodded as he settled down on the left side of the bed. Rebecca joined him from the right side, and she had to laugh. "Colonel Redmond, it is all right. You do not have to sleep on the very edge of the bed."

"I want you to have plenty of room, Miss Rebecca."

"And I want you to enjoy sleeping in a big bed, and you cannot do that on the very edge, holding tight to keep from falling off." She reached out and took Charlie by the shoulder, pulling him back into the bed.

As Charlie rolled over on his back, their faces were only an inch apart. His eyes were still the most amazing thing Rebecca had ever seen, and those lips seemed to have a powerful attraction all their own. Slowly Rebecca licked her own lips as they watched each other. "Charlie," *I wonder if I sound as breathless as I feel.* "I...unh...I..."

A look of pain and longing flickered through those sky blue eyes, and then the stern, determined Colonel was before her again. "Good night, Miss Rebecca."

"Good night, Colonel Redmond."

Charlie woke in the middle of the night, an unfamiliar weight against his shoulder. Rebecca had curled herself around him in her sleep, using Charlie's body as a warm and safe pillow.

Oh, Lord, help me. She is so beautiful and so trusting. I would wake her, but I fear our current position would embarrass her immensely.

Charlie was careful to stay very still, holding Rebecca gently as she slept. He wanted to believe that perhaps this was the first time Rebecca had slept soundly, and more importantly, safely, for a long time. If, in her sleep, she naturally sought the comfort of a warm body beside her, who was Charlie Redmond to take that from her?

Get a grip on yourself, Redmond. She is probably dreaming of her lost husband right now, thinking him back in her bed. He gently slipped his arm around Rebecca, and she snuggled in more closely.

Besides, how long has it been since you have held a beautiful woman in your arms? How easy is it to imagine that such a lovely woman would find you attractive, that you could have the love of someone like this? You know better, but for the moment, where it hurts no one, it is so lovely to imagine.

Saturday, October 29, 1864

Charlie rose with the first gray light of pre-dawn, carefully sliding his body from beneath Rebecca's, and slipping his still warm pillow into her arms to replace the warm shoulder she had been using as the resting place for her head. He had always made a habit of rising before the troops, to be there as they faced the day and let them know he worked by the same standards he expected from them. He dressed and slipped out of the house.

He returned to his command tent, which was a brisk five-minute walk through the early morning air, and began his morning ritual. It started with a careful and thorough shave. When he first started, it had seemed so ridiculous. Why should a woman shave? But it did make a difference. He had realized a long time ago that women do have facial hair—very fine and light, but nonetheless there. So he had started shaving; it would not do to have a thirty-four-year-old Colonel with peach fuzz on his cheeks. Today, it soothed him, reminded him of his role, put him back into the day-to-day activities of the life he had followed for the past nineteen years.

Every day, rain or shine, he reviewed and drilled with the men. In part, he believed, it kept them in line, and in part, it was important to holding his command. He had found that regimental commanders who were not connected to their troops had higher casualties than those who were. But that was just the argument he gave the public. More importantly, it grounded him, reminded him of the man he had become and of the role he must play every day.

Rebecca had shaken his world. Those little traditions helped him return to reality.

~

Saturday, November 5, 1864

Colonel Redmond reviewed his morning dispatches. General Sheridan had ordered him to find secure winter quarters for his troops, near the rail lines. Although it was still warm, winter was drawing near and it was an order he had been expecting for several days.

His men had been driven hard. In March, they had been ordered east to join with the remnants of the 13th Pennsylvania. Since then, they had faced Jubal Early's forces several times, as well as engaged in a number of minor skirmishes. It was time to hunker down for the winter and try to recover their strength. He finished the dispatches and orders, then called for Jackson.

"Jocko, I need to do something special for Mrs. Gaines."

"By God, Colonel Charlie! You spend a few nights with the wench, and you need to do something special?"

"Jocko! That will be enough of that Master Sergeant!"

"Sir?" Jackson was the picture of military readiness, standing at attention.

"I wish to ask Mrs. Gaines for permission to winter over on her property. When I do, I want to show her that the regiment will take care of her while we are here. From the looks of things, the war has been extremely hard for her."

"Yes, Sir." Jackson maintained his façade of perfect military demeanor.

Charlie looked at him with no small irritation. He needed Jocko's help. He was, after all the expert when it came to charming women.

"At ease, Master Sergeant."

He could hear the irritation in his Colonel's voice. "Sir."

"Jocko, are you going to help me here, or do I flap in the breeze all by myself?"

"Sir, I am not sure what you mean, Sir."

The Colonel sat back in his camp chair and regarded his batman for a long, speculative moment. "Fine. If this is how it must be, then so be it. Sergeant Jackson, would you lay out my dress uniform? I expect your presence in dress uniform this evening to serve us at supper. Please request the mess chief to join me. When you have conveyed the message to Mess Sergeant Jamison, return here, day dress, ready to deliver an invitation. Dismissed."

"Sir, yes, Sir." Jackson snapped a crisp salute.

"And Sergeant, when you are ready to talk, send Jocko in."

That did not go as Charlie had expected. *I swear you could cut the disapproval in here with a dull butter knife.*

He searched his field desk for the finest piece of paper he had for a simple note, an invitation to dinner. In his best hand, the copperplate that was drilled into Charlotte at Mistress Amelia's School for Girls, he carefully penned the invitation.

Col. Chas. Redmond requests the pleasure of your company for an alfresco supper,
at dusk this evening, beside the pond.

At the foot of the back lawn was a lovely pond, complete with willow and small seating area. It was the perfect place for a picnic. Having a regiment of Yankee soldiers take up residence in your home for the winter was not typically a welcome occurrence to a Southern landowner, so he would have to do what he could to make it more palatable.

As he finished folding and sealing his little note, Mess Sergeant Jamison tapped at the tent pole, requesting entry. Jackson was behind him, still stiff as a board, but clean and fresh to deliver the invitation.

"Come in, Jamison, Jackson. Have a seat, Sergeant." He waved Jamison to the small campstool opposite his desk. Then he turned to Jackson. "Deliver this to Mrs. Gaines, Jackson, and wait for a reply, please." Jocko took the note and set off, still displaying his disapproval by his exacting manners.

Charlie could only shake his head as he returned his attention to Jamison. "I know it is short notice, but I want to prepare a special dinner for Mrs. Gaines; something with a little elegance, to be served outdoors down by the pond. What can you do for me?"

"Well, Colonel, most of what I have is normal mess food—beans, rice, salt pork. But one of the men likes to fish. Let me see what he and I can come up with—some bass or trout. The streams and ponds around here ought to have something."

"Sounds good to me. You know I like fish. Just do the best you can, Sergeant. And some of my special coffee? A bottle of brandy? Maybe some fresh greens or fruit?"

"I will do the best I can, Colonel."

"Thank you, Sergeant. I have every faith in you."

Charlie spent the time waiting for Jackson to return worrying. Worrying that Rebecca would not want to see him after last night, when he was almost certain she had awakened in his arms.

Concerned that she would want more than he could give.

Anxious that she would betray him to the men.

Afraid that she would hate him for wanting to winter here.

Apprehensive that she might think he was just using her to give his men a safe haven.

Fretful that she would send him away.

Mostly, alarmed about what he would say to her tonight if she accepted his invitation.

Rebecca watched as the soldier walked purposefully across the main yard towards the house. He was a compact, redheaded man, with broad shoulders and a neat waist. He sported a tidily trimmed mustache and long sideburns. He stopped, squaring his shoulders, then removing his hat and gloves.

"Sergeant Jackson, Ma'am." He offered her a smile and a little salute. "Colonel Redmond sends his regards and has asked that I deliver this to you." He offered her the folded note.

She stepped toward him, taking the letter from his hand and smiling like a schoolgirl. She felt a blush rise to her cheeks as she read the note.

"Colonel Redmond requested I wait for an answer, Ma'am."

Rebecca cleared her throat gently, refolding the letter, and then she looked to the Sergeant. "You may tell Colonel Redmond I shall be delighted to dine with him tonight."

"Thank you, Ma'am." Jackson returned his hat to his head, stood at attention, and turned on his heel to return to camp. *Eyes as green as Irish clover. No wonder our Colonel is so smitten by her. The lady is charming, and very easy on the eyes.*

Rebecca smiled to herself as she watched the Sergeant walk away. She chewed the inside of her lip, realizing she would have to find something to wear that would be appropriate for dinner with the good Colonel.

Returning to the house, she headed straight for her bedroom, opened the wardrobe, and looked at what remained of her clothes. They were very out of style, but in reasonable condition. She considered a green dress that had been her brother's favorite. He always said it set off the color of her eyes. Then her attention turned to a rose-colored dress. It was two tones of deep pink, and the cut was off the shoulder. It was a little daring, but she pulled the dress from the wardrobe and laid it on the bed.

She looked at the bed; the one she had been sharing with the Colonel during the previous nights. It had been years since she had slept so soundly. When she had awakened that first morning, she had been a touch disappointed to find the Colonel gone. She was more surprised, however, to find that she was firmly ensconced around the pillow on which Charlie's head had rested. She found a great deal of comfort from holding it and learning the scent left behind. Cuddling Charlie's pillow had become a morning habit in the past few days.

She shook herself for just a moment, realizing that her thoughts of the Colonel were not exactly proper. He was a Yankee officer, serving with the enemy, and one with a very dangerous secret. A secret Rebecca would keep, but also one that should keep her from thinking these things about him.

What Rebecca could not understand was why she was arguing with herself over this issue. She could enjoy the Colonel's company while the troops camped on her land, but anything more would go against everything she had been taught was proper. Still, she could not help but smile, feeling butterflies in her stomach when her mind's eye pictured those piercing blue eyes and that very charming smile.

Oh, God!

~

Charlie saw Jocko through the open flap, walking toward his tent. He had a strange look on his face, one Charlie had never seen before. He looked almost reverent.

"Colonel C?"

"Yes, Jocko."

"I am sorry. I was wrong. She is a true lady."

"Yes, she is, Jocko. So?"

Jocko smiled at the look of anxiety on the Colonel's face. "Oh, and yes, she would be honored to join you for supper, Lucky Charlie. I will get your dress uniform ready. You need a bath."

Charlie thought wistfully of the lovely bathing room, the tub, and hot water up at the main house. But for this evening, he must be the Colonel, as right and proper as he knew how to be. For this lady deserved to be treated with dignity and respect. He might sleep with her in his arms tonight. *Please, God, let me hold her tonight.* The thought came unbidden to his mind, and startled him just a bit with its intensity. But she still deserved all the grace he could give her in the midst of this hell.

Jocko gathered Charlie's kit and stumped off to clear the bathing area for him. Jocko made his demand for privacy out as an officer's privilege. Little did the troops know. Charlie gave Jocko a few minutes to prepare, then he followed.

As Charlie bathed, Jocko set up to shave him again, a soothing ritual and a kindness from Jocko in their little conspiracy of deceit.

Seeing Jocko set up his shaving gear set Charlie off again as he bathed carefully in the cold, clean water of the stream. He realized he wanted to do more than just ask this woman to shelter them this winter; he wanted to woo her, to charm her. Yet, who was he to woo a woman? A soldier from the side of the enemy. Eventually, orders would come and he would go off to where he was told, to fight whomever he was told.

I am just a weapon to be aimed blindly at the enemy, not seeing the humanity, the flesh and blood, the mothers and fathers and lovers who will mourn when I am successful. I am a soldier, one whom no one will mourn if I fall. Indeed, a soldier who will be castigated and stricken from the rolls of the regiment when I die and am discovered. I am no man to be her champion, to give her children and a home. Who am I to woo her?

And who was she, who in a matter of a few days had made his body, which had always been obedient to his mind, cry and ache constantly for her touch? He had been satisfied. The Army was his home, had been his fate, his future, and most of his past. He had not wanted anything else. Now he was a five foot eleven inch vessel of barely restrained hunger and want.

How could she do this to me? In that first night of innocent seeking, looking for warmth and protection from someone she trusted? I should not do this. I should not offer her the form without the substance. For I will have to leave, and what kind of hurt will I inflict when I do? But I cannot not woo her. My head says no, but everything else compels me to do so.

The cynic, that pragmatic voice in his head that had helped him to survive undiscovered all those years, told him it was just a dream. He had been at war for too long, and now before him was the Eden everyone dreamed of—a beautiful home, beautiful land, and a beautiful woman.

Be gentle with her. Take what she offers freely. Leave with no regrets and no ties. The worst is yet to come, and no one knows where, or how, they will die, not even Lucky Charlie.

CHAPTER 3

SATURDAY, NOVEMBER 5, 1864

Charlie returned to his command tent to change. Jocko had laid out his dress uniform, carefully brushed and pressed. Boots, belt, and leather straps were polished to a gleam, and each metal fitting and buckle was burnished.

"Well, Jocko's done his best to make me look good. Now, if only I can maintain the image as well." Over the years of being alone, he had developed the habit of talking aloud, often to just relieve the quiet solitude of his life. He kept his voice to a low murmur, so others could not overhear him. It was still a somewhat distracting habit for those who worked around the Colonel.

With care, he donned the uniform. The tight moleskin breeches with the broad yellow stripes down the sides tucked into his dress boots. A carefully tied waterfall cravat topped his crisp linen dress shirt. The tight weskit with the yellow facings that spoke of a master horseman went over that. The issue uniform was completed by the blue frock coat with red facings and the silver eagles embroidered on the shoulders that announced Charlie's position as regimental Colonel. On top of that went the one piece of non-standard issue material, a rich red silk sash, wrapped twice around his waist, and tied so the fringe brushed the top of his left boot. The wide belt that held his sword went over the sash. He tucked a pair of fine kid gloves into his belt, and slipped his hat under his arm. Using the small mirror that hung on his tent pole, he checked his hair, brushing it into place.

"Ah, the image of the perfect officer and gentleman. But not the kind of man she could ever really want." With a suddenly bleak look in his eyes, Charlie squared his shoulders and strode up to the main house, his hat, and to be honest, his heart and hopes in his hands.

As he walked up toward the house, he could tell that Jocko and Jamison were already at work. The lawn around the main house had been scythed and trimmed. Surely, the lawn behind the house leading down to the pond had received the same treatment. As he approached the portico, Jocko came bustling around the corner of the house. In his hands was a lovely bouquet of freshly picked flowers, late blooming asters and ferns. "For the lady," he said. "Ye cannot go in there empty handed, Colonel C."

"Thanks, Jocko, but I had something more substantial in mind for this evening. Like negotiating to make this our winter camp."

"I do not care what the business part is, Colonel C. Miss Rebecca is a lady, and you will treat her like one. Now, take my advice and take the flowers."

Charlie snorted at the cocky little bantamweight's vehemence as he took the bouquet. Well, he had managed to charm an amazing number of women.

Charlie's boots rang heavily on the brickwork of the portico as he mounted the steps and knocked politely on the great door. One of Jamison's assistants, clad in his dress uniform to play the proper footman, opened it. "Miss Rebecca is in the back parlor, Sir." Charlie followed the soldier cum footman to the parlor door.

Rebecca wore the lovely rose-colored dress that laid low on her shoulders and set off her fair complexion. The dress complimented her figure well. Charlie stood for a moment, gripping the flowers in his right hand, unable to summon a single word or thought. To Rebecca, he looked like a teenaged boy paying court to a lady for the first time. Her impression was closer than she knew.

As the silence between them stretched to an uncomfortable length, Rebecca realized they would remain there like a pair of statues if she did not do something. She rose from the chair in which she had been sitting, watching the beginnings of the sunset over the western hills and Sergeant Jamison's minions swarming over her property. Gently, she took the flowers from Charlie's hand and gave them a sniff, looking at him over the top of them with flirting eyes.

"Good evening, Colonel Redmond. Your men have been here much of the afternoon, and I must say they have done wonders in just a few hours."

Shaking himself, Charlie remembered his manners—finally. He took her hand in his own and gently brushed his lips over the back of her fingers. "It is our honor, Ma'am. You have extended your hospitality to me and my men; we could do no less."

An ironic laugh was forced out of Rebecca at that. "Sir, if you were representative of all of the Northern officers and men I have seen in these terrible times, there would not have been a war in the first place. But then, you and I would have never met."

Charlie gulped. She was flirting with him. Flirting. That evil little voice in his head started to coach him. *Ah, time to be the gallant, Colonel Charlie. Surely you can find something charming to say, you fraud.*

"Then, Madam, much as I regret this conflict, I would willingly have gone through the very gates of hell for the privilege of meeting you." A gentle smile curled his lips.

She looked up into his eyes. Dressed as he was, standing in such a strangely shy, yet attentive posture, he was surely one of the most handsome men she had ever seen. His face was slightly weathered, tanned, and with small creases around his eyes caused by years in the sun and wind, but they only served to set off the eerie blue-gray eyes that were almost silver. His hair, dark as a raven's wing, had the first hints of gray at the temples. The only thing missing was facial hair; every other man she knew sported some hirsute adornment. Yet, she knew beneath that masculine exterior was skin that was warm and soft, like the palest ivory velvet. The dichotomy that was Charlie Redmond fascinated her.

The young trooper who was serving as footman for the evening cleared his throat at the door. "Supper is ready whenever you care to adjourn to the pond, Sir."

"Thank you." Charlie spied Rebecca's shawl thrown across the back of the davenport in the small parlor. He caught it up and gently settled it around her shoulders, then offered her his arm to escort her to dinner.

She slid her hand into the curve of his arm, and together they followed the young trooper back to the hall and out of the back door. The smell of freshly cut grass rose up as they strolled toward the little plaza by the water. Jamison had set torches on poles around the area. A small table was set under the willow, with candles and a cloth. Two chairs from the dining room had been brought down for them.

Rebecca was stunned by how lovely the men had made the grounds look through the day's labors. She had done her best to keep things neat, but the men had really outdone themselves. "It is lovely, Colonel. I have always wanted to have this as a place for alfresco suppers."

"Miss Rebecca, your property is beautiful. I cannot imagine anyone who had this land ever wanting to leave."

"I must admit I do love this land. But I fear that with no income, and no way to create income, when things have settled, and it comes time to reckon with the taxman, I will lose it."

Just at that moment, Jamison brought the first course to the table. He had found some musk melons, and had carefully wrapped paper-thin strips of country ham around bite sized slices of the sweet fruit. They savored the choice tidbits as the sky darkened to a vivid palette of sunset pinks, purples, and reds.

"So, tell me about this land. What do you grow here?"

Rebecca laughed. "We used to grow horses. And hay, alfalfa, timothy, some grain and feed corn."

The rest of the meal was spent discussing the advantages of this rolling land, stitched with small creeks, guarded with small stands of first growth forest that provided shelter from sudden storms. They spoke of various breeds of horses, the advantages and disadvantages of each. Rebecca loved the gentle beasts, and had been heartbroken when her own special mount, a spirited thoroughbred mare, had been conscripted along with the rest of the family's herd.

Supper was a success. As promised, Jamison had found trout from a nearby stream, fresh greens, and a lovely squash that he had steamed. One of the scouts had brought in a young deer from the western hills, which he had roasted. Dessert was apples braised in brandy, gently seasoned with cinnamon from his own personal horde of spices. When the meal was over, the troopers removed the remnants, leaving Rebecca and the Colonel alone.

As they sat in comfortable silence, enjoying a cup of Charlie's own special coffee and a small glass of brandy, Charlie steeled himself to broach the true reason for the evening's elegance.

"Ah, Miss Rebecca? I would like to ask you something, and maybe offer you a solution for some of your troubles."

"I hate to say this, but how can a Yankee officer help me with my troubles?"

"Well, we need a place to winter. Your land is ideal; there is plenty of pasture and water for our horses, and room for my men to have reasonably comfortable quarters. It is close to the rail lines, but protected. In return for letting us stay here, we will put your barns and stables back in shape, and will provide you with some basic brood stock—some mares, a good stud stallion, some asses so you can also breed mules."

"Why, Colonel Redmond, if I did not know better, I would think you were trying to take advantage of my person, and offering me this as your payment." She turned away from him, so he could not see that he was being teased as she tried to evaluate the offer he had just made her.

"No, no, I did not mean it that way, really, Miss Rebecca. I just..." Charlie stopped, helpless before what he feared was her injured sense of honor.

She turned to face him again. Gently, she covered his hand, lying loose and open on the table, and looked into the sad eyes of the person before her. "Let me think on it, Charlie. Let me think on it. Now, it is getting chilly, and we both have much to do tomorrow. Will you escort me to the house?"

He rose and held her chair. Quietly, he took her hand in his own and folded it over his arm. Silently, the two of them walked up to the house. It was quiet; the troopers had returned to their own billets. A lamp had been left lit in the hall, and a few others were lit upstairs.

Charlie escorted her to the foot of the stairs, intending to let her go and then return to his own tent. Each night, he had offered to leave her and return to his own narrow camp bed. But each night, Rebecca had other ideas. Tonight was no different. As he stopped at the foot of the stairs, she said, "Put out the lamp, Colonel."

"Miss Rebecca?"

"You shoulder needs tending."

"Miss Rebecca, Jocko can take care of it. I do not want to impose."

"I told you, while you are here; you sleep in a real bed, not that camp cot. Come along."

His mind told him it would be infinitely better if he went back to his cot. The experience of waking in the middle of the night with her in his arms was terrifying. It was fire, fear, and yearning. He knew if this continued, the wanting would grow beyond his ability to handle it. But the desire was already there. Just to hold a beautiful woman in his arms was like heaven—a few moments when he could escape from the hell, the fear, and the hopelessness of his life. Charlie turned the small wheel that lowered the wick, and followed her up the stairs.

~

Sunday, November 6, 1864

As the first pale light of pre-dawn lit the sky, Charlie awoke. Once again, the blonde lay safe within the circle of his long, wiry arms. Once again, Charlie's night had been shortened by the awareness of her warmth and gentle presence, and what little sleep had been possible was illuminated by dreams of what, in Charlie's mind, could never be.

Slipping from the warmth of her embrace and the down comforter that covered them both through the chill morning air, Charlie pulled his clothes on, leaving the boots for downstairs in order to not awaken the sleeping woman. He resisted the urge to place a kiss on her forehead before reaching for the doorknob. This morning, he was unsuccessful in his efforts to be quiet. As he was about to slip out the door, sleepy green eyes blinked open.

"Good morning, Colonel Redmond." A sly, soft smile played around her lips.

"Good morning to you, Miss Rebecca. I am sorry. I did not mean to awaken you. It is very early, so go back to sleep, dear lady."

"Oh, I am awake now—and not because of you. I feel more rested than I have for as long as I can remember."

"Well, then, I will leave you to your morning ablutions. I have to tend to my flock of lost boys out there, and we have a staff meeting this morning. But perhaps this afternoon, you would do me the honor of joining me for a ride? I would like to talk more about the request I made last night."

"Colonel Redmond, I love to ride. But as you know, I have no horse."

"I believe one of my mounts will take you. I have used her before as a woman's mount, and she goes sweetly under a sidesaddle. You do have a saddle, I hope, for I do not normally carry such equipment in my kit." Charlie's self-deprecating smile was endearing.

"Yes, I still have my saddle. It is the one piece of tack that was not requisitioned for the war. But I fear I still cannot join you."

"Oh." Charlie's voice was flat. He turned away from her to fiddle with his cravat, hiding the pain that welled up in his chest at the rejection. He had known it was coming; he just had not expected it so soon. "Then I am sorry I imposed on you." The dreams and fantasies of wintering over here in this place, with this charming woman, evaporated in that instant.

Rebecca heard Charlie's controlled withdrawal. She softened her voice, somewhat embarrassed by the situation. Rising slightly, holding the covers modestly over her body, she smiled. "It is not that I would not love to join you, Colonel Redmond. The problem is that I cannot get into my riding habit by myself, and my lady's maid ran off some time ago."

He turned back to face her, a playful smile flirting around his lips. "Well, my dear lady. That can be remedied if you are willing to let an old soldier play lady's maid. I did, once upon a time, know how to do these things."

Rebecca, blushing a little, smiled again. The idea of a real ride after so many months with no mount thrilled her. "Then, Sir, I will see you after lunch? And we will see if you can handle buttons as well as you handle reins."

Rebecca made the bed; unconsciously, she lovingly smoothed the pillow Charlie used, a slight smile playing on her lips the entire time. She was truly excited about the thought of riding later in the day. She felt almost giddy at the prospect. Not only would it be wonderful to have a horse under her again, she could not imagine more charming company than the Colonel.

She tidied the room, then dressed for the day. Before leaving her room, she retrieved her riding habit, placing it on the bed to be changed into when Charlie returned to the house.

She enjoyed a nice breakfast of more fruit and cheese that the Colonel had thoughtfully provided, and considered where to start her day. Looking out of the back door, she saw Jocko bringing a group of men toward the house. Smoothing her apron, she stepped out to the back porch.

"Good morning, Sergeant," Rebecca greeted him as he climbed the steps. Rebecca knew that if it were possible she would have to form some sort of friendship with this man. He was important to Charlie, and she knew his opinion of her would go a long way in cementing her friendship with the Colonel.

"Mornin', Ma'am. Colonel Redmond has sent us to continue with the repairs to the property. Where would you like the men to start?"

She smiled. She was not quite sure what her answer would be. She was sure Charlie had ideas about where the men should be working. "That is entirely up to you, Sergeant."

"Well, then, Ma'am, I will set some of the boys off to the barns to start there. Is there anything you need here at the house?"

She at once thought of the roof. "Sir, there is a small problem with the roof, over the kitchen."

"Then a couple of our boys will take care of that for you."

"Thank you, Sergeant."

Charlie walked back to his command tent in the soft light of dawn. His step was light, as was his heart. He felt full of energy, even though he had slept very little that night.

There was still hope that this would be their winter quarters. There was still the chance his little fantasy of peace and a home could be played for at least a few weeks.

He slipped silently into his command tent. Jocko had been thoughtful; laid out on the bed was his normal day uniform, cleaned and ready to wear.

The Colonel lit the oil lamp on the command desk and dove into the paperwork that always accompanied the movement of troops. Requisitions for supplies, for ammunition, for winter boots and blankets and medical supplies and new tents—the lists were endless, and the need for supplies never fully filled. The number of shysters who supplied the Army was appalling, and often the quality of the supplies they did receive was shoddy at best.

He sighed deeply as he scratched his forehead while sorting through the reports. Sometimes the best he could do for his boys, no matter how hard he begged, borrowed, and called in favors from the past, was not enough. The last batch of boots they had received for the troopers were made of green leather—as soon as they got wet, the boots shrank and became stiff as planks. Well, if they could winter over here, the men could do some of their own repairs. It would not be enough, but it would help.

Completing the requisitions, Charlie turned to the daily report to Sheridan and his command officers. He was very careful in his wording, as he described to his commanding officer the site he hoped to use as his winter camp.

Nov. 6, 1864
   Outside of Culpeper, Virginia
   Lieut. General Philip H. Sheridan
   Department of the Shenandoah

Dear General Sheridan,

As you recommended, I have been looking for a sound site for the 13th Pennsylvania to winter over. I believe I have found such a site, and am in discussion with the owner to facilitate this process.

We are currently camped outside of Culpeper, surrounding the railhead here. The position is excellent for a number of reasons. By controlling the railhead, our troops can control any shipments going either north or east out of Charlottesville. This position is something of a crossroads and positions our forces to be able to respond quickly to any requirement here on the eastern face of the Blue Ridge Mountains. We are only one day's hard ride from Fredericksburg, should the entrenchments there require our support.

The land here is designed to support horses. There is extensive pasturage and small creeks with clear, fresh water lace the land. In addition, it is a protected area, with rolling hills that extend out from the Blue Ridge, providing sheltered dells and soft valleys.

The men I brought east with me are settling in well, and the 13th is reintegrating slowly after the devastation of The Wilderness campaign. I have been extending myself, as always, to ensure the men have what they need, or as much of what they need as I can get them, given the problems that the War Office seems to be having with suppliers.

If you could, please remind your supply officer to check into the last problem with shoes and boots we had. My men cannot have rawhide footwear for the winter.

The site I have selected to house my headquarters is the home of a young woman who was widowed by the war. The facility was a stud farm, with excellent barns and stables already present. Although there is nowhere near enough stabling for all of our mounts, it will provide us with the space to care for the injured animals properly.

In addition, there are extensive outbuildings that can be used to house our injured staff and as starting points for building out our half-timbered winter tents.

General, although this part of Virginia has been more physically damaged than some, the inherent richness of the land, with proper husbandry, offers the residents a hope for a reasonable life after this terrible conflict concludes. I would like to provide our hostess with the means to meet the conditions of the new order that will inevitably emerge after the armistice is reached. We have several mares, both horse and ass, that will never be sound enough to serve the Army again, but would be ideal brood mares to put this horse farm back into operations after the war. The 13th Pennsylvania has a tradition of taking care of the civilians who support them, as do I as their latest Regimental Commander. I seek your support for this plan.

Assuming I can negotiate a reasonable agreement for the winter housing of our troops here, I would like to request that Dr. Walker be assigned to my staff again. Many men are still suffering from the results of their respective battle experiences. Some of the men in the original 13th Pennsylvania have lingering injuries from The Wilderness campaign, and some of my original boys from the 49th Ohio still suffer the effects of malnutrition and parasites that resulted from that hell before Vicksburg. Her skill as a long-term care physician would be welcome.

I hope to complete the negotiations with the local residents within the next few days and be able to focus my energy on settling the men for the winter and establishing appropriate patrols to support the efforts to keep supplies from heading east to relieve Petersburg and Richmond.

Cordially

Chas. Redmond

Regimental Colonel

13th Pennsylvania Light Cavalry

"Well," he mumbled to himself. "That pretty much said it all. I know Phil Sheridan will assume I have taken a shine to the lady. And he will be right. But that pretty much makes the argument for the location." He had not mentioned that he intended to leave one of his personal mounts as the stud for Rebecca's little herd.

Reveille had sounded while Charlie was writing his dispatch to General Sheridan. He folded and sealed the document, dropping it into the dispatch pouch that hung on the tent pole, and set off on his usual morning rounds, starting with breakfast with the troops at the general mess or at one of the many small cook fires around the camp.

Mid-morning found Charlie reviewing the picket lines. He found the head hostler and the farrier in deep conference.

"Good morning, Tarent, MacFarlane." Both men snapped crisp salutes to their commanding officer. "What have we here?"

"Major Montgomery's primary mount, Sir. Appears she threw a shoe, and he rode her 'til she was dead lame. Her hoof is split—bad. Nasty rips where the nails came out, and the frog is bruised as well. There is swelling up into the leg; I cannot tell how bad it is right now."

MacFarlane, the farrier spoke up. "Yes, Sir. I agree. The only thing we can do for her now is bind the hoof, tack a shoe on to help keep it together, and keep the horse in a loose stall. The hoof is too damaged for me to be able to do anything with a special shoe."

"Is not this the third or fourth horse Montgomery's been through in the last couple of months?"

Tarent nodded vehemently in agreement. "Aye, Sir. He is hard on the horses, he is, Sir. He took another one from the reserves this morning." It was clear that neither Tarent nor MacFarlane approved of the man's horsemanship. "Permission to speak freely, Sir?"

"Yes, Tarent." Charlie absentmindedly scratched up under the injured horse's mane, one of those places horses loved to be tended.

"Something has happened to Major Montgomery, Sir. Before The Wilderness, he was one of our best officers, always caring for his horses. Now he rides like a crazy man—and he is hurting horses right and left."

"Thank you, Tarent, for your honesty. I will keep an eye on him, and do what I can. On a different issue, gentlemen, I would like to take our hostess out for a ride this afternoon. This looks to me to be a good place to settle in and winter over, and I would like to try and work something out with her. Your assistance will be appreciated. I believe Shannon is sidesaddle trained, if she is sound. If not, something with enough spirit to give Mrs. Gaines a good ride, that can handle her sidesaddle, but not so hard mouthed that she will have to saw away for control?"

"Aye, Colonel, this would be a good winter over. A hell of a lot better than last year's, if I may say so." Last winter, MacFarlane had been with Charlie, standing in the mud before Vicksburg.

"I saw her sidesaddle in the tack room, Colonel. Not much else there, but I have been looking over the stables. I think there is room for as many as fifty horses in the stables, and plenty more pasturage." Tarent had been with the 13th since its inception, but had taken to the new Regimental Colonel as soon as he saw Charlie's way with horses. "I will check on Shannon and, to be sure, I will find Mrs. Gaines a proper mount, whether Shannon or another. When do you want the horses delivered?"

"Why not say about two o'clock at the main house, Tarent? That gives me time to get through the officers' mess and take care of some other odds and ends."

"Aye, Sir. I will be there with both of them at two."

As he walked away from the picket lines back toward the officers' mess tent, Charlie thought seriously about what Tarent and MacFarlane had said. Montgomery was a bit of a problem. What Charlie had seen led him to believe Montgomery was one of those things he detested—an arrogant man who liked to intimidate those with less power than himself. His treatment of Miss Rebecca and of his latest mount was, as far as Charlie knew, typical of the man. But Tarent said that he had been a good officer before The Wilderness. What had happened to create this cruel, harsh man with no regard for others, man or animal? Well, maybe Elizabeth and Walt would be able to help when they arrived. Together, they were almost as good at healing broken souls as broken bodies.

Charlie entered the mess tent a few minutes after lunch service had begun. Lieutenant Colonel Richard Polk, Charlie's adjutant, was away on detail to Sheridan's supply depot, trying to sort out the problems they had experienced with some of the materials recently received—including the damned boots. Most of the men at the table were his field officers, each leading a company of between fifty and seventy troopers. There were several staff officers as well. Montgomery was missing.

"Good afternoon, gentlemen." Charlie seated himself at the head of the table, and immediately a plate of simple beans, rice, and pork was set before him. "Let us get right to it today, as I know we all have much to do. Company A, report, please."

Charlie worked his way around the tables, receiving updates on the status of each company and their various duties. There were the normal issues—supplies, problems with the boots, a few lame horses, a few men under the weather, and the long-term problems of men with serious injuries slowly returning to health. Charlie had intentionally blended the men together, so that some of the forces from the western troops were included in each of the companies, to bring them back to full strength.

After all of the officers present had briefed the Colonel on the status of their companies, Charlie asked after the missing Major Montgomery.

There was a rustling around the room. Most of the men present had heard Montgomery's comments the previous night as the man was polishing off another bottle of redeye whiskey. He had seen the lady up at the main house and wanted her for himself. His words had been harsh. "Who is this damned Colonel to move in and take over our Pennsylvania Regiment? It is bad enough that the man is a prude, but to embarrass me in front of that damned rebel whore is unforgivable. I will have the woman, and a Bucks County man to lead the regiment, or I am gone from here."

"I see. None of you are willing to tell me? Is it because he is one of your own, and I am the stranger imposed on you by the War Office? Or is there something else I should know?"

At that moment, Montgomery's lieutenant came bursting into the tent. "Excuse me, Colonel, but the medic is needed." Charlie nodded to his chief medic. Albert Samuelson was not officially enlisted, but instead was part of the Surgeon General's medical forces. Because of his quasi-military status, he was afforded the honors of a junior officer.

"Who needs the medic, Lieutenant?"

"Major Montgomery, Sir. His horse went down under him, Sir. I am afraid it is pretty bad."

"We will talk of this later. Get your Major taken care of now. I will be along in a bit."

As the medic and the young lieutenant left, Charlie turned to the other officers in the room. "So, will you tell me now?"

The senior officer from the original Pennsylvania troops, Major Swallow, cleared his throat. "Well, Sir, Montgomery's not been right since The Wilderness. He lost almost all of his forces in one day—men he had grown up with, friends and family. He used to be a gentle man. But since then, his hatred of Southerners has obsessed him. To him, the women are whores, the men are bastards. He has had a problem with you from the beginning 'cause he thinks you are a Southerner from your accent. Then you defended the lady up at the house. That was sort of the last straw for him. He was in his cups last night, and then up early this morning to take his company out."

Charlie listened without comment, and with a perfectly blank, neutral face. "Thank you, Swallow. Do any of the rest of you share Major Montgomery's concerns or attitude?" Charlie stood and walked the room, looking into the eyes of each man there.

"Do any of you question my commitment to the Union, which I swore to uphold when I took my oath nineteen years ago, and have reaffirmed every four years since then? Do you think that because I have the accent of a South Carolinian, my love of this nation is any less than yours?" Charlie's voice was deceptively gentle. The questions were asked as if he were genuinely puzzled and trying to figure out the situation. The barbs were buried deep.

He continued pacing the room, looking into each man's eyes, an open look of questioning on his face. Ruminatively, he continued, "You know, I signed on in Philadelphia in 1845, and faced the blood and rain and sweat and fear of Buena Vista in 1847." He moved to the next man.

"There were forty-seven hundred of us. Santa Ana had over twenty thousand men. Still, we won." As he looked into Major Andrews' eyes, the man flinched at those odds.

He moved on. "From there, I worked my way up in the Army, one step at a time. When we stood in mud for weeks in front of Vicksburg, where I was born did not matter."

Charlie watched as several heads dropped, each man had his eyes focused on the table before him.

"When I first met with you in the hospitals and reserves in Maryland after The Wilderness, you seemed to welcome the fact that we wanted to keep the 13th intact, and fill your ranks with experienced troops rather than disband your regiment. Where I was born did not matter."

The Colonel paused for a moment and swallowed before continuing.

"When we stood with General Sheridan at Cedar Creek, it did not matter. When your guts seized up because you were drinking bad water, and I saw to it that you were all cared for, it did not matter. When our own turned on us at Brandy Station, where I was born did not matter. So if you have a problem with me now, tell me."

Charlie had completed his circuit of the mess, and stood behind his seat at the table. A long silence gripped the tent, as these men, who had been through hell and back, recognized that their new Colonel had seen things and done things as horrific as they had in defense of the Union. An embarrassed rustling and surreptitious eye contact among some of the senior officers was all Charlie needed to see. In a much gentler voice, he released them from their discomfort.

"Gentlemen, shall we assume this conversation never happened, and was never needed? Now, we all have much to do. For your information, I am off to see what I can do about securing us at least decent winter quarters. I plan to check on Montgomery before I go."

Charlie walked out of the mess tent, stopping to have a word with one or two of his officers as he went. If Montgomery had let his obsession get out of hand with the troops, Charlie needed his commanders to find it and dig it out before it created irreparable rifts in his organization. In the spring campaign ahead, these men would have to work together as a well-oiled machine. It was time to start making sure there were no broken cogs in the workings.

He hurried over to the infirmary where the medic was working feverishly over Montgomery. The damned fool had ridden out on an unordered scouting trip while he was still drunk. His batman was there, looking grim and disapproving. His lieutenant was looking sickened.

Charlie caught the medic's eye and got a neutral shrug in response to his unspoken question. Montgomery's condition was questionable at best.

The lieutenant was fading. He was sweating and a sickly shade of nauseous green. Charlie took the young man out of the infirmary tent. "Tell me what happened."

"Major Monty was...I do not know. He was not right. He drove us all at a hard pace this morning, like he was looking for something or someone." The lad stopped to gulp at the water Charlie offered him from the small cistern beside the door. "There was a fence that he drove his horse to—it was not a coop, it was a hard fence—stone base and rails. The horse—that big buckskin gelding the Major rode as a backup—you know the horse, Sir, I have seen you ride him— anyway, the horse refused. He turned him and tried again. The horse refused again; and the second time, he threw Major Monty."

That glazed look came over the boy's face again. His voice came out as a dull monotone as he spoke. "Major Monty grabbed the reins and hauled the horse's head around, then took his crop to the horse —from the ground. He cut him—all around the head and neck. Cut him hard with the crop. Finally, the horse reared up and pulled the Major up with him. He fell back, and the horse kicked out. I could not see exactly what happened next, but they both went down, with the horse on top. When I cleared the horse, the Major was in terrible shape. The horse was in worse. He had a broken leg and one eye was gone. I had to put him down." The boy dissolved in tears.

Swallow came up just then, and took the lad under his wing. The boy was Swallow's younger cousin. Charlie surrendered the lad to him gratefully.

It was time for Charlie to go and attend to Rebecca. He took a deep breath. The short time it would take him to walk to the main house was a welcome respite. He needed the time to think. He needed the time to prepare for the afternoon. Cleaning up the mess that Montgomery created would have to wait until he had settled the regiment for the winter.

CHAPTER 4

Sunday, November 6, 1864

Charlie straightened his uniform and brushed the dust from his coat and trousers as he walked up to the house. *The next few hours will be critical*, he thought. *Perhaps Miss Rebecca will make her decision.*

As he got closer to the house, he remembered the duty that lay ahead of him, to serve as Miss Rebecca's personal maid. The thought of her standing before him in just her chemise and slip was enough to make his hands sweat.

Manfully, he strode to the front door, and was, as usual, greeted by one of his own troopers. *I have to do something about that*, he thought to himself. *She deserves to have some help around here that is hers, not one of my boys doing double duty.*

"Miss Rebecca is upstairs, Sir. She asked me to ask you to join her in her sitting room."

"Thank you, soldier." *Sitting room? Oh, yes, next to her bedroom.*

Charlie walked up the stairs, feeling trepidation in the face of his upcoming task. To touch her bare skin, just to touch her and find out if her skin was as soft and velvety as it looked in that pink dress. The idea was making Charlie slightly crazy.

He entered the sitting room and closed the door behind him, frowning slightly because Rebecca was not there. However, the door to the bedroom was ajar. Softly, he rapped on the door.

"Come in, my elegant Sir." Rebecca's voice was filled with laughter. The prospect of the ride had made her bright with anticipation.

Opening the door just enough to let him pass, Charlie slipped into the room. The vision before him stopped him cold for a moment.

She was standing in the sunlight streaming through the windows. In the light, her golden hair, pinned up for riding, formed a halo around her head. The bare skin of her neck and shoulders had a soft glow, and was set off by the simple white chemise and slip she wore. Charlie's mouth went dry; his throat seized up, and breathing was, for a long moment, not possible.

"Oh, Colonel, I am so excited. It has been so long since I have been able to ride. Please, give me a hand here so we can be on our way."

The Colonel nodded dumbly.

The habit was laid out on the bed. It was a lovely green velvet, with a full skirt and a tight bodice that buttoned up the back. Charlie sorted out the skirt, then knelt and held it for Rebecca to step into. Her hand on his shoulder, she stepped into the pool of velvet. He could feel the warmth of her touch through his woolen coat, her thumb barely grazed his ear lobe, sending a shiver running down his spine, and he had to work to control his hands. That was hard enough, but with her body so close to his, he could smell her. Her body exuded a unique blend of lilacs and musk that made his stomach clench painfully.

Charlie stood, drawing her skirt up over her hips and tying the strings that held it around her slim waist. His fingers trembled, making it hard to hold the bow tight.

Rebecca stepped away and drew the jacket onto her arms, settling the fabric over her shoulders. She stood there, waiting for Charlie to button what looked to be about a hundred tiny buttons that would draw the fabric snuggly around her slender frame. She looked over her shoulder at him. "Well?"

"Uh, yes. Sorry. You are lovely in green, my dear lady." *You are lovely in anything. Your shoulders glow in the sunlight. Your hair is like spun gold. I would lay my lips on your neck and think I was in heaven.* Charlie shook himself out of the haze of desire that gripped him at the sight of her, and began the slow process of buttoning the garment.

The waist was tight, but that was not too difficult. The cotton chemise was there as a buffer between Charlie's trembling fingers and Rebecca's warm skin. As he moved up her straight, strong back, the chemise ended, and he brushed his fingers against her skin, feeling the heat of her body, the silk of her, as he continued to fasten the small buttons. By the time he finished the last button on the high collar, he was sweating and trembling.

They stood there for a moment, his hands resting gently on her shoulders. She turned her head and softly brushed her lips over his fingers. "Thank you. You make the best lady's maid I have ever had."

Charlie stood there, unable to move for a moment. From somewhere in the distance, they heard the neighing of a horse.

"Come on, Colonel Redmond. The horses await us."

Charlie shook himself and stepped forward to take Rebecca's hand and escort her downstairs to their mounts.

"**O**h, my. She is beautiful!" Rebecca went to the solid mount that was obviously prepared for her. In the afternoon sun, Shannon's coat looked almost golden, her mane and tail a soft buff blonde lighter than her coat. She was a good-sized horse, built like a warmblood but with the gentle eye of a saddle bred. And at over sixteen hands, Rebecca's head did not top the amiable beast's withers.

Rebecca stood waiting expectantly for Charlie to lift her into the saddle. He took a deep breath to steady himself and laid his hands gently around her slim waist. She set one hand on the saddle, the other on Charlie's shoulder. "Ready?" he asked. She nodded confidently, and he lifted her gracefully into the saddle.

She settled herself in and adjusted her skirt to lie comfortably.

Charlie stepped away and ducked under his own mount's neck. In the moment when he was hidden from her gaze, he pulled his handkerchief out and wiped his sweating forehead and upper lip. The heat that consumed his body was not from the weather—that was cool and crisp. The woman beside him, on the other hand, made fire tear through his veins with even the most innocent of glances.

Rebecca took a moment to put on well-worn riding gloves. "Come on, Colonel. Let me show you my land. It is the most beautiful place in the world, I do believe."

"Well, then, Miss Rebecca, which way would you like to go?"

"That is entirely up to you, Colonel. I am at your disposal."

"Then, Ma'am shall we make a circuit? I have seen the northern and eastern parts of your property, but I am sure there is more." Charlie nudged his horse into an easy walk down the carriageway. Rebecca joined him and they rode to the road knee to knee, chatting as their horses walked along companionably.

"There is much more. I am sure you will find all kinds of things that will interest you."

"I am sure I will. I have lived with horses for many years, Ma'am. From what I have seen, this is the most beautiful horse country I have ever been in."

"Well, as I said before, Sir, I have never been out of Virginia, but I cannot imagine a more beautiful place."

"I thought Bucks County, Pennsylvania, where I did my basic training for the Army, was spectacular horse country—rolling hills, sweeping pastures and plenty of water, but there is something about this place that is truly special. I have not been able to decide if it is the colors, the mountains like lavender ghosts in the west, or something as intangible as the quality of the air that make this place so unique."

"Indeed. There is just something very special about the land here. My father always told me when I was growing up, that God first created Virginia; then he did everything else."

Charlie chuckled at that conceit. "Well, Ma'am, perhaps he was right. All I know is that even with the neglect of the past years, this is the loveliest land I have ever seen. The only thing I miss is the smell of the ocean."

They reached the end of the drive and turned right onto the dirt road that ran off to the southwest. Behind them lay the road to Culpeper and the encampment of the 13th Pennsylvania; before them lay fields that had been allowed to go fallow in the years since the war began, for lack of anyone to plant and tend them. Charlie saw a land rich with possibilities, nurtured over the years by loving hands, but now being slowly reclaimed by nature. All this land needed was some tender husbandry to become a spectacular horse farm again.

Rebecca drew him out of his contemplation of the vista before him. "I suppose, through the years you have seen many interesting places."

"Well, I have been all around the United States. Most places were pretty much the same—an Army camp or fort, with the opportunity to go into town occasionally. But I grew up in Charleston, which is a beautiful city with a spectacular harbor. I have spent some time up in New York and along the Canadian border, some time in Pennsylvania, and a tour of duty at Fort Pulaski in Georgia."

Charlie's voice changed subtly, as he recalled the places he had been and seen in the past three years on the western front. "Then I have been out along the Mississippi, but that was different."

"Why? What made it different?"

In a very tight voice, he responded, "I was at Vicksburg, Ma'am. It was not the way to see the Mississippi lands at their best."

"I am sorry, Colonel. I certainly did not mean to pry."

"No, Ma'am. You did not pry. It is just that Vicksburg was a terrible time." Charlie took a deep breath, shaking off the more gruesome memories that came to his mind whenever the subject arose. "I will say that the Mississippi River is an amazing thing. I have never seen such power, such an awe-inspiring sight. It is like the greatest highroad you have ever seen, multiplied a hundred times. But it is also alive, this great, powerful beast rolling along."

"Then maybe one day, you will go back there, so you might enjoy it properly."

"Perhaps, Miss Rebecca. Would you like to visit such places?"

"Oh, why, yes, of course. I am just not sure what the future shall bring when the war is over. So, for the time being, I must think of the here and now, and not concern myself with dreams of distant places and new people."

Charlie's heart went out to the woman who was facing a future no one could predict, with no allies, no resources, and no hope; just an implacable determination to survive. "Well, Ma'am, I hope you will consider my offer. It is meant to provide you with the means to have, at least, a sound foundation on which to build when the war is over."

"I have thought about it, Colonel. I must admit, at first I was hesitant. Then I realized you need a place to winter, and my land could only benefit from being used again. I am not sure what some of the local gossips will have to say about it, but I find I really do not care. If you would like to stay for the winter, Colonel, I would be very pleased."

Somewhere in Charlie's heart, another small window of hope and gratitude opened. "Ma'am, I would be more than happy to stay. My men and I need the rest, and this is a lovely place. We hope not to inconvenience you, rather perhaps to help you get the place back in shape."

"Colonel, I will gratefully accept any help you wish to give. However, I can only imagine the amount of work your men will have to do to prepare your own camp. I do not want to be a burden to you, Sir."

"It will be no burden, I assure you. I was hoping to use your stables, barns, and other outbuildings for part of our winter quarters—that would allow us also to put them back into shape for your needs." Charlie paused, concerned that his personal desires were perhaps inappropriate, then continued, "I was wondering. Is there a farm office I might be able to use for my office, rather than using my tent over the winter?" He hoped the office was in the main house, as some were. It would mean he could be closer to her. And being closer to Rebecca was a prospect that Charlie found very attractive.

"There are many empty buildings you could use. Please choose whichever one will suit your needs."

Ah well, perhaps I asked for too much. "I was also thinking of bringing in a full medical staff. I am not sure if you were aware of it, but half of our regiment was at The Wilderness and the other half are survivors of Vicksburg, so medical attention continues to be very necessary. I had thought to offer the medical services to the community as well, to perhaps do some small bit to ease the strain of our presence."

Rebecca's gentle smile lit her face. Directed at Charlie for the small kindness that he was more than able to offer, it lit his heart. "I must admit, Colonel, every time you speak, you amaze me. You have such a kind heart. You really care for those around you. You are a very special person, Colonel Redmond. I will also tell you now, that no matter what may happen in the future, I feel honored to have met you. I wish it could have been under different circumstances."

Charlie's response was far more serious than Rebecca expected. "Ma'am, I am a career soldier. Contrary to what most people think, we career soldiers may be more devoted to the idea of peace than anyone else in society, for we know the alternatives first hand. This war has been a terrible thing for our country, pitting brother against brother, father against child. I would give anything if the political leaders of our nation could have found another way to settle their differences. Yet I must say, had it not been for this war I would never have met you, and my life would be poorer for that."

In that moment, Charlie was all male, a charming gentleman. "You certainly do know how to turn a lady's head, Sir. Somewhere there must be a lady waiting for her gallant Colonel to return."

Rebecca's words ripped through the Colonel's soul, once more reminding him that what he appeared to be was a façade to the rest of the world. Because of that, there was no hope of a life outside the Army, for a home, or a loving wife. Rebecca could not see his face, as he had nudged his horse a step or two ahead of hers, but a painful yearning and emptiness darkened his features for a moment. In a low voice, laced with his own personal sorrow, he responded. "Nay, Ma'am. I am a solitary soul. Seemingly meant to walk along alone, for as you know, there are few who would join with a man such as I."

Rebecca plowed on; oblivious to Charlie's pain and consumed by her own curiosity and fascination with his situation. "I will admit the idea is new to me, Colonel. But, I am sure there are others who would be delighted to share their life with you. You should not be alone. You deserve only the best things life can bring you."

Her words cut like a knife. *I deserve exactly what I have. Nothing. No hope. No love. I am a thief in the night, stealing what little shreds I can, because I know that no woman who knows the whole sordid little story would ever want the likes of me. I have to stop misleading her like this.*

Aloud, he answered her gently. "Would that I and others could agree with you, Ma'am. Were you to know..." Charlie's voice trailed off for a moment. He cleared his throat, seeking to change the subject quickly; any further discussion would be more than even his stoicism could endure without cracking.

"The land here looks to have been under cultivation at one time. Is this where your family grew the corn and such?"

"Yes, we grew that which was required to keep the horses healthy and happy. Our surplus, we sold in town. It has been a long time since it has been planted."

Rebecca looked out over the fallow land, seeing it in her mind's eye as it had been before the war had changed everything. A soft chuckle escaped her lips. "My mare, Ginger, would often find her way out here to try the early growth. It used to drive my brother and my husband to near distraction. She definitely had a mind of her own, and a taste for sweet corn."

"You loved that horse very much, I think."

"I did. She was a wedding gift to me from my father. My husband tried to claim her as part of my dowry, but I let him know right away that she was mine and belonged to no other."

"May I ask?"

"You may ask me anything, Colonel."

"What happened to her?"

"Ah, well, she was taken from me when they started commandeering things to help the war effort. The Confederate soldiers took everything that was not nailed down. What you found me with is most of what I was left with."

"Oh, my dear lady, I am so sorry. I wish there were some way I could make all of the pain go away, as if it had never occurred. Alas, I cannot. But my men and I will do what we can to at least leave you and this community in more comfortable circumstances when we depart."

There was an awkward pause before Charlie changed the subject. "On a lighter note, Ma'am, how do you find Shannon as a mount?"

"You are very kind, Colonel, your company is very soothing. I do so enjoy it. And Shannon is a fine girl." She gave the mare a firm and loving pat on her broad neck. "She is very well behaved, and I can tell she is a smart one, as well. I am sure if given the chance we would find her happily tasting the sweet corn."

The Colonel laughed heartily, "She has a love of the tender shoots that will become the husks—very hard on a corn crop is my Shannon girl. She goes sweetly, Ma'am. If you were up for it, I think you would find her gaits smooth and exhilarating."

"Colonel, with you as my guide, I believe I am up for almost anything."

"Well, Ma'am—this is a lovely swath of pasturage we are coming on to the right. Shall we ride toward the mountains for a bit? And you can put her through her paces."

"That would be lovely, Sir. I must admit to feeling a bit selfish in not wanting to return home. This fine animal and your tender company are so delightful; I would so enjoy extending our ride. If you do not have business to attend to?"

"Miss Rebecca, I am at your service for the entire rest of the day and evening. Come, Ma'am, your horsemanship is outstanding—I will race you to that copse."

Without another word, Rebecca spurred Shannon to a gallop. Mane and tail floating, muscles rippling, the big mare showed her paces willingly. Rebecca reveled in the joy of the moment, the freedom, the wind in her face, and a strong, responsive horse beneath her.

Charlie just caught up as they reached the small copse of trees that surrounded Gaines Run. Rebecca was laughing with pure pleasure, her skin flushed from excitement and the crisp air. A strand of hair had come free in the rush of the gallop across the field. The sight was enough to make Charlie's hands tremble with the desire to reach out and smooth that lock of pale hair back into place.

Slightly breathless, Rebecca turned. "Colonel, I believe our mounts have earned a drink and a rest. Let us walk for a bit."

"I am at your service, Ma'am." Charlie swung down from his mount, Black Jack, dropping the reins to ground tie the well-trained beast. He stepped over to Rebecca and offered her his arms to help her dismount. She could have let him put his hands around her waist and lift her down. Instead, she placed her hands gently on the Colonel's shoulders, and allowed herself to be lowered to solid ground by sliding into his arms. She stood for a moment looking into blue eyes that went wide, startled and showing their owner to be at a loss for what to do next. She lowered her own eyes, blushing just a touch. "Thank you, Sir."

For a moment, that same endearing look of innocence she had seen the night before when he stood at the door of the parlor, flowers in hand, flickered across his features. Then the Colonel returned, charming and polished.

"Ma'am, it is entirely my pleasure. Time spent in your company is a sanctuary such as I have not known before."

"You flatter me with your kind words." Looping her arm through Charlie's, she set them off at a slow pace.

Charlie gathered up the reins and led the horses with his free hand. In a very gentle voice, Charlie responded, "No, Ma'am, I do not flatter you. To me, being here with you is a little touch of Eden to a lonely soul."

"Then I am very glad you came. And I am even happier you are staying for the winter. I, too, have been alone for too long, Colonel. Could I...I mean would you...you be available for supper tonight?"

"Ma'am, I would be honored to join you. I can think of no place I would rather be."

"That is wonderful, Colonel. Neither can I."

"Shall we ride again, Ma'am? The afternoon is slipping away."

Rebecca nodded her agreement. If she was to host Charlie at dinner, she had to get back and find something worth eating.

Charlie clenched his jaw a bit and stepped up to lift her into the saddle again. The warmth of her slender waist between his hands, the pressure of her hands on his shoulder sent ripples of wanting through his frame. *Dear God, how this woman touches me; and yet I think she does not know...*

The ride back to the manor was uneventful. They followed the winding course of Gaines Run, past the kitchen garden, with herbs and vegetables that were the mainstay of Rebecca's diet in these hard times, past the small farrier's and overseer's cottages. Finally, the run spilled out into the pond at the base of the long rolling lawn and gardens that graced the rear of the main house.

They walked around the pond, admiring the mountains in the distance and the lovely colors of fall that were just beginning to paint the trees in brilliant oranges, reds, and yellows. As they approached the house, Rebecca reminded Charlie that his services as a lady's maid would be needed once more.

Oh, Lord. Dressing her was hard. Undressing her is going to be worse. I am a gentleman. I am a gentleman. I am a gentleman.

Charlie rushed through unbuttoning the lovely, tight jacket of Rebecca's riding habit. He slipped the ties of her skirt, and then backed away, trying not to look at the soft skin of her shoulders, the tender curve of her neck. "Uh, I forgot, I need to go and check on Montgomery. I will be back in time for supper." He turned to go, pausing at the door. "Thank you for a truly delightful afternoon, Miss Rebecca. I hope we can repeat it soon."

As he rode away from the house, Charlie slumped in his saddle. *How can I keep doing this? I have got to get that woman a lady's maid, or I will die before the end of the year.*

He hurried back to the camp, dropping the horses off with one of the troopers at the picket line, then making his way directly to the infirmary. He entered quietly, looking around to catch the medic's eye. Samuelson moved to him silently, and motioned for both of them to step outside. "I am sorry, Colonel. There has been no change. He took a massive blow to the head, as well as to the chest and shoulders. One arm is broken, as are several ribs. I have set the arm. I am afraid, with the swelling, that he may have a skull fracture. There is nothing we can do but keep fluids going into him a little at a time, hope we do not drown him in them, and wait."

Charlie shook his head. "Well, do the best you can. Oh, by the way, Mrs. Gaines has agreed to let us winter over here, so we will be setting up a proper hospital. I have asked headquarters, and hope Dr. Walker will be joining us."

Samuelson's face lit up. Charlie was not sure if the pleasure his chief medic took in Dr. Walker's company was because of the doctor's skill and kindness, or because of her friend and sometimes medic, Mr. Whitman's imminent arrival.

Working his way through the camp, Charlie stopped and talked with various members of his regiment—a sergeant here, a trooper there, checking on his men as he moved through the camp, naturally reaching out to ensure that he had a personal relationship with each man.

By the time he returned to his own tent, Jocko had been there before him. Obviously, he had been up at the main house and knew where the good Colonel was supping that night. Laid out on his cot was Charlie's only suit of civilian clothing, a walking suit of soft wool in a dove gray. Lying beside the clothing was a small bouquet of flowers and a twist of coffee. Charlie smiled. Jocko was such a confirmed romantic. With the memory of the day's gentle touches still tingling through his body, Charlie set off to see if he could be a gentleman without being a soldier.

Rebecca could only smile as Charlie entered the house. She was amazed to see him in his suit. She did not even try to wipe the beaming smile from her face. She noticed that a bit of Charlie's hair had fallen down over his forehead, and for the briefest of moments she was tempted to reach out and smooth it back into place. However, she found her hands otherwise occupied when he handed her a bouquet of fresh flowers. "Thank you, my dear Sir. They are lovely."

"You are most welcome."

"Come, Charlie, dinner is ready."

She led him to the back parlor, where she had set up a small table near the window. The room was softly lit with a lamp and candles. Rebecca let Charlie settle down at the table, and then she began preparing him a plate.

"Miss Rebecca, I can do that."

"Nonsense, Charlie, let me. I rather enjoy it." She finished the plate, setting it in front of him before taking her own seat.

Charlie watched her prepare her own food, then settle a napkin across her lap. She looked at him and smiled. "Would you like to say grace?"

He nodded, reaching across the table to take her hand. Once the prayer was given, he expected her to move her hand, but to his great surprise, she did not.

"I want to thank you for the ride today. It was delightful. Your Shannon is a wonderful animal. I would dearly love to have a beast from her line."

"You handle her as if you two had known each other forever. It is a testament to your riding skills. I have never seen a lady such as yourself who handles the reins so well."

"I grew up on horses. Before I was old enough to ride my own mount, my father would take me on his. He said I was holding the reins before I was walking."

"It shows."

"After dinner, I have a surprise for you."

"For me? Ma'am, really you should not have gone to so much trouble."

"Trust me, it was no trouble. Now eat your dinner. Then we will have some of that wonderful coffee you brought, and I will give you your surprise."

After supper, Rebecca settled Charlie on the davenport in front of the fire while she made coffee. Returning to the parlor, she found him with his head back and his eyes closed. Placing the tray on the table, she touched him on the knee. "Are you tired, Charlie? Would you rather go to bed?"

He sat up immediately. "Oh no, Miss Rebecca, I am fine. The fire was just so comforting."

"It is nice. I must admit I would not have been able to get it started if it had not been for one of your young men. The flue was stuck. He wrestled with it for quite a while before it came free. Then

I am afraid he found himself covered with soot. He was quite the picture."

"Which man was it?"

"He said his name was Corporal Duncan Nailer."

Charlie gave a knowing nod. "Duncan is a good boy. I assigned him to the stables to help with the horses. He was expecting to fight again after The Wilderness, and I think he has resented me for not allowing it, but there is something about him that is not quite right. He seems, I do not know, slow. I am told he is quite an excellent soldier, and certainly his record indicates that, but somehow I wanted to protect him a bit."

"I noticed that, but I think it is just that little stutter he has. I am sure he has been tormented all his life because of it."

"I know some of the men have commented, which is why I put him in the care of my hostler. He is a kind, gentle man who takes each young man and treats him like a son."

Rebecca poured coffee, handing a cup to Charlie, and then she got up, and moved to the mantle. She paused for a moment then pulled the item down, tucking it behind her back. "Charlie, I have something for you."

"Rebecca?"

She turned, looking down at him. Then she removed the book from behind her back. "I found this yesterday, and I thought you might like to read it."

"Oh, Miss Rebecca." He took the book, running his fingers over the soft leather cover. "I really cannot -"

"Of course you can. You mentioned to me that you enjoyed philosophy. I am afraid I do not have any volumes of that nature, but maybe you will enjoy this. It is a collection of poetry."

"I am sure I will find it very enjoyable." He gave the davenport a pat with his hand. "I believe I would enjoy it more if you would allow me to share it with you. May I read a few pages?"

"Oh, that would be wonderful. Your voice is very soothing, perfectly suited for readings."

Charlie laughed. "I am sure my men would not agree with you, Miss Rebecca, but I would be delighted to read for you."

Rebecca prepared her own coffee, and then got comfortable on the davenport next to Charlie. He smiled when she sat very close to him, turning beautiful green eyes to him in expectation.

"Well..." He cleared his throat gently. "Yes, let us see here."

Charlie glanced to Rebecca; she was relaxed, with her eyes closed and her hand resting gently on his leg. He had been reading for almost an hour when he noticed her breathing had gentled considerably.

"Miss Rebecca?"

"Hmm? Yes, Charlie?" She had a slightly dreamy look on her face as her eyes opened to look at him.

"Would you like to retire?"

She sighed. "Well, as much as I hate to admit it, I am rather tired. I do believe our lovely ride took more out of me than I had anticipated."

"Then, dear lady, I will take my leave of you so you may —"

"Leave? You mean you will not be staying?"

"I —"

"Charles Redmond, let us please put this behind us now. I offered you the use of my bed while you are here, and I would think you would understand that is meant for every night; I should not have to invite you every evening."

The Colonel could not stop the reddening of his cheeks; he just hoped it was not readily visible in the low light. "Yes, Ma'am, I will remember."

"Good. Now shall we adjourn upstairs?" She stood, offering her hand to him. "I am sure we will both sleep very soundly tonight."

Somehow, I doubt that my dear Rebecca. You have no idea of the things you do to me when you lie so close at night. He shook his head and allowed himself to be led upstairs.

Rebecca took her sleeping gown and went into her sitting room to change, leaving Charlie in the main room to get dressed for bed.

He was quick about it, wanting to be in bed by the time the lady returned. He had just pulled the covers up when she came back in. He swallowed hard when she passed in front of the window and the moonlight showed her body through the light material of her gown. Even in shadows and silhouette, her figure made him lose his breath. He was sure if there were ever a time when he might be graced with actually laying his eyes upon her, his heart would beat out of his chest.

Rebecca got into bed and rolled over to face him. "Good night, Charlie."

"Good night, Miss Rebecca." He turned over and lowered the wick on the lamp, putting the room in near darkness, except for the moonlight from the window. He nearly jumped out of his skin, and the bed, when he felt her touch his shoulder.

"Charlie? I forgot to ask. How is your shoulder?"

"It is fine, Miss Rebecca, really."

"You are sure?"

"Yes, Ma'am. I am definitely sure."

"Sleep well, Charlie."

He lay there listening to her breathe, hearing the soft sighs and moans as she shifted to get comfortable. He intentionally slowed his breathing and closed his eyes, trying to relax. He was nearly asleep when he felt it happen; she rolled over and curled up next to him. It was all he could do to keep from whimpering. Instead, he just took a deep, calming breath and prepared for a long night.

Rebecca felt strong hands on her shoulders. Resting there, comforting her, making her feel safe. She could feel warm breath in her ear and on her cheek, soft lips caressing her neck.

She closed her eyes, just letting all these pleasant sensations wash over her body. She could not stop the soft groan that left her lips. Her breathing picked up, her lips grew dry as she pulled in deep breaths to try and calm her racing heart.

"Rebecca..."

"Oh..." she moaned, leaning back into the body behind her. Her

hands traveled to the arms that encircled her waist from behind. She stroked the skin, realizing for the first time that they were both unclothed. The skin under her hands was warm and soft. The touch was gentle in a way she had never experienced before, and her body was responding in kind.

"So lovely..." the voice whispered in her ear, as soft lips tenderly kissed her neck and jaw.

She closed her eyes, reveling in the feel of the gentle touches and the soft words. She reached back, caressing the side of her lover's face. She could feel short hair and smooth cheeks. She moaned again, when lips kissed the tender flesh of her palm. "Please..."

The hands that circled her waist slowly moved over her body. One caressed her stomach, while the other left blazing trails from her hip to her shoulder. Rebecca's senses were on overload. She did not understand the way her body was reacting; she could feel her pulse racing and her stomach fluttering wildly. "Oh, God..." she gasped when she felt tender fingers, brush over her nipple, causing it to go painfully hard. She could swear there was fire running through her veins, but it was delicious in its intensity. She did not know what she wanted exactly, but she knew she did not want this to stop.

"So soft..." the deep voice burred in her ear, as hands continued to roam her body, touching her in ways she did not know were possible.

Rebecca felt as if she would die from want. She wanted to turn around and face her lover; she wanted to know who it was making her feel so wonderful. Slowly she turned, and then suddenly her lover was gone.

Rebecca's eyes opened, her breathing ragged, her body still responding to the dream. She shifted to try and dampen some of the feelings coursing through her. When she did, she realized she was in Charlie's arms, held close to the strong body.

Her first reaction was to move away, so she would not disturb the Colonel, but she could not force herself to do so, and she ended up moving closer, allowing herself to find comfort there. She did not understand all the things that were in her mind. All she knew was that at this moment she was warm and safe for the first time in years.

Charlie laid quietly in the big bed, listening to Rebecca's breathing slow to that deep, regular tempo that indicated sleep. As she had each night before, she rolled to face away from him, cuddling into his arms. He rolled onto his side and curled around the smaller woman, sheltering her in his arms, comforting her sleeping form with the heat of his own body. The aroma of her hair filled his nostrils with the memory of lilacs. Slowly, he drifted into sleep.

Slowly, he ran his hands over her slender form, caressing the curve of her arm, the sweep of her back from her shoulder to that lush flaring of her hips and the soft curve of her nether cheeks. Slowly, he traced the line of her spine through the thin fabric of the nightgown clinging to her warm body. His hands brushed her silken hair from her slender neck. Slowly, using a touch that was barely there, he began tasting the smooth, soft skin at the base of her neck, across her shoulders, and up to the tender spot behind her ear. The pressure of his breath on her skin was more profound than the delicate touch of his lips.

He gathered her deeper in his arms, stroking soft circles on her firm stomach, sliding his hands over the sweet swell of her hips and up the front of her thighs. Her head rested on his right shoulder, and that lucky arm curled around her body, the tips of his fingers lightly stroking the tops of her breasts through the thin gown, venturing lower and lower until they just barely swept over hardened nipples.

As he continued to stroke and caress her, the nightgown seemed to melt away. Her silken skin lay under his fingers, the palms of his hands, his lips. Tenderly he tasted the skin of her neck and shoulders, the elegant lines of her shoulders and spine, the fullness of her firm derriere, then turned her towards him and sampled the silk of her breasts, the planes of her belly. He worshipped her body with his hands and lips, his tongue and, very gently, his teeth. He breathed her name like a prayer "Rebecca."

Charlie awoke suddenly. His arms were around Rebecca, whose hands lay over his own, affirming the tender grip she had on him.

Charlie's heart was pounding, unbound nipples pressed against Rebecca's shoulders through the cotton of a nightshirt and the flannel of Rebecca's gown. The heat in his belly was trying to consume him. Though Rebecca's touch was gentle, it was if she had placed shackles on Charlie's wrists, binding his arms around her body. Charlie pressed his forehead against the back of Rebecca's neck and sighed softly into her hair. The rest of the night was spent suspended in this most exquisite torture.

CHAPTER 5

MONDAY, NOVEMBER 7, 1864

Charlie rose before sunup. This night had been both better and worse than the preceding ones. Rebecca was beginning to invade his dreams as well as his heart, and the results were enough to put the usually even-tempered Colonel into a serious state of melancholy.

He gathered his clothing, pulling on his chest wrap, shirt, trousers, and coat. The rest of his clothes he bundled under his arm. Barefoot, he hiked back to his command tent, relishing the cold on his feet almost as if it were some sort of self-inflicted penance.

At this hour, the bathing area was always deserted. Charlie posted the sign that indicated the bath was in use, and then quickly submersed himself in the cold stream. A rough shave left him with a small nick on his chin, the price of his own shaking hand. Whether the trembling was from the cold or from his memories of the previous night was not a question Charlie wanted to consider too closely.

He prepared to don his day uniform—the outer shell of an officer. A wry, bitter smile played around his lips as he donned the undergarments that hid his true gender, and added a certain amount of padding to emulate the appendages of a man in his tight britches. The evil little voice in his head taunted, *One more piece of the fraud. Ah, Miss Rebecca. When I wear the trappings of a man, I am one to you. You flirt, you tease, and I respond as any true gentleman would. Yet divest me of my trappings and appearances, let me stand before you as a woman, and I am just a sister, safe and trustworthy. Perhaps I represent the best of both worlds to you—a charming masculine companion and a safe bed partner. I wish you understood what you are doing to me, dear lady, but I can never explain, can I?* Charlie put on his clothes for the day, and with them, his role as the dedicated Colonel.

He settled at his desk for his usual morning routine—reading and writing the dispatches, attending to the paperwork of command. The afternoon would be spent going over the supplies issues and planning the things needed to ensure secure winter quarters for the men. Also, Polk was due back today. With a little luck, his Second-in-Command might have found some cigars. His own stock had been stolen in the brush up at Brandy Station.

The morning dispatches included a telegram from Sheridan. It was terse, as usual, but exactly what Charlie needed to hear.

Permission granted. Negotiate fees. NMT 100 / month. Walker arrives Wednesday.

Well, first things first. The daily dispatch to headquarters had to be written and posted with the riders. He had established a chain of outposts along the way, so that communications between them could be sent quickly and more completely than the terse communication necessitated by the telegraph system. Post riders changed horses every hour, and thus could cover about twenty miles an hour instead of the more sedate six or seven hours that distance would take if the same mount was ridden all day.

Nov. 7, 1864
    Outside of Culpeper, Virginia
    Lieut. General Philip H. Sheridan
    Department of the Shenandoah

Dear General Sheridan,

As discussed, Mrs. Gaines has consented to allow the 13th Pennsylvania to winter over on her property. I will immediately negotiate terms with her, and assume we will issue demand scrip for the hundred dollars per month for November through March, as is customary. Considering the economic conditions here, I am certain this will represent a welcome influx of income for the community.

I further assume you have given Polk the necessary budget for setting up winter quarters. If not, please forward such information to me with the next dispatch.

As is policy, we will seek to build positive relations with the local civilian population. In terms of the condition of the land and facilities, this area has been more affected by the war than most other sections of northern Virginia I have seen. It may provide a foundation for beginning the re-constitution of our nation. As such, I will follow the guidelines set down by the President and General Grant for reconstruction of relations. It is my expectation that our mixed troops will be successful in establishing cordial relations with at least some of the civilian population.

Thank you for re-assigning Dr. Walker to our regiment. She is from this area and will be key to our efforts to form effective relations with the local civilian population. As usual, the 13th Pennsylvania will extend what support we can in terms of labor, medical care, and interaction to the community.

I must report a sad event within our forces. Major Montgomery, who has led one of the 13th Penn. companies since the regiment was created, has been badly injured in a riding accident. The injuries include a severe head trauma, and we are unable to predict the outcome at this time. I have written to his family, informing them of his condition, and will continue to monitor and advise you and his family of his status.

Integration of the forces from the remnants of the 49th Ohio into this regiment continues at a slow, but reasonable pace. I am confident our forces will be at full strength and working effectively as a team by the spring campaigns. The decision to distribute the men within the existing companies appears to have been a sound one.

We begin the process of settling into winter quarters immediately. I expect to be ready for winter inspection, no later than the fifteenth, assuming funding and resources are provided promptly.

Cordially
    Chas. Redmond
    Regimental Colonel
    13th Pennsylvania Light Cavalry

Once the necessary paperwork was filed, Charlie slipped into his old work clothes, intending to take a run through the extensive grounds before the lunchtime mess meeting with his officers and the afternoon of planning with Polk.

Although he had tried, Charlie had never found a running companion. Most of the men thought their Colonel's habit of regularly running long distances strange. He found it provided two benefits that they would never understand. First, it helped him keep his body weight down, his wind up, and his body structure more like that of a man. Second, he had found, quite by accident, that if he stayed more muscular and exercised intensely and regularly, it seemed to stop the regular monthly courses that plagued normal females every month. When he stopped exercising, his body resumed the irritating monthly cycle of a woman.

Running alone did present certain risks. Were enemy scouts to find a regimental colonel without escort, they would immediately attempt to capture or kill him. When he ran, he dressed as a regular trooper, with hobnail boots, britches, and a short, belted tunic. Unlike his officer's uniform, with its skirted, double-breasted frock coat, this uniform left nothing to the imagination. Charlie made sure that in every way, he presented the profile of a man.

He set out for a long run, heading east away from the encampment. He passed north of the main house, behind the stables and close-in paddocks, across an old hump-backed bridge over Gaines Run, and into the eastern pasturelands on the far side of the pond. After several days of not running, the exercise was a welcome relief, letting his body relax into the old rhythms, his eyes became his sentinels, watching for anything out of the ordinary and freeing his mind to deal with the problems of the day. By the time he had completed his circuit, passing over the log footbridge south of the pond and back up across the bottom of the back lawn to the stables, he had settled his mind to the task of planning for the winter camp, shoving the dream and the reality of the previous night to the back of his mind. For a while.

Richard Polk and his detachment rode into camp just as Charlie returned from his run. "Polk! Good to see you. Meet me in my tent as soon as you can. We are wintering over here." *Ah. A distraction. Something else to think about other than Rebecca and last night's dreams.* Charlie dunked his head in a bucket of water, and then hurried off to meet with his Executive Officer.

Polk swaggered into the command tent. "Greetings, oh fearless commander. I bring gifts from the great warehouse at headquarters —more cigars. And a small keg of that brandy you like so much." Polk's sense of sarcasm was irrepressible. With that cheerful greeting, he pulled up a small campstool and perched on the other side of Charlie's field desk. He took a portfolio out of his dispatch case and spread the papers in front of him.

"All right, I started by royally chewing out that greedy ass major at supply for sending us uncured leather boots. We went downhill from there and I am fairly certain at one point he called me a prick. But after two days of haranguing him and personally going through the supply depot and selecting what we needed, I expect a supply train to show up before the end of the week." Both men gleefully opened the small box of cigars, lit up, savored the first taste of the fulsome smoke, and set to work.

By time for the noon mess and the daily stand up with the rest of the command staff, Charlie and Polk had worked through all of the major plans for setting up the winter bivouac. Additional supplies would be needed, and Polk, with the regimental quartermaster, would attend to getting them by hook or by crook. The announcement was made at lunch, and each company had its marching orders.

By midafternoon, the entire regiment was swarming over the Gaines Cove property, sorting, cleaning, digging latrines, and generally setting things in order. Charlie set off to oversee the clearing of the stables.

Mrs. Williams entered the mercantile with a purpose. This was a very serious issue; somebody would have to find out if what she had been told was the truth. She stopped at the counter, waiting for the slightly frazzled man working behind it to notice her. Finally, he looked up.

"Mrs. Williams, what can I help you with today?"

"Nothing from the store, thank you, Mr. Cooper. Is Mrs. Cooper home?"

"Why, of course. Last time I saw her, she was in the kitchen. Please go in, if you like." He gestured to the door leading to the residence attached to the store.

"Thank you, Sir."

She entered the house, and he looked up to the heavens. "Lord, help us if that woman has latched on to something."

"Grace?" Mrs. Williams called as she moved down the hall.

"In here."

Mrs. Williams entered the kitchen, pausing to put her hands on her hips. "Grace, have you heard?"

The other woman turned around, wiping her hands on a towel. "Apparently not, Margaret. What has you so upset?"

"I was told this morning that Rebecca Gaines has Yankee soldiers on her property."

"Yes? So? What would you have Rebecca do, Margaret, take on a troop of Federal soldiers herself? You know there is not much she could do to stop them." She moved across the room and poured two cups of coffee.

"I understand that. But would you like to explain why in the world she was out riding yesterday with the Yankee Colonel?"

Mrs. Cooper was duly scandalized. "She was not!"

Mrs. Williams nodded as both women took a seat at the table to drink their coffee and have a proper gossip session. "She was out riding with him yesterday. Walking arm-in-arm with him, strolling like they were betrothed."

"Are you sure it was Rebecca Gaines?"

"Positive. Reverend Williams' errand boy was out fishing yesterday, and he saw them. Said she was dressed in a green velvet riding habit. Think of it, the widow of a Southern war hero gallivanting with a Yankee Colonel. It is shameless. And to top it all off, it was Sunday. She did not even attend services, but she was out with this man, doing God only knows what."

"Surely you do not think..." The rest of the question went unasked, but its meaning was quite clear.

"I think anything is possible. She has obviously forgotten her dear, departed husband, who fought and died for the glory of the Confederacy. Who knows what kind of things she is doing with that Yankee?"

"Do you think we should go see for ourselves? I mean, it is one thing to take the word of a boy, but it is entirely another thing to see with your own eyes."

"Yes, oh absolutely." Margaret nodded emphatically, "I do believe a visit out to Gaines Cove is certainly called for."

"Perhaps if Rebecca is under some sort of duress, we can find a way to help her."

"It is our duty as good Christians."

"Of course. I find it difficult to believe a good woman like Rebecca Gaines would willingly take up with Yankee rabble. I am sure there must be some sort of force being used against her."

"Do you think the Colonel and his troops have..."

"Oh, I hope not. I would hate to think of such a thing."

"Well, then I shall fortify our number by gathering a few more of the ladies from the church, and we shall just go out there and see for ourselves."

Thursday, November 10, 1864

"Sergeant Jackson?" Rebecca called from the back porch.

"Yes, Ma'am?"

"Could I borrow Corporal Nailer for a few minutes? I have two chests I need to bring out of storage."

"I can get those for you, Ma'am." Jocko climbed the steps, and then held the screen door for her. "After you, Ma'am."

"Thank you, Sergeant." Rebecca led the man to a storage space under the stairs. "They are in there. Two cedar chests."

He opened the door, looking in to find the items she was asking for. He pulled the first chest out and placed it against the wall. Then he pulled out the other and hoisted it into his arms. "Where would you like it, Ma'am?"

"In the parlor, I think."

Without another word, he took the first chest into the room, and then returned to pick up the second. As he placed it by the first, she followed him into the parlor. "There you go, Ma'am. Is there anything else?"

"No, Sergeant, but thank you very much."

"Welcome, Ma'am. If you need anything else, just let me know."

"I will."

Once he was gone from the room, she opened the chests to check the condition of the clothes inside. Her year of mourning her husband had ended on the fifteenth—the anniversary of the Second Battle of Auburn—and she was relieved. It would be nice to wear a little color in public again.

I think Charlie would love that blue dinner dress.

She stopped suddenly and considered her last thought.

Colonel Redmond. Charles Redmond. Charlie. Kind, gentle, sweet Charlie.

She considered the Colonel, tall, elegant, charming, as handsome a man as she had ever seen. She lifted the blue dress from the first chest. Looking at it, she smiled. Yes, Charlie would like this dress.

The more she considered it, the more confused she felt. There was no denying all those wonderful things about Charlie were true. However, there was that single something about the good Colonel that should not even allow her to think of him in such a way. On the other hand, she readily admitted to herself it was difficult not to think that way.

She realized why it was so easy to think of Charlie like that. The Colonel, for all intents and purposes, was a man. He lived every moment of his life as a soldier, riding and fighting along with the men he commanded. He had never had the opportunity to be a woman. *Perhaps he never wanted to.* She considered silently, slightly started by the thought.

She shook her head to clear her thoughts. Perhaps she had simply been alone for too long. Any companionship was a welcome diversion from the loneliness of her life.

She sighed and looked into the chest again, her eyes falling upon her wedding gown, the gown she had worn when she had married Mr. Thaddeus Gaines. A true man in every sense of the word, but most definitely not a gentleman like Charlie.

He had been indifferent to her most of the time, caring little for her or her feelings. It was only when she could serve his needs that he showed her any attention at all.

If he was entertaining prospective business partners or important members of the community, she was paraded out to be the perfect wife. When he had been drinking and wanted his more carnal desires satiated, she was expected to lie in his bed and perform her martial duties. His touch actually made her skin crawl, but as her mother had told her on her wedding day, it was to be expected and, if nothing else, tolerated.

He was never gentle, always taking what he wanted until he either collapsed on top of her or passed out. When it was over, she would always leave his bed, take as good a wash as she could, and then retire to her own room. Where, most of the time, she would curl up in a ball, hidden under the covers, and cry herself to sleep, hoping she would not be subjected to his brutality again anytime soon.

She was actually relieved when she found out that her husband had been seen in the company of less than respectable ladies. It had even been whispered that he had taken a number of the young slaves as well, although given his attitude toward the servants they did have; she suspected that was just rumor.

He treated his horses better than his slaves and, in her opinion, would not stoop to relieve himself with either. While she was saddened for the ladies of ill repute who had no other option than to surrender to him—for she could only imagine how he might treat them—she was relieved for herself. When he was finding his release elsewhere, she did not have to worry about him coming to her.

What made it worse was that her brother knew how she was treated but was powerless to stop it. He did not dare stand up to the head of the household. Once when she had been treated to a rough course from her husband that had left her bruised and hurting for days, her brother had threatened to do something about it, but Rebecca had calmed him down, telling him it would only make it worse for her. Her husband would most certainly take his revenge on his wife if her brother confronted him. Andrew had held her and sobbed, he told her he was ashamed of his failure to protect her, but she knew that given their situation, they had no choice but to submit to Gaines and his demands.

With tears in his eyes, her brother had agreed. And from that day forward, he had done everything possible to make his sister's life more bearable. They would share walks and go riding together, talking of their hopes and dreams. She smiled and sniffed, holding back the tears when she thought of her brother's dreams of travel and adventure. He wanted to travel, see new places, and meet new people. Rebecca was sure her brother would have left long before the war had it not been for the misery of her marriage. He stayed to protect her as best he could and, in the end, he had died for his selflessness.

Reaching further into the chest, she removed a small jewelry box. All her jewelry was gone now, but this box held treasures of far more importance. Cracking the lid, she removed a piece of paper and unfolded it.

September 13, 1862

Sharpsburg, Maryland

Dearest Sister,

I take the time while we have a break, to write and let you know I am well. They put me in the cavalry, telling me that my experience will serve the Confederacy well. I hope so.

I think of you every day, dear sister, wishing there was more I could do for you. I know you are unhappy, and while I am proud to serve, I wish I were still there with you.

I am sending some of my pay to you. I beg you, Rebecca, keep this money to yourself. You may find yourself in a position where you will need it. I will send more from each pay, as I have no real needs here. The Army provides everything I require.

When the war is over and I return home, we will take a trip together. We will go wherever you wish, to some place new and exciting. Just keep thinking about where it is we will go, and save the money for that.

I will be home soon, dear sister. Until then, please take care of yourself.

Love,
Your brother, Andrew

She wiped the tears from her cheeks and unfolded a second piece of paper. She looked down at the crinkled paper. It was dated September twenty-second. There it was, in the middle of the second column. This casualty list from September seventeenth had her brother's name on it. It was the last trace of him she had. His body had not even been returned home. He was buried someplace on the battlefield of Antietam, Maryland, far away from home. All she had left were these two pieces of paper, and the memory of how had he looked the morning he left.

She remembered the day she had been given the list. Her husband had presented it to her, and then told her it was the nature of war, and not to waste time crying over it. But she had cried, cried until he grabbed her by the arms, giving her a sound shake and reminding her that she was still his wife, bound to him and him alone. He told her that her brother had done what every good Southern man would do, and that she should be proud of him, not crying for him like a whimpering child.

At that very moment, Rebecca had realized her life was over, that she was truly alone in the world with only that man, whom she detested more with every passing day. When her husband had been called to serve, she had felt an odd combination of fear and relief. The fear came from the fact she would now be unprotected, and the relief that she would not be subject to him any longer.

She had never wished him any harm, and was truly saddened when he too had been killed; but deep in her heart, she felt as if the last year of her life had been a lie. She had worn the dark colors, as polite society had expected of her, but her heart never could truly mourn the loss of her so called husband.

Of course, his death had brought a completely new set of problems for her. After finding out Mr. Gaines had been killed, most of the slaves had taken the opportunity to run away. The ones who did not were taken away later, along with most of her belongings, when a band of renegade soldiers came through looting, and worse.

Because her land was backed up against rail lines, she had been subjected to her share of soldiers from both the North and the South. But this time, it was different; and the one thing that made it different was Charlie. Not only because of his secret, although to her it was only a minor part of it; more important was his courtliness and consideration. She admitted to herself it fascinated her, but she found herself hard pressed to think about it too much. She did not want to make any assumptions that might embarrass or upset the Colonel.

The plain and simple truth of the matter was that Rebecca Gaines enjoyed the company of Colonel Redmond, and she would do whatever necessary to continue building a friendship. Not only did she like being with him, he made her feel safe. Safe because of his strong presence and personality, and safe when he shared her bed, knowing that he would never harm her.

She folded the papers, putting them back in the box. She started to put the box back in the trunk, but thought better of it and placed it gently on the mantle above the fireplace. Returning to the chests, she removed a few of her favorite dresses, then combined the remaining clothes into one chest. At the very bottom of the empty chest, she found a small wooden box. Retrieving it, she opened it to find her father's pocket watch. She was delighted at this discovery, having thought it lost some time ago.

"Oh, Papa, I wish you were still here. I think you would approve of him." Tracing her fingers over the watch, she smiled at the gold timepiece, and then gently closed the lid. It too was placed on the mantle next to the box that held her brother's letter.

Sunday, November 13, 1864

Rebecca hauled her personal laundry into the washroom off the kitchen and prepared to clean the garments. A loud crash just outside made her curious. Taking a bucket, she went outside on the pretense of fetching water. She nearly laughed aloud when she saw a tilted wagon, and Charlie covered in a goodly amount of grease. Charlie and two of his men had apparently been changing a wheel on the wagon when one of the men lost his grip, sending the bucket of wheel grease down on their commander. She could tell he had been working just as hard as his men, and now that his uniform was covered in black splotches, he looked quite pitiful.

As he wiped the grease from himself in large handfuls, he did not notice Rebecca on the porch. He tried to replace most of the slippery paste into the bucket that had fallen when the wagon tipped.

"Colonel Redmond," Rebecca giggled as she set her water bucket down and walked out into the yard. "I dare say it is going to take a very strong lye soap to clean up that uniform. And even then, the smell may never come out. I hope you were not fond of that particular set of clothes." She unconsciously looked him over from head to toe, blushing when she reached the apex of his trousers. Yes, there were things she really wanted to know about how he managed his deception so well. Perhaps she would find the courage to ask him some evening when they were alone.

"These things happen." He smiled, slightly embarrassed as he wiped yet another huge glob of grease from his shirt. Charlie looked at the small woman. She had shadows under her eyes and her face was streaked with dust and, he suspected, tears. "Miss Rebecca, you look tired. Would you like to join us in the officers' mess for supper this evening? I cannot promise anything special, but at least it would save you from cooking for yourself."

"Colonel, I would be honored. And not having to cook tonight would indeed be a blessing!"

"Excellent. Then shall I call for you at, say, sundown? I rather need to finish this and then clean up." Charlie looked ruefully at his grease-smeared clothing.

"I shall be waiting for you, Colonel."

Charlie went back to work with the men and quickly finished replacing the wheel on the wagon. As the cotter pin was driven in, the good Colonel shrugged and grinned at his men. "Other than the small incident with the grease bucket, good job lads. Get cleaned up and have a good dinner. Tomorrow is going to be a long, hard day."

Trudging back to his own tent, Charlie hailed Jocko. The batman took a look at his charge, who was definitely the worse for wear. "Been having a battle with a wagon wheel, I hear. Looks like the wheel won."

"Thanks, Jocko. I need all the support I can get. How about letting the mess know Miss Rebecca will be joining us for dinner, and then meeting me at the bath shack? I have to get this grease off me. Between the sweat and the grease, I feel like a pig that has been rolling in a wallow."

Jocko's laughter was heard trailing behind him as he set off quickly to carry out the necessary errands and collect a clean uniform for Charlie.

The news that Mrs. Gaines was joining the officers' mess for dinner ran through the camp like wildfire. By the time Jocko got to the bathing shed with Charlie's clean uniform, every officer in the camp was lined up and waiting for a turn.

"Relax, boys, you will have plenty of time to pretty up. The Colonel still has to go and collect the lady." Jocko could not help but laugh at the eager young men. Dinner with a lady—even a rebel lady—was a treat.

Jocko entered the shed with Charlie's clothing. "Well, Colonel C, you have some competition out there. Every man jack of them is chafing at the bit to come in here and pretty himself up."

"What do you mean, competition, Jocko? She is our hostess, a charming lady, and one to whom I have been a gentleman and a friend. Anyway, as you well know, there is nothing more possible there."

"I only know what I see, Colonel C. And I see you trying to woo her, and I see her responding. You may have found more here than you bargained for."

Charlie raised a skeptical eyebrow at Jocko's romantic notions, and pulled on his uniform. With a shrug, he settled his coat over his shoulders and strode out of the shed. Interestingly, his face was a bit pink, but whether it was from the harsh soap he had used to remove the grease or from Jocko's comments was hard to tell.

"It is all yours, boys. See you at dinner. And remember your manners."

~

He made two stops on the way back to the house to escort Rebecca to dinner. The first was to the Mess Sergeant's domain, the great tent that housed the cooks for the regiment. Much to his relief, dinner was comprised of another small deer one of the scouts had brought in and some locally caught fish, rather than the usual Army ration of beans and salt pork.

His second stop was at the infirmary tent to check on Montgomery's condition. There, the news was not as good. The man was still unconscious and unresponsive. Trickling water into his mouth caused a reflexive swallowing, but that was about all the response they could get. "Thank God, Dr. Walker will be here soon. Maybe she will have a solution." Charlie agreed wholeheartedly with his medic.

Arriving at the main house just a few minutes later than he had planned, Charlie found Rebecca waiting for him in the small parlor at the rear of the house. He wrapped her shawl around her shoulders and offered his arm.

As one, the gentlemen of the regiment rose as Charlie escorted Rebecca into the mess tent. They clustered around her, escorted her to the seat of honor, and each in his own way showed her that Northerners could be attentive gentlemen, too. There was a festive atmosphere in the tent that night, and Rebecca rose to the occasion, flirting with some, listening with gentle sympathy to others, and being motherly or sisterly to the youngest members of Charlie's staff.

As the evening came to an end, Richard Polk quietly took Rebecca aside and handed her a hundred dollar chit. "It is for the first month's rental on the use of your property, Ma'am. I hope it is sufficient, but our budget does not allow for what the land is really worth."

Rebecca looked at him slack jawed for a moment. "Um. Thank you, Colonel Polk. I did not expect this. We hear so many tales of commandeering..."

"No, Ma'am. The 13th Pennsylvania always honors its obligations, one way or another. This is fair money, Ma'am, given honestly and openly. Payment you deserve for your kindness."

"Well, thank you, Colonel. I know you are aware it is most gratefully received."

With that, the two parted, one to return home, the other to prepare the rosters for the following day's activities, but a cautious understanding and respect had been planted between the two, one that would grow and serve them both well in the coming weeks and months.

"Miss Rebecca, may I walk you home? You look tired."

"Of course, Colonel Redmond."

Charlie gently draped Rebecca's shawl over her shoulders, then offered her his arm. They set out on the short walk back to the main house. Quiet reigned between them as Rebecca considered the hundred dollars in her reticule and what it could mean for her future. Finally, Charlie ventured a safe little conversational foray. "It has gotten chilly tonight, Ma'am."

Rebecca stopped for a moment and looked up at the night sky, blanketed with clouds. "Yes. I believe the chill is giving us fair warning of things to come." Rebecca once again put her arm through Charlie's.

"Miss Rebecca, I believe this place offers more shelter than my men and I have seen for a long time. We are all very appreciative."

"You are quite welcome. I must admit that when you asked to use the property, I certainly never expected to receive recompense. These funds are a most welcome resource. Thank you for arranging it."

"Thank General Sheridan when he comes to inspect, and he will —he always does. President Lincoln has issued orders that we are to do our best to help rebuild normal relations with our Southern citizens, particularly the civilian population. He is well aware of the difficulties that lie ahead in reconstructing the Union once this war is over."

"Do you ever take credit for anything you do, Colonel?" She gave his arm a playful tug then slipped her hand into his.

The small, chilled hand in his was more than enough to still Charlie's tongue. For a moment, he could not quite remember how to talk. All he wanted to do was to shelter the woman beside him as tenderly as he was sheltering the hand she had given. He shook his head slightly, then smiled gently. In the dark of the night, with clouds covering the moon and stars, their way was lit only by the lantern he carried. She could not see the wonder on his face.

"Umm, I take credit when credit is due, Ma'am."

"Credit is due, Colonel. Accept it. Enjoy it. Could I interest you in a hot cup of tea to ward off this evening chill? Perhaps we could build a fire and talk for a bit."

"I would be honored, Ma'am. Your company is always gratefully enjoyed."

"Wonderful. You can start the fire while I make the tea." She laughed softly. "Terribly domestic of us, do you not think, Colonel Redmond?"

"My dear Miss Rebecca, if you must know, I have never been domestic with anyone since I joined the Army. It is more comforting than you know to do so now with you. Which room would you like to have tea in, Ma'am?"

"The parlor."

"The front one or the rear one, Miss Rebecca?"

"Rear, I think. It is warmer than the front, and if the clouds move out, we might be able to see the moonlight on the pond."

"My pleasure, Ma'am." Charlie opened the front door for her. He lit a candle from the lantern he was carrying, and then a couple of lamps in the hallway. Handing her the lantern, he asked, "Shall I come with you to get the tea things from the pantry?"

"No, do not be silly. I know the pantry so well I could go in total darkness and still find what I need. You go tend the fire and then relax. You worked very hard today. I am surprised you are not on the verge of collapse."

"And you, my dear lady, look just as tired. I will have the fire going in two shakes of a lamb's tail, and then we can both unwind."

Entering the small parlor at the back of the house, he was pleased to note the wood box was filled and there was plenty of dry tinder. It even looked as if the fireplace had been cleaned. The boys had been busy. He laid the fire, putting loose tinder at the base, then laying the logs and packing moss into the crevices to speed up the process of creating a nice steady, warming flame. Within minutes, the fire had caught and a bright flame lit the small room.

A few moments later Rebecca entered with a tray, which she placed on the small table by the davenport. She smiled at Charlie, standing by the fireplace, watching the fire like a proper Southern gentleman. If it were not for his uniform...Rebecca found herself longing for Charlie's suit.

"You are in luck, Colonel. I managed to find a little honey. Would you like some in your tea?"

"I will share it with you, Miss Rebecca. I must confess, I have a bit of a sweet tooth." He thought for a moment, a shy smile softening his face. "You know, you keep giving me these little gifts. I think you will spoil me, Ma'am."

She fixed his tea, taking him the cup, gently caressing the back of his hand. "In just a short time, Colonel, I have discovered I rather enjoy spoiling you." She returned and fixed her own tea before taking a seat on the davenport.

Just that touch, coupled with the words, set Charlie's hand to trembling. Rather than rattle the teacup—or even drop it—he set it on the mantle to cool. For a moment, the shy boy was back in his eyes; then the Colonel returned. "Well, Ma'am, if I were a selfish man, I would say that you could just keep on spoiling me." He paused then and looked at her, his eyes lit with something she had never seen before. "I think I would like to be a selfish man, just a bit."

"Then please do. I will say that I, too, am being a little selfish. I think I may distract you a bit too much from your duties, by asking for so much of your time, but for some reason I just cannot dredge up an ounce of guilt."

"Ma'am, you know you can call upon me any time, and if it is at all possible for me to come to you, I will." There was an odd moment of intensity between them, and then Charlie picked up his teacup and took a sip, savoring the flavor and the hint of sweetness.

Rebecca looked into her teacup, trying to decide if her next question was beyond the bounds of their newly formed friendship, but she decided to press on. She really wanted to know Charlie and this was the only way. She looked to him with a shy smile. "Charlie, may I ask you a personal question?"

"My dear lady, you may ask me anything, and I will endeavor to answer you with all honesty."

"How do you do it? I mean, your disguise. Surely there must be times when it is difficult." She felt a heat rising to her cheeks as she tried to find the proper words. "I mean...how do you...umm..." She shook her head, more embarrassed than she had anticipated. "Well, I mean what about things such as relieving yourself," she finished in a rush, nearly so embarrassed she thought she might burst out laughing, though it was not a laughing matter.

A blush started at the tips of Charlie's ears and worked its way across his features and down to his collar. It was fortunate he had swallowed his sip of tea before she asked, otherwise, he might have sprayed it all over from pure shock.

He took a deep breath and remembered the promise he had made just seconds ago. "Well, in camp, Jocko and I have arranged that one of the privileges of command is privacy for such things. And in the field, well, there are always bushes—and I hurry." A weak grin, more nerves than humor, lit his face.

Rebecca burst out laughing, she simply could not help herself; but she quickly regained control. However, the grin was still firmly on her lips and a mischievous twinkle in her eyes. "I am sorry,

Colonel. I just cannot fathom you being that quick in those tight breeches." She cleared her throat gently. "Like the ones you had on today."

"Ah, well, um. They are not as bad as you might think. And a little talcum goes a long way in getting them off and on quickly." He grinned back.

All right, she could see she was just going to have to be blunt, because the suspense was too much for her. "That does not explain certain, um, attributes that are so readily on display when you are wearing them." She tried hard not to smile, but she could not help it; and she knew her face was bright red.

Charlie's blush renewed itself until his face was as brilliant as the flames flickering around the logs in the fireplace. "Well, you see, I, um, I am fairly handy with a needle, you see, and I, um, well, I make my own under things. A little artful padding and a snug fit..." He could not continue, and stared up at the ceiling looking, perhaps, for some divine intervention in this conversation. Still he plowed manfully on.

"It is not really that hard." With that, he could not help it. He scrunched his face up and closed his eyes, turning a truly amazing shade of red as he realized exactly how many ways what he had just said could be interpreted.

Perhaps the floor could open up and swallow him.

Rebecca did choke on her tea when he made that last comment. Half-coughing and half laughing, she added playfully. "I see. Well, I must say, Colonel, you do yourself proud."

Charlie dropped, boneless and awkward, into the chair opposite her and started laughing. The utter ridiculousness of the lengths to which he would go to mask his situation, to be unexceptional, to alleviate suspicion had all been revealed in a couple of simple questions. He could either laugh until the tears ran down his cheeks, or cry.

Gaining some small modicum of control, Rebecca pressed on. "I am sorry, Colonel. I did not mean to embarrass you. Perhaps I have asked too much. I am sorry."

"No, Miss Rebecca—you ask obvious questions, and ones that I have never had a friend who was close enough and trusted enough to ask, let alone for me to answer them. Carry on, brave lady. All my secrets are yours to bare." At the moment, Charlie looked like a young boy caught in some indiscretion and being brought to task for it.

"Oh, you are a brave man, Colonel," she teased a bit. "There are so many things I want to know. I am amazed at what you have done. I find it simply fascinating, and I do not mean that in a bad way. But what you have accomplished is truly astonishing. Would you mind explaining to me, how you...umm...find companionship."

The look of pain and loneliness that skittered across Charlie's face at that question was enough to take Rebecca's breath away. In a low, tight voice, he responded, "Mostly, I do not. When the loneliness grows too vast I guess I am just like any other man. There have been a few...very discreet professional women who have given me surcease when...things became more than I could bear alone." In a lower voice he added, "And I cannot believe I am talking about women of ill repute with a lady of your standing. Please, please forgive me?"

Rebecca rose from the davenport, walking over and kneeling down in front of him. She took his hands in hers, running her thumbs over the backs of them gently. "There is nothing to forgive, Charlie." She continued softly. "I asked and you answered. You were very honest and forthright. Please do not be upset. Do not be concerned about any answer you have given me." She reached up and palmed his cheek. "You are the most incredible person I have ever met, Colonel. I wish I had a tenth of your strength."

He closed his eyes and pressed his cheek more firmly into her hand, savoring the touch, storing it in his memory. Every inch of his body begged to be the skin her warm hand caressed. Without opening his eyes, he turned and reverently laid his lips in her palm. In that moment, Charlie Redmond lost his heart. He whispered into her palm, "I have no strength, only fear. I am a creature who has lied and cheated to survive. You are the strong one, dear lady."

"There you go again, refusing to take credit. I am going to have to work on that, Colonel Redmond." She did not stop to think about her next action; it came from the heart and it just happened. She leaned up and placed a soft kiss on Charlie's cheek. "I wish it were in my power to make you truly happy, Charlie. I would live the rest of my life trying."

That one kiss burned into Charlie's soul. He could not breathe, he could not move. Part of his heart cried out to take her into his arms, the other sat in stunned fear that he would awaken, that this was another dream like the one that he had had the previous night, and if he moved it would disappear.

Slowly his eyes opened, and he looked into the moss green ones before him. A vista of peace lay in those eyes. All of the hope he had ever had, all of the dreams he had ever dreamed were there before him. "You do, dear lady, you do."

She smiled and caressed his cheek one last time. She wished it were true, that she could make this wonderful, noble person happy. But she knew in her heart someone like Charlie would never be happy with her. For a brief moment, she wished she were more. "Come, Colonel. It has been a long day, and I think we are both exhausted. Let us go to bed."

He was struck dumb; he had no words to respond to the gift she had just given to him. Charlie knelt to bank the fire, and then followed her from the room, hungering just to remain in her company. Of course, she could never truly love one such as him. She was a woman, a widow who had known the touch of a true man. But if he could somehow be allowed to stay close to her, to be in her company at least some of the time, then maybe that long bleak life after his time with the Army was up would be bearable. Maybe.

~

Charlie was dozing when he felt her tremble in his arms. Then, when she began whimpering and crying, he was fully awake. He moved his arm that had been around her waist and propped himself up on his elbow. He wondered what she might be dreaming about that would make her cry out and struggle with the quilts.

The overwhelming look of pain on her face made Charlie's heart break. He wanted so much to take the pain away from her, to make everything all right. Maybe for the moment, maybe for tonight, he could.

Gently he touched her shoulder. "Rebecca? It is all right; it is only a dream. You do not need to be upset."

Still she struggled and cried in her sleep. When she crossed her arms over her body as if she were protecting herself, Charlie pulled back, wondering if he was the cause of her distress. Suddenly her eyes opened and she gasped in panic, sitting up suddenly, looking around to get her bearings. Finally, she saw Charlie. "I am sorry," she sniffed. "I did not mean to wake you. I will go to the davenport."

"You will do no such thing. Please," he placed a gentle hand on her arm. "Lie down, and rest." He coaxed her back, then ran his fingers through her hair. "You are safe here. No one will hurt you."

"Thank you."

He let his fingers drift down to wipe the tears from her cheeks. "Will you share with me what has upset you so?"

"I was dreaming of my husband."

Charlie's heart sank yet again. "I am sure you miss him."

"No." She shook her head, the tears welling up again. "I know I am sinful for saying this, but I do not miss him."

"No??"

"No." She looked to Charlie, expecting him to leave her. When he did not move, she thought it safe to explain. "He did not love me, Charlie. He...he...never loved me." She began crying again, this time moving closer to him, seeking comfort there, hoping he would not turn her away.

He opened his arms and she curled into them with her head on his shoulder, her tears soaking the cotton of his nightshirt. Charlie could tell that the woman was trying desperately to regain control. "It is all right," he whispered. "You are safe. Go ahead and cry. There is no one here who will pass judgment."

CHAPTER 6

MONDAY, NOVEMBER 14, 1864

Sheridan threw Charlie's report over to his executive officer, Colonel Angus McCauley. "What do you think of this?"

McCauley read it, then looked at Sheridan. "Charlie Redmond wrote this?"

"Yup. Looks like our perfect officer and gentleman may finally have decided to shift the emphasis from officer to gentleman. I think I will have to conduct my formal inspection as soon as possible. He has either fallen for the land or the lady, and I am damned if I can tell which, but I sure want to find out."

"Well, Sir, even though he may have his head in the clouds, from the looks of his reports, he has found a good place for the troops. It has got everything—pasture, water, places for the men to be at least partially sheltered from the weather, room for a real hospital, and he has secured the rail head. We will not have too many problems provisioning them. I believe General Grant used Culpeper as his headquarters for a short time last spring. Thank God, we will not have to use horse and wagon. I have enough problems with the troops outside of Haymarket."

Sheridan took the report back and scanned it again. "Oh, by the way, McCauley, what about those boots? Did you and Polk sort that out?"

"As well as we could, Sir. The materials the War Department sends us are often substandard. I sometimes suspect our purchasing agents are Southern saboteurs, but then I have to look again. They are just crooks."

"Well, see what you can do for them. The 13th Pennsylvania has taken more punishment than almost any other cavalry regiment in the entire army. I would like to try and take care of them as much as possible."

"Yes, Sir." McCauley made a note in his already full list of orders for the day.

"You know, McCauley, this war is going to be over soon. And the President has issued orders that we are to begin reconstruction of the Union as quickly and painlessly as possible. Considering the amount of anguish and animosity this war has engendered, I think our good Southern gentleman might be just the thing to help the process along. Make sure you see to it that Charlie has all of the resources, supplies, personnel, and money he needs. Make it real money, not military script. That will probably help, too. Also, I will issue orders that will allow Dr. Walker to treat the locals using Army supplies. We must do whatever we can to rebuild relations with these folks."

Sheridan glanced over some papers on his desk, apparently focusing on other issues. He then looked at his calendar. "And see what you can do to clear my calendar around the end of next month. I want to go see this paragon Charlie has found—the woman or the land."

∽

Morning broke clear and bright, which, given the night they had both endured, was more irritating than welcome. Lack of sleep on Charlie's part, and for Rebecca, the sting of tears that had flowed until there were no more, made the first light of dawn feel like knives in their sensitive eyes.

"Miss Rebecca?" Charlie called gently as he tried to untangle himself and his soggy nightshirt from what felt like Rebecca's death grip. "Dear, I have to get up now. Duty calls."

Rebecca relinquished her hold on Charlie, moving away, feeling embarrassed at her outburst the previous night and ashamed she had made the Colonel witness to it. "Yes, of course. I am sorry."

He reached out and caught her hand in his larger one. "Do not be sorry. I am not. Your trust is one of the most precious things I have ever been given." He tenderly kissed the back of her hand. "You honor me more than I can tell you."

"Thank you. For everything." She smiled at him, wishing she could make him understand what feeling safe for the first time in years truly meant to her. "But, sir, I do believe you have men who require your orders, and I am sure I must have a thousand things to be done here."

"We both have a thousand things to attend to if we are to settle this bunch of ruffians I call a regiment for the winter. I think that the first thing I need to do is to create a relationship with the local merchants. And you, dear, need to get some help out here. Why do you not accompany me into town this afternoon?"

"Town?" She smiled and chewed the side of her bottom lip. "Oh, it has been ages since I have been to town. I am not sure I would know how to behave in proper society." Rebecca hesitated. Her year of mourning was over, and it was finally acceptable for her to return to society on a limited basis. But to be seen in the company of a Yankee was beyond the pale.

Charlie saw the hesitation and realized that the problem was not going to town, but going to town with him. "Well, perhaps some other time when it is more convenient."

Rebecca looked at him, startled as she realized he was hurt by her hesitation. She thought of the reaction her neighbors would have if she appeared in his company, and in that moment realized his friendship was far more important than the opinion of the ladies of Culpeper. She smiled. "But, yes, Colonel, I would love to go to town with you. Perhaps I can get some badly needed supplies. Maybe get the items to fix you a proper dinner."

"My dear lady, if I could have a plate of pirleau again, I would be in heaven. I may have lived with Yankees for the past twenty years, but I still love my Southern foods. Would it be convenient for me to pick you up after lunch?"

"Yes, Colonel Redmond, I would be pleased if you did. Thank you."

"Oh, we found a little basket cart in the stables. If the boys have it fixed this morning, I will hitch Shannon to it and we will go in style, if you like."

"I must warn you, we shall be the talk of the town. You wait until you meet some of those old hens."

A rakish grin illuminated Charlie's normally gentle visage. If he had had a moustache, he would have been twirling the ends. "Oh, my dear, I relish the thought."

She laughed softly as she stood and put on her robe. "Is that a bit of a wicked side I see coming out, Colonel Redmond?"

Charlie's Southern accent was normally rather understated, but the next words out of his mouth made it unmistakable he was from that French-flavored city in South Carolina. "Why, ma chère Madame Rebecca, whatever gave you the idea that I would be anything other than a perfect gentleman?"

She laughed harder, the memories of her bad dreams fading away like the early morning mist. "Yes, Sir, I do believe you have just a little evil streak, and I must say I find it utterly charming."

"Well, my dear, if you find it charming, then perhaps I can find the means to sway the local hens as well—no?"

"Oh, Colonel, I am absolutely sure you will find the older hens as tough as leather, but a few of the younger ladies will have their heads turned, I am sure."

"Miss Rebecca, I am, as ever, a perfect gentleman. I would not consider taking advantage of a young, innocent woman. Now a mature, confident lady of means and birth—that certainly does get my attention."

She smiled again; she could not help it. The normally reserved Charlie was actually flirting with her. Now it was up to her to do what any woman of proper Southern breeding would do: flirt back, then leave. "I will keep that in mind, Colonel Redmond." She licked her lips just slightly. "Now, if you will excuse me." And with that, she left the bedroom.

Charlie grinned to himself as he quickly donned his uniform to start the day. His gentle teasing and flirting had broken the shroud of grief and pain that had surrounded Miss Rebecca all night. Whistling to himself, he clattered down the stairs and off to the camp, anticipating an absolutely delightful afternoon in her company. *And the Devil may take the biddies and their opinions.*

The two went their separate ways that morning, each in a far more positive mood than the tasks before them would seem to indicate was reasonable.

Charlie worked with Polk and his company commanders to finish the detailed plans for the winter camp. They agreed to spread the companies across the property, so each would be able to deal with their own horses, maintain their own cook tents, and have at least some space. This would also put fewer demands on the land, and allow them to keep their horses safe from the inevitable civilian attempts to "borrow" one or two.

They decided to half-timber the tents, providing reinforcement against snow or heavy rain, as well as providing additional insulation to augment the heavy canvas. Each troop would also build a small berm around the outside of the tent, burying the edge of the canvas in the ground to prevent the wind from getting up under it, or even worse, under the ground cloth that served as the floor of the tent. The berms would also divert any flowing water away from the interior of the tents. Charlie issued orders for the men to work as quickly as possible. So far, the weather had been kind, but it was November, and the mild temperature and clear skies could not go on forever. Anyway, Charlie figured that the lumber would come in handy for Rebecca when the troops departed in the spring.

Troopers with specific skills were identified from each company to help prepare the stables as an infirmary for injured horses, the large stone barn as a hospital, and the overseer's house as Charlie's headquarters. Samuelson was in charge of preparing the hospital, and was given one of the regiment's precious Franklin stoves to keep the space warm for the sick and injured. His first concerns were to get the barn clean, and to take steps to create a special area that could be kept immaculate to use for surgery. Dr. Walker was particular, and he did not want to disappoint her.

In the midst of this flurry of activity, Charlie found time to have a word with Tarent and MacFarlane about the little basket trap he had seen the day before, ensuring it would be ready for the afternoon trip. He also checked with Sergeant Jamison, who had already been into town to obtain fresh, specialty supplies and to retain the services of a few local hands to help with the transportation of goods from the railhead to the camp. What Jamison had to say about the conditions in the colored part of town concerned Charlie. It seemed that emancipation without work for these people was not a particularly beneficial situation. Charlie made a note to warn the company commanders to be on the lookout for petty thievery, and to be stern but not harsh about it. On the other hand, it did suggest that he would have his pick of potential servants for the main house.

Rebecca also had her hands full. Jocko had seen to it that she had a small number of troopers, led by Corporal Nailer, to continue the clean up and refurbishing of the main house. There were rooms that could shelter the extremely ill and provide a safe, quiet residence for Dr. Walker and her staff. The winter kitchen had a full stillroom attached to it, where medicines could be prepared as well. All of this had to be put in order. She sent the troopers up to the attic to discover anything that might be useful in terms of old furniture, bedding, and other items. The troopers even set up a small carpentry shop to allow them to either repair what was usable or to rough together additional beds, chairs, and tables to fill the voids.

Once she had gotten the boys to work, she spent a good bit of time going through her kitchen and basic supplies. Care was taken to create a list of all of the things she absolutely needed from town, and a few things that she did not really need, but had been missing. Last, but not least, she carefully looked over her supply of spices and vegetables, making sure she had everything she needed to make a beautiful chicken pirleau. It seemed such a simple dish, but it was much more complex than most people thought. Rice with chicken, onions, green peppers, celery, saffron, tomato sauce, chicken broth, and sweet chilies gently steamed together was a classic Charleston dish with which she wanted to treat her Charlestonian Colonel. It was her way of repaying him in part for all of the truly lovely things he had done for her.

As the morning drew to a close, she fixed herself a small bite of lunch and then went to decide on what to wear. Her first foray into town after her year of mourning had to present the right image. She must not be too forward, but no longer a woman in the black weeds of deep grief. To be honest, getting rid of what she knew in her heart was a hypocritical adherence to social norms was a blessing. And black had never been her best color.

She chose a lovely blue-gray walking dress, modest in cut, quiet in color, acknowledging that the "acceptable" colors for the second year of widowhood were all soft, cool shades of blue, gray, and lavender. But it was also the walking dress that most flattered her own coloring, the blue bringing out the gold in her hair, the green in her eyes, and the soft pinks of her skin and lips. She wanted to look good for

Charlie, and to put the biddies—ripe for any tidbit of gossip—in their proper place.

~

Tarent and MacFarlane had outdone themselves. The little basket cart was shining. Shannon was too, groomed to a high golden gloss. A few ribbons added, and the little trap would have been perfect for a May Day parade.

Charlie almost matched the little rig. He had dressed carefully; every part of his gear was shining with polish, carefully brushed, or starched. He had surrendered his usual headgear for a rakish slope brimmed hat with a curling egret feather, which was properly fluffed. He was, indeed, the picture of a dashing cavalry officer.

Sliding into the seat of the trap, he clucked to Shannon, and together they went off to present themselves for Miss Rebecca's approval. As they trotted up to the main house, Rebecca came out onto the portico. Charlie's eyes lit up with frank appreciation. She was lovely.

"I say, Colonel Redmond, your men do wonderful work." She moved down the steps, stopping to give Shannon a good scratch on the nose. "How are you today, my lovely girl?"

Silently, Charlie stepped down and offered her a hand up into the cart. As she settled herself, he spoke reverently. "You are breathtaking, my dear."

"And you, as always, Sir, are as handsome as may be."

He settled himself into the cart beside her, and the two set off.

"Thank you, Ma'am. I do try to maintain the appropriate image —especially when I am about to enter the lions' den. I call this my Daniel costume."

"You will do just fine, Colonel. I have the utmost faith in you." Rebecca chanced a glance at him before making her next comment. "I would like to offer you an apology."

"Miss Rebecca, I told you this morning, you have nothing to be sorry for. I am flattered you trust me enough to turn to me in your grief."

"Yes, but I did not mean to make you uncomfortable. I took some things out of storage yesterday, and I suppose doing so released a few less than pleasant memories."

"You did not make me uncomfortable, Ma'am. You honored me with your trust. I hope you know that I am always available if ever you need a willing ear or a solid shoulder."

"Thank you. So few people would understand my feelings about my late husband. Not many people would take well to hearing that I did not love him and that I was not happy in my marriage." She looked to Charlie, realizing that he might think her callous to speak in such a fashion about a soldier killed in battle. "I do not mean to sound harsh, but for me marriage was not a pleasant experience."

Charlie's eyes darkened. He knew well what being in an unloving family relationship could do to one's spirit. "I hope he did not hurt you. Indifference is hard enough to bear, and you, my dear lady, are not one who deserves such pain of the soul."

"Well, he was...master of the house. I knew my place, and I was not expected to want or achieve anything higher. I was the perfect show piece."

His voice was very low. "Did he hurt you?"

"That is no longer of any importance. Let us just say I knew my role well and learned how to do what was expected of me."

Charlie's jaw tightened as he tried to control the sudden swell of anger he felt toward the late Mr. Gaines. She certainly did not need his wrath; she only deserved his tenderness. Yet, the idea that this beautiful, vital, passionate woman had been ill-used and cast aside touched the deepest wells of anger within his soul.

"So you see, Sir, occasionally I am plagued with night terrors. I just wish you had not been subjected to them."

When he could speak calmly, he tugged Shannon to a halt so he could turn and look her in the eye. In that moment, he was not the dashing Colonel, nor even the charming gentleman. He was, like her, the survivor of abuse, willing to do whatever necessary to get by.

"Miss Rebecca, I may understand more than you know. If you need to talk, if you need to cry or rail or anything else, I am more than willing to listen to you, and help you to purge your soul of this."

She laid her hand in his, giving it a gentle squeeze. "You are very kind. I am sure that in your company, all these unpleasant things shall pass."

He lifted that trusting, gloved hand to his lips and reverently kissed it. "Miss Rebecca, if it were in my power, I would take it all away today. Alas, it is not. I can only offer you my understanding and my honor to protect you from it happening again."

"That is more than I have a right to hope for, Colonel." She caressed his cheek. "Simple words cannot express how much..." she paused, stopping the first word that came into her mind, but allowing the next, "this...means to me."

No words came to Charlie's heart, just the honest desire to protect this woman, who was braver than he ever could be. She had stayed and endured. He had run. Before her quiet courage, he was humbled again. He looked deep into her eyes, wordlessly offering his soul and his support, then he clucked to Shannon to move on. "Shall we go and brave the biddies? I am sure, after all you have endured, you are more than equipped to handle them."

Charlie stopped the buggy right in front of the mercantile. He climbed out, made his way around to Rebecca, and gave her his hand to assist her out. Out of the corner of her eye, she saw them. She rolled her eyes then looked to the Colonel. "Cluck, cluck, cluck," she whispered, giving him a wink.

He turned at the waist, to find two women watching them with their mouths practically hanging open. He turned back, wrapping Rebecca's hand around his arm. "May I escort you?"

She tried to stifle a giggle, but was not entirely successful. "My, my, Colonel, that evil streak just keeps getting longer and wider." She walked with him to the front door of the store. "But I also know you have things to do here in town, so please, Sir, take care of your business. I assure you I will be fine."

He looked down at her, feeling very protective. "Are you certain?"

"I am positive."

"As you wish, Ma'am. I will be back shortly."

"Take your time, Colonel. I am just going to get some supplies."

The blue eyes twinkled as he glanced again at the hovering onlookers. "Enjoy yourself, Miss Rebecca."

Smiling mischievously, she replied, "I will, Colonel."

She watched him walk back to the buggy and climb in, and she continued to watch as he drove down the street. Then she turned to find the ladies still watching her. She gave them a little wave then turned for the store.

"Why, Mrs. Gaines," Mr. Cooper walked around the counter to greet her. "It has been so long. How have you been?"

"Like everyone, Mr. Cooper, I have just been doing my best to ride out the current troubles."

"You look well, Mrs. Gaines."

"Thank you." She looked around the store, finding it better stocked than she had expected. "There are some supplies that I need."

"Why, of course. Have you a list? I will be happy to fill it for you."

She handed him the list she had made, and he unfolded it and looked over it carefully. His eyes widened, and he looked back to her. "This is a rather long list, Mrs. Gaines."

"Do you not have the items?"

"Yes, Ma'am, I have most of this, but it is going to require a goodly sum of money."

She smiled as sweetly as possible in view of the fact that the man had just insulted her. "Yes, Mr. Cooper, I realize that. I hope this might make a difference to you." She handed him the chit Colonel Polk had given her. "As you can see, I have funds coming; I trust that will be sufficient to reopen my account."

Mr. Cooper scratched his chin while he considered the paper. "I am not sure, Mrs. Gaines. This is not money, Ma'am, and it is also drawn from the Yankee Army."

"Indeed it is, considering it is a regiment of Federal soldiers on my land and not Confederate troops."

"Ma'am."

She held up a hand. She was going to get the things she needed, and maybe one or two things she did not need. And most of all she was going to get everything she needed to make Charlie's supper. "Mr. Cooper, I will tell you what, you reopen my account, and if I do not come in and settle with you within ten days of the date on the chit, you may come out to Gaines Cove and pick five acres of my land that will suit you."

"Excuse me?"

"You heard me, Mr. Cooper. I have complete faith that I will receive the funds promised me; however, if you are that nervous about it, then you may take your pick of five of my best."

"On your word?"

"On my word, Mr. Cooper, and you know the Gaines word has always been good." Rebecca may not have truly mourned the loss of her husband, but she was not above invoking his memory and standing in the community for a little advantage. "Do you think I would tarnish my husband's good name? And after he gave his life in the war?"

"Of course not!" He was shocked she would think he would suggest such a thing. "I will take care of this for you, Mrs. Gaines, but it will take me a few minutes."

"Take your time, Mr. Cooper. I am in no hurry." She made sure to retrieve the chit from his hand and tuck it away in her reticule.

While the shopkeeper scurried around pulling things from the shelves, she took the opportunity to look around. She moved first to a display of tobacco pipes. Thus prodded, she remembered that when Charlie had come to get her for dinner the night before, he had smelled faintly of tobacco. It was actually a very appealing smell on Charlie. Of course, she was beginning to wonder if there was anything about him she did not like.

She moved over to a small bin that held partial bolts of fabric and looked through them, lifting them one by one. As she continued to browse, she heard at least two women come through the door. She smiled to herself and simply waited.

"Why, is that Mrs. Gaines?"

Rebecca nearly laughed aloud when she heard Mrs. Cooper speak. She fingered a piece of blue cloth, giving it serious consideration.

"Why, yes, Grace, I do believe it is."

The blonde rolled her eyes before plucking the bolt from the bin and pulling it into her arms as she turned to face them.

"Mrs. Cooper, Mrs. Williams, how good to see you again." Rebecca liked Grace Cooper and had always gotten on well with her, but Mrs. Williams, the minister's wife, had most certainly always been a thorn in Rebecca's side. *You old bat. You say one word about Charlie, and I will...*

"You, too, Mrs. Gaines. Tell us, what brings you to town?" Mrs. Williams asked, with a disapprovingly raised brow.

"A buggy," she said in all seriousness, never breaking eye contact with the minister's wife. Mrs. Williams had made their strained relationship worse by commenting in mixed company about Rebecca's failure to get pregnant within the first year of her marriage. The woman had implied that because of this, Rebecca was somehow less of a woman. This, coupled with the way her marriage was going, was just one more thing that made her feel like chattel.

"Yes, we saw it being driven away by that," Mrs. Williams paused, crinkling her nose as if she smelled something distasteful, "man."

"Oh, you mean Colonel Redmond. Colonel Charles Redmond?"

"Rebecca Gaines, do not dare tell us you are on a first name basis with him."

She ran her hand over the soft linen in her hands. "Why, yes. Yes, I am." She watched as the disapproving looks crossed their faces. "And I must say, he is one of the most charming men I have ever met."

She thought they were going to swallow their tongues as her words began to register. She realized Charlie was not the only one with an evil streak. She knew she should stop, but she just could not.

"He is also a fine horseman, and he has a beautiful voice for reading poetry. If you ladies will excuse me?" She brushed past them, moving to the counter where Mr. Cooper was boxing up her purchases. "Mr. Cooper, this partial bolt, how much would you want for it?"

He looked at the fabric. "Well I suppose I could let you have it for, let us say five cents. It is an old bolt."

She placed it next to the box running her hand over it. "I think he will love it," she murmured.

"Excuse me?"

"Nothing, Mr. Cooper. Would you happen to have any cinnamon? I forgot to put it on the list."

"I think I might have some around here somewhere. Going to do a little baking, Mrs. Gaines?"

"I am thinking about it." She smiled, and then turned to the ladies. "Colonel Redmond is very fond of baked apples."

"If you do not mind my asking, Mrs. Gaines," Mrs. Cooper came up beside her, "what is it like, having all those soldiers on your land"?"

"It was certainly most unnerving when they arrived, but even in these two weeks, I have grown quite accustomed to them being there.

As a matter of fact, Colonel Redmond and his men will be wintering on my land. They will be here for several months."

"And I suppose," Mrs. Williams piped up, even though Rebecca wished she had swallowed her tongue, "we will have to put up with them coming into town and taking what they want."

"Not at all, Mrs. Williams, Colonel Redmond is very careful of his men. He will make sure they do not bother you."

"Rebecca," Mrs. Cooper whispered, looking around to make sure no one could hear her, "you are all right, are not you? You are not being forced..."

"Oh, no! Colonel Redmond and his men have been perfect gentlemen. They have even been helping me get Gaines Cove back into order."

"You are taking assistance from Yankee rabble?"

"Mrs. Williams, I figure since it was the Yankees that did this to us, why should they not fix it?"

"Cannot argue with that," Mr. Cooper snorted, as he began writing Rebecca's bill.

"I suppose they have been in your house."

"Several of them, several times. And if you must know, the Colonel and I dine together every night. Is there anything else you would like to know, or do you have enough to put through the rumor mill?"

"Why, I never!" The older woman turned on her heel and stormed from the store.

"That is not what my overseer used to say," Rebecca mumbled.

Mr. and Mrs. Cooper burst out laughing. Rebecca just shook her head.

"Now, Rebecca," Mrs. Cooper laid her hand on the blonde's arm in a motherly fashion, "it is all right to tell us. Are you really safe?"

"I am very safe, Grace. I promise you." She placed her hand on the other woman's, giving it a tiny squeeze. "If I were not fine, I would tell you and ask for help. Colonel Redmond and his men really have been perfect gentlemen. But thank you for being honestly concerned for my well being and not just looking for things to gossip about like that old hen." She jerked her chin in the direction Mrs. Williams had just departed.

"Oh, I cannot guarantee I will not gossip, but at least I can gossip about the truth."

"That is all I ask. You know if she has the chance to tell her version of it, I will be at the mercy of every soldier on my land."

"She does seem to remember things in her own unique way."

While Rebecca was meeting the social challenges of her little community, Charlie drove on to one of the areas Jamison had described as the colored town. A horrible little spot on the map called Slab Town by the locals. He was greeted with the sight of a small clutch of shacks, patched together from whatever scrap was available, with raw sewage running in open gutters and gaunt figures already huddling over small fires because they did not have enough clothing for even this mild November day. The wind had picked up a bit since he had set out with Rebecca, and gray clouds were starting to scud in from the northeast. He made a mental note to himself that this situation would have to be cleaned up, or there was a chance of serious illness, as well as unrest and petty crime.

He stopped in the middle of the little town within a town and announced in his best field commander's voice, "I am looking for some folks. I need a cook, a lady's maid, a housekeeper, and a general handyman." Immediately, virtually every able-bodied adult was lined up in front of him, looking hopeful.

"All right. Cooks first." Four women stepped forward, and he quickly interviewed each of them. One young woman was a standout. Sarah had been an assistant cook for the Gaines household before Rebecca's marriage. She had then been sent to the Washington household of a distant cousin of the late and unlamented Mr. Gaines to finish her training, and combined the skills of a traditional

Southern cook with some of the latest French styles. Her older sister, Beulah, had obviously been a big woman until the shortages of the war forced her to trim down. But she still had the muscle and solid build that Charlie associated with a good housekeeper, mostly because that had been the build of the mammy in his own childhood home. Reg stood up and requested the position of handyman, offering skills with both basic carpentry and cleaning, as well as a bit of experience with horses. Since both women seemed to feel he was a good Christian man and a hard worker, Charlie nodded his agreement.

That left the selection of a lady's maid for Rebecca. None of the people before him had any skills in this calling of the more elite servant class. But one girl caught Charlie's eye. She was young, perhaps fifteen or sixteen, skinny as a rail, and clearly shy. What got his attention was the way she had tried to take care of herself. In this pigsty of a shantytown, her dress was clean and neatly pressed, her hair was carefully braided and combed, and she had tied it back with a bit of grosgrain ribbon that was shiny with age but still carefully tended. Lizbet was what the others in the group called her. And Lizbet became the fourth servant Charlie picked.

He gave them instructions to go to the mercantile and get a new suit of clothing each, including shoes and a winter coat, get their belongings together, settle any affairs they might need to attend to, and report to the main house by the end of the week. The terms were simple. First, they had to satisfy Mrs. Gaines. They had to be honest, clean, neat, and orderly, and do the work given to them. Assuming the work was satisfactory, he would pay them each a dime a day, payable twice a month, plus food, shelter and a new suit of clothes, including shoes, twice a year. They would get Sunday mornings and one afternoon during the weekday off to attend church and take care of their own affairs.

Those who were not hired looked so dejected that Charlie could not just leave. "Today, I have hired four of you. I have every expectation that we will find ways to create gainful employment for as many of you as possible. Until then, you may see my mess chief, Sergeant Jamison, or one of his men every day at dinnertime for a bowl of rice and beans. No one will be turned away. There may also be day work available from time to time while we are here in winter camp. I will set up a tent at the edge of the camp to which you can report every day to find out what work is available. Any day worker will be paid according to his or her skills. I wish I could do better for you." With that, he left, eager to be gone from this depressing place.

He set a brisk pace back to the mercantile where he was to collect Rebecca. The condition of the Negroes in that miserable collection of shacks offended him. They may have been slaves at one time, but they were still human and part of the community. Surely, the good people of Culpeper could have done something for them. *Ah, but charity begins at home, and these ex-slaves are not worth the bone thrown to a starving dog, according to some. Well, let us see just how much we can shake these good folks up.* Charlie was as loaded for bear as Rebecca.

Pulling up before the store, he looped the reins around the brake handle on the little trap. Shannon was so well trained that she was just as good when driven as she was when ridden. She would stand, waiting for his return, and more than willing to resist any attempt to get her to move by any other individual. He brushed the dust off his coat and hat, and prepared to make a grand entrance into the store that served as a social center as well as a primary resource to the community. As he dismounted from the cart, he was acutely aware that every person there on the little main street was watching him. *Give 'em a good show, Charlie.* He slowly looked up and down the street, seeking to make eye contact with every single person there. A small, wry smile twisted his mouth slightly, but did not reach his eyes. Not one of the folks watching him had the nerve to face him head on.

He stepped into the store. While he did not actually have to duck to enter, he did anyway, giving the impression of being taller than he actually was. He pulled his gloves off and tucked them into his belt. His hat came off with a flourish and took up residence under his left arm. Everyone in the main room came to a dead stop, staring at the tall man standing in the door whose presence filled the room.

A quick glance at Rebecca's face told Charlie she was not a happy woman. While she was smiling politely, there was a guarded look to her eyes and a slightly pinched quality to her mouth that told him something was amiss. He smiled at her and bowed slightly. "Mrs. Gaines, I await your pleasure, Ma'am."

He bowed to Mrs. Cooper, and stood waiting for an introduction.

Rebecca shook herself. "Forgive me, Colonel. Mr. and Mrs. Cooper? May I present Colonel Charles Redmond? Colonel Redmond is the regimental commander of the troops who are currently staying on my property. Colonel Redmond, Mr. and Mrs. Cooper are my dear friends here in Culpeper."

Charlie bowed over Mrs. Cooper's hand and rumbled in his lowest voice, "Enchantez, Madame. I have heard complimentary things of you, but they cannot compare with the charm of making your actual acquaintance."

Rebecca looked at Charlie with a slightly surprised look. The accent was back in full force, and Charlie was not giving the folks in the store even a moment to do anything other than respond politely to the very formal, very Southern gentleman standing before them, even though he was wearing Union blue.

Turning to the shopkeeper, the Colonel advanced and offered his bared hand. "Ah, Mr. Cooper. I have heard very good things of you, Sir, from my quartermaster. Please be assured, I have been advised by my commanding officer that we will convert to a cash, rather than scrip basis within the next ten days. Your cooperation with my staff has been greatly appreciated."

Reaching into his coat pocket, Charlie pulled out his personal wallet. "I have retained some servants for my comfort as we winter over here. It is my intention to pay them on a monthly basis, but for them to be equipped to serve my needs, they must be properly clothed. I hope you do not mind that I have sent them to you for their necessities, Sir. If I may, here is fifty dollars as an initial payment on my tab." He laid two golden double eagle twenty-dollar coins and a handful of silver dollars on the counter.

Mr. Cooper's eyes bulged. He had not seen that much real cash coming from one customer in a long time.

"Sarah, Beulah, Reg, and Lizbet should be visiting shortly. Please, Mr. Cooper, if you will, take proper care of them. I would like them each to have a new suit of clothing, shoes, and a winter coat. Thank you." Mr. Cooper could only stand there and nod.

Charlie turned to Rebecca, who was enjoying this bravura performance. "Mrs. Gaines? Are you ready, or shall I wait?"

"No, Colonel, you need not wait. The things I need immediately, I have all boxed and ready, and Mr. Cooper has promised to send me the rest of my supplies."

"Then, Ma'am, as soon as Mr. Cooper's clerk has loaded the trap, I will be most happy to drive you back to your home before I return to camp."

He turned to Mrs. Cooper, and bowed over her hand. "Ma'am, I trust we will meet again." A polite nod to Mr. Cooper, and Charlie extended his bent arm to Rebecca.

Escorting her to the trap, they waited, chatting about the weather growing colder as the slightly rattled clerk loaded the boxes and packages in the back of the trap. The Coopers and the other folks in the store, straining to overhear the conversation between the dashing Colonel and Mrs. Gaines, trailed them to the boardwalk to bid them farewell. Charlie settled Rebecca in the little cart and carefully tucked the lap rug over her knees, before climbing in and clucking Shannon into action.

As soon as they were out of earshot of the overwhelmed citizens of Culpeper, Rebecca laid her hand on his arm. "Lovely act, Daniel. The lions may yet be tamed."

They rode home with Rebecca regaling him with stories of the absurdity of her neighbors, all of the lovely, ridiculous, salacious stories that every small town has about its denizens. They laughed together gently over the silly situations that small town self-righteousness can create. As they approached the manor, Charlie brought up the subject of house servants. Rebecca had assumed that he had hired help for the camp, and had not paid too much attention to the specifics. She was due for a surprise.

"Miss Rebecca, I have done something without your permission. However, with all of the strains my troops and I are placing on you, I feel it is only fair to provide you with some help, other than my troopers, to manage the house. So, I have hired some staff for you. If you do not like them, or do not find them acceptable, I will be very happy to find others that are more suitable."

"Thank you, Colonel, it is very considerate of you, but I am afraid I cannot afford servants at this time. I have taxes to consider and..."

He put up his hand. "Oh, no, Miss Rebecca, I did not mean to place this burden on you. These folks are for my convenience, to ease the load I have placed on you. I will attend to all their needs; they are coming to attend to yours. Please say you will accept this, I cannot bear to think that I am placing a strain on you in anyway."

Rebecca flushed. The financial constraints that prevented her from hiring any help were magically gone because of this man, and there was hope for her future after the war. How much did she owe him? How could she repay him, and with what?

The storm that had been threatening all afternoon broke just as they returned to the manor. Cold rain and a driving wind hit hard. Charlie left her to rejoin his men and oversee the efforts to meet this sudden storm and minimize any damage. She went to her room and changed into her daily work clothes, thinking that with this storm, Charlie would need a warm, hearty meal. Within a matter of minutes, a young trooper appeared at the kitchen door. "Colonel asked me to tell you that he doubts he will be available for dinner, Ma'am. The men need him now."

So, instead of creating the lovely pirleau she wanted for Charlie, Rebecca put a pot of soup on to cook. When he finally did manage to make it to the shelter of the house, he would need it.

CHAPTER 7

MONDAY, NOVEMBER 14, 1864

Charlie had returned Rebecca to the main house, escorting her to the door, and then hurrying off to the camp. He had hoped the weather would hold for a few more days; he had not been so lucky. Within minutes the storm hit with full force. The rain pounded down and the wind howled out of the northeast, ripping at the canvas of the tents not yet reinforced for the winter. Anything not securely tied down was either snapping in the near gale force wind or had disappeared already.

He turned Shannon and the little trap over to one of Tarent's troopers, and stomped into the officers' mess that also served as the situation room for his senior staff. Polk was there, along with Jocko and Major Swallow of Company A. The rain that had hit like a sledgehammer had soaked all four men as they gathered to coordinate activities.

"A quick rundown, gentlemen." Charlie wiped rain from his forehead and face with the palm of his hand as he dropped his sopping hat into a pile of others near the stove. "Swallow, how are we doing with getting the injured and sick into the stone barn?"

"Colonel, we have not completed preparing the space, but I have men transporting the wounded and sick from the infirmary tent over to the barn. We have rigged a sort of enclosed sledge to take them over there one at a time, bed and all. I also have men stationed around the infirmary tent to make sure it does not blow down."

"All right, Lieutenant. I assume you need something else, or you would not be here. What is it?"

"Well, Sir, if we could have a couple of the mules, I think we will be able to go forward more quickly."

"You really think you could get mules to cooperate in this weather?"

"Colonel, we should try. It is a better option than having the men struggle with pulling sledges themselves in this weather."

"Jocko, get MacFarlane and see what you two can do to help with this. And, Swallow? Do not sacrifice what works for your new scheme. Use another carrier with the mules. I do not want a bolting mule to destroy the sledge you are using now."

Swallow nodded his agreement and hurried out.

"Aye, Colonel C. I brought you your mucking clothes. Figured you would be here."

"Thanks, Jocko."

Jocko followed Swallow out of the tent. The Colonel had always made it clear; his most important issue was the welfare of the men.

Turning to Polk, Charlie addressed the next most pressing issues: the condition of the horses and the supplies.

"Well, Richard, how bad is it likely to be?"

"Sir, Tarent and some of the boys from Company D have moved the injured animals into the old stables. Company B is out trying to make sure that the horses in the paddocks and fields are all sheltered and that there are no fence breaks."

"That is a relief. Small blessings that this place is already designed for horses. Did Hoffstader's boys manage to finish walking the fence perimeters before the storm broke?"

"I honestly do not know. They were out in the field all day, and Hoffstader was with them. They have not yet reported."

"Have you sent anyone out to check on them and give him a hand if he needs it?"

"Not yet."

"We will get to that as soon as we can, then. How are the men's quarters faring? Anyone on duty battening down the tents?"

"Major Andrews commandeered Company F and H, as well as his own boys, to try and secure the troops' quarters. He is looking pretty harried."

"Good man, Andrews. What about the supplies? Did you get the new shipment under safe cover?"

"Mostly. Jamison and his boys have the worst job. If those beans, the rice, or the salt pork get wet, we will have a real problem. I have put all of the rest of the men available on getting the supplies stowed in the various buildings around the farm, and trying to protect whatever is left that they cannot manage to stow."

"Well, let us split our efforts, my friend. You want the infirmary or the mess tents?"

"Take the infirmary, Colonel. Some of the original boys from the 13th still do not know you. It will help. Anyway, I am used to heaving sacks of supplies—it is what I do every time I go back to headquarters to harangue the quartermaster's boys."

Polk hurried out, and Charlie tied off the tent flap to gain a few quick minutes of privacy to change. He pulled on the heavy woolen britches and tunic, belting them tightly to provide himself with at least partial protection from the wind and rain. He traded his plumed hat for a battered old kepi, and set out to help move the wounded men to shelter.

The afternoon merged into a night of cold rain and high winds. Once the injured men were settled, Charlie set out to check on the horses. Two had broken through an old, rotten section of fence, trying to find shelter from the wind in the stand of trees on the other side. Working with Hoffstader's men, the Colonel helped to calm the injured beasts. Tarent did the best he could for the animals, with Charlie's assistance, but for much of those miserable, cold, wet hours, Charlie could be heard cursing under his breath about the loss of the veterinary surgeon.

The next near disaster could have been much worse. The regiment had not been in camp long enough to establish a pattern of drainage ditches. The mess area was inundated with a constant wash of muddy water across the floor, first under the tents' ground cloths, and then over the top. Anything on or near the floor was in danger of being soaked. The men worked desperately to get the sacks of beans and rice, flour and oats up above the water. In the end, the only casualties were one sack of flour and a number of pairs of boots. The uncured leather that had been used to make them had started to shrink as soon as they got wet.

The night wore on with similar problems cropping up. One row of tents was flattened when the first one was caught by the ripping wind and took the rest of the canvas structures around it down in an ugly domino effect of tent pegs and poles, guy ropes and ripped canvas.

On Charlie's orders, Jamison took over the summer kitchen, thus securing a safe place where fires could be lit and maintained. Throughout the night, the cooks produced kettles of coffee and cauldrons of soup. All they could do was give the men something warm to sustain them through the bitter night.

Rebecca spent the rest of the afternoon and evening cleaning and putting things away. She felt she needed to get the house presentable before Dr. Walker and Mr. Whitman arrived. She had to admit she was very excited about meeting Dr. Walker. The idea of a woman doctor astounded her. She had so many things she wanted to ask her.

It would be nice to have someone to talk to who might understand some of the things she had begun feeling recently.

She also prepared soup, and kept it warm through the evening. Charlie would need it when he came in. She listened to the storm picking up. The temperature had dropped, and the rain had started. She knew it was an early winter storm settling in for several hours. Living in the area all her life, she knew how nasty these types of storms could get.

After making sure she had fires started in the parlor and bedroom to keep the chill out of the house as much as possible, she returned to the kitchen to find the leak in the roof had returned and was relentlessly letting rain pour into the room. She found a large tub and placed it under the leak as best she could, and hoped the rain would let up before the kitchen flooded.

As she surveyed the damage around her, it happened. It all started crashing in on her. She sat down in the chair at the table and started totaling everything up in her head. She had a regiment of Federal troops on her land. She had agreed to let them stay for the winter. She was sharing her bed with their commander, who had quite the secret to hide. More staff was expected, and they would need to be housed in a residence that most certainly was not ready to receive guests. The damn roof was still leaking. And she was not entirely positive, but she was pretty sure she was falling in love with Charlie Redmond.

She put her face in her hands and just sat there, not quite able to understand all that had happened in the last several days. *I have to pull myself together and just do what needs to be done. I cannot let myself think like this. There are so many reasons I cannot feel this way.*

She stood, moving to the window to watch the troopers running in the rain to perform their duties. She sighed, and her heart and mind laughed at her. She found herself fighting her own demons, just as, had she but known, Charlie fought his. *Then there are a few good reasons why you should. But Colonel Redmond most certainly would not be interested in a widowed woman, a woman who was never much of a wife to a man who lost his life fighting in the war. You are a woman who could not even properly mourn him. You did not love a real man, how could you consider loving this freak of nature?*

"Stop!" Rebecca growled out loud, shaking her head to clear it. She took a deep breath, then returned to the soup she was preparing for Charlie.

It became clear, as afternoon became evening and evening became night that Colonel Redmond would not be returning to the house. Rebecca kept checking at the windows for any sign of him. She paced incessantly back and forth and from room to room, trying to find something to occupy her mind so she would not worry about him. Soon she realized how futile the effort was. She simply was going to worry about him, and there was nothing to be done about it.

To try and calm her frazzled nerves, she fixed a cup of mint tea and took a book into the rear parlor. She settled near the fire and began reading, but soon realized that over the course of the last few nights, she and Charlie had done the same thing in this very room, and it only made her miss and worry for him more.

Finally, she decided to go to bed, but once she was settled there, the overpowering essence of Charlie lingering in the sheets and bedcovers made rest difficult and sleep impossible. She rose from the bed; and, taking a warm quilt and Charlie's pillow, moved to the rocking chair next to the window, from whence she watched the shadows of movement from the camp where she knew Charlie was out working on this horrible night.

Tuesday, November 15, 1864

Around dawn, Polk and Charlie met over a quick cup of coffee that looked more like thick ink. At least it was warm and there was no grit or mud in it.

"How bad is it from your point of view, Richard?"

"Not anywhere near as bad as it could be, Sir. I think your luck is holding, at least somewhat. We lost one wagon—broken axle—but managed to save the supplies in it. I have a bunch of boys with sprains and turned ankles. And the damned boots they sent us are a real problem."

"From my end, at least the sick and wounded are safe and dry, which is more than I can say for the rest of us. We lost a few tents, and those troopers' personal effects are all soaked, but it could have been worse. We also have a few injured horses."

"Well, it is a good thing Dr. Walker was delayed by the weather. We certainly would not have been ready to greet her properly."

Charlie raised his eyebrow at that comment and grunted noncommittally. *Which one of us would have had to "prepare" to greet Elizabeth? I wonder what is going on there.* The two men stood together, silent, contemplating the work that would have to be done to repair the storm damage. At least the wind had died down, and the rain was now just a steady, soaking downpour. Cold, gray morning was illuminating a scene of mixed mayhem and mud.

"Well, guess we better go start fixing the damage." Charlie tossed the dregs of his coffee into the mud.

"Yes, Sir, boss, Sir." Polk grinned through his mud-spattered beard, and they went back out into the muck.

The day proceeded with methodical misery. Every foot of fencing in all of the paddocks and fields was checked, and several critical sections were repaired. Each horse had to have its feet cleaned of the mud and debris packed into its hooves, or the troopers would have to deal with hoof rot and bruises from small stones trapped in the mud. Racks were built to keep all foodstuffs above water level, and the men were set to work building a series of berms and drainage ditches around the camp to try to keep the ground a little drier and firmer.

The Colonel had been up since before dawn of the previous day, and had been soaked continuously in rain and icy mud for a full night and day. It was time. As the sun set, Charlie finally took himself up to the main house to check on Rebecca, and hopefully catch a quick bath and a few hours of sleep.

Charlie came around to the back of the house. He knocked on the door of the winter kitchen hoping that someone—Rebecca or Duncan or one of the new servants—was there to let him in. He was muddy and wet, and he did not want to tramp the filth through the main house.

Rebecca was there, just sitting in a rocking chair beside the open fire. A pot of soup was set on a spider at the edge of the glowing coals; a kettle was simmering, ready for tea. The soft knock on the door roused her from her thoughts, and she rose quickly and opened the door, hoping it was him.

"Colonel Redmond. Come in. My Lord, you are soaked! Here, let me help you." She threw a woolen blanket around his shoulders and led him to the chair beside the fire. "I have been so worried about you. When you did not come in last night, I...I thought perhaps you had been hurt." As she spoke, she bustled around the room, catching a mug and filling it with the broth from the soup kettle. She thrust the hot cup into his hands. "Drink up, you need the warmth. I hope you got at least a little sleep last night, Charlie. My Lord, you cannot stay in those wet things, you will catch your death of cold."

Charlie just sat there as she rushed around and clucked away like a mother hen. Every part of him felt frozen, sore, battered, and stiff. Sitting in a warm place, with the cup of hot broth cradled between his hands and warming his frozen fingers helped some. He knew he needed to get clean and dry, but, at the moment, movement was beyond him.

Rebecca stopped and looked at him closely. "Colonel? Charlie?" He looked up at her. "I have hot water ready to fill a bath for you, and then a warm bed. Let me help you." He nodded in tired agreement. The idea of her helping him to undress made Charlie uncomfortable. Hell, the idea of anyone helping him to undress made Charlie uncomfortable.

Usually Jocko pulled his boots off for him and then left him to his own devices. But he had sent Jocko to bed hours ago, and right now, there were no other alternatives.

Rebecca pulled the small tub in front of the fire and half filled it with water from the boiler, topping it with cool water from the cistern pump until it was warm but not hot. Given how cold Charlie's skin was to her touch, she knew a bath that was too hot would be painful.

She then carefully eased the blanket from his shoulders. Kneeling in front of him with her back to him, she lifted one booted foot and gave it a hard tug, pulling the mud-encrusted leather from his foot. The other boot was more stubborn, and Charlie had to brace his sock clad foot against her back to give her enough leverage to pull it off.

She turned to him expectantly. He silently drained the mug of broth. "Thank you, Miss Rebecca. I can handle the rest myself."

"I do not think so, Colonel. Let me help. You still have stitches in your shoulder, you are cold and wet and muddy, and I doubt if you have the energy to take care of yourself properly." She stepped close to him and began efficiently unbuttoning the heavy wool tunic he was wearing. Embarrassed, Charlie looked down at the fingers working the buttons through the stiff cloth, then sighed as they unbuckled his belt. The tunic came off quickly, then the sodden cotton shirt under it; her hands just as efficient with the bindings that were so much a part of Charlie's life.

Rebecca stepped back from the tall figure standing before her, dressed only in breeches and socks. The contrast was startling. In one moment, Charlie changed from being a tall, lean, well-built man to being one of the most elegant and unusual creatures Rebecca had ever seen. There were muscles in Charlie's arms and chest, similar to a man's but more fluid, more graceful. The breasts were small and firm, with the nipples erect in the cool air. She could see the definition of each muscle around Charlie's ribcage and of his belly. The skin under his shirt was pale, almost translucent, and lightly marked with blue veins. For a moment, it was as if she were looking at a beautiful carving of an ancient Amazon warrior, executed in the finest marble. Rebecca forgot to breathe for a moment. Charlie slowly turned the most remarkable shade of red, starting with his ears, working its way down his body, and disappearing into his breeches.

Rebecca shook herself. "Turn around and sit on this stool. I need to look at that shoulder." Carefully, she examined the injury. It was healing cleanly, with no sign of the infection that had been there when she first saw it. While the scar would always be there, it was now a healthy pink, not the angry red it had been when she first treated it. "I think I can take the stitches out." She fetched her embroidery scissors from her sewing basket and used them to snip the stitches, pulling out each one carefully.

"There. Now you can soak your whole body in the tub without having to worry about keeping the stitches dry. In you go, Colonel."

Charlie turned his back to Rebecca and quickly shed the breeches and socks. Transformed again, she slipped into the tub. The warm water against her cold skin prickled and burned for a few minutes until her body started warming up. She relaxed, sliding down and curling into a ball, allowing herself to sink into the water up to her neck. She closed her eyes and rested her head on the edge of the tin bath. The wonder of the woman who had done this for her made Charlie's heart beat a little faster, and kept her awake when sleep should have already claimed her. A silent prayer of thanks went up from Charlie's soul to the God that at times had been her only confidant and companion. *She waited for me, made me soup, made a safe place for me to get clean. And she was worried about me. About me! Oh, Lord, thank you for giving me this time with her. Thank you for letting her look at the entirety of me and not turn away in disgust.*

Charlie shivered in sudden shock. Rebecca had taken a soapy washcloth and stroked her shoulders and neck with it before dropping it over her shoulder. "Here, my dear Colonel. You still look like a mud puppy."

Charlie sat up in the tub and began to scrub herself clean. Rebecca could not resist watching those limber muscles move under the surprisingly alabaster skin. Her eyes fell again on the old scars crisscrossing Charlie's back. *What kind of man could have done such a thing to him? To her? Oh, Lord, I have got to figure this out.*

"Tilt your head back, Colonel." Rebecca eased her confusion by doing what she had always done. Going to work on the thing at hand that most needed care, and hoping the rest of the situation would sort itself out eventually. Right now, getting the mud out of Charlie's hair was the most obvious thing that needed to be done.

The bath was concluded as quickly as possible. Each had their reasons for wanting to hurry through it. Charlie did not want to embarrass herself any more than she already had. And if Rebecca kept looking at her and tending to her in her current state of undress, the arousal she inspired in Charlie would be more than a little uncomfortable, even in her current state of exhaustion.

Rebecca wanted to touch Charlie, to explore the feel and texture of those muscles and skin, because he was, without question, the most fascinating thing she had ever seen, combining the best of both genders. Charlie was a strong woman, a delicate man, or maybe something entirely different.

For now, the nightshirt that had been warming by the fire was Charlie's immediate objective. To get dry and warm, and covered, and then get some sleep were all that he was capable of.

Rebecca insisted he get another mug of broth, which he took with him as they went upstairs to the bedroom. She had built a small fire in the room, and it had burned down to glowing coals. Shoveling a few into the bed warmer, Rebecca ran the copper pan under the covers, warming the cool sheets before Charlie gratefully tumbled into the bed. He was asleep within seconds of his head touching the pillow. She gently tucked the comforter around him and stood beside the bed just looking at his face, relaxed and somehow innocent in sleep, regardless of the horrors he had seen.

Then she turned, banked the fire, and went downstairs to try and rescue his mud caked clothing.

Charlie's dream began much as it always had when he was hurt, tired, or sick as a child. He had not had this dream in almost twenty years. She was small, still wearing the short white dress and stockings of a very young child. And there were warm arms around her, a soft shoulder to rest her head on, and a safe haven when the world was too much for a little girl. A low voice, softly accented, would sing, sometimes in French, sometimes in English, and sometimes in Scottish Gaelic all the songs the child loved.

The water is wide, I cannot get o'er
Neither have I the wings to fly.
Give me a ship that can carry two,
And both will cross, my love and I.

The child looked up, trusting and safe, into the pale blue eyes of one long missed person.

"Maman."

The ice-eyes smiled.

Charlie faded back into dreamless sleep.

Thursday, November 17, 1864

Rebecca woke quite early, for some unknown reason. Clearly, it was still very dark out, and Charlie was still curled up behind her with a strong arm wrapped around her waist. Actually, truth be told, it was she who always initiated the contact once they were both in bed. She would lie on her side and listen until Charlie's breathing slowed to a constant rhythm, and then she would roll over and get as close as she dared without waking her companion.

She did not realize how much she had missed and craved the warmth and comfort of another body until Charlie began sharing her bed. To her surprise and, once that passed, her great delight, the Colonel always moved closer as well, wrapping her in strong arms and making her feel very, very safe. It had been years since she slept as well as she did when he shared her bed.

And two nights ago, when he had not come in because of the storm, she had not only worried about the officer, but she realized she missed him as well. She had been unable to fall asleep for the longest time, finally falling asleep in her rocking chair, wrapped in the quilt they shared and clutching Charlie's pillow firmly to her breast.

Now she heard a recurrence of the noise that had disturbed her slumber. It was him. There was a quiet but very persistent wheeze coming from the Colonel that was not his normal soft snore. Slowly Rebecca rolled over and placed a hand to Charlie's face. The skin under her palm was so hot it was almost painful to touch. Moving away gently, she got out of bed, and quickly lit a lamp to really get a good look at her companion. His skin was reddened considerably and slight beads of perspiration lay across his forehead.

"Good Lord, Charlie, I told you, you would catch your death out there in that storm." Moving to the other side of the room, she poured a basin of water from the pitcher and collected cloths from the cabinet underneath. Taking them back to the bed, she placed the cool damp cloths on Charlie's forehead and neck.

The Colonel stirred, coughing as he came further into wakefulness. It did not take long for him to realize he felt ghastly. He had not felt this bad since Jocko had assured him it was all right to "have just one more" when they had visited the local bar outside of St. Louis, Missouri that housed an establishment of quiet or, in some cases, not so quiet pleasure.

"Ungh..." was all he could manage before trying to lick impossibly dry lips with a horribly dry tongue.

Gently, Rebecca brushed a moist cloth across Charlie's lips to help the process. "You are sick," she whispered needlessly.

He was very well aware of the fact he was sick. If it were not for the tender caring of the woman at his side, the good Colonel would wish himself dead, so he would feel better. His body was hot; his chest, head, and stomach hurt as if he had been kicked by the biggest horse in the stables. Closing his eyes to keep the room from spinning and his stomach from roiling, he merely nodded his head. Gently.

"Guess who is staying in bed today, Colonel Redmond."

The thought of protest crossed his mind. Then the rolling sensation heaved through his stomach. The protest tucked its tail between its legs and dutifully lay down in the corner of Charlie's mind.

"Jocko..." he rasped, softly for fear of another coughing jag.

"You leave it to me, Charlie. I will see to it that we get word to Jocko."

"Thank you."

"And in the meantime, Colonel Redmond, you will stay in this bed, and you will do everything I tell you to do. I currently outrank you."

"Yes, Ma'am." Charlie just really felt too bad to argue. Besides, he was learning rather quickly that Rebecca Gaines had a stubborn streak a mile wide, and when her mind was set on something, it was just better not to argue, because when she was riled, Rebecca could talk the ear off the Devil.

A smile curled at the Colonel's lips when another cool cloth was placed across his burning forehead and gentle fingers combed through his damp hair. He could feel her breathing on his cheek and hear her whispering in his ear. "Rest, Charlie, I will be right back with something to help your chest."

Unable to open his eyes for fear of what would happen to the contents of his stomach, he listened as she left the room. He could hear a slight creaking of the stairs as she descended them.

He pushed down the covers, feeling far too hot with them on. A shaky hand traveled to his nightshirt, and he felt the wetness that had been absorbed from his sweating skin. He moaned as his hand dropped back to the bed. Turning his head slowly, he could see it was still very dark out; and he wondered what had wakened Miss Rebecca.

Then he realized he must have been fussing in his sleep and awakened her. He listened as she made her way back up the stairs. She entered the room, holding a plate with a steaming towel on it. He wanted to tell her he would be out of her way soon and that he would go back to his tent until he felt better, but the words just would not pass through his dry mouth and thick tongue.

Suddenly he had no choice but to open his eyes when he felt the buttons being opened on his nightshirt. He turned his head and looked at her with wide, startled eyes.

"Relax, Colonel, it is only a mustard plaster for your chest. It is all right, I am not going to hurt you."

Being hurt was the last thing on Charlie's mind, the first being the gentle touch of this lady's hand as she applied the medicine cloth to his chest. They never broke eye contact the entire time it was being done, and Rebecca's sweet smile reminded him all was well. He need not worry; he was just as safe with her as she felt with him. She would not disclose his secret or betray his trust.

"Relax," she whispered again.

His mind began to reel from her tender touches, as she continuously replaced old cloths with fresh wet ones to cool his fevered brow. He closed his eyes, absorbing the comfort she was offering. It had been a very long time since someone other than Jocko or Dr. Walker had taken care of him. He imagined that the man who would eventually have Rebecca as his wife would be the luckiest man alive. Charlie only hoped that whoever it was would have the good sense to cherish this woman. He relaxed even further, knowing he was falling asleep and unable to stop it.

Rebecca watched as Charlie's eyes closed. She could not help but smile. She did feel sorry that the Colonel was sick, but she felt good that she had been able to relieve some of the distress and allow him to fall into a peaceful slumber. She brushed her fingers through damp hair, smoothing it back.

"Rest well, my dear." She placed a tender kiss on the Colonel's forehead, lowered the wick on the lamp, and quietly left the room to let him rest.

As the sun came up, Rebecca saw Sergeant Jackson, riding up to the house. She placed the pot of mint tea she had been preparing for her patient on a hot plate on the stove, then moved to the back door. Opening it, she smiled at Charlie's friend as he climbed the steps.

"Good morning, Sergeant Jackson."

"Good morning, Ma'am. I am here to inquire about Colonel Redmond. He has not returned to camp this morning."

"Yes, Sergeant, I know. Colonel Redmond is quite ill this morning. He is upstairs asleep."

"Ill?" Jocko's brows came together. "Should I send for the medic?"

"No, Sergeant. It is a cold. A bad one, I am afraid, but just a cold. I can take care of the Colonel. There is no need to bother your medic. He is upstairs in the master bedroom if you would like to go see him. I am making him some mint tea. I doubt he will be able to hold down much more than that."

"Yes, Ma'am. I do need to speak with him."

"Up the stairs, the door on the east side right at the very top."

"Thank you, Ma'am."

She returned to tending to the tea, listening to the sound of Sergeant Jackson's boots as he climbed the stairs.

Shortly after the sergeant had left to carry out the Colonel's orders for the day, Rebecca prepared a tray of mint tea and warm, soft bread. Returning to the bedroom, she found Charlie rolled on his side with his back to her. "Colonel?" she inquired softly so as not to wake him if he was sleeping.

Very slowly he rolled over, opening bloodshot eyes and gracing her with a weak smile. "Miss Rebecca."

"I brought you a little breakfast."

"I do not think…"

"Hush. You need to understand that while you are under my care, Colonel, you will do as I say."

He nodded slowly. "Yes, Ma'am."

Placing the tray on the floor, she helped him sit up, with his back against the headboard. After fluffing his pillows and straightening the blankets, she picked up the tray and placed it across his lap. "This is just mint tea with a little honey. It will ease your stomach. Try and eat a bit of the bread, too." Before taking a seat on the bed next to him, she poured the tea. "Come on now. Just a little, to make you feel better and help you keep your strength up."

Charlie found the tea extremely soothing. He had not really noticed until now, but his throat was raw, and sore as well. He closed his eyes, savoring the faint aroma and the soothing steam from the cup. That was, however, an error. As soon as he did, his head started spinning. Panicking a bit, he opened his eyes and thrust the cup into her hands. "Uh. Basin. Please."

Rebecca had been expecting this unfortunate turn of events, and quickly placed a basin at the side of the bed and helped him roll onto his side, with his head just slightly off the edge of the bed. She sat patiently and rubbed soothing circles on his back as he tried to decide if he were going to be sick.

Taking careful, deep breaths, Charlie focused on the top of the small chest of drawers across the room from him until his rebellious stomach decided the tea was acceptable and would be allowed to remain. He allowed himself to roll back onto the pillows and collected himself.

"Thank you. I was afraid it was not going to stay put. You have been so kind to care for me, Miss Rebecca." Just those few words seemed to tire him.

"It is my pleasure, Colonel. It is the least I can do for you. I want you to rest and get better. Your men are going to need you." *And I am going to need you.* The thought startled Rebecca for a moment, but she realized it was true. She and Charlie had started a hen war in town, but she was not going into the battle alone. And then, there was just the fact she found his mere presence in her life, somehow comforting.

"Perhaps I could try a little more tea? Your kind attention cannot help but make me feel better soon, Ma'am."

Charlie lay there, trying to be gallant. Well, trying to be civil. Just talking was a strain. *Maybe the bed would just absorb me. It would feel better than this.*

Rebecca helped him with the tea, smiling gently, wishing there was more she could do for him. "The good news is, the storm has abated. A little too late for you, I am afraid."

Charlie groaned. "Oh Lord. My men. How are my men? Did Jocko come by? Is Polk taking care of them? How much damage?" He tried to sit up, but determined arms held him back into the warmth and safety of the bed.

She ran her fingers through his hair, causing him to stop struggling against her attempts to make him lie back in bed. "I know you do not feel well, Charlie, but do you not remember Sergeant Jackson coming by earlier? You sent him off with his orders for the day."

Without thinking, Charlie leaned his head into her hand. He felt so miserable, and her touch felt so good. He wanted to just lay his head on her breast and be held like a child. A vague memory flitted through his mind, of a lovely, delicate woman with dark hair and laughing blue eyes who had held him in her lap when he was small and sick, and that had made things better.

After that dark lady of his memories had left, there had been no one who took care of him when he was sick. Until now. Unbidden, and unwanted, tears came to his eyes.

"Oh, Charlie," Rebecca soothed. "It is going to be all right. You just need to rest. I will take good care of you; you need not worry about a thing." She just wanted to hold him, make him feel better and make him believe her words.

He cleared his throat and blinked rapidly, leaning back against the pillow again. "Oh yes. Yes. I remember. The damage is not as bad as I feared." Turning to look into her eyes, needing at least a little more contact, he felt an aching loneliness that, coupled with his illness, made him more miserable.

The look in his eyes was one she had never seen before. It was the look of a child, a lonely, lost, miserable child. Then he dropped his eyes, lifted her hand, and tenderly kissed the back of it. "Thank you. Perhaps I could handle a little bread?"

She broke off small pieces of bread, feeding them to him from her own hand. "Is there anything more I can do for you? You will ask me if there is, will you not? Do not make me guess, Colonel. It is hard telling what I will do to you if left to my own devices," she teased gently as he took another bite. In a very small voice, punctuated by his careful chewing and swallowing of the small piece of bread, he responded, "I do not know what to ask. Usually when I am sick, I just stay in my tent and Jocko brings me water every so often."

A coughing fit took him for a moment, but the tickle in his throat was eased by another sip of the tea Rebecca gave to him as she supported him in her arms. "Eventually, I get better."

When he lay back, he continued to eat the bread she willingly fed him, savoring the feather light touch of her fingers against his lips.

"Well, you will need more than water to get through this. If you can think of anything, and I mean *anything*, that will help you, do not be afraid to speak up."

"Please, just stay with me." It was out of his mouth before he could stop it. Just being with her made him feel better. It had been so long since anyone cared for him, just for him; and he craved her companionship like a dying man craves water.

"I swear to you, Charlie, I am not going anywhere. I will be right here with you, I promise."

He caught her hand and brought it to his cheek. It felt so cool and so soft. His voice was husky, but she could not tell if it was because of the cold or something else. "You are so kind to me, Miss Rebecca. I am sorry to be so childish and demanding. I just..." He looked into her eyes as he slowly, reluctantly, let go of her hand. Weakened by the cold and fever, shaken by the impact of the memory of his mother who had died when he was only four, all of the pain and loneliness and despair of his life showed in that moment.

"Hush, now, do not be ridiculous. You are not being the least bit demanding. And I told you, I enjoy taking care of you. In a few short weeks, you have given me back something I did not realize was missing. It is nice to have someone who needs me again."

"I did not mean to impose, but it does feel good to be tended. I... I have not had anyone take care of me like this since I was very small. You could spoil me. Why, if this is how you take care of sick people, I might have to get sick more often." A weak attempt at humor was about all Charlie could manage just then, but he had to do something. He was desperate to get the relationship back on a more even keel, or he was going to break down and beg to be held.

Rebecca sighed, shaking her head. It was becoming clearer with each passing day, Colonel Redmond was a tough nut to crack. "Colonel, let us get one thing very clear. You are not imposing." There was so much she wanted to say, but she was not sure how much was appropriate right then. She had only known him for a short time, but she was beginning to feel as if she had known him forever; and as much as it amazed her, she really did feel affection for him.

"I care about you, Charlie, and I want to see you better very soon. You have an inspection coming up, and I hope to bribe you into another wonderful ride before the weather turns completely miserable."

"Well then, Ma'am, I will surely get better quickly under your care, and Shannon is always there to be at your service."

He smiled wanly at her and went on. "But, Miss Rebecca, we have taken over your farm, your life, we have made things uncomfortable for you with your neighbors, and I have taken over your bed and used your bedroom as a sick room. If that is not imposing, then what is?"

She smoothed the blankets at his chest. "It is not; trust me when I tell you this. If it were, you would most certainly find yourself in your tent on a very hard cot." She looked out the window. It was still very early and Charlie needed to rest. "I think you need to sleep, Colonel. And I could most certainly take a catnap. Would you be terribly uncomfortable if I settled in on my side of the bed for a bit of rest?"

As she lifted the tray off the edge of the bed and took his empty cup, Charlie shifted position. "Of course, Miss Rebecca. It is your bed." Almost under his breath, he added, "And I am always comfortable when you are beside me." As she settled into the bed, he reached out and took her hand in his, holding it gently.

CHAPTER 8

FRIDAY, NOVEMBER 18, 1864

Rebecca placed the washcloth on the rim of the basin. She glanced back at Charlie who was finally sleeping peacefully. She had gotten very little sleep the previous night. The Colonel had been tremendously fussy, thrashing about in the bed. She had done everything she could, including sitting up most of the night, continually wiping his forehead and neck with cool cloths.

She reached for her chemise, slipping into it before putting on her dress. She had considered taking the time for a proper bath, but did not want to be away from Charlie for that long. So, she had simply prepared a basin, stripped out of her clothes, and had a quick washing.

As she buttoned her dress, she watched Charlie. He curled up and rolled over, reaching to her side of the bed and pulling her pillow to him. She could not help but smile. For some reason she was still trying to understand, that action made her very happy.

She finished dressing, then went to his side, giving him a tender kiss on the cheek. "Sleep well, Charlie. We have another long day ahead of us."

~

She left the room, going first to the rooms that would house Dr. Walker. They were as ready as they could be, but were by no means all that Rebecca wished they could have been. Her home had once been beautiful, but the demands of the war had reduced it to a mere shell of its former glory.

Knowing there was nothing more she could do to the rooms, she closed the door, then went downstairs. She was putting the kettle on to boil when there was a rapping on the back door. She opened it to find four faces staring at her—three women and a man, each of them holding two small bags.

The young man spoke first. "Mrs. Gaines?"

"Yes."

"Yes, Ma'am." He pulled his hat from his head. "I am Reg." He gestured in turn to each of the women he was with. "This is Sarah, Beulah, and Lizbet. Colonel Redmond told us to come to you."

"Ah, yes. Come in." She allowed them in, appraising them as they stood before her. Charlie certainly knew how to pick servants. "Well, I will tell you that I am just starting to put Gaines Cove back in order, and it will require very hard work to do so. You are not afraid of hard work are you?"

"No, Ma'am," Reg answered for them. "We are very grateful to you and the Colonel for the work. We promise to do right by you and the Colonel, Mrs. Gaines."

"And the Colonel and I will do right by you." She gestured to the stairs. "You will find quarters upstairs on the third floor. Go put your things away, then come back down so I can get you started. And be very quiet going up the stairs, the Colonel is not feeling well and is still resting in bed this morning."

"Yes, Ma'am."

Charlie slept until mid-morning, when he was awakened, not by Rebecca as he had expected, but by Jocko, who came bustling in with a pan of hot water and a shaving kit.

"Well, Colonel C. How are we feeling this morning? Bright and chipper, I trust."

Charlie regarded his batman blearily. This degree of chipper was less than wonderful when Charlie still felt like he had a ton of wet bricks on his chest. Particularly when he had been hoping to see gentle green eyes, and instead was looking into brown ones that twinkled maliciously.

"We will be having company today. Colonel Polk needs his orders; Dr. Walker is arriving; and 'tis time for you to be the Colonel again. So I thought I would come over and fix you up."

Charlie groaned. "Just be gentle. I feel like I have been dragged through hell and back."

"A nice shave and some clean clothes will fix you right up again, I promise."

Charlie lay back and closed his eyes as Jocko bustled around him, lathering his face and then methodically removing the lather and the whisper of facial hair. Years of shaving had coarsened some of those very fine facial hairs so that Charlie did have a little bit of a beard, so it was a real necessity now. The two were silent as Jocko applied the brush full of soap froth, and then began removing it and the soft stubble with the straight edged razor.

As Jocko shaved him, Charlie turned to his oldest friend for some advice. The dream of his mother the previous night had shaken him more than he was willing to admit, even to himself, and Rebecca's gentle tending had added to his confusion.

"Jocko, am I wrong to play the role I do?"

"What do you mean, wrong, Charlie? You are a damned fine officer. You take care of your men, you get the job done with minimal casualties, and you are a fine tactician. You win battles. If you appeared to be a woman, you could not do the things you do at all. They would not let you."

Charlie snorted. "Well, I have been being a soldier and a man for so long; I do not think I could go back to wearing skirts if my life depended on it."

Jocko stopped for a moment and looked his old friend and commanding officer in the eye. "Charlie, for you to survive, you had to be a man, to act like a man, look like a man, and think like a man. You even seek out company like a man. In every way that counts, you are one. So why torment yourself?"

Charlie and Jocko were silent for a minute. Charlie thought about the raw truth in what Jocko had said. It was true; to survive, Charlie had to be a man. Most of the time, he thought of himself as a man. It was only in the safety and seclusion of his room, late at night when he had undressed and released the bindings around his chest that he remembered just what he really he was. It was sometimes confusing and it was usually terrifying. Staring at a reflection that did not match what his mind told him it should be. There was no way to explain that kind of disorientation in a way that would be considered socially acceptable in most circles.

Jocko's mind had traveled elsewhere. "So, you wore skirts? Now that is a sight I would pay money to have seen. Long hair, too? My, my, Colonel C. Were you the proper young Southern lady? I think not." With a snicker and a flourish, Jocko finished shaving Charlie by splashing his face with bay rum.

"All right, boss, time for you to get up and out. I brought your uniform. There is warm water in the basin, so get yourself up and dressed. When you are ready, I have set up a desk in the back parlor, and there is a nice warm fire going. Miss Rebecca has said you can use it as your office until you get better. Colonel Polk will be here at nine, and Dr. Walker is due in on the train at ten thirty. Your dispatches are waiting for you, as well as the reports from each company."

"Thank you, I think. Now go on. I will be down in a bit."

Charlie hauled himself out of bed. He was still feeling feverish and shaky, but the needs of the regiment were more important than his desire to lie in bed for the day. A quick glance at his pocket watch told him he needed to get a move on to meet Polk. Jocko had been thoughtful. He had brought the uniform trousers instead of the usual riding britches, and the soft, low cut dress boots that went with them instead of the snug knee-high riding boots. Even so, just getting dressed tired him out. He sat on the edge of the bed for a few minutes before tackling the stairs.

Finally, he carefully worked his way down the stairs. He met Rebecca coming out of the small parlor just as he was approaching the door. She took his arm and walked back into the room with him.

"I wish you could stay in bed for another day or two."

"To be honest with you, so do I. However, the needs of my men must be met, regardless of how I feel."

"Well, at least you can stay warm in here. I found a woolen shawl my husband used on cold days to help keep you warm. And I just put a pot of that mint tea you like on the hob. And if you get too tired, you can lie down on the davenport. There is an afghan you can use or the lap rug if you need them."

"Thank you." He glanced around at all of the things that Jocko and Rebecca had done to make him comfortable. The neat pile of handkerchiefs on the corner of the table that had been converted into a desk brought a smile to his lips. "I see you have thought of everything. Would you join me in a cup of tea?"

"Thank you, but no. I understand Dr. Walker is arriving today, and the servants you hired have arrived this morning, so I need to get them to work and make things ready. I will have a light lunch prepared for her and whomever she brings."

"Ah, Miss Rebecca, there is a close friendship between Dr. Walker and Colonel Polk. I would think they would both appreciate it if you included him in your luncheon plans."

Rebecca's right eyebrow rose, and a slightly amused look played over her features. "By all means. Colonel Polk is a—charming gentleman. By the way, Corporal Nailer has been a Godsend.

Duncan has found every piece of old furniture in the attic and the storerooms, and repaired and cleaned everything that could be made usable again. It feels like I have a furnished home again, even if nothing matches."

"I am glad for you. And I will be sure to commend him for his efforts. I noticed you still have a problem with the kitchen, though."

"Yes, well, the wind took the patch off almost as soon as it started raining."

Rebecca's face looked strained. Charlie did not know what had affected her so: whether it was the stress of dealing with all of his demands, the pain of having her home taken over, or something else entirely.

"Miss Rebecca, I am sorry we have imposed on you so. If there is anything we can do to lessen the burden, please..." He trailed off, at a loss for words, but sensing the small woman's distress.

She responded gently, "No, Colonel, you and your men have done nothing to cause me distress. If anything, you have offered me a reprieve, a chance to build a new life for myself. For this, I am deeply grateful."

"Rebecca, I hope you know I would do anything in my power to make your life less painful, less difficult. I am at your service whenever you need me."

The raw honesty of Charlie's offer shook Rebecca's fragile control. She became a bit brusque to mask her reaction. "Well, Sir, with guests coming, I must be about my business." She walked briskly to the door, and paused as she was leaving. "Please, Colonel Redmond, do take care. Do not push yourself any more than you absolutely must." With that admonition, she quietly closed the door.

Charlie seated himself at the makeshift desk and drew the dispatch case in front of him. But instead of opening it, he just sat staring at the door that Rebecca had just closed, seeing the tired look in the woman's eyes, the almost lost look that haunted her today, and wracking his brains for something to make her feel better.

Finally, he poured himself a cup of the tea she had left him and proceeded to plow through the dispatches and reports before his meeting with Polk.

Promptly at nine o'clock, Polk rapped on the door and Charlie called for him to enter. Without rising, he waved his adjutant to a chair as he finished reading the last report.

"Well, Richard, it looks like we could have sustained much worse damage than we did."

"Yes, sir. We have a number of sprained ankles, and a number of colds amongst the men, but nothing serious. We have five injured horses, but none had to be put down. We are still looking for about half a dozen missing horses and one missing mule. The best news is that, except for a couple of sacks of flour and a barrel of salt pork, our supplies are all fine. The bad news is, every single pair of those lousy boots Supply sent us have fallen apart or turned into solid blocks. With the wet weather, we are scrimping, using old boots and lining them with whatever we can get, but it is not good."

"All right. Telegraph the Quartermaster General, with a copy to General Sheridan as urgent. In the meantime, is there any tanned leather around? We could make moccasins and line them with straw or something to at least keep the men's feet dry and warm. Check with Sheridan; and what about checking with Mr. Cooper? This area was once all cattle and horse farms. Maybe there are still some cured hides around. And see if there are any men with skills as cobblers or leatherworkers."

"Yes, Sir. We will do the best we can."

"How are we progressing on putting in drainage and winterizing the tents?"

"The storm certainly defined the current water flow patterns Sir. I have four companies at work on digging ditches and building berms around the tents themselves. We have not yet received the wood for the rough timbering. It is waiting for us at the rail yard, but the road is still too muddy to transport it."

"Keep up the work, and get those timbers in as quickly as you can. I do not want a repeat of the last couple of days. Now, on another subject, what is the word on Montgomery?"

"Samuelson is concerned. He has not yet regained consciousness. You put water or broth in his mouth, he swallows; you tickle the soles of his feet with a blade, he twitches; but that is the extent of his responsiveness."

"I would hate to lose him. I am glad Dr. Walker will be here today."

"Um, Sir, that leads me to another question. Dr. Walker is due in this morning."

"I know." The commander nodded seriously.

"I would like permission to go meet her train."

"I had assumed you would." Charlie looked down at the papers in front of him to hide the slight smirk that came to his lips. "Perhaps you would take Samuelson with you. Just to fill her in on the status of the men, of course. And to provide a companion for Mr. Whitman, if he is with her. Escort them here, as I believe Miss Rebecca has planned a light lunch for them and plans to host them in the main house."

"Certainly, Sir."

"And you are invited to lunch as well, Richard."

Polk had the grace to blush slightly. "Thank you, Charlie. And thank Miss Rebecca for me."

"I assume you can convey your appreciation to the lady herself, Richard. Now, off you go. You have much to do between now and ten thirty."

"Yes, Sir!" He saluted briskly.

Polk walked out the door, closing it gently behind him. Charlie slumped in his chair, leaning back and closing his eyes. Just the effort needed to read the reports and meet with Polk had drained what little energy he had.

A gentle tap on the door failed to rouse him from the gentle doze into which he had fallen. Rebecca entered, followed closely by Corporal Duncan Nailer, who was embarrassed by having to report to the Colonel directly. The heavy clump of Duncan's hobnail boots roused Charlie.

"Miss Rebecca? Duncan? What can I do for you?"

Rebecca looked upset, Duncan looked determined. He spoke first. "S-si-sir, about the k-ki-kitchen. I have looked it over c-ca-carefully, and we really need to put a new r-roof on it. Otherwise, it will just c-co-continue to spring leaks. I talked to Sergeant Wise, who s-said we had the materials. So, I want about f-four men to help me rip the r-roof off and r-re-replace it. I f-f-figure it will only take a c-co-couple of days with the right men."

"Colonel, I cannot let you do this. This is my property, and I am responsible for taking care of it."

"Duncan, pick your men and get the job done before the weather changes again. Dismissed."

Duncan looked between his Colonel, who looked rather pale and drawn, and Miss Rebecca, who looked like a thundercloud about to break. He sketched a quick salute to the Colonel and hastily retreated from what looked as though it would be a messy skirmish.

"Colonel Redmond! What gives you the right simply to make decisions about my house, about my choices, without even consulting me?"

Charlie closed his eyes and let her anger wash over him. He did not have the energy for this. In a flat monotone, he responded without opening his eyes. "It needed to be done—and done before we get another storm. This is the only way it could be done promptly."

"Colonel Redmond. You are not the master of this house, you are my guest. And I at least have the right to contribute to these decisions."

The master of this house. Dear God, I wish I were. I wish it could be so.

"Yes, Miss Rebecca. I know I am not the master of this house." He opened his eyes and looked at her, holding her gaze with sick, tired eyes. "And I certainly know I am not your lover, let alone your husband. But you are the one who wanted my protection. This is one of the results."

She opened her mouth to respond, then looked closely at him once more and abruptly closed it again. "Charlie?" She passed her hand over his cheek and forehead. "Charlie, are you all right?"

"No. I am sick. I am tired. I am drained." *And I am trying to do right by you, and you are busy giving me what for and throwing it in my face.* "You are welcome for the new roof."

Her hand on his cheek was more pain than he could take at the moment. He turned his face away from her, sick in heart as well as in body. He wished he could be the man she needed and deserved, but he was not and never would be. The voice in his head, the one he hated and feared, crowed with glee.

You see, you miserable fraud. Even your kindnesses are not needed, not wanted. You know that when this war is over, when they no longer need a lackey to do the dirty work of war, even that pitiful little usefulness will be gone. Give it up, Charlie Redmond. You are only useful to the dogs of war, and when they are kenneled this time, so shall you be.

The familiar, hollow ache in his chest, the one he had lived with for all of his adult life, burst into full flaming agony. It was all he could do to sit still. The urge to curl into a shaking ball around that burning emptiness was all consuming.

"Charlie. What is it, Charlie?" Rebecca was contrite. She had not meant to hurt him, and then suddenly it was as if he just... went away for a minute.

He took a deep breath, trying to get himself back under control. He looked up at her, and for a fleeting moment, she could see the soul-killing anguish in his eyes before the usual gentle and polite Colonel returned. "I am sorry, Miss Rebecca. I did not mean to be sharp with you, nor to take away your prerogatives around the house or the farm. Can you forgive my presumption?"

"Colonel, if anyone should apologize, I believe it is me. I did not mean to rail at you like that. I am afraid I am just tired. And there is so much to do before Dr. Walker arrives." She took him by the arm, wrapping her hands around him. "Charlie, you need to rest, dear man. Please, please at least lie down for a bit until luncheon?"

Her touch was still fire. The gentle solicitude of her voice was an agony. Between the recent dream of his mother and the moment when Rebecca had gone from gentle concern to angry lashing out because he had crossed the line of acceptable behavior, Charlie was now deeply mired in his darkest melancholia. A part of him wanted to reach out to her, like a wanderer lost in the desert seeking the peace of an oasis. The rest of him knew, beyond any doubt or hope, that such sanctuary was not for him.

He let her help him to the davenport, and laid back, exhausted as much by his own pain as by the illness. Gently, she tucked him in and left him lying with his eyes closed, hoping he would sleep for a bit. As the sound of the latch clicked home, the first of a long stream of silent tears ran down Charlie's face.

An eager Polk stood at the small railroad station in Culpeper, looking north up the line for the smudge of smoke that would tell him the train was coming. He had sent one of the quartermaster sergeants looking for cured leather and another looking through the rosters for skilled leather crafters. Now he was waiting for her.

The normally jovial, calm gentleman paced up and down the platform, hands stuffed deep in his coat pockets, tromping to and fro like an expectant father, chewing rather vigorously on the stub of his cigar. Samuelson sat quietly on one of the three benches on the platform, watching the Colonel as though he was a circus exhibition or taking part in some sort of competitive sport.

Finally, Samuelson could stand it no longer. Quietly, he went into the stationmaster's office and inquired on the latest notification of progress of the supply train with the small passenger car tacked on at the end. The stationmaster's report was terse. The train had taken on water in Warrenton about an hour ago and was expected in approximately ten minutes. Samuelson thanked the man courteously and stepped back out to inform the pacing officer.

On hearing the news, Polk threw the stub of his cigar onto the cinders of the tracks. "Why can we not get the damned trains to run on time? Somebody ought to be able to do something as simple as that." He lit another stogie and went back to pacing.

Eleven and a half minutes later, the supply train pulled into the station and moved up so the passenger car was even with the platform. Immediately, Polk was at the door, ready to hand the lady down. Samuelson followed a step or two behind.

"Dr. Walker, I am so glad to see you. How was your trip? Not too tiring, I hope. You are looking well. Is this a new traveling suit? It becomes you, Ma'am." Polk hustled about, gathering her cases and talking non-stop.

The diminutive, dark haired woman with the soft brown eyes just smiled gently, waiting for the Colonel to wind down a bit. "Good morning, Colonel. You are looking well, and the trip was uneventful, thank you," she answered all of his questions smoothly.

Samuelson smiled shyly at Mr. Whitman as he disembarked from the train. The two men silently shook hands.

Dr. Walker turned her attention to Samuelson. "Good morning, Mr. Samuelson. I trust we have no pressing cases demanding our immediate attention."

"Well, Ma'am, there is one case I wish you would examine fairly soon. A head injury, I am afraid."

"Ah, yes, those can be quite difficult."

Polk broke in. "Dr. Walker, Ma'am, our hostess, Mrs. Gaines, has prepared a luncheon and a suite for you in her home. Would you not like to get settled before you attend to medical issues?"

"Gentlemen, my oath comes before my comfort. Let us go and see this case that has Samuelson so concerned. Then we can enjoy the social amenities."

The three men hauled various cases and trunks from the train to the waiting carriage. Tarent had managed to get a larger open carriage back into working condition in time to collect Dr. Walker and her traveling cases, most of which contained medical tools and drugs. Stowing them in the boot, Samuelson offered to drive back to the farm. Whitman rode beside him on the driver's bench, while Polk joined Dr. Walker.

The trip back was quick, with Samuelson managing to avoid the worst of the rain-induced ruts in the road. Each couple spoke quietly of personal things, catching up on news of mutual acquaintances and one another's activities. As soon as they reached the stone barn that was now the infirmary, the gracious lady transformed into the efficient physician.

"Let us take a look at your most serious cases, Mr. Samuelson."

"There is only one urgent one, Dr. Walker. It is Major Montgomery. He was kicked in the head by a horse. We have some reflex activity, but he has been unresponsive since the accident."

Quietly, Whitman opened the black satchel he always kept handy; the one that contained the doctor's most commonly used tools. A candle, quickly lit, was placed inside a small, directional lantern with a focusing lens. This was used both to light small areas, like the insides of the ear, and to check the reaction of the patient's pupils. Dr. Walker took her listening horn and checked Montgomery's heart and breathing, then took a small tool that looked like a tiny rowel spur and ran it over his palms, the inside of his wrist, and the soles of his feet.

Finally, she carefully examined his head, probing with gentle fingers all around the inflamed area. Shaking her head, she turned to Samuelson and Whitman. "Gentlemen, we will have to perform surgery—and even then I do not know if we can save him. How long will it take for you two to set up the surgery and create as clean an area as possible?"

Samuelson spoke up. "Ma'am, I have already been preparing a surgical area. With Mr. Whitman's help, we should be ready for you by mid-afternoon."

"Fine. I will meet our hostess and get a little rest; then we shall do what we can for this poor man. Oh, Whitman, do get yourself something to eat. You will need the strength."

The Colonel and the lady waited as Whitman and Samuelson unloaded all but the personal baggage from the carriage, then Polk drove Dr. Walker up to the main house.

They were met at the door by Beulah and were immediately joined by Rebecca, who had been waiting in the front parlor. Quiet introductions and greetings were exchanged, as Rebecca explained about Colonel Redmond's incapacity. As Beulah hustled off to get Reg to unload the personal baggage and take it to the guests' rooms, Dr. Walker offered to check on Charlie, both in her capacity as a physician and as an old friend. Polk excused himself for a few moments, to send a couple of messages back to the duty officer of the day.

Quietly entering Charlie's office cum sick room, Dr. Walker was shocked to find him lying on the sofa, looking drained and exhausted. "Hello, Charlie."

She surprised him. He sat up abruptly, a move that caused his touchy head to pound for a moment. "Elizabeth. I am sorry, you startled me."

She sat beside her old comrade. "So, tell me. How are things going—really? You look very tired."

"Oh, it has been a tough few days, Elizabeth. I am very glad you have come. I need your help, old friend—in so many ways."

"Well, Montgomery seems to be the first problem. I am going to have to operate as soon as possible if we are to have any hope of saving him."

"I was afraid of that. When will you do it?"

"This afternoon, if at all possible. I do not want him to deteriorate any more than he already has. Even so, it may be too late. Head injuries are very tricky."

"Well, whatever you need, my dear lady, whatever you need."

"What about you, Charlie? Is there something bothering you other than a cold?"

"Ah, we will talk about that later, if you do not mind. Focus on Montgomery first, my friend. But before that, I believe our hostess, Mrs. Gaines, has prepared a luncheon for you. We should not keep her waiting."

"Yes, I met her. She seems a lovely lady. It will be nice to have a Southern woman to talk with again."

"I hope you two can be friends."

"Yes, well, from the looks of it, she and I have about the same approach to taking care of Colonels who will not take care of themselves. I can smell the mustard plaster and the mint tea. My prescription for your ailments, Colonel, is that you continue to follow your hostess' instructions."

A shadow flickered across Charlie's face, then his usual polite mask slid into place. "Of course, Doctor. As you say. Now, shall we go in to luncheon?"

Charlie rose and offered his arm to the diminutive woman. Since she was barely five feet tall, Charlie towered over her, presenting a strikingly romantic picture. Both Polk and Rebecca stiffened a little as the two entered the dining room, arm in arm, laughing at some riposte that one of them had made to the other. Charlie did not notice; Elizabeth did, especially Rebecca's response. *My, my. I wonder if there is something there. Well, there is no one who more deserves loving care than our Charlie, but can this proper Southern lady handle our boy?*

Luncheon was a bit stilted.

After coffee, Rebecca offered to escort Dr. Walker to her room to rest, and Polk and Charlie lingered outside the front door to share a cigar, an act that turned out to be less than intelligent on Charlie's part, as it set off a violent round of coughing that left him feeling drained. Rebecca, descending from the upper floors, heard his raucous hacking and stepped out on the portico. She shooed Polk back to his duties, then hustled Charlie into the back parlor.

A dose of mint tea, a new mustard plaster, and some very focused fussing later, and Charlie, swathed in a lap rug and woolen shawl, was settled before a warm fire with pillows at his back. "You need to rest, Colonel Redmond. Would you like me to read to you?"

"You need not inconvenience yourself, Miss Rebecca. I will be fine here."

"It is not an inconvenience, Colonel. I often read to myself after lunch: poetry, philosophy, or the Bible. It soothes me. When my brother was alive, we would read aloud to one another, and I grew into the habit. It is one I would happily renew."

"As you wish, my dear lady. The sound of your voice alone is soothing to me. And anything that interests your agile mind will be enlightening, I am sure."

Rebecca looked at Charlie with some concern. The gentle informality of the last few days had been replaced with his most courtly manners. Perhaps the good doctor had more of a relationship with Charlie than she had thought, and he was distancing himself because his lover had arrived. But that did not make sense. Charlie had said he was not involved with anyone—he had been quite clear. Perhaps she had rebuked him. Ah, well, she knew she would never win the love of someone as generous and good as Charlie. So, these moments together were to be savored. And savor them she would.

"I have been reading some of the Apocrypha to the Holy Bible. I find there are some interesting additions to the stories we all learn in our normal religious studies. Would that interest you, Sir?"

"Just continue from wherever you left off reading. I have read them, and find them quite fascinating. A reminder would not be unwelcome."

"This is the additional Chapter Fourteen to the book of Esther, then.

"*Queen Esther also, being in fear of death, resorted unto the Lord: And laid away her glorious apparel, and put on the garments of anguish and mourning: and instead of precious ointments, she covered her head with ashes and dung, and she humbled her body greatly, and all the places of her joy she filled with her torn hair. And she prayed unto the Lord God of Israel, saying, O my Lord, thou only art our King: help me, desolate woman, which have no helper but thee: For my danger is in mine hand."*

Charlie listened carefully to the words. It seemed to him that Rebecca might find her own situation reflected in these words. The deep losses of husband and family this cruel war had inflicted upon her were suddenly there before him. He knew she had first put aside her widow's weeds when he had invited her to ride with him. He continued to listen to her reading.

"And now we have sinned before thee: therefore hast thou given us into the hands of our enemies, because we worshipped their gods: O Lord, thou art righteous. Nevertheless it satisfieth them not, that we are in bitter captivity: but they have stricken hands with their idols, that they will abolish the thing that thou with thy mouth hast ordained, and destroy thine inheritance, and stop the mouth of them that praise thee, and quench the glory of thy house, and of thine altar, and open the mouths of the heathen to set forth the praises of the idols, and to magnify a fleshly king forever."

As she read, Charlie's evil voice forced him to draw comparisons between Rebecca and the queen she was reading about. *Dear God, what if she thinks that she is in bitter captivity with our presence? Have we abolished the order that God ordained for this country, or are we right in claiming the Union to be paramount? Even so, has this been worth the price people like her have had to pay? I am different, I am just a soldier, doing my job—but look what this war has done to her and others like her. I do not know. I just do not know. I wish I could take away her pain.*

As Rebecca read on, her voice soft and soothing, the exhaustion of his illness and the emotional turmoil that had battered him throughout the night and morning caught up with him. Charlie slid into a light sleep. As his breathing changed, she quietly closed her Bible and moved to his side. She straightened his shawl, covering his chest more completely, and smoothed an unruly lock of hair back from his forehead. Softly, she laid her lips on his forehead, pleased to feel that his temperature, although not yet normal, had fallen. Settling into a chair beside him, she sat and watched his sleeping face, holding his hand tenderly in her own. She roused a little as she heard Dr. Walker leaving, then returned to her vigil as the shadows of late afternoon and then evening slowly claimed the little parlor.

Dr. Walker stretched, and flexed her hands. The surgery on Montgomery had been very demanding, and had gone on far longer than she had expected. She had found a depressed area of skull, with small splinters surrounding the indentation.

She had carefully trimmed the broken section of bone, removing the little shards and then replacing the large section so that it would eventually merge back into the rest of the skull. He was fortunate; the thin membrane that protected the actual brain was unbroken. Hopefully, with the pressure from the break removed, the swelling would start to diminish and he would survive. It was still too early to tell.

Richard was waiting for her. As Samuelson and Whitman tended to the patient, he wrapped her in his own greatcoat and half walked, half carried her back to the main house. There, Sarah was waiting with warm soup, bread, and fruit, along with a pot of strong, sweet black tea. The doctor ate as much as she could, then Richard carried her upstairs to her room and turned her over to Lizbet for the night.

A similar repast had been carried to the back parlor. Rebecca woke Charlie, who was embarrassed by sleeping the afternoon away. She soothed his concern, reminding him he was ill, and that the best cure for what ailed him was sleep. They shared the simple meal sitting before the fire, and spent the evening speaking of effortless things:

poetry and literature they had both read and enjoyed, music they liked, and even foods they preferred. Once more, they found they shared a great similarity in tastes and sensibilities.

Unusually, Rebecca was dreading bedtime tonight. She feared that with Dr. Walker's presence, Charlie would choose to sleep on the davenport, rather than with her. The thought of trying to sleep without those strong arms around her was almost frightening. Finally, Charlie yawned.

"Miss Rebecca, you must be tired. Shall we retire?"

"Oh, Colonel, I am sorry. You are still ill and I have kept you up 'til all hours. It was just that I was enjoying our conversation so."

"Well, come upstairs. We can continue our chat for as long as I can keep my eyes open, at least," he laughed softly.

"Are you sure, Colonel?"

He raised a brow. "I am very sure, Miss Rebecca, unless you have reconsidered our arrangement."

"No!" she blurted out faster than she intended. "Everything is fine. I...I... Well, it is not important." She stood, offering him her hand. "Let us go to bed."

Saturday, November 19, 1864

Charlie woke early the next morning. His fever had abated, and though his head was still congested, his throat no longer felt like someone had poured acid down it, and his lungs had lost their wet bricks.

Time to get back to work. Just too many things needed to be done after the storm for him to lie about in bed for another day.

In the dim light of dawn, he slipped from under the covers and went looking for his clothing. Jocko had brought over at least one change of clothes for him. Rustling through the wardrobe in the corner, Charlie made just enough noise to wake Rebecca.

"Colonel Redmond, what do you think you are doing?" She threw the covers back, getting out of bed quickly.

"Oh, Miss Rebecca. I am sorry, I did not mean to wake you."

"Nonsense, do not worry about that, but please answer my question."

"Well, it is morning. I usually get dressed and go to work in the morning, Ma'am." Charlie was amused. She reminded him of a bantam rooster—or maybe a hen—when she was in this mood.

She took his shirt from his hand. "Get back into bed, Charlie."

"But, Rebecca, I sat up in the parlor yesterday and took it easy. And I am feeling much better today, really I am."

"Colonel Redmond, whether you like it or not, you are still not up to snuff, and I want to make sure you are completely better."

"I assure you, Ma'am, I am feeling much better. I will be fine. And if I do feel a little less than full force, I promise you, I will sit and rest." Unfortunately, his attempt to depict the image of the hale and healthy gentleman was somewhat marred by an explosive sneeze, followed by another coughing fit.

"Oh yes, I can see you are the picture of health. Now, do not make me resort to violence to keep you in the house," she teased. "I do believe in your current condition I could give you what for. I may be small, but I am fierce." The scolding was softened by the smile on her face.

He groped for a handkerchief and sat in the rocking chair to regain his breath. "Well, perhaps I am not yet fully recovered. But I do feel much better, and the men really do need me."

"I am very well aware of everyone who needs you, Colonel." She brushed her fingers through his unruly hair to offer him some comfort. "I will make you a deal."

He looked into her eyes expectantly. The feel of her fingers in his hair was very pleasant indeed. Somehow, in the past two days, a barrier had been crossed.

"If you promise to behave and stay in the house today, you may retain the office here in the house for your permanent office and hold your meetings here where the staff can tend to you properly."

"Yes, but I know you prefer the back parlor as your own personal refuge. Perhaps your husband had an office with a separate entrance? Or the farm manager? Here in the main house, but not in the middle of your daily life? If there was a room like that, I would like it very much."

"There is a manager's office that has a separate entrance. You are most welcome to use it, if you wish"

"Thank you, Miss Rebecca. This way, the back parlor remains private. I know how much time you spend in that room, and how lovely the view is in the late afternoon as the setting sun is reflected in the pond. I would not want to take that from you, dear lady."

"You are not. And using the manager's office, I will not even know you are there, Sir. So it is no bother at all."

Charlie stepped closer to the woman standing before him, and caught her hand in his own. The care she had given him, the things she had thought of and offered for his comfort and convenience, all touched him in places no one had ever reached. "I cannot even begin to tell you how much I appreciate what you have done for me and to my men. I promise you, I will do my best to make our stay as comfortable for you as I can."

"You have already given me more than you will ever know, Colonel Redmond." She paused for a moment then slowly stepped closer and embraced him, holding him for a long moment. "More than you will ever know."

Charlie's arms had encircled her automatically. The feel of her arms around him, the soft silk of her hair against his cheek, the warmth of her slender body against his own was heaven. He felt as though he had been given a brief taste of Eden, as though she heard the words in the silence of his heart and had answered them. When she stepped away, the sense of loss was so great he wanted to cry out. He tried to speak, and had to clear his throat. "Miss Rebecca." He could not express what he felt in that moment. Instead, he simply bowed over her hand, pressing it to his lips in a long, tender tribute.

The two came to a truce, and Charlie had permission from the lady of the house to hold his first staff meeting in the manager's office. To have a place where his men could gather and stay reasonably warm was a blessing. It was amazing just how cold a large tent could get in the winter.

Together, Charlie and Rebecca went downstairs to sample Sarah's breakfast cooking. They entered the morning room, traditionally used by the family for informal meals like breakfast, to find Dr. Walker already there, and happily eating Sarah's lovely, fluffy drop biscuits with butter and honey. Appropriate greetings were exchanged, while Rebecca poured cups of coffee for Charlie and herself. She then settled at the small table with the two old friends. Elizabeth watched the pair with a twinkle of amusement in her eye. Clearly, these two had a connection. It remained to be seen just how intense it was, and whether Charlie would have the courage to act upon it.

"Ah, Mrs. Gaines. I must thank you for the lovely hospitality you afford me. I cannot tell you how much more pleasant it is to have a room and a bed of my own than the tent I use when out in the field with the boys."

"Dr. Walker, please, call me Rebecca."

"And you must call me Elizabeth, as Charlie does."

"It is my pleasure, I assure you. I have been alone in this big old rambling place for so long, that company is most welcome. I trust you slept well?"

"Most assuredly. Colonel Polk was kind enough to escort me back to the house last night when I finished surgery, and I was so exhausted that I simply retired after a light supper. I know it was not the most polite action, but I was sure you would understand."

Charlie broke into their chat. "So how did the surgery go, Elizabeth?"

The physician's face shifted into a focused look of concern. "He had a compressed skull fracture. I have cleaned the wound, relieved the pressure on the brain, and removed a number of bone splinters. Now it is a matter of time. He may stay as he is until something like pneumonia takes him, or he may begin to recover. It really depends on how strong he is."

"Thank you for your efforts, Ma'am. I will write his family again, providing them with at least some information as to his status and prospects. If you do not mind looking over the letter before I send it, I would deeply appreciate it."

"Of course, Charlie. I know how hard these things are for you, my friend." Elizabeth gently patted his arm.

A pang of jealousy shot through Rebecca as she watched the easy exchange between the two. The closeness of their friendship, shown both in the fact they were on a first name basis and in the casual touch, burned into her. She wanted that kind of easy intimacy with the Colonel.

"So tell me, Elizabeth, how did you and Colonel Redmond meet?"

Elizabeth glanced at Charlie, a little concerned over inadvertently revealing more than perhaps the Colonel would like.

"It is all right, Elizabeth. She knows." There was a calm self-assurance in the statement that was a testament to Charlie's faith in this woman's discretion.

One eyebrow rose with that knowledge. *What is there between these two? Charlie only came to me out of absolute necessity. I thought I would have to drag his secret out of him. He has only known Rebecca for a few days and still he speaks of her knowing with so much confidence. Has our good, austere, and isolated Colonel fallen?*

"To be honest, we met as doctor and patient. Charlie was injured and needed help. He sought me out, hoping I would understand and keep his trust. From there, we became friends."

As the three of them sat and chatted politely over breakfast, Beulah escorted Colonel Polk into the room.

"Good morning, Miss Rebecca, Doctor Walker, Colonel." Polk's manners were still impeccable. He stood there fidgeting with the brim of his hat.

"Please join us, Colonel." Rebecca motioned to Beulah to get the Colonel a cup of coffee.

"Thank you, Miss Rebecca." He turned to the physician. "Did you sleep well, Doctor? I was concerned about you last night. You seemed so exhausted. You know," he admonished, "if you wear yourself out, I would not...you will not be able to help any of the men," he finished rather lamely.

"Thank you for your concern, Colonel. I truly appreciated your waiting for me last night and escorting me back to the house." She smiled very gently at the flustered officer. "Your concern and care for me, is always appreciated."

Rebecca watched these two, then glanced at Charlie. The look on his face almost made her giggle. He had leaned back in his chair and was watching the two of them like a satisfied, well fed cat. The look of benign amusement in his eyes, coupled with the small smirk that twisted his lips, immediately conveyed the message. *Elizabeth and Polk. Charlie had said they were an interesting pair. This definitely had possibilities.* The stab of jealousy receded, and instead Rebecca thought that perhaps, just perhaps, Elizabeth would be someone she could talk with.

Elizabeth and Polk came to something of an impasse, with neither of them willing to move forward in their conversation nor willing to break their eye contact. Charlie raised an eyebrow and decided to break the tension.

"Polk, I am glad you are here. I have a couple of issues I would like to discuss with both you and Dr. Walker." The two broke their gaze and looked at Charlie inquiringly. Rebecca hid her smile behind her coffee cup.

"We have a couple of morale problems to deal with. First, Dr. Walker, I have orders to try to build bridges to the civilian community. President Lincoln is aware this war cannot continue for much longer. The end is inevitable." Both Polk and Elizabeth nodded their agreement, as did Rebecca. "He wants us to do whatever we can to lay the groundwork for a relationship with the civilian population that will make the reconstruction of the Union as painless as possible, given the circumstances."

"I would like to offer the people of Culpeper County access to our medical services, plus whatever else we can provide them. Can you organize such an effort, Doctor?"

"Well, I can certainly organize the resources, but I have no relationship with the people here. I have not lived in the area for years, and when I did, it was down in Charlottesville." She turned to Rebecca. "Perhaps, you could assist in this process? Surely providing medical care for your neighbors is not an issue related to which side of this conflict you support, but instead can be framed in terms of being a good neighbor."

Rebecca nodded, placing her cup on the table. "I would be delighted to assist you, Elizabeth. There are many good people here who just need a helping hand to get back their good standing. But I must warn you, there are some very sharp beaks in Culpeper."

"Excuse me?"

The Colonel laughed. "Miss Rebecca is referring to what she likes to call the biddy brigade."

The doctor and Polk both burst out laughing. Charlie looked to Rebecca, but did not even pretend to try and hide the grin on his face.

"Oh you!" she scolded, giving him a playful slap to the hand. "The doctor will think dreadful things of me if you tell such stories."

"Then do not say such things," he teased, causing further laughter.

Elizabeth glanced down to the table, noticing that Rebecca had not moved her hand from Charlie's after lightly tapping him, and that he had wrapped his fingers around hers. *They are not even aware they are holding hands. What they have is so natural, they do not even notice. Oh Charlie, you have found yourself quite a lady here. Be strong and hang on to her.*

Charlie turned to Polk. "What about ways in which the men can create some relationship with the locals? Would you think they would accept help in getting their properties back in shape for the spring? Perhaps checking and fixing fencing, roofing, barns, and such? I would think the men might actually enjoy doing such things, as it is certainly better than sitting around being bored, and they might find it comforting to be able to do something familiar."

"I also think it would be a good way to help erase some of the lines drawn between the original troops of the 13th and the men from the 49th who we have used to build the regiment back up to full force."

"Your opinions are most welcome. Miss Rebecca. What do you think about the citizens' willingness to accept such support?"

"As I said before," she moved her hand from Charlie's to pour him another cup of coffee, an action that went totally unnoticed by Charlie, but most certainly was observed by Polk and Walker, "there will be those who will gratefully accept the help. Then there will be others who will be obstinate and half-witted."

She continued fussing with his coffee, adding just a touch of sugar then stirring it in before placing it back in front of him. It was all Elizabeth could do not to laugh out loud when she watched Charlie pick up the cup without even looking at it. He just knew it would be there.

Oh dear, Charlie. You have managed to fall in love. She glanced at Rebecca, who was watching Charlie. *And she adores you.*

"Well, Polk. I think you have your work cut out for you in terms of building civilian relationships. On a different subject, I am concerned about some of the issues that raised themselves the other day. In particular, how common is Montgomery's attitude among the men?"

"I have asked the company commanders to explore this issue carefully, but because of the sensitivity, I wanted to have the reports given verbally. I expect to have the information at today's staff meeting."

"And the issue of the integration of the men into a solid team?"

"That is also on today's agenda."

"Then, my friend, we need to go hear what our officers have to tell us."

"I will bring them around to your office at one o'clock, after the noon mess, Sir."

"Oh, I am not going to be using the overseer's cottage as an office after all. I will use the office here in the main house. You can use the overseer's cottage as your facility, and put the quartermaster in with you. That would probably be more convenient for you, my friend."

"Well, I am not going to argue about an office with a real roof and a good clean-burning hearth. Thank you, Sir. Where shall I have the staff assemble, then?"

Charlie knew Rebecca was listening in on their conversation. He looked at her and received a smile of confirmation. "Ah, I will have Beulah show you on your way out. Oh, and have the dispatches brought to me there."

Charlie turned to Dr. Walker. "Perhaps, Elizabeth, you will join me for lunch and give me your views on the state of our infirmary and our injured?" She nodded her acknowledgment and smiled at Rebecca. Polk was waiting at the door to escort her to the infirmary. "Until later then, my friends."

CHAPTER 9

SUNDAY, NOVEMBER 20, 1864

The day had been more tiring than Charlie expected. Perhaps it was his own illness, perhaps it was the dreams that had plagued his fever-ridden sleep the previous nights, and perhaps it was the enormity of trying to heal the rifts between the Federalists and the Confederacy, even on the small level of the community of Culpeper County.

He sat on the cedar chest at the foot of the bed and pulled off his half boots. The coat and weskit were neatly folded on the coat rack already. He slid out of his trousers and folded them over the bar on the coat rack. Standing by the hearth, staring into the fire, wearing only his shirt and socks, he stretched, twisting back and forth trying to relieve the knots in the muscles of his back and shoulders.

Rebecca came to the door, holding a bottle of liniment Elizabeth had given her to help Charlie's cold. Seeing him there, mostly undressed, she paused. She nearly dropped the bottle, but managed to hold on to it. "Colonel?"

Charlie started, turning around quickly. "Oh, Miss Rebecca. I am sorry. I did not realize you were there." He blushed slightly, then realized she had seen pretty much all of his body at one time or another.

"It is all right." Rebecca swallowed hard. "Um, Doctor Walker was kind enough to give me this menthol rub for your cold. She said I should give your back a thorough rubbing with it."

Charlie's blush deepened to a charming shade of red. "Um, it is not necessary. I am feeling much better. And I am sure you would rather not sleep with a bedmate that smells like a medicine chest."

She stepped into the room and closed the door. "I really think we should follow her orders if you are going to recover fully." She bit the inside of her lip to keep from smiling.

"Um, I guess that means you need my back bare?"

"It would make the job a bit easier, yes."

Charlie looked very much like a startled deer in the moment before it bolts. "And you would like me to be somewhere that you could get at my back?" *With your hands.* "With the liniment."

"Yes." She could only smile now. "Why do you not take off your shirt and lay down on the bed?"

The blush continued to grow, turning Charlie's face a lovely brick color. Charlie turned away from her, facing the bed, and slowly took off his shirt. The strong shoulders, tapering down to a slim waist and trim hips emerged hesitantly. From behind, Rebecca could see the simple cotton underpants he wore, and the band around his ribs that constrained his breasts.

Rebecca took a deep breath to try and calm her racing heart. *Oh, Lord.* She could only stand there and find Charlie nothing but astounding. "Let me help you." She stepped forward, licking extremely dry lips before placing the bottle on the nightstand and reaching for the bindings that would free the Colonel and bring the woman's body completely into being.

Charlie closed his eyes. Her hands on his skin were warm and gentle. Alone, this moment was one of freedom, when the bands around his chest were freed and he could breathe deeply, releasing

Charlotte, if only in private. Before this woman, it was a moment of extraordinary fear and anticipation. With the transformation from Charlie to Charlotte, would she be repelled? Charlotte's voice was loud in his head, reminding him of just what an abomination he was. *She should be. You have lived as a man for so long, Charlie Redmond; you have forgotten what it is to be a woman. Except for moments like this, when you emerge from your costume and your role, and face the truth of who and what you are.* His breathing was shallow, and every muscle in his torso tensed. It was as if she held him in her hands.

Rebecca's hands were actually shaking. She took slow, deep breaths to control everything she was feeling as she unwrapped Charlie's bindings. The urge to touch this beautiful creature before her was overwhelming. Once the bindings were dropped to the floor, Rebecca whispered, "Lie down." She recognized the timbre of her own voice, but hoped the reason for it would escape Charlie.

Rebecca's whisper shot fire through Charlie's body. The combination of Rebecca's touch and her voice were almost enough to make Charlie lose control. She wanted to turn around, to take Rebecca in her arms, to feel her skin against her body. Charlie lay down on the edge of the bed; face down, with her head cradled in her crossed arms. A deep breath, let out slowly, helped her to gather herself and her rampaging emotions. "Is this how you want me?"

Oh, dear God, give me strength. Rebecca wanted to tell Charlie "No," and then figure out exactly how she did want her. Instead she picked up the bottle and poured a little of the oil into her hands. "That is fine." The words came out almost as a squeak.

Charlie nodded. "Uh, would you mind covering my legs? It is a little chilly in here." Chilly was not how she was feeling. But maybe a little modesty would help. Maybe. Some.

"Thank you. It is a little nippy in here." Charlie buried her head deeper in her folded arms. *Maybe I can slip up to Washington for a few days. Maybe that would help. If I just got some of this wanting out of my system, it might be easier. Who the hell are you kidding, Charlie?* The voice in her head was back, making it a little easier to manage the feelings in her belly. *She could not want you. You are no man, just the image. No woman like her could ever love an abomination like you. Why look at you—the only time you have ever been touched is by whores. She is just kind. That is all it is, just a kindness from a lady who is far too good for the likes of you.*

"Tell me if I hurt you," Rebecca said before laying her hands on the flesh before her. Her breathing hitched when she first touched Charlie. Despite the scars, the skin was smooth and warm, and Rebecca felt a unique sensation settle deep in her belly as she began a gentle massage.

Charlie could not help it. She could not stop it. A long groan was forced from deep within her. The feel of Rebecca's hands gently kneading her shoulders and the heavy muscles in her back was infinitely sensual. Her breathing became deeper. Goosebumps pulled her skin tight. Her nipples hardened so that the pressure of the sheet beneath her was almost painful. "You can use a little more pressure." Her voice was tight. It was all she could say at that point. Anything else and Rebecca would know.

Rebecca did as Charlie asked, deepening the pressure. She licked her lips again. She desperately wanted to lean over and place a kiss on the soft skin in front of her. "Better?"

Another groan emerged as her hands moved to loosen the tight knots in Charlie's shoulders. "Oh, yes, wonderful. You have wonderful hands. I do not think I have ever felt quite this good."

Rebecca felt as if she would faint at any moment. Another groan out of Charlie and she would be lost to her forever. "I am glad I make you feel good." She could not help it when the statement came out almost as a low moan of her own.

The answer came without thought, straight from Charlie's heart to her lips. "You make me feel better than I ever have before." *Oh, God. Did I say that? Was that me? She will run, she should run. Oh, hell.*

The blonde smiled and further increased the pressure on Charlie's back. Shifting her weight so she would be more comfortable and have much better access, she said, "Charlie, may I tell you something?" She knew this would do it. It would either make or break them, but she could not stand the uncertainty one moment longer.

"You know you may." Charlie was savoring every moment, every touch, every caress, committing them to her memory to be taken out, examined carefully, and cherished when Rebecca finally rejected her.

Rebecca took a deep breath, hoping this was the right thing to do. "I think you are quite undeniably the most attractive person I have ever seen."

Her words broke Charlie's haze of pleasure. She snorted. "How can you say that? I am neither man nor woman, but instead some weird half way creature." A shiver passed through her body. *How can she say such a thing? Can she not see what you are?* The little voice goaded her, tormented her.

"No." Rebecca lay down next to Charlie, but kept making small soothing circles on her back. "Look at me, Charlie."

Charlie rolled to one side so she could look into Rebecca's eyes. What she saw took her breath away. Charlie looked at her like a child, filled with pain, waiting to be hit yet again. Charlie had stopped breathing, and Rebecca could feel the goose bumps rising all over Charlie's skin. She could feel the muscles in Charlie's back, which she had worked so hard to relax minutes before, tighten up again, turning in to bands of steel.

"You trust me, do you not, Charlie?"

She nodded her head, her eyes locked on Rebecca's.

"You know I would never lie to you?"

Again, she nodded, holding her breath, waiting.

"Then you must believe me when I say this to you, Charlie. I see in you the best of both. You are strong like a man, a charming gentleman; and yet you are the most beautiful woman I have ever seen. You remind me of a classical sculpture of an ancient goddess."

Something in her words touched an empty little place within Charlie. Her face relaxed a bit. In a very soft voice, Charlie finally found words. "Thank you, dear Rebecca. No one ever told me that I was beautiful. I was always too tall, too ungainly, too gawky. As a man, I was too whippy, too thin. Your words seem very strange, but very nice." The blush was back in full force.

"Anyone who has said those things to you should be ashamed. You are the most striking person I have ever seen. And since I have said this much, I feel I must continue. Is that all right?"

If anything, the blush deepened. Charlie nodded. If she did anything more, she might try to crawl into Rebecca's arms, and that would never do.

"I am telling you this because I want you to understand. I am more than a bit confused by all of this, Charlie. And I am working very hard to figure it all out." Rebecca made a long languid stroke up and down her back that was deliberately sensual. "I hope I can find a way to express to you how much you mean to me, how much I have come to care for you. But this is new and very different to me on a variety of levels, and I just ask for your patience."

With the stroke up and down her spine, Charlie froze. Her eyes closed, and her brow furrowed slightly as she concentrated on Rebecca's words. *Care for me? She cares for me?* When Charlie's eyes opened again, Rebecca found herself looking into lakes of pure silver. "I am here, Rebecca. However you want me. Whatever you want from me. You have only to reach out and I will be here."

Rebecca's hand moved from her back to her face, caressing her cheek. She watched her for a long moment, then leaned in and gave Charlie a very soft, chaste kiss. Right on the lips. She lingered for a brief moment, allowing the sensations to settle so she could work through them later.

Sweet Jesus. The heat roared through Charlie, ignited by that gentle touch. Every muscle in her body tightened. A light sheen of sweat broke out on her forehead. Rebecca could feel the trembling in Charlie's body through the bed. If she had held that kiss for a second more, Charlie would not have been able to prevent herself from gathering Rebecca in her arms and keeping her there. She looked into Rebecca's eyes, her soul naked and vulnerable before her.

Rebecca looked carefully at her. She graced her with a shy smile. "Thank you, Charlie."

"Thank you, dear Rebecca."

Charlie cleared her throat. "Um...Rebecca? I, uh, I need to do something here, or I will either embarrass myself or frighten you."

She looked at him, not understanding. "Charlie?"

"Ah, I need to get some clothes on."

"Oh yes, of course, let me get you a night shirt." She rose from her spot on the bed and retrieved a freshly washed shirt for Charlie. She laid it on the bed, and then, even though she really did not want to, she turned around to afford her some privacy. "You would not have frightened me, Charlie."

Charlie could not stand it. She needed to feel Rebecca against her body again, if only for a moment. She stepped behind Rebecca and very gently drew her back against her chest. She slid her hands down her arms and then softly wrapped them around her waist, holding her close, burying her face in her hair, savoring the warmth and smell of her.

Rebecca's mind flashed to the dream she had had. Suddenly it was crystal clear. She laid her hand over Charlie's and leaned back. "I feel things when I am with you that I have never felt before," she whispered, closing her eyes and enjoying this connection. She wished Charlie would touch her as she had in her dream.

The feel of Rebecca's body leaning against her naked chest, her shoulders brushing against her nipples, was driving Charlie crazy. "If I do not let go of you, I will beg you here and now to make love with me. And I do not want that. I do not want you to decide I am not what you want. I need you to be sure." She hoped Rebecca understood what she was trying to say.

Rebecca gasped before opening her eyes. "If you do not let go of me, you will not have to beg. But I am grateful for your patience,

Charlie. I want to share so much with you, but I need to understand so much more."

Charlie's heart was pounding so hard she felt light headed, but she did not let go of Rebecca. Slowly, gently, Charlie ran her hands over Rebecca's slender waist and up the sides of her ribs, as if was memorizing her. Charlie leaned down and placed a tender kiss on Rebecca's shoulder where her nightdress left it bare. "Sweet lady, when you are ready." Then Charlie stepped back, caught up the nightshirt and quickly pulled it over her head. She was breathing hard, her hands itched with the desire to hold Rebecca, and she felt as if there was a gaping hole in her chest that Rebecca's slender form had filled. "When you are ready."

The two of them settled into bed, both a little shy, both a little awkward. Charlie caught Rebecca's hand and brought it to her lips. "Ready for sleep?"

She chuckled. "Not really, I am sorry. If you would like to sleep, I can go downstairs for a bit."

"No, I am not exactly sleepy myself. Something about a backrub, I believe."

Rebecca blushed. "I was not trying to...well...you know." She giggled, then scrubbed her face to try and rid it of the blush. "Can we talk for a bit? Or I could read."

"Stay here and talk, if you do not mind. I love learning about you, and I find you are one of the few people I am comfortable with talking about myself."

"There is so very little about me to know. I am afraid you know most of it all ready. Tell me something about yourself. Tell me why you joined the Army."

Charlie settled a pile of pillows against the headboard and relaxed, opening his arms for Rebecca to cuddle against him. "This is very nice, dear." A satisfied hum came from the small woman who was resting her head on his shoulder.

"I promised I would tell you how I got the stripes on my back."

Rebecca looked up at him, startled. She had asked for the story of how he had joined the Army, never guessing there was a link.

Charlie continued in a quiet voice. It was almost a monotone, lacking emotion. Rebecca was concerned. It was as if he had gone away and left only his voice, recounting the events of the past.

"I was born in Charleston, South Carolina in 1829. My father, Mark Russell Redmond, was a merchant who provided all manner of goods and equipment for the merchant fleets that sailed in and out of Charleston. He was a big man, a black Scot, with a stern visage and a tight fist for money. My mother, Emelia Huger DuBosque, was from one of the French Huguenot families, small, delicate, with laughing blue eyes and coal black hair. They were quite a striking pair, I am told. I do not remember my mother well, as I was only four years old when she died of yellow fever. Mostly I only remember little snippets, like fragments of dreams. I missed her terribly for many years."

Charlie stopped for a moment, the recent dream about his mother still very fresh in his mind. He realized the lovely woman cuddled in his arms was the first woman other than his mother who had held him just because she wanted to. He tightened his grip on Rebecca slightly, wondering at the feel of her.

"After my mother died, my father became engrossed in his work. He became more and more distant, and more and more harsh. As I grew, it became obvious that, while I had my mother's coloring, I had his build. At fifteen, I was tall, gangly, awkward, and nothing like the image of a Charleston lady. I think he had hoped I would grow up to be like my mother. All I know is that everything I did disappointed him. It was a very lonely childhood."

Charlie paused there. When he resumed, his voice was even more distant and controlled. "I can still remember the day as if it were yesterday: the weather, the words, the sounds and smells. It was cold and overcast. It was raining, a needle-fine drizzle that seemed to cut right through your skin. I had just returned from taking Papa his luncheon at the mercantile. I settled in front of the big fire in the winter kitchen to dry out my wet hair and dress. Mamie, our cook, had given me a cup of warm soup to help take the chill off.

"As I was drying out, Joshua, the errand boy for our mantilla maker, Madame Prévost, brought in my new Sunday bonnet. I remember thinking, "I do not know why I bother to frequent the city's best hat maker; Father always says I look like a boy in girls' clothing regardless of what I wear." But back then, I kept trying to be the daughter my father wanted.

"I remember looking closely at Joshua as he set the hat box down in front of me. He was barefoot and coatless, soaked and shivering from the cold. Mamie brought him a cup of hot soup and a towel, scolding him for dripping all over her nice, clean floor.

"It was pretty funny watching Joshua try to towel off and drink the soup at the same time. The soup won; he drained the cup quickly, while barely managing to get some of the bigger drips with the towel.

"I opened the hatbox and just looked at the bonnet. It was lovely, but I remember thinking then that a pretty hat was not sufficient to make me the lovely lady my father wished for. I was still tall, gawky, bony, and too much of a tomboy.

"I remember thinking that Joshua looked as though he was not getting enough to eat. He was thin, too thin even for a boy of his age. I wondered if Madame Prévost was having problems. The last bout of yellow fever had severely restricted Charleston's social activities, and I suspected that her business had been hurt badly. I thought the cold snap would help, as yellow fever is a warm weather disease. Perhaps the winter season would be good for her. But at that time, I suspected that her servants were going on short rations.

"I asked Mamie if we had any butt ends of bacon, fatback or shanks or a hambone we could give Joshua as recompense for his errand. She agreed with me that he looked like he was not getting enough to eat. But she warned me that if I took anything out of the meat locker, there would be hell to pay for it with my father. I did it anyway, and promised her that I would take responsibility.

"We gave the poor boy another cup of soup and sent him on his way with a small package of fatback and the butt end of a ham. It was so sad to see how tightly he clutched that package of scraps to his chest, as if it were a treasure to be carefully guarded.

"I walked upstairs with my new bonnet, and as I did, I remember hearing a loud commotion out on the street. I looked out of the hall window and saw Father there, holding Joshua by the scruff of the neck. There was a lot of yelling going on. I rushed out of the front door, hoping to somehow ease the situation. Unfortunately, my father was in full righteous rage. He called Joshua a thieving nigger, a sneak, and a variety of other choice epithets."

Charlie paused for a moment. The next part of this story was one of the most painful times in his life. Rebecca was mesmerized. Charlie so rarely opened up like this. She knew instinctively that any story he recounted with this much detail was intensely important. All she could do was hold Charlie's hand tenderly, to give support and encouragement. She did not dare say anything for fear she would disrupt this healthy outpouring of long concealed pain.

Charlie took a deep breath and continued. "I intervened. I told my father that Joshua was not a thief. His response was not what I expected. He said, 'If he is not a thief, then someone else is. I gave no permission for meat to be taken from my home'."

Charlie's voice became oddly determined. "You know, I could have lied that day. I could have let Joshua take my father's wrath. But I chose to be truthful. I paid dearly for that truth.

"I told my father that I had taken the meat and given it to Joshua in return for him bringing me the hat. My father's response shocked me to my core. I expected him to be annoyed, let Joshua go, and give me a lecture about being too generous with the family's resources. Instead, he told me, 'Then you are a thief. For whether it be you or this little wretch, someone is going to pay for this."

"I could not believe it. The man standing in front of me was not my father. This man, with his face all red, the veins in his neck bulging, and the eyes of a rabid dog, was not the calm, stern father I knew. I was terrified, and rightfully so. My father literally tossed Joshua into the gutter, where he grabbed the package of meat and skittered away through the crowd. Papa stalked to the front door where I was standing, took my arm and threw me into the hall, slamming the door behind him.

"He asked if I took his ham. I said yes.

"He asked if I had permission. I said no.

"He asked me if I understood that taking something without permission was theft. I said yes, and asked what I could do to make amends."

Charlie was almost rigid. Rebecca was trying not to cry from the pain that was radiating off his body at these harsh memories.

"He said, "You, daughter, will pay the price that any thief would pay. You will be out in the courtyard in half an hour." I had never heard him sound so cold, so angry or so distant.

"Punishments in the courtyard were major events. Every member of the household, down to the lowest slave in the stables, was required to attend. I thought he would do what he usually did, shame me in public for being such a failure and disappointment as a daughter. I was wrong.

"Thirty minutes later, to the minute, I was standing in the courtyard. He kept me waiting there, in the icy rain, for what felt like another ten or fifteen minutes. By the time he came out wearing his oilcloth slicker, I was soaked. I looked into his eyes, hoping to find some trace of fatherly tolerance there. Instead, I saw eyes as cold and gray as the cobblestones under our feet.

"Then it got worse. He commanded me to strip off my shirtwaist. I was horrified. He wanted me to stand before these people in nothing but my chemise and my skirt. I did as he commanded, for I knew that whatever my punishment was to be, it would be even worse if I continued to disobey him. Then he drew his hands from behind his back and I saw the whip."

Rebecca cringed. Charlie was very still beneath her, but she could feel his heart pounding. Rebecca took Charlie's hand, which she had been holding and stroking, and held it to her own heart, trying to give her friend some small amount of comfort.

"He announced my crime, naming me a petty thief. Then he ordered the head stableman to tie my hands to a tall post in the courtyard usually used to tie horses, which doubled as a whipping post when necessary.

"After the first blow from the blacksnake whip, all I can remember is burning, searing pain and overwhelming shame. My father was beating me like a recalcitrant slave in front of the entire household. I have no idea how many times he struck me. I wrapped my hands around the ring on the post and hung on. I refused to crumble, to beg, or to fall. After it was over, all I can remember is Mamie tending to me.

"I honestly do not know if the whipping or the medicine in the welts afterward hurt worse. I do know that sometime during the course of Mamie cleaning the welts and cuts on my back, I passed out. Even with the immediate treatment, several of the cuts became infected. I was feverish for several days, drifting in and out of awareness. Eventually, I rejoined the world, my back a mass of scabs. The first thing I remember asking for was some water; the second was if my father had been to see to me. He had not. Evidently, attending on a thief was sufficiently repugnant to him to prevent him tending to his daughter.

"That was what made me leave. To him, I was never the child he wanted, could never be the daughter he expected me to be, and after the whipping, I was obviously no better than a petty thief. I knew I could not stay any longer, but my choices were limited; I had few skills. I could try to get a job as a dressmaker or a haberdasher, as my sewing was fine, but my embroidery left much to be desired. I could become some kind of teacher for children, though I was hardly the model that most mothers and fathers wanted for their little girls, or I could be the world's ugliest prostitute. I never was very comfortable trying to be a proper lady. I saw my cousins and the boys in the neighborhood in clothes that they could actually run and ride and climb in, while I had to put up with crinolines and stays. My female cousins would gush on about this hat or that dress pattern. I was bored to tears. I tried so hard to fit in, and I failed so miserably, that I thought if I could pass as a man, things would be easier. I waited until my back healed, then I cut my hair, got a couple of suits of boys' clothing, and signed on to a ship bound for Philadelphia, working as a mess lad. Once I got to Pennsylvania, I realized that with the troubles in Mexico brewing, the Army was the best available choice.

"In January of 1846, President Polk declared war on Mexico. By the end of the month, I had enlisted in the Army in Philadelphia. After some basic training, I was on my way west, to join the ranks of cannon fodder. After that, I got lucky."

The pain that had driven him to become Charlie instead of Charlotte, the agony of betrayal by his own father, and the unending feelings of inadequacy were written all over Charlie's face and, Rebecca realized, on her beloved's soul. She did not know where to begin to heal such deep wounds, or if she had the means to do so, but in that quiet moment, she swore in her heart to try.

～

Wednesday, November 23, 1864

Charlie looked between the two women, who were laughing and obviously enjoying each other's company very much. This morning, the good Colonel felt very out of place at the breakfast table and, being a career soldier, knew when a tactical retreat was in order. He took the last drink of his coffee and placed his napkin on the table.

"Well, ladies, if you will excuse me, I have a meeting to get ready for." He stood, waiting to be excused.

Rebecca nodded with a smile while Elizabeth merely grinned. She found this whole thing extremely amusing. She could see she had her work cut out for her here, and it was more than just taking care of the sick and wounded.

Once Charlie was gone, Elizabeth could not resist any longer, especially after observing Rebecca watch Charlie walk out of the room. The doctor could not help but chuckle. Rebecca looked at her quizzically.

"Oh, Charlie...he is such a gentleman. And he has absolutely no inkling of the impact he has on others."

"You are very right, Doctor. I can never seem to get him to accept credit for his good deeds and kind heart."

"My dear, I suspect he may be allowing you to see more than most. He is without doubt the most private person I have ever met," the doctor said.

"Not that you can blame him. He has to be very careful. If someone were out to hurt him, discovering his secret is all it would take."

"That is certainly true. I must confess, Charlie confuses even me at times, and I think I know more about people like him than most."

"Like him?" Rebecca hoped the good doctor would enlighten her. Maybe it would help clear up some of her own confusion if she understood Charlie a little better.

"You must know that there are all kinds of people in the world, Rebecca. Most follow the traditional path of man and woman. Others prefer the company of their own gender, and still others seem to have been born into the wrong bodies, and have the characteristics of one of the opposite gender. This has been true throughout all history, though not often spoken of."

"And how would you think of Charlie? I mean is it not a matter of circumstance that has made Charlie what he is? Could he not, well, change? I mean if he were to leave the Army and start over again? Please help me to understand. There are so many things..." She dropped her eyes, sighing deeply, and staring into her coffee cup.

"So many things? Perhaps, Rebecca, it would be easier if you just asked me. I think we both care very much for Charlie, and he has so few people he can call friend."

Carefully, the blonde raised her eyes and looked at the doctor.

She could see concern and new friendship looking back at her. "I think I care for Charlie very much," she said quietly.

"And the way you care for him confuses you?" Elizabeth's concern was obvious in the tone of her voice and the open honesty of her face.

"Yes, very much. I look at him and I see everything I need and want, yet I know I should not feel that way."

"When you look at Charlie, who do you see, Rebecca? Do you see the Colonel, the gentleman, or the woman underneath the image? It makes a huge difference, you know. And it probably makes a huge difference in why you think you should not feel the way you do."

"That is just it. I see both. One moment, he is the gallant and charming Colonel, and the very next minute he is entirely a woman. I am so frustrated because I am simply attracted to him, and all of that does not matter to me; yet there is a voice that keeps telling me that what might be, could never be."

Elizabeth looked at her new friend for a long moment. She felt sure that even if Charlie had not been forced to assume the identity of a man to survive, he still would have sought the love of a woman to complete him. She also suspected that, for Charlie, the years of hiding his real identity, coupled with whatever circumstances had driven him to destroy his identity as a woman, had left him believing that he would have to be alone for the rest of his life. Rebecca's concerns would only feed those insecurities.

"Dear lady, I personally do not believe that caring for someone is ever wrong. But I also know society does not agree with my point of view. You will have to make that decision for yourself, if you have any desire to keep Charlie in your life."

Rebecca laughed at the situation. "Doctor, I believe the community would be far more scandalized if I took a Yankee officer as a lov...uh...well..." She cleared her throat. "I do want Charlie in my life. I mean, I understand it has been only a short time, but God help me, there is just something about him that is undeniable. Elizabeth, do you believe in love at first sight?"

Elizabeth broke into gales of laughter at Rebecca's first sentence. "Rebecca, you are sleeping with the man. The whole camp knows the Colonel sleeps at the main house, not in his tent. And they all assume you two are lovers. It was one of the first things I heard about you. I thought it was a case of Charlie doing one of the silly things he does occasionally to try and bolster his masculine image." She looked at the now blushing Rebecca. "There is more here than just Charlie's image, is there not? And I assume that the rumors are not true...but some part of you wishes they were?"

"The rumors are not true. We do sleep together, but it is entirely platonic, I assure you." Rebecca's brows came together in contemplation. "Unless you consider the fact that I wake up in his arms every morning less than platonic. And I must admit I am having very unusual feelings and dreams since meeting Charlie."

Elizabeth sighed deeply and walked to the window, looking out over the gentle, rolling land. What she saw was not the beautiful land, but the memory of Charlie's face, torn with pain and emptiness on the one occasion when they had talked of relationships and the future, the time after the war. She had seen the look in Charlie's eyes as he looked at this young woman. The amount of pain her friend might have to face was terrifying. She drew another deep breath. "Rebecca, Charlie is the most honorable person I have ever known. But he was hurt very badly a long time ago, and I suspect has never healed from that hurt. Our mutual friend believes he is fated to be alone in the world. I have never known anyone who was more deserving of being loved and was more capable of giving love, but I fear for him. To be honest, I fear for him because of you."

"Me? I would never hurt Charlie." Rebecca felt tears well in her eyes and her heart at the mere thought. "I would never hurt him. I promise you, Elizabeth."

"Rebecca, if you offer your love to Charlie and then find the good opinion of society matters more, you will hurt him very badly indeed. I am just asking you to be very sure before you do anything. I think Charlie would prefer the company of women no matter what happened in his life. But the circumstances that forced him to give up his true identity have made it even harder for him. Please be gentle with him."

Rebecca nodded her understanding. "I know that. That is why I am so confused. I know I should care what other people think, but when it comes to Charlie, I just cannot. I do not care that his men think we are lovers, and I do not care that the entire community of Culpeper is sure that the Colonel and I are carrying on an illicit affair. I enjoy his company; and I simple drown in those eyes every time he looks at me. I have never felt anything like this before in my life."

"Rebecca, are you sure you are not simply responding to the company of someone who is charming and attentive, and who has eased your loneliness after your husband's death?"

"I know my feelings for Charlie are real, born from caring for him. Does it matter why they have manifested themselves?"

"It may. Many times I have seen people who have been beaten down by the effects of war and who need to affirm the reality of life through passion. If that is the case, then you may find your feelings for Charlie will fade as life returns to something more normal."

"I do not believe that will be the case." She bit her bottom lip, fighting tears. "I love Charlie. I want to be with him. I want him with me."

Elizabeth wrapped her arm around the woman's shoulder. "Rebecca, why are you crying?"

"I am just so confused. I know I love him. I think he cares for me. Why must this be so hard?"

"Sometimes loving someone is very hard, my dear. But loving one's self is often even harder. For both of your sakes, I am asking you to examine your feelings closely. Are you falling in love with Charlie, or with the idea of Charlie?"

The look Rebecca gave Elizabeth was truly confused. She shook her head, hoping that would help, but it did not. "I do not understand. What?"

Elizabeth thought for a moment, trying to find the best way to express a rather complicated set of thoughts. She sighed, and then started trying to explain her concerns. "You were married to a gentleman with position and rank in the society here. The war took that away. It took away your family, and it basically took away your home. You have been surviving here alone for how long?"

"I was married, but he was no gentleman. And my life, such as it was, was over long before the war. Yes, I have been alone a long time, and I am tired of being alone, but I want to share my life with Charlie."

"I hate to ask you this, but what do you really know about Charlie that makes you so sure you want to be with him? Is it possible that it is because he is charming, gentle, courtly—in fact all the things that are written about in the romance novels? In other words, is it the image of Charlie, which you know he has so carefully created, that attracts you?"

Rebecca began to feel utterly defeated. "Perhaps," she said softly. "I could never win him. He needs someone who..." She smiled her bravest smile. "But I will remain his friend, and I will continue to see to his comforts as long as he is here."

Elizabeth felt the defeat in the slender shoulders under her arm. "My dear lady, I have not said a word about how Charlie may or may not feel. I am asking about how you feel. I assure you, you are exactly the kind of woman Charlie finds compellingly attractive." *What is going on here?* She had asked Rebecca about the genuineness of her feelings for her dear friend Charlie, and all of a sudden, she had turned into one of the most sadly defeated souls Elizabeth had ever seen.

"Elizabeth, you ask valid questions that I cannot answer. I love Charlie. Why, I am not sure, but I do. I was a miserable failure as a wife, and I am only deluding myself to think I could..." Rebecca wanted to escape and just go have a good cry. She slowly pulled away from the woman. "I promise you, I would never do anything to hurt him."

"Rebecca." Elizabeth's voice was gentle, but commanding. "I do not know what was done to you to make you believe you were a failure as a wife, but I do see how you care for Charlie—and for all of us here—during very difficult times. I also see his face when he looks at you when you are in the room, or even when someone just mentions your name."

"Yes, but maybe that is loneliness, too. He tells me he has been alone for a long time, that he has no one. I am sure after the war, he will find someone..." Rebecca's heart nearly stopped beating at the thought of Charlie not being with her. But she knew Elizabeth was right, and she knew her own failure would only come back to haunt her. Charlie would need a strong woman with a very special outlook on life to have anything even close to the happiness he deserved.

"Rebecca, I do not think you are a failure, either as a lady or as a wife. You treat Charlie very well indeed. And I am very sure that if he won your heart, you would be a perfect partner for him. I have to confess, I was much more concerned with you finding the, umm, novelty of who Charlie really is to be just that. A novelty. And that the attraction you feel for my friend might pale when the fact of never being able to have children, to have a family of your own, became real for you. If your love for him were to fade, I think it would hurt you both very much. I look at him when he thinks no one sees him. I see his face when he looks at you. If you find yourself to be truly in love with Charlie—with the woman as well as the man —I think you will make him a very happy person."

Elizabeth moved forward and hugged Rebecca again. "My dear, that is as much as anyone can ever ask for. To love and to be allowed to love for who you are, not who you appear to be. Charlie is, without question, a gentle and attentive friend, and when you are ready, I think he will be a spectacular lover and husband. In my opinion, this is much more a question of whether he can accept your love as being genuine and lasting, than it is one of your fear of being inadequate."

"I would do everything in my power to prove that to him, every day. I do not want you to worry for your friend, Elizabeth, although I know you do. Charlie's love is the greatest thing I could have in my life. Given the opportunity, I believe we could make a wonderful life for ourselves. But I want Charlie to be with me because he loves me. I could not stand being with another who did not love me."

"I see the love he bears you. Longing is painted on his face and burns in his eyes when he looks at you. I suspect he is very afraid of not being enough for you, afraid you will find a real man who fills your needs better than he can."

"I want no other," Rebecca admitted softly. "Charlie makes me feel as no other could. I know the differences between what I have felt before and what I feel now. I am sure I could never feel that way about a "real" man. Part of my love for Charlie is, that being a woman; she has tenderness and understanding that no man could ever have."

"Then keep exploring how you feel. Go slowly. Be sure. There is nothing about Charlie that is abnormal, just unusual. And very lonely. I thank you for your trust in me. It means a great deal to me, both because I felt an instant affinity with you, my dear, and because I care deeply for Charlie."

"I know." She smiled, slightly embarrassed. "I will admit when I saw you and Charlie together for the first time, I felt a great deal of jealousy. May I ask you a personal question, Doctor?"

"Certainly. I cannot imagine getting much more personal than we already have," Elizabeth laughed. "But if you are going to ask me personal questions, please address them to Elizabeth. Dr. Walker must always maintain her air of professional detachment, and I somehow suspect you do not want that from me."

Rebecca took a deep breath and plunged forward into territory she never imagined herself in. "Elizabeth, were you and Charlie ever lovers?"

"Would it bother you if we were?"

"Ah, well, no. Because I have no claim on Charlie." Rebecca felt tears rise in her eyes again and desperately tried to hold them back. Elizabeth's evasion of the answer made her fear the worst. "But I certainly would not want to be a disruption to you if you were. We both know the same thing. Charlie deserves to be loved and cared for, and if you are the woman to do that, then I only want him to be happy."

Elizabeth saw what she had hoped to see—a real, honest commitment to her friend's happiness. She reached out, and with the fingers of her left hand, gently lifted Rebecca's face so they were looking eye to eye. Handing her a soft linen handkerchief, she spoke with gentle compassion. "No, child, I have never been, nor will I ever be, Charlie's lover. I am his friend, one who cares deeply for him, but I prefer the companionship of another."

"Thank you." She wiped the tears from the corner of her eyes. "I really think I am falling desperately in love with your friend, Elizabeth."

"Then, dear, take your time, and be sure. Charlie is a patient man —and a gentle woman."

"I will, but thank you again. You have helped me a great deal. It is very nice to have someone to talk to. Someone who truly understands."

"All it takes is the willingness to see what is there, rather than what society dictates. I see this as being no different from my desire to be a physician, when society said that only men should be doctors."

Rebecca had to chuckle as she finished wiping tears from her eyes. "I hate to argue with a lady of your standing, but I think it is a little different, Doctor."

"In some ways, Rebecca, your situation is easier than mine. Charlie has been Charlie for so long, he will never be anything else. If you choose to be with him, you will not have to cope with explaining why you chose the company of another woman. From all outward appearances, you will be a normal couple. You, my dear, will have to deal with choosing a Yankee, but the rest will be between just the two of you. I must handle all of society struggling with the idea of a female doctor."

"Your point is well taken. You are just as amazing as Charlie. I am very glad you have both come into my life."

"I suspect that you will have many questions along the way. I am sure that you and I will have more of these little chats, my dear. I look forward to them. You have no idea how much more pleasant it is to consider the condition of someone's heart instead of the condition of someone's mutilated body."

"I do have one request of you, Elizabeth."

"Anything, my dear."

"For the time being, until I am surer of myself and my feelings, I would ask you to hold our conversations in confidence."

"I would not think of violating this confidence. I am glad to see you taking my advice, taking your time and wanting to be very sure of your feelings."

"I will. The last thing I want to do is cause Charlie more pain."

Elizabeth just smiled and patted Rebecca's hand.

CHAPTER 10

WEDNESDAY, NOVEMBER 23, 1864

Charlie and Richard spent the morning going over dispatches, reports, inventory lists, and the host of other paper work that was part of keeping a regiment of almost a thousand men and fifteen hundred horses fed, clothed, housed, and healthy.

"Well, Richard, how do you think we are doing? What things have to be tended to most urgently? Will we be in trouble for the winter?"

"We need to get the ditches finished, and we need to get the wood in place to half-timber the tents. We have started getting the infirmary in good order. Samuelson and Whitman have been haranguing every man assigned to do it right, 'the way Dr. Walker wants.'"

"What about supplies? Have we taken the steps needed to keep them dry? And has anyone checked on it?"

"Yes, Sir, Colonel, Sir. Of course, we have, Charlie. You know me better than that."

"I am sorry, Richard. I think being down sick has gotten to me more than I expected. I feel like I am being a mother hen and my chicks have all run away."

Richard laughed at that. Charlie as a mother hen was a difficult image for him to conjure up. "More like a stallion keeping his herd in line, I would say."

"So, tell me, what progress have we made on Project Boot?"

"Mr. Cooper has a search out to find leather, and I have found about seven men in the troops with at least some leatherworking skill; including one boot maker, and an assortment of men with experience in patching saddles, harnesses, leather furniture, and other types of leather goods. We will get by. I also sent another scathing letter to the Quartermaster General's office about their buying practices."

"Well, 'tis all we can do for now. Have we done an inventory to determine which men need boots most urgently?"

"I expect to get that back from the individual companies today or tomorrow."

"Fine. Well, off with you, my friend. We both have full plates today. I have to write my report to Sheridan, and then I will come out and do the rounds."

Rebecca was laughing as Sarah told her how Mrs. Williams had come into the mercantile while they were being fitted for their clothes. The cook managed to do a fairly reasonable imitation of the snooty woman that simply had Rebecca in hysterics.

"I know it is not right to feel that way, Mrs. Gaines, but for a minister's wife, she is not a very charitable woman."

"Sarah, you need not apologize to me. I have had my fill of Mrs. Williams. She was less than charitable in her attitude toward the good Colonel Redmond the other day."

"The Colonel? Why? He is a very kind gentleman."

Rebecca did not even try to hide the smile on her face. "I know." She looked down at the soft blue cloth in her hand, which was slowly taking the shape of a new shirt. It made her feel good to be doing this. Charlie had given her so many new things; she hoped the new shirt would be a small token of her gratitude. She was taking special care with a seam when Beulah entered the kitchen.

"Mrs. Gaines?"

"Yes?"

"There are a group of ladies from town here to see you. I have shown them to the front parlor."

"Oh Lord!" Rebecca placed her sewing in the basket and stood, straightening her dress. "I am sure they are here to see what gossip they can collect." She sighed. "Sarah, will you please prepare a tea tray for my," she paused, nearly choking on the word, "guests."

"Of course, Ma'am. It will be ready jiffy quick."

With that, Rebecca headed for the lions' den, wishing "Daniel" were home.

Charlie walked into the area Company D had staked out as its own. The men were toiling away at digging ditch works around their encampment to handle run off in the event of another storm. Others had started the process of cutting corner poles to timber the tents. When the planking became available, they would construct rough cabins inside the walls of the tents, and pack straw, hay, or some other insulation between the boards and the canvas. The canvas would repel water, the boards would stabilize the structure against wind and help keep the interior of the tents a little warmer than the outside. Berms around each tent served to seal the bottom edge and keep the wind out, as well as diverting water around the tent and into the drainage ditches.

The men were busy, focused on getting the job done, and only slowly did they realize their commanding officer was with them. A ragged salute worked its way slowly through the encampment.

Charlie waved them into a small group around him, and pulled over an empty barrel to sit on. He looked around the faces surrounding him. Some he knew from old days; some were new to him, men of the original Pennsylvania muster. Some faces were welcoming, some were shuttered and neutral, and a few—thank God only a few—were overtly hostile. His work was cut out for him.

"Gentlemen, I want to report to you that Dr. Walker performed surgery on Major Montgomery to relieve the pressure on his brain. While it is too soon to be sure, as head injuries are very dangerous, she feels he has at least a reasonable chance of recovering completely. I for one am very concerned about Major Monty, and very relieved we had the good fortune to have such a fine surgeon available to help care for him."

Murmurs, some of them relieved, some muttering things like, "Served him right," went around the group of men. That the "Served him right" comments were coming from fellow Pennsylvanians was enlightening to Charlie.

"Men, for a moment, let us forget rank. Major Monty has a problem. We all know it. I do not think he was quite right after The Wilderness." Nods of agreement went around the circle. "I have seen this kind of thing before, and it is hard to handle. Hard for the men who suffer from it, and hard for their friends, too. Monty was a good soldier and a good officer. The pain and guilt of losing so many of his men, I think, overwhelmed him. Tell me, did he ever talk about it with any of you?"

One gnarled old sergeant spoke up. "Monty was my boss back home, Colonel. He used to get together with us boys pretty much regular, but after that battle, all he did was sit in his tent and brood, usually with the help of the ol' jack. I swear, that man could drink stuff that would rot your guts out, and then get up the next morning and ride hell bent for leather all day."

Another one took up the story, "Yes, he would, but damn, he

treated his horses like they were made of iron, not flesh. Before the war, he was the best horseman in Bucks County—horses just loved that man; but lately, he has been driving them to do things horses were not meant to do. I do not blame that horse for kicking him. I have been wanting to do the same myself sometimes."

"Gentlemen, I believe your Major had something break inside his soul after The Wilderness. It is going to take all of us to help him see that he is not to blame—that no individual is to blame—for what happened. And we all have to realize that the civilians we are dealing with today are not the men you faced in battle. The men who served with me at Vicksburg know what I am talking about. Discuss it amongst yourselves, and come to me or Colonel Polk if you have any questions."

Charlie looked around the circle of men, catching the eyes of those who had served with him on the western front. Small nods of agreement and support came from them. He knew he had their backing.

"Now, gentlemen, for the time being, I am not going to name a new commander for this company. You have a commander, Major Montgomery. With support from Colonel Polk, Major Swallow will continue to act as your temporary commander, in addition to leading his own company. We will worry about a new permanent commander for Company D if, and only if, Dr. Walker feels Major Montgomery is not going to be capable of resuming command for the spring campaign. If you need anything, or just need to talk, you know I have an open door to any man in this regiment. Please feel free to come by my office. I am using the farm manager's office in the main house. The entrance is at the northwest corner of the ground floor."

Charlie stood and straightened his coat. "By the way, gentlemen, we will be conducting a gymkhana this year before Christmas. The company that wins the most overall points will serve as color guard in the spring campaign, and the individual trooper from the company who wins the most overall points will serve as the color bearer. I expect a good showing from Company D. Do your Major proud, men."

Charlie accepted the departing salute, then walked toward the infirmary. *Well, that went better than I expected. Loyal to a fault, those boys are, but they did see what was happening with Monty. Maybe my boys and the gymkhana, between them, will pull those troops together. I can hope.* A small grin lit his face as he opened the door to the barn that had been converted to an infirmary. He went straight to the surgery, where Elizabeth and Samuelson were tending to Montgomery.

"How is he?" Charlie asked quietly.

Elizabeth looked up, a little startled. "Oh, I did not hear you come in. He is doing about as well as can be expected. His eyes are a little more reactive, and the swelling seems to be going down. That is all I can hope for right now."

"Well, I just talked to his troops. Seems they had seen changes in his behavior before this event, so even if he does survive, we have our work cut out for us. Battle shock, I would say, the raging kind, not the suicidal kind."

"Yes, I have been thinking on that. Samuelson gave me the background. With your permission, I would like to try something. "

"You know I support you in whatever you decide, Doctor."

"I want to make sure the only people who care for him when he becomes conscious are people with Southern accents. That would be Samuelson, Rebecca, and any others I can find."

"I will put Polk on finding any other men in the brigade with Southern accents who can serve as medics. But I suspect he will be pretty abusive and uncooperative."

"That is the point. He had made all Southerners into demons to be destroyed. I want to create a dissonance—having the very people he hates be his caretakers. He will be torn, between gratitude for their care and his hatred. I am hoping the dichotomy will give us the opening we need to really help him."

Whitman spoke from the corner. "I will help as well. You know, I have a way of listening and talking with people which has been quite effective."

The others in the room could not help but laugh at Whitman's comment. "Mr. Whitman, as long as you have been tagging along after me, you have had a way with words. It must be the poet in you, good Sir."

Charlie stepped over to look into Montgomery's face. His head was swathed in white bandages, his features at rest. This man could not be more than twenty-four or twenty-five years old, yet he had seen so much death and destruction that it had overwhelmed him with hatred. The cost of war included this man's soul. Charlie shook his head.

"Come, Elizabeth, let us look in on the other men."

Rebecca paused just outside the doors, gathering herself for a fight. Opening the doors, she stepped inside and closed them behind her. "Good afternoon, ladies. Welcome to my home." She looked at each woman in turn. Mrs. Cooper gave her a polite smile. Mrs. Williams once again appeared as if she had something unpleasant under her nose. Her eyes grew wide when she saw the next two ladies, Miss Katherine Reynolds and Miss Mary Simms, both of them young and single. She knew why they had come and, she did not like it one damn bit.

"Rebecca, we came to make sure you were indeed all right," Mrs. Cooper offered.

"But we can see that you are living well," Mrs. Williams all but sneered. "Your home is being refurbished, and you have a house full of new servants —"

Rebecca raised her hand, interrupting her. "Colonel Redmond has his men helping with much needed repairs to my home, and I would hardly call a staff of four a houseful. Besides they are here for the Colonel's comfort more than mine."

"Where is the Colonel?" Mary asked with a gleam in her eye.

"Charlie," Rebecca let all of her jealousy and possessiveness tumble out just in pronouncing his name, "is out with his troops, tending to his camp."

"Mrs. Williams was sure we would find him sitting before the fire sipping brandy and smoking a cigar," Katherine giggled.

Rebecca looked directly at Mrs. Williams. "Had you come a little after supper, you might very well have done so. The Colonel does enjoy a cigar, and he has impeccable taste in brandy."

"Rebecca, have you lost your senses? You act as if you have feelings for this man," Mrs. Williams countered.

"Do I?"

"You do. It is shameful."

"No, it is not. But do you know what is? You, Mrs. Williams, your self-righteous condemnation of something you know nothing about. What gives you the right to come into my home and —"

"Rebecca." Mrs. Cooper broke in and stopped the young woman's tirade. "We are only concerned for your safety."

"You may very well be, Grace, and I appreciate that, but others are not so kind." She looked at each woman. "Colonel Redmond is a gentleman, and he has graciously offered to help the community of Culpeper as much as possible. His chief physician, Doctor Walker, has offered to give of her services to our community."

Reg had gone running hell bent for Charlie as soon as Beulah had told him of the unexpected "guests." He found Charlie and Elizabeth visiting with the men in the infirmary, Elizabeth to assess their condition and Charlie to bolster their morale. A quick word with Reg, and Charlie knew Rebecca was in trouble.

"Excuse me, Dr. Walker, may I have a private word with you?"

The two hurried to the end of the makeshift ward, "What is it, Charlie?"

"It seems the local morals committee is paying us a visit. Can you join me to help give them a new perspective?"

"You go ahead. I will be there as quickly as I can."

~

Charlie hurried back to the house. Slipping up the back stairs, he stopped to pull on his day dress uniform—sword, sash, and all. Dressed in his "Daniel" costume, he was ready to enter the lions' den. Stealing back downstairs, he circled around and entered by the front door. Hearing the murmur of the visitors' voices, punctuated by the deceptively low tones of Rebecca's voice that he knew was her version of anger, he straightened his tunic and entered the room.

Rebecca was reaching the end of her rope. She wondered briefly if Charlie's men could put a new roof on the entire house, as she was about to go off like a keg of gunpowder when Charlie entered the room

"Excuse me, Miss Rebecca. I did not mean to interrupt your tea, but I have a request from Dr. Walker." Charlie's Charleston accent was back with a vengeance.

"Charlie." She got up immediately, nearly running to him. She took a deep breath and just let it happen. She put her arms around his neck and gave him quite the complete welcome home.

For a moment, he was stunned. As Rebecca settled back into the arms that had risen automatically to embrace her, she looked up into his eyes. Charlie blinked at her like an owl suddenly blinded by a bright light. A slow smile then played over his features. "Bonjour, ma chère, ça va bien?"

"I have been better, Daniel," she whispered into his ear. "I am very glad you are home." She pulled back just a bit without letting go of his neck. "Come, my dear Colonel Redmond, let me introduce you."

He let her slide down in his arms until he could take her arm in a more traditional hold, and allowed her to introduce him to the ladies in the room.

"Ladies, may I present Colonel Charles Redmond, originally of Charleston, South Carolina? Colonel, I am sure you remember Mrs. Cooper. This is Mrs. Williams, Reverend Williams' wife. And Miss Reynolds and Miss Simms."

He first addressed Mrs. Cooper, bowing over her hand and lightly brushing her knuckles with his lips. "I am charmed to see you again, Madame. Your husband has been quite professional in his dealings with us, and I appreciate it. I also know you and your husband have been good friends to Mrs. Gaines, and I am deeply grateful for that."

He turned to Mrs. Williams and similarly bowed over her hand, murmuring "Enchanté, Madame. I look forward to seeing you at church when my health and the demands of my command permit."

Finally, he turned to Miss Reynolds and Miss Simms, summing them up immediately as young women on the hunt, and dismissing them as quickly. He bowed to both of them, "Ladies, the honor is mine." Through all of this, the Southern accent, spiced with the bits of French that were part of his heritage, was blatant. He stepped back to stand beside Rebecca.

"Your health? Are you ill, Colonel?" Mrs. Williams inquired, causing Grace to snort her amusement.

"Madame, I was stricken with a touch of pleurisy after that terrible storm last week. Fortunately, Miss Rebecca and Dr. Walker provided sound medical care, and I am recovering."

All eyes returned to Rebecca, who led Charlie to the love seat so they were sitting side by side. "He is a very grumpy patient, too. It was all I could do to keep him in bed."

Charlie smiled gently at Rebecca, "Ah, chère Madame, for you I would do many things, even allowing you to tend me when I was ill. I am very grateful, I do assure you." Turning to the other ladies in the room, he continued. "You know, Miss Rebecca has joined with Dr. Walker to try and plan ways to offer good medical care to the whole community. I would appreciate it, ladies, if given your standing in the community; you would let folks know we will be available to provide such medical support when needed? Oh, and I hope you will be able to meet Dr. Walker before you depart today."

"Colonel, are you suggesting that good Southern people take help from Yankee rabble? It would be a disgrace to allow such a thing. Maybe Rebecca Gaines does not mind sharing her home, and obviously her bed, with you, but I have no desire to take anything from you." The minister's wife was nearly out of her chair by the time she was done.

"Margaret!" Mrs. Cooper looked to Charlie and Rebecca with pleading eyes.

Charlie's voice, low and quiet but powerfully commanding, broke through the woman's tirade. "Madame, you will not besmirch Miss Rebecca's name in her own home. Yes, I am staying here. But I have not taken advantage of her, and I will not. I will court her and woo her, and if I am fortunate, I may win her. And I assure you, as an officer and a gentleman, I will always treat her with honor and respect. I am just as much a Southerner as you. I was born in Charleston and, as you can hear, retain both the speech and the manners of my native state. Our physician, Dr. Walker, grew up in Charlottesville, not forty miles south of where we stand. Neither of us are Yankees. We are people who believe in the sanctity of the Union—a political difference."

Rebecca gripped Charlie's arm to calm him down. She could see the veins in his throat and temples beginning to stand out. She did not wish him upset just as he was beginning to feel better.

Charlie took another step forward to stand directly in front of the sputtering, bigoted woman. "I find your attitude surprising in one who claims to be a good Christian woman. For does it not say in Ecclesiastes, 'The words of wise men are heard in silence more than the cry of him that ruleth among fools. Wisdom is better than weapons of war: but one sinner destroyeth much good.' It seems to me, Madame, that you have failed to learn the lesson of the Good Samaritan."

"That may be, Colonel, but you chose to stay with the Yankee army when the Union split, so you are no less than a traitor to your own people. And as for Rebecca Gaines, she has made her own bed, she must lie in it."

"Madame, each of us had our choices. General Lee was offered the position of Commander of the Army of the Potomac. He chose to serve with Virginia. Did you know he freed all of his slaves before he committed to the Confederacy? Each of us who served as career officers faced that decision. Each of us had to decide for ourselves, which was more important: our individual states, or the Union of those states. My mentor chose his state. I chose the Union. It was the most difficult decision of my life. I am no more a traitor than General Lee. I am simply a man who chose differently."

"Colonel," Mrs. Cooper stepped forward. "I must apologize. Not everyone shares the same belief as Mrs. Williams, and I feel in my heart that the help that you and Rebecca are offering will be gratefully accepted."

"I am most appreciative, Mrs. Cooper. Please convey my honest commitment to maintain as cooperative and constructive a relationship as possible. I have issued orders that any man of mine who harasses or in any way importunes the people of Culpeper will be severely punished. I have also ordered that any request for assistance, be it medical or otherwise, be met immediately. We are here for the winter, and I believe we should live as neighbors, in good will and understanding. The prodigal son was welcomed with open arms and feasting. We can do no less, Madame."

"I will convey your intention, Colonel Redmond, thank you. Now I do believe we have taken enough of your time. Please, when you have time, bring Dr. Walker by my husband's shop. I most certainly look forward to meeting her." She turned to her companions. "Ladies, I believe it is time we left Mrs. Gaines and the Colonel to their evening."

Rebecca patted Charlie's back and escorted them out. She returned a short time later, closing the doors. "Well, that went well."

"That went well? The wife of the local minister practically called you a whore, and you say that went well?"

She laughed as she crossed the room and settled on the couch. "Charlie, it is not like I did not set them up for it."

"Ah, yes. Would you care to tell me what that was about?"

She motioned him to the couch. "Come sit with me. We need to talk."

"Yes. Indeed we do. I do not think I have walked into a situation like that in my entire life. I cannot stand anyone saying things like that about you."

"Firstly, my dear Sir, I could care less what they say about me. Dr. Walker was very good at making me realize that. Secondly, while I will admit I kissed you, in part, just to annoy that old bat, the main reason I kissed you is that I wanted to. I have wanted to for days."

"You have kissed me before, dear lady. I admit, today's kiss was certainly more... stirring. You may most assuredly do it again, but I would prefer it if you did it to please yourself or to please me, not to offend the biddies." Charlie softened this stern request with a rather shy smile.

"Fine." She leaned over, took his face in her hand, and kissed him. Kissed him for her pleasure and his. She was gentle, but left no doubt in his mind she would go wherever he wished to lead her.

Charlie pulled her into his arms, his emotions running high, torn between overwhelming tenderness and a rush of passion and desire that left him shaking. He held her close and, cradling her head in his hand, slowly lowered his head to return her kiss. Just as his lips brushed hers, the door banged open and Elizabeth stalked in, fuming.

"Drat that bigoted, high and mighty, self-righteous woman." Obviously, Dr. Walker and Mrs. Williams had met. Elizabeth then registered the scene she had walked in on. "Oh...Oh! Uh. Excuse me.

I am sorry. I did not mean to intrude, but Charlie asked…" Elizabeth tried to back out of the door.

Rebecca smiled, pulling away from Charlie, but patting his leg to reassure him. "It is all right, Elizabeth. Come in."

The doctor came into the room. "So, I take it the lovely Mrs. Williams came out to check on you, and brought a little Charlie-bait with her. How bad were you?"

"We were good. Mostly," Rebecca chuckled.

"Mostly? Charlie, was she good?"

Charlie grinned and shook his head.

Elizabeth looked at the two of them. They both looked rather sheepish.

"Oh, Charlie was very good." Rebecca raised her brows, patting his leg again.

"True. I was very good. I did not pass out from surprise."

"I am afraid I was a little naughty," Rebecca admitted.

"I am afraid, my dear Rebecca, you convinced Mrs. Williams that you and I are conducting our own version of the Hell Fire Club's rituals, perhaps with our own satanic orgies on Saturday evenings."

Rebecca sighed, slipping her hand into his. "If I am going to burn in hell, Charlie, I will not mind it if I am with you."

Elizabeth looked sternly at them both. "Well, my dear friends, if the two of you burn in hell, I suspect it will be for malicious taunting of unsuspecting bigots. Keep it up, and you may give the poor woman apoplexy. I really did not like her color at all."

Both Charlie and Rebecca burst out laughing. They needed that after the visit.

"Now, if you will excuse me, I would like to get cleaned up and get a little rest before dinner."

They watched their friend leave, then Rebecca turned to Charlie, "Now, where were we?"

He smiled gently and drew her back into his arms, "I believe, Mrs. Gaines, I was about to do something I have wanted to do for a long time." Slowly, tenderly, passionately, and possessively, Charlie kissed her, putting into his touch all the wanting and yearning he had in his soul.

Rebecca responded to Charlie's gentle touch and his slow demonstration of affection. She had never been kissed that way before in her life, and she could not help the moan that rose from her depths as Charlie continued to kiss her. Her entire body tingled, alive with feelings she had never felt before. It was as if Charlie was touching her very soul with his kindness and tenderness.

Her eyes remained closed when Charlie's lips left hers, and she immediately felt the loss. She was brought back to her current surroundings by the gentle hold Charlie had on her face, as he reverently cupped it between his hands. Slowly her eyes opened and she looked at his smiling face. At that very moment, Rebecca Gaines lost her heart completely.

Without a word, Charlie leaned back against the couch and pulled Rebecca into his arms, holding her there close to his thundering heart. Rebecca was more than willing to be there.

Polk looked around the dinner table. All three of his companions were strangely quiet, but all were smiling like the cat that ate the canary. He watched with fascination: Miss Rebecca would look to the Colonel, then lower her eyes like a schoolgirl with her first crush. The Colonel, on the other hand, kept his eyes mostly locked on his plate, while trying to hide the smile on his face. Polk looked to Elizabeth, who had a thoughtful look on her face.

"Did I miss an amusing story?" he asked, sipping from a glass of wine.

Charlie gave his Second-in-Command a glance. "No, Polk. I assure you there is nothing funny going on."

"Then why are you all smiling?"

"We are not." Elizabeth offered him a gentle smile.

"Absolutely not," Rebecca said, hiding her own smile behind her dinner napkin.

"Uh-huh," Polk replied skeptically, once again looking at each of his companions in turn.

"Richard," Charlie spoke up before further prodding could embarrass any of them, "shall we step out on the porch and have a cigar?"

Rebecca laid her hand on Charlie's arm. "Colonel, please, go to the parlor and have your cigar. It is very chilly out tonight. I will prepare a digestive we might all enjoy if you and Colonel Polk would be so good as to start a fire."

Charlie rose from the table. "Our pleasure. Come along, Polk."

Rebecca waited until they were gone from the room before turning to Elizabeth. "I am in love."

Elizabeth smiled. "You are sure?"

"Absolutely. Oh, Elizabeth, when Charlie kissed me today..." She stopped and just shook her head, her smile bright. "I had no idea affection could be like that." She leaned forward as if to tell a deep secret. "So tender. So passionate. I felt wanted and needed, and very loved."

"I am happy for you, Rebecca. I truly am. Just remember our dear Charlie is fragile, and he is opening his heart for the first time in his life. Be gentle."

"I promise."

~

"All right." Polk nudged Charlie's shoulder, handing him a cigar when he looked up from his place in front of the hearth. "Now that we are away from the ladies, perhaps you will tell me."

Charlie finished tending the fire before standing and lighting his cigar. "What would you like to know?"

"Damn it, Charlie, do you have to be so stubborn all the time?"

"Was that a rhetorical question?" The Colonel smiled, taking the first puff of his cigar.

"You are intentionally trying to drive me insane."

"No, I am not, my friend. I am just getting accustomed to the fact that I have done something here in this beautiful country I have never done before."

"And that is?"

"I believe I have had my heart captured by our hostess. I do believe I am falling in love with Miss Rebecca."

Polk blinked, not believing the words coming out of his friend's mouth. "Love? Charlie, just because you have found a little...um, relief, with the lady is no reason to get silly over her."

"Richard, would you call your friendship with Elizabeth 'silly'?"

"No, but Elizabeth is not a Confederate widow. She is a member of our own regiment. Charlie, this is dangerous. You are a career Army officer. You know as well as I do that you are on the short list for a fort command in the western territories when this is over."

"I have been in service to this country for almost twenty years. I am tired. Tired of the killing. Tired of the mud. Tired of the blood, and the heat and the cold. Tired of having no place I can call home. For the past four years, I have killed men and boys who are from my own country, my own state, even. I do not belong anywhere any more. I want a place where I belong."

"And you think you belong here, with her? I am not trying to cause you distress, my friend. I am just playing devil's advocate. How does she feel about you?"

"She is taking it slowly and carefully, but I think she wants me. Wants me to be here with her. At least, I hope so."

Polk sat down in the chair nearest the fireplace and just shook his head. "I have known you for over thirteen years, Charlie, and this is the first time I have ever heard you talk like this." He looked up at his friend. "So what are your plans?"

"This is so new, we really have not had time to make plans. I think the war will be over soon, so I will see my duty out with it, then we will have to see."

The Second-in-Command sighed, and then smiled at his friend.

"Well, Charlie, if this is what you want, and she truly makes you happy, I wish you the best of luck."

"I knew you would, my friend."

"Of course. It will be my pleasure to watch you find someone else who will put up with your bullheaded ways. I hope the lady has better luck with you than I have had."

Charlie laughed out loud, a full, rich laugh unlike any Richard had ever heard from him before.

"Yes, I do think this lady is good for you."

Elizabeth cleared her throat as she and Rebecca entered the room. "I hope you boys are done talking about us."

The men executed courtly bows. "Never, Mesdames, never when there are such lovely ladies to fascinate us." Charlie was being the charming Charlestonian.

Elizabeth shared a smile with Rebecca. "Such romantic gentlemen we have before us."

"Indeed." She winked at Charlie before setting the tray on the table. "They do know how to turn a lady's head. I know Colonel Redmond certainly turned a couple earlier today."

Both men remained standing by the fireplace as the ladies settled themselves. "And which heads would you be referring to, Miss Rebecca?"

"Well, it seems two of Culpeper's young ladies seem to have an eye for our charming Colonel."

Charlie's right eyebrow rose. "I hardly think so."

Rebecca giggled at his response. "Please, Colonel Redmond. Those two were eyeing you like you were the entrée at a banquet." She poured a glass for him and held it out. "The moment you said hello, they simply melted."

"More likely they wilted under Mrs. Williams' onslaught."

Elizabeth chuckled. "I heard them whispering about you as they were leaving. Miss Reynolds thinks you are just the most handsome thing she has ever seen, and Miss Simms thinks you have wonderful blue eyes."

Charlie blushed. "Clearly the result of an extended dearth of masculine company. Were we at peace, they would not have looked at me twice."

Now it was Rebecca's turn to laugh. "Right." She tried to quell the laughter by sipping her brandy. "Colonel Polk, has Colonel Redmond always been fanciful, or is this something new?"

"Charlie has always been a modest gentleman, and rarely one for the ladies."

"Then I believe I am doubly honored to have caught the Colonel's eye."

"My dear lady, you have caught more than my eye." Charlie dropped to his knee beside Rebecca's chair and gathered her hand into his.

She smiled, feeling him run his thumb over her hand. "Have I?"

He looked into her eyes and asked, "Can you doubt it, dear heart?"

Rebecca reached out, tracing her finger down his cheek. "Not when you look at me like this." She brushed her thumb over Charlie's chin. "You have indeed won my heart."

He gathered her hands in his and turned them, tenderly kissing the palm of each. Elizabeth and Polk quietly slipped out of the room, leaving the two lovers to themselves.

Rebecca removed her dress, placing it in her sitting room for Lizbet to collect for laundering. Dressed in her chemise, she returned to her bedroom and turned down the bed. She puttered around the room absent mindedly, readying it for the night, while waiting for Charlie to come in. He had gone to the infirmary with Elizabeth to check on the condition of Major Montgomery.

She pulled her nightgown from the dresser and placed it on the bed, then slowly began undoing the buttons of her chemise. She slid it from her shoulders then, gathering it at the waist, she bent to push it to the floor. Stepping out of it, she turned to find Charlie standing in the doorway.

Suddenly she was frozen, the sound of her heart pounding loud and hard in her ears. A huge part of her hoped the Colonel would take advantage of the situation by laying his hands on her.

He stood like a statue, looking at her, drinking in the beauty of this woman with his eyes, torn between offering her the privilege of privacy and taking her in his arms then and there.

Finally, he remembered to breathe. "Rebecca?"

The sound of his voice broke her entranced state. Startled, she reached for her nightgown, and quickly pulled it over her head. She could not look at him; her embarrassment and shame were too great.

Charlie stood there the whole time, his breathing shallow. He was trembling. The voice in his head was alternating between screaming at him for being an unmannered, ungrateful clod for taking advantage of her like this, and laughing at him for dreaming that she could really love him. Between the aching want that burned through his chest, and the black truth that he could never have the love he so craved, it took everything that Charlie was to remain standing. He wanted to curl around that searing pain and try to find some surcease, if only for a little while.

"Forgive me, Colonel. I did not hear you come in." She kept her eyes on the floor, too embarrassed to look at him. *He must think I am shameless for letting him catch me like that.*

Charlie looked up at her, confused, in pain. She was saying something to him. He could not quite understand the words coming from her mouth. All he could see was that she could not look him in the eyes. "Ahhh. Uhhh. I am sorry. I did not mean to intrude." Somehow, he had to get away, but he could not seem to get his feet to work.

"You did not intrude. It is your room, too. I should have changed in the other room." She gestured to the door. "I am sorry, I did not mean to embarrass you."

He swallowed, hard. Somehow, he needed to get his voice back, his control back. "You did not embarrass me, dear. It is just that you are so beautiful, you take my breath away."

She blushed at the compliment. *I am beautiful? Oh, he has been alone too long.* "You are very kind to say such things."

He took one step toward her. His voice dropped to a deep rumble. "I am not kind. I am truthful. You are beautiful." He knew that if she but had the courage to look, she would see the truth of those words shining out of his eyes.

At last, she did look to him. She smiled, trying not to cry at his kindness. "Charlie, you are the first person ever to tell me that. Is it any wonder you have won my heart?"

He saw the tears threatening to fall, the pain in her eyes. Like a moth drawn to a candle flame, he moved close, gently cupping her chin in his hand. He whispered to her, caught in a moment of awe and longing. His longing burned in his chest. Here was the only cure for the pain that ate his soul away. "Rebecca, dearest lady, you are beautiful. Your face is beautiful, your eyes are as lovely as the new green of spring, and your body draws me so that I want to hold and caress and protect you for the rest of my life. And your heart and soul are pure beauty." He knew she saw him as a man. He knew that when the reality of loving one such as he sunk home, she would leave him. He knew when she did; she would take with her more than his heart. She would take his soul, too.

She placed her hands on his chest, looking at him to try to make him understand her simple words. "I love you, Charlie. And I want to know if you will do something for me."

"I will do anything you ask of me."

"I know what I feel for you is true, Charlie; that I love you. I know what that means and all that goes with it. I need you to trust me, to help me, to go slow and easy. I have desires I have never felt before, and I find them a bit frightening. I need to learn to deal with them."

He reached up and tentatively cradled her shoulders in his hands. On his face was a look that tore at Rebecca's heart. It was the look of a lost and lonely soul, wanting so much to please and to be loved, totally bewildered about what to do, and terrified of doing something wrong. She could feel him trembling under her hands lying lightly on his chest. "Whatever you need. Whatever you want."

"Then," she looked down and then back up, a furious blush heating her cheeks, "when we go to bed...would you, would you hold me?"

"I have to confess something. I wake in the night sometimes with you in my arms." Shamed at his own weakness, he lowered his eyes from hers. "I know I should have moved away, but I could not. I could not let you go. Yes, I would very much like to be able to hold you and know that it is what you want." In a much smaller voice, he added, "And I crave the warmth of you."

She smiled, placing a hand gently under his chin to make him look up. "A time for confessions, my dear. Once I know you are asleep, I roll as close to you as I can. I long for your warmth and strength. I feel very safe in your arms."

A shy smile lit his face. "Then you shall have my arms around you for as long as you want them, dear lady."

"Charlie?"

He quirked an inquiring eyebrow at her.

"Let us go to bed."

"Do I have time to change clothes? I am a little overdressed." All of a sudden, standing there in his uniform, was nervous as a cat.

"Yes, of course. I will go and brush my hair. Call me when you are ready." She leaned up on her toes and placed a gentle kiss on his lips, then left for her sitting room.

Charlie moved quickly to strip himself of his uniform. As he released the binding around his breasts, the voice came back again. The transformation from male to female was once again complete. *Ah yes, she does love her strong, gentle Colonel Charlie. But, that is not who holds her at night, is it? You are not the person she is falling in love with. She is falling in love with the image you created—she is falling in love with a fraud. Certainly, you can give her what she thinks she needs for now. Companionship. Comfort. A warm body at night. She has missed these things, and you are there, convenient and safe.*

And what will she think when you ask for more? When you want her to touch you? When your womanhood is obvious to her hands and eyes? What then?

With a heavy sigh, Charlie washed up at the basin then pulled on his nightshirt. He spent a few moments on purely domestic issues. With a shovel full of hot coals from the fireplace dropped into the warming pan, he carefully heated the sheets to make their bed a warm and comforting space. He fluffed the pillows, and smoothed the sheets, then stepped to the door. "Rebecca?"

The door opened slowly. Rebecca looked to Charlie with a shy smile. Rebecca ran her hand over her hair, which she had been brushing non-stop for the last few minutes. She giggled nervously. "Charlie."

Charlie extended his hand to Rebecca and waited for her to enter.

Rebecca took Charlie's hand, hoping that she could control the shaking in her own hands. She tried, but just could not wipe the silly smile from her face.

A soft smile lit Charlie's features, and he lifted Rebecca's hand to his lips, whispering a touch of lips over knuckles. He helped Rebecca into the high bed, then banked the fire to burn slow and warm all night, doused all the candles and lamps except for one, and climbed into bed.

Rebecca waited for him to move closer, not wanting to upset him by doing something inappropriate. She felt like a new bride, only this time she was enjoying the slight giddiness.

Carefully, Charlie moved toward Rebecca, and then gently slipped one arm under her shoulders. "Is this all right with you?"

"It is perfectly all right," she sighed, and cuddled as close as she could. "It is wonderful."

Charlie shifted and drew her tighter against his chest. He buried her face in Rebecca's hair and savored the unique smell of it, with hints of lavender from her shampoo. A small sound, almost like a whimper, escaped from his lips.

"Charlie, are you all right?" Rebecca started to pull away. "Should I move? Have you changed your mind?"

"Shhhhh. I am fine." Charlie drew Rebecca gently back to his chest. "Please, do not leave. I... I need to..." Charlie's voice almost broke. He tried again, in a much smaller voice. "I need to be close to you." Rebecca could feel the tension in him. A fine, subtle tremor quivered through the muscles of his body. He could not tell Rebecca that having her in his arms eased the burning hole in his chest, in his soul. That his internal demons warned him this would not last, and Rebecca would someday walk away from him. That he was memorizing every moment, every sensation to take out in the future and examine like a cherished prize. That he knew that someday these memories of Rebecca in his arms would be the only thing he had, and he would use them to both sustain and torture himself for the rest of his life.

Rebecca hummed, getting closer to him. "I love this, Charlie. Love being close to you. Feeling you hold me." She looked up timidly. "Will you do something else for me?"

"Anything." Charlie managed to make his response sound almost normal. It was not easy.

"Kiss me."

Charlie's eyes fluttered shut. His breathing stopped for a second. Then he slowly shifted, bringing his body around so that Rebecca rested in the curve of his arm as he held himself above the smaller woman. As he did, Rebecca shifted to slide her arm under Charlie and around his back. With his free hand, Charlie caressed Rebecca's face, then cradled her head in his hand. Charlie lowered his face to Rebecca's, then very slowly, and very gently, their lips met. It was a dream of a kiss, a reverent salute, sweet and tender, and undemanding.

"Mmm," Rebecca moaned, smiling a little. "That was...so nice."

Charlie stayed hovering above Rebecca's body for a moment.

Then he laid his face in the crook of Rebecca's neck and wrapped his arm around her waist, pulling her closer still. "Oh, yes."

Rebecca's heart was hammering in her chest, and her body was feeling sensations she had never before experienced. "Oh, yes," she echoed, her hands running over Charlie's back.

Charlie felt as if he was suspended halfway between heaven and hell. Rebecca's touch was like fire. Her innocence was a bastion Charlie refused to assault. Nothing had ever felt like having Rebecca in his arms, warm, compliant. Her affection was so tender, it brought tears to his eyes. The heat from her body ignited Charlie's core. The knowledge that this would all be taken from him someday beat at Charlie's soul. He was helpless in Rebecca's arms.

Happy and safe, Rebecca settled in and closed her eyes to enjoy the security of this moment. Her breathing settled in to the soft, regular rhythm of sleep.

I lie here, holding this beautiful woman in my arms, my body hungering for more than simply the holding of her. Oh God, dear God, what have I done?

It has been so long, and she feels so soft and sweet. She feels so right in my arms. I want to stay here. I want the damned war to go away. I want this to be real. But tomorrow I will rise, and eventually orders will come and I will have to ride away.

Will I take her heart with me? I will leave my soul behind. Dear God, what have I done?

I want to stay. I want to winter here in this beautiful place with this beautiful woman, and pretend this is not the winter camp of an army at war, but instead a fine horse farm, breeding the most beautiful animals in the state. A happy home, a place where others may come and be safe.

Please, God I am so tired. I just want to lie in this lovely soft bed, holding this lovely, tender woman, and rest. I want to rise in the morning and have it all be real. I want to have a life that is not mud and miles, sweat and stuffy tents, waiting and being afraid, bleeding, death, and more mud. Always mud. Sometimes brown, sometimes red with the blood of men and horses, but always mud. What would it be like to have a home, to have the love of a woman like her? But it cannot be, can it?

That hated voice in Charlie's head spoke into the darkness—that voice of the proper Southern woman, of Charlotte. *You gave up any hope of real love, of family, of a normal life that day when you left, did you not, Charlie? That day when you killed me.*

Charlie is not real, you fool. Charlie is your armor, the place you hide. You can never marry. You cannot raise a family. What woman would want you, Charlie—really want you? You are no man. You act like one, you talk like one, you dress like one, but take away the title, the clothes, and you are not one. When the reality sinks in, she will not want you.

Yes, you are safe. You are worlds better than the men out there who will use her and hurt her. You are better than that. You are safe. For the simple price of her body, you give her protection from violation or worse. And you are novel—something she has never felt before—her dirty little secret she can take out on cold nights and remind herself that once she was naughty and bad and wicked and sinful. On those nights when the dullness and drudgery of her life are more than she can stand. That is what you are good for, Charlie Redmond.

Something stirred in Charlie's soul. Some small light of hope had been kindled in the tenderness of this night, of Rebecca's trusting love. For the first time, Charlie answered that taunting voice. *What if you are wrong? What if she really does love me? Have I not paid my debts? Is it so impossible that two people can find some comfort, some love in this world? I do not care what it costs. I am going to try. And I will be here. I will love her. I will give her whatever she is ready to accept from me. For as long as she wants me.*

When sleep finally came, Charlie had a small, hopeful smile on his face.

CHAPTER 11

Thursday, November 24, 1864

Rebecca rolled over, reaching for Charlie, who was long gone from the bed. She smiled and stretched, allowing the memory of the previous night to wash over her. Her body still felt his touch, and she relished it, "Oh, Charlie."

Sighing, she rose from bed and called for Lizbet. She was slipping into her dressing gown when the young woman entered the room. "Yes, Ma'am?"

"Have you seen Colonel Redmond this morning?"

"Yes, Ma'am. The Colonel rose early and went to camp. He said to tell you he would return for lunch."

"Thank you. Could you please draw a bath for me?"

"Yes, Ma'am. What would you like to wear today?"

Rebecca smiled, an indulgent look crossing her face. "Something bright and pleasing. I feel good today, Lizbet, and I want the world to know it."

The young woman smiled, crossing to the wardrobe. "I would

guess Colonel Redmond is feeling very good today as well, Miss Rebecca. He had a very bright smile on his face all through breakfast this morning. I have not seen him eat so much since we arrived. Sarah said if his appetite stays like this, he will need to have his uniform altered."

The blonde snorted at the thought. Knowing what she did about Charlie and his uniform, she could only imagine what kind of alterations he could make.

Charlie looked around his tent and the furnishings that had been packed up. Jocko was placing the last of his things in a crate. "Well, it will be nice to have the spare tent," the batman mumbled as he moved the crate to the opening.

"If you would like, Jocko, you can take it for yourself. Give yourself the treat of a little privacy."

"And what do you think the boys would do without me yelling at them?"

"Give me a medal for getting you out of their hair?"

Jocko looked to his friend. "So tell me, Colonel C, what has you acting like a man reborn overnight?"

Charlie smiled gently. "I found a healing to a part of me that has been wounded for so long I did not realize it still hurt."

"And I take it this healing happened in the company of one Miss Rebecca?"

"Well, she has been tending to my injuries and illnesses."

Jocko gave his friend a sly grin before turning away and adding, "I think she is tending to more than your physical body, Charlie; she soothes your soul. Do you have any idea how much you smile now?"

"Who me? I always smile when I am relaxed. You just rarely see me relaxed. Seriously, though, old friend, she is a very special lady, one I hope I will be allowed to see grow old."

"Is it that serious now? What are you thinking, Charlie?"

"Between us, I am thinking that when this conflict is over, I will take my twenty year retirement, and come back here and properly woo and marry the lady. If she will have me."

"Marry the lady?" He turned around, the shock registering clearly on his face. "You are serious?"

"I am."

"And what does the lady say about this?"

"I do not know. I have not asked her."

"Marriage? Good Lord, Charlie, has it slipped by your good senses that you have only known this lady for a month?"

"No, it has not. That is why I am taking things slowly, and why I will not take any radical action until the war is over."

"I hope for your sake, and the sake of the lady, you know what you are doing, Charlie. I want you to be happy; I do not want you to be hurt. And I do not want to see the lady hurt, either."

"Nor do I, Jocko. I want her to be cared for and loved as she deserves to be." A wistful look came over Charlie's face. "And if someone came along who could do that better than I..."

"Well, I doubt that will be the case. I think you are the man for the job, Charlie. Now all we have to do is get you through this war in one piece so you can come home to your lady." Jocko gave a quick laugh. "Of all things I thought we would be discussing about the end of the war, this was not among them."

"Jocko? You and I started at the same time. What had you planned to do when your time in the Army is up?"

"Colonel C, I have lived in the Army all my life and I am sure I will die in the Army. I will probably be sent off to some post where they need a hotheaded Irishman to keep the boys in line."

"Well, my friend, if you change your mind, I will find a way to keep you occupied."

"Oh, is that so? You think you and the lady will need a hotheaded Irishman to help you keep the place going?" He smiled and crossed his arms over his chest. "Or maybe you want me around to protect you from the lady. I know she is almost as hard headed as you are."

Charlie threw his head back and laughed. "My friend, maybe I am just trying to keep you from destroying the morale of the western forces—'cause none of them will be able to keep up with you. More seriously, the time after the war will be hard, very hard. We could use your charm and your skill."

"Well, I suppose Virginia is just as good a place as any to settle. Some mighty pretty ladies in town that will be husband hunting after the war." He winked. "Might even find myself a lovely just like you did."

"Well, let us see what we can do to help make the end of the war less painful—at least for a few folks."

"I will be right there with you, Colonel C. Just like always."

Charlie slapped Jocko on the shoulder. "Good plan, my friend, good plan. Now, let us go see how the boys are doing at getting ready for winter."

~

"Ma'am?"

Rebecca turned to find Corporal Nailer and several other troopers carrying various trunks, boxes, and crates. "What can I do for you, young Duncan?"

"Th-the-these things belong to the Co-co-colonel, Ma'am. Sergeant Jackson told us to fetch them up here. Where sh-sh-should we put them?"

"Well you may put his command items in the manager's office and his personal things at the foot of the steps. I will have Reg take them upstairs."

"Yes, M-ma-ma'am."

She held the screen door for the men to pass through, then she stepped out on the porch for a breath of fresh air. She turned when she heard the soft clomping of a horse. Charlie was riding toward the house slowly, obviously enjoying the crisp autumn air.

"Why look at you, Colonel Redmond. Out for a lazy ride?" She smiled as he climbed down from his mount.

"No, Miss Rebecca. I have been out riding fence this morning to see how repairs are coming."

"Are they suitable?"

"Indeed. My boys are doing a fine job."

She held out her hand. "Come, Colonel. Sarah has prepared a wonderful lunch for us."

"If it is all right with you, Miss Rebecca, I will be having my officers in for a meeting after lunch," he said, as he wrapped her arm through his.

"I told you the manager's office is yours. You may do with it what you will." She gave him a coy smile. "It is only fitting that the gentleman of the house should have his private office."

Charlie stumbled slightly. *The gentleman of the house. I think I like that. A lot. Right. You think you can play this role forever, Charlie Redmond? What are they gonna do when you slip, and someone finds out just what you are.*

Shut up! I have lived this successfully for nineteen years. I am not about to slip up now. "Thank you, Rebecca. You offer me a home and a place, when I have not had either for many years. I am more grateful than I can tell you."

Immediately after lunch, Charlie adjourned to his new office. The staff officers gathered for their daily meeting, some grousing and some being amused that the Colonel did not join them in the mess, opting for joining the lovely lady instead of his scruffy officers. Overall, Charlie's choice of luncheon companion did him no harm in the men's eyes. If anything, they were proud of their Colonel, who had suddenly manifested as a lady's man. It had certainly squelched the rumors that the Colonel preferred the personal company of men.

Charlie could not help but smile as he heard the quiet whispers among the men as they filed in for the meeting. He hid the smirk with a twitch of his lips.

"Well, gentlemen. Welcome to my new office. Shall we begin? Company A, report."

The meeting went on as expected. The issues of wintering in, regimental morale, and immediate needs were all discussed at length. Finally, Charlie announced that the regiment would hold a gymkhana, a traditional series of competitive events that demonstrated various aspects of horsemanship. Appropriate awards would be made to all of the winners. Charlie's staff agreed this would help to meld the troops together into a cohesive team, a critical factor for his patched together regiment.

As he escorted the staff to the door and sent them on their way to attend to afternoon duties, Charlie looked around at the office, piled with boxes of papers, many of which he needed to read and file. It was a long, boring afternoon that stretched into evening and a supper hastily eaten from a tray at his desk.

Rebecca was upstairs in her sitting room, reading, when Charlie finally finished and came to find her. "All finished with your paperwork?"

"For today," Charlie sighed, taking a seat on the settee to remove his boots. "I learned very quickly when I became an officer that there is never an end to the paperwork. That is one thing I shall not miss about the Army." He turned and looked at her. "Actually, I do not think I will miss anything about the Army."

"I am sure all your training will come in very handy in getting our farm up and running again."

"I am sure it will. Between knowing how to keep the books and manage insufficient supplies, and figuring out how to keep a herd of horses going regardless, I think I might be good at this."

"I think," Rebecca set her book aside, "you will be very good at this. I do believe we will have the finest program in all of Virginia."

"I hope so, dear lady. I would love to give you all of the comforts you deserve."

"Charlie, having you here with me is the only comfort I desire."

"Beloved, I will do my very best to be here for you. You know I have responsibilities to see to until the war ends, but I promise, I will take very, very good care of myself."

For a moment Rebecca's heart stopped beating, her breath caught in her throat as the thought that Charlie might not come home ran through her mind. She reached over and placed her hands on Charlie's shoulders. "You must come back to me, Charlie. If you do not I...I shall not be able to go on. Promise me you will not take unnecessary risks."

"Having you to come back to is the best incentive I could possibly have for being very, very careful. They will not call me Lucky Charlie any longer; they will call me the cowardly Charlie." He laughed gently and pulled her into his arms, "My dear, I will do everything in my power to come back to you. I want to have time to explore our relationship and to discover all that is possible for us."

She sighed, nodding at his reassurances. "I know you will." She opened her eyes and looked at him. "But we have a while before you will have to leave. So there is no need to worry about it now."

"Will you be waiting for me when I return? I hope so with all my heart." Charlie released his hold on her, and slid from her side on the settee. Holding her hand in his, he knelt at her feet.

"You know I will, Charlie. Please do not doubt that."

He looked up at her. She was struck by the look of fearful hope in his eyes. "You know that I love you with all my heart."

"And I you, my dear Colonel."

He swallowed, hard.

She was worried about his color; suddenly he looked very pale. Clearly, whatever he was trying to say was not easy. "Charlie?"

The voice spoke up. *Charlie, you fool. Why are you even... Shut up! She loves me. I have to believe she loves me.*

"Rebecca. Mrs. Gaines. Dear lady. I do not have a lot to offer." *God, help me. This is so much more difficult than facing a charging line of pike men.*

"What is wrong, Charlie? Please tell me."

He looked down at her hand, so small and delicate in his own. *Damn. I do not even have a ring.* "Rebecca." He drew a deep breath. "When I return after this war is over, would you... would you consider doing me the honor..." His throat closed for a moment.

Rebecca looked at him expectantly. She did not want to assume what he was going to say, but that giddy feeling in the pit of her stomach was back. "Yes?"

"Would you consider doing me the honor of being my wife? I know someday a real man may come along that will meet your needs, but until then, please. I would do whatever you want, be whatever you ask of me, whether that be friend or lover. Please?" There. It was out. The scariest thing he had ever done was over. The nasty little voice had stayed quiet. Now all he had to do was wait.

She smiled, cupping his face in her hands; she leaned forward, placing a kiss on his lips. "Yes. Yes, Charlie, I would be honored to marry you, but on one condition."

He looked at her, waiting to learn her condition. She had seen that expression on his face once before—the look of a child who did not know if they were going to be hit or hugged. Yet, for all of that, there was hope in his face.

"That you never speak of stepping down again. I love you, Charlie. I want you. There will be no other."

A look of wonder dawned on his face as her words slowly seeped into his brain. He caught both of her hands, pressed them together, and covered them with light kisses. "Thank you. I love you so, my dear, dear Rebecca." He turned the palms of her hands up, and placed reverent kisses in each one. "I love you."

He pulled the small garnet ring from his little finger, the only thing he had of his mother's, and gently placed it on her finger. "I am sorry, but I have not had time to go to a jeweler to get you a ring. This was my mother's; would you wear it until I can get something more appropriate?"

Her hand covered her mouth as she gasped. "Oh, Charlie, I love you, so very much, but I cannot take a ring that belonged to your mother."

"Why not? When we marry, everything that is mine will be yours. And you already own my heart and soul."

"Charlie, that ring belonged to your mother. You should keep it close to your heart."

He smiled at that. "My darling, if it is on your finger, it will be closer to my heart than it could ever be on my hand."

She was beyond words. Very gently, he leaned forward and gathered her into his arms. They stayed like that for long moments, his kneeling form embracing her gently. Finally, the awkwardness of his position forced them to shift, but the tenderness remained. It was a night of tender caresses and softly whispered words of love.

~

Monday, November 28, 1864

Charlie rose early, as was his habit. The illness that had plagued him had also kept him from his regular routine of exercise, something that was critical to maintaining his public deception. The work uniform he habitually wore for running in was clean, much to his relief. He disliked taking any chances.

He ran the longer version of his circuit, behind the stables, around the small pond, up Gaines Run, back down the other side of the pond, and back across the stream. It was roughly ten miles, across sometimes rough country. It felt spectacular, with the cool air keeping him from overheating too badly, but not so cold as to be uncomfortable. He missed the morning officers' mess, because of the duration of his run. As he approached his office, thinking perhaps

Beulah could bring him something from Sarah's now fully functional kitchen, he was quite startled to notice Reverend Williams' carriage approaching, not the main entrance to the house, but the side entrance to his office.

He waited for the carriage to stop, flushed, sweaty, hair ruffled by the wind, wearing the tight breeches and short tunic that were his regular running clothes. He forgot that the breeches showed every detail of his anatomy, including the padding he used to sustain his masculine image. To the two women in the carriage, he was indeed the image of a stalwart man in that moment.

Mrs. Williams sniffed. "He just stands and waits, in all of his dirt."

Grace Cooper was much more realistic, "What would you expect him to do, see us coming and run to get a bath and clean clothes?" To herself she thought, *My, my Rebecca, I do see what you mean. He is absolutely delicious looking.*

Charlie stepped to the side of the carriage and offered a hand to the ladies. "Good morning, ladies. If you care to come into the office, I will send for some tea. To what do we owe this early morning visit?"

Mrs. Williams ignored Charlie's hand and his offer. "Colonel, we will not stay. I just wanted to let you know that we are starting to get an influx of refugees from your war. What are you going to do about it? We have no resources to take care of these...these waifs."

"Refugees? How many, Ma'am?"

Mrs. Cooper cut in, fully aware of how little information Mrs. Williams could convey when she was on one of her righteous streaks. "Colonel Redmond, in the past twenty-four hours, we have seen seven groups of refugees, mostly women and children, come to the steps of the church looking for sustenance and shelter. We have given them soup and a roof in the form of the church, but with winter coming on, we cannot care for these people. Since you so generously offered to help, we hoped you would be able to do something."

"Of course, ladies. We will do whatever we can. Can you tell me if there are any buildings available that could be turned into refugee quarters?"

Mrs. Williams sniffed. "I do not know about such things. You would have to ask my husband or the other gentlemen in town. And furthermore, these people are your responsibility, not ours."

Charlie looked down for a moment. Something about this woman just plain irritated him. "Well, then, Ma'am. We will find a way to take care of them. I will have my quartermaster attend to it as soon as possible."

"See to it, Colonel. See to it." Without further comment, Mrs. Williams urged the horses on, leaving Charlie standing at the side of the road. He shook his head and walked into his office.

Refugees meant more people, more people meant more cots, more blankets, more shoes—damned shoes—more medicine, more food, more clothing, more space, more firewood, more of everything. He was having enough problems getting supplies for his own men. But he had promised.

A long letter went out that morning to General Sheridan, explaining the situation. Food he could do at least something about, such as organizing hunting expeditions into the great forest on the lower slopes of the Blue Ridge. But the rest of the things he would need to care for these people would have to come from Supply. Charlie had the mess deliver lunch to his office, and the meeting with his officers was long and querulous that day, as they wrestled with the problems this would present to their already over-extended resources.

By the time late afternoon arrived, he was tired of the demands of command. A quick trip over to the infirmary confirmed Montgomery was not yet conscious, but was slowly showing signs of returning to the world of the living. Charlie and Elizabeth spoke briefly, both concerned that at his current rate of recovery, Monty would suffer one of the common ailments of hospitalized people— pneumonia or pleurisy, and succumb to that before his head had time to heal sufficiently for him to return to consciousness.

Feeling somewhat overwhelmed, and still dressed in the uniform he had worn to run in so many hours before, Charlie decided to quit early. Anyway, there was nothing more he could do until he heard back from Sheridan.

Charlie entered the parlor where Rebecca and Lizbet were going through the chests Rebecca had recently gotten out of storage.

The maid lifted the wedding gown from the chest. "Oh, Miss Rebecca, it is beautiful. What should I do with it?"

Rebecca considered the gown. "Just launder it and pack it away. I have no need for it."

"But..."

"Please, Lizbet, trust me with this." She smiled and patted the young woman's arm, before looking up and seeing Charlie in the door. "Colonel, you are finished early today. That is good, I hope." She gave Lizbet a pat on the shoulder to send her on her way.

"The mountain of paperwork was pretty tough today. I think I have a headache just from reading all of the excuses from the Quartermaster General's office." He flopped into a chair in front of the fireplace. "I also had some visitors from town today. There are some serious problems starting to arise because they are getting a constant stream of refugees from some of the areas that are now under siege. We will have to do something about it."

Rebecca slid up behind him and began a firm massage of tight and tired muscles. "Then maybe an early supper and off to bed for a good night's rest? We can worry about other things tomorrow."

He really had not paid much attention to Rebecca's interaction with her maid when he came in, but something was not quite right here. Something in her voice signaled some strain or concern. "Rebecca, dear, what is bothering you?"

"Oh, it is nothing, Charlie. Just trying to vanquish some old demons." She took a deep breath and continued to rub his shoulders.

"Would you like some tea? I will have Beulah make some fresh for you?"

"I think that tea and some quiet talk would be good for both of us, dear. Old demons are something you and I can dispel together."

"Then take off your boots and get comfortable, while I see to it." She gave him a kiss on the cheek before leaving the room.

Charlie pulled his boots off and slipped on the pair of carpet slippers Rebecca had found for him. He thought carefully on what he had seen as he came in, and remembered the dress. It had been white, with a good bit of lace. *Oh God, it was her wedding dress. I hope she is not missing her husband, and regretting her relationship with me.* Charlie was feeling more than a little nervous, waiting for her return.

Within a few minutes, they were seated side by side, sipping warm tea and resting, watching the flames in the fireplace. Rebecca glanced to Charlie. "Better? How is your headache?"

"Yes, love. Just being with you is enough to ease my stress."

"I am glad." She reached over and intertwined her fingers with his. "How is winter camp coming? Is everything coming together for the men?"

"You know it is. You want to tell me what has you upset and what you are avoiding, love?"

"I fear you are getting to know me too well. I assure you it is nothing. Simply old memories, but now is not the time to look back. Now is the time to look forward. We have much to plan for when you come home to stay."

"Rebecca, darling, we both have ghosts in our past. We will have to face many challenges in the future, as well. I think it would serve both of us to find those things that lurk in our memories and expunge them—both for ourselves and for our future." His gentle tone softened the bluntness of his words.

She looked down at her teacup. "It is my husband." She looked to her lover. "I swear to you it is not important anymore, Charlie. I do not know why I let it bother me so."

"Love, if it bothers you, it is important. Tell me. Let us lay that ghost to rest together, dear." *As long as that ghost is around, eventually he will come between us. And I swear, if I can do anything to dispel that, I will.*

Yes, certainly, you will, Charlie—the knight on the white horse, displacing the real man with the false one.

"He hurt me, Charlie." She blurted it out before she had a moment to think about it. Now her biggest fear was that he would view her as damaged goods and want to be as far away from her as possible. She prepared to let him walk out of her life.

Hurt her? He hurt her? His first reaction was anger. Immediately, he realized she did not need his anger, she needed his understanding and love. Instead of lashing out, he gathered her in his arms. "I am so sorry. I do not know how he hurt you, or even why, but I do know you could never do anything to deserve to be hurt."

She fought tears that threatened to overwhelm her from his tenderness. "Thank you," she whispered.

Charlie braced himself, knowing perfectly well that when anyone had faced a painful and violent situation, talking about it was important. Time and again, he had sat and coaxed stories of pain, and fear and bewilderment out of his men. He could do no less for this gentle woman. "Can you tell me about it?"

"I do not know what to tell you, Charlie. It was an arranged marriage; we certainly did not love each other. He was several years older than I was. He made it quite clear from the very beginning that my place in this house was at his pleasure and his leisure. I tried to be a good wife, Charlie, I really did, but very little seemed to please him."

He was very careful. The tone of her voice told him there was much more behind these simple statements. "I am so sorry; it sounds like a very lonely and sterile existence. Perhaps if you continue, you will feel better."

She seemed to be thinking back, and slowly detaching herself from the present to pull up those old memories. "He used to decide everything for me, including what I was allowed to eat and wear. One time I spilled something on my day dress, and I changed my clothes. When he came in, he was furious," she paused, trying to sniff back the tears. "He grabbed me by the arm and took me to the wash room. He ripped the clean dress off me and made me put the other back on..." she stopped, her face twitching and lips quivering with the memory.

The image that came to Charlie's mind was clear. The deceased and unlamented Mr. Gaines clearly had tried to control her, and may have enjoyed humiliating her. He was very familiar with such harsh treatment. In fact, Gaines was sounding painfully like his own father after his mother's death. Gently he stroked her back. "It is all right, my dear. You are safe now; just let it go. Give the memories to me, and together we will put them in the past."

"He...ah...he used to tell me I was worthless and stupid, and that I was lucky to have him. That I was fortunate he took pity on me and married me. That he provided me a home and food and the clothes on my back." She wiped away a tear. "He was furious when I did not give him a child in the first year, and that is when it started."

Charlie softly stroked her back. He kept his voice low and neutral and continued to gently probe, trying to give her a safe space to let out all of the pain and all of the shame that went with such treatment. "Love, was it always like this, or did something happen that marked the start of this... harsh behavior?"

"When my father arranged the marriage, I know he thought I would be all right, or he never would have done it. But from the very first day, my husband started telling me how he only married me because my family needed the prestige of being related to the Gaines family. That was not true, by the way. That if he had his choice he would have picked a pretty woman, but I looked good and strong and would be well suited for giving him a son every year. And when I did not, he started drinking; and then the beatings started." She gave a little laugh. "My family thought I had become the clumsiest human being on Earth. I was always having an "accident" of some type. He told me if I ever said differently, he would kill me and then say he caught me with a stable hand and did it in a moment of passion."

Strong arms held her gently. If she had broken down and sobbed, it would have been easier, but this flat, almost emotionless narrative, broken only by a little, painful, embarrassed laugh, frightened Charlie beyond words. It suggested she actually believed the bastard's lies. "Rebecca, look at me, please."

She looked up, tears pooling in her eyes. "I swear, Charlie, I tried to be a good wife to him, and I will try for you, I promise." The tears finally gave way and rolled down her cheeks.

He held her gently and yet firmly. "Rebecca, look at me and listen to me very carefully. I want you to know that everything I am going to tell you is the absolute, unflinching truth."

She nodded. But the frightened woman who lived in the back of her mind was waiting for Charlie to tell her the same things. Her heart told her it could be, would be different with him. "Yes?"

"To me, you are the most beautiful woman I have ever seen. I can get lost in your eyes; I joy in the sight and feel of your hair; your skin is like silk against my hands and lips. You have shown over and over how gentle you are and how caring, for me and for others. I am awed that you have managed to keep your home together as you have, facing the ravages of war alone. I am humbled by your bravery and your courage. The problem is not you, dear. It was never you. It was him."

"I have lived as I was taught by my parents, Charlie. To be kind, to care for others. I have lived by those teachings. I have only done what I need to. I am not special, I just want to love and be loved. I did not think that was wrong. But he made me feel like it was. He made me feel like a worthless whore, sometimes. He used to tell me that is what I was when he forced himself on me. That I was nothing more than a brood mare, like the ones we kept in our stables."

Charlie held her close and stroked her hair. "He was wrong, beloved. He was so very, very wrong. There are some people in the world, people who are dead inside and who only feel alive when they can make someone else hurt. That is the only time they can actually see that they can affect others. I do not understand it, but I have seen this on occasion. It is evil, reprehensible in every way, but it does happen. And these angry, broken people go through life hurting others, just as a rabid dog will lash out and injure anything or anyone that gets in its way. I am so sorry you fell into his hands, my heart. And I am even sadder that you bear the scars of his illness. But it was never your lack, it was his, I promise you."

He cleared his throat and then plunged on—into the area that was hardest for him. "My love, I know what kind of scars someone like that can inflict. I told you about my father, some. How he beat me. What I did not tell you is how he acted for most of my life. When my mother died, I think something in him died, too. Somehow, he was angry at the whole world; and since he could control me, he took it out on me. Finally, I could take it no more, and so you see me as I am. I chose to give up my identity, everything I was or could be, to escape. You had the strength to remain true to yourself and withstand his sickness."

"Oh, Charlie, I never would have had your courage. The courage it took to leave and never look back. I do not think you ran way. I think you were very courageous in doing what you did. Had my husband not left and died when he did, I am not sure I would have survived much longer. After Andrew was killed, I really did not have a reason any longer." She caressed his cheek and smiled. "But now I think we were brought together from our terrible pasts. We both have so much that makes us different, that we understand each other as no one else could. And I promise you that I will spend the rest of my life doing my best to give you the happiness you deserve."

"All you need to do, my dear, is to do your best to be happy for yourself. I love you. I want what is best for you. I will give you everything I can, and everything I am to keep you safe and give you the kind of life you deserve."

She laughed as a thought crossed her mind, and she looked up to him. "Are you prepared for the sympathy you will receive when it becomes apparent that your wife cannot give the distinguished Colonel children?" She laughed again, wiping the tears from her cheeks.

"For you, my dear, we will attribute our lack of offspring to a war wound."

"You most certainly will not." She grinned, "The town whispers about my inability now. May as well let them think that still."

"They would know differently, if the right man came into your life. I will not do that to you, dear," his heart cried.

"You are the right man, Charlie. There will be no other. I have learned what love is, and I intend to hold onto you for dear life."

As darkness fell, the two sat drained, cuddled together, and quietly rejoicing in the simple comfort they offered one another's wounded souls.

CHAPTER 12

Tuesday, November 29, 1864

Rebecca paced outside the door of Charlie's office. He was still in his midday meeting, and the fact she had been summoned made her wonder what was going on. In the time that he had been there, he had never called her to his office when he was working.

She twisted her hands nervously, waiting for the meeting to end and the officers to leave. Finally, the door opened and the officers filed out, each of them smiling and offering various greetings to the woman.

"Good day, gentlemen," she smiled back, before peeking into the office and rapping on the doorframe. "Charlie?"

"Come in, Rebecca, and please, have a seat." He rose from his desk and stood while she settled herself. "I know I am being a little presumptuous in asking you to join me here, but since this is official business, I thought it might be easier. We have a problem in town, and I hope you can help fix it. There are refugees showing up from some of the harsher battle zones. The most charitable Mrs. Williams made it very clear that the people of Culpeper do not have the resources to help these folks. While I do not believe her, I do not know where to start."

"My goodness, for a woman who does not want or need our help she certainly was quick to bring this problem to us."

"Yes, well, she coerced your friend, Mrs. Cooper, into riding out here and dropping this in my lap. Got an eyeful, too, as I had just finished my morning run."

Rebecca chuckled, picking a piece of lint from her dress. "Charlie Redmond, you keep it up and I will have to beat the women of Culpeper off with a stick. But before that, I suppose we should try and figure out what it is we can do to help. Your men have taken over most of the buildings. I am not sure we have room for more people. Unless you have any ideas." She smiled at him. "You know I am always open to your suggestions."

He tugged at his earlobe for a moment, obviously a little uncomfortable with what he was going to suggest. "I was thinking that if each of the leading families in Culpeper took one refugee family into their homes, and I saw to it that there were extra rations, extra blankets, that sort of thing, we would be able to handle much of the influx. You have a big house here, with lots of bedrooms that are not used. I was hoping you would set an example for the rest of them."

"Ah, I see. Well, yes, I suppose we could take in a few of them, Charlie. But it will require lots of work to ready the house. Are your men finished enough with camp that you could allow them to lend a hand? I could not expect Duncan and Reg to do all the work."

"I could give you a squad of men—what do you need? Or do you want to leave that to Duncan?"

"We will have to make sure the rooms are clean, and find a way to prepare beds and storage. I think we will have to find and install stoves in some of the rooms. The fireplaces warm the house enough if you have proper clothing to ward off the chill, but I imagine these people will not have much. And Charlie, if there are any men among them, I am afraid we will have to find spots for them with your troops. I just would not be comfortable having strange men residing in the house with displaced women and children."

"My dear, I am afraid that if there are any men among them, I will have to look very closely to see if they are enemy spies. As for the clothing and cleaning, I can do something about that. I am not sure I can find stoves, but we can make sure there is enough wood to keep all the fireplaces going, and I can get raw woolen material—nothing fancy, mind you, but at least I can get the material."

"They are probably sick, and half starved, too. Will Dr. Walker and her staff be available to offer medical care?"

"Absolutely. Elizabeth brought extra drugs with her, and we have several medics working under Samuelson and Whitman who can provide care. I am worried about taking care of the women; they may feel uncomfortable about day-to-day care from a man. We could hire more of Beulah's family to help."

Rebecca nodded. "All right, Charlie. We will do what we need to do to handle this problem. I suppose I should make a trip into town to see about this situation. Maybe the Coopers will be willing to help us with some of the supplies we will need, if they have them. May I have Duncan take me into town this afternoon? That will give me time to talk with Elizabeth first, if she is available." She shook her head. "I must say Colonel, your arrival has made life interesting."

"If you would like, I would be happy to drive you myself. I suspect it would be a good thing for me to meet with Mr. Cooper, Reverend Williams, and Mayor Frazier. That way, Duncan can get the crews working on the basic clean up and such."

She rose from her chair and moved to him, gracing him with her brightest smile. "I would love to have you take me." She gave him a sweet little kiss. "But now I should go see if I can find Elizabeth and speak with her. I will also get Duncan started, if that is all right with you."

"Tell Duncan that I will authorize him to select the ten men from the troops he feels will best help him. Polk knows about the problem

—all of the company commanders were informed of it at the staff meeting, so he will have all the cooperation he needs. When do you think you will be ready to go?"

"I think I can be ready in two hours. Is that convenient for you?"

Charlie rose from his chair and stepped over to stand very close to her indeed. He ran one finger under her chin and lifted her face to his, whispering, "Anything you want is fine with me, darling." A soft kiss sealed the agreement.

She smiled when the kiss ended, rubbing her hand up and down his arm, taking a deep breath between clenched teeth. "Yes. I will have to get myself a big stick while I am in town, too."

He looked confused. "A big stick?"

"Yes, for beating the women away from my charming, gallant Colonel," she teased with a wink.

"You know you have no problem there. No matter how many women are around, I only have one in my heart."

She tugged on his uniform, then smoothed the front of it. "Hmm...you just remember that, Charlie Redmond. I am afraid I have discovered I have a bit of a jealous streak."

"Well, love, you do have green eyes." He smiled into those eyes, enchanted and a little stunned that anyone would actually be jealous and possessive of him.

"Yes, I do." She gave him another quick kiss and sighed happily. "But now I must take them and find Doctor Walker. I will see you in two hours time."

~

"This room will serve nicely as a ward where we can put several beds, but I am concerned about the chill." Rebecca waved her hand around the room as Elizabeth looked on. "I hope I will be able to find a spare stove in town. Are we going to need to set up a room for you to use as an examination room?"

"Yes, I should have one. It does not have to be as sterile as the surgery. If I need to perform surgery, I will want to do it there anyway, rather than try and move my tools around. A small, warm room would be good."

"There is a small room at the end of the hall we can have Duncan and the men prepare." She released a deep breath. "I never thought I would be turning my home into a half-way house for refugees, but Charlie is right, if we are going to heal this wound, we need to set the standard. It will also make it easier for him when he comes home."

Elizabeth looked at Rebecca questioningly. "You two are very serious now, are you not?"

She nodded, trying to convey her sincerity to the doctor. "In confidence I tell you this, Elizabeth. Charlie has asked me to marry him when this war is over. And I said yes."

Elizabeth's hand covered her gaping mouth. When the power of speech had returned to her, she blurted out the first thing that came to her rather acerbic mind. "Well, you certainly have an interesting definition of taking it slowly and carefully."

Rebecca straightened, a bit thrown by the doctor's reaction. "I realize it is quick. But I assure you, I love Charlie and will spend the rest of my life trying to make him happy and give him the life he wants. Is there something else? Do you not think Charlie and I should be together?" Rebecca's stomach fluttered, and she felt her body tingle with nervousness. She knew Charlie valued Elizabeth's opinion, and if she had reservations, that might be enough to change his mind about returning. Once he was gone, she would only be able to wait for him to return, if something or someone changed his mind, he might never come back.

Elizabeth thought for a moment. "I am sorry. You know my tongue gets the better of me at times. Yes, it is quick. I suppose my concern is that the two of you may be getting involved because you are both lonely and each of you offers the other things you need very badly—safety, tenderness, a sense of belonging, an anchor in a very uncertain time. But if you and he are sure, well then, my dear, I will dance at your wedding."

Rebecca smiled, feeling the tears in her eyes recede. She took Elizabeth's hand, giving it a squeeze. "My dear, had I married my first husband for such good reasons, I might have loved him, but I did not. I assure you, I adore Charlie. I feel for him as I have never felt before. We are very sure about our feelings, but I would ask you to speak to him about it as well to make sure. We would love for you to dance at our wedding."

An evil little grin sidled onto Elizabeth's face. "So, does this mean that the rumors are now true?"

Rebecca immediately flushed deep red. "Elizabeth! I cannot believe you would ask such a thing." She tried to pretend she was shocked, but failed when an equally wicked grin perched on her lips. "No. I have some concerns of my own to deal with, and I am not quite ready to take that step. I am not sure Charlie is, either."

The blonde patted her friend's hand. "And now I must go fetch the Colonel. We are to go into town. Will you and Colonel Polk join us for supper tonight?"

"I would be glad to join you. As for the good Colonel Polk, you will have to ask him yourself. I certainly do not control his social calendar."

"I think for the opportunity to dine with you, Elizabeth, the Colonel would forego a meeting with Lincoln himself."

Elizabeth just smiled. "I will see you at dinner, then. Please suggest to Charlie that he invite Richard, if you want. I will work with Duncan and his lads to start getting this in order."

"Thank you. We will be home in a few hours. If you need anything at all, just let Beulah or Reg know and they will fix you up."

"Thank you, dear. Enjoy your visit with the biddies."

Charlie helped Rebecca into the little carriage. Shannon stood like a proper lady, waiting patiently for the drive to begin. Charlie carefully tucked a blanket around Rebecca's legs, then climbed in next to her.

She was quick to move the blanket so it was settled over both pairs of legs. "Shall we, Colonel? Let us see if we can get a few more tongues wagging."

He snapped the reins before glancing at her. "I do believe, my dear, you enjoy taunting the biddies."

"Colonel, would I do something like that?" she asked with the most sincere voice she could muster under the circumstances.

"Yes. Yes you would." He clucked his tongue and gave the reins another snap, sending Shannon into a gentle, but quick trot.

She looped her arm through Charlie's. She had discovered she did so enjoy being with him and being able to touch him. "What would make you think such wicked things about the woman you want to marry?"

"Why, dear, it is simple. It is your spirit and spunk, your sense of humor, and the rebel in your soul that I do so love."

"I am glad we have found each other. It seems that something good has come out of this dreadful war."

Charlie transferred the reins to one hand so he could cover Rebecca's hand with his own. "You have given me so much, my dear. You have given me a future when I had none. I love you."

I am giving him a future? Can he not see it is me he is rescuing from an unknown fate? We will be together when this is over, and we will both have something we never could have expected. "Oh, Charlie, I love you, too. You have no idea how much." She cuddled as close as she could to him, resting against his side.

He settled in, just enjoying the contrast of the crisp fall air and the warm loving woman beside him. It was a moment to capture and hold, like a gem in his heart.

"Charlie, I want you to know something very important."

The tone of her voice captured his total attention. "What, my dear?"

"I loved my brother as a sister should, and I loved my parents as a daughter should. I have never loved another the way I love you, the way a wife should love a husband. I want you to know that. I want you to take that with you and let it keep you safe, so you can come home to me."

The honesty of her words took his breath away. He pulled Shannon to a stop, and then turned to the small woman beside him. Reverently he took her hands in his larger ones. "I promise you, I will do everything in my power to come back to you, dear. I must go; I have given my oath. But no man ever had as much reason to come back alive as I do to come back to you. You know if you ever need me, for anything, all you have to do is call; and if I am at all able, I will come to you."

She raised his hand to her lips and brushed his knuckles over her cheek. "I know you will have to leave, and believe me it will be the hardest day of my life, letting you go. But I know you are going to come home; and I will be here waiting." She gave a sad little smile, trying to hold back tears that wanted to fall as she thought of him leaving. "I will be making wedding plans. You will wonder what you have gotten yourself into, my dearest Charlie."

He softly wiped her tears away, brushing his thumbs over her eyelids. "That reminds me. I need to make a trip to Washington. And I need to know your ring size, love."

"Oh, Charlie, do not spend your hard earned money on something like that. I only need you. I could wear a band of copper, and to me it would be the most precious thing because you gave it to me."

He smiled. "I am not a rich man, but I have had few expenses in the last twenty years, and have accumulated enough to be more than comfortable. Anyway, I want you to be able to announce to the world that a man of substance has claimed you. If for no other reason, it will set the biddies on their ears. Will you want gold and diamonds? Perhaps an emerald for your eyes?"

She laughed, cuddling closer to him. "Whatever you desire, my love. And if you want to set the hens clucking with your choice, I will be more than happy to flaunt my good fortune." She looked up at him, her brows drawn together. "Well, now, that was not very charitable of me, was it?"

Charlie threw his head back and laughed. "My dear, look at what you are doing—taking in a broken down old Colonel, a whole regiment of boys, and some stray refugees—and you think you are not charitable. Mrs. Williams needs to take lessons from you."

"Oh, my dear, you are many things." She gave him a little leer. "Broken down and old are not among them."

They continued into town, and as they approached the church, Rebecca straightened and patted Charlie on the leg. "Let me off here, dear. I would imagine this is where I will find everyone I am looking for."

"I will go on to the courthouse first, then visit with Mr. Cooper, and meet you back here. I want a word with Reverend Williams, myself."

"I will be here, and with any luck, I will not blow up and take the roof off the church." She gave him a wink.

"Darling, be gentle. The refugees are our concern, not the biddies. And remember, Mrs. Williams will have all her allies around her here. It is not a good idea to walk into an enemy camp single handed if you are not carrying a white flag."

"Hmm, good advice from an expert. I will remember that, Colonel Redmond. Now have a good chat with the gentleman. I promise to be as kind as possible."

"And I promise to come riding up with the cavalry, just in case you forget the rules of truce talks." Charlie pulled Shannon up in front of St. Stephen's Episcopalian Church and stepped down from the trap to hand Rebecca down. As he did, he whispered in her ear, "And be good."

"Why, Colonel Redmond, I thought you would have learned by now," she paused and ran her hand over his arm, "I am always good." She laughed, then turned on her heel, and walked toward the church.

Feeling a little dazed, and a lot teased, Charlie climbed back into the trap and headed up the street to the little red brick courthouse, where he knew he would find Mayor Frazier. Time to be the gentle conqueror again.

~

Rebecca entered the church to find the sight before her heartrending. There were women and children huddled together under thin blankets around the fireplace and a small stove. No one was talking, and the only sound was the occasional whimper of a frightened child.

"Oh dear," she sighed. "Well, Daniel, this is quite a battle we are going into." She looked around and saw Mrs. Cooper coming from the back. She raised her hand in hello as she made her way over.

"Rebecca, I am so glad to see you."

"Grace, I did not know things were this bad. When did they start arriving?"

"A few days ago. I just do not know what we are going to do with all of them."

Rebecca scratched her chin, looking around the room. "Colonel Redmond and I are preparing Gaines Cove to take as many as we can handle. That will be twelve or so. We hope by doing this, others who have room will also take some in."

"You are a gift from God, Rebecca. I was at a loss as to what to do with them. Reverend Williams, of course, offered the church for as long as it was needed, but Mrs. Williams had a right fit, and said we did not need the burden of cleaning up after them so we could have services on Sunday. I swear to you, Rebecca, I do not know what that woman is going to do when she is at the Pearly Gates and St. Peter asks her to name one good deed."

Rebecca tried not to laugh and quickly placed her hand over her mouth. "Grace! As a very wise man just told me, 'be good.'"

"Would that very wise man be the good Colonel Redmond?"

"It would." Rebecca took her friend by the arm and turned her around for a bit of privacy. "Tell me, Grace, what is the general consensus about the Colonel and his men? Can we expect any real problems, because the Lord in Heaven above knows we have enough problems already."

"No, I do not think so. Most folks know that their being here is actually a good sign. We hope that this will all be over soon."

"Colonel Redmond believes it will be, but at what cost I am not sure; and I am afraid to consider it too seriously."

"What more could it possibly cost us? They have taken everything we had."

"Grace, in all this destruction and this horrible time, I have found something very important, and I cannot bear the thought of losing it."

"What have you found dear?"

"Love. I have found love."

"You and the Colonel?"

"Yes. He is truly a wonderful man who, if I am learning to understand him correctly, hates this conflict just as much as we do. He simply wants it to end so he can come home and have a life."

"A home and a life with you?"

"Yes. Please, Grace, be happy for me. I am finally going to have a good life with Charlie, and he is only going to be an asset to our community."

The older woman smiled, "Of course I will be happy for you, child. Your mother and I talked many times before she passed, and all she ever wanted for you was your happiness. She knew you were never happy with Mr. Gaines, and right before she died, she was going to ask you to come home."

"I could not have done that. I would have disgraced my entire family. But now I have a chance at happiness, and I am going to take it."

"You should. Colonel Redmond is, umm..." she smiled. "Well, let us just say I will expect to see you with child within a few months."

Rebecca managed not to laugh out loud. "We will see." She turned back to the women and children. "We need to get these poor souls settled over at Gaines Cove. Having a sense of stability would be good for them, I think. Corporal Nailer said we could probably be ready to take them by tomorrow evening."

"We have some old down mattresses we can send with them to help until new supplies can be gotten."

"Wonderful. Maybe the Colonel can have his men make some rough frames to keep them off the floor."

"If you need anything like hammers and nails, let me know, and I will see what I can get Mr. Cooper to scare up at the store."

"Thank you. One of my concerns is keeping them warm enough. Do you think we could take the stove from the church? You still have the fireplace, and the building only needs to be warm for services."

"We can ask the elders. And you know I have a say there, and I will certainly take up your cause. If we are not going to care for these people here, we should support those willing to take them in; and you have more than enough in your life right now. I certainly do not know how you keep giving of yourself like you do."

"It is as my mother always taught me, Grace, 'Do unto others.'"

"Mrs. Williams had better not hope it comes back tenfold."

Charlie tied Shannon at the hitching post in front of the courthouse. He walked into the brick building, which housed the county's records, the small county courtroom, and the office of the city administrator. Virginia was rather odd: counties and towns did not overlap, so there were separate administrations for each. However, with the catastrophic reduction in Culpeper's population, the mayor had taken over what little administration was possible for both county and town. He quickly sought out the office of the mayor and knocked lightly on the door.

"Come in." The voice bidding him enter was brusque and a little squeaky. Mayor Horace Frazier was an old man, grown crotchety with age, rheumatism, and the stresses of the past four years. Charlie entered the small, cluttered office, barely warmed by a tiny iron stove in the corner. The place was an invitation for a fire; there were ledgers and papers piled everywhere.

The mayor looked askance at the Colonel standing awkwardly in front of him. "Well, what do you want? As you can see, the only thing I have plenty of is old paper. If you want it, you are welcome to it. Otherwise, make it quick."

"Mayor Frazier, I understand we have some refugees, and that we may be facing an influx of more in the future. I would like to form a joint civilian/military committee to work together to find places for these people, provide medical care, and see to it that they have at least basic food, clothing, and a warm place to stay."

"Bluntly, Colonel, neither the city nor the county of Culpeper has any resources left. We have not enough to feed our own people, let alone support some ragtag collection of refugees. We might be able to find room in some of the houses around here, but nothing more. Most of the houses that stand empty are badly damaged. You would have to repair them if you want to use them. Put your committee together: Reverend Williams, Mr. Cooper, some of the others around here might be willing to help. I suggest you talk to the ladies; they are more equipped to figure these things out. But expect no official support from me. You can only get so much blood from a stone."

With that, the Mayor turned back to studying the papers in front of him. Charlie had clearly been dismissed.

Exiting the building, he gathered Shannon's reins, but instead of remounting the little trap, he walked, leading the horse down the main street to Mr. Cooper's shop. As he passed the few people on the street, he cordially tipped his hat and bowed. Every one of them pointedly ignored him. Tying off the patient horse, Charlie went into the store hoping to catch Cooper alone. He was not so fortunate, and waited patiently until the customer was served and departed. The whole time, the woman who was buying a spool of thread, looked askance at him. She left quickly, clearly uncomfortable about being seen with the Federal officer. Charlie sighed. Forging relationships was not going to be easy.

Mr. Cooper was open and cordial; a distinct relief after the reception Charlie had gotten from the others. "Colonel Redmond, to what do I owe the pleasure of your visit today?"

"Good day to you, Sir. Mr. Cooper, I will get right to the point. I want to organize a joint civilian/military committee to deal with the refugees and with those in the community who need assistance this winter. However, given the reception I have gotten so far, I have about as much chance of doing so as I have of ending the war tomorrow."

"Well, if I may be perfectly honest, Colonel, you are the conqueror. You have to expect a certain level of resentment and resistance."

"I know. I have to tell you, Cooper, this is far harder than facing a battle. In battle, you know your enemies and your friends. You can see the lay of the land. You know what your resources are, and where reinforcements can be gotten. Here, I am lost. I feel like I am forever about to step into a tiger trap, usually in the form of the most innocuous looking woman.

"Well, Colonel, these are Southern ladies. They know more about covert warfare than any man ever will." The merchant laughed at his own joke. "Seriously, Sir, I think if you and Miss Rebecca keep on the path you are on, providing support consistently, being there when needed, offering things for which this community has been desperate but too proud to ask, they will come over. One at a time, but they will come over. Mrs. Cooper and I are certainly aware of what you are trying to do, and will do our best to support you. It is time for this conflict to be over and for this country to look to healing itself. What you are doing is important to that end."

"I think so. But I seem to be in the minority." Charlie reached into his inside coat pocket and retrieved a cigar. "Mind?"

"Not at all."

Charlie could see the wistful look on the merchant's face. "Want one?"

"Yes, that would be very nice."

The two men enjoyed their cigars together for a few minutes, discussing the logistics of supplying both the refugees and the most urgently needy in the community. Charlie felt more confident in his plans as he cordially parted with Cooper. And perhaps he had made his first male friend in the community, which he knew was vital to his own future after the war.

Rebecca had made a list of those who would be coming to the house. She had four women with seven children and one more on the way. The pregnant woman was several months from giving birth and already looked ill and drawn. Rebecca wanted to get her to Dr. Walker as soon as possible. The woman's daughter, a tiny girl of between eighteen months and two years of age, hid behind her mother, peeking out to give Rebecca a bright smile with tiny teeth showing through pink gums.

The blonde knelt down and offered her hand to the child. "It is all right sweetheart; I am not going to hurt you."

The girl's mother helped her daughter toddle to Rebecca. "Her name is Emily."

"Hello, Emily. How would you and your mama like to come and stay at my home for a while? I know a very nice gentleman who will show you a horse."

The baby smiled. Rebecca knew the child was probably shy with strangers, but the little smile made her heart swell. She looked to the girl's mother. "What is your name?"

"Constance, Ma'am. Constance Adams."

"I am glad to meet you Constance. Please, I am Rebecca." She gestured to the woman's slightly swollen midsection. "Is your husband a solider?"

"I am widowed, Ma'am. My husband was killed at Seven Pines." She caressed her stomach. "And I am afraid that this child is because of a group of renegades I had the unfortunate luck to..." She stopped, lowering her eyes, shame written all over her face.

"Constance, do not dare be concerned what I or anyone else might think. You are doing what every good mother does; you are caring for your children. They are gifts from God. Now that you have shared with me, let me share with you. I will never have children. Not that I do not want them, I do, so very much; but I am afraid it will just never be possible for me. I know there will always be an empty spot in my heart because of it. We have lost so much because of the war, we must cherish what we have been given; and you have been given two children. Love them as only a mother can."

"Thank you, Rebecca, I will."

"Good. Now if I send a young man to get you tomorrow, will you be ready to travel? It is not far to my home."

"Yes, Ma'am. I will be ready. Thank you."

The last stop was the most critical. Without the backing of the Reverend Williams, any hope of creating the kind of relationship with the community Charlie envisioned was futile. He left Shannon in front of the church and walked around to the rectory to knock on the door of the minister's office.

"Come in."

Charlie eased into the little den. It was neat and orderly, in a comfortably shabby sort of way. A small fire in the fireplace took the chill off the room. A large, battered desk dominated the area, but there were easy chairs around the fireplace where one could sit and talk. The minister was searching in his bookshelves, looking a little distracted, and wearing a dusty shawl over his shirtsleeves and waistcoat.

"Ah, Colonel Redmond. Come in. Come in. Please, have a seat. I would offer you something, but I am afraid Mrs. Williams is over at the church, and I have no one here to —"

"No, thank you, Reverend. I am fine." Charlie gently intervened in the man's rambling welcome. He sat in one of the chairs in front of the fire.

"I will get right to the point, Sir." The Colonel explained his plan once again. He concluded with a simple plea, "Without your support, Sir, I am perfectly aware that I have no chance of creating this bond between my men and your citizens."

Soft blue-gray eyes, slightly bleary from reading without the correct glasses, regarded him seriously. "Sir, you realize that you have the attitude of folks, such as my own wife, to overcome?"

"I do, Sir. That is why I have come to you. Your voice, raised in behalf of brotherhood, will be of great benefit."

"Well, as you have seen, I cannot even control my own wife. To be honest, I cannot see where I will be of much use to you in swaying the others in this community who share her attitude. But in the spirit of Christian brotherhood, I will do what I can."

"That is all I can ask, Sir."

"And I expect similar cooperation from you. For example, I expect to see you in church on Sunday—this coming Sunday, and every one thereafter. Of all the people whose souls need guidance and sanctuary, you, as a soldier and a leader of men, are certainly in need of God's gentle protection."

"Sir, I was raised as a Presbyterian. However, if it serves my goals, I will certainly attend your services."

"God does not make distinctions among sects, Colonel. God only makes distinctions between men of good will and those of evil intent."

Charlie rose and nodded. "Then I will see you on Sunday, Sir."

Very thoughtful about what Reverend Williams had said, Charlie walked slowly from the small church office in the rectory to the main building. His hands were going to be very full in the coming months, if the conditions and the attitudes the minister had described were to be met and shifted. Perhaps he and Rebecca together would be able to find a way to sway some of the stalwarts. Perhaps not. But for now, there were women and children who needed help, not only those who were refugees, but also within the community. *Damn this war. Damn it all to hell. Too many innocent people have paid far too terrible a price. I pray for it to just be over.*

Entering the church, Charlie stopped for a moment. The quiet in this sacred space was not the same as the one encountered at a Sunday service; instead, it was the quiet of people whose souls had sustained more battering than they could stand. It was the quiet of a beaten dog, cowering, waiting for the next blow and lacking the will to fight back any more. In the midst of this, Rebecca, with her gentle caring and her stubborn will, shone like a beacon.

He moved quietly, stopping to give quiet words of encouragement, praise the beauty of a child, the bravery of a young boy trying hard to be adult before his time. Finally, he reached Rebecca, who was talking to a frail looking young woman with a young girl peeking out from behind her skirts. He bowed courteously to the woman.

"Mrs. Gaines? I am sorry to interrupt, but do you have a moment?"

"Of course, Colonel."

The two stepped away to the side of the church, where their softly spoken comments would not be overheard. "How bad is it, Rebecca?"

"Well, it could be worse. We can handle everyone who is here now. That young woman I was talking with, she does not look good, and she is having another baby in a few months. I want Elizabeth to look at her as soon as possible."

Charlie shook his head and sighed. "Trying to carry successive pregnancies in a short period of time without plenty of healthy food is a recipe for problems. I fear we will see more. And as bad off as these folks are, there are people here in the county that are only slightly better off—they have a roof over their heads but damned little else."

"We will get them out to the farm and settled, I am sure that will help. Right now, they are just scared. As for the others…"

"I am concerned there will be more refugees. And from everything I can determine, there are no resources here to help them except a roof, maybe, and many of those in abandoned buildings leak. God, Rebecca, what are we going to do to get the local folks to help? Cooper is a good man, but Reverend Williams tells me that his wife's attitude is far more typical than the Coopers'. I am just not sure what needs to be done here. We have already taken over Gaines Cove—you are rapidly running out of space." The good Colonel was babbling. Charlie, Lucky Charlie who could figure his way out of any battle situation, was at a total loss.

Rebecca laid her hand on his arm, giving him a gentle smile. "Charlie, we will manage. My house is large, and we can in take a few more bodies. We will be fine. My dear, I do believe that together we can accomplish anything. Come with me, and I will show you one very good reason to believe."

She led him back across the room and lifted Emily into her arms. "Colonel Redmond, I would like you to meet Emily." She smiled at the child, then looked to Charlie. "Emily, this is the gentleman I told you about. He has a very pretty horse I am sure he will show you." She tilted her head to the baby's mother. "And this is her mother, Constance Adams. Mrs. Adams, may I introduce Colonel Charles Redmond."

The woman slowly lifted her hand, sizing up the Yankee Colonel as she did. "It is a pleasure to meet you, Colonel Redmond. I want to thank you and Mrs. Gaines for coming to our aid."

Charlie gently took her hand in his. "It my pleasure, Ma'am. It is the least we could do." He was struck by the similarity between the two women—and the differences. They were of similar height, build, and even facial shape. But, where Rebecca had a rosy, healthy look to her, it was obvious to even the most casual observer that Constance Adams was not a well woman.

The small child looked into the face of the man with blue eyes and black hair, similar to her own. She had a vague memory of a man who was like him, but dressed in gray, not blue. One finger hooked into a soft lower lip and a lisping voice asked hesitantly, "Papa?"

With a strange combination of tenderness and grief for this little, trusting soul who already was forced to face the harsh reality of the world around her, he lifted Emily from Rebecca's arms. "No, little one. I am not your papa. But I will be your friend. My name is Charlie. Can you say Charlie?"

Rebecca smiled at the scene in front of her. "You look so much alike. It is little wonder she thinks you are her papa."

The baby pulled on Charlie's tunic, bringing her face to his. "Papa."

He chuckled, a little embarrassed. "No, honey. Charlie. I am Charlie."

The child continued, undaunted. "Papa!"

The officer looked helpless and more than a little embarrassed. Looking beseechingly at Rebecca, and then at the child's mother, he mumbled, "I do not know why…I am sorry, I do not mean to make this awkward."

Constance watched the Yankee Colonel with her daughter. He was gentle and tender with her. The woman wondered if he had children of his own that he was anxious to get home to. She considered this thought and found herself thinking of the Colonel as just as much a victim as she was.

"Looks like you have a new friend, Charlie." Rebecca took the baby and held her close. "Or at least another admirer." She winked at him. "I promise not to get jealous over this one." She gave the baby a kiss on her forehead. "Time to go back to your mama, sweetheart."

As Rebecca started to give the child back to her mother, the baby reached for Charlie. "Papa!"

Blushing under the intense gaze of the small child and the rather bewildered looks of her mother, Charlie looked to Rebecca for help. Not seeing any assistance coming from that source, he turned to the woman holding his young admirer. "Ma'am, your daughter seems to have taken a shine to me. And you look like you could use a warm place and perhaps some medical attention." He turned to Rebecca, and asked plaintively, "Perhaps they could come back with us now, and we could send for the others tomorrow?"

"Of course, Charlie. We will make room for them tonight. I think Emily has decided you are her new papa." She laughed and turned to the baby playing with her hand. "Excellent choice, my dear. Mrs. Adams, I will be happy to take her while you get your things together."

"Thank you, Mrs. Gaines."

"Please, call me Rebecca."

"Then you and the Colonel must call me Constance."

Once again, the child was passed to Rebecca, but she continued to stare and smile at Charlie.

Charlie waited patiently for the woman to gather her belongings, such as they were. All the time, he flirted with the little imp in Rebecca's arms. In his mind, he thought of how perfect Rebecca looked with a child in her arms and how insufficient he was as a partner. He could never give her this joy. His heart sank deeper and deeper. The ugly little voice in his head laughed maliciously.

Rebecca noticed the shuttered look that had come over the Colonel's face. "Charlie? Are you all right?"

He looked down at his feet, and then out over the other refugees huddled in the church. "Yes, I am fine. Just thinking."

"I know it seems very daunting, Colonel, but I am sure we will make it through just fine." She adjusted the child in her arms so she could touch Charlie's shoulder. "We just have to do our best."

The eyes that met Rebecca's were filled with sadness and regret.

"We will do our best. I just hope our best is enough." *I hope my best is enough for you, my love, my heart, for there are so many things I will never be able to give you.*

Rebecca could see something was terribly wrong. She reached out and cupped his cheek, not caring who might see them. "Oh please, Charlie, do not worry. Everything will be all right. You have to believe that."

Before he could respond, Emily let out a loud laugh and lunged for him, wrapping her arms tightly around his neck. "Papa. Good."

Charlie caught the tenacious, flying child in his arms. "All right, little one. I have you. Or more accurately, you have me. Miss Constance? I am afraid your daughter is very persistent." He smiled at her shyly. "I hope you do not mind. I truly do not want to usurp her father's place."

The woman smiled. "Colonel, my daughter is happy for the first time in months, and it is you that is making her happy. She is very determined. I do not mind that she calls you "Papa." I hope it does not bother you."

"Well, Ma'am, when her father does return..."

"He will not be returning, Colonel. He was killed at Seven Pines."

"I am sorry, Ma'am. You have my sincerest condolences."

"Thank you, Sir." She lifted her small bag, which Rebecca took since Charlie had his hands full of determined baby.

"Tell me, Charlie," Rebecca giggled, "how do you intend to drive and hold the baby? I do not think we are going to be able to pry her out of your arms."

"We are just going to have to do our best." He softened the echo of her words with a gentle smile. The four unlikely companions walked out into the crisp fall air. Charlie walked over to the hitching post and very seriously introduced Shannon and Emily.

Her little hand reached out to the broad white stripe down the big horse's face. "'Orsy. P'etty 'orsy." Charlie looked at the two women watching him.

Rebecca did not even try to hide the huge smile on her face. Charlie looked so natural with the child. She assisted Constance into the buggy, then moved to Charlie. "Maybe she will sit on my lap next to you on the way home." When she held her hands out, the baby shook her head and tightened her arms around Charlie again.

"No!" The child simply refused to be separated from him.

"Or," Rebecca smirked, "you could hold her and I could drive."

"Or I could drive one handed. It is not like I am driving a full team. Shannon will go on verbal commands only."

"As you wish, Colonel. I say, you do have a way with the ladies, do you not?" she teased. "I wonder what Sergeant Jackson will have to say about this." The blonde climbed into the buggy. "I imagine he will be very amused."

Charlie groaned. Jocko had been slipping around quietly. He was not quite sure who was really running the house, Rebecca or Jocko. He was very sure the two of them had created some kind of agreement, since his clothing was always there and ready, his office was impeccable, and whatever he needed was normally at hand. But Jocko himself had managed to stay scarce lately, except for the ritual morning shave. Charlie made a mental note to check on the activities of his batman. Carefully balancing the bundle of energy in his left arm, Charlie climbed into the little trap, gathered up the reins in his right hand, and clucked Shannon into a sedate walk towards home.

Upon returning to the farm, Charlie dropped his passengers at the house and excused himself to go brief his officers. He could only smile and promise his littlest friend he would be back soon. Emily was not a happy child. She was very vocal about it, shouting, "Papa. No go!" as the Colonel drove away.

The crying child brought Beulah and Lizbet to the door right away. "Good Lord, Miss Rebecca, who do we have here?" Beulah asked, as Emily's sobs for Charlie lessened to hiccups and sniffs against Rebecca's shoulder.

"This is Mrs. Adams and Miss Emily. They are going to be staying with us for a while. Let us get them settled." She smiled at Lizbet. "Please take Mrs. Adams' bag to the room on the second floor next to Dr. Walker's, and have Reg start a fire in there."

"Yes, Miss Rebecca." The young woman did as she was bid.

Rebecca then turned to Beulah. "If you would find Corporal Nailer for me, we need to figure out what Emily here can use as a crib."

"Yes, Ma'am. And Sarah has a fresh stew and hot tea in the kitchen."

"Thank you." Rebecca turned to Constance. "Come, let us get you some solid food while your room is put together."

"Miss Rebecca, I really do not want us to be a burden to you. If you will just tell me where my room is, I will happily go there and be out of your way."

"Nonsense. You have to eat, and it is wonderful to have the company. I am starting to feel like maybe everything will be all right again. I know it is going to be a long road, but the fact that we are coming together again is evidence we are ready for the healing to begin." She took the woman's hand. "Come on now, you will love Sarah's stew. It is the best in the county."

Rebecca watched indulgently as Constance finished a second bowl of stew. It was apparent she had not been eating properly. The blonde was sure she had been giving young Emily such food as she could get. The baby sat quite happily in Rebecca's lap, chewing on a hardtack biscuit and trying to sip from a cup of cooled tea.

"Constance, in light of your condition, I think you should stay in a private room with its own fireplace and close to Dr. Walker."

"That is too much. I cannot accept more than you can comfortably offer."

"Then do not argue with me, because I can comfortably offer this to you." She looked down at her little friend. "Besides, Colonel Redmond resides in the house as well, and I think Emily will enjoy being near him."

"She certainly did take to him right away, did she not? I have never seen her act that way with a man before."

"The Colonel is a very special gentleman, and Emily knows that."

The back door opened, and Charlie and Elizabeth stepped inside. Emily was quick to squeal her delight. "Papa!" She squirmed until Rebecca put her down, and she made her way over to Charlie to tug on his pants leg. "Papa. Up Papa."

The look on Elizabeth's face was priceless. She tried not to smile as she sized up Charlie and his new little friend. "Something you forgot to tell me?"

"No," he grumbled, even while hugging Emily. "The little one just seems to have picked me as a surrogate father."

Elizabeth smiled and gave an amused nod. "I can see that."

"Papa. 'Orsey, Papa."

"We will see the horsy later, little one. Right now, Charlie needs a cup of coffee."

Rebecca was quick to get up and pour Charlie a cup of coffee, while performing the requisite introductions between Elizabeth and Constance. "Elizabeth?" she offered, holding up another cup.

"Maybe later, Rebecca, thank you. Right now I thought I would have a look at our newest patient." The doctor smiled at Constance. "Charlie, do you think you can keep little Emily occupied while I take care of her mama?"

He looked down at the child who was quite happy chewing on the button of his tunic. "I think we can manage."

Emily did perk up a bit when her mother stood up, but relaxed back against Charlie when she was assured mama would be right back. She picked up her biscuit from the table and offered it to Charlie. "Bite, Papa."

Charlie just sighed, completely unsure what to do next. "No, thank you. You eat that. I will have my dinner later."

"Speaking of which," Rebecca handed the baby a slice of apple, "a couple of your men brought Sarah a nice brace of rabbits, so we are having roast rabbit for supper. Would you like to invite Colonel Polk?"

"Would Elizabeth like me to invite Colonel Polk?" Charlie had to ask past the piece of apple Emily was trying to put in his mouth.

"I think the Doctor would be delighted."

"I will see to it then." Charlie looked down at the little girl, who looked back with adoring eyes. She smiled and reached up, pulled herself up, and grabbed Charlie's cheeks.

"Papa good!" she squealed, then kissed Charlie on the cheek.

The Colonel had the grace to blush, but not enough time to react to the fact his batman had just come through the kitchen door in time to see the little brunette continuing her sloppy kiss to Charlie's cheek.

The Irishman burst out laughing. "A little young for ye, I would say, Colonel C."

CHAPTER 13

WEDNESDAY, NOVEMBER 30, 1864

Supper was—different. The addition of a toddler to the household caused unexpected disruptions in a number of ways. The addition of a toddler who refused to let go of the Colonel added to the excitement. Charlie found himself liberally sprinkled with mashed squash and some undefined cooked cereal. For the fastidious Colonel, this was something of a rude awakening. Charlie had never dealt with the messy aspects of day-to-day childcare. It was a revelation. He handled it with surprising good cheer.

After supper, Charlie and Rebecca watched as Constance put the little imp to bed. They adjourned to Rebecca's back parlor, where, after a polite cup of after dinner coffee, Charlie excused himself to go write some needed dispatches.

In the quiet of his office, Charlie built a small fire to disperse the chill of the evening. For long minutes, he sat in the soft light of the fire, staring at the flickering flames. He forced himself to focus on the requirements of his position. That habit ran deep: duty before all other things. Consciously, he pushed his confusion and, if he was honest, his rising frustration about his relationship with Rebecca to the back of his mind. Confronted with the hostility of the citizens, their abject poverty, and the wave of refugees from the war, Charlie was overwhelmed. He knew he had to do more than just find food and clothing for these people to last the winter. He had to find a way to help them start rebuilding their lives, if only on a basic level.

He lit one lamp on his desk, drawing paper before him to write his dispatch to Sheridan.

November 30, 1864
 Outside of Culpeper, Virginia
 Lieut. General Philip H. Sheridan
 Department of the Shenandoah

Dear General Sheridan,

Appropriate steps are being taken to settle the 13th Pennsylvania into their winter quarters. As discussed, we have set up our infirmary with a surgery for Dr. Walker. She is well pleased with our arrangements.

The heavy nor'easter that moved through the region several days ago has done little lasting damage. Colonel Polk's supply and inventory reports are attached.

Montgomery has undergone surgery. We wait anxiously to discover if the surgery was successful. His situation highlights one of the greatest challenges I face this winter, that of creating a cohesive regiment out of the battle-scarred remnants of two very different forces. I find that my personal history and heritage, as well as my accent, contributed to the problems of integrating these troops. Some of the Pennsylvanians cannot seem to overcome the impact that my Charleston accent has on their faith in my leadership. It will be an interesting process.

Yet a greater challenge faces us in the coming weeks and months, one that I am sure every officer who is wintering in conquered territory is facing. The citizens of this community are beaten down, bereft of resources and lacking in the basic elements of human survival. All they had has been taken from them, either by forces moving across their lands, or because the few people remaining have been unable to tend to their properties. To this is added an influx of refugees, primarily women and children escaping from the front line regions around Richmond and Petersburg.

I recognize that the influx of additional personnel brings with it the threat of an influx of agents of espionage. I have discussed security and silence with my officers as we consider ways to deal with this latest challenge.

General, we have to provide at least a modicum of support to the people here. They have no food stores, no proper winter clothing, no money, or resources to repair their homes against winter cold. Some do not even have the tools or strength to gather wood for the fireplaces to warm them this winter. Nor do they have the means to till the ground or plant for the coming months. General Grant, in his stay earlier this year, said he thought Culpeper was the most devastated part of Virginia. I believe he was correct, given the abject poverty I see all around me. A thriving town of over fifteen hundred people has been reduced to perhaps a hundred or a hundred and fifty tenacious survivors. I cannot help but think we owe these people some shred of hope.

I have started creating community service details. This is beneficial in several ways. It allows me to build teams that include both Ohioans and Pennsylvanians, encouraging the integration of my command. It also allows us to create personal links to the people of the community. It is very hard to hate the Yankees who come and repair your roof, stock your wood shed, repair your fences, and till the ground for the spring, asking for nothing in return but a drink of cool water to ease the sweat of honest labor.

Yet I lack the resources to address the most pressing and immediate needs. Something as simple as a supply of flour, beans, rice, and salt pork to share with the citizens would go a long way to improving things here. Woolen goods would also help, as these people lack clothing for the winter.

I believe we could make a huge step forward in our relationships with the civilians if we could add one more resource to our support for the community. If we had seed stocks that we could make available, we would be able to help them reestablish their basic economy. More than anything else, this would serve to give them hope and a vision for a future that is not as bleak as they currently expect.

Your direction and assistance in these matters would be greatly appreciated.

Cordially
    Chas. Redmond
    Regimental Colonel
    13th Pennsylvania Light Cavalry

Having addressed what he could for the evening, Charlie's thoughts turned to the situation with Rebecca. The peculiarities of people baffled Charlie; and the woman was driving him crazy. Everyone thought the two of them were lovers in every sense of the word. He had made his intentions clear: he would marry her if she would have him, would offer her all of the protections of his honor, name, estate, and love. But physical intimacy beyond mostly chaste kisses and tender embraces was not part of their relationship.

They talked often, sharing their history, their fears, their hopes, and dreams. They slept together every night, where she lay beside him, sweet, warm, and trusting. Her hands caressed him gently, never overtly sexually, but often very sensually. She cuddled into his arms and reached out for him in her sleep if he left the bed. Sometimes Charlie thought she wanted more than his gentleness, and sometimes it was clear she was terrified of greater intimacy. But whatever she wanted of him, he had given his word they would progress at her speed.

Dear God. Please help me. Every time she touches me, every time she looks at me with those trusting, welcoming eyes, I can feel it all through my body. She inflames me and there is no way to quench that fire. I do not want to frighten her, but I have to do something. Anything.

The evil little voice in his head just laughed at him.

Charlie shook himself. Perhaps a brisk walk in the chill night air would help cool his need, at least for the time being.

He banked the fire and extinguished the lamp. Shrugging on his lighter overcoat, he stuck a couple of cigars in his pocket and went out into the night to pace until he was more tired than desirous.

His brisk strides took him down to the lovely little terrace overlooking the pond. There, sitting huddled in the cold under the willow, he found Mr. Whitman, quietly smoking an old pipe and just watching the shadows dancing over the wavelets generated by the light evening breeze.

Whitman looked up as the Colonel approached. "Good evening, Sir. What brings you out at this time of night?"

"A host of night demons, Whitman, a host of them. What about you?"

"Ah, well, my friend Samuelson finds himself held to the bedside of Major Montgomery. We have been trading shifts to keep watch on him. I was not yet ready to sleep, and so came here to perhaps do a little thinking."

Charlie laughed. "In your case, you are either composing poetry or thinking of things I am not sure I want to know. On the other hand, you could be doing both."

"Does that mean you have read my little efforts, Colonel?"

"I have indeed, I have indeed. The poetry is outstanding, but I fear that many of our more..." he paused, searching for the right word, "...our more tradition bound brothers and sisters may find it difficult." Charlie and Whitman had found common ground the previous year when Whitman had assisted Dr. Walker in treating Charlie for a minor injury.

Whitman laughed a slightly bitter laugh. "Well, the soul of a man is his own, yet so many have sold their souls to propriety. Neither of us will ever find a place in that world of propriety, will we, Colonel?"

"No, Whitman. I fear you are right. I fear there is no place in this world for the likes of us."

The two men sat on the cold stone, each smoking their chosen form of tobacco, both staring into the infinity of reflections in the broken moon mirrors of the pond.

Charlie shrugged off his immobility. "Come, this is a cold place to ponder the indifference of the world. There is a bottle of good French brandy in my office and a fire in the hearth. Will you join me?"

"Colonel, I would be honored."

The two men walked in companionable silence back up the lawn to the private entrance to Charlie's office. He built up the fire until he had a cheery blaze, then shed his coat. Whitman broke out the brandy and glasses Charlie had pointed out to him.

The two settled into comfortable chairs before the fire, refreshed their tobacco, and sat quietly, savoring the brandy. Whitman broke the silence.

"Good quality brandy is hard to find."

"Yes, well, I have an associate in Washington who keeps me supplied when he can."

"Must be a very good friend."

"He is as a good a friend as I pay him to be," Charlie laughed. "You can get anything for the right price, my friend."

"Ah, I would beg to differ, Colonel. The important things in life you cannot buy for all the money in the world."

"True enough. And sometimes the important things in life are unattainable."

"So, Colonel, what are the important things in your life? I would think, from what I have heard of you and Mrs. Gaines, that you are well on your way to attaining what every man dreams of."

"Ah, Whitman that is what concerns me. I fear that I may well be dreaming, and will awaken one morning to find myself back in my tent, alone, surrounded by mud and miserable men, with no hope for the future beyond another day of waiting interspersed with bloody conflict." Charlie knocked back the last of his glass of brandy and poured himself another.

"It seems you and I have the mirror image of one another's fear, if I may be so presumptuous."

Charlie raised an eyebrow, waiting for Whitman to continue.

"You, Sir, have your dream before you and you fear you may never be able to grasp it. I have held my dream and find it slipping away to the duty that makes him who he is."

"Samuelson?"

"Yes."

"Well, at least you know where you stand."

The two men looked at one another, then by unspoken consent, silently toasted their respective loves. Once again, glasses were refilled.

"Yes, well, I may know where I stand, Sir, but I certainly miss knowing where my head will lie—on a cold pillow or a warm shoulder." Whitman's smile was rueful.

"I have read your works, Sir. And I am not clear that a warm shoulder is exactly where you choose to rest your head." Charlie's grin was licentious.

"Ah, Colonel, you must be referring to:

I mind how once we lay, such a transparent summer morning;
How you settled your head athwart my hips, and gently turn'd over upon me,

And parted the shirt from my bosom-bone, and plunged your tongue to my bare-stript heart,

And reach'd till you felt my beard, and reach'd till you held my feet."

"That was the quatrain that came to mind."

"Colonel, I presume, but I think I know your heart. For did I not capture it when I wrote:

I am the mate and companion of people, all just as immortal and fathomless as myself;

(They do not know how immortal, but I know.)

Every kind for itself and its own—for me mine, male and female;

For me those that have been boys, and that love women;

For me the man that is proud, and feels how it stings to be slighted;

For me the sweet-heart and the old maid—for me mothers, and the mothers of mothers;

For me lips that have smiled, eyes that have shed tears;

For me children, and the begetters of children."

Charlie stood, restless and angry with himself and the world. Another brandy was poured and consumed. "Yes, indeed. There is the crux of the matter. For I am one who has been a boy and who loves women. For me, I can never be the begetter of children. But she, she deserves to have that; she deserves the family and the ability to leave a legacy that I can never give her. And what is the reason for intimacy but to beget a legacy."

Whitman looked at the brooding man before him. While his senses were slightly numbed by the alcohol, the pain of the figure standing there was obvious. "Colonel, there are more reasons for two people to come together than just to produce children. What you are describing is intimacy, when two people come together because their hearts call them together. You know that the propagation of children does not require intimacy, only the physical act. And you know the physical act without intimacy is nothing more than release. But when intimacy is involved, then the heart and the soul are involved, then physical pleasure is unlike anything you have ever experienced."

Whitman paused, considering the nature of the woman in question. From the little he knew of her, Rebecca seemed to him to be a careful, clear thinking woman who would go to any length to please her Colonel. "Your lady will come to realize that, Colonel. Just as you will come to realize that there are more ways to build a family and leave a legacy of love than through the begetting of children."

With that, Whitman finished his brandy. "I leave you, Colonel, to consider the nature of love. It is broader and more varied than most believe." Quietly, Whitman donned his cloak and slipped out of the office, leaving Charlie standing and ruminating before the fire.

With a deep sigh, Charlie finished the last of his brandy and banked the fire. He walked upstairs to the main floor, and pulled off his boots before mounting the stairs. Stopping in the small sitting room outside of their bedroom door, Charlie slipped off the rest of his clothes. Naked, he slid into the room he shared with Rebecca. She was lying, half turned toward where he usually slept, hugging his nightshirt to her. Her face was relaxed, her breathing even and slow. The fire in his belly that plagued him almost non-stop now flared again. More of Whitman's words came to mind.

Undrape! you are not guilty to me, nor stale, nor discarded;
I see through the broadcloth and gingham, whether or no;
And am around, tenacious, acquisitive, tireless, and cannot be
shaken away.

Charlie looked at Rebecca's face, at the lovely form hidden only by the light flannel of her nightgown. *Yes, I am around, tenacious. To me you are not guilty. You are not stale, nor discarded. You are the most beautiful woman I have ever seen. Oh, Rebecca, I ache for you. I burn for your touch. I hunger for your passion.* She slid into bed beside Rebecca, and looked at her, illuminated in the soft moonlight from the window and the faint glow of the banked embers in the fireplace. As she looked at her, her hands slowly began stroking her own body. She gazed on her loved one's face, imagining it was Rebecca's hands and not her own that were caressing with her. In a matter of minutes, she arched into her own hand, and softly cried Rebecca's name. With the most urgent of the flames eased for at least a moment, the brandy took over. Sliding her arm around Rebecca's sleeping form; Charlie fell into a deep, dreamless sleep.

~

Thursday, December 1, 1864

Charlie awoke early and went for his usual morning run. As was becoming his habit, Jocko prepared a hot bath in the bathing room, and was enjoying a cup of coffee while waiting for the Colonel to return.

Charlie stomped into the bathing area, sweating and limping slightly. He had fallen over a root and slammed his knee into the ground. His mishap, coupled with a mild hangover the run had not managed to clear completely, meant that he was not in the best of humors.

"Good morning, Jocko." He growled his greeting, barely civil in his current mood.

Jocko knew better than to get in Charlie's way when he was in this kind of a mood. "Morning, Colonel C."

He stripped off his work clothes, and threw the trousers over the modesty screen to Jocko. "See if you can fix them."

Jocko looked them over. One knee was shredded and slightly bloodstained. The trousers would have to be replaced. Jocko sighed. Sometimes Charlie was hard on clothes.

Charlie emerged a few minutes later, clad in shirt, breeches, socks, and weskit. Shaving was performed in silence. When Jocko was finished, Charlie turned to him. "Do you have any commitments today?"

"Just the normal, Sir."

"Good. Get Black Jack saddled up, get yourself a horse and a note pad, and meet me out front in a half hour. Send Polk to me before you get the horses."

"Yes, Sir, Colonel, Sir." Jocko was not inclined to be Charlie's whipping boy when the universe had served up the normal reaction to an overdose of the grape.

"Being a little overbearing this morning, am I?"

"A bit, Sir."

Charlie laughed a wry and self-deprecating chuckle. "Well, I will tone it down. Thanks for the warning."

"Oh, by the way, Sir, why Black Jack? Lately, you have been riding Shannon."

"I am leaving Shannon for Miss Rebecca. I believe she and Duncan will go into town today to collect up the other refugees."

"Oh, aye. I did hear tell of that. A little admirer of yours gave it away."

"Enough of that, Sergeant." He softened the admonition with a grin.

"So what do I need a horse and notepad for, Colonel?"

"You and I are going to tour the county and try and figure out just how badly off these people are."

"You and I alone?"

"Yes, you and I alone."

"Charlie—have you lost your mind? You will be the biggest target these folks have had in ages. What if somebody recognizes you? They are as likely to shoot you as speak to you."

"I know that. But we will never get anywhere if we go with an armed entourage. We ride alone. Sidearm only."

Jocko shook his head. He loved Charlie like a brother, was unfailingly loyal to him, but sometimes he knew his boss was just plain crazy.

Jocko turned to leave.

"And Jocko?"

The batman turned to look inquiringly at Charlie.

"Do not dawdle. We need to get a move on. I will be in my office."

~

Charlie finished dressing quickly. He wanted to be out of the house and on his way before Rebecca made her way down for breakfast. In fact, he wanted to put as much distance as possible between them this morning. Maybe if he pushed himself hard enough and limited their encounters, he could, somehow, manage, a little, to control the desires she aroused in him. Maybe.

While waiting for Polk and Jocko, Charlie prepared his orders for the day. Polk had been briefed on the plans for work details to support the civilian population the day before, and would handle the daily staff meeting and the transfer of the refugees. The company commanders would have to manage a great many details to implement Charlie's wishes. Polk's meticulous mind made him a good second. He was outstanding at patiently handling these kinds of administrative details.

Polk entered his office first. "Thanks, chief. I needed to be rousted out at the crack of dawn. Why can you not wait for reveille like a normal person?"

"Because I cannot ask the men to get up unless I am waiting for them."

Polk poured himself a cup of coffee from the pot that Sarah delivered to the office every morning. "So, what is so urgent that I am here before breakfast?"

"I am riding out to see for myself what needs to be done to pull this county together and set its people on the road to return to the Union. We have to survive winter here, and so do the civilians. I am taking Jocko as my clerk."

"So you want an escort. I will go rustle one up."

"No. We are going alone."

"Sweet Jesus, Charlie. You are crazy."

"No, I am not. If I go with a guard, I know for a fact they will not talk to me. If I go with just Jocko, they may recognize that I am not coming to try to take anything from them. This way, I have at least a hope of them listening and talking."

Like Jocko minutes earlier, Polk just shook his head. Charlie had been known to pull off some hare-brained stunts in the past. He just hoped his commander knew what he was doing this time.

The day was brisk and clear. Black Jack, Charlie's big black stallion, had not been ridden for days. Due to a slight bruise to his hock, he had been at pasture since they had arrived. He was full of energy—nervous, jittery, and full of beans. Everything distracted him. He shied at the slightest provocation. In fact, Jack's mood fit Charlie's exactly.

Jocko was mounted on an ugly old buckskin with a foul temper and the endurance of a dray. Between them, they had the means to cover a great deal of ground in a short time. Just as Rebecca was coming down the stairs for her breakfast, she saw the two men set off at a brisk canter down the main drive.

Charlie had spent some time the previous evening examining the map of Culpeper County. Dividing it roughly into four quadrants, he decided to start in the eastern portion. He had planned a loop that took him to Alanthus, through Brandy Station, over to Kelly's Ford, down to Lignum and back through Stevensburg. It was a brisk day's ride. If all went well, he would be back in plenty of time for dinner.

Alanthus was his first stop. Having left so early, Charlie and Jocko rode into town just as the small general store was being opened. It was always the same: the local general store was the gathering place for news and gossip in every small town Charlie had ever been in. Charlie and Jocko left their horses tied at the rail and entered quietly. The soft buzz of normal morning banter faded to a cold and hostile silence as the people in the small building realized who had just joined them.

"Good morning, ladies and gentlemen."

Silence.

"My name is Colonel Charles Redmond, of the 13th Pennsylvania Cavalry. We are wintering over in Culpeper, and I am conducting a tour of the area to determine what we can do to assist you. My men are prepared to do basic repairs, fix fences, chop firewood, or winter-till fields to prepare for the spring. All we ask in return is that you be willing to recognize that we are all citizens of the same country, the United States, by signing our oath of allegiance. I have issued strict orders that no men of mine are to harass or show any disrespect toward you or yours. If such an event does occur, please come to me and I will ensure the individuals responsible are appropriately disciplined.

"Now, Sergeant Jackson and I are conducting a survey of the work that needs to be done so we can assign men with the correct skills to assist you. Is there anything we can do to help you out?"

The men and women in the small store looked at one another, confusion combining with hostility toward this crazy Yankee.

Finally, one man stepped out. "Colonel. We are Virginians. We need no help from you. Please take your troops and leave us in peace."

"I have no one with me but Sergeant Jackson. We will be around town for a little while, and either he or I will be through periodically, so please feel free to speak to either of us if you need something. Otherwise, I bid you good day."

Charlie and Jocko walked out of the store and turned the corner. The Colonel grinned at his partner and leaned up against the wall of the store. A pair of cigars came out of his breast pocket and he offered one to Jocko, making a sign for silence at the same time. Jocko looked at him like he had lost his mind, until he heard the voices coming out of the nearby window.

"My God. What did that man think he was doing here?"

"He has courage, I give him that. Walking into enemy territory all alone."

"I would rather accept assistance from the devil himself than let some Yankee see how hard it has been."

"I do not know about you, but I would rather have a fire in the fireplace this winter than sustain my sense of pride. Anyway, think of it this way—Yankees doing servants' work seems pretty appropriate."

The arguments went on, each of them having something to say. After listening for a few more minutes, Charlie motioned to Jocko to come away from their listening post. Slowly they strolled down the one street of the village, looking at the handful of shops and offices, noticing that every building at least needed paint, and most needed some kind of repair. Several houses no longer had a woodpile, or had only a very small one. Jocko made some notes as they strolled. Finally, like so many small towns, Alanthus had a little park. They stopped in it, choosing a sheltered place to sit and wait. They did not have to wait for long.

A woman approached them hesitantly. Charlie rose and doffed his hat politely, waiting for the lady to speak.

"Colonel. Did you really mean what you said about helping?"

"Yes, Ma'am, I did."

"I really do not know how to ask this, but I just have no idea what else to do."

"Well, Ma'am," he said very gently, "we have all seen what war can do to people. There is no shame in asking for our assistance, for I do believe that we are all our brother's keeper."

"My husband was killed at Gettysburg, and the one servant we did have ran away. I fear that without help, I will have no wood this winter."

Jocko stepped up. "Ma'am, I am John Jackson. I would be happy to make sure personally that you are prepared for the winter."

"Pleased to meet you, Sergeant Jackson. I am Esther White. My, what a lovely accent you have. You are an Irishman?"

"Yes, Ma'am, that I am."

"Then, Sergeant Jackson, I look forward to seeing you soon. And I am very grateful for your assistance."

"Ma'am, I will be there as soon as the Colonel permits."

Charlie inserted himself into the little tableau between Jocko and the attractive widow. "Mrs. White, will Monday be soon enough?"

"Why yes, Colonel. That will be fine. I have about half a cord of wood left, which should last me until then."

"We are at your service, Ma'am."

Charlie and Jocko bowed to the lady and quietly departed. As they mounted up, Charlie commented, "You know, Jocko, you will find plenty more where she came from." Jocko just grinned.

The rest of the day proceeded in approximately the same pattern. The level of hostility varied, depending on the degree to which the individual town had been affected by the war. Brandy Station was particularly hard, as they had recently fought a skirmish there. Kelly's Ford was rather strange, as the local residents, who had provided ferry services for both Federal and Confederate forces, viewed Charlie's presence with indifference.

But the message was going out. In every town, the fact that Charlie chose to ride with only his clerk as his escort made an impression.

～

Friday, December 2, 1864

Rebecca watched as Constance left the breakfast table with Emily. She smiled as the child talked of "Papa" all the way out of the room. Papa and Colonel Polk had already left for the day. Charlie was back out early to continue his mission of canvassing the county. This left Rebecca and Elizabeth sitting at the table.

"Emily certainly has fallen for Charlie." Rebecca smiled, pouring them both another cup of coffee.

"Yes, she has, has she not? It is amazing to watch Charlie play papa. I personally expected him to have apoplexy over the mashed squash and cereal."

The blonde smiled. "Secretly I think he loves it, even if he is a little unsure of it all. Last night while we were having tea after dinner, he kept talking of Emily. I think he is just as smitten."

Elizabeth detected a note of something not quite right or

comfortable in Rebecca's tone. "It is startling how much she resembles him."

"Yes," she agreed before sipping her coffee. "Charlie could certainly pass for her father. They even have the same chin." She leaned back in her chair and played with her napkin. "He would make a wonderful father."

"And you, my dear friend, would make a truly wonderful mother."

"You are very kind, but I am not sure about that. Not that I would not love to try, but you have seen the affinity the child has for Charlie. It is astounding. She certainly does not light up like that when I walk into the room. And given the choice, she would much prefer Charlie's lap to my own." Rebecca sighed. "But she does have her mother near."

"Rebecca, think on this for a minute. That child's affinity for Charlie is for one reason and one reason only: he looks like her daddy. And she misses her daddy more than she can express at her age." Elizabeth thought for a moment. "You know, you resemble her mother somewhat. If her mother had gone away when she was eleven months old and then you appeared in her life and were gentle and loving, she would adore you the way she adores him. You would be the mother she misses returned to her."

"I suppose that is true." Rebecca smiled at her friend. "But whatever the reason, that child is totally in love with our Charlie. He manages to charm the ladies, no matter what their age." She drew a deep breath. "Elizabeth, I have a question and I do not know who else to turn to for the answer. Do you mind?"

Elizabeth looked at Rebecca closely. She appeared concerned, confused, and embarrassed all at once. *Ah. Another round of lessons from the unconventional doctor. Well, this should be interesting.* "Of course not, Rebecca. I told you that you could ask me anything, and I would do my best to answer you honestly."

Rebecca moved from her seat to the one occupied by Colonel Polk over breakfast, the one closest to Elizabeth. "Uh... I must admit I am not sure how to put this. It is about...intimate matters."

Elizabeth bowed her head and patted her lips with her napkin; that is what proper ladies did when they wanted to hide a smirk. *Introductory same gender intimacy. This should be interesting indeed.* "Yes? I will certainly help if I can. After all, is that not what doctors are for?"

"Oh Lord." Rebecca ran her hand over her face in a vain attempt to remove the blush. "You see, marital duties with my husband were just that, duties. I never actually enjoyed my couplings with him." She took another drink of her coffee waiting to see what that admission would bring from her friend.

Elizabeth's professional face was firmly in place: kind, accepting, understanding, and non-judgmental. "I know that is true for many women, unfortunately. Their husbands fail to take the time or effort to teach them that intimacy can, and should, be an expression of deep love for both partners."

"I am sure it would have helped if we had loved each other." That was out before Rebecca thought about it. She shook her head. "I am sorry; I am getting off course here. Obviously, I want to ask you about something else. You see, Charlie and I have agreed to take things slowly. And since then, at night we have been cuddling and sharing small kisses..." She looked to the doctor trying to hide her smile. "I have discovered I rather like that."

"I would imagine so. Charlie can be very gentle and very tender. So what is it about this that bothers you?"

"Oh, that does not bother me!" She was quickly defensive. "I really do enjoy it and Charlie is very patient, but I am afraid I may be hurting him."

Elizabeth had a crystal clear picture in her mind of a rather excited Charlie trying very hard to be gentle and to restrain himself. She suspected under that very controlled surface lay an extraordinarily passionate soul, one for whom tender kisses and chaste embraces would be little solace indeed. "Hurting him how, dear lady?"

"Umm..." She blushed a deeper red. "He is never going to forgive me for knowing this. Night before last, I retired before he did, as he had paperwork to do. He came up some time later and came to bed. He thought I was asleep, but I was not. He smelled of cigars and brandy." She bit her lip and looked to her friend.

"Well, perhaps he stopped to have a drink and chat with one of his officers. I understand gentlemen often do such things." *Where is this going? Just because Charlie had a brandy with one of his men did not indicate he was hurting in any way. In fact, I know he often reaches out, a man or two at a time, to build more solid relationships with his staff.* "I do not see how that leads you to believe he may be hurting."

"Well, you see, when he came to bed he was naked." She looked directly at the table and waited.

Elizabeth waited patiently for Rebecca to continue. Clearly, a little goading was going to be necessary. "Was that a problem for you, dear?"

"No. Actually, I find Charlie," she leaned over and whispered so no one save them would hear, "in all her glory, quite enchanting." She sat back up and continued at a semi-normal level. "He got into bed and lay next to me. I let him think I was asleep but I watched him, while he umm...well..."

"While he?" *Oh, this is prime. Charlie, Charlie, what have you gotten yourself into?*

"While he," Rebecca was sure she was going to die of embarrassment, "he pleasured himself."

Elizabeth's nose twitched. She bit her lower lip. Laughing in the face of Rebecca's obvious discomfort would clearly not do. *So. Charlie had a bad night, had a couple of drinks with one of the other gentlemen, went to bed to lie beside a beautiful woman who is sleeping peacefully and who Charlie desires to the core of his soul, and had to do something to relieve the pressure a little.* "How do you think this is hurtful to him, my dear?"

"Oh dear," She shook her head. "I must be doing something wrong...if he needs to...I do not know...you know, that." She blushed and hid her face behind her hand. "He called my name."

"Then perhaps, dear Rebecca, you are doing something very right. Has it occurred to you that Charlie desires you deeply and respects you enough to keep his passion at bay until you are ready?"

"But, umm, is that normal?"

"Is what normal? Needing to relieve a little of the pressure of a deep, persistent desire, or being willing to wait patiently until you are ready both to accept and return his passion?"

Rebecca really liked Elizabeth, but the woman's refusal to answer a simple question was maddening. She laughed; now the situation was getting too silly for words. "Do that...you know...what Charlie did."

"I assume he masturbated. And further, that as he reached release, he called out your name. If I were you, I would be very flattered." Elizabeth smiled. "All it means is that he wants you, desires you, and is doing what he needs to do while he waits for you to feel the same for him."

"So I should not be worried?" She chewed on her lip. "I have just never been subject to such a thing. I thought something was wrong."

Elizabeth looked at her friend with some concern. "Dear woman, have you never felt the joy that desire, that a loving touch can bring? Have you never explored your own sensuality? That is all Charlie was doing. I suspect that he either wanted to touch you, caress you, and bring you intense pleasure; or he was fantasizing about your doing that to him. What made you think something was wrong?"

Rebecca felt like a girl, embarrassed and confused. "No, I have never felt that way. The only thing I have found I enjoy is lying with Charlie. My husband...well let us say, I have never heard sounds like I heard out of Charlie night before last."

"Well, dear, from what you have said, I suspect your husband was one of those sad people who get pleasure from controlling others. Charlie, on the other hand, is a very giving soul. And at his core, he has the sensibilities of a very passionate woman, not a man. The most intimate and binding love of all is one that encompasses the heart, soul, and body. Your Charlie is willing to give you all of those things, as soon as you are willing to accept them."

Rebecca nodded and took Elizabeth's hand. "Thank you. You know I have no desire to hurt him. I just wanted to make sure he was all right."

"I suspect the worst thing that he has to deal with right now is some frustration. He can hold you, but is not free to express the range of his love for you. He will survive, with the help of some cold baths and a few late nights like you had that night. You might find him running more, or doing other things to tire himself physically. You are doing exactly the right thing. Accept what love and physical affection from him you are comfortable with. Take each step slowly, and build your relationship on trust and friendship so that it will last through the years."

"Umm, one other thing? That night after Charlie was asleep, I got a very unusual feeling very deep in my stomach, and I was wondering," her voice cracked and she had to clear her throat, "if that is all right."

"Was the feeling unpleasant, or just unusual—a tightness perhaps? A tingling sensation or a swollen sensation? And did you notice if your heartbeat jumped a bit, or other parts of your body became sensitive?"

"It definitely was not unpleasant. And yes, I felt all those things. It took a good quarter hour for my heart to stop beating so loudly I could hear it in my ears. And when Charlie rolled over and wrapped me up in his arms, all I could do was whimper."

Elizabeth drew a deep mental sigh, while holding her external appearance neutral and gentle. *Oh, Lord, a virgin trying to teach a formerly abused woman something about intimacy is not my best skill. Charlie, my friend, I certainly hope you have more experience than I do in the actual act, because I am working from the textbook right now.* "I believe, my dear, that your body was responding to him—to the physical desire he has for you and to the desire you have for him. Those feelings are all part of becoming sexually excited. You were aroused by Charlie that night."

Rebecca laughed. "Well, that is new." She shook her head. "I cannot believe I have to ask these questions. I am a grown woman for Heaven's sake. One who has been married and widowed. You would think I would have some clue."

Elizabeth softened from her clinical self. "Rebecca, you are a grown woman who had a harsh and unloving husband, and who is now confronted with a relationship that is, to say the least, outside of the boundaries of "normal," whatever that is. Of course you have new things to learn."

Rebecca was quite pleased with the way everything had come together in a single day. Duncan and his men had done a tremendous job refurbishing the rooms that would house the refugees arriving later in the day.

Mr. Cooper had rounded up men to deliver the wood stove from the church and a few mattresses. It had only taken a couple of men from Duncan's crew about two hours to get it properly installed and vented.

While Rebecca was glad to help where she could, she had to admit, at least to herself, that the thought of having strangers in her home was a little daunting. She had no idea what to expect. She was also concerned for Charlie; his off-handed comment about spies worried her as well.

They might only be women and children but nothing was impossible at the moment. From listening to Charlie and Colonel Polk talk in the evening, she knew the Confederacy was desperate to mount a final strike in the hopes of winning a war long since lost.

She made a mental note to herself to watch and listen to

everything very carefully. She would not let any harm come to Charlie or his men.

She was walking toward the front of the house when she heard the little voice. She followed the giggles to the front parlor where Constance was busy with Emily, who was perched on a chair looking out the window.

"Papa!" the child yelled, and banged on the glass pane.

"Oh, does someone see Colonel Redmond?"

"Yes, Ma'am. The Colonel is standing out front with a few of his officers smoking a cigar." Charlie and Jocko had just returned from their daily trip, dusty and tired, but in good humor. They had stopped to talk to several of the company commanders, who had been walking down the drive from the rail yards.

Rebecca smiled, moving to the window to see Charlie with Polk and a few others. He was laughing and looked very relaxed. She let an evil thought germinate for just a moment. "Em, would you like to go see Papa?"

The baby's eyes grew wide when she looked to Rebecca. "Papa!" she yelled, before banging on the window again.

"Well, come on then, before you break the window." She scooped the baby up in her arms and headed for the front door. Pulling it open, she stepped out on the front porch.

"Papa!" Emily squealed and clapped her hands.

Charlie just dropped his head and shook it slowly from side to side. He turned around and waved to them, his smile a cross between affection and total embarrassment.

"You have someone who is desperate to see you, Colonel," Rebecca chuckled, as she lifted her skirt and descended the steps. "I was afraid she was going to break the glass in the parlor window."

The moment he was within reach, Emily lunged for Charlie. "Papa. Kiss Papa."

Charlie's men stifled laughs as their commander was graced with a sloppy baby kiss and a fierce hug.

The Colonel cleared his throat. "Gentlemen, may I introduce

Miss Emily. She and her mother are going to stay with Mrs. Gaines for a while."

Each man in turn said hello to the baby, all the while barely managing to restrain their smiles.

"Papa." Emily patted Charlie's chest. "'Orsy?"

"I promise to bring Shannon by for you to see later today, little one." He looked to the men. "She only loves me for my horse."

Saturday, December 3, 1864

Rebecca, Constance, and Emily enjoyed a light lunch together, and then mother and daughter retired to their room for a nap. Rebecca made the rounds of the house looking for last minute things to be done, but found nothing. That helped her peace of mind considerably.

Going into the kitchen, she found Sarah and Beulah preparing large pots of soup. "Hmm, something smells good." She peeked in one of the pots, then found a spoon in her hand. She smiled at Sarah before tasting the soup. "Ooo that is very good. What is that?"

"'Tis only ham and bean soup, Miss Rebecca. Corporal Duncan brought the beans, and Mr. Cooper supplied a little ham for flavoring."

"Sarah, you have done wonders." Rebecca could not resist taking another taste of the soup. "And what are you making, Beulah?"

"Sarah convinced me to make cornbread. We are going to have a lot of extra mouths to feed this evening."

"And every evening for some time to come, I think," Rebecca agreed.

"Miss Rebecca?"

"Yes, Sarah."

"Colonel Redmond mentioned the possibility of hiring a few more people, especially since he is talking of opening the north wing and rebuilding the stables. I was wondering if he still wants to do that. I have several family members who are eager for work and good food."

"I believe he is, but you will have to speak with the Colonel about that. You may speak with him this evening after supper."

"Yes, Ma'am."

Reg entered the kitchen and gestured to Rebecca. "Ma'am, Mrs. Cooper and Mrs. Williams are here."

Rebecca looked to the ceiling and prayed to God to give her strength. "All right, let us go greet them. Where is Daniel when I need him most?"

"Ma'am?"

"Nothing, Reg. Let us go see what is to be said today."

They walked to the front of the house where the ladies were getting out of their carriage, which had been followed by a wagon carrying the refugees from town.

"Good day, ladies." Rebecca greeted them as she watched everyone get out of the wagon with Reg's help. "Gaines Cove is ready, and we welcome you all. Sarah is preparing hot soup and tea for you, and Reg will show you to your rooms. There is a warm fire and a warm, dry bed for each of you."

She moved to a boy of about ten years old. The look on his young face made Rebecca's heart ache. "What is your name, son?"

"Jeremiah, Ma'am. Jeremiah Carter."

"Well, Jeremiah, I am glad to see a young man here."

"I have been taking care of my mama since Papa was called away."

"I am sure you have. And I am sure you will be a great help. There are a lot of things for a young man to do around here."

Jeremiah looked back to his mother. "Will that be all right, Mama?"

"Of course, son. You may help where Mrs. Gaines needs you. It is the least we can do to repay her for her kindness."

"You owe me nothing. But I think it will be good to keep young Jeremiah busy."

"Yes, Ma'am. You know how boys can be."

"Indeed I do. My brother Andrew was the one that our father had to keep busy lest he found himself into something that was best not gotten into." She ruffled the boy's hair. "Then start by helping everyone get settled."

"Yes, Ma'am."

The blonde turned to the boy's mother. "Please call me Rebecca. And you are?"

"Samantha Carter."

"I am glad to meet you, Samantha. I wish it were under better circumstances. Welcome to my home. Now go ahead with Reg and get yourself settled. I will be in directly."

She watched as the group went to the house. She would have to take the time to get to know all of them. She turned back to Mrs. Cooper. "Well, Grace, this is a start."

"Yes, it is, Rebecca. We are grateful."

Mrs. Williams sniffed. "My husband tells me we can expect to see you and the Colonel at services this Sunday."

Oh Lord, Charlie, what have you gotten us into now? Are we to show up at church as a couple? Rebecca smiled. "If that is what the Colonel said, Mrs. Williams, then yes, we will be at services on Sunday. I look forward to it, as circumstances have kept me from attendance for some time."

CHAPTER 14

SUNDAY DECEMBER 4, 1864

Charlie roused the entire household early on Sunday morning. He had promised, and he meant to keep his word. They would all be in church, wearing their best, and presenting themselves as proper members of the community. Polk, half of his company commanders, and all but one of Samuelson's medics were coming as well.

Rebecca wore a discreet dove gray dress, while Charlie was in his Daniel costume, as was Polk when he came to join them. Elizabeth was in stark black and white, appropriate to her professional standing. Between them, Rebecca and Lizbet had found appropriate Sunday clothing for all of the ladies. Even the servants were gussied up for the day. As the wagons and carriages were filled with the representatives of Gaines Cove, four more officers rode up, all in their best, to serve both as escort and representatives of the regiment.

The churchgoing citizens of Culpeper did not know what hit them when this entourage rode into the churchyard.

Into the church marched Rebecca and Charlie, along with

Elizabeth, Polk, Constance, and Emily. They sat down in the Gaines pew at the front of the church, one of the few real benefits the late and unlamented Mr. Gaines had provided Rebecca. Emily sat between Constance and Rebecca, with the two gentlemen taking the end positions.

Behind them came the twelve refugees, the women, and children staying at the farm. Four officers and four of the regiment's medics escorted them. They took their places in the unassigned pews at the rear of the building. The servants made their way upstairs to the balcony. At breakfast, Charlie had told Sarah and Beulah to recruit three more servants to help take care of the influx of refugees and sick people. A wave of hushed whispers rippled through the balcony as those two very efficient women looked for the right staff among their friends and relations.

Mrs. Williams, sitting at the organ to the side of the apse, drew a hissing breath between her teeth. *How dare they come into this church as if they were a family—these interlopers, these traitors to the glorious intent of the founding fathers?*

A sweet little voice rose above the hushed whispers that were circling around the church. "Papa. Papa." Em was trying to crawl across Rebecca's lap to get to Charlie.

"Hush, Em. We are in God's house. You must be respectful and quiet in God's house." Constance gently admonished her little girl.

"Yes, Mama." The little girl settled into the crook of her mother's arm.

Mrs. Cooper and the rest of the choir filed into their position behind the organ. She smiled to herself as she saw Rebecca sitting with her Colonel. The little black haired imp beside Rebecca could, indeed, be Colonel Redmond's child. But then, Mrs. Carter was also dark haired.

"That child called that monster Papa. And Mrs. Carter allowed it. What has happened to all of the good Southern women in this town? Corrupted by those damned Yankees. Look at that little slut sitting there in dear Mr. Gaines' pew, that noble hero of the cause, as if she were proud to be there with that Yankee. It is disgraceful, I tell you, absolutely disgraceful."

"Margaret Williams, you watch your mouth. I do declare, one of these days you will be struck down for your blaspheming. I happen to know that Mrs. Gaines has every right to sit there, and that Colonel Redmond has only the most honorable of intentions. He may have chosen for the Federal cause in this war, but he is still a good Southern gentleman."

At that point, Reverend Williams entered and took his position before the altar. Mrs. Williams pounded out the final chords of the processional. Further conversation was postponed until after the service. The laggards filed into their seats, and with the appropriate amount of rustling and coughing, the congregation came to order. The exhortation, read by one of the elders of the church, and first hymn proceeded normally.

Then Reverend Williams stepped into the pulpit, and someone very different emerged from the mild, slightly bumbling man who Charlie had seen before. Williams was something rare—a minister who truly believed in the power of the God whose word he preached, and who allowed that power to flow through him when preaching.

"Our text for the day comes from Ecclesiastes, Chapter nine, verses ten through eighteen.

"*Whatsoever thy hand findeth to do, do it with thy might; for there is no work, nor device, nor knowledge, nor wisdom, in the grave, whither thou goest.*

"*I returned, and saw under the sun, that the race is not to the swift, nor the battle to the strong, neither yet bread to the wise, nor yet riches to men of understanding, nor yet favour to men of skill; but time and chance happeneth to them all.*

"*For man also knoweth not his time: as the fishes that are taken in an evil net, and as the birds that are caught in the snare; so are the sons of men snared in an evil time, when it falleth suddenly upon them.*

"*This wisdom have I seen also under the sun, and it seemed great unto me:*

"There was a little city, and few men within it; and there came a great king against it, and besieged it, and built great bulwarks against it:

"Now there was found in it a poor wise man, and he by his wisdom delivered the city; yet no man remembered that same poor man.

"Then said I, Wisdom is better than strength: nevertheless the poor man's wisdom is despised, and his words are not heard.

"The words of wise men are heard in quiet more than the cry of him that ruleth among fools.

"Wisdom is better than weapons of war: but one sinner destroyeth much good.

"Through fate and chance, we have faced a time of war. Now, that time of war is coming to an end for us and we must find a different way." The good minister spoke passionately and compassionately on the ravages of war and the prices all had paid for it.

"But then, are we not all at war against evil thought, against lack of compassion, against letting the matters of the body politic overwhelm the matters of the soul?" His sermon went on to look to the future and he spoke of a conflict that would come to end all conflicts, that each man, woman and child would have to face for themselves.

And then he spoke of what would happen if a wise man who came among them and offered them peace and a chance for a new future, of how the voices of fools who could not let the time of war pass into the time of peace might drown the words of wisdom. For wisdom is spoken softly, and wise words heard only in the silence of a peaceful heart.

Reverend Williams talked on, reaching many of the people in his audience with the compassion in his plea. Emily was far too young to listen. She looked around the church, enjoyed the light through the window, sucked on her fingers for a while, and started squirming. Constance's pregnancy was beginning to show; holding a squirming toddler was uncomfortable, so Rebecca took the little girl in her arms. She promptly cuddled up in Rebecca's lap and fell asleep.

With the sermon over, the congregation stood for the second hymn. Reverend Williams' prayer asked for the silence of the heart to hear words of wisdom in this time of change. The hymn roused the little girl, who was usually cranky and fussy when she first woke. Charlie quietly lifted the child from Rebecca's lap and held her through the hymn. She went back to Rebecca while the collection plate was passed. Charlie dropped a silver dollar into the plate, and Rebecca reached into her reticule for a smaller silver coin. For a moment, Charlie wondered at how much women could get into those small, frilly pouches, then he noticed that many of the people in the congregation had nothing to offer, and if they did have an offering, it was usually just a penny.

The final hymn and the benediction were over, and it was time to file out of the little church. Constance was looking tired, and Elizabeth and Polk were both being solicitous of her. Charlie simply took Emily back into his arms and walked out, politely greeting anyone who would deign to speak with the Yankee invader. The first to greet him was the good minister. Mr. Cooper was there, as well. Surprisingly, Mayor Frazier was also there to acknowledge the Colonel and his entourage.

The ladies, led by Mrs. Cooper, clustered around Elizabeth and Rebecca, who by now had taken Emily from Charlie's arms. The little girl was the center of a great deal of oohing and aahing. She was ecstatic at the attention, and was being very charming.

As the ladies were admiring the little girl, Miss Reynolds noticed the ring on Rebecca's left hand and pointed to it. As the other women in the group realized what that ring implied, there was a moment of stunned silence so profound the gentlemen looked up to see what was wrong. Then all of the women broke out at once, some envious, others unsure of the propriety of marrying the enemy.

Mrs. Williams, having divested herself of the robe she wore as the organist, came charging into the group, obviously prepared to condemn the conqueror and his harlot, when her husband stepped in front of her. In a firm, carrying voice, he turned to Charlie and announced, "I see congratulations are in order, Colonel. When do you plan to have the happy event? You know, I expect to officiate."

Charlie grinned, Rebecca blushed, and Mrs. Williams looked like she was going to explode. All in all, it was a very successful Sunday.

~

Wednesday, December 7, 1864

Rebecca entered the room quietly, closing the door behind her. She moved to Montgomery's bedside and looked upon his sleeping form. "Good evening, Major. I will be sitting with you for a time. Dr. Walker has asked that we talk to you in the hopes you will respond. But since I do not know what to say to a gentleman such as yourself, I thought perhaps I would just read to you."

She pulled a rocker close to the bed and raised the wick on the lamp for more light. Taking the Bible from the table, she opened it. "Let us start at the beginning, shall we, Major?" She cleared her throat as she adjusted the lap rug over her legs. "Genesis, Chapter One. In the beginning..."

Rebecca rubbed her eyes. She was not sure how long she had been reading. She would pause occasionally to give the Major a sip of water as Elizabeth had instructed. She placed her ribbon marker in the Bible and stood up to stretch tired muscles. Moving to the window, she could see it was very late.

The moon was high in the sky; thin gray clouds passed over it, causing shadows on the land. Rebecca realized that was how she felt right now, like a shadow had been cast over her heart, since Charlie seemed to have been so distant the last few days.

She looked at the ring on her finger, playing with it. "Oh, Charlie, if you have changed your mind, you need only say so," she sighed, her thoughts plunging her into darker despair with every moment. She was about to retake her seat when the door opened and Samuelson came in.

"Good evening, Miss Rebecca. I am here to spend the rest of the night."

"Thank you, Samuelson."

"Has there been any change?"

"No, I am afraid not, but he is taking water regularly. Just small sips, but he does swallow it."

"That is good." The man regarded the woman before him. "Miss Rebecca, I think you need to rest. You look exhausted."

"Perhaps. It has been a very difficult few days." She patted his shoulder. "Good night, Sir, I will see you tomorrow."

She left the room and headed for her bedroom. Stepping inside, she saw the bed was still empty, that Charlie had not yet come to bed. She left the bedroom and went downstairs.

Entering the kitchen, she prepared a pot of tea, fighting tears the entire time. Picking up a piece of bread, she started to bring it to her lips, but found she had no appetite and replaced it in the basket.

Taking the tea, she went to the rear parlor and settled in her rocker by the window. Pulling a shawl over her shoulders and a blanket over her legs, she sipped her tea as she watched out the window. It was not long before she felt her lids getting very heavy, but rather than go face their bed—which was cold and empty—she let sleep claim her in the chair.

Charlie spent the evening documenting the problems he had found throughout the county. He indulged himself in a quiet half hour before the fire with a cigar and a glass of brandy. Finally, he slipped into the hall and sat on the bottom step to pull his boots off. Holding them in one hand, he crept up the stairs and eased into Rebecca's private sitting room. There he stripped off the rest of his clothes and pulled on his nightshirt. Dousing the last light in the room, he eased the door to the bedroom open. He nearly panicked when he realized she was not in bed as he expected.

Quickly, he looked around the room. No, the rocking chair was empty. He went back into the little sitting room. Maybe she had fallen asleep on the davenport; but that, too, was empty. He hurried downstairs and then saw the faint light under the door to the back parlor. There she sat, wrapped in a shawl and lap blanket, asleep in her chair by the window.

Softly he went to her. Moving slowly and gently, he gathered her up in his arms. She did not fully waken, but wrapped her arms around his neck and burrowed her head into his shoulder with a contented sigh. Carefully, he carried her upstairs to bed. He tucked her in on her usual side, and then slid in beside her. She rolled over, seeking his warmth in her sleep. Entwined, satisfied for the moment to feel his arms around her and the sweet smell of her in his nostrils, they slept.

~

Thursday, December 8, 1864

Rebecca woke slowly and reached for Charlie, who was already gone. She sighed and rolled over on her back staring at the ceiling. She was not sure what had come over Charlie in the last few days, but she wondered if it had something to do with the other women who had come to live with them. Perhaps he found young Constance and little Emily far more appealing. After all, this was a woman with children; and it was clear that Charlie adored Em. Pushing the thoughts from her mind, she tossed the covers back and sat up.

Lizbet entered the room and opened the curtains. "Mornin', Miss Rebecca. What would you like to wear today?"

"I do not care," she answered quietly.

Lizbet looked at her mistress. "Are you all right, Ma'am?"

"I am fine. Just very tired."

Rebecca moved to the window while Lizbet bustled around the

room laying out her clothes. She looked out over her land, wondering where Charlie had gone. "Has Colonel Redmond left for the day?"

"Oh yes, Ma'am. The Colonel was up and out very early this morning. He had breakfast with Miss Constance, Miss Emily, and Dr. Walker before he left."

"I see." She heard her own voice crack as she sniffed back tears. It looked like Charlie was making some changes. She could not think of a reason why he would not have awakened her.

Rebecca dressed quickly, then went to Major Montgomery's room. She slipped inside to find Elizabeth tending to her patient.

"Oh, I am sorry I did not mean..." She started to back out.

"No, no, Rebecca, come in. I am nearly finished here."

"How is he?"

"Improving. I see some movement behind his lids now. That is a very good sign."

"Elizabeth, did Charlie seem all right to you at breakfast this morning?"

"Oh, yes. You should have seen him helping little Em with her breakfast. It was adorable."

She smiled, even though she felt her heart breaking. "Good, I am glad. He did not wake me this morning."

"Well, we were all up very early. One of the hazards of life around the military."

"And Constance?"

"One of the hazards of being pregnant." Elizabeth chuckled, pulling the blankets over the Major.

"I am sure." She moved closer to the bed and handed a cool cloth to Elizabeth. "Do you know where the Colonel has gone off too this morning?"

"I believe he is finishing his survey of the needs of the county. You know, he is really very serious about trying to lay the groundwork for an effective reconstruction."

"Oh yes, I know. These people do not know how lucky they are it was the Colonel who arrived and not someone else."

"He said something about wanting to get it done so that work could begin before the first snow."

"A valid point. We could get snow any time now, and the weather has started turning." She wondered how long she could make idle chit chat. She felt as if she was dying inside, and all she wanted to do was think of something else and figure out how she could let Charlie go.

"He told me privately he wanted to get this done, and get things settled into a routine so he would have more time to spend with you."

She smiled and gave a little nod. Apparently, Charlie had not explained to Elizabeth there might be a change in his plans. "That would be nice."

"Rebecca, what is wrong?"

"Oh, nothing. I am sure that, given time, it will work itself out." She drew a deep breath. "There is just so much to be done."

"Rebecca, look at me."

The blonde squared her shoulders and looked to the doctor. "Yes?"

Elizabeth looked at Rebecca very closely. There were deep shadows under her slightly bloodshot eyes. Her color was pallid, and there was a tiny tremor to her hands. "You are pushing yourself too hard. If you are not careful, you will be on my list of patients. I recommend a good meal or two and several naps."

Rebecca nodded. "Yes, of course, Doctor, I will see to it." She gave her friend a squeeze on the shoulder. "Thank you for your concern."

"So, do you want to tell me what has you not sleeping and eating properly?"

"You know, Elizabeth," Rebecca lied, "there is just so much work to be done. We have the refugees to care for and the Major to look after while he recovers."

Elizabeth looked with concern at her young friend. Something was amiss here, but she could not put her finger on it. Rebecca looked as though she was neither sleeping nor eating properly, and Charlie had simply looked like hell this morning. His eyes had a haunted look in them, and during breakfast he had kept looking with longing to the door or up toward the ceiling.

"Well, my dear, you will not be able to do anything if you push yourself to the point of illness."

"I promise to take care. As a matter of fact, I will go down now and see if Sarah might still have something to eat."

As the young woman turned to leave, Elizabeth watched her carefully. There was something in her stance, something in her walk that projected overwhelming sadness. For long moments after the door had closed, Elizabeth continued to stare at it. *Drat. I am going to have to talk to that man. Something here is very far from right.*

Rebecca stood on the back porch looking down toward the camp, wishing Charlie were home so they could talk. Then she considered that she had no right to say anything to him. She would just have to wait until he came to her.

The sight of Corporal Nailer brought a smile to her face as she waved to the young man. "Good morning, Duncan."

"Good m-mo-morning, Miss R-rebecca."

"And what are you up to on this brisk morning?"

"A-actually, Ma'am, I am h-here to c-collect Jeremiah. We are going f-fishing this m-m-morning to see if we can have f-fresh bass for d-dinner tonight."

"That is very kind of you to look after the boy like that."

"My p-pl-pleasure."

"You are a good man, Duncan."

The young soldier ducked his head as he tried to hide the blush. "T-th-thank you."

Rebecca jumped when the screen door banged shut and Jeremiah ran past her to his new friend. She chuckled at the boy's enthusiasm.

"Be good boys and have good luck. I am looking forward to fish for dinner tonight."

They both waved to her as they headed for the pond. She sipped her tea, aware of the warmth of it as it slid down her throat, and the coolness of the air, and the pain she was feeling. Finishing her tea, she returned to the house to see who needed tending this morning.

Rebecca left Montgomery's room once Constance had arrived to take over for a while. The young woman could not do a lot of the chores because of her condition, but sitting with the injured man was something she could do. Emily was napping and would be for at least an hour. Rebecca promised to take charge of the child when she woke.

She paused briefly at the top of the steps, feeling a bit dizzy. Steadying herself with the banister, she started down the stairs, but paused after the first few steps. She shook her head, feeling the room beginning to spin just a little. Then everything started to grow dim. A moment later, everything went dark.

Reg walked into the main hall, on his way to carry a load of wood to the back parlor. Miss Rebecca was lying in a crumpled heap at the foot of the stairs. "Oh Lord, Miss Rebecca!"

He looked around, then ran upstairs to find Doctor Elizabeth. He knew better than to try and move Miss Rebecca.

"Doctor 'Lizabeth. Doctor 'Lizabeth!" His cries roused everyone in the house.

Elizabeth rushed out of her consulting room. "What is it?"

"It is Miss Rebecca, Ma'am. She has fallen, and I am feared she is dead."

Elizabeth grabbed her black case and came charging out of the office, a grim look on her face. Reg danced behind her, wanting to help and not knowing how. They returned to the hall, where everyone was gathering. The children were crying at the furor, the adults were looking horrified and ineffectual.

Elizabeth dropped to her knees beside Rebecca's limp body and quickly checked her pulse and respiration. Both were thready, but reasonably normal.

She looked up at the gawking onlookers. "Get those children out of here and settle them down. Reg— you go find Colonel Polk and get Colonel Redmond back here immediately. Lizbet—go get her bed ready. Sarah, Beulah, go get two heavy blankets. I want you to put them together into a sling so we can get her upstairs without jostling her."

As people moved to fulfill Elizabeth's orders, the doctor carefully examined her patient. Nothing appeared to be broken, although Rebecca would have some spectacular bruises. The one that concerned her was the large lump and rapidly darkening bruise on her right temple.

The three women gently straightened Rebecca's limbs, moved her onto the makeshift stretcher, and transported her to her bedroom.

Reg ran into Polk's office at full speed, nearly taking the officer off his feet as they collided. "Whoa, boy! What is so urgent you cannot knock and enter properly?"

"Colonel Polk, Sir, it is Miss Rebecca. She has fallen and Doctor 'Lizabeth sent me to get you to get Colonel Charlie back here immediately."

"Easy, lad. Is Miss Rebecca going to be all right?"

"I swear I just do not know, Sir," the man wailed. "I thought she was dead there on the stairs."

"All right. Can you ride?"

"Yes, Sir. I ride good. Mr. Gaines used me to exercise the horses."

"Fine." Polk turned to his aide, Captain Harriman. "Get two

horses, one for you and one for Reg here. Saddle up for a hard, fast ride. Meet me at the Colonel's office, and I will be able to tell you where to go."

Polk hurried over to Charlie's office, where he knew his boss had been plotting his surveying trips. He hoped the maps were still on the desk. As he entered the office, he saw the maps on the staff table. With a sigh of relief, he looked them over and figured out Charlie's plan for the day.

As Harriman and Reg entered, he showed them the map. "Here, he was going to start at Fordsville, then Leon, Tryme, Novum, Reva, and then Griffinsburg and Pelham Manor. He left just after dawn this morning, so I would go directly to Reva, then either catch up or back track until you find him."

The two men nodded and set out at a hard pace.

Upstairs, Elizabeth finished her examination of Rebecca. Lizbet and Beulah made the young woman comfortable, stripping her of her daywear and putting her in a nightgown.

"Well, my dear, you did work yourself into a swivet. And unfortunately, I cannot let you just sleep." Gently, Elizabeth set about reviving the young woman. Slowly, Rebecca returned to awareness.

"Uh...steps..."

"Uh, steps indeed. I told you to go take a nap."

"What...what happened?"

"You fell. I would imagine your lack of food and sleep left you a bit dizzy. The rest, as they say, is history."

Rebecca raised her hand slowly to her throbbing head. "Hurts."

"I am sure. You have a lovely bruise and a nice little concussion. So now you will stay in bed, drink fluids, rest, and one of us will wake you every hour for a while, just to be annoying."

"Charlie..." She let her eyes close as a tear escaped from the corner of one.

"I have sent for him, dear." She wiped the tear from the young woman's cheek with a gentle thumb. "I expect him back within a couple of hours." Elizabeth fussed over Rebecca briefly. "And when he gets here, please be kind."

"Yes. But he is...busy."

"Rebecca, if I know Charlie like I think I do, what he has been doing is trying to control his own feelings. Remember what you told me about the night he went drinking with one of the men?"

"Yes."

"Well, if he is trying to get his desire for you under control, he might want to put a little distance between you. He may be embarrassed about that night."

Rebecca's eyes closed yet again, and she nodded. Her head hurt, and the thought that Charlie wanted distance made it hurt worse. "I understand."

"I honestly do not think you do, dear. I think our good Colonel, who has been so in control of his life for so long, is spinning very much out of control around you."

A long pause lay between them, and then Elizabeth added, "The problem is probably that he just cannot figure out how to keep his hands off you."

Rebecca turned teary eyes to her friend, smiled, and reached for her hand. "I love him so. I only want him to be happy."

Elizabeth soothed the hair back from Rebecca's bruised forehead. "And he loves you. I am very, very sure of that. I have never seen my old friend like this over anyone. And to be honest, I never expected to see it, either. I know you two will find a way to make your relationship work. Now, you rest. Close your eyes and I will keep watch and wake you in an hour."

～

Reg and Harriman rode like demons. They found Charlie and Jocko in Novum.

"Colonel Charlie!" Reg cried out as soon as he saw the tall man.

Charlie looked startled. "Reg, what is it?" The only reason the servant would be there was if something had happened at the house. "Is Miss Rebecca all right?"

"No, Colonel Charlie! She fell down the stairs, and Doctor Elizabeth sent me for you."

Before the words were out of Reg's mouth, Charlie was sprinting for Black Jack. He pulled himself up into the big stallion's saddle and shouted back at the three men standing behind him. "Follow as you can." Then he took off for home.

The miles melted under Black Jack's steady ground-eating gallop. Riding cross-country, Charlie arrived at the farm in slightly over an hour, covered in dust and Black Jack's lather.

Distraught, he flung himself out of the saddle and threw Black Jack's reins to some trooper; he did not notice who it was. Up the steps to the portico and through the door, he charged, barely stopping to drop his sword, hat, and gloves in the hall before he roared up the stairs to Rebecca's door. There he stopped, frozen, terrified of the worst. And since he had considered every possible scenario in his frantic ride home, he was already prepared to find her dying or even dead. *If she is, it is your fault, coward.* Carefully, he opened the door and slipped into the room.

Elizabeth rose as he entered. There was anguish and fear in his eyes. "Shush, Charlie. She is fine. Nothing that a few days of rest and some good food cannot fix. She has a mild concussion, and needs to be wakened every hour until tomorrow evening. Other than that, my dear, she is fine."

Timidly, Charlie asked, "May I see her?"

"Of course. I think it will do you both a world of good if you awaken her."

"But I am filthy. I should get cle..."

"So? She needs you, Charlie. Go to her."

Charlie approached the small, still figure in the big bed very timidly. He knelt next to the bed and stroked her cheek with his fingertips, and softly called her name. "Rebecca? Darling? Rebecca, honey, wake up, please?"

Slowly her eyes opened and she focused on him, smiling as soon as she realized he was real. "You came."

"Of course I came. Oh, honey, I am so sorry. Are you all right?"

She moaned a little and smiled as much as she could. "I love you, Charlie; please do not stay away..." She knew she could not hold the tears in her eyes. She just felt so bad, and the stress had finally become too much for her.

He swept her up into his arms and held her close. He cradled her head against his chest and softly rocked her. "My love, my dear heart, I did not mean to hurt you. I am right here, where I want to be; where I need to be...with you."

"Stay." She gripped his shirt. "I promise...to...do my best."

"Darling, you always do your best. Do you understand how much I love you? Do you know I cannot think straight when I am with you, that I dream of you during the day, that I want to touch you whenever I am near you, and when I touch you I want to hold you, and when I hold you it takes everything I am not to lie down and worship you?"

She cuddled into him. "I love you. I am sorry, for being silly. I thought you had decided against me and did not know how to tell me."

He laughed, a little, nervous, relieved sound. "My God, love, I am so sorry. I was having trouble trying to control myself." In a much lower voice, rich with hunger, he added, "I want you so much, I think I am going crazy sometimes. My hands itch with wanting to touch you. I promised to go at your pace, and I was afraid I was going to break my word to you. I ache with desire to worship and love you."

"Then let us agree to go at a natural pace, not mine. We will be together and whatever happens, happens because we love each other. I do not want you to be uncomfortable any more than you want me to be uncomfortable. But I do not like not being with you when we can, Charlie. Our time together right now is short. I want all the time we can manage."

"Then you shall have me every minute I can spare from my command." He kissed her very softly. "Now, Elizabeth tells me you need to rest, and I know I need to clean up. I will be back and wake you again in an hour, darling."

She held his hand almost afraid to let him go. "I love you, Charlie."

Charlie looked deep into her eyes. "I love you, Rebecca. With all that I am, I love you. Rest, my love."

Charlie held her hand and stroked her head until she slipped back into a gentle sleep, then he hurried down to the bathing room where someone had thoughtfully filled the tub with warm water and laid out some clean clothing for him. He quickly scrubbed the sweat and dirt from his body and pulled the clean clothes on, all the while listening to the voice in his head berating him.

Look at yourself, Charlie. You tell her you love her, promise to be there for her, and the first thing you do is you run away and hurt her. But then, is that not what you always do, Charlie? Run away. If you cannot handle a situation that is painful or frustrating, you run away. You ran away from your father, you ran away from your home, you ran away from who you really are, and now you are running away from her just because you cannot keep your libido in check. You are a coward, Charlie Redmond. And if you stay with her, what are you going to do? Hum? I can tell you what you are going to do. You are going to keep running away, you are going to keep hurting her. You know why? Because that is what you always do.

Charlie shook his head and argued with the voice. Alone, his old habit of talking out loud to himself returned. "No, that is not how it is. I needed to do the survey of the county. And I needed a little space. The worst thing I did here was I did not think —"

That is exactly right. You did not think. You never do. You just run when things get too uncomfortable for you to handle. Oh, sure, you are physically brave. That is why you are such a good soldier—because you do not think there, either. You do not think about what might happen, you just plod along doing what the commanders tell you to, and watching men and boys get hurt and killed.

"Oh, no. You cannot say that. There are too many times when I have gone against orders or found innovative ways to follow them that have saved lives, not taken them." Slowly, it was dawning on Charlie that every so often, the bitter voice in his head was simply wrong. Could it be the voice was wrong about Rebecca and him? Charlie was beginning to have a glimmer of hope. "Enough. I did something that was foolish, but not evil. And maybe in relationships, things happen that are painful at the time. But we can talk, and work things out, because what we have together is more important than the hurt of the moment.

You tell yourself that, Charlie-boy. You tell yourself she can really love a pervert like you. That she can withstand the hurt you will give her in her life with your lies and your running away. And when she leaves you because loving you hurts too much, then you tell me I was wrong.

Just then Charlie heard a ruckus in the entrance hall. He emerged, towel still in hand, dressed in trousers, shirt and vest, barefoot and irate that someone would make noise that might disturb Rebecca. It was Polk, along with Harriman, Jocko, and Reg, finally having returned from Novum.

He gave them all a baleful eye. "Quiet. You will disturb her."

Jocko spoke up. "So, is Miss Rebecca all right, Sir? We were all worried."

"Miss Rebecca is fine. She has a mild concussion and is resting. Go get cleaned up. Jocko, please check on Black Jack; I rode him rather hard. Now, off with you all. We will speak tomorrow." With that, Charlie stalked back upstairs, leaving them whispering among themselves.

Reg volunteered to go check with Beulah and find out the real story. The other three retired to the front steps to share a cigar and wait for word. The report was soon delivered, at least, the bare bones. Harriman looked at a loss, but Polk and Jocko each vowed to do whatever he could to lessen the load on Miss Rebecca. She had taken on caring for so many of them, that they could only return the service.

Slipping into the bedroom, Charlie stood at the side of the bed, gazing down on her sleeping form, so innocent in repose, and marred by the purple bruise on her forehead. His mind went to the bruises Mr. Gaines had placed on that small body in anger, and the voice in his head started up again.

Gaines battered her in anger. Look at her face. You batter her with your fear. Is one any less painful than the other?

He knelt beside the bed and pressed her hand to his lips, almost in a prayer. "I promise you, my love, I will do everything in my power to keep from hurting you again. I know I will not always be successful. I know going back to war in the spring will be agony for both of us, but I have no choice. I can promise to do my best to be safe and to come back to you whole. And I can promise I will always let you know what I am thinking and feeling, so you will worry as little as possible." He arose and gently began waking her again.

In a sleepy voice, she responded. "Charlie?"

"Yes, love. I am right here."

"Ummm, come hold me, please."

He shed his vest and slipped into bed, clad in trousers and shirt. He settled her body against his shoulder and went through the short series of tests Elizabeth had said she needed to have administered hourly.

Warm and safe again, Rebecca slipped back into sleep as soon as he allowed her to. For the rest of the night, Charlie held her, awake and caring, rousing her every hour to check for any sign of damage from the concussion.

Friday, December 9, 1864

Around dawn, Elizabeth entered, to find him valiantly fighting sleep, still holding the sleeping woman in his arms.

"How is she?"

"She seems all right. The headache is easing, and her vision seems to be fine." He smiled appreciatively at his old friend, and slid out from under Rebecca so Elizabeth could conduct her examination. As Charlie moved, Rebecca grew restless, whimpering in her sleep and clearly looking for something. He smiled gently and a bit humbly; Elizabeth stifled a laugh. Her examination was quick but thorough.

"My friend, she is doing fine. With a little sleep, she will be as good as new. I would say that it is time for you to get some sleep, as well. Richard has things well in hand, I am sure."

Charlie nodded and walked Elizabeth to the door. He stripped off his trousers, and crawled back into bed wearing his shirt and underwear. The two curled around one another, and sleep took them both until early afternoon.

Rebecca woke first, happy to be cradled in Charlie's long arms. She lay there quietly, her eyes closed, savoring the feelings of safety and peace she felt when they were wrapped together like this. Slowly, she opened her eyes and looked up into Charlie's face. Even sleeping, his features showed the stress of the past day; a slight frown cut a furrow between his heavy eyebrows. In the slanting afternoon light that slipped between the edges of the curtains, she could see the fine, silver hairs that were starting to mark his temples. Her slight movements were enough to awaken him; he looked back into her eyes with all of the love and concern she ever hoped to see.

"Good morning, sleepyhead, or should I say good afternoon?"

"Good afternoon, my noble pillow. I am glad you got some sleep, dear."

"How is your head this afternoon?"

"A bit tender, and I still have a touch of a headache, but otherwise, not too bad."

"And the rest of you, dear?"

"The rest is probably a bit tender, too, but I am too comfortable here with you to really notice it."

"Then, obviously, you must stay where you are most comfortable." Charlie settled his arms around her more securely to reinforce his offer.

They spoke of little things: their dreams for the time after the war of building a great stud farm; of having a home that would be open to their friends, a gracious place where all would be welcome; of having a life together that suited them both. Their talk turned to their pasts, as Rebecca spoke of the time before the war and of the horse farm on which her parents had raised her. Finally, she asked Charlie how a raw recruit had become a career officer.

"That, my love, was a matter of sheer luck. And perhaps a case of being in the wrong place at the wrong time. It was Mexico. There were forty-seven hundred men serving under Zachary Taylor. Santa Ana, with twenty thousand troops, backed us into this maze of canyons the locals called Buena Vista. There were lots of little dead ends and no obvious way out. The cliffs that bordered them were sheer, and looked too high to climb. Just to make matters worse, it was raining, and the cliffs were slick with mud. But climb them we did, using ladders and ropes, mostly. Through the night, we climbed, mostly in the dark, with our work lit by occasional flashes of lightning and the fires from Santa Ana's camp reflecting off the clouds. I had made sergeant by then, and our lieutenant had been killed in the skirmishes that backed us into that hole in the first place. A captain came by and appointed me acting lieutenant in his place. We abandoned the horses, and used pulleys to haul some light artillery up the cliffs. By morning, most of our troops were hidden up on top of the canyon walls. When Santa Ana's troops entered the canyon, intending to cut us down, we let loose on them. Santa Ana signaled a withdrawal. They said I had served well, and confirmed my brevet as permanent. They even sent me to school at the Academy. Now that was an experience, let me tell you."

"The Academy?"

"Yes, up at The Point."

"You graduated from West Point?"

"Yes. A couple of the junior officers convinced General Taylor and General Scott I was officer material, so when the war was over in 1848, they sent me. It was rather strange, actually. I was a bit older than most of the boys at the school, and I had already seen action. So they gave me a private room, thank God, for I am not sure how I would have handled things for the time I was there if they had not done so. They let me take extra classes instead of summer encampment, because I had already seen action, so I went through the curriculum in three years instead of four. When I graduated, the Commandant gave me the rank of captain, since I had gone in as a lieutenant. All in all, it was a good time for me."

"You must know just about all of the officers in the Army, then."

"My dear, between the Mexican War and this conflict, the career officers could all fit in this house for a party. I think we all know one another, either because we were at school together, fought together in Mexico, or served together at one point or another. I think that may be part of why this war has been so terrible. We do know one another, and to some extent, we can anticipate what the other side will do because of that. It is very hard to fight against men you have known for twenty years as comrades in arms." Charlie grew silent, lost again in the pain of this war. He had served under Lee, had gone to school with Early, taken classes from Grant and Jackson. These men were his friends, and to some extent, the only family he knew. Now, they prepared to face one another across the final battle lines.

Rebecca gathered him into her arms, just holding him, trying to ease the bleakness that thoughts of the war and of his friends on both sides had brought to his soul. "Someday," she whispered, "it will be over. And we will be able to rebuild at least some of what we have lost."

CHAPTER 15

Saturday, December 10, 1864

As Charlie slipped out the door after lunch, little Em tried to follow him, which resulted in the little girl falling and scraping her hand and knee. Her cries grew louder as she cried for Papa while shaking her hand.

Rebecca, who had been watching Charlie's departure, was quick to scoop her up and take her to the kitchen to get her calmed down and cleaned up. The child sniffed and wanted to continue with her fit, but under Rebecca's loving care, she found it very difficult.

She did, however, continue to look toward the door for Charlie. "Papa gone," she sniffed, watching as Rebecca cleaned her knee with a warm cloth.

"Papa will be back for supper, Em. He has work to do."

"Work?"

Rebecca chuckled and turned the little hand over to clean its palm. "Yes, Papa work."

Em looked to her hand, then to Rebecca, and she raised it. "Kiss."

"Of course." Rebecca planted a tender kiss on the little hand. "Better?"

She was rewarded with a hug around her neck. The child yawned and fussed with her scraped hand, then started playing with a ribbon on Rebecca's dress while leaning against her knee. It was obvious that Em was struggling to keep her eyes open.

"Sleepy, Em?"

"Em not sweepy."

"I think maybe you are. I am. Let us go up for a nap, little one. Your mama is already napping; you can lay down with her." She picked the child up, cuddling her close as she made her way upstairs.

After Em was safely tucked in with Constance, Rebecca went to check on Montgomery. Samuelson was with him when she entered the room. She crossed to the bed and sat down on the opposite side of the bed from the orderly. Then she took Montgomery's hand. "Major? Major Montgomery? Sir, if you can hear me, squeeze my hand."

She looked down at his hand in hers and waited. She sighed and looked to Samuelson. "If you dare tell on me for what I am about to do, I will..."

"Ma'am?" Samuelson had a bemused look on his face, having no idea what Miss Rebecca was planning.

Rebecca turned her attention back to Montgomery. "Major, Colonel Redmond wanted me to pass along to you that you have done enough lollygagging in the infirmary, and it is time for you to get back to your command."

She waited again, then smiled when she felt a tentative squeeze to her hand. Samuelson's eyes went wide as he saw her reaction. "It worked?"

"So it would seem." She patted the man's hand. "I will go tell Dr. Walker."

She left the room, going to Elizabeth's examination room. The doctor was in the process of trying to get a small boy of about five to open his mouth so she could finish her examination. "Now come on, Marko, open up and let me see why your throat is hurting."

With lips clamped firmly shut, the boy shook his head. Rebecca chuckled and joined Elizabeth. She knelt down and placed her hands on the boy's legs. "Marko, do you like horehound drops?"

He regarded her cautiously, and then nodded.

"If you let Dr. Walker look at your throat, I will take you to the kitchen and we will find you a couple. I think I remember seeing Sarah tucking a few away."

His eyes lit up. "Really?"

But it was too late. The moment he opened his mouth, Elizabeth stuck the depressor in and had her look. When she was finished, she smiled at the boy. "Now that was not too bad, was it?"

"No, Ma'am."

"All right, young Marko, my prescription for your ailment is two horehound drops and some hot tea. I think Miss Rebecca can take it from here." She helped him out of the chair and handed him over to Rebecca.

"Anything serious?" the blonde asked Elizabeth while holding his hand

"No, just a little raw from the influenza everyone had. He will be fine."

"Good. I will just take Marko down to Sarah. I just saw Major Montgomery. He is starting to respond, and I think you may wish to look in on him."

"Really? Thank you for letting me know. I will check in on him directly."

Once Marko was settled, Rebecca then tended to everyone else, making sure the chores were getting done and nothing was being left undone. She joined a few of the ladies in the washroom and spent close to two hours helping with the washing of linens. She took a full basket outside to the line and had just started hanging them, when she looked up to find Charlie walking toward the house from camp.

"Hello, love. Why, pray tell, are you out here hanging laundry? Do I need to get more servants?"

"No, you do not, my dear. I am hanging laundry because it needed to be done and everyone else is occupied with runny noses and chamber pots." She gave him a little grin. "Considering my options, I chose laundry."

"I just spent twenty four hours sitting up with you because you worked yourself to collapse. I will not have that happening again."

She straightened up from the laundry basket and smiled at him. "My, my, Colonel Redmond, you certainly are solid in that opinion. What would you have me do, let these people sleep on dirty linens?"

He swept her into his arms in a very protective embrace. "I would have you tell me when the work is too much and let me get you more help. You, my dear, are the mistress of this house. Your job is to supervise."

She chuckled, running her hands over his shoulders and giving him a kiss on the cheek. "I love you, Charlie, but the fact remains that right now we do not have a spare pair of hands, and the laundry still needs to be hung. So, unless you want to do it," she gave him a wink, "you had better let me get back to it, so I can wash up before supper is on the table."

Charlie pulled off his riding gloves, stuffed them in his belt, grinned, and started pinning linens to the line. "As I said, I will do it myself rather than have you back in bed from exhaustion."

She laughed and pulled the linen from his hand. "Charles Redmond, you are the master of this house, and I will not have you doing woman's work. Good Lord, Charlie, what would your men say if they saw you hanging laundry? Sergeant Jackson would never let you forget it." She gave him a playful look that dared him to challenge her. Then she reached up and ran her fingers through his hair. "You need a haircut. I will tend to that after supper. Now really,

Charlie, I promise this will be the last thing I do today, and I am yours for the rest of the evening. Perhaps we can see if Colonel Polk and Elizabeth would like to play whist this evening."

Charlie smiled down at her. "A haircut, humm. All right, on one condition."

"Yes?"

"We let Richard and Elizabeth entertain themselves tonight and the two of us spend a little time together."

"Will you hold me in your arms and read poetry to me?" She looked at him with total adoration

"I will. And stroke your back and tenderly kiss you, as well. A right, proper romantic evening."

"Why, Colonel Redmond, you do know how to turn a simple country girl's head. Sounds wonderful. We have a date. I think the haircut can wait until tomorrow."

To set the mood, Charlie immediately launched into quoting one of his favorites, the English courtier, soldier, and poet, Philip Sidney.

Loving in truth, and fain in verse my love to show,
That she, dear she, might take some pleasure of my pain,
Pleasure might cause her read, reading might make her know,
Knowledge might pity win, and pity grace obtain —
I sought fit words to paint the blackest face of woe;
Studying inventions fine, her wits to entertain,
Oft turning others' leaves to see if thence would flow
Some fresh and fruitful showers upon my sun-burned brain.
But words came halting forth, wanting invention's stay;
Invention, nature's child, fled step-dame Study's blows,
And others' feet still seemed but strangers in my way.
Thus, great with child to speak, and helpless in my throes,
Biting my truant pen, beating myself for spite,
Fool, said my muse to me, look in thy heart and write.

～

Charlie was preparing the fire in the rear parlor, having just dismissed Beulah after giving her authorization to bring another three members of her family up to work at the farm. Colonel Polk knocked, and then entered the room. "Charlie, do you have a minute?"

The commander's shoulders slumped; he had promised the evening to Rebecca and really did not want to go back on that promise. "What do you need, Richard?"

"I promise you it will only take a minute or two. I have reports you need to see before I dispatch them."

"All right." Charlie joined him at the door just as Rebecca came in. "Dear, I have one small thing to tend to, then I will be right in, I promise."

She smiled and caressed his cheek. "All right, Charlie." She then looked to his friend. "Do not keep him too long, Colonel Polk."

"No, Miss Rebecca. It will only take a minute."

"Very well. You know, Charlie, I think I will meet you upstairs," she told him with a twinkle in her eye that gave him great pause.

"All right. I will be up directly." Trying not to think about it, he turned to his Second-in-Command. "Come on, Polk."

Once the men had left, Rebecca adjourned upstairs. She found her orders had been followed precisely, and by the fire in their room sat a tray with hot tea and sweet rolls. She finished preparing the room, and when she was satisfied, she had a rather nice little spot created by the fire.

Spreading a couple of heavy Army blankets, she covered them with the quilt from the bed to take some of the hardness from the floor. Then she changed her clothes and slipped into her robe. After that, she took her hair down and gave it a quick but thorough brushing, so it flowed freely over her shoulders. Then she sat down near the fire and waited.

~

Charlie and Polk adjourned to the office for a brief review of Polk's reports to the Quartermaster General.

Charlie shook his head. "I swear, I believe these idiots are using the war just to get rich. The quality of some of these woolens is such that I would not give them to slaves. Flaws, holes even. How do they expect us to keep an army moving on this garbage?"

"I do not make the stuff; I just complain about it."

"Well then, keep complaining." Charlie signed the documents, then said, "If there is nothing else?"

"No. Go spend time with your lady. I would say she has something planned for you."

Charlie smiled contentedly as he walked back to the rear parlor. Rebecca was no longer there, and the fire was banked. Smiling in anticipation of spending quiet time alone with his lady, he mounted the stairs to their room. Opening the door, he looked into the sitting room. No Rebecca. But the door to their bedroom was cracked, and there was a soft light coming through. He stepped into the room and was confronted with the most beautiful vision. There she was, dressed in a soft robe, her hair loose and shining around her shoulders. His chest went tight; his hands itched to touch her. He took a deep breath and let it out slowly, trying to get a little control over his suddenly pounding pulse. "My love, you are beautiful."

She smiled and ran her hand over the blanket. "I dare you come over here and tell me that." She gave the floor next to her a pat. "I have something sweet over here, and you did promise me a romantic evening."

Charlie ran his finger under his collar to loosen it a bit, then walked over and settled onto the quilt next to Rebecca. "My love, you are beautiful," he repeated, answering her challenge. He lifted her hand to his lips, then turned his head and caressed it with his cheek.

"And you are the most charming, handsome thing I have ever seen." She leaned over and gave him a tender kiss.

Her lips left his, and for a moment, he remained immobile, his eyes closed, savoring and memorizing the silken warmth that had touched him. When he did open them, Rebecca was looking into eyes that were the silver of the moon on a summer night.

"Would you get out of your uniform, Charlie? We should both be comfortable this evening." She ran her finger down his cheek. "I have plans for you, dear man."

"What would you like me to put on, dear? You know I am yours tonight, and every night for the rest of my life."

She tugged at the button of his tunic. "I do not care what you wear, but this," she tugged again, "is far too much cloth between us."

Charlie choked a little at her suggestion. He needed to know more of what she wanted. "Just the jacket, or should I put on my nightshirt and robe?"

She chuckled at his apparent nervousness. "Get ready for bed, Charlie. I promise I will not bite."

Unlike their normal routine, where Rebecca afforded him some privacy as he transformed, he could feel her eyes burning into his shoulder blades. A blush started at the tips of his ears and burned its way down his body. Slowly, he removed his cravat and unbuttoned his shirt, sliding it off his shoulders. The wrappings around his chest came off, freeing both his small breasts and the woman under the disguise. The transformation from male to female was almost complete.

He slipped her breeches and underwear off, and pulled a clean, white nightshirt over his head. Donning the robe, he tied the belt. Charlie turned to look at Rebecca's face, unsure if the woman by the fire wanted who he was now.

Rebecca held her hand out. "My beautiful Charlie."

Charlie let go of his breath in a soft sigh, retrieved a little book from the pocket of the tunic, and returned to sit beside Rebecca. He was feeling a little shy and a lot hopeful.

"Charlie," Rebecca dipped her head just a bit before looking back to her companion, "I am not really in the mood for poetry at the moment." She gave him a beguiling smile.

Very gently, Charlie covered Rebecca's hand with his own much larger one. "What are you in the mood for, sweetheart?"

Her blush deepened, and her smile grew wider from embarrassment. "I was hoping, maybe we could, well…" She looked up. "Well, I really want to explore a few things with you."

Charlie's blush matched Rebecca's, but he moved gamely forward. In a voice made husky with sudden wanting, he responded, "I am always here, always open to anything you want. Ask, and if I am capable, it is yours."

"Are you sure? I do not want to make you uncomfortable, but I think it is time for me to learn more about the feelings I have when I am with you, feelings I have never felt before."

Rebecca felt a fine tremor pass through Charlie's body. What Charlie wanted was to take Rebecca in his arms; to make Rebecca scream with pleasure; to hear his own name cried out in that moment when the universe exploded into a myriad of crystal rainbows. "Darling, my heart, my soul, and my body are all yours to do with as you wish."

She nodded her understanding. "I have a confession to make. Before I got sick, there was a night when you came to bed. You thought I was asleep, but, well, I was not." Rebecca leaned in and kissed Charlie again. "It was that night these feelings began stirring, and I have had them every day since; and they only get stronger with each passing day." She kissed him yet again. "I am told it is because you excite me, Charlie."

Charlie drew a deep breath, in part to quell the embarrassment at knowing Rebecca had listened as he eased the ache between his thighs that night. Then Rebecca's words soaked into Charlie's brain. *I excite her?* Charlie drew Rebecca into her arms and gently returned the kisses. "And you excite me beyond words, my love."

Rebecca's breath caught in her throat as she felt Charlie's hands on her and the sensations started in her body with a vengeance. "I want to explore a little." She tentatively ran her hand over the outside of Charlie's thigh. "I need to touch you, Charlie." The tremor ran deeper; Rebecca could feel it under her fingers.

"I am yours."

It was just a breath against her ear, but she could hear it down to her soul. "I am not sure how far this will go, you do understand that? And I certainly do not want to tease you, so if you would rather not, I will understand." She stilled her hand on his leg until she received an answer, because she really had no desire to make him miserable.

At the moment, Charlie did not care where the exploration went. All that was important was that Rebecca was touching him. He swallowed convulsively and repeated, "I am yours. However you want me."

Rebecca smiled and took another kiss. She slid her hand up Charlie's side, then to his shoulder, until she started back down the front of his robe. She paused in her movements just as her hand reached the slight swell of Charlie's breast. She broke the kiss and looked to him for permission.

His eyes were silvered with desire; he could not control his body's reactions. Still he looked at Rebecca and shyly smiled and nodded.

The small woman slowly let her hand travel the rest of the way. Touching Charlie's body was delightful, and she was truly glad she decided to explore her desires. Her hand lingered at Charlie's breast and then slowly closed over it, feeling it and learning the feel of his body. She moved her hand and slid it under Charlie's robe, needing to get still closer.

With her free hand, she placed Charlie's hand on her own hip. "It is all right, Charlie, I need your touch, too," she whispered, feeling a little nervous.

Charlie's breathing was rapid and shallow. His eyelids fluttered to half closed as Rebecca's fingers closed around his always sensitive breast. Charlie could feel his nipples tightening until they ached. Charlie's hand gently stroked up Rebecca's side, a long, sensuous stroke that traced from her hip, along her waist, up her ribs and came to rest with Charlie's thumb stroking the tender skin beneath her breast. "You are so beautiful."

His words and his touch sent chills all through Rebecca's body. "God, Charlie, I have never felt anything like this before. It feels so good." She brushed her thumb over Charlie's hardened nipple. She realized her own were becoming erect and very sensitive.

Charlie's body curled around the hand that was driving him insane. Each stroke of Rebecca's thumb sent lightning bolts through his body. Charlie dropped his head to Rebecca's shoulder and tenderly kissed her neck.

Rebecca's head moved to the side giving Charlie as much room as he needed to nibble and caress the hollow of Rebecca's throat. A soft moan left Rebecca's lips, and her eyes slid shut. Rebecca felt dizzy. Knowing that sitting upright for much longer was not an option, she began lying back, making sure to hold tight to Charlie. "Yes," she moaned again.

Charlie slid his arm under Rebecca's shoulders and eased her down to the quilt. Never taking his lips from the throat and shoulder, Charlie softly covered Rebecca's body with his own.

"I love you, Charlie," Rebecca gasped, as she tugged on the belt of Charlie's robe and slipped it from his shoulders. "Tell me how to please you."

"My love, my love. Anything." Charlie slid his hand around Rebecca's breast. "Just touch me. Hold me."

She moved to Charlie's neck and began exploring there with her lips. She loved the feel of the soft skin under her lips. It amazed her how loving and tender this was, and how much she wanted to be here with him. Her.

Rebecca's touches were first tentative, then tender and intimate. They drove Charlie to the point of no return. "Oh, God, please, please," Charlie moaned. Charlie's wrapped his hands around Rebecca's shoulders, holding on for dear life. He buried his head against Rebecca's shoulder. "Please."

"Yes, Charlie, it is all right, my love," she whispered in his ear. "I have you, darling, let go. I will protect you."

For a moment or an eternity, Charlie lay rigid in Rebecca's arms as the universe exploded through his body. Then he sank, boneless, onto Rebecca's shoulder. Reverent, shattered, Charlie whispered in Rebecca's ear. "Oh, God. Oh, love."

Rebecca's arms wrapped around him and she sighed to herself, quite satisfied she had pleased Charlie. "I love you," she whispered. "I will never love another like I love you."

Charlie was embarrassed. "I am sorry. I did not want to startle you or push you too much. It is just that every night I have held you and wanted you and... I love you so much, Rebecca," and in a smaller voice, "I need you so much."

"Shhh..." she comforted her, gently stoking his back and combing fingers through hair that still needed to be cut. " I wanted this, too, Charlie. I wanted to know if I could please you, make you happy. You have helped me understand a great deal tonight with your gentleness and your patience."

"Patience? You touch me and... It was unlike anything I have ever felt before, dear heart."

Rebecca worked her way from under Charlie and shifted until she was lying in his arms, her head resting on his shoulder and her hand slowly tracing over his stomach. "I just needed to know I could please you. That I would be enough for you." She did not quite know how to explain her feelings. She cuddled closer, feeling Charlie's arms tighten around her. "I felt like such a failure in my marriage. My husband did not desire me. He did not love me, and I never pleased him." She fought hard against the tears that wanted to spill.

Charlie hugged her close when he felt rather than heard the sob Rebecca choked back. "Mr. Gaines was a fool. You are amazing, dear woman. Your compassion, kindness, and ability to give of yourself in these uncertain times when it would be easy to turn your back on all those around you is astounding."

"I think you are biased."

"My dear, I am very biased. You are beautiful, and I desire you very deeply. Your touch excites me, your kisses set me on fire, and now I find I have not the strength to resist you even for a moment when you hold me and want me."

"I will admit that I was confused and unsure of it all. But when I opened my eyes and you were there, everything became so clear. I realized I could never find what I have with you with anyone else. I intend to hold on to you forever."

"I will be yours for the rest of my life, dear. But what confused you, love?"

"All of it. You were here and so charming, wonderful and kind. You were what I dreamed of for a life and a home. But, Charlie, you have to admit that ours is not a conventional relationship. I had to know and understand that. That everything I wondered about just did not matter. I love you; it matters not to me that you are a woman under your disguise. But I had to find that. I had to understand that it just does not matter to me."

"What convinced you, darling? I have always thought that because I was not what I seemed, that I was something that our society reviles, I thought I would spend my life alone. You are a miracle to me."

She sighed and pulled herself up to look into Charlie's eyes. "I cannot tell you what it was. Maybe it was your kindness, your tenderness, your fierce loyalty to service and duty." She shook her head. "I do not know. All I do know is that whatever it was, I have fallen head over heels for you. I cannot wait for our life to really begin together. I will be proud to take your name and call myself your wife."

"And my gender? What of that, dear? You know there are things I can never give you, things that most men do not even have to think twice about."

"I assume, my dear, you are speaking of children? You should know that if we want them badly enough, and are faithful, one way or another, we will be blessed with children. But if having children should never come to pass, I will still happily live my life with you. You are my family now, Charlie. All that I have. All that I want."

"Rebecca, my love. You are the family, the love I dreamed of and thought I could never have. You are the miracle in my life."

"Then it seems that we have everything we need." She giggled and poked him in the ribs. "Maybe one of these days I will even live down the stigma of having married a Yankee."

Charlie rolled over onto his back and covered his eyes. "Ah, the shame of it all."

Rebecca chuckled and pulled Charlie's hand from his eyes. "I am sure I will survive it."

Charlie rolled onto his side so he could look directly at Rebecca. "Are you really? You know, it could get unpleasant." He stroked Rebecca's cheek. "I do not ever want to cause any unpleasantness for you."

The blonde ran her hand down Charlie's arm. "My dear, I have survived a war. Nothing can be as unpleasant as that. I believe our life together will be wonderful."

The gentle stroke raised goose bumps on Charlie's skin. His voice became husky again. "What of you, dear heart? As much pleasure as your touch brings me, I would love to give you that pleasure also."

Rebecca shivered at the thought and smiled. "Charlie, what I want from you right now is to be with you. I love you, and I want to experience everything you have to offer; but I must admit I am nervous. No one has ever touched my heart and my body like you do."

Very gently, Charlie stroked Rebecca's arm, caressing the tender skin on the inside of her elbow and wrist with just the tips of his fingers. "I am right here, love. All you have to do is ask me, and if I do something you are not comfortable with, then you must tell me straightaway. I would never want to hurt or frighten you."

She nodded, a nervous smile still playing on her lips. "I have a question for you."

"Anything, love."

"The other night...when you...well..." She had the good grace to truly blush and look away for a moment. "How often do you do that?"

Charlie blushed from the roots of his hair to the tips of his toes. He laid his head down on Rebecca's shoulder and rested his hand gently on her hip. In a choked whisper, he finally figured out how to answer. "I used to do it occasionally, usually when being lonely got too bad. Now, um... when the need to touch you and be touched by you gets to be more than I can handle without breaking my word to you." He lay there, expecting her to draw away.

She sighed and held Charlie as close as she could. "I just wondered. I have never...uh...well, I have not."

Charlie ran his hand from Rebecca's hip, up her ribs until his thumb again rested on the tender skin under her breast. "What do you feel, dear heart? You talk about 'these feelings,' so tell me about them."

She gave a small nervous laugh. "My heart beats faster, my stomach flutters wildly, and I get a warm feeling all over my body."

Charlie traced small circles on the very sensitive skin with his thumb. "Does this bother you?"

She released soft sigh and her eyes closed slowly. "No. Not at all."

"Tell me what you feel. Tell me what you want."

"I feel warm all over. My heart is beating so hard I feel light headed..." She licked her lips, trying to breathe normally, "I do not know what I want. I have never been asked."

Softly, Charlie caressed her body through the thin material of Rebecca's nightgown. "You can use your imagination, love; and if you find you do not like something, tell me."

Rebecca gasped softly. "I do not know anything other than being..." She stopped, refusing to say the word. She knew Charlie would never hurt her as she had been hurt before, but still she had no idea of what brought her pleasure; and she was afraid this fact would disgust Charlie. Fear was starting to war with the new feelings of arousal.

Charlie stopped immediately. "Tell me, love. I want to know. I need to know what you are feeling, and more importantly, what you are afraid of."

Rebecca noticed immediately that Charlie had stopped touching her. She smiled and tried not to look disappointed. "My husband never cared how I felt. Never cared that he hurt me. Never tried to be tender. I am afraid I really do not know much about the more intimate matters of life. Especially with someone like you, who is so kind and gentle with me." She laughed a little. "If you came in, pushed me to the bed and did what you would, that I would understand."

Softly, Charlie started stroking Rebecca's cheek, neck, and shoulder. "I want to come to you with gentleness, and with all my love and tenderness. I want to gently explore every inch of your body. Then I want to bring you to the absolute height of physical excitement and passion, so that at least for a moment, you will know how much I love you, how much my heart and soul and body long to be linked to yours"

"And I want that so much. I am just afraid I will not please you."

Gently but firmly, Charlie drew Rebecca's face so she had to look into his eyes. "There is nothing you can possibly do that will not please me. All you have to do is touch me and a fire runs through me. You kiss me, and I ache for you. When you entwine our bodies together, so close, so sweet, I soar to heaven."

"Is there not some part of you that would like to have a wife who is more versed in loving? Who is not terrified that she is going to do something wrong? I am truly damaged goods, Charlie."

He dropped his head and very gently kissed directly over Rebecca's heart. "I want no one other than you. And you, I want very much. You are no more damaged goods than any other woman with no experience of loving. Few women have experience in loving another woman. I think I would like to try and heal the hurt he dealt you, sweetheart."

Charlie slipped his arm around Rebecca's shoulders and drew her close, so the length of his body fit against Rebecca's from shoulder to ankle. He left his hand resting motionless on Rebecca's breast. "I am right here, love."

"I know." She placed a kiss on Charlie's neck. "Thank you. Are you sure this is all right?"

"I am very, very sure. I would spend my whole life just holding you, if that is what you need."

She snuggled closer, wrapping herself around him. "I am going to need more. I am just not sure what that is. I know it sounds silly."

They lay facing one another, with Charlie holding the smaller woman tenderly in the crook of his arm. With his free hand, Charlie gently caressed Rebecca's body, carefully avoiding the obvious places, and focusing on her arms, back, and shoulders. He placed soft kisses all over Rebecca's face. "Be gentle. This is the safest place in the world. Let yourself enjoy my body touching yours."

Rebecca nodded and gave Charlie a kiss. "All right. I trust you."

Charlie's hand continued to stroke gently. "Are you all right?"

"Oh yes, now that I know I am supposed to feel this way," she whispered in his ear. "I am all right."

"You are very all right, my love." Charlie continued to hold and caress her, gently, tenderly; hoping his gentleness and undemanding love would be the healing for the injuries this gentle woman had sustained.

CHAPTER 16

Monday, December 12, 1864

"Charlie, sit down."

He looked at the chair she had placed on the back porch. "Umm, Rebecca, dear heart, you know Jocko usually tends to these things for me: shaving, haircuts, you know, the basics."

"Yes, I know; and I also know eventually the good sergeant will not be around to do it and you will just have to trust your wife to tend to these things. Now sit."

He continued looking at the chair, but made no movement toward it.

She approached and waved the scissors under his nose. "What is the matter Colonel Redmond, do you not trust me?" she teased. "Surely, an Federal Army Colonel is not afraid of a tiny Southern woman with a pair of scissors."

"No, of course not, dear. It is just that I have certain ways I like things, and Jocko knows them." The look on her face made it clear that his preferences and old habits were not a sufficient excuse. "And I have invited Jocko to come back with me when the war is over."

"Yes, and I am sure he will have more important things to do than cut your hair. Now sit down, Charlie." She pointed to the chair with the tip of the scissors. "I assure you I know how to cut a gentleman's hair. I did it for my brother and my husband, and I did not scalp either of them."

"Yes, Ma'am." Charlie capitulated meekly and sat down.

Rebecca chuckled and settled a towel around his shoulders. "The way you are acting, you would think I planned to lop off your ears." She picked up a comb and began running it through his hair.

"No, dear, it is not my ears I am concerned about."

"Then what would it be?" She pulled a length of hair between her fingers and made the first cut.

"Um. My reserve? My sense of propriety? My ability to keep my hands off you?"

She laughed, making another cut. "Good Lord, Charlie, I am cutting your hair. How could you possibly find that in any way intimate?" She leaned over and whispered in his ear. "Now, if we were in our room..."

"My dear, just being this close to you and having you run your fingers through my hair is seriously distracting."

"Think of something else. Think about putting up a tent or better yet, sitting down to a lovely Sunday tea with Mrs. Williams."

He chuckled, making very sure to hold his head still. After all, she was holding a large pair of very sharp scissors. "You certainly do know how to dampen a fellow's ardor, my dear."

"Hopefully, I will learn how to build it as well." She made another cut just as Jocko rounded the corner.

The Irishman stopped in mid step, his eyes went wide, and he laughed. "Well now, what do we have here, Colonel C?"

Charlie ignored Jocko for a moment to respond to Rebecca. "You do, my dear, you already do."

He then looked at his batman with a slightly sour look on his face. "Obviously, a haircut. She felt that you had failed to tend to me properly."

"Oh, now, is that so?" Jocko looked to Rebecca, who just smiled and shook her head. The batman knew he was being played with. "Well, if you would bother to come back to camp once in a while instead of staying up here at the house like a proper gentleman, then I might find time to give you a haircut."

"Rebecca, dear, do we have a closet where we could stash this reprobate so he can do his job properly?"

"I am sure we could find a space, but, you know that after I get done with you, I could always cut the sergeant's hair, too. He looks like he is about due for a trim himself."

Charlie's eyebrow rose and an evil little grin played around his lips. "Yes, my dear, I do believe my batman is looking a little shaggy around the edges. And there is the matter of a certain widow he met on one of our rides, one whom I suspect he would like to impress."

Rebecca looked to Jocko. "Is that right? Have you found a lady to woo, Sergeant? If that is the case, then we most certainly should fix you right up. I am sure Sarah would be happy to boil water so I could give you a shave, too. I still have Mr. Gaines' razor. Of course it has not been used in years and may be a little dull, but I am sure that you would tolerate a nick or two; and I know Colonel Redmond has some wonderful cologne we could put on you."

"Ah, thank you, Miss Rebecca, but I am perfectly capable of shaving myself, Ma'am. And Tarent usually gives me my haircuts."

"And you usually cut the Colonel's hair." She gave Charlie a little nudge even as she continued to torment the batman. "Times are changing, Sergeant. I think having a lady cut your hair would be a nice change." She evened up the hair at the back of Charlie's neck. "I am sure the Colonel would be happy to help."

"Why, Jocko, I am sure that Miss Rebecca would be more able to give you the kind of hair cut any lady would find attractive, instead of looking like Tarent put a bowl on your head and trimmed off anything that stuck out. Just let her finish up mine and you can have this chair."

Jocko looked around nervously. "You know, I think I hear Duncan calling." He gave a crisp salute. "Have a good day, Colonel, Miss Rebecca."

It was all Rebecca could do to hold in the laughter as Jocko managed to exit rapidly without actually running away. "What is it about a woman with scissors that a man finds so dangerous?"

"Perhaps, dear, any woman with scissors is in a position to um... create an instant eunuch... or at least a symbolic one. Men are so proud of their hair and beards, that it may as well be the other appendages. And you know how protective men are of certain portions of their anatomy."

She chuckled again as she began working around his ears. "I know it is important enough that you find it necessary to add some rather impressive padding to your trousers."

"Well, love, that padding does not hurt either your standing or mine in this community."

"This is true." She very carefully trimmed the hair from behind his ear. She gave him a tap on the shoulder when he squirmed. "Hold still. As I was saying, Mrs. Cooper is impressed."

"My love, the only person I need to impress with my skills and ability as a lover is you. The padding is not for you; it is to protect you. Of course, if you like the things such equipment can do, I can at least provide a simulacrum."

She stopped just before the next cut. "Excuse me?"

Charlie blushed. "I, uh, I can, uh, use a, uh, prosthesis if you like."

She stepped around and looked at him for a moment before going back behind him. "You have done this before?"

"No, but, um, I have heard of such things. And I believe I know where I can get one, if that is what you would like." Charlie's head dropped, his chin on his chest, his voice low. "I want to be as much of a man as you need me to be."

Rebecca rubbed his shoulders and leaned over to whisper in his ear. "Charlie, in the privacy of our bedroom, you are exactly what I need you to be. I think you are the most beautiful thing I have ever seen, and I love touching you and having you touch me in return." She kissed him on the cheek. "I trust you to show me what things are possible there, but I desire only you."

Charlie looked into her eyes, hoping to see truth. "Just me? I am enough for you?"

"Yes, my dear Charlie. Just you. You make me happy, and you are more than enough for me."

Charlie grinned happily. "Well, then, I guess I shall just have to learn how to live with that."

She went back to the haircut. "Yes, I guess you will. I am sure you will adjust quite nicely." She ran her fingers through his hair, checking the cut. "Now, are you going to hold still while I take the razor to your neck, or do I have to tie you into that chair?"

Razor? My neck? Blunt razor? "I will be very, very still. I promise. Please, do not slip. My neck is very sensitive."

She took the razor and ran it over a leather strop. "I promise not to cut your throat, Charlie, and I was only teasing about the razor. It is quite sharp." She handed it to him. "See for yourself."

"No, dear. I trust you." He bent his head forward, exposing his neck to her hand and blade.

At that moment, as Rebecca put the blade to Charlie's skin, she realized how much he really did trust her. If she were a Confederate spy, she could easily cut Charlie's throat, and there would be nothing anyone could do about it. She very carefully and very lovingly began to scrape the short hairs from his neck. "I love you, Charlie."

He waited until she was through trimming his neck, then he turned to look into her eyes. "I love you, Rebecca. I trust you with everything I am and everything I have. I trust you with my honor."

"I promise to keep it safe and protect it, and you, until my dying day, Charles Redmond."

Charlie closed his eyes and savored the moment.

Once Charlie's haircut was finished and Rebecca released him from his torture, she sent him on his way and carried the chair back into the kitchen. Sarah was tending the fire in the boiler. She looked up and gave Rebecca a little smirk. "Do not worry about it, Miss Rebecca, men start squirming in the chair as youngsters when their mama cuts their hair, and that is one of the things they never outgrow. My mama used to say it was because they all thought they were like Sampson."

Rebecca laughed. "I can see that. I hope Colonel Redmond does not think of me as Delilah."

She had stepped back out on the porch to collect the things she had left there, when a commotion drew her around the corner of the house. There she saw Duncan and another trooper in the midst of a fistfight. "Boys! Stop this!" She left the porch and ran to the men. "Stop this!" She wanted to try and separate them, but knew she would not have the strength to stop these two men who were intent on hurting each other.

She moved to the back of the house and yelled as loud as she could, "Charlie! Sergeant Jackson!"

Charlie was just entering his office, scratching at the little hairs that had inevitably slipped under his collar. He turned and ran around the house, looking for Rebecca, sure she was in trouble when he heard her yell.

Jocko had been to his tent to gather his belongings and was hauling them back to take over the little room Beulah had told him was to be his own. He dropped his belongings in the mud and started running.

When Rebecca saw Charlie come out of his office, she pointed to the other side of the house. "Oh, Charlie, you have got to stop them!"

He looked to where Rebecca was pointing. Duncan was rolling in the mud with what looked like one of the Pennsylvania troopers from Montgomery's company. Fortunately, Jocko was on the way to the scene from the other side.

The two men moved quickly. Charlie literally lifted Duncan off the larger man. Davison, a trooper with a history of aggressive behavior, was up and after Duncan again in a heartbeat. Jocko grabbed Trooper Davison and pinned his arms behind his back.

Rebecca stayed well back, and watched as the two men pulled the fighters apart from each other. It was all she could do to stay back and let Charlie handle the situation.

The Colonel's command voice rang out. "'Tenhut!" Both men realized their commanding officer was present. They snapped to full attention, eyes forward, one with a blackened eye, and the other with a bloody lip.

Charlie stalked around both of them. "All right. Which one of you wants to tell me what is going on here?"

Both men remained stubbornly silent.

"All right. Duncan, you are the last man I would expect to break the rules about fighting in camp. What happened?"

"Sir, n-nothing, Sir." Duncan's eyes strayed to Rebecca, then back to his commander.

Charlie caught the look. He stepped behind Davison. "What about you, Trooper? What have you to say?"

The man all but growled his answer. "Nothing, Sir."

"You are both aware that fighting is a punishable action?"

"Yes, Sir," they answered together. Duncan swallowed hard.

"Which one of you started this?"

Duncan stepped forward without a word.

Duncan's one glance to his fiancée had told the whole story. Charlie's eyebrow rose. Duncan Nailer was the gentlest man in the whole regiment. Whatever Davison had said about Rebecca must have been harsh. Charlie nodded. "I assume that something was said or done that inspired this behavior."

"I threw the first p-p-punch, Sir," Duncan responded. "It w-was my f-fault."

"Duncan, go to my office. Wait there for my judgment. And wipe your feet before you go in. I do not want mud on everything." He turned to Davison and just waited.

Duncan double-timed it around the house to wait for the Colonel. Davison continued to stand at attention, eyes straight ahead.

"Since I know Duncan well enough to know that he would not throw a punch without some provocation, do you want to tell me what you said?"

Davison's eyes strayed to Rebecca, and then he looked hard at Charlie. "I said she was a whore."

"You realize you are speaking of my fiancée." Charlie's voice was hard and flat.

"You deserve her." His lip curled before he added with a sneer. "Sir."

Charlie's temper was rising rapidly, though he had learned long ago to curb it. Instead, a deadly calm settled over him, one that Jocko recognized as the most lethal of all of Charlie's moods. "Really? Would you care to tell me, Mr. Davison, just why you hold that opinion?"

"She is Southern trash. Makes sense you would find your way into her bed."

"Does that mean you believe I am Southern trash as well, Mr. Davison?"

The man said nothing but continued to glare at his commanding officer. Then he took a deep breath. "They should not have given you command. You are a Southern sympathizer. Look at what you are ordering us to do for these rebels. I would rather cut my own throat than chop one piece of wood to keep them warm."

"Are you aware, Trooper, that we are following orders issued by our Commander-in-Chief himself?"

"Not all people agree with him, either. They started this war, let them suffer for it."

"We are going to resolve this issue today." He turned to Jocko. "Muster the regiment. I want full attendance, in formation, in the north paddock in fifteen minutes." Turning back to Davison, he commanded, "You, Sir, will be free to state your opinion at the muster. I expect you to state it succinctly and as a gentleman. Know that I will personally speak for the other side of this issue."

Charlie called one of the staff sergeants from his old regiment over. "Sergeant, guard this man. He is under arrest for fighting in the encampment. Further charges, specifically dereliction of duty, may be brought."

While the regiment gathered, Charlie stalked off to his office to deal with Duncan.

"Well, what do you have to say for yourself, lad?"

Duncan stood ramrod straight, in front of Charlie's desk. "Sir, I am s-s-sorry for f-f-fighting."

"So how many of your fellow troopers have the same opinion of our situation as Davison?"

"Sir?"

"Mr. Davison just informed me that he referred to Miss Rebecca as a whore. He went on to inform me that I should not have been given this command because I am a Southern sympathizer. I assume that he said something similar to you."

Duncan's eyes dropped to the floor for a moment, then he looked back up. "Yes, s-s-sir. He said insulting t-things about M-m-miss Rebecca, and he..." The boy stopped and shook his head.

More gently, Charlie urged him on. "Tell me, Duncan. I cannot fix it if I do not know what I am facing."

"Davison said appalling things about Miss Rebecca that I would r-r-rather not repeat, and as f-for those other th-th-things, Sir, I know t-that s-s-several of the men in Major Monty's c-co-command grumbled around about them."

"I assume he called Miss Rebecca a whore. Anything worse than that?"

Duncan looked very uncomfortable and squirmed under Charlie's gaze. "He s-s-said..."

"Go on, lad. I am not angry with you. In fact, if it had been me, rather than you, I might be in the uncomfortable position of having to discipline myself."

Duncan laughed a little. Then he stood up straight and looked at his commander. "He said she should be taken out into one of the f-f-fields and shown what a good Northern man could do for her, instead of s-sh-sharing her bed with you. Then he made c-co-comments about what Miss Rebecca might do." He took a deep breath. "I tried to ignore him, Sir, but w-when he t-t-talked about h-hurting Miss R-rebecca I just c-co-could not let that g-go."

"I understand, Duncan. I would have done exactly the same thing you did. What about the problems he seems to be having with me as his commander?"

"Sir, m-men grumble. N-not all of them m-mean half the th-things they say, but D-davison is j-ju-just mean, Sir. Always has b-b-been. If Major Monty were in c-co-command, he would find s-something wrong there, t-too. You j-ju-just have m-more for h-him to h-hate, Sir."

"All right. Your punishment for fighting will be levied at the muster. Time for us to go."

Charlie walked out with Duncan behind him just as Polk came charging up. "Colonel, what has happened?"

Charlie stalked toward the assembly point. "You will have to conduct the action review. Seems Mr. Davison has a major complaint about me, as well as a desire to insult our hostess—rather grossly, I might add."

"Rebecca? My Lord, what could someone possibly have to say about Rebecca?"

"Evidently that she is Southern trash, a whore, and that she should find out what a good Yankee man can do for a woman instead of sharing her bed with me. By the way, I am a Southern sympathizer who does not deserve command."

"My, my, Charlie. Did you start the war, too?" Polk chuckled, trying to wrap his mind around this whole blow up, and also trying to figure out why Charlie had not whaled on Davison for what had been said about Rebecca. "And what did young Duncan do, back there?"

"Whaled on Davison. Wish I could have."

"Davison said these things to Duncan? Does not seem like a bright thing to do. Anyone with eyes can see Duncan has a horrible crush on Rebecca."

"He said similar things to me." Charlie's voice was dead flat.

"Oh, Charlie, I am sorry. What are we going to do about this?"

"You are going to give Davison a chance to voice his opinion. I am then going to point out a few facts. At which point, any man who agrees with Davison will be invited to go elsewhere. Immediately. Dishonorable discharge for dereliction of duty and failure to obey the orders of the Commander-in-Chief."

"All right. We will deal with it. Tell me, did Rebecca hear this?"

"To be honest, I do not know."

"I hope not. She has been very kind and does not deserve this disrespect."

"No one does."

The two men arrived at the muster point. "All right, Polk. It is your show."

The Second-in-Command took his place in front of the troops, walking back and forth slowly. "All right. Seems you boys need a chance to get some things off your chest. And if you want to do that, we are going to give you a chance right now." He turned and looked into the ranks. "But before that, Colonel Redmond has a few things to say to you."

Charlie stepped up and stood before the men. Slowly, he swept his gaze across all of the assembled companies, making eye contact with individual men he knew to be troublemakers and malcontents. Some avoided him; most looked at him with some degree of curiosity.

"It seems some of you may have objections to the relationship I am trying to build with this community and with some of the work details to which you have been assigned. I also understand you may have problems with individuals, either among our hosts or within this command. This is your chance to voice your opinions."

He paced in front of the troops. "Before you do, however, you should know that the 13th Pennsylvania is operating on direct orders from the Commander-in-Chief, which are validated by both General Grant and General Sheridan."

"Colonel Polk will be conducting this process, as I have a personal interest. Therefore, I will only speak as a member of the regiment, not as your commanding officer, until such time as it is appropriate for me to perform my duty."

Polk took a step forward. "You heard the Colonel. Any man who has something to say about our situation can say it now, or report to me in my office within the next half hour. But let me tell you, gentleman, I will not tolerate derogatory things being said about Mrs. Gaines. If you have something to say about the Colonel or me, say it now. Nothing else will be tolerated."

He looked to Charlie, who was clenching his fists. "Anything else, Sir?"

"Davison, I told you that you would have a chance to speak your opinion. You may do so now. Publicly."

Clearly, Charlie was going to bring this issue to a head.

"I do not have anything to say that the men loyal to the Union do not already know. That woman is a whore, and you are a sympathizer."

"Any man who agrees with Mr. Davison is free to step forward."

Polk watched with some curiosity as twenty men fidgeted about, and then fifteen or so stepped forward.

"Quartermaster. Pay these men their quarterlies and their muster out pay. See to it they have civilian clothing. Show them as mustered out of the 13th Pennsylvania as of this date. Go in an orderly fashion; leave the battle lines, and your release from duty will not be noted as for cause. Create any disruption, harass any civilian in any way, and you will be charged with disobeying a direct order, dereliction of duty, and shown as a dishonorable discharge. Am I clear?"

The men just looked to each other and stared at Charlie, not believing what had just happened. "You cannot do that!" one of the men in the back yelled.

He turned to the regiment. "Oh, yes, I can, Trooper. This regiment will obey the orders of President Lincoln. As such, we will begin the process of reconstructing the Union. The civilians of this community are not armed opponents. They have done nothing to warrant this hostility. General Grant himself, when he bivouacked here last spring, said this was the most devastated portion of the country he had seen and that these people deserved our support and assistance if they were to successfully return to the Union."

Charlie went on to address the other critical issue, his own commitment to duty. "I have personally served this country for twenty years. I stood at Buena Vista and lived. Some of you have been with me since that time. I stood at Vicksburg. Some of you were there during that bloody hell. I will stand with you as we end this conflict. But I will not have it said that the men of the 13th were ever anything less than honorable gentlemen.

"And Trooper? I can do more than that. The penalty for failure to obey a direct order from your commanding officer during wartime is death."

A sudden chill fell over the restless crowd. The tone of Charlie's voice made it perfectly clear he was not threatening them. Instead, he was simply stating that he would have absolutely no compunction about applying the ultimate punishment, should the situation warrant it.

Polk signaled to a few armed troopers acting as sentries, and they began rounding up the few men who had stepped forward. "Anyone else want out now? This is the time to speak up."

Charlie stood with his arms crossed and his expression etched in stone.

They watched, but no one else had anything to say, except for Duncan, who raised his hand. "Sir?"

"Corporal Nailer?"

"You t-t-told me I would find out my p-pu-punishment for fighting, Sir."

Charlie turned to the rest of the men. "Davison called Miss Rebecca a whore and called me a Southern sympathizer. Nailer fought with Davison. I will entertain suggestions for what should be done to Mr. Nailer for this infraction."

"He should be forced to eat Sergeant Jackson's rabbit stew," someone piped up from the back, causing a roar of laughter from the rest of the group.

"Now that is punishment. Other suggestions?"

None of the men seemed too keen on naming a punishment for one of their own. They shifted back and forth.

"Well, since Mr. Nailer got into trouble for defending Miss Rebecca, I think assigning him as her permanent bodyguard seems appropriate. Of course, that means he is always on duty, one way or another. What do you think, Colonel Polk?"

Polk cleared his throat and hid the smile behind his hand. "I think that is a good idea, Sir. He can accompany Miss Rebecca into town and the likes, when you are unavailable."

Charlie turned to the troops. "Gentlemen, what do you think of that idea?"

"I have seen Miss Rebecca when she is riled up about something. I feel sort of sorry for Nailer, Sir," one man at the end of the row offered. "Nothing worse than a Southern lady having a full blown conniption."

"All right, men. Unless one of you still has a problem with President Lincoln's orders or with my command?"

They answered all at once as a proper unit, as one man. "No, Sir!"

"Then, gentlemen, our orders are to find a way to get the citizens of Culpeper County through this winter in one piece—and along the way, maybe make the reconstruction of the Union we have fought for so long and hard a little easier."

The men shifted a bit, expecting to be dismissed. Instead, Charlie talked quietly with Polk for a moment, and then turned back to the troops. "While I have you all here, I have another announcement."

They formed back up, waiting to hear what else their commander had to drop on them.

"As part of our holiday celebrations, I hereby announce a formal gymkhana, to be held on the twenty-second and twenty-third of this month. I will want all of the classic equestrian games of a gymkhana, and some competitions for marksmanship and swordplay. The winning company will serve this spring as my personal guard and the vanguard of the regiment. The man with the most points within that company will serve as the color bearer. There will be appropriate prizes for the winners of each event. Gentlemen, it is an opportunity to hone your skills as soldiers, horsemen, and members of a crack fighting team. Events will include the traditional and cross-country endurance races, horsemanship, and demonstrations of skill with saber, lance, rifle, and side arms. We will invite the civilians of the community to observe our games. You have a fortnight to practice. I expect every one of you to participate in some event."

A cheer went up from the men. Such events were usually fun, and they enjoyed the challenge. Anyway, showing off to the locals sounded like a good idea.

Charlie smiled. The men were distracted from their latest crisis, and there seemed to be universal approval for the gymkhana. "Dismissed."

The men disbanded and returned to their various duties with a buzz of excited chatter.

Rebecca stripped the linens from the bed. Part of her wanted to be mad and upset over what had been said about her, but she could not be. The fact of the matter was, she could understand why Charlie's men would think such things. What did make her angry were the nasty things that had been said about Charlie.

She put the old linens in the basket and placed new ones on the bed, remaking it quickly. "Fools, can they not see how hard he is working to make things better?" she grumbled, as she continued puttering around the room.

"Papa?"

Rebecca looked up to find Em standing in the doorway. She went over and scooped the little girl up. "What are you doing here sweetheart, and where is your mama?"

"Mama sweep. Em want Papa."

"Oh, honey, I do not think right now is a good time to disturb Papa. Let us go down and have some apple slices."

"Apple!" Em bounced around in Rebecca's arms.

"Yes, Ma'am."

She carried the baby downstairs, meeting Elizabeth at the bottom. "Good afternoon, Rebecca."

"Good afternoon. Care to join Em and me for some tea and apples?"

"I would love to. I have finished my rounds. Tell me what happened just a little while ago."

"One of the troopers got into a fight with Duncan. Apparently he had some unkind things to say about Charlie and me, and Duncan took him to task over it."

"Oh dear." Elizabeth looked down the hall at Charlie's office. "Give me a few minutes, and then you and Em come join me in Charlie's office."

"Do you think that is all right?"

"It will be more than all right. And very necessary." Elizabeth turned on her heel and went to Charlie's office, knocking on the door.

"Come."

Elizabeth entered the office and closed the door behind her. "I knew it," she said as she crossed the room and settled into a chair.

Charlie was sitting at his desk with his head in his hands. He looked up sourly. "What?"

"That you would be in here brooding."

"Well, what would you have done? I had rebellion in the ranks. I tried the nice way. It did not work. How many more men believe as those reprobates do and do not have the guts to say so?"

"I know, Charlie, trust me. This must be very difficult, but sitting here brooding over it is not going to help. You and Richard are very good commanders. You will handle it, I am sure."

"And to have them use Rebecca as the excuse. I made her a target, and they took the shot. So how much of this really is my fault?"

"You made her a target? Did she not ask for your protection?"

"Damn it, Elizabeth. I could have offered her my protection without sleeping in her bed."

She smirked at her friend. "No you could not. Charlie, I love you. We have been friends a long time, and I am very fond of Rebecca; I think she suits you. But Charlie, she did this to herself by inviting you into her bed."

"Are you saying that little..." Charlie bit back what he was going to say, "was justified in calling Rebecca a whore?"

"No, I am not saying that at all. No one has that right. But the simple fact is, people think you two are carrying on a torrid affair; and as a result, people have formed opinions about a widowed woman who is apparently giving her body to the Yankee Colonel."

"So which one of us is worse—the traitorous Southern woman or the devil Yankee Colonel? And God help me, I am more than eager to make her an honest woman. You know that, Elizabeth."

She chuckled again. "Charlie, Rebecca is an honest woman, a good woman. And you are no more a devil than Mr. Whitman," She paused and rethought that with a smile. "All right, you are no more a devil than I am. This war has caused many hard feelings, Charlie, and you have to know your men are tired and are going to lash out. I think the plans we discussed for the winter gymkhana are wonderful, and will go a long way to boosting morale. Remember, these men miss their wives and children and sweethearts, and they see you up here with Rebecca and you seem so happy. They must resent that."

Charlie closed his eyes and then buried his head in his hands again. *If they knew. If they only knew what I go through to keep them clothed and fed, to get them the care they need when they are sick. They are like my children. When they face the enemy and die, cut down like cattle. When I have to write their parents, their wives. When I see them lying in the infirmary, missing an arm or leg.*

"Elizabeth. I cannot do this anymore. When the ceasefire is declared, I will muster out as quickly as I can."

"Charlie, I know this has been hard on you. I know you are happy here with Rebecca and are looking forward to coming back and starting a life with her. I want that for you both, I want you both to be happy. But you must know there are people in the community who feel exactly as some of those men do. They are not going away. And chances are, they are going to be more verbal about it. You cannot come to your office and brood every time something like this happens. You will sink into despair; and I assure you, Rebecca will grow tired of it. You have to be prepared to be strong and make a stand."

"I know you are right, Elizabeth. But, damn it all! It feels like I have had people hating me all my life." In a much sadder voice, a lost voice, he added, "What is wrong with me, Elizabeth?"

"My dear friend, there is nothing wrong with you. Do Richard or Jocko hate you?"

"No," came the sullen reply.

"Do Whitman or I hate you?"

"No."

"Does Rebecca Gaines hate you?" She gave her friend a grin and a wink.

"No." Charlie got a wry look on his face. "You are trying to back me into a corner."

"Not at all. I am just pointing out that there are people who love and care about you. And, save for Richard, all the rest of us know exactly who you are, Charlie; and not one of us hates you for it or anything else. Moreover, one of us loves you because of it. I hate to break this to you, my friend, but if you were 'wholly male,' I do not think you would have had such good fortune with Rebecca."

Charlie looked at Elizabeth with vast confusion. She had just put forth an idea that had never occurred to him.

"I mean, I gather from things that have been said, that she was treated badly, true?"

"Yes." Charlie spoke slowly, his mind working overtime to try and process what Elizabeth was suggesting. "She was abused terribly."

"By her husband, a man in every sense of the word. She told me what kind of life she had with him. That he all but forced her when he wanted to. She has never known tenderness from a man. I think if you had been a typical male, she would have been far more skittish. Tell me Charlie, did she invite you to share her bed, before or after she found out?"

"After." Charlie looked wary. This was an entirely new perspective on the situation.

"I will bet you a month's pay that if you had been a man in every sense of the word, you would still be sleeping in your tent. Rebecca loves you because you are not a man, in every sense of the word."

Charlie slumped back in his chair, his mouth literally hanging open. Scenes were running through his head, scenes of the two of them together, of Rebecca telling Charlie how beautiful he was, how important his tenderness was to her.

"Charlie Redmond speechless? My, my, I will have to write this down in my journal."

Charlie looked up at Elizabeth. "So you think she really wants me?"

Elizabeth smiled. "That is easy, Charlie. Yes. I know she does. Anyone who looks at her can see that."

"But... I mean. The first time we had dinner, she challenged me to convince her. She wanted me to be a gentleman. She treats me like a gentleman. She wants to be my wife."

"She is a very bright woman, Charlie. She knows you will have to continue to be a man to the outside world, and she is adapting to that so that she will not accidentally reveal your secret. But when you are alone, and especially when you are alone in your bedroom, what are you there?"

Very slowly, a smile of extraordinary serenity spread over Charlie's features. "That is the only time when I am just me."

"Right, and has Rebecca ever turned away or been repulsed when you are 'just you'?"

A blush rose up Charlie's cheeks. He was remembering her desire to touch and please him, to learn that she could please him. "Apparently not."

"Indeed. So, my dear friend, get rid of the gloom and doom and prepare to get on with your life with this wonderful woman."

There was a well-timed knock on the door. Charlie was grateful because he could tell Elizabeth was about to go off on a rant.

He grinned at Elizabeth. She had a habit of reading him riot acts when he got too morose. Avoiding them was always a good thing. "Come in."

The door opened and Em bolted in, running as fast as her little legs would carry her to Charlie. "Papa!" she screamed as she giggled and flung herself at him.

Rebecca carried the tray in, trying not to laugh.

Elizabeth smiled at her friend. "Does she hate you, Charlie?"

Charlie looked at his friend and shook his head, while coping with a small, dark haired, blue-eyed monkey who was rapidly climbing his body. "Elizabeth, you are a unrepentant manipulator. Em, do not chew on Papa's buttons." He tried to rescue his uniform from her ever-inquisitive hands and mouth.

Rebecca laughed as she poured tea for all of them. "She's teething, Charlie. What do you expect?"

"Papa good."

"I swear, I am going to soak a piece of rawhide in honey to give her something to chew on that does not involve my brass buttons. My expensive brass buttons."

When Charlie raised his voice, Em's movement stopped and her lower lip poked out as tears formed in her eyes. "Papa?" she choked out.

"What is it, little one? You are a good girl, a very good girl. Just do not chew on my buttons." He smiled at her and reached into his pocket, pulling out a piece of soft un-dyed leather that he had picked up to work into a braided hair piece for Rebecca. He could get more where that came from. "Here, little one. If your teeth are hurting, you can chew on this."

She took the leather and turned it over in her hands then offered it to him. "Papa bite?"

Elizabeth was doing her best to hide the smile on her face, but failing. Rebecca handed her a cup of tea, then placed one in front of Charlie.

Very seriously, Charlie folded the strip of leather in half long ways and took a solid bite in it, leaving very clear indentations in the leather.

Rebecca laughed and relieved Charlie of Em. "Papa's silly?"

Em straightened in Rebecca's arms and gave her a very serious look as she grasped her leather in her hand. "Papa good."

Charlie laughed. "Well, ladies, do you believe the youngest member of your sorority, or have I managed to totally demean myself in your eyes with my little display of temper?"

Elizabeth chuckled. "You know how I feel, Charlie."

Rebecca leaned over and kissed him on the cheek. "And I think you are good, too."

Em simply refused to remain with Rebecca. "Papa hold Em." She reached for him.

"Demanding, are you, little one?" He shifted to accommodate the little girl. "I suppose it is all right. Aunt Rebecca's had you for hours." Charlie sipped his tea, then lowered the cup and held it for Emily to taste. She preferred her tea with lots of milk and a little honey. His was too dark and bitter for her. She made a disgusted face, and then started chewing on her piece of leather.

Rebecca settled down in a chair next to Elizabeth. "Charlie, Duncan is not in a lot of trouble, is he?"

"No, dear. In some ways, he is something of a hero. Most of the men are pleased their usually anti-social Colonel has found a lady and clearly wooed and won her. A sign of masculinity, I believe. Duncan did exactly what at least half of them would do: he stood up for his commander's lady. And, you must realize, he sees his punishment as more of a reward. I did listen in, you know." Charlie absently picked up a piece of apple and offered it to Em while he spoke.

The baby took the apple and sucked on it, making a long, happy humming sound. Rebecca smiled at the picture of Charlie with the baby. "Well, I am glad he is not in serious trouble. I would have felt bad if he had been. Duncan's a sweet boy."

"Duncan is a grown man, with a rather serious crush on you, my dear. Step gently with him, please."

Rebecca blushed. "Oh, Charlie, you are being silly. Duncan is just a boy."

"Rebecca, dear, Duncan is twenty five years old, and has served in this regiment since the beginning of the war. He has been wounded in battle three times, and has won multiple commendations for bravery. He is most decidedly a man, a very gentle, caring man. I have only held him back because of the degree of damage he took at The Wilderness."

"All right, I see your point. I promise to be good. He reminds me a bit of Andrew."

"Actually, dear, I am more concerned about you hurting him than anything else."

"Hurt him? Charlie, I would never hurt him."

Charlie looked to Elizabeth for help. Rebecca just did not understand what Charlie was trying to tell her.

"You brought it up, Charlie," Elizabeth giggled.

He groaned, and provided Em with a piece of cheese to crumble on his coat. "If you look at him as a boy, you are liable to treat him more casually than if you see him as a man. He may mistake casualness for intimacy and invitation, and believe he means more to you than he does. It would be painful for him to get his hopes up and have them dashed."

"Charlie, Duncan is well aware that you and I are engaged. But I promise you, my dear, to be very careful with him."

"Thank you, love." Another piece of apple was provided to the small child in his lap, and the combined apple juice and childish drool mixed with the cheese crumbs on his tunic to make a pleasantly gooey paste that fascinated Em. She proceeded to use it to draw random shapes on Charlie's chest.

Rebecca just shook her head, and Elizabeth stood. "If you will excuse me, I need to go check on Montgomery. Things are looking much better on that front, Charlie. I think we will see him open his eyes in a day or two."

"I do hope so. Having him come around, both physically and emotionally will do much to resolve the problems we have been having with morale." Emily continued to use the mixed cheese crumbs and masticated apple to decorate Charlie's jacket. The normally immaculate Charlie did not even seem to notice.

"We will make him better, Charlie." Elizabeth waved at Em, who was now trying to put her mush-covered fingers in Charlie's mouth.

"Papa bite."

Charlie let the child slip the decidedly questionable cheese and apple goo into his mouth, sucking gently before he let her fingers go. "More apple, Em? I know you are doing your best. Both of you are doing your best with him. I do appreciate it."

Elizabeth could not stand it any longer. "Charlie, you do realize you are being covered in mashed apples and cheese?"

He looked up at her. "Yes. I believe that is rather normal behavior for a young child. Jocko has been giving me these long suffering looks for what she does to my uniforms, but I really have not found an alternative."

The Doctor looked accusingly at Rebecca. "You do realize that this is because of you. Before he met you, he would not have let a child within fifty feet of his uniform."

Rebecca smiled and shrugged. "There have been lots of interesting changes since Charlie got here."

Em shook her head and cuddled into the crook of Charlie's arm.

"Nap time, little one?"

Em shook her head again and burrowed deeper into Charlie's shoulder.

Charlie took his large handkerchief out of his pocket and cleaned up the little girl's face and hands. "Cuddle up, little one. I will keep you safe; and when you are asleep, I will carry you up to bed." He looked at the two women in his office and smiled serenely.

CHAPTER 17

Wednesday, December 14, 1864

Whitman settled into his chair at Major Montgomery's bedside. It was late, and he had volunteered to sit with him through the night to give Samuelson a much-needed break.

Adjusting the lamp so he would have enough light, he took a sip of his tea and began working on his newest poem. As he composed careful lines, he heard Montgomery groan. Setting his pad aside, he moved to the edge of the bed.

"Major?"

Montgomery groaned again and his eyes opened. He looked confused and in a great deal of pain.

"Good to see you, Sir. Let me go get Dr. Walker."

He took the lamp to make his way across the hall to Elizabeth's room. He knocked on the door, then pushed it open just slightly without going in. "Doctor, the Major is coming to."

Elizabeth woke quickly, sitting up and rubbing sleep from her eyes. "Come in, Whitman."

He pushed the door open further and entered the room. "Montgomery is coming to."

"Excellent." She got up and pulled on her robe. "Let us go see the gentleman."

Returning to the room, Whitman stood back and watched as Elizabeth worked with her patient. "Should I wake Colonel Redmond?"

"Actually, yes. I think he will want to know this."

He excused himself, then went to Charlie and Rebecca's room, knocking firmly on the door. After a moment, Rebecca opened the door. "Yes?"

"Miss Rebecca, Dr. Walker sent me. Major Montgomery is coming to. She thought the Colonel would like to know."

"Of course. We will be right there." She nodded to him and closed the door. Then she went to the bed and gently shook Charlie's shoulder.

Charlie rolled over from the pillows and slowly opened her eyes. "Yes? What is wrong, sweetheart?"

"Nothing. Dr. Walker sent word. The Major is coming around."

"Wonderful." Charlie got up right away and pulled on his robe. "Let us go."

Entering Montgomery's room, they watched as Dr. Walker tenderly took care of her patient. "How is he, Doctor?" Charlie asked, stepping forward.

"Well, come see for yourself."

Charlie got closer, looking down on his officer. Montgomery's eyes slowly tracked to him. The Colonel smiled. "Good to have you back."

The man did not speak. He just closed his eyes. Elizabeth tucked the blanket around him and stood up, taking Charlie by the arm, away from the bed. "It is going to take time."

"Elizabeth, how aware do you think he is now?"

"It is hard to say, but I believe he understands what is being said. That was apparent when he gripped Rebecca's hand the other day. I am sure at this moment he is confused and in a lot of pain, but the fact that he is responsive is a very good sign."

"I want to make sure that all he hears from now on are Southern accents. Not just you and Rebecca, but find everyone with a Southern accent, male and female, and pull them in to sit with him."

Elizabeth nodded. Rebecca joined in. "I am sure we can provide him with constant care. I think that the ladies who are here will be happy to help."

"It is going to be a long hard road with him, Charlie. I know I suggested this plan, and I will implement it as long as it does not upset him so much as to endanger his health," Elizabeth said.

"I agree with both of you. However, I also think that his problems may be as much emotional—left over from The Wilderness —as they are physical. I would like to try and handle both issues if possible."

"And we will. For tonight there is not much we can do besides let him rest. Whitman and I will remain with him, and if there are any further changes, we will let you know. Now, you two need to get back to bed."

"Thank you, my dear. How I handle Montgomery will be critical to morale—especially after that little demonstration of temper I had the other day."

"I know." Elizabeth laid her hand on her friend's arm. "We will make sure he gets the best care possible, and that the men, especially his men, know that you are doing your best for their major."

"What would you say about him having a few visitors—as long as they were not his caretakers?"

"I think that it would be good for him to have one or two a day, as long as it does not tire him out. Men from his troop could be beneficial as long as they speak positively about the happenings in camp."

"That would be good. If I can find men who will speak enthusiastically about the relationship with the locals... even better."

"Yes, absolutely. Positive reinforcement will be needed to aid in the healing process. Perhaps we could also ask Reverend Williams to pay a visit."

Charlie chuckled at that. "As long as you do not invite his wife."

Elizabeth laughed as well. "I think she is secretly sweet on you, Charlie," she teased, giving Rebecca a wink when the blonde woman stifled a chuckle herself.

"Well, if that is all that we can do tonight, shall we all try and capture a little more rest before we face tomorrow's demands?"

Elizabeth laughed as Charlie ignored her comment. "Yes, by all means go back to bed. If there is any change, I will wake you."

"Elizabeth, let Whitman watch. I have a vested interest in keeping you healthy."

"Charlie, I am a doctor. I promise to take care of myself, but the care of my patients comes first. I promise to rest, but I want to stay with him for a bit longer."

"All right. I will check with you in the morning. And do get some sleep, my friend."

"I will. Good night, Charlie, Rebecca."

Thursday, December 15, 1864

Constance took the afternoon watch. When she was first asked to sit with a wounded soldier, she had thought nothing of it, until she had walked into the room. Being confronted by one of the men who had assaulted her was a terrible shock. In fact, it had been so overwhelming that she could not speak of it, or even allow herself to think of it for quite a while. When she finally allowed herself to consider Montgomery's presence in the same house, she realized that it was a test from God; a time for her to truly discover the meaning of forgiveness.

She sat close to the bed, working on a small sleeping gown for the baby that would arrive in a few months. Even though it was only mid-afternoon, the sky was so overcast that she needed the lamplight to see. She was roused from her work when Montgomery asked for water.

She poured a cup and very gently helped him take a few small sips. He focused on her when she took the cup away. "Where?" he managed to croak.

"You are at Gaines Cove Farm, Major Montgomery. You sustained a head wound from an injured horse, and we have been caring for you here."

He grimaced with pain. "Should have...let me die."

"Major Montgomery, everyone here has been quite committed to your survival. I do wish you would join us, Sir." She gave him another sip of water and carefully arranged the pillows behind his head.

"No." He closed his eyes and licked his lips. "Would rather die."

Constance smoothed the hair back from his forehead. "You know, I do understand. There was a time not too long ago when I wanted to end it all as well."

He looked to her, wishing he had the strength to knock her hand away. He did not need the comfort of Southern trash. "You should want an end."

"No, Sir. I should not. I have one child by my husband, who died at Seven Pines, and another one on the way—a 'gift' from one of the men who came through wearing the uniform of the 13th Pennsylvania. Which one, I am afraid I cannot tell you. This child, regardless of his father, deserves a life."

"You are suggesting..."

"Sir, I am implying nothing. I am stating that men from this regiment forcibly outraged me. As a result, I am now pregnant. Prior to that day, no man except my lawful husband had ever touched me, and that was done with love. Believe me, I was as defiled as you, with your hatred of all like me, could wish. So you, Sir, have no excuse for wishing to be dead." She did not say anything about Montgomery's presence that day, the day that his men had forced her and this man lying in bed before her had sodomized her.

"Why? Why not revenge? Or has that Southern bastard influenced you, too?"

"It is very simple, Major. The Good Book says it best of all. 'And unto him that smiteth thee on the one cheek, offer also the other.' Your men assaulted me, defiled me, and in doing so, defiled themselves. This anger and hatred will continue until the good Lord's words are heeded."

"So did Redmond take them to the post? He would stripe the back of a good Northern man, to protect the sensibilities of a Southern," he paused and his next word came out as a snarl, "lady. How can you believe they defiled themselves?"

"Colonel Redmond does not know, nor will he ever, at least from me. I realized that 'Unto the pure all things are pure: but unto them that are defiled and unbelieving is nothing pure; but even their mind and conscience is defiled.' I was a good wife, loving and loyal to one man. I had done nothing to bring this abuse upon myself. The men who abused me did not see me as an individual, but instead saw only with the hatred and evil in their own minds and hearts. They will have to live with the results of their actions, bearing the guilt and defilement in this life and paying the price for their defilement in the next."

"You are as much of a fool as that bastard Redmond."

"And you would risk your soul in hell so that you can enjoy your anger and guilt now?"

"I saw my men cut to ribbons, they did not deserve to die. I wish we could wipe out your kind."

"And I have seen my home, my husband, and my family destroyed because you chose to come here—to my land, to my home —and do your damage. I do not remember the Southern forces invading Pennsylvania until long after your men had managed to cut terrible swaths through the people and land of Virginia."

"You chose this war. You deserve what happens."

"How, Sir, did we choose this war? We chose to secede from the Union, a right we had under the Constitution. You chose to persecute us for exercising our legal rights. And how, Sir, did I choose to be the object of your men's evil intent?"

"I fight to keep the Union together. I am not responsible."

"And if I were to identify them to you, and you were to find that they are men under your command?"

An uneasy memory of Davison and his cronies came to the Major's mind. "It cannot be undone now, can it? Maybe you will get lucky and the child will die; then you will not have to live with the reminder."

"I would not want the child to die, because the child did not break the commandments. The child is pure. The poor men whose anger overcame the purity of their souls are the sinners here, not this child. You see, Sir, I do not hate you. I pity you and your men. For you are small, and consumed with hatred. You will spend the rest of your days being eaten away by the beast in your souls, unless you let go of your anger and see the reality before you."

"No pity. Nothing from Southern trash."

"Sir, the good book says 'To everything there is a season. A time to kill, and a time to heal.' Whether you like it or not, this is your time to heal. You may fight it, you may resist it, but your time, Major Montgomery, has come. We have had our time of war. It is now time to think on peace."

"I want to die. Leave me alone."

"Tell me, Sir, why you wish to die?"

"I should have died at The Wilderness. I would rather die than spend one more minute under Redmond's command."

"Have you plowed such iniquity and sown such wickedness that you deserve to reap the same?"

"I want the peace that death brings."

"Were you the cause of your men's deaths?"

"I led them into hell."

"And you faced the same chances of dying as they did?"

He closed his eyes and seemed to be remembering that time in his life. "I should have."

"Why do you think so?"

"Because that is what a commander does. Now I have been subjected to Redmond. I cannot stand that bastard. I would cut his throat if I had the strength."

"Dear me. What has Colonel Redmond done to earn such enmity?"

"He breathes, the Southern sissy. You share his bed, too, or is he only bedding the whore who owns this place?"

"Ah, poor man, your own heart must be so impure that you must see sin everywhere you look. No. I am not sharing his bed. I believe he sleeps with his wife-to-be. And from what I understand, General Grant does not find him a coward in any way."

"Oh, the perfect officer and gentleman." Despite his weakness, Montgomery's sneer was acidic. "He plans to marry her? That is the first smart move I have ever seen him make. Now at least he is thinking about taking land."

"I would not know what his commanding officers think of him. I only know what General Early said about facing him. I believe he said, 'Grant sends Redmond after me because he is the only man with the courage to face me head on.'"

"Redmond is a coward. He lets Southern troops escape and hates to kill his own kind."

"Whatever leads you to say that, Sir? I had understood that Colonel Redmond only recently assumed command here."

"I have heard things about your wonderful Colonel. He is so... pathetic. I am sure he prefers the company of men."

"My, jealousy is certainly an ugly emotion, Sir."

"Jealousy? Me jealous of Redmond? Ha."

"It certainly sounds like you are. Perhaps your problem is that women do not find you as attractive. Or are you one of those men who need to dominate a woman—like your rapist troops?"

"I have no problems with women. And a man has rights with his woman."

"If a woman consents. What of those who do not consent? Like me? Did your men have a right to force me?"

"A man has needs."

"Ah, so force is justified then?"

Montgomery did not deign to answer that. He just sneered at her.

"My, what a fine representative of your precious Union you are, then, Major. I believe that forcible outrage of an innocent woman is a hanging offense in every state in your Union."

"Then have Redmond hang me."

"Are you saying you have committed this outrage, Sir?"

"I have a wife. I have taken what I wanted when I wanted it."

"From her or from others?"

"It does not matter and is none of your concern."

"Ah, then you have never been loved. I feel sorry for you. You have never felt the exhilaration when a woman comes to you, craving your touch, aching for your love. You have never known the true pleasure of a woman's tender touch. You poor, poor man."

"The world is a cruel and heartless place, and one must survive."

"Ah, I remind you that those who live by the sword shall die by the sword; and as for those of us whom men call meek—well, we shall inherit the earth."

"You can have it. Now leave me alone."

"Sleep, sad Sir. One of us will watch over you as you recover." Constance sat quietly, watching over the man who had himself once watched over her as his men violated her repeatedly, then joined them.

Rebecca sighed and ran a cloth over her face in preparation for bed. It had been a long day, and she was looking forward to getting some rest. She hoped Charlie would be up soon. She really wanted to relax in her lover's arms and let the frustration of the day melt away.

She smiled when she thought of Charlie. Rebecca's body tingled from head to toe at the thought of being close to him. She shivered, keenly aware that her body was now responding to the mere thought of Charlie. She looked down to find her nipples had tightened painfully. "Oh, Charlie," she groaned, as she moved to the bed and climbed under the covers.

Charlie's day had been long and difficult. He had spent much of the time filling out all of the paperwork necessary to justify his summary discharge of men and to notify the other commanders in the area to watch for them, as their behavior was unpredictable. He was looking forward to stripping away all of the trappings of his position, getting cleaned up, and then finding some quiet comfort in Rebecca's arms.

He came into the bedroom already stripping off his coat. In the weeks they had been together, he had grown comfortable with having her witness his nightly transformation.

"Good evening, darling." He looked over and smiled at her, already cuddled into bed with the comforter pulled up to her chin and tucked in around her shoulders. "How was your evening, beloved?"

"Long and lonely without you. I am very glad this day is done. Major Montgomery is going to be quite the handful. His attitude is positively hateful."

"I knew he had problems. How bad is it?"

"Well, he will not talk to me at all. He practically threw the soup that Whitman brought him across the room, and I suspect he was very unkind to Constance today. She has been somewhat upset since her time with him."

Charlie rolled his neck to ease the stiffness. From the bed, Rebecca could hear the slight crunching as the bones settled into place. He sighed. "I may just have to get him somewhat better, then send him home. God save me from vindictive idiots. Can you or Elizabeth talk with Constance tomorrow and find out what happened?"

"We have already discussed it, and one of us will try to talk to her. Being upset is not good for her baby, so we want to try and help her. I will make sure you know anything we find out."

Charlie walked over to the bed and leaned down to kiss Rebecca's forehead. "Thank you, love. I am not sure if you were not better off before we came; we have put you through so much in the last weeks."

She took his hand and intertwined their fingers. "We have been through it together." She gave a little tug. "Now get undressed and come to bed."

Charlie went back to the washstand and used the jack he now kept beside it to pull off his boots. The weskit and cravat followed, so he stood in his shirt, breeches, and socks. With his back to her, the transformation that liberated Charlie and always enthralled Rebecca began. He pulled the braces off his shoulders and then pulled his shirt and singleton off over his head. The breast bindings came off next, and Charlie quickly ran a damp cloth over her body to wipe away the remainders of the day. She swept her breeches, underwear, and socks off in one bunch, and draped them over the rack beside the washbasin, reaching for her nightshirt in the same motion. With a simple sweep, Charlie dropped her nightshirt over his head and padded over to crawl into bed.

Rebecca curled into his arms immediately and placed a kiss on his throat. "I missed you."

Charlie ran his hands over the fine, soft flannel that covered Rebecca's back. He kissed the soft blonde waves at the crown of Rebecca's head, as that was the only part of her Charlie could reach with his lips. "Ah, I see. But I am here now, love."

Rebecca blushed and buried her head in Charlie's shoulder. "Hush," she teased, giving him a poke in the ribs. "It is not my fault I am having these reactions, it is yours."

"And what reactions are you having, beloved?" Charlie's nose twitched. He could feel goose bumps rise on Rebecca's flesh wherever his fingers touched.

"You evil thing, you. You know what is happening." She giggled and scooted closer. Then she took Charlie's hand and placed it on her breast. "See."

Charlie's hand gently covered the full breast with the very taut nipple at the center. He flattened his hand and lightly brushed the tip of the nipple with the palm. "Oh, you mean this? I thought perhaps you were just chilled."

"I am...not chilled," she managed to gasp as her body arched into Charlie. "I am many things, but I am not chilled."

The same hand that had been teasing Rebecca's nipple slid under her chin and drew her face up so that Charlie could kiss her. And kiss her he did; slow, long, languorous, searching kisses, exploring every inch of her lips and her mouth.

Rebecca moaned and enjoyed the kiss, taking Charlie's hand and putting it back on her breast.

Charlie continued the kiss, and softly caressed Rebecca's breast. When breathing became necessary, Charlie's lips slid to Rebecca's ear. "Does this make you want more, darling?"

"Oh yes!" She wrapped her hands in Charlie's hair. "Much more." She placed several little kisses where her lips could reach. "Will you teach me?"

"We will teach each other, darling. Every person is different, or so I am told. Everyone has parts of their body that are sweet to touch— and no two people are the same."

Rebecca took a deep breath and reached under the blanket, and placed Charlie's hand on her hip. "I want to learn about pleasure, Charlie."

Charlie ran his hand over the sweet curve of Rebecca's hip and up to her slender waist. "I think the first thing that you need to discover is what feels good for you.

"Show me how."

Later, as they were drifting off to sleep wrapped comfortably in one another's arms, Charlie thought to himself, *I am home. I am finally home.*

Friday, December 16, 1864

Rebecca sat at the breakfast table, finishing what everyone considered a huge breakfast. Charlie had sat through the first part of the meal with a silly grin on his face. Elizabeth watched them, but decided to wait until Charlie had left for the day before she said anything.

She chuckled as she leaned back in her chair and watched out the window as Charlie walked down the path with something of a bounce in his step, splashing happily in the puddles that the rain continued to expand, and then turned back to Rebecca.

"Well?"

Rebecca looked up from the coffee she had just poured. "Well what?"

"So what has you two grinning like a pair of baboons?"

Rebecca blushed. "Why, Doctor, I have no idea what you're talking about."

Elizabeth raised her eyebrows. "Something happened that I do not know about, or I too would be stretching my grinning muscles like you two are."

Rebecca tried to hide her grin, which only widened. "I assure you, the Colonel has been a perfect gentleman.

"And have you been a perfect lady?"

She was nearly laughing now, but trying very hard to keep from it. "I like to think so, yes."

"Shall I take it that the two of you are discovering a new aspect of your relationship?"

"I believe that would be a safe assumption on your part, Doctor."

Elizabeth laughed softly and shook her head, then went back to brooding over the information she had gleaned from Constance in the early hours of the morning.

Rebecca took note of the obvious shift in her friend's demeanor. "What is wrong, Elizabeth?"

"I had a long talk with Constance this morning, a very long talk. Seems that our Major Montgomery was awake and feeling hostile last night."

"Ah. Constance did not seem right last night, but she was tired when I saw her and I did not want to push her for information. "

"It seems that in his present state, Montgomery is just as vicious towards both Southerners and women as Charlie said he had been before the accident. He is also overtly hostile, as well as suicidal."

"I was afraid of that. He is not a kind man. What did he say to her?"

"Evidently quite a bit, including but not limited to suggesting that she deserved being forced by his men because she was a Southerner."

Rebecca was appalled. "His men? My Lord, do you mean to tell me that the men who did this are members of Charlie's troops?"

"Evidently. And although he did not say specifically, I would say that our Major might know who did it. Charlie does not know about this, and to be honest, I am almost afraid to tell him. Not because of what it would do to Charlie or to the men, but because of what it would do to Constance."

"Those men need to be punished. If they are not, any woman they choose is next. It could be you or me, and what would happen to Charlie, Richard, and Constance then?"

"You are right, I suppose. I just hate dragging Constance through this. Perhaps Montgomery, in his anger and arrogance, will provide us with more information."

"We will give him a few days, but if he does not tell us anything else, I will have to go to Charlie. I am going to be his wife; he trusts me. If he found out I knew this and did not tell him, he would never forgive me."

"Rebecca, Constance knows that the men who outraged her were from the 13th, but it was before Charlie took command."

"You know Charlie as well as I do, even better, I am sure. You know that it would not matter to him when it happened; he would want to know of this regardless. He would want to see those men punished."

"It would be hard on him. The penalty for such an outrage is hanging. And he would see that sentence carried out, because he could do nothing else."

"I know that. I do not want to hurt him, but look at Constance, look at Em. You know the men who did this may have seen her here at the house. Maybe they do not remember her, or maybe they do. If they do, can you imagine what kind of things are being said about that lovely woman, who has had to endure far more than any of us have?"

"As a doctor, I am pledged to save lives, to do no harm; but this is a hard decision. In this case, what I have learned is supposed to stay with me, part of doctor—patient confidentiality. But, if this information is not shared, it could eventually cause another, even more painful rift than Duncan's little fight."

"Doctor, I will not hide this from Charlie, but I will help you try to get more information out of the Major."

"And we will have to get information from Constance gently. I fear that more than I fear grilling the arrogant Montgomery."

"I know. We will not do it right away, but it has to be done."

Both women looked grim. "You know, I think I will discuss this with Richard. He may be able to handle it more effectively than I, and I would be much more comfortable not breaking my physicians' oath directly. Constance's history and Montgomery's delirious ramblings are protected by that oath."

"Yes, I think he could be of valuable assistance to Charlie with it."

"Perhaps I can convince Richard to take this issue on himself, and handle the military side of it. In that way, though Charlie will have to sit in judgment as regimental commander, he can stay clear of it. Otherwise, he may find that this issue simply polarizes the troops further."

"That sounds like a very logical thing to do. And maybe he could deal with it in a quiet manner, only letting those who need to know, be privy to the information."

"Let us hope. See what you can do about getting Constance to talk with you, please. I really hate being in the position of being pulled in two different directions."

"I will. I will talk with her today. We are supposed to take Em to the pond for a picnic. I will talk to her there."

"Thank you, Rebecca. It is an impossible situation for me to be in. I am not supposed to share the confidences of my patients, yet what these two, separately and together, have told me has the potential for harming so many others if some action is not taken."

"I know, and I would never ask you to betray a confidence; but if I can get the information from one or both sources, I am bound by no honor other than that as Charlie's wife."

Elizabeth stopped short. "Charlie's wife? So you really will marry him?" She shook her head, knowing that the two were swept away by their relationship but still concerned over whether this wartime romance had a chance to last for the long term. "Have you decided on the date?"

"Yes, of course we are getting married. I told you this was a serious relationship. We have not set a date, yet. I do not know if it will be before he goes back to battle, or when he gets back."

"If I know Charlie, he will want to do it before he goes. He will want to make sure that if something does happen to him, you will be taken care of."

"That does not matter to me. I just want him to come home."

Elizabeth smiled. "You know, he is called Lucky Charlie. I think it is because he always considers the worst case and prepares for it. That way, having prepared for it, he somehow manages to keep it from happening. At least that is what he says."

"He had better be very careful. I expect him to come home and help me get the farm running again. Do you think he will be happy here, Elizabeth? He will not get bored, will he?"

Elizabeth looked out the window over the rolling land, perfect for raising healthy horses. She looked back at the shy, eager woman beside her. "Rebecca, I do not think that Charlie will ever be bored living with you. Challenged, perhaps, but never bored."

"I hope it is good challenged and not bad challenged."

Elizabeth laughed, the first uninhibited laugh that Rebecca had heard from her. "It is very good challenged, my dear. Very good indeed."

"I am glad you approve. I know you are one of Charlie's closest and dearest friends, and your opinion is important to him."

"Rebecca, we are both seeing a Charlie that I have never seen. He is open, he is laughing, he is happy with you. Even with all the burdens on him right now, he is laughing. And I think he feels very loved."

"After last night," she paused and smiled, "he should."

Startled, Elizabeth looked at Rebecca for a moment, then a slow blush traveled over her features. Rebecca had sounded so sultry and so satisfied that just her tone of voice was embarrassing. *Damn. Sometimes this being a virgin is just a plain annoyance.*

CHAPTER 18

Saturday, December 17, 1864

Saturday was the first day that had been clear in almost a week. Charlie needed to get outside, to smell the clear air without the constant odor of ashes, burning wood, and damp wool.

His need to get out of the house was urgent; he also needed time alone with Rebecca to resolve an issue that had been gnawing at his conscience for weeks. What better way than to take his love on a ride through this crisp, early winter morning.

With that plan in mind, he slid from the bed into the chill morning air and briskly dressed in his work clothes, knowing that the little sounds of him moving about would rouse his fair-haired lady.

"Good morning, sweetheart. Look, it is a beautiful clear morning."

Rebecca rubbed the sleep from her eyes and smiled at him. "You are very chipper this morning."

"Oh, I am, my dear, I am. I am sick and tired of rain; I swear I have no idea which way to turn. I need to be out and about today. So, will you join me for a ride this afternoon? I can have Shannon ready for you right after my staff meeting."

"I would love to go for a ride. It will be nice to get away from the house and have some time just for us."

He stepped over to the bed and slid his arms around her, holding her gently and kissing her forehead. "Then I will be here promptly. Ummmmm. Have I told you that I love how you feel when you have just awakened? You are so warm and soft."

"Hmm, is that so? Could be because I sleep so close to you that I steal all your body heat?" She smiled and nuzzled his neck. "I suppose it would not be possible to talk you into coming back to bed?"

"I was going to go run. You know how much I need to keep in shape, love. It would not do for the Colonel to start growing hips and a rump, now would it?"

She could not help but chuckle, even as she kept her arms around him and her nose buried in his neck. "No," she sighed. "I suppose not. I guess we should both get a start on the day; then so we can go riding with a clear conscience."

"Then, dear, I will call for you promptly at one thirty. I think I will take a longer run than usual, since it has been so long, have my bath, and then breakfast in the office. I want to clear as much away as possible so we can have an undisturbed afternoon. Could you ask Sarah to arrange it?"

"Of course. Your bath will be ready when you get back. I suppose I should go check on the Major this morning as well."

"I would appreciate it. I hope that placing him in debt to Southerners for his life will help shift his attitude."

"I hope so, Charlie, but he is very bitter and very angry. I do believe he would see us all dead if he had the strength."

"I was afraid of that. Well, if nothing more, I have the grounds to send him home without raising the enmity of his troops any more than I already have. We may even come out the heroes in this for saving his life."

"I do not want to be a hero; I just want to help the poor man to get better. I will try my best to change his mind about us, but I must tell you, once he is stronger, if he is still in his current state of mind, I think it would be prudent to have an armed trooper outside his door. I would hate for him to burn the house down around us."

Charlie's eyebrow shot up toward his hairline. "That bad? I knew he was angry, but I did not realize his hatred was so entrenched."

"It is. I believe he could be very dangerous."

"I will have a guard placed on his door this afternoon. I also need to discuss this at the staff meeting today. Between that little expulsion the other day and Montgomery coming around spitting enough nails to frighten you, we still have a problem."

"I know, and thank you. I will feel safer, and I am sure the other ladies will as well."

"Then of course we will put a guard on him. I will quietly ask Polk to use only men who served with me in the 49th."

"Thank you." She gave him a little kiss on the cheek.

By now, Charlie was fully dressed in the outfit that most amused Rebecca: the one with the short, belted jacket, tight pants, and hobnail boots. Just to amuse her, he asked, "Do I look all right?"

"Oh yes, you do...very all right." She nearly leered at him.

"Well, love, I will see you at half past one." A quick peck on the cheek, and he was off.

For Charlie, the morning went by quickly. There was some consternation over Montgomery's attitude. Fortunately, none of the other officers shared his point of view, or, if they did, they were not admitting to it. The orders were clear: reconstruction was to be effected gently and peacefully. Before he knew it, one thirty arrived and Tarent was outside the front door with Black Jack and Shannon both saddled and ready to go. The horses were full of energy; the cool weather after days of rain and mud had them in as exuberant a mood as their owner.

Charlie stood, hat in one hand and reins from both horses in the other, smiling, and ready to go.

The door opened and Rebecca stepped out on the porch, pulling on her riding gloves. "Why, good afternoon, Colonel."

"Good afternoon, dear lady. Are you ready to ride?"

"I am very ready simply to spend the afternoon with my charming Colonel. I do not care where we go or what we do."

"Then come along, and we shall run away for the day." He lifted her into the saddle, his hands lingering for a moment on her trim waist, then made sure she was settled and in control of the frisky mare. He swung up onto Black Jack's back and played the big stallion for a few minutes while the horse danced and fidgeted; then the two of them set off around the house toward the bridge over Gaines Run and the orchards and pastures east of the pond.

"I do believe Shannon needs to get out more," Rebecca chuckled as she gave the feisty beast a pat on the neck.

"Tarent warmed them up for us, so I would say a good run would be in order." The two of them entered the big pasture behind the stable yards and gave both horses their heads. Running neck and neck, knee to knee, they covered the half mile or so to the tree line in good time. Both were laughing with sheer joy at the end of the run.

"Oh, Charlie, that was wonderful!"

"It was indeed." He pulled Jack to a sitting trot, and Shannon followed suit automatically. Drawing in a huge lungful of fresh air, he turned to her, grinning like a willful boy full of mischief. "What do you say we just keep riding east?"

"East, west, I do not care, as long as we keep riding. We can ride in small circles for all I care at the moment. I am just glad to have the time together."

"Then we ride, dear." He tightened his grip on Jack's sides and they were off. They came around through the strip of woodland that bordered the run then turned west, and rode across the old wooden bridge, breaking out into a long run of grassland that led toward the foothills in front of them. The profile of the Blue Ridge was hazy purple in the distance.

Rebecca was amused by her fiancé's behavior. The normally

dignified Colonel was grinning with the pure joy of being out. He was playful and almost as twitchy as his horse, playing tag with her as they rode by coming close, touching knees, and then picking Jack's pace back up. For this little while, the mantle of command and all of the burdens that came with it had lifted. He seemed like a young man, so full of life and energy was he.

"You know, Jack would make a fine stud. I believe we could get good money for his colts."

"I rather had that in mind, love. He has been put to stud on a couple of occasions, and the line ran true. And, just in case you were wondering, both Jack and Shannon are mine, not the Army's."

"I am very glad to hear that, Charlie. I was rather hoping I would not have to petition President Lincoln to buy Jack out from under you."

"Another gallop to get the beans out of these two?"

"Where you go, I will follow." Rebecca shot him a saucy grin.

"Then perhaps I should call you Ruth, not Rebecca." And with that jibe, he touched his heels to Jack's side and was off running again.

She smiled and shook her head, sending Shannon after the frisky pair ahead.

The ride continued until it was clear the horses needed a rest, and perhaps some water. Charlie found a small glade, with a rill that chuckled over moss-covered stones and a couple of fallen logs that would serve as seats for them. He slid off Jack and lifted Rebecca down from her saddle, and then ground tied the horses near the water and a small patch of grass. He pulled a blanket from the roll behind his saddle, and a small packet with a flask, apples, and cheese from his saddle pack.

With the ground still soaked from the rain of the previous days, a small outcropping of rock beside the fallen logs offered the only really dry area in the glade. He spread the blanket over the rock, making a rustic table, and using the log as a bench, and offered her his hand. "A small treat, my love?"

She smiled at him. "You think of everything?"

"Well, actually, I have something I want to talk with you about." He was nervous and fidgety.

"What? You know you can talk to me about anything." She placed her hand over his, giving it a gentle squeeze.

"Umm... well, I was thinking, about our future, about all the things that might happen. And I have found that if I, if I, umm, plan for the worst case, um, it usually helps. It keeps bad things from happening." The last came out in a rush.

Rebecca looked at him, trying not to get upset. "Please, do not think like that, Charlie. Nothing bad is going to happen. I believe that. You have to believe that as well."

"I do believe it. But what I have found is that if I do all the things I have to do in case the bad things happen, then they do not happen. I know it sounds superstitious, but it has worked for me for twenty years, and it is extremely important to me. You are the most precious thing in my life now, and I want to make sure everything is taken care of before I go, just in case. Please?"

"All right, Charlie. You know I am willing to do whatever will make you feel better."

He caught her left hand in both of his and tenderly kissed her fingers, then lingered over her hand, looking at his mother's small garnet ring. "You know, this hand represents the only people who have ever truly loved me, I think."

"Charlie, I love you with all my heart and soul, but there are others who love you as well. You have very dear friends who care so very much for you."

"I know. But that is not the same, is it, love?" Charlie took a deep breath. "So, Rebecca, will you marry me before I am called back to service?"

She could only smile tenderly at him and stroke his cheek with her fingers. "Of course I will."

Charlie was wearing his childlike look, part impish, and part bashful. "I talked to Reverend Williams. He could marry us on the twenty-eighth of January. I was hoping you could be ready for a small wedding that quickly. Could you?"

"The end of January? My goodness, that is not a lot of time, is it?" She considered it for a moment, then nodded slowly. "Yes, I am sure I can enlist enough help to be ready."

Charlie caught her other hand up in his and covered them both with delicate kisses. "You. Have. Made. Me. Exquisitely. Happy."

"And you, my dear Charlie, have made me happy beyond words." She looked up suddenly. "Oh my...oh my... " She looked a little pale.

"What is it, darling?"

"This will be a military wedding, will it not? Charlie, I know nothing about military weddings."

"My dear, this will be whatever kind of wedding you want. Reverend Williams has agreed to officiate, and I am sure that Polk and the boys will want to honor us, but if you wish, we could have a civilian wedding. I will even get a new civilian suit, if you want me to."

She smiled and shook her head again. "No, no not all, Charlie. I think you will look absolutely dashing in your dress uniform. I just need to make sure that everything is perfect. I would not want anyone to think you have married below your station."

He shifted so that he could pull the small woman into his lap. "I am the interloper here. I just want it to be good enough for you." He could feel her trembling in his arms. "My love, are you chilled?"

"You, Sir, are an important commander in the Federal Army, very trusted and apparently highly spoken of in the circles of high command. I have been talking with Elizabeth, Charles Redmond. I know more than you think. I am shaking partly from the chill and partly from nerves."

"You, madam, are the most beautiful woman I have ever seen, the owner of a fine property, and a woman of such spirit and intelligence and breeding that any man would be proud to call you his wife. And if you are chilled, I have a flask of brandy. Would you like a sip?"

"Why, Colonel Redmond, are you trying to get me drunk so you can take advantage of my person?" she teased, tugging on his tunic.

"Sweetheart, I have no desire to see you back in a sick bed, so I took the precaution of bringing a little medicinal brandy. And if I were going to take advantage of you, I would have done so already. I do believe you may have attempted to take advantage of me on occasion, though," he laughed, as he poured a shot of brandy into the little silver cup that formed the lid of the flask.

She laughed as she took the cup and sipped the brandy. "Well, now, my reputation will be completely undone if people find out I have been trifling with the Colonel, taking advantage of him in ways that I never thought possible." She finished the cup and smiled at Charlie as she held it out for more.

He refilled her little cup, and leaned in to whisper in her ear "Love, you may trifle with me all you wish. I am yours to command in all things."

Charlie's breath tickled her ear, and she giggled like a schoolgirl. "You have no idea what that does to me."

"Oh?" His voice sank to a rumbling purr. "Then tell me, darling. You can tell me anything and everything."

"Oh, Charlie," She sighed, as she again sipped from the cup. "You just excite me all over. Before you came, there were nights when I was afraid to go to sleep, for fear of what the next day would bring. Now, I cannot wait for night so I can be with you and be in your arms. And I look forward to every morning because I know it will bring us joyous new discoveries." She took another drink and licked her lips.

Charlie's lips, so close to her ear, dropped to place light, teasing kisses on her exposed neck. "My future is with you, dear. It is a future I dreamed of and never thought I would find. And here you are: loving, feisty, adventurous, and so beautiful it makes my heart stop. I love you, Rebecca."

"I love you, too, so very much." She turned and wrapped her arms around his neck, kissing him quite soundly.

He savored her kiss, flavored with brandy, spiced by the crisp air. He responded with teasing nips and strokes with just the tip of his tongue.

Rebecca moaned. She was feeling just a tad lightheaded. She was not sure if it was from Charlie's kiss or the brandy, but she decided that it did not matter. Another strong shiver ran through her body, but she knew that was from the kiss.

He whispered in her ear, "Love, we either have to stop, or we have to make a commitment to go on and the devil take anyone who stumbles upon us. For I crave your touch past words to tell you."

Rebecca pulled back and looked at him. "Go on? Outside? My, my, Colonel," she laughed. Nothing like that had ever been suggested to her before.

"My love, if you keep teasing me like this, I probably would not care if the entire regiment were watching."

"Charlie!" She blushed and buried her face against his neck. "I cannot believe you said that."

"And would you prefer that I could resist you, dear?" This teasing was more fun than he had anticipated.

"You need not resist me, but that was just scandalous." She smiled, running her hand over his chest. "I am glad you cannot resist me," she said sincerely before kissing him again.

He groaned and sank into her kiss. When he could speak again, he looked into her eyes. "This is wonderful, darling, soon-to-be wife of mine, but I think it is getting late, love. And it is getting colder. We need to get back. To our nice, warm room. To our nice soft bed."

Rebecca's laugh could only be described as sensual. "Oh yes, that is an absolute must. Our nice...warm...bed."

He stood and pulled her up into his arms. She came to him fluidly, almost boneless, and for a moment the two stood, wrapped close, just savoring the feel. "Time to go, dear."

"By all means, dear man, lead the way. But do it very slowly. I am afraid I may be just a tad tipsy."

"Stand here, while I gather up our blanket. I shall get you home in one piece, I promise." Quickly, Charlie gathered up the blanket and the remains of their afternoon snack and stowed them in his saddlebags. The last thing to go into the saddlebag was the silver flask. "One more?"

"You are trying to get me drunk," she teased, even as she accepted the cup.

"I am trying to keep you from getting sick from the cold. And I will take the last of that, if you do not mind."

She handed him the cup. "If you insist."

Charlie lifted the cup in silent toast to his bride and tossed back what was left, then stowed the flask. He whistled for Shannon and she obediently came to him, allowing him to lift Rebecca into the saddle. "Take care of my girl, Shannon."

"Your Shannon is a very good girl. I am sure she will see me safely home."

Jack was a little less cooperative, having stood patiently while Charlie packed his gear. He danced a step or two as Charlie swung into the saddle. They set off at an easy pace, riding knee to knee, as much to make sure Rebecca was not too inebriated, as to enjoy the closeness of her company.

She reached across and took his hand. "I promise you, Charlie, I will not embarrass you by falling out of the saddle."

The trip home was uneventful. They arrived at evening mess, so there were few men around the stables. Charlie was left to groom the horses himself as his companion looked on.

He settled both horses into the holding stalls and began with Shannon, pulling off her saddle, bridle, and saddle pad, and setting them onto the racks to be cleaned. The mare received a rough currying, with special attention to the area under the saddle pad that was damp with sweat, followed by an apple as a reward for good behavior. He led her to her regular stall, where she settled down peacefully to munch some hay. Then he returned to tend to Jack.

Rebecca watched Charlie, with a look that was half smile and half leer. She was feeling the effects of the brandy to her very toes, and she wanted to play. She walked over and leaned on the wall, watching him. "Do you have any idea how handsome you are?"

"I am certainly glad you think so, my love, as you will have to look at me for many years to come."

"I do think so, very much." She slowly moved to the front of the stall and close to him.

He was focused on brushing Jack down and did not realize that Rebecca was coming closer and closer. "I will have to stay healthy and hale for you, then."

"Oh yes, it is a must," she purred as her hands came to rest directly on his tightly muscled bottom, which she proceeded to give a long loving rub. "Hurry, Charlie, that nice warm bed awaits us."

Her hands on his rump were the last things he expected. Her hands kneading his buttocks were almost more than he could take. For a moment, he froze; then his forehead dropped onto Jack's near wither. In a very low, warning tone, he queried, "Ah, Rebecca, dear?"

"Yes, Charlie, dear?"

He did not have to turn around to see the smile on her face; he could hear it. "We will be able to go inside sooner if you, ah, refrain from —"

"From?" she teased further, giving his bottom a little pinch.

"From playing with my body," he whispered.

She removed her hands and put them up playfully. "Your wish is my command."

He groaned. Under his breathe, he muttered, "I could dream." He quickly finished grooming Jack, gave the big horse his favorite treat, a carrot, and led him to his stall. "There. Shall we, Ma'am?" He offered her his arm to escort her decorously to the house.

She winked and took his arm. "We shall, Colonel."

As they walked out of the stables, they could hear sniggering behind them. Charlie turned and looked.

Standing at the corner of the barn, were three members of the Pennsylvania contingent of the regiment. They gave their commander very impressed looks. "Very nice, Colonel," one yelled.

Another was laughing so hard Charlie thought that he might pass out.

The next trooper waved. "Now we know why they call you Lucky Charlie!"

Charlie's first impulse was to call them down for being disrespectful, until he felt Rebecca's silent chuckle. Instead, he grinned, threw the men a casual salute, and walked on with the beautiful woman on his arm giggling softly.

"I think your status with your men just went up tenfold, Colonel."

"Well, perhaps it will put some lie to the rumor that I prefer the company of men." A cheerful grin lit his features. Little did any of his men realize the full meaning of that statement.

"Well, then, I suggest we just finish off that rumor right now." She pulled Charlie to a stop and threw her arms around him, bestowing a deep kiss upon him. When they parted, she looked back to the men who were staring, slack jawed. "Have a good evening, gentlemen."

Charlie looked back, winked, and smiled. "Gentlemen, meet my fiancée."

She whispered, "Protecting my reputation, Charlie?"

"Always, my dear. I prefer not to have you referred to as the Colonel's whore. They will refer to you as the Colonel's lady, or they will not enjoy their lives."

"I love you, Charlie. You are my hero."

The two of them walked into the house just as the ladies were preparing to go in for dinner. They rushed upstairs to clean up from their ride. Charlie used Rebecca's small sitting room as his dressing room, while Lizbet helped her mistress out of her riding habit and into a dress more appropriate for supper at home. In a matter of minutes, they were ready to join the other inhabitants of the house for a warm meal.

Charlie escorted Rebecca to her place at the foot of the table, and then took his own seat at the head. The two of them had easily fallen into the patterns of a more courtly and traditional time. Elizabeth shook her head and smiled softly to herself. *Yes, Charlie is well and truly hooked. Master of the house suits him.*

They all bowed their heads to say grace, then Beulah and Reg began serving the soup. Charlie started conversation by inquiring after the day's events. Young Jeremiah Carter piped up excitedly, "I went fishing and caught dinner for us!"

"Well done, young Sir. And what kind of fish are we having?"

"Corporal Nailer said they were the nicest bass he had seen in ages."

"I like bass very much. Thank you for your contribution to the table."

Jeremiah glowed. The tall Colonel may have been a Yankee, but he was also a nice man, who always spoke to him politely and let him eat with the grown-ups, a privilege he had not enjoyed in his own home. Then the reality of the situation descended on him again. He remembered that Charlie and Duncan were the enemy, and retreated back into his normal sullen silence.

As Jeremiah's fish was being served, the ladies all "oohed" and "ahhed" over his catch. When the praises for the lad had died down, Rebecca spoke up. "Ladies, I have a great favor to ask of you."

The ladies turned to her with looks of interest on their faces. Miss Rebecca had offered them sanctuary; being able to repay her in some way was a welcome opportunity for these proud women.

"As I think you know, the Colonel has asked me to be his bride, and I have consented. Alas, the demands of the times have created a situation where urgency is more important than propriety. We have set the date for January twenty-eighth."

A buzz went round the table. The twenty-eighth was so soon, and with Christmas and the New Year ahead, it gave them very little time to prepare for a wedding worthy of their respected host and hostess.

Rebecca continued, "Ladies, I will need the assistance of every one of you to ensure this wedding is all that we can make it." She smiled charmingly at each of the women at the table. The buzz turned into an instant cacophony, with words like "dress patterns," "lace," "flowers," "cake," and "wine" all bubbling up to the top of the din. Charlie and Jeremiah looked at one another in mild panic. By mutual consent, the man and boy both skipped dessert, excusing themselves to go and hide in the back parlor, where Charlie chewed a cigar to shreds while he played a game of checkers with the boy.

As the two were finishing their game, one of the new servants, another of Beulah's cousins, knocked on the door. "Colonel, Sir, the little one refuses to go to bed without seeing her Papa. Miss Constance told me that she thinks you are her daddy, and I swear I do not know what else to do with her." As she was speaking, little Emily squirmed in her arms, trying to get down to go to Charlie. The look on Emily's face was one of quiet determination.

Charlie held out his arms to the little girl. "That is all right, Tess." He turned to Jeremiah. "Will you excuse me while I settle this young'un down?"

Jeremiah looked on with wide eyes. Yankee officers were supposed to be devils who ate small children for breakfast. This one was a gentleman who treated him like a guest and a grown up, and who comforted little Southern girls who mistook him for their father. He was not the ogre Jeremiah had been taught to expect. Still, Yankees killed his father. The boy was getting more and more confused. All the things he had been told did not match his own experience. Duncan was kind, almost like an uncle; and the Colonel was a gentleman with an accent more obviously Southern than his own. As he watched, he thought about his own father, killed only a couple of months before at Winchester.

While Jeremiah brooded, Charlie took Em into his arms. "Were you a good girl today?"

"Um huh." One finger went into her mouth and she cuddled against the scratchy blue wool covering his shoulder.

"My good girl. You ate all your supper?"

The little head nodded. Charlie looked inquiringly at Tess, who smiled and nodded as well.

"So why were you being naughty when Tess told you it was time to go to bed?"

"Want hugs, Papa. Miss Papa. Em not sweepy." Em yawned and cuddled into his shoulder.

Charlie smiled and held the little girl closer. She wrapped one hand around one of his buttons; sucked on her finger a little, then promptly feel asleep on his shoulder. He held her for a few minutes to make sure she was sound asleep, kissed her on the forehead, and then handed his small bundle back to Tess. "Thank you, Tess. Tuck her in well."

"I will, Sir."

"Good night."

The young woman left the room carrying the child. Jeremiah sat in his chair, looking thoroughly confused.

Charlie watched the boy, waiting patiently for him to speak. Since he had arrived, Jeremiah had been sullenly polite, distant, and obviously angry, both at the Federal troops—because he blamed them for his father's death, and at his mother—for demanding that he be a gentleman and mind his manners. Perhaps the boy was finally ready to talk openly with him.

"Why does she call you papa? You are not her father; you are just a damned Yankee passing through." Jeremiah had been dying to ask him this very cutting question for a while, but had not found the courage before tonight.

"I think it is because I look something like her own father, and she misses him."

"Why would she want to call a Yankee papa? I would never do a thing like that. It insults the memory of her father."

"Jeremiah, she is just a little girl who does not understand or care about North and South, Yankee and Confederate. She just misses her daddy. I look like him, am kind to her, and make her feel safe. I like to think that if her father were alive, he would appreciate the care I give his daughter in his place."

"Sir, my father would not appreciate it if I called a Yankee "papa." He would be offended and feel betrayed. My father fell at Winchester, fighting with Jubal Early against your side."

Charlie was a little startled. Jeremiah already had a number of confusing problems to deal with. The possibility that his father had been killed by one of his own men in the heat of battle was something that he needed to address, and quickly, or this mercurial and proud boy might find himself in a great deal of trouble very soon.

"So tell me, Jeremiah, do you understand why we are at war?"

The youth gave him a very startled and confused look. "Everybody knows why we are at war."

"Do they really? Why do you think we are at war?"

"Because you Yankees are evil and tried to take our Southern way of life away from us. You tried to free all the nigger slaves and make us work in factories like you make your shanty Irish slaves work in New England."

"If that is true, then how did the war start?"

The boy looked unsure. "Uh, Yankees shot at innocent Southerners down in Charleston, South Carolina?"

"What if I were to tell you that is not why we are at war. And that the first shots of the war were fired by Southerners? Jeremiah, men go to war for many reasons. But the fact that we have gone to war does not make one side right and the other wrong, nor does it mean that one side are all devils and the other all angels. It just means that we disagree, and have failed to find a peaceful way to resolve our differences."

Charlie stopped for a moment. The confusion on Jeremiah's face showed him that he was not getting through to the boy. An inspiration came to him.

"Tell me, Jeremiah, have you ever gotten into a fight with someone at school?"

Looking a little abashed as well as startled by the sudden change of topic, Jeremiah responded, "Yes, Sir. And I caught the very devil for it, too. The teacher gave me what for, and when I got home, my da gave me a good licking and sent me to my room without supper. He said I was raised to be a gentleman and a Christian, and that I should find a way to settle my differences without fighting like a common street urchin."

"Well, wars are what happen when large groups of grown men do exactly what you did in that school yard. The biggest difference is that when grown men fight, like the Federal and the Confederacy troops are doing now, instead of a few bloody noses, thousands of men are wounded and killed. War is a terrible thing, a time when we fail at being gentleman and good Christians. A time when we cannot find a way to resolve our differences by talking, and resort to fighting like common street urchins."

"But you are a soldier. Your job is to fight."

"That is certainly true. And if you ask the career soldiers—the ones who have devoted their lives to the Army, as I have—you will find that the biggest proponents of finding peaceful settlements to our differences are the very men who are willing to fight if necessary. I think I am a soldier because I know if a fight starts, I can help end it more quickly. That way, I can help keep the damage to a minimum."

"That is not what I heard my father saying. He said we should whip you all back to the North." The boy did not add the rest of his father's statement "like dogs to their kennels." Somehow, he felt that would be disrespectful of this imposing soldier, who said the strangest and most puzzling things.

"Perhaps, Jeremiah, your father was behaving the same way you did when you got in the fight at school."

Charlie let the boy sit and consider that idea for a while. After a long pause, Charlie steeled himself to say what needed to be said. "Jeremiah, I want you to hear this from me, and not overhear it out in the camp. Our troops fought at Winchester with General Sheridan's troops, against General Early. I do not know, and to be honest, no one will ever know, if your father was killed by one of my soldiers. But I do know that the men who fought—on both sides— fought bravely and honorably. Your father was one of the unlucky ones, sacrificed to our inability to find a peaceful resolution to a very difficult problem. I am very sorry."

The boy sat in stunned silence. No tears came to his eyes. Somehow, this was not what he had thought war was about. War was supposed to be noble and glorious, not about grown men who could find no better way to solve their differences than by shooting and killing one another. But as he thought about it, he could see how his father sounded just like the boys at school, blustering, and threatening and cocky. Before he could say anything or gather himself to react with anything other than a sort of numb confusion, the parlor door opened and the ladies filed in, all still chatting eagerly about the wedding plans. Charlie and Jeremiah looked at each other, and by silent, mutual consent, returned to their quiet games of checkers.

Sunday, December 18, 1864

Charlie was up early and cheerfully about his business, preparing the troops for the gymkhana, cheering the boys on, and doing a bit of practice himself, since he was one of the finest horsemen in the regiment.

Rebecca attended to her usual morning responsibilities— meeting with Sarah, Beulah, and Reg to organize the servants' activities, and with Elizabeth, to coordinate care of the two refugees who had rather severe colds, exacerbated by malnutrition. Elizabeth was also concerned with Constance's condition. Her energy was declining, and she was requiring more rest just to get through the day. This pregnancy was straining her already depleted resources, and both Elizabeth and Rebecca were deeply concerned. Finally, there was the issue of Major Montgomery, who vacillated between being arrogantly abusive and morbidly suicidal.

This morning it was Rebecca's turn to spend time with the wounded man. As she approached his door, her sewing basket in hand to pass the time, the guard warned her that the major was in a particularly unpleasant mood.

Rebecca entered the room and settled herself in the rocking chair beside the window. "Good morning, Major. I trust you slept well."

Montgomery rolled over and faced the wall.

"I am glad to see you moving around a little. I am sure that lying in bed all day must be uncomfortable."

That foray into polite conversation received a non-committal grunt as Montgomery jerked at the covers to try to get more comfortable.

Rebecca took some soft blue material out of her sewing basket. She had cut it into a shirt for Charlie and was methodically sewing fine overstitched seams to make sure it was strong as well as warm. "Perhaps one of the orderlies would have time to help you with a bath later today. That might make you more comfortable."

"Madam," he sneered, "the only thing that would make me comfortable would be to be out of your house and out of this godforsaken nest of rebellious vipers."

"Sir, given that your mistreatment of your horse was the cause of your injuries, you should be grateful that this 'nest of rebellious vipers' has been able to offer you another chance at life."

"Madam, I did not ask for another chance at life. It was thrust upon me, no doubt so that Charles Redmond could torment me with yet another piece of evidence of my 'unjustified animosity' toward Southerners."

"Well, Sir, it is true that President Lincoln and General Grant have ordered the Colonel to begin the process of reconstruction in this area. I believe that the Colonel is simply following orders in his behavior towards the residents of Culpeper."

"Oh, so are you suggesting that General Grant ordered the Colonel to take you to bed, or are you just one of the benefits that will be available to Northern officers when the war is over?"

Rebecca gritted her teeth. Charlie had asked her to be civil no matter what this man said, and civil she would be. Just barely. For as long as she could stand being in the same room with the vile pig. "Sir, my personal relationship with the Colonel is just that. Mine. I rather suspect that my husband-to-be would not particularly appreciate your comments, though." She paused for a moment. "As a matter of fact, there is an issue of a criminal charge being investigated."

"Oh, yes. Your gallant Colonel Redmond. I think you should know that he has done this before."

"Really? And who might the unlucky woman have been, Sir?"

"Why, I must confess, I have seen him become involved with at least a half a dozen women. And each time, he has conveniently been called back to service just before the final commitment is made. That man has avoided more altars than battles. I even suspect that he has more than one by blow populating the countryside. But you will not find the good Colonel paying for his bastards' upbringing. As I understand it, what he does when things get too close for comfort is to run to his whore in Washington."

Rebecca was having a hard time listening to this man's vitriolic lies. Part of her wanted to slap him silly, and perhaps do permanent damage to his already injured brain. The other part wanted to laugh in his face, knowing intellectually that part of what he was ascribing to Charlie was physically impossible. The rest based on what both Charlie and Elizabeth had told her, was patently untrue. How to break through this sea of rancor was beyond her.

"That, Sir, from a man who, I understand, enjoys watching women being forced, and then taunts them with the memories of the event, is beneath contempt."

"You cannot prove anything, you greedy little whore. It is my word as an officer and a gentleman against the word of that little lying, Bible quoting bitch. I am quite sure that no board of inquiry would ever accept her testimony. As for you, you pitiful little slut, play your games with the Colonel. Let him take care of you, draw him in, and when you know what his orders are, I am sure you will pass them on to your rebel cohorts. As for Redmond, he is not only a Southern sympathizer; he is a damn fool who has no more right to lead this regiment than I have to be King of England."

Rebecca was appalled at the ocean of hatred roiling out of this man's mouth. He strained to pull himself up in the bed, and glared at her. "Yes, indeed, you little slut. I wanted you the minute I saw you. I wanted to throw you down in the hall and tear your skirt off. I wanted to show you just what a good Pennsylvania man could do to a woman. I could not decide if I was willing to look at your face as I took you and taught you what a real man was like, or if I wanted to turn your face to the floor so I did not have to watch you whimper and whine. You would have been just like your little friend, Constance. You would have whined and cried and screamed, but secretly, you would have loved it: the feel of a real man inside you, controlling you. Just like she did. She begged for it, you know. By the time the third man was through with her, she was so sloppy and open that I had to take her in the ass just to feel something. You would like that, too, would you not, you little slut?"

The blue shirt lay ignored in her lap, as she fought the urge to expel her breakfast on this vicious, twisted excuse for a man. All of the pain and horror of her life with Gaines came back to her, as she recognized the same qualities in Montgomery as she had seen night after night with her husband. Slowly, she rose from her chair, the shirt falling unnoticed to the floor. Deliberately, she advanced to face him directly, staying just barely out of arm's reach, emboldened by her own new found knowledge and by Montgomery's incapacity.

"Major Montgomery. I believe I have just heard you confess to being a party to the forced outrage of Constance Adams."

"I believe you did. And I dare you to attempt to prove any of it, slut. My word against yours. My confession, as you call it, is pure hearsay that no court in the country would accept."

"You pitiful excuse for a man. You know nothing but force and the lust for power. You abomination. You are no better than my husband, that raping, whoring, drunken bastard. If it had been up to me, Sir, I would have let you lie there and die in your own blood and gore. Were it not for Colonel Redmond getting Dr. Walker down here in time to operate on you, you would now be dead and burning in hell where you belong."

Neither of the two occupants of the room had noticed when the door had opened a few minutes earlier, nor had they been aware of both Charlie and the trooper assigned to guard Montgomery's door standing there listening to this damning exchange.

Charlie stepped into the room as Rebecca delivered her condemnation. In a low voice, he simply said, "Enough. Both of you." He dropped his hands onto Rebecca's shoulders, and could feel her shaking with rage. "Major Harrison Montgomery, you are under arrest for the malicious outrage of Constance Adams, self-confessed, and with the confession witnessed by myself and Trooper Abel Franklin, as well as Mrs. Rebecca Gaines. Trooper Franklin, I will send someone to relieve you forthwith. I request that you immediately provide your testimony as to what you have heard today to Colonel Polk, so that it can be fully documented. I remind you, Major Montgomery, that a verbal confession, witnessed by two standing members of the regiment, is considered by the Military Code as being as valid as a written confession. There is only one penalty for such a crime. We will convene a Military Court of Inquiry as soon as I can get General Sheridan here to officiate. Would you like me to send for a minister to tend to your soul?"

"Well, Redmond, you have what you wanted—a legal way to get rid of me, the only man in the whole regiment who would willingly stand up to your Southern sympathizing and your treasonous actions against the Union of the United States. You should have just let me die, and no one would have been the wiser."

"I suggest that you save your comments for your counsel and for the court, Montgomery." He turned to Rebecca, who was white faced and trembling. "Gather your belongings, Mrs. Gaines. I will escort you to your quarters and send someone to take your testimony."

CHAPTER 19

SUNDAY, DECEMBER 18, 1864

Charlie gently escorted Rebecca to her sitting room and settled her into her favorite chair before the fireplace. "My dear, I must attend to a couple of things." He rang briskly for Reg, and as he waited for the man to appear, quickly penned two notes. One was for Polk; the other was to Major Swallow. The two notes were essentially the same, outlining the results of the afternoon's confession.

Reg slipped into the room. "You rang, Sir?"

"Yes. Deliver these two notes as quickly as possible. Run. And if you see a trooper—any trooper—on your way, send him to me immediately."

Reg tugged his forelock and scurried from the room.

He returned to Rebecca's side, concerned over the shuttered look on her unusually pallid face. "My love. Are you all right?"

"I am fine, Charlie. Just angry."

"Want to talk about it, dear?"

"I do not know what to say. I simply cannot believe he could be so arrogant about what he and those men did to Constance, and I am ashamed of the way I feel toward him."

"I heard you, tell him that he was no better than your husband. Is that what Gaines did to you? What they did to Constance? And why should you feel ashamed, love? He is despicable."

She lowered her eyes, unable to look at his gentle face. "Yes," she offered softly before looking back at him, tears in her eyes. "I should not have said those things to him. It makes me as despicable as he is to wish such things."

He took her into his arms. "My dear, to want to exterminate vermin is not despicable, it is human. That you should suffer such treatment at the hand of your husband, who had vowed to protect you, certainly qualifies Mr. Gaines as vermin in my mind. Listening to Montgomery spew his venom and clearly enjoy the impact it was having on you was enough to make both Franklin and me feel physically ill."

She sank into his arms with a sigh. "I must admit it had much the same effect on me." She took a deep breath and sat up, wiping her eyes, giving Charlie a little smile. "Do you not have things you should be attending to?"

"I sent messages to both Polk and Swallow, and expect a trooper at the door shortly to take over from Franklin. Until then, I am yours, dear."

"What will happen to him?"

"He will be hanged. There is no alternative. I will have to have Sheridan down here to conduct the court martial, as I believe if I sit the Board of Inquiry, it will be questioned."

She gave a slightly frustrated laugh. "Ironic. We spend weeks saving his life, only to have it taken from him."

"He condemned himself. To be honest, I almost suspect he did it on purpose. I have often seen officers spiral down into suicidal guilt and anger when they lose too many men, and Montgomery certainly fits that pattern. Unfortunately, there is little or nothing we can do about it. If Franklin had not been witness to the confession, I do not know if I would have made the charge or not. Perhaps he could have been saved, perhaps not. Certainly, Constance has room in her heart for forgiveness. Montgomery does not have the same in his. Mostly, he cannot forgive himself."

"Charlie, we are going to have to be very careful with Constance. She is not well. The pregnancy is very difficult. I am afraid that this could make it more so."

He sighed deeply. He had seen Constance growing paler and more fragile as her child grew within her. "I do not want this to become a circus. I have a confession; I have a senior staff officer, I have two witnesses. I believe we can keep it quiet and simply transfer Montgomery to Sheridan as soon as he can be moved. I hope that Davison and his boys took my advice and left the area. I will put a notice in my dispatches to keep an eye out for them, as well. I can only imagine what conducting the trial here would do to morale, let alone what it would do to Constance. It is a very ugly picture."

"It is indeed an ugly picture." She rubbed his arm. "I really am concerned for her. Elizabeth is taking very good care of her, but there is only so much we can do. Lizbet, Tess, or I have Em almost all the time. Constance is so weak she cannot look after the baby. It is a good thing that child adores you so; some nights you are the only one who can calm her down."

Charlie smiled indulgently. "She is a charming little imp. And I have noticed that lately she seems to go to you as much as she comes to me. Rebecca, what will happen to Em if Constance..."

"Dies?" She shook her head. "I am not sure. She has no other family that I am aware of."

"Would you..." He floundered. He loved the little girl dearly, and knew that Rebecca did too; but to ask her to consider adopting a child who still had a living parent, when they were not yet married seemed to be both tasteless and something of an imposition. On the other hand, he would certainly be proud to raise the little scamp if her mother succumbed under the hardships of pregnancy.

"What, Charlie?"

"Well, um, if Constance, um, does not, um, survive her, um..." He flushed a bit. This was one of the strangest ways he had ever considered to gain a family. Perhaps planning parenthood was not a bad thing. "Well, if Emily is left alone, would you consider raising her?" he finished in a rush.

"Me? Oh, Charlie, I..." she paused, then smiled at him. "No, Charlie, I would not raise her. We would raise her. You would be a wonderful Papa. She is quite her Papa's little girl now."

"I meant us, love." He blushed, starting with his ears and spreading over his face. "I know it is not the normal way to acquire a family, but I also know you want one. And I do not wish Constance ill, but you know how I am. I always figure that if I plan for the worst case, well then: if it happens, I am ready; and if it does not happen, I have been lucky."

"Of course." She cupped his cheek. "I am sure all will be well."

Charlie luxuriated in her touch, cuddling her close for a few minutes. As they sat quietly, a hesitant knock sounded at the door. He rose and went to talk quietly with the trooper for a few minutes, then returned to her side.

"You know, dear, there are many orphaned children who will need love and care. What do you think of adopting children after we are married?"

She smiled. "Hmmm, a whole herd of children for the good Colonel to corral along with the horses?"

Charlie held her close as he laughed. "My dear, if I can keep these unruly troopers under control—at least most of the time—I think I can handle children. How many were you thinking of, darling?"

"Oh, I do not know." She gave him an evil grin. "We can just keep going until we run out of bedrooms."

He laughed a full, hearty laugh. "My dear, clearly you are intent on making sure that I keep my exercise program up and maintain my image. For with that many children underfoot, I will no doubt have to do a fair bit of weight lifting just to carry them all around with me." With that, he kissed her soundly. "It sounds like a lovely plan, my love—a whole house, full of laughter and growing young'uns. All because of our love." He gently tickled her. "And you will be able to keep your lovely figure as well, my dear, without the risks or drain of pregnancy. I think it sounds like a perfect plan."

~

Monday, December 19, 1864

A light frost covered the grass, and Charlie's boots made the stiff blades crunch as he ran his morning route around the stables and the exercise rings behind them. The men had laid out various practice courses, and several groups were already clustered around the drawings of the various jump patterns for the events. In the center of the largest exercise ring, some of the men were already sparring with saber and small sword. Some were practicing classic cavalry maneuvers: attempting to thrust a javelin through a small ring hanging from a swinging beam, and using sabers to pick up rings from the ground, all while riding at a brisk clip.

Off in one corner of the main paddock, all of the company commanders, except Montgomery, were holding an impromptu conference of some sort. Casually and very quietly, Charlie walked up behind them, curious as to how well his plans for inspiring both teamwork and a bit of good-natured competition within the regiment were going.

Braddock of Company H, and the only company commander who had served with Charlie on the western front, was holding forth to the others. "Look, we all want to win the honor of both the vanguard and the colors. That means we are going to have to get the men to work together, regardless of whether we are from the old 13th or the remnants of the 49th. And my Ohio boys are more than willing to do so. So tell me what I have to do to get these stiff necked Bucks County boys of yours to pull together?"

Swallow, the most senior of the Pennsylvanians, stroked the pencil fine beard at the tip of his chin for a moment. "Well, you know Colonel Polk has been working with Montgomery's boys in Company D. He set up an internal review, where each man voted to decide which members of the company would compete in which events, the object being to put together the team that was best equipped to win the overall competition. You know what a mess Monty had left that company in. I swear, before Polk took them over, I was breaking up fights almost every night. He has them working together pretty well now."

The other members of the little conference nodded at Swallow's advice. Hoffstader piped up, "Yes, it is working. I have had a good bit of luck with mixing up the teams that have been repairing the fencing. All it took for me was to find the thing we all had in common; and for my boys, taking care of the horses was the thing."

"Well, just being able to stay in the fight, especially after what the Rebs did to us at The Wilderness, was enough for my boys. I swear, giving command to that upstart Wilson was the stupidest thing I ever saw." Major M'Cabe, who still had not completely healed from the grapeshot he had taken in the shoulder, spat to emphasize his disdain for the young, arrogant general who had led an entire division of Federal cavalry into hell because he was too stubborn to take proper precautions.

Young Avery, who had taken command of Company I after The Wilderness Campaign, looked glum. "Have you been watching the fellows from Company D? They are driving hard, every one of them. I swear, I think they need to prove something after both Monty and that idiot who called Mrs. Gaines a..." He trailed off, loath to repeat the insult. His companions relieved him of that burden by nodding sagely at him. "Anyway, I think they want to prove themselves. So they are all pushing hard."

Swallow and several of the other commanders laughed. "Yes, lad, that would be the kind of thing Polk would put them up to. Prove that Monty and his little clique were just that—a little splinter group, and that the rest of them are good, God fearing, hard riding, well trained soldiers."

Maguire looked back and forth between Swallow and Braddock. "What about the Colonel? What do you think he will do? Will he play favorites, either for his old troops from Ohio or for Polk's boys?"

Braddock laughed. "Lucky Charlie play favorites? That man has always been the most "by the book" officer I have ever heard of. No, he will definitely not play favorites. But watch out. He has been known to compete personally in the individual events, and he is absolutely deadly out there."

Swallow added, "I think the man could ride a horse through hell and back without breaking a sweat. And Tarent and MacFarlane both think he walks on water when it comes to horses."

Major Byrnes, ever the regiment's black sheep, finally grew bored with this discussion. "Gentlemen, there are three days left before we all go out there and either prove we can stay on a horse or make asses of ourselves. What do you say to a little wager?"

Charlie smiled. His officers were on the right track, and where they went, he was sure the men would follow. Quietly, he slipped away. He had promised Duncan some pointers and private practice with the small sword.

The evening was crisp; the fire was warm. Elizabeth had gone to bed early after a particularly trying day. Two of the men, practicing for the gymkhana's mounted lance competition, had managed to overextend themselves. The result was two broken legs, one broken arm, and a number of bruises. MacFarlane and Tarent were both unhappy as well, as two horses were decidedly upset. Not injured, just upset.

Charlie had spent the day alternating between writing extensive dispatches to Sheridan about Montgomery and the related problems within his command, and working with the men as they practiced. He was tired, but edgy and not yet ready for sleep. More to the point, he had finally realized that Christmas was only a week away and he did not know what gift he could get for Rebecca.

The two of them sat together in the back parlor sharing an after dinner coffee and brandy, as well as the details of their respective days. Charlie obliquely broached the subject most on his mind.

"Say, did you know that some of the men have been making toys and such for the refugee and neighborhood children?"

"That is very sweet. I am sure the children will be delighted with new toys. Em discovered an old rag doll of mine a few days ago and refuses to give it up."

"I saw it clutched in her arms when I went in to say goodnight. She is very beguiling with it. Does it have a name?"

She laughed, nearly losing her brandy through her nose. "I am afraid I was never very talented in that respect as a child. Mother always told me I called it "Doll." Em, however, has christened it "Em." Quite original I think."

Charlie laughed. "Ah, yes, she is certainly the center of her own universe, is she not?"

"I do believe that you also share that special place in her heart. She loves you so much."

"And I love her." Charlie looked at his lady almost shyly. "But you, my heart, are at the center of my universe."

"And you are mine, love." She placed her glass down and took his hand. "Are you tired yet? You have had a very long day."

"Not yet, love. I just need to spend a little time with you. It was a rather harrowing day. I am more tense than tired, I fear." He took a sip of brandy. "I have obtained some lengths of good sound worsted, and thought they might make good Christmas gifts for the ladies."

"Oh yes, that will be very nice indeed. Some of these ladies have not had anything new in a very long time. I must say, Charlie, I think that Christmas is going to turn out to be wonderful this year."

"And what of you, my love? What would you like for Christmas?"

"I honestly had not given it any thought. I am just glad to have you here with me. But I suppose, knowing you as well as I do, if I do not give you an answer, you will never rest. So, let us see...it is too late to do anything about it this year, but maybe next year we could replace my mother's piano."

"You play, my love? I do enjoy listening to piano music. It is so soothing.

"I can play. Not as well as many, but enough so that I enjoyed it."

"What happened to it?"

"I am afraid we had to sell it, when things got difficult. Mr. Cooper gave a very fair price for it in a time when he most certainly did not have to do so."

"He is a very generous man. I wish that things were different; I could see him being highly successful if the situation were more benign. Did you know that when he was encamped here last spring, General Grant commented that this was the most devastated section of Virginia?"

"I know. But now that the war is going to be over soon, we can start rebuilding. You have given us an excellent start."

"I mean to give it everything I have once I muster out. This is your home, my dear. I cannot help but want to return it to prosperity, if for no other reason than to make you happy."

As he spoke the words, Charlie's mind was spinning at a rapid rate. Perhaps Cooper still had the instrument, or knew where it was. If he could get the actual piano back, it would be delightful. He made a note to talk with Cooper personally on the following day. If not in time for Christmas, perhaps the piano could be his bride gift.

"With you at my side, I shall always be happy, Charlie."

Tuesday, December 20, 1864

The gymkhana was just a few days away. Charlie decided it was time for him to check in with the men, and remind them that whoever won the competition, they were all his men and all under his eye and his care.

He told Rebecca he would be eating with the men that night and set out, dressed in his simple tunic, breeches and boots, without the normal markings of his rank, to measure the pulse of his regiment.

As dusk fell, he walked into the compound that Montgomery's boys had built. Their tents were all shored up with rough planking; berms and ditches controlled the flow of water around the little enclave; and there were cheerful fires burning in the small squares that defined the clusters of tents. A group of men was gathered around one such fire, carefully roasting a brace of rabbits that a trooper had brought down with a sling. A small barrel of ale was being tapped and shared.

Charlie joined the men, sharing a mug of the ale and chatting with them. He asked what they had received in the mail shipment that had come in the day before, and congratulated one of them on the birth of his first son. With friendly banter, Charlie moved on to visit more clusters of men throughout the encampment. He would share a joke, a story, congratulations or commiserations as appropriate, and with each stop, he encouraged and challenged the men to do their best in the competition. There was not a soldier in the regiment who did not want to win the honor of bearing the colors. It was the most dangerous position in the entire regiment, and the most glorious and honorable. Charlie made it clear that the only way to earn that coveted position was through teamwork and excellence.

By the time he had finished his rounds, he was exhilarated. It was clear that the efforts to unify these two disparate forces were starting to work. The men were excited. They were functioning as teams, with each company working together to field the best, most competitive team they could in the upcoming games. He was also a little more relaxed than usual, as he had shared a glass of beer, albeit a small one, with just about every group of men he had visited.

He slipped into the house quietly, as many of the inhabitants were already abed, and pulled his boots off at the foot of the stairs. Carrying them in one hand, and using the other to grasp the balustrade, as his balance was a little impaired, he made his way up to Rebecca's room.

She was sitting before the fire, dressed in her nightgown and a robe, brushing her long hair that glowed red in the fire's flickering light. To Charlie, she looked like a heavenly being, with a halo of red-gold light around her. His hands itched to touch her, his heart hammered in his chest.

She turned to see him enter the room on less than steady feet. She stood and slowly walked toward him. "Charlie, are you all right?"

"Absolutely, my dear. I simply shared a glass or two with the men as I chatted with them." In a softer voice, he added, "You are utterly bewitching tonight, my love."

She took a step back from him after getting a good whiff of the beer he had been drinking with his men. Her stomach roiled and she felt dizzy. "I am glad you had a good time." She tried not to sound as upset as she felt, but visions of Gaines' drunken fumbling came flooding back to her.

Charlie watched Rebecca backing away from him in confusion. The expression on her face was one that he normally associated with an unpleasant smell. *Do I have something on me? I took my boots off, but did I sit in horse droppings?* He looked down at himself, a little befuddled. No, there was nothing untoward on his uniform. "Rebecca? Did I do something wrong?"

Remaining silent, she shook her head, but turned back to the table and took her seat as she tried to keep her tears from falling. "Of course not," she choked, trying desperately to keep the emotion from her voice, but failing miserably.

He shook himself, trying to clear his head. This was not what he had expected. The evening had been highly successful: his men were in good cheer, and they were coming together as a team. Christmas was ahead of them, and he and Rebecca were about to celebrate it together for the first time. Everything should be fine. But the evidence in front of him said something was not fine.

Moving slowly and speaking very gently, he approached her. "Darling, tell me what is wrong. You know if I can, I will fix it. If I cannot fix it, at least we will share it and by doing so, halve the pain." By the time he finished his little speech, he was standing behind her, softly caressing her shoulder.

She swallowed hard and tried not to flinch at his touch. She realized there was no reason to have such a reaction; as always, his touch was kind and tender. "Beer," she whispered quietly.

Beer? It made no sense to him. Of course he had been drinking beer. That is what his men drank at night. Well, it did have a strong smell. While he had not had that much to drink, and had certainly come to bed more inebriated from his evenings of chatting with Whitman or Polk over a few glasses of brandy, he probably did smell of it. "You have a problem with beer?"

Judiciously, he backed away from her. Perhaps the smell offended her. She might not like the smell of beer, but he still could not figure out why it should make her cry. Charlie backed up to the door, and stood there looking like a child being sent to his room and not knowing why. "Please tell me what is wrong, dear."

Keeping her head down and her eyes on the hands in her lap, she turned and offered the only explanation she could. "He drank beer."

He? He who? Oh, hell. Gaines would drink beer then come to her. It had to be. She associates the smell of beer with the pain of Gaines' unwelcome attentions.

"Darling, I am sorry. I had no idea..." He trailed off, at a loss, not knowing what to do or say to make things different. He had climbed the stairs wanting Rebecca with every fiber of his body. Yet in the matter of a moment, somehow, he knew he was no better than Gaines. "I will leave you until I no longer smell of something that reminds you of so much pain."

He turned to leave, his shoulders slumped, his head bowed with shame. A few beers, a night with the men, and he had turned into something he detested—the same kind of man his father was, that Gaines was.

The voice in his head was back in force. *See. It is in you, too, like a poison, like an insidious evil that you can never escape. You do not deserve this woman, and you know it. Especially now, if the first thing you think of after a couple of beers is to come and bed her, regardless of her feelings, regardless of what has been done to her in the past.*

Rebecca rose from her table and moved to the bed. Every single ghost that haunted her told her to let Charlie go and sleep off his drunk elsewhere. But her heart made different demands. She got up and went to the door, peering around to see if he was still upstairs. He was standing at the top of the steps, looking down them as if he were trying to decide if he could manage them.

"Charlie?"

"Yes, Rebecca?" he responded, without turning around. If he had, she would have seen the tears in his eyes that blurred the stairs before him.

"Please, please come back. I am sorry. I did not mean to..." She stopped, not sure what she wanted to say. "Please come to bed."

He took a deep breath. "So am I, dear. I did not know. Let me get cleaned up, and I will join you."

"No. Please come now. You are not him. I should know that. I should know that what was wrong with him will not be wrong with you. You have never been anything but kind and loving to me, Charlie. Please, just come back."

He sat abruptly on the top step of the stairs. In a low voice, made rough by suppressed tears, he started to confess. "No, dear. You do not understand. I am exactly like him. I had a few beers with my men, and all I wanted to do was take you to bed. I had no more thought of what you wanted and needed than I did of what Shannon or Black Jack wants when I put them out to breed." In a much smaller, broken voice he added, "I have become what I tried to escape. I am so sorry."

Rebecca took a few tentative steps toward him. Some sense of fear remained that his temper would snap and she would be slapped back. But her soul told her to move forward, to offer support and comfort to its other half. Slowly she sat down next to him, wrapping the hem of her nightgown around her feet to keep them warm and resting her chin on her knees. "I love you, Charlie."

"I love you, Rebecca. I would give anything to have not hurt you tonight. I promise, I will not drink beer any more, since it bothers you, darling." He was babbling and she knew it. Every so often, he simply turned into a scared, miserable child—trying so hard to please, and so afraid of failing.

She reached over and took his hand, bringing it back and holding it tight in her lap. "I never loved him, Charlie. I have never been in love before," she smiled at him and brushed the hair back from his forehead with her free hand, "until now. I know you did not mean to hurt me; and, to be honest, I had never realized what the smell of beer would do to me. I did not know I would react that way."

He did not say anything. He sat very still. As she caressed his forehead, his eyes closed, and he leaned into her hand. She could feel his pulse pounding in his wrist and see it in the veins at his temples.

"Now let us go back to our room and get ready for bed. Everything is fine, my love."

He stood and followed her back into the bedroom. He went immediately to his side of the room, stripped his clothing off and bundled it into a tight wad, which he carried back into the sitting room and left by the door for Lizbet or Jocko to pick up in the morning. Rebecca grew concerned as his bedtime washing seemed to go on for longer than usual. When he finally did climb into the bed, the smell of mint was quite strong. He lay still, remaining on the far side of the bed and facing away. "Good night, love. Sleep well," He offered, in the same subdued voice he had used by the stairs.

Rebecca sighed and rolled over to his side of the bed. She draped her arm over his waist and kissed the back of his neck. "I love you, Charlie. Good night, my love."

~

Wednesday, December 21, 1864

Reg was carefully polishing the woodwork in the front hall. Preparing a house for Christmas was a Southern tradition that Beulah was strict about. The house had to look perfect for the callers who would inevitably troop through to see how much Miss Rebecca was benefiting from the Federal Army's presence. A loud rapping on the front door startled him out of the trance he had settled into as he carefully rubbed bees' wax into the balustrade.

Hastily stuffing the rag he was using into his pocket, he smoothed his hair as best he could and opened the door. Before him stood a short, wiry man with close-cropped beard and hair, dressed in a very dusty Yankee uniform. There were three stars on the man's shoulder.

"Colonel Redmond, please."

Reg closed his jaw with a snap. "Yes, Sir. Come in, Sir. Can I get you something, Sir? Who shall I tell him is calling, Sir?" Reg knew he was babbling, but the sight of those stars, plus the brass on the shoulders of the small group of men behind this little man had put him into a panic.

"You may tell him General Philip Sheridan is calling."

"Yes, Sir, General, Sir. Would you step into the parlor, Sir, and let me build a fire for you and your men? Are you sure I cannot get you or your men something, Sir? Some tea, or maybe a brandy or..." Reg trailed off, realizing that he could not open the door to the parlor, bow, pull on his forelock and look like a rational, properly trained house servant all at the same time.

"Is there a problem?"

"Oh, no, Sir. Right away, Sir. I will just go and get him, Sir."

At that moment, the door from the small family dining room at the back of the hall opened and Charlie entered, carrying young Em. He had just finished feeding her lunch, a significant amount of which had found its way onto the front of his blue frock coat.

Charlie looked into Phil Sheridan's eyes and nearly panicked. A slow blush worked its way from his ears across his face. "Good day, General. I was not expecting you, Sir."

The General did an extremely good job of hiding his amusement at seeing one of his finest officers covered in unrecognizable mush. He took a deep breath. "Apparently not, Colonel Redmond."

Charlie first tried to salute, but with a squirming child in his arms, it was less than effective. He then started to offer his free hand to the General, but noticed that it was still lightly dappled with mashed apples and cereal. He hastily wiped it off on the skirt of his coat and settled Em more securely in the crook of his left arm, to complete the greeting.

While Sheridan managed to keep a straight face, Colonel McCauley was not so successful. A muffled snicker could be heard coming from behind the hand that McCauley had clamped over his mouth. Other members of Sheridan's entourage could not resist the impulse, either. Here was one of the most pristine, "regular Army" members of Sheridan's staff: covered in gruel, with a squirming child in his arms; sporting a blush that would do credit to a schoolgirl; and no hope of regaining his regimental dignity in sight.

"Um, Reg, would you please take Em to Miss Rebecca? And while you are at it, please ask Beulah to bring us some lunch." He turned to Sheridan. "I assume, General, that you have not yet eaten?"

The General removed his hat and looked the Colonel in the eye. "Lunch would be most welcome."

Charlie handed the squirming child to Reg. Or rather, he tried to hand the child to Reg.

Em shook her head furiously and grabbed his collar. "No! Em stay with Papa."

At that moment, a voice floated down from the second floor. "Charlie Redmond. Where is that child? It is time and past time for her bath and her nap."

The snickering got even more pronounced. Not only was Charlie covered in a child's lunch, he was also obviously, seriously henpecked.

This was a sad fate for the Army of the Shenandoah's premiere cavalry commander, a man they had all thought was a confirmed bachelor.

"Have you other plans, Colonel?" the General asked, trying to contain the grin threatening to break across his lips.

"Um, no, General. Actually, I just finished lunch myself and was going to get cleaned up and go back to my office." He turned towards the stairs and raised his voice. "Miss Rebecca. Rebecca, you might wish to join us, as we have guests." He continued to hold the child, who had attached herself like a small leech to his coat collar and was peeking over her own shoulder at the men in her hall.

Rebecca dried her hands on a towel she had prepared for Em's bath. Before she even poked her head into the hall, she called. "Guests? Oh, who in the name of God would have the bad manners to call just before a holiday?"

"My commanding officer and his staff." Charlie's response was very flat, devoid of any expression or emotion at all. Rebecca had learned that tone was a very bad sign.

She took a deep breath and quickly glanced into the mirror as she removed her apron and tossed it aside. *Oh wonderful. Charlie is going to have my hide for this.* "I will be right there, Colonel Redmond."

Reg, in the meantime, had retreated to the kitchen, where he had helped Sarah and Beulah quickly assemble trays with ham, breads, pickles, and cheese, as well as a huge pot of hot tea for the officers. They carried the rough lunch into the main dining room, and threw open the doors, inviting the officers in to eat. Charlie let out a very relieved sigh. Now, if only Jocko had seen them coming and managed to grab a clean coat for him, he might be able to rescue some shred of dignity.

As Reg opened the doors to the dining room, Rebecca descended the stairs. The gentlemen of Sheridan's entourage all drew themselves up to greet the lady of the house. Snickers were muffled, although several of the men could not help continuing to grin.

"General Sheridan, gentlemen, may I present our hostess and my fiancée, Mrs. Rebecca Gaines?"

Rebecca tried to present herself as the proper hostess and a lady worthy of the distinguished Colonel. The very first thing she did was relieve him of Emily and then smile at the General. "General Sheridan, gentlemen, good day to you, Sirs, and welcome to my home."

The gentlemen bowed politely to the lovely, somewhat flushed young woman before them. The child in her arms squirmed and reached out for Charlie, fussing and whimpering. "Papa. Want Papa!"

Charlie stepped in. "Gentlemen, we have put together a hasty lunch for you. If you would step this way, you can ease your hunger while Mrs. Gaines and I attend to this particular... small, and very demanding citizen."

"That is all right, Colonel Redmond; please attend to the General and his men. I will see to our Em and return shortly."

"Thank you, Miss Rebecca." With a look of relief, Charlie turned back to the officers in the hall and led them into the dining room. Beulah had thought to provide a pile of warm, damp towels in a basket on the sideboard to let the men wipe the dust from their hands and faces. "It is a chill day, gentlemen. There are hot cloths, hot tea, and some fine brandy to warm yourselves." Reg was tending the fire, stoking it from glowing embers to a warm flame. "So, General, have you come in response to my request, or do you have other business with the 13th as well? We would be honored if you would join us for the Christmas feast."

"I will indeed, Colonel. I wanted to see for myself this Eden you had found for the winter. Your letters about the beauty of the land made me want to see it for myself. I also wanted to see the condition of the civilians you have told me about, and what progress you have made in unifying your regiment."

McCauley cleared his throat. "Um, General, there was the matter of that paperwork you were waiting on, as well."

Sheridan smiled a dour half smile. "Oh, yes. Thank you for reminding me. Just a little bit of administrative hoopla to attend to, I think."

Charlie looked at Sheridan with a puzzled expression. Paperwork? He was certain that he and Polk had submitted everything that they were supposed to. But then, the ongoing adventure of trying to get quality supplies from the Quartermaster General was always a challenge.

"Well, Sir, I am sure we can clear up any questions you may have. I will send for Polk while you eat."

"No, Colonel, do not bother Polk. You will be responsible for answering the questions I have." The General turned his back to the Colonel and picked up a plate as he looked over the food placed before them. "Looks like your Mrs. Gaines is a very capable hostess, Redmond."

"Yes, Sir, she is. She has found homes and productive work for a number of refugees, and has helped to organize the ladies of the community to do what they can to help themselves and the refugees survive the winter. It has been hard for her, I confess, for some of the locals see her as a traitor for associating with us, but she has been magnificent."

Sheridan picked a few things for his plate and slowly turned to face his officer. "Your fiancée, aye, Colonel Redmond?"

Charlie drew himself up to his most erect and dignified, an effect that would have been a perfect demonstration of his pride in his lady, had it not been marred by the now drying and flaking bits of gruel on his uniform left from Em's lunch. "Yes, Sir, my fiancée. Mrs. Gaines has done me the honor of consenting to be my wife. We plan to announce it officially at the New Year, although many of the local folks already know. It will be a small wedding, probably before the spring campaign, as is appropriate for her second marriage."

"I suppose congratulations are in order, then. Will the new Mrs. Redmond be joining you when you go west?"

"When I go west, Sir? I had understood that General Wilson was finally chosen to go west. I hoped that I would be able to remain here." There was a hint of a squeak in Charlie's voice. McCauley and Brigadier General Merritt, standing behind Sheridan at the buffet, overheard the conversation and snorted to one another.

"Yes, of course. West, that is where the excitement will be after the war, Colonel. Certainly, you want to be where you are needed the most. I have two or three burgeoning forts that I think you would be just right for. They are just getting started. Not much in the way of luxury or comfort, but if you can survive the Indian attacks, I am sure you will be fine."

Rebecca swept into the dining room at that moment. "Oh, my. The West! I hear it is very exciting—rugged and natural."

Charlie stood there with a bemused look on his face. "The West. Yes. Well, Sir, I believe we need to see the current situation to an end before we start thinking of Indian attacks, Sir."

Sheridan could only smile at the couple as Rebecca took her place next to Charlie and looped her arm through his. The General could tell he might be able to bait the Colonel, but he would not succeed in luring his lady. "Yes, Redmond, I do believe that is the wisest course of action. Very good, Sir."

"I look forward to it, Sir. Now, I believe I asked if you and your staff would be joining us for Christmas. Miss Rebecca, do you think we could find places for these gentlemen?"

Rebecca smiled and caressed Charlie's arm as she looked at the General. "Of course, Colonel Redmond. I will have Reg and Lizbet prepare rooms immediately. We are honored to have the General in our home."

Sheridan smiled at Rebecca. "Thank you, Ma'am. My men and I are honored." Sheridan gestured to McCauley, who stepped to his General's side and handed him a packet of papers. "But I have a question, Ma'am. Why do you persist in referring to Charlie as 'Colonel'?"

Rebecca blushed and looked to Charlie, then back to the General. "To be honest, it just seemed like the thing to do."

"Madam, it is customary to refer to officers in the United States Army by their proper rank." He handed the packet of papers to Rebecca. "Perhaps you should review these documents?"

Her heart jumped to her throat, fearing she had made a serious mistake in front of Charlie's commander. She swallowed hard and took the packet of papers. "Of course, General. I do apologize if I have offended." She glanced to Charlie, hoping that he was not too horrified.

Charlie was totally confused. Had his summary dismissal of the men who had objected to the orders to begin the process of reconstruction come back to haunt him? Had he been demoted? Was that why Sheridan was talking about the western forts? Was he going to be banished to some nameless, primitive stockade in the western plains, never to be heard from again? If that was the case, it was time for him to tender his resignation. He looked around at the other officers in the room. Several were Brigadiers; the rest wore the same eagles on their shoulders he had on his. Most were younger than he was. Charlie was afraid that his twenty years of honorable service were about to end because of one moment of righteous anger. He nodded to Rebecca to open and read the documents.

Rebecca slowly opened the envelope, and with shaky hands removed the papers and began reading. After a moment, she looked to Sheridan. "Really, General?"

"Really, Mrs. Gaines." He nodded gently.

By now, every man in the room was watching the tableau among the three of them with some degree of interest. Every man also had a glass in his hand. The man before them was one of the finest field commanders in Sheridan's force, and had finally been recognized by the War Department as such.

Rebecca nodded, and slowly folded the papers and placed them back in the envelope. Then she looked to Charlie. "I am sorry. I did address you incorrectly." She paused, continuing as she failed to keep the smile from her face, "Brigadier General Redmond."

Slowly, the reality of what she had said soaked into Charlie's consciousness. A serious look came over his face, and he drew himself up to full attention, saluting General Sheridan. "Thank you, Sir." Somehow, in that moment, the bits of Em's lunch, the embarrassment, and the teasing were all forgotten.

Rebecca smiled with great pride.

Someone handed glasses of brandy to Sheridan and Rebecca.

"Congratulations," he paused and smiled at the couple before him, "General Redmond. Let us pray that with your leadership and determination, we all find an end to this conflict soon, so you may return home to your lovely bride. Gentleman, please raise your glasses to Brigadier General Redmond and his lovely fiancée."

Charlie smiled broadly. "Thank you, gentlemen. General, if you and your men would like to finish your lunch, Miss Rebecca and I will see to quarters for you. When you are ready, we can begin your review."

"Fine. Oh, and Redmond? You might want to change into a clean coat."

CHAPTER 20

THURSDAY, DECEMBER 22, 1864

Sheridan was a hard driving commander. On the first morning of the gymkhana, he called Charlie and Polk into conference just as reveille sounded. McCauley trailed along with a large dispatch case in either hand. The four men spent two grueling hours going over the requisition and supply problems that had plagued Charlie since he took over command of the 13th. They ate while they went through the ledgers and collected correspondence, trying to find solutions to the basic problem of preparing the 13th for a key role in the spring campaign. Before they were finished, Charlie's desk was piled high with papers and books.

"Well, Redmond, as near as I can tell, you have about three quarters of what you need right now."

McCauley added, "And we are scheduled to ship the rest over the course of the next month."

"With all due respect, General, Colonel, the quality of materials we have received is, for the most part, atrocious. If one item in four is actually usable, I would be surprised. Polk, did you get those samples ready for me?"

"Yes, Sir. Duncan and Jocko worked for half the night pulling samples from every one of the lots in the stores."

"Well, have them bring them in. General, Colonel, I want you gentlemen to see just what kind of supplies your quartermaster has been sending us."

Polk rose from his chair beside Charlie's desk, stuck his head out the door, and spoke a few words to the trooper standing outside. Turning back into the room, he picked up a roll of butcher's paper and spread it over the large table Charlie used for his staff meetings.

First, Duncan hauled in small bags of flour, meal, and salt pork. Behind him, Jocko lugged in several pair of boots, breeches, and tunics. Silently the two men filed out, returning immediately with more sample items. Several blankets, a jumble of tack, various pieces of metalwork, and a pair of saddles came next. Finally, Duncan and Jocko carried in a large roll of heavy canvas, which from its clean, unstained appearance had obviously never been used.

Charlie started with the food supplies. He opened the bag of corn meal and poured it onto the table. "Gentlemen, take a look. One in four bags of meal come in with these little fellows riding along." The little pile of yellow meal was moving, alive with small white grubs. As he poured the flour on the table, he added, "Of course, they are clearly additional meat for the men. I have no idea what these are, although I suspect they are rodent feces." There were small, rod-shaped black specks mixed in with the flour. "However, neither of these will kill my men. It just gives them a bellyache. Of course, there is the nausea my mess crew suffers from having to deal with it. This, on the other hand," he continued as he opened the third food package, "will kill." As he spoke, he rolled a piece of salt pork on the table, green with mold and moving with maggots. The stench was sickening.

Jocko stepped over and tore the paper off, carrying the offensive materials out of the office. Both Sheridan and McCauley looked slightly green. The salt pork had been a bit overwhelming.

Charlie turned to the uniforms and blankets. "As you can see, gentlemen, the blankets are pitiful." He rolled out three blankets, each of which had holes that were clearly flaws in the basic cloth, rather than from wear. The uniforms were no better. "I cannot keep my men warm with clothes and blankets like this." He nodded to Duncan, who unrolled the canvas tent. The roof of the tent was stitched together with a seam that was not completed because the canvas was thin and could not hold the stitches well enough to even try to patch it. It was obvious the tent would leak under the lightest of rains. "Nor do we have dry tents for them."

He laid the tack on top of the woolens. "The leather they send us for the horses is no better. Sometimes it comes in green with mildew. Of the last three batches of saddles that came in, almost half had broken trees." He pointed to the obviously unusable saddles. "But the worst is the boots. We got an entire shipment of cavalry boots made out of rawhide. Do you know what happens when a rawhide boot gets wet? Let me tell you. It shrinks, and turns rock hard. We had to cut these off four of our men. They were desperate; they had no boots, so they tried to use what we had. It was very unpleasant, to say the least."

Charlie walked over to his gun cabinet and withdrew two carbines and a pair of pistols. He walked back to the table and held one of the pistols between two fingers by the grips. He gave the pistol a brisk shake. The pistol rattled and a small metal pin fell out. It was the only thing holding the trigger in place. He laid the other pistol beside its mate and opened the breeches of the two carbines. Neither of them had firing pins. "Of course, it does make it difficult to engage the enemy when we have no weapons that will fire."

Charlie looked at his General. "Sir, I submit that if we are to engage the enemy this spring, we will have to be properly supplied. The only resources that have been of the consistent quality needed to properly supply this force have been the horses provided by Cavalry

Services. General Wilson's efforts to organize our mounts were clearly successful. Why can we not have the same quality effort from the Quartermaster General's office?"

Sheridan looked to McCauley. "What have you found, Angus? Is this typical of what our troops are getting?"

"I am afraid so, Sir. No one has presented such a...forceful case before, but we have consistent problems with our suppliers."

Sheridan thought for a while, then turned back to Charlie. "Well, General, I believe that your personal plans will require that you make a visit to the capital in the not too far distant future. I will prepare some dispatches for you to deliver, and suggest you take your little demonstration with you. I am sure General Meigs will be fascinated. I have known the man for a long time and find him to be honorable and well intentioned. I cannot say the same for some of the men in his command. In the meantime, I will do what I can to see to it that you get better quality supplies in the future. McCauley, please make a note that every single batch of materials for General Redmond be manually inspected before it is shipped. In fact, see to it that everything we get from the Quartermaster General is inspected. And feel absolutely no compunction about sending back anything that is substandard. Am I clear?"

"Yes, Sir." The look on McCauley's face would have been humorous if the situation had been any less grave.

Sheridan's voice was silken as he went on. "And McCauley?" His adjutant looked up. "I will hold you personally responsible should any more shipments to the 13th or any other regiment under my command contain any substandard products." McCauley looked rather like a startled deer. It appeared that his lucrative case of selective blindness was now a thing of the past.

There was a long silence in the office, and then Sheridan slapped his hands on his thighs. "Gentlemen, I believe there is a contest about to start. Shall we go cheer the men on?"

~

As the officers arrived at the main paddock, Major Swallow was posting the official rules and scoring standards for the gymkhana. Each event would have individual winners; the judges for the event, drawn from the officers' ranks, were also tallying the overall placement of each company. As Charlie had announced, the company with the most total points at the end of the two-day event would take the vanguard; the individual with the most points would be the color bearer. Within the regiment, these positions were the highest honor to which any trooper could aspire. There were also personal rewards for the winners of each event, all designed to help make the life of the winning trooper and his friends a little more pleasant. Hams, small kegs of brandy, fine coffee, tobacco, and a handful of passes to visit home for a week with travel orders on one of the supply trains were waiting, ready to reward the winners.

The men had already assembled their teams in the big pasture. They had set the fences and brush jumps for a variety of cross-country races. These first events of the gymkhana were traditional races, each covering between two and three and a half miles, over rolling terrain. There were water hazards for some of the races, created by crossing shallow sections of the stream that ran through the pasture, wood jumps, and brush jumps designed to look like the hedges that were common separators between fields.

The men had built some small stands, somewhat protected from the weather and the chill breeze from the north. Each had a few chairs, tables, and a small brazier to provide some warmth. These stands were for the officers and guests. Most of the residents of Culpeper had turned out in their best finery, such as it was, to watch the events. In addition, Sergeant Jamison and his mess crew had put together a small feast, with hot soup, ham and biscuits, coffee, tea, and a small mountain of apples for the men and guests to sample.

The races started with the shorter, easier stretches. The first was two miles, over wooden fences, with no water hazards or blind jumps. The best of the younger horses were being tested, with a fairly large number being fielded. Each company was represented by at least one rider, and in a couple of cases, two. The race went without incident and the rider from Company A just nosed out one of Company D's men for first place. A brief hiatus allowed the judges to clear the field and reset the course flags.

The next race was also short, again only two miles, but over brush jumps designed to look like hedges. This race was also well contested. When jumping over wooden fences, the horses had to clear the fence completely; but when jumping over hedges, the smart horse and rider actually went through the top of the hedge, keeping as low to the ground as possible while still clearing the obstacle. It was always an exciting race, and one with more than a little risk associated with misjudging the jump. Too high, and you lost ground; too low, and you ran the risk of the horse stumbling and throwing the rider. The young horses being used for this shorter distance were just learning that fine line.

The race was running cleanly until one of the riders from Company C misjudged the second jump. The horse's left cannon dragged through the brush, and he stumbled as he landed, sending his rider directly over the horse's head. The trooper tucked and rolled, as he had been taught. His mount gathered himself and managed to jump over the fallen rider, then continued to run the race. Several of the race judges ran to check on the fallen rider, who rose, with a bruised ego but otherwise unharmed, having only had the breath knocked out of him. Others raced to catch the riderless horse.

The mount was having none of that. He was running with his herd, a young, dominant stallion. Winning the race was as important for the horse as it had been for his rider. He took each jump with ease, gaining steadily on the lead horse. By the time the race was over, the young stallion had outrun every mounted animal in the race and eluded the judges' attempts to remove him. Riderless, he crossed the finish line first, then pranced, and kicked his heels in pleasure at his accomplishment. The crowd laughed and cheered at his antics. Unfortunately, without a rider, he was not qualified to win.

However, all of the young gallants within the troopers' ranks made a mental note to try to claim this fine young fellow as their own regular mount.

The next four races proceeded with minimal incidents and no disastrous injuries. One horse pulled a hock, another bruised her knee from a bad landing, but there were no broken bones. The riders were not quite so lucky, as one rider managed to dislocate his shoulder and another broke a collarbone. Dr. Walker and Samuelson tended to the human casualties, while Tarent and MacFarlane managed the equine patients.

A late lunch was enjoyed by all, with a bit of strained socializing between the Culpeper citizens and the officers from both Charlie and Sheridan's commands. Mayor Frazier and General Sheridan retired to a quiet corner where they were seen having a very intense discussion on the condition of the county. Words like "seed stock" and "winter supplies" were heard drifting from their conference.

Finally, Mayor Frazier stood, the veins in his forehead standing out. "General, how do you expect us to recover? We were a thriving town with over fifteen hundred citizens. Now we are less than one hundred and fifty old men, women, and children—with no resources and no hope for the future. Where do you think we will find the means to do anything other than starve, freeze, or rot away this winter?"

Sheridan looked startled. Frazier rejoined Mr. and Mrs. Cooper, who were chatting with Elizabeth and Rebecca. Charlie, dressed in breeches, boots, and short tunic because he had been serving as a mounted race judge and was also to ride soon, was quietly tending to the ladies, bringing cups of hot tea for them. Sheridan had started towards what he hoped would be a more accepting group when the next race was announced. He sighed, and made a mental note to discuss the situation with Charlie later.

The seventh race of the day was exciting. Only one entrant from each company was allowed. Each team put forward their best rider and horse for this demanding course. It had both brush and wood jumps, a water jump, several combination jumps, and a blind drop in the three and a half mile span. Because of the difficulty of the course, the company that won would receive double points in the cumulative total, and the individual winner would receive a two week pass—long enough to catch the supply train for an extended visit back home.

Every rider was keyed up for this critical race. The first start was called back, as one horse broke early. After some milling around to calm the horses, the flag dropped again.

Nine horses and riders broke cleanly this time. For the first mile, they ran in a tight cluster, with two and three horses running side by side, almost in formation, over the first jumps. As the horses moved through the water jump, one rider's stirrup leather snapped, startling the horse and nearly dropping the rider. He hung on manfully, righting himself in the saddle and continuing.

The blind jump forced the riders to spread out a bit, since controlling the horses as they dropped the four feet of the jump presented more risk than a regular jump. As the riders started to spread, young Duncan, riding for Company H, moved into second place. Through the combination jump, he held his position, then let his rawboned buckskin have his head for the dead run to the finish line. After more than three miles of hard riding, this last spurt to the finish line was a measure both of the endurance of the horse, and the skill of the rider in husbanding his mount's energy. The final sprint was close; the rider from Company D was determined to prove his mettle as well. Montgomery's men had something special to prove. They were determined to show they were just as good or even better soldiers as any in the regiment, regardless of the problems Monty and his cronies like Davison had created. Riding neck and neck with Duncan, Raiford from Company D kept repeating to his horse, "We gotta win. We gotta. Go, boy." Subtly, gently, so the judges could not see, Duncan eased back on his mount, giving Raiford the lead. More than most, Duncan understood.

As the winners from the seventh race were being recognized, Charlie stepped behind Duncan. "Pulled him a bit, did you?"

"No, Sir. He j-j-just did not h-have as m-mu-much left as I thought."

"Right. Well, you are a good man, Duncan. A good man. I would be proud to have you carry the colors for me."

"Well, Sir, you n-ne-never know. There are st-still tomorrow's c-co-contests."

Charlie smiled and moved away. It was time for the officers' race; he was riding, although if he and Jack won, the rewards and points would go to the line officer that placed first. The officers' circuit was a complex double figure eight around the course, followed by a long straight on the outside track. The race was a little over three and a half miles, a test of both the rider's skill and the horse's endurance. The field was limited to one officer from each company plus one officer from the general staff. As the riders assembled, Charlie noted that the young lieutenant who had brought word of Montgomery's injuries was riding for Company D. He nudged Jack over to stand beside the young man and wished him luck.

Jack was full of energy. All day he had watched the other horses race, while Charlie held him back. From Jack's point of view, this was unfair. Now he had a chance to show off, to prove he was the dominant stallion in this herd. The General had his hands full as the horses lined up for the start. The flag dropped and Jack was off before he had a chance to do more than settle in the saddle.

Jack took the lead immediately, trying to shake off Charlie's attempts to hold him back and conserve some energy for the sprint at the end. As far as Jack was concerned, Charlie could tell him where to go, but they were going there at Jack's pace.

The pace the horses set was brutal. Charlie constantly tried to check Jack's speed, but the big black just took the bit between his teeth and charged on. Jack sailed through the first series of jumps, and leapt into the water, throwing a huge spray of icy foam behind him as he plunged ahead. The horse had been watching; he knew that the blind drop had a long, down-sloping flat after it. He sailed long over the drop then gathered himself for the combination jump.

Jump, stride, stride, jump, stride, stride, jump. Then Jack was off to the final straight with only two jumps to go. Charlie let himself look back for a moment.

Right off Jack's left flank, the young lieutenant, Major Swallow's cousin from Company D, was hanging on for dear life. His mount was heavily lathered; the boy was sheet white and his jaw was locked, but they kept the pace. The two horses—one coal black, the other a light chestnut almost a hand shorter than Jack—fairly flew over the ground, brushing through the last two jumps as though they had wings. The rest of the field was almost ten furlongs behind, but it did not matter. This was an issue of honor, of excellence, of rising to the challenge.

Jack refused to let the smaller horse take the lead. The big black reached deep into himself and found the energy for a final sprint. The chestnut still kept pace, and they crossed the finish line with Jack in the lead by less than a length. As the lieutenant's mount swept across the line and tracked into the cool down zone, the boys of Company D literally mobbed their young officer. They raised him to their shoulders and bore him off to preside at the dinner of roast venison that went to the winner of the officers' race. Tarent personally took charge of the light boned chestnut, checking to make sure that the dead out run had not blown the beast.

Charlie wiped the sweat from his forehead then rubbed Jack's nose. "Good boy. You just had to have your head, old fellow." MacFarlane took the reins from Charlie as Sheridan, Rebecca, and a host of others swept up to the winner's circle. McCauley was noticeably absent, no doubt handling the myriad of details Sheridan had dumped in his lap as a result of the morning meeting.

"Well done, Redmond," the General grinned at his commander. "Now, we shall see if you can resolve some of the other problems we face as well as you rode this race."

Charlie smiled ruefully at Rebecca and shrugged. His General had called.

The light of day had long since waned as the four men sat amid piles of papers, rolled maps, assorted tax ledgers, and empty coffee mugs. Charlie was still dressed in his breeches and field tunic, smelling of a combination of horse sweat, cigars, and the smudge from the fireplace that was not drawing as well as it should. When the wind blew from the southwest, the chimney always backed up. It was but a small inconvenience to an experienced field officer, as having an office with a fireplace was a luxury.

"So, Charlie, if you get the seed you asked for, do you think you can at least give these folks the basics to get started on the road back?"

"Yes, Sir, I do. Most of my men have been quite willing to help these people rebuild."

Polk added, "To be honest, Sir, I think they are glad to be doing something other than fighting or sitting around waiting. For many of them, it feels a little like being at home to be mending fences, winter-plowing fields, and repairing roofs."

"Well, that is good. But I am still worried about the more vehement elements of this little society."

"That continues to be a problem. But one at a time, we are bringing them over."

"Well, if you can bring Mrs. Williams over, it may constitute a miracle." McCauley had listened politely to Mrs. Williams during the luncheon earlier that day. She had managed to offend every Union officer present.

Charlie snorted. He stood and stretched. "A brandy, General?"

"Yes, thank you."

Charlie looked inquiringly at the other two men, then poured brandies for each of them. A silence hung in the room, as they had one more issue to deal with and none of the men wanted to broach the subject. Montgomery.

Finally, Sheridan addressed the problem, starting with the summary dismissal of Davison and his small group of cronies.

"You know, Redmond, I have confirmed your dishonorable discharge of Davison and the others, but I still worry about them. They are just the kind of men to stay in the area and prey on the locals. Keep a sharp eye out." Sheridan considered his brandy for a moment, then added, "And if they do cause trouble, turn them over to the civilian authorities, you hear me?"

"Yes, Sir. However, Sir, I believe I am part of the civilian authority here right now, as the regional representative of the U.S. Government."

"Yes, but get Frazier and the others involved. I am afraid if those renegades do create trouble, it will be serious trouble. I would rather see the locals handle any capital crime."

Sheridan finished his brandy and held his glass out for another tot. "As for Montgomery, I am afraid there is no option but to hold a court martial. Since you two, Swallow, Mrs. Gaines, and several of your men are all witnesses, I will not have any of you sit on the panel. Merritt and Colonel James will serve with me, and you, McCauley, will serve as the defense advocate. Howard will serve as prosecuting officer. If Montgomery is well enough, we will hold it immediately after Christmas." Sheridan finished off the second brandy in one swallow. He hated having any of his men come to trial, especially an officer, and on such vicious charges. "Now, with that settled, gentlemen, shall we clean up and join the ladies for dinner?"

Jocko had thoughtfully hauled a bath up to Rebecca's small sitting room so Charlie could bathe without having to share the bathing room with Sheridan and his staff, thus maintaining his masculine image.

As Charlie sat in the small tin tub before the fire, Rebecca pulled her sleeves up and captured the washrag. She began scrubbing her back thoroughly. "I swear, Charlie, I have no idea how you do it. You wear a singlet, a shirt, a vest, stock, and a coat and still you get mud all down your back."

"Jack was very affectionate when I visited him in the stable. He drooled on me and, I assume, shared some of his chewed up hay. It itched all through this afternoon's meeting with Sheridan and McCauley. It was all I could do to stay in the room and not rub up against the door jamb."

Rebecca laughed, the image was too funny: Charlie trying to discreetly scratch his own back against the fireplace or the door jamb like a big bear, while looking cool and collected in front of his commanding officer.

"So, dear, you disappeared after the races. Did you and the General have another epic session?"

"We did. Much of our discussion was centered on what to do about Montgomery. I am afraid Sheridan will want you to testify. He intends to hold a court martial just after Christmas, before he returns to his own headquarters. Do you think Montgomery is well enough for that?"

Charlie could not see the look on Rebecca's face. The idea of testifying at any time was distasteful; the thought of repeating Montgomery's vitriol in front of a room full of Federal Army officers was downright revolting. However, for Charlie's sake, she would. "Montgomery is hale enough, and, of course, I will testify. I suppose it is necessary."

Charlie turned to look at Rebecca. The look on her face told the story. "I will talk to him again. Perhaps we can get by without you."

"Thank you, but if it is necessary, I will do it."

Charlie rose from the bath. The sight of her beautiful body, gleaming wet, shining in the firelight was enough to distract Rebecca from her brooding concern over Montgomery. Charlie looked at Rebecca as she dried off, recognizing the lustful looks with which she was being graced. "That, dear, will have to wait until later. The General and his staff will be expecting us to join them for dinner."

"Oh, la. You think just because you are beautiful when you are naked, I cannot resist the impulse to touch you. Just you wait, Charlie Redmond. I have as much willpower as the next."

Charlie dried off and went into the bedroom to retrieve her clothes. "Well, dear, you have more willpower than I do, for I swear, I cannot resist you when you are naked."

The two of them proceeded to dress quietly. Finally, just as they were about to go downstairs, Charlie thought to ask again. "So, do you think that Montgomery is ready for the trial?"

Rebecca looked thoughtful. "Well, he is regaining his strength and can be up and about somewhat; but I have no idea if his mind has the strength to understand what is really happening. Elizabeth will have to be consulted."

"I know she will, and I dread it. We could be in a situation where she saved his life just to have him hanged. I know her. She will not be happy."

❧

Friday, December 23, 1864

Day two of the gymkhana was far more military than the previous day. Racing and horsemanship had been the focus of the first day; on the second, weapons skills were the theme. At this point in the competition, the men of Company D were tied for the lead with those of Company A. A young man from Company A was leading in the personal points, with the soldier, Raiford, from Company D who had run neck and neck with Duncan in second place.

The competition opened earlier than on the previous day, as there were numerous and more varied events scheduled. At the opening ceremony, Charlie led the senior officers in a demonstration of precision formation riding. The sight of those beautiful horses was stirring—moving in step, wheeling and turning, weaving back and forth, all under rigorous control by officers who barely moved as they conveyed their commands to the mounts under them. The only sound was the crisp tattoo of the horses' hooves on the hard ground as they moved through their silent routine.

As a finale, the officers formed their mounts into a single, perfect line facing the audience. As one, the horses bowed to the audience, while their riders doffed their plumed hats. The silence continued for a long breath, then the audience broke into sustained applause. Though these officers were the enemy, the people of Culpeper were horse lovers, first and foremost. The demonstration was an awesome presentation of equestrian skill at its best.

There were three types of contest scheduled for the day. In one area, men on foot demonstrated their marksmanship with both carbine and pistol. In another, they demonstrated their skill with sword and saber. But the most exciting contests of the gymkhana were mounted events.

The men competed in pairs, with one competitor eliminated at each pass. The first competition was one that demonstrated the rider's skills in lance work. Rings were laid on the ground at intervals; each horseman had to collect as many rings as possible on the tip of his lance, while preventing his opponent from collecting any.

Typically, this competition resulted in a number of bumps and bruises, and the occasional unseating, but no serious injuries. There were a number of competitors, with the less experienced troopers going first. Wielding eight foot long bamboo lances with blunted tips, the early contenders provided some excitement and some amusement as several of the younger men managed to unseat themselves by overextending out of the saddle. As the competitive field narrowed to the more experienced men, the demonstration of equestrian skill and dexterity drew rounds of loud applause. At the end, somewhat battered and bruised, a grizzled career trooper from Company B stood grinning as General Sheridan himself awarded him the first prize, a small keg of good brandy.

Swordplay was the next of the equestrian events. In this competition, the pairs of men again used their weapons to retrieve items from the ground. However, they were required to cross sabers at least once with each pass. Even though the competitors used blunted sabers and were usually careful to use only the flat of the blade, there were a few cuts and scratches that kept Samuelson busy through the late morning and early afternoon. Unexpectedly, the young man, Raiford, from Company D excelled in this arena, as he had in the hand-to-hand saber contest earlier in the morning.

The last mounted events were demonstrations of marksmanship, first with carbines and then pistols. Three targets were mounted at varying distances from the course. Each rider had to complete the course in a specified period of time, shooting at the targets as they rode by. Points were awarded for both the speed at which the course was ridden and the accuracy of the shots. Here Duncan, Raiford from Company D, and the winner of the lance competition were all serious competitors. After three passes, the men were tied. Sheridan and Charlie looked at one another and decided to reward all three, giving each of them both the prize and the points for first place. Jamison scrambled in his stores to find two extra hams for them.

The final competition was the sharpshooters' demonstration. Here, a number of the troopers from Bucks County, men who had grown up hunting for their primary meat supply, excelled. Duncan led the Ohio boys. Of the Pennsylvanians, Raiford, the young man from Company D, was far and away the leader.

As the marksmanship competition ended, Hoffstader, Polk and McCauley all huddled over the scoring table. The winning company was clear. Company D had placed in every single event. They would be under Charlie's personal command, the vanguard company for the coming campaign. The position of flag bearer was more problematic. There were three men who had demonstrated consistent personal excellence; their scores were very close. The career trooper from Company B, Raiford from Company D, and Duncan from Company H were all in the running.

Charlie joined the scorekeepers and looked over the results. He then faced the waiting troopers, drawn up into formation to hear the results.

"Gentlemen, as we have all seen, Company D has outdone itself, and the rest of you, in performance over the last two days. As promised, Company D will have the honor of riding as the vanguard of the 13th Pennsylvania for the spring campaign. In addition, gentlemen, I offer you the services of Sergeant Jamison for your dinner this evening. Enjoy the feast."

He then called the three individual winners forward. "These three men have distinguished themselves in all aspects of this contest. Their scores are so close, that it is very difficult to distinguish among them. I award each of you a two-week pass, with access to the rail system so that you can go and visit your families. I ask that you be back in camp no later than February first. In addition, since I cannot clearly declare one man the overall winner, I have decided to name Raiford of Company D the flag bearer, while Nailer will serve as my personal aide and Thomson will serve as Colonel Polk's personal aide. Congratulations to all of you. And now, gentlemen and guests, please avail yourselves of the refreshments that we have prepared. I wish all of you a very merry Christmas."

Charlie stepped down, escorting the three winners back into the crowd of their fellow troopers. It pleased him that he had seen a combination of both Ohio and Pennsylvania troops working together. It seemed his plan for creating a cohesive team was working.

Saturday, December 24, 1864

Charlie rose early the next morning to see several ambassadors of good will off on their rounds. Some of the men who had been on the various work details around the county had seen the plight of the women and children living in this barren war zone. In their spare time, a number of the men had made small toys for the children and various housewares for the women. The groups of men set off in high spirits to deliver their gifts.

Charlie and Jocko joined one of these groups for the first few miles of their Christmas journey. Charlie wanted one thing more for the Christmas decorations—a sprig of mistletoe to enliven the festivities. As the men rode, they searched the treetops, barren with winter, for that bright flash of green that signified the parasitic plant's presence. Finally, in an old oak, gnarled by time and wind, they saw the clump of green, speckled with white berries.

The ball of greenery was far too high in the old tree for even the lightest and most nimble of the men to climb to it. Charlie pulled his pistol, took careful aim, and fired. The foliage exploded, with sprigs of green falling like rain. Jocko scrambled off his horse, gathered the mistletoe, and carefully wrapped the best sprigs in his handkerchief. Charlie was thrilled. His men were amused.

A gnarled trooper chewed on his pipe stem, watching his commander behave like an excited boy. "Yup, General, Sir. Just look at what happens to a fella when a pretty lady falls into his life."

Another trooper joined the gentle ribbing of their usually stoic commander. "Yeah. He goes out and starts shooting at trees."

Charlie grinned good-naturedly. "Well, boys, it certainly gives me a good excuse to kiss the lady."

The men rode on their way, laughing and joking at their General's expense. Charlie and Jocko headed back to the house, grinning and planning where they would plant their little green bits of Christmas cheer.

Corporal Nailer and Reg were covered in a fine powder of snow. Duncan's face was red, and a fine mist of sweat had turned to frost in his blond eyebrows. Reg was just as flushed, his dark skin almost plum colored with the combination of cold and exertion. Jeremiah danced around both men as they struggled to bring in the huge, long needled pine tree they had cut and hauled across half the paddocks on Gaines Cove farm. Unfortunately, Duncan had promised Jeremiah he could pick the Christmas tree. The boy wanted it to be perfect, so the two men had trudged several miles, hauling a sledge and trying to keep warm.

The two men struggled to set the tree in the stand that Duncan had built and set it up in the great hall. Jeremiah's excited voice brought the entire household to the hall.

"Ladies and gentlemen, it would seem these fine men have found a beautiful tree for our first Christmas celebration." Rebecca paused briefly, giving Em a kiss on the temple as the baby clung to her. "The first of many happy celebrations at Redmond Stables." She waited, hiding the grin and wondering when people would make the connection. It had been quite a week for Charlie.

Elizabeth, standing with Polk and admiring the beautiful tree, looked at Rebecca with a gentle smile. Charlie had his hands full; several of his troopers had followed Duncan and Reg into the hall, bearing great boughs of holly and greenery. One small, agile fellow quietly handed Charlie a sprig of gray green leaves with fine white berries, tied with a small red ribbon. The two men grinned at one another. They had gone to some lengths to find the Christmas mistletoe, and Charlie had plans for this particular sprig of greenery.

Sheridan did hear Rebecca's comment. "Yes, indeed, Miss Rebecca. I look forward to spending many happy days here at Redmond Stables when the war is over. That is, of course, if I am still welcome here, Charlie."

Charlie and Jocko were preoccupied with stringing a rope of long leaf pine over the entrance of the front parlor. Absentmindedly, Charlie agreed. "Of course, General. You and McCauley and the rest of the men will always be welcome, will they not, Miss Rebecca?"

Rebecca decided he was truly hopeless, as he had not yet noted the reference to Redmond Stables. She smiled at her love. "Absolutely, General." She hugged Em close to her and smiled at Elizabeth, who was on the verge of full-fledged laughter at her friend's predicament.

Charlie very carefully tied his little sprig of mistletoe into the rope of evergreen. "Indeed. I have always hoped to have a home that was open and welcoming to my friends. I am very grateful Miss Rebecca shares my sentiments." He moved to one side. "Say, Polk, would you and Elizabeth step over here and tell me if you think the tree is straight? I think it may be leaning somewhat."

Polk joined his commander. He looked at the tree with his fists resting on his hips. "Looks fine to me Charlie. Are you blind as well as deaf?"

Charlie looked at Polk with a bit of confusion? "Deaf? No, I am not deaf. What makes you say that?"

Polk was laughing so hard he had to take a step back and lean against the wall to keep from falling down. Elizabeth stepped up and looped her arm through Charlie's. "My dear friend, where do you intend to live after the war?"

Charlie flushed a bit. "Well, I was planning to make this my home. You know that."

"Difficult to do from the frontier, would you not think, General?" Sheridan was quick to bring a glass to his lips to hide his grin. Charlie Redmond was a good man, even if he was a little slow on the uptake sometimes.

Charlie flushed a deep red. "Um. Well, you know, General, by next summer I will have spent twenty years in the Army. I was thinking that when the conflict is over, I might better serve by helping this community recover from the effects of the war. After Buena Vista, the West just does not hold much appeal to me."

"Well, if you are determined to retire, Redmond Stables seems like the perfect place to do it."

"Redmond Stables?" Charlie's initial confusion turned slowly to recognition as he looked to Rebecca.

"Yes, Charlie. Redmond Stables. The home of General and Mrs. Redmond. The finest horse farm in all of Virginia." She moved to his side and placed a kiss on his cheek. "My wedding gift to you, darling."

Charlie stood there under the mistletoe he had carefully hung for Polk and Elizabeth, with the impression of Rebecca's lips on his cheek, looking rather like a pole axed ox. Everyone in the room was silent as they watched realization dawn on Charlie's face.

Jocko swirled a measure of good whiskey in his glass as he watched his friend. Taking a deep breath, he leaned over to have a word with McCauley. "General Sheridan made a good choice with that one. Charlie Redmond is a fine man. Irish, you know. Member of a very famous clan."

McCauley looked to the batman and raised a brow. "Really?"

"'Tis true. Largest clan in Ireland. The clan O'Blivious."

The batman's words dropped into the silence like a rock shattering the calm of a pond. It did not take long for Sheridan's assistant to get the joke, and soon he was laughing with Jocko as the two men poured another drink. Slowly, the meaning dawned on the rest of the guests, and a slow ripple of realization ran through the room. When all eyes turned to them and the laughter had died down again, Jocko looked over the crowd. "Pay no attention to us. Go back to your party. General Redmond has plans for that sprig he just hung." The batman gestured to the doorway.

Richard Polk, who had inevitably gravitated to Elizabeth's side during the conversation, stepped up. "Move aside, my friend, and let the rest of us take advantage of the tradition." Charlie and Rebecca stepped away from the doorway, moving to the side to speak quietly together for a moment. Richard, still laughing, drew Elizabeth with him to stand beneath the white berries. "Merry Christmas, Doctor Walker." With that, he kissed the normally formal and proper lady heartily on either cheek and then fleetingly on the lips.

"Merry Christmas, Colonel." She smiled and leaned up a bit to return the kiss, but not the ones bestowed on her cheeks. "A very Merry Christmas, Richard," she whispered against his lips. Then she pulled back before the occupants of the room could accuse her of taking advantage of the Colonel.

Before anyone commented on the obvious relationship, Phil Sheridan, who was usually a rather taciturn gentleman, stepped up beside his old friend and offered a gentle kiss to her cheek. "Merry Christmas, Elizabeth."

"Merry Christmas, Philip." She took his arm and allowed him to escort her into the crowd.

Charlie stood in the shadow of the Christmas tree, facing Rebecca and gently holding her hands between them. "Redmond Stables?"

All around them, people began the bustle of trimming the tree, with ribbons, tiny white candles, delicate glass ornaments that Duncan had found in the attic, and strings of berries and popcorn that the ladies and Jeremiah had been making for several days.

"Yes, Charlie. I think it is only fitting. I filed the papers this week. Half of the land is now yours. It is the only thing I have to offer you, other than my love." She blushed, running her hand over his tunic.

"My love, you have given me something I never thought I would have. A future, filled with love and hope. I love you, Rebecca Gaines." As the plain pine tree was transformed into the living symbol of Christmas, slowly Charlie's face began to reflect his growing faith in his dreams becoming reality.

The tree was trimmed, the house was decorated, and as darkness closed in, all was in readiness for the evening. The adults of the house retired to their various quarters to rest and dress for the dinner, while the children were herded off to the old schoolroom to share dinner, Christmas pudding, and games before bedtime. Charlie had driven Sarah and Mess Chief Jamison to distraction about preparing a Christmas Eve dinner that would honor his commanding officer and impress the local citizens he had invited. As the clock chimed seven, the civilian guests arrived at the house. Reverend Williams and his wife had joined the Coopers in their buggy. Mayor Frazier had accompanied them, riding on his old nag.

Reg was dressed as befitted the butler of a fine house. He met the guests at the door, and with Lizbet's assistance, relieved them of their winter wraps. Charlie and Rebecca were waiting for them in the formal front parlor, with a warm fire dancing on the hearth and a selection of hot beverages—milk punch, and brandy—to dispel the chill of their evening drive.

Charlie was in full Southern gentleman mode, dressed in his formal evening uniform with his new stars shining on his shoulders and wearing his South Carolinian heritage like a medal on his chest. "Good evening, Mrs. Williams, Reverend."

"Good evening Col…"

Before Mrs. Williams could finish, Rebecca cleared her throat and Reverend Williams gave his wife a not so polite nudge.

"General Redmond," she acknowledged, with a slight tilt of her head.

"Old bat," Rebecca grumbled under her breath.

"Mrs. Cooper, you look lovely tonight. Cooper, good to see you again."

"Thank you, General." Mrs. Cooper winked at Rebecca. "You look radiant this evening, my dear. I do believe being in love agrees with you."

Rebecca tightened her hand on Charlie's arm. "It does. It truly does."

Wordlessly, Cooper reached out and shook Charlie's hand, silently grinning his congratulations.

Charlie turned to Frazier, who was rubbing his hands. "Damned cold out there, General. Hope the dinner is worth it."

Charlie laughed. "I assure you, Mayor, the dinner is as good as both our cook Sarah and our Mess Sergeant could make it."

"Sarah Coleman is your cook? Ah, well then, it should be worth the frigid trip."

At that point, Sheridan, McCauley, and Polk entered the room.

"May I introduce my commanding officer, Philip Sheridan, and his adjutant, Colonel McCauley? I believe you all know Colonel

Polk." While some informal introductions had been made at the gymkhana, not everyone present had met one another.

Introductions were flowing like wine when Dr. Walker and Whitman escorted Constance Adams into the room. Rebecca noticed immediately the young woman did not look well and straight away made her a place to sit near the fire.

"Are you all right?"

"Thank you, I am feeling somewhat better. And the company will do me good. It is very hard to lie abed all day while so much is going on around me. And I must confess, I have always loved Christmas."

Quietly, Whitman slipped over to stand beside the frail woman. A gentle, knowing look passed between the big, shaggy haired man and the small, perfectly coiffed woman. Rebecca turned to the rest of her guests.

"Ladies and gentlemen, please enjoy each others' company tonight, and let us rejoice in the love and friendship we have all found in this time of hardship. Let us pray for a quick end to the conflict that keeps us from our loved ones. May this be the first of many happy Christmas celebrations in our home." She turned and smiled at Charlie. "And I would like to take this moment to say how happy and proud I am of my betrothed, the newly commissioned Brigadier General Charles Redmond."

Phil Sheridan took the floor. "Charles Redmond has served this country with distinction for many years." Sheridan walked over to stand beside the officer. He indicated one of the medals on his officer's chest. "Indeed. He won this for his heroic action at the Battle of Buena Vista during the Mexican conflict." Sheridan faced Charlie. "You were only sixteen at the time, I believe, and a newly made sergeant, when you stepped up and led your men to safety after your lieutenant and captain were both killed." He turned back to the rest of the guests. "You may not be aware of this, but Charlie served under Captain Lee at Buena Vista. As a matter of fact, he attended West Point on Lee's recommendation." Glancing back to Charlie, he asked, "I believe you also served with Lee at Fort Pulaski, in Georgia, did you not?"

"Yes, Sir. He was Colonel Lee at the time, and I must say, I learned a great deal from him. I believe he has long been one of my greatest role models. When I had to choose between nation and state, I went to him for advice. He told me to follow my conscience and my faith, as he himself would do."

"Well, Charlie, I wish that Robert had chosen the same way you did, but I honor him for his choice." He turned back to the assembled guests. "I believe General Redmond has long since earned his stars. So tonight, let us celebrate our host and his generosity and courage, as is appropriate in this season of remembering God's most precious gifts."

Charlie was appropriately humble, blushing at Sheridan's praise. Reg peeked in through the parlor door, offering Charlie respite from being the center of attention. "Thank you, General. Now, ladies and gentlemen, I believe supper is ready. Mrs. Williams, may I escort you in?"

The woman nodded politely and took Charlie's proffered arm. Rebecca smiled and took the arm offered her by General Sheridan. The General said quietly, "Charlie is a very lucky man. I hope you both will be very happy."

"Thank you, General. I think we will."

Polk claimed Elizabeth's hand, and Whitman very gently escorted Constance in to dinner.

The room was lit with a multitude of small white tapers and decorated with fresh evergreens, holly, and ivy. Charlie seated Mrs. Williams to his right, taking the head of the table, while Rebecca took her position at the foot of the table with General Sheridan to her right. The others found their places at the table, each marked with a beautifully lettered card in a small porcelain holder. Beulah and Reg served the opening course of potted trout, followed by a delicate soup of clarified chicken broth with winter greens. The main course followed, a fine rack of venison. At first, conversation was traditionally formal, with the weather, the crops grown in the area and other comfortably neutral subjects being discussed. But as the guests grew more comfortable with one another, conversation turned to the condition of the economy and land around Culpeper.

As Reg cleared away the plates from the main course, Mayor Frazier leaned forward. "General Sheridan, as I said the other day, when the war started, Culpeper was thriving. The county was rich with productive farms and several of the best stud stables in Virginia. Since then, the armies of both sides have rolled through this county over and over, churning the crops to mud, tearing down the fences, stealing the horses—so we have no breeding stock left, no seed, no nothing. There are less than one hundred fifty people left in Culpeper who were here when the war started. The rest have died in battle, been killed by marauders, died of disease brought on by lack of good food, warm clothes or medical care, or left because there was no way to make a living here."

Sheridan responded thoughtfully, "This part of Virginia has paid a terrible price for this conflict. As you know, General Redmond is under direct orders to do everything he can to help you rebuild."

Mrs. Williams could not hold back her anger. She interrupted abruptly. "All of this pain and suffering is your fault, General Sheridan—yours and all the Yankees like you who have torn our rights from us and tried to take away our glorious heritage and way of life."

The guests held their breaths. Such vitriol was an unheard of breach of etiquette. And while all of the guests present might not have agreed with the politics the Federal officers represented, they had accepted the invitation from Rebecca Gaines knowing full well that General Sheridan was the guest of honor.

Mr. Williams finally stepped in. "Mrs. Williams, remember yourself. I am now, and always have been, a man of peace. I expect you to respect my position, and to respect our hostess and her guests." He turned to Rebecca. "Mrs. Gaines, please accept my sincere apologies for this outburst." He then scanned the rest of the assembled guests. "I, for one, welcome intelligent discussion of how to return my community to the health and prosperity it once knew. For that, I am grateful to you, Sir, for your honest concern. Now, I fear I must excuse my wife and myself. She clearly is not herself this evening."

Charlie stood. "Certainly, we all understand, Reverend Williams. I will see to it that Mr. and Mrs. Cooper return home safely. I am sure we all hope that Mrs. Williams is feeling more herself tomorrow."

The rest of the evening was subdued, with dessert, a lovely presentation of poached apples, served quickly. Shortly after, Polk volunteered to see the Coopers home.

Elizabeth and Whitman helped Constance upstairs. The stress of the confrontation had drained the young woman. Finally, Charlie and Rebecca stood together beside the Christmas tree, their guests having all retired to their respective quarters or homes.

"Well, my dear, that went reasonably well, do you not think so?" Charlie stood behind Rebecca and wrapped his arms around her waist.

Rebecca reached back and caressed Charlie's cheek. "I think so, General. You were a charming host. However, I am afraid that Reverend Williams is going straight to hell for telling such lies."

Charlie threw his head back and laughed. "Are you suggesting, my dear, that Mrs. Williams was very much herself this evening?"

"Very much. Good Lord, Charlie." Rebecca turned to face him. "I am surprised she lasted as long as she did. I noticed she managed to hold her tongue until after dinner."

"Well, dear, she may be a shrew, but she is not a fool. And she does enjoy a good meal. So consider it a compliment to Sarah's skills."

"I suppose so." She yawned, then sighed. "I am tired, Charlie, and I have had enough contemplation of the despicable Mrs. Williams for one evening. Take me to bed."

"Willingly, my beloved." Charlie swept Rebecca up in his arms and proceeded to march up stairs. "Shall we go and enjoy the first of many Christmas Eves together, my love?"

"We shall, dear." She held close to him as they went up the steps. "You know, I have never made love with a General before."

"Well, darling, you will tonight. But I fear we will not be able to sleep in late tomorrow, for I heard little Em telling Lizbet she wanted to get up early to see what "pwesents" Father Christmas had brought her. "

CHAPTER 21

Sunday, December 25, 1864

Charlie was curled around Rebecca's body, keeping her warm through the chilliest part of the night. The first silver light of false dawn had just begun to lighten the shades when he woke with an uncomfortable feeling of being watched. Very carefully, he untangled himself from Rebecca, moving quietly so as not to awaken her. Slowly, he rolled over and opened his eyes.

A pair of serious blue eyes topped with tousled black hair looked back at him. "Mewwy Chwistmas, Papa." Tess had admonished the little girl that asking what Father Christmas brought her was not polite. Good little girls said "Merry Christmas." Today, Em wanted her presents as quickly as possible, so being good was very important.

Two little hands appeared at the edge of the bed. The bed was too high for her to climb into without help. "Up, Papa," she demanded. "Em cold!"

Charlie reached one arm out. Two very cold little hands wrapped themselves around his wrist, and he pulled the child up onto the bed and under the covers with him. Considerable squirming resulted as the giggling child happily settled in and quickly managed to maneuver herself to the warmest spot in the bed—between Charlie and Rebecca. Rebecca's first conscious awareness of the morning was a pair of very cold little feet tucked against her side.

Without rolling over the blonde murmured, "We have a guest."

Em cuddled against Rebecca's back. "Mewwy Chwistmas, Mama 'Becca."

Rebecca rolled over and wrapped the little girl in her arms, giving her a kiss on the forehead. "Merry Christmas, Em. Do you know how early it is? Could you let Papa and me sleep just a little more?"

Em knew she was not allowed to go down the big stairs by herself, but Papa had told her last night that someone called Father Christmas was going to come and put a surprise under the big tree just for her. She did not quite understand why he was going to do this, but that did not matter. What mattered was that she was getting a big surprise, and she could not wait to get down there and see what it was. Excited blue eyes looked back at Rebecca. "No, now."

Charlie, who normally rose at this hour anyway, was thoroughly enjoying watching Em wrap Rebecca around her little finger. Usually, he was the object of the child's demands; this time, Rebecca was definitely in the child's sights.

Rebecca looked to Charlie, who was watching the exchange with a huge smile on his face. "Oh, you hush up, Charles Redmond!" she scolded, with a smile of her own.

"Does that mean I should get up and stoke the fire, dear? I could put your kettle on the hob as well, if you wish." He was all sweetness and solicitation, but there was a wicked little gleam in his eye.

"Yes, I think that is exactly what that means, you evil man. Em and I will just stay nice and warm, all tucked away in the down. You may fetch us when the room warms up." She paused and smiled at him. "Considerably."

He rose and shrugged into his robe. A little searching was necessary, as the carpet slippers that normally resided right beside the bed where he could step into them had somehow gone wandering. Finally, he knelt down and rummaged under the bed, dredging the slippers back from where two small, bare feet had kicked them as their small visitor had climbed up his arm. As he stoked the fire, coaxing flames from the banked coals and carefully feeding more wood to heat the room, he heard giggles and some very high pitched squeals coming from beneath the covers.

He filled the kettle from the pitcher, set it on the hob, and walked back over to the bed. There were no heads showing, but under the down comforter there was quite a bit of suspicious movement. "Are you two having a command conference in there?"

"Yes, we are, Papa," came the muffled reply that Charlie knew had to be Rebecca. "We are discussing what Father Christmas may have brought you this morning."

"Oh, dear. I hope I have not been too bad this year, or he may have brought me sticks and coals."

The covers came whipping down, and Em giggled and squealed, "Papa good."

"And what about you, Em. Have you been good, or did Father Christmas bring you sticks and coals?"

"Em vewy good," she giggled, then suddenly got a very serious look on her face, glancing back and forth between them. "Yes?"

Charlie smiled at the child. "Em is very, very good." He reached down and caressed the top of her head. "Papa thinks you have been very good indeed."

"But Papa may just get coal for teasing you, Em. What do you think of that? Does Papa get coal?"

"No, Mama 'Becca. Papa good. Papa get kisses." The child held her face up to Charlie, all puckered to deliver one immediately.

Rebecca laughed as Charlie was graced with what could only be called a wet, sloppy baby kiss.

But that was not sufficient for the child. Papa deserved kisses from everybody, as far as she was concerned. "Mama 'Becca kiss Papa."

"Have you been a good boy, Charlie? Do you deserve a kiss from Mama 'Becca?" She gave him her best coy smile.

Charlie looked deep into Rebecca's eyes. In an instant, the moment had shifted from lighthearted play to deep intimacy. "I think that is for you to say, my love."

Without a word, she leaned over and graced him with a kiss. Em was quite pleased to see Mama 'Becca and Papa sharing a kiss, until she had been stuffed between them just a little too long for her comfort. She pushed on Charlie. "Papa kiss Em."

Charlie drew back from Rebecca's lips and promptly kissed the little girl soundly on the forehead. His eyes never left Rebecca's. As the kiss ended, he murmured, "Merry Christmas, my beloved."

The kettle on the hob began to whistle. With a lingering smile and a soft caress that started with Rebecca's cheek and passed over Em's head, he turned and poured the water into the teapot.

Rebecca rose, carrying the child with her, and went to sit before the fire. She poured tea for the three of them, liberally dosing the child's with honey and cream. Charlie splashed some of the water from the kettle into his washbowl and began lathering his shaving brush. Em watched, fascinated, as Charlie spread the thick lather over his cheeks and chin.

Em squirmed out of Rebecca's lap and made her way across the room. Once next to Charlie, she tugged on his robe. "Papa?"

"Yes, little one?" Charlie spoke a little absent-mindedly, as he stropped his razor.

This was not nearly good enough for the little girl, and she only tugged harder on Charlie's robe. "Papa!"

Charlie stopped in mid-strop. "What do you want, Em?"

"Down, Papa."

He crouched down until the two of them were face to face. "Yes?"

Em immediately put her hands in the thick foam covering his face. She then squealed with delight and clapped her hands together, covering them both in the foamy white froth. Then she took what was left on her own hands and smeared it on her face. From her spot near the fire, Rebecca roared with laughter.

Charlie, with soap in both eyes, groped for a towel, squinting at the howling Rebecca through the tears in his eyes. "Ahhhh," he sighed, "that stings." He turned to the child in front of him. "And you, little one. Shaving soap is for men, not little girls."

Not to be deterred, Em managed another handful of soap, which went promptly into her mouth. This only served to make her gag and then to cry as bubbles foamed out of her mouth.

Charlie's head dropped onto his chest, smearing more shaving soap over his nightshirt. Since it was already covered in soapy foam, what did a little more matter? He took the towel that he had used to wipe his own eyes, wiped the foam from the child's lips, and fumbled for the glass of water he kept on the bedside table. "Here, honey. Take some water in your mouth, swish it around, then spit it into the bowl." A few tries resulted in both of them being soaked, and a rather subdued little Em curled in Papa's arms. "See, honey. I told you that shaving soap was not for little girls." Charlie looked at Rebecca, a plea for rescue in his eyes.

Rebecca put down her tea cup and crossed the room, relieving Charlie of a quietly whimpering Em, who now hiccupped a couple of times before wiping her runny nose all over Rebecca's nightgown. After settling down next to the fire and cuddling the child, Rebecca looked up to Charlie. "How many children did we want again?"

He grinned ruefully. "As many as you want, dear."

"Very tactful, General Redmond. Non-committal, but tactful."

"Well, dear, I think that we might start with whatever the good Lord gives us, and go on from there. Speaking of which, do you think Lizbet is up and about yet? This little one needs to get dry and dressed, as I believe that Father Christmas may have paid us a little visit."

Rebecca stood up, careful not to jostle Em very much. "I am sure she is. You finish getting dressed, and I will see to it."

Charlie rang for Lizbet, and then finished shaving and dressing, while Rebecca carried the child back to her room. When Rebecca returned, he was dressed, not in his uniform, but in his gray civilian suit.

"Why, Mr. Redmond. You are the most handsome thing I have ever seen." She walked over and kissed him on the cheek. "Hmm and you smell good, too."

"All for you, my love. I thought I would attend church today as the newest member of the community, rather than as the local military government. I will let Sheridan take that role for a change. Now you, Ma'am, need to get dressed, or we will again have an impatient little one tugging at our knees—and heaven only knows what mess she will create this time."

"Yes, Mr. Redmond. Right away, Sir," Rebecca teased, as she drew open her wardrobe and removed a light blue dress that had been fashioned just for this occasion. "Will this do?"

Charlie looked tenderly at his lovely fiancée, barely noticing the dress but entranced by the joyous smile on her face. "My dear, it will do very well. Shall I help you?"

Rebecca laughed and held her gentleman at arm's length. "I am supposed to be getting dressed, Charlie. If you help me, we will miss Christmas morning and church. Then we will have both Em and Mrs. Williams calling for our heads."

"Oh, Lord. One of them I can handle; both of them would be far too much, even for me."

Charlie left the room as Lizbet entered to lace Rebecca into her dress. He collected a now dry and dressed Em and headed out of the door. "Well, little one, shall we go and admire Father Christmas's handiwork?"

Charlie and Em met General Sheridan on the stairs. "Good morning, Sir."

"Good morning, Redmond. Merry Christmas. And Merry Christmas to you, Miss Emily." Sheridan had found out about the child's relationship with Charlie from Polk. "I can smell the coffee from here, so I assume breakfast is ready."

"Yes, Sir. She has become accustomed to my early hours. I think we may see more than just the usual early birds at the breakfast table this morning."

The three of them proceeded downstairs. As they passed by the tree, with the presents spread out beneath it, Em got upset.

"Papa! Pwesents!"

"Breakfast first, Em."

Em looked to her Papa, back to the tree, and back to her Papa. "Pwease?" Sheridan muffled a snort behind the disguise of coughing as Charlie was confronted with the pouty lower lip.

Charlie reached into his pocket and pulled out a small package. "See this package? Father Christmas gave it to me, and told me that it was the first thing you should open, but that you had to have your breakfast first. Now, you know you have to do what Father Christmas asked."

Em sighed and laid her head on Charlie's shoulder. "Yes, Papa. Em good."

"Well done, Redmond. I have always found bribery to be very effective."

Charlie smiled. "I have always believed that reason and negotiation are far superior to force, Sir."

The three proceeded to the dining room, where, as had become their habit, Charlie settled into his chair with Em on his knee. Two dishes were set before him, one with his breakfast, the other with Em's cereal. Sheridan eyed Charlie as he finished tying Em's bib around her neck and silently handed him an extra napkin. "You may find this useful. If I had known about this meal-time practice, I would have had a bib made for you, as well."

"Yes, well, my batman has been very... tolerant of the situation."

Dr. Walker swept into the room, giving Em a peck on the head before taking her seat. "Good morning everyone." She glanced around the room. "Where is Rebecca this morning, Charlie? She is not ill is she?"

"Not at all. We had a little... adventure this morning with Em that delayed her dressing. I expect her any moment."

Elizabeth chuckled as she placed her napkin in her lap and poured a cup of coffee. "I will not even bother to ask."

Em took the opportunity to take her spoon and dig it into her cereal bowl, gathering a large clump, which was immediately offered to Charlie. "Papa eat."

"That is Em's. Papa will eat his own breakfast." Charlie took a forkful of eggs. "Ready?" The child nodded and together the two of them took their first bite of breakfast.

"Good morning everyone, and Merry Christmas." Rebecca smiled broadly as she came into the room, first giving Em a kiss then placing a kiss on the top of Charlie's head before taking her seat at the opposite end of the table. "Where are Colonel Polk and Mr. Whitman this morning?"

"Right here, Ma'am." The two gentlemen entered and both immediately went for the coffee pot. Evidently, there had been some private celebrating the night before.

Charlie looked to Sheridan with a grin and winked. "Say, Richard?"

Richard looked at Charlie with bleary and slightly bloodshot eyes. Cautiously, he responded. "Yes, Charlie?"

"I noticed that some of the men were a little ragged on the mounted lance exercises. They need a bit more instruction before we assemble the honor guard to escort the General to church. Do you think you can handle it? A brisk ride will do you good."

Richard simply looked at his so called friend, his mouth hanging open a little as he cradled his coffee cup in both hands. "Um, Charlie, could you..." Richard simply could not go on; he needed his coffee.

"Could I what, Richard?"

Elizabeth did a fine job of hiding the grin on her face; then she cleared her throat and attempted to help her friend out of his mess. "Ah, Charlie, Richard is looking a tad under the weather to me, and as your regimental physician, I must ask you to rethink that request."

"Bless you, woman," Richard whispered, but everyone at the table heard it and roared with laughter. Even Sheridan was enjoying the teasing this morning.

More people joined the breakfast table. Jeremiah was particularly excited—trying very hard to act like an adult, and hoping so much that he had been given the fishing gear he wanted. Duncan had gotten him addicted to that particular manly sport.

Rebecca watched as everyone enjoyed his or her breakfast. As soon as she was finished, she retrieved Em from Charlie's lap so he could at least drink his coffee in peace.

"Mama?"

"Oh, your mama is laying down, little one."

"Mama sick?"

Rebecca's heart went out to this child. She was old enough to know something was wrong, but not old enough to know how serious the situation was.

"Yes, sweetheart, I am afraid so. But we are doing everything we can to make your mama better."

Em wrapped her arms around Rebecca's neck. "Em love Mama 'Becca."

"Mama 'Becca loves Em, too." She gave the baby a kiss and looked to the table, which had suddenly grown very quiet watching the interaction between them. "Shall we adjourn to the tree and see what Father Christmas has left for us?"

Jeremiah leapt from his chair, almost overturning it. Fortunately, Whitman was right beside him and caught it before it could crash to the floor.

Whitman quickly excused himself and ran lightly up the steps. He tapped on Constance's door. "My dear, I thought you might like to see your daughter have her first real Christmas. May I carry you down?"

"Oh, thank you, Mr. Whitman. I do believe I feel strong enough to join the festivities, if only for a little while."

Whitman, who was a bear of a man, let the frail woman arrange her clothing, then simply lifted her in his arms, carried her downstairs, and settled her in a comfortable chair near the fire.

Laughing and chatting, the rest of the company rose from the table and proceeded to the main hall of the house. There, Lizbet, Reg, and Beulah had been busily lighting all of the tiny candles carefully tied to the branches of the tree. It looked like a fairy tree, all sparkles and shining little lights. Jeremiah immediately plunged into the packages under the tree, sorting through the ribbon wrapped packages for one with his name on it. His mother reminded him of his manners.

"Jeremiah, as the youngest of us, other than little Em, could you do the honors and hand out the gifts?"

"Papa!" Em squealed and clapped her hands, reaching for Charlie as soon as he took his place between Rebecca and Constance.

Without breaking his conversation with Sheridan over the horse stock the cavalry was getting for the spring campaign, Charlie took the child into his arms and settled her on his lap.

While her Papa was preoccupied, Em seized her opportunity and started rummaging through his pockets.

He pulled the small package out of his pocket. "Were you looking for this, little one?"

"Pwease, Papa? Em good."

"Here you are, then." Em carefully opened the small package, a packet of the horehound drops and benne seed candies the little girl loved.

She happily placed a piece of the candy in her mouth, and then gave Charlie a kiss on the cheek. "Mmm, good."

Jeremiah handed out the gifts, chafing under the need to wait before he could open the good-sized box bearing his name that rattled when he shook it. All of the gifts were distributed. Charlie had his blue shirt that Rebecca had made, Em had a new hand carved rocking horse and a new doll, as well as a new dress, and all of the others in the circle of friends had at least one or two small presents in their hands. Jeremiah was engrossed in examining all of the little bits and pieces of fishing tackle the rattling box contained. Charlie, checking his watch, told Rebecca her gift would be delivered at precisely nine o'clock. Em looked around and noticed that only one person had no gifts; General Sheridan was sitting with empty hands.

"Papa? Down pwease."

Charlie set the small child on the floor and made sure she was steady on her feet. He watched her, curious as to what had put that determined look on her face.

Em walked slowly over to Lizbet and retrieved her doll, Em, from the woman who looked after her for so much of the time. Slowly and carefully, she walked to General Sheridan and stood between his legs. She offered him her favorite doll. "Chwistmas."

The normally stoic General looked into the earnest face of the little girl in front of him. After four years of being at war with the people she represented, that one touch of genuine, childish generosity touched him deeply. He realized he could not refuse her gift, nor could he take her doll.

Very gently, he took the doll into his hand. She was worn, well loved, threadbare, and clearly this child's most cherished possession. Very seriously, he looked at the little girl. "Miss Emily, Em is a very special gift, and I thank you very much. But I have to ask a favor of you. You know I am a soldier?"

She looked back to her Papa who encouraged her with a nod, and then she looked back to the man before her and gave him a nod as well. "Like Papa."

"Yes, like your Papa. Well, soldiers have to live in some strange places. Sometimes those places are not very good for special gifts like Em. So, would you keep her safe for me?"

Em smiled and decided that Phil Sheridan's lap was a nice place to be. She proceeded to climb up. Once she was settled, she took Em back and gave the doll a hug, before giving the General a hug of his own.

Charlie smiled at the little girl and then checked his watch. It was a quarter to nine. His gift to Rebecca was due in fifteen minutes, and then they would all have to leave for church. "Folks, I hate to end the festivities, but we need to leave for church in a few minutes, so if you have anything you need to do, gather your wraps and put your gifts away; we should be getting along."

Lizbet took Em from Sheridan and hustled her upstairs to get her bundled up for the ride to church. Rebecca watched as everyone moved around getting things settled. She looked at the tree then to Charlie who was looking out the window. "Charlie? What has you so preoccupied this morning?"

"Oh, my dear, I have to confess, I am a little nervous. I hope you like your Christmas gift."

"My gift? Oh Charlie, you have already given me so much. You should not have..." She just shook her head. "I think you are going to spoil me, Charles Redmond."

"That, my love, is the plan." Charlie looked out the front window again. MacFarlane was coming up the path leading Shannon, who was beautifully groomed, with braided mane and tail. She was proudly pulling a lovely little basket carriage that was trimmed with red ribbons and greenery. Charlie smiled and turned to Rebecca. He caught her cloak up in his hands and held it for her. "Your gift has arrived, my dear. Will you join me?" Throwing his great coat around his shoulders, he escorted her out the front door. "My dear, your horse, and carriage."

Rebecca could not help but laugh as she placed her hands in Charlie's pocket to keep them warm. "She is beautiful, Charlie. Perfect for a trip to church this morning."

"Rebecca, I am not sure you understand. She is yours. Your horse. Your carriage. Merry Christmas."

"Oh, Charlie, I...I cannot take Shannon from you. She is a wonderful horse indeed, but she is yours, darling. I..."

"Shush, dear. Shannon loves you. You love her. I have Jack. She is yours. And, darling, in about a month, I will stand before God and man and declare that I endow you with all my worldly goods anyway. So, please accept her as an advance deposit on that pledge."

Rebecca chuckled and kissed him on the cheek before leaving his side to go and pay special attention to her new horse.

He stood and watched the two of them together. It was perfect. It was one more piece in the life he was determined to build with this lovely woman.

Tarent and MacFarlane drew up in two large wagons set with hay bales covered in blankets. As they arrived, the various members of the expanded Redmond Stables household emerged from their rooms, pulling on wraps and coats, the ladies checking their reticules to make sure they had a little something for the offering plate, the gentlemen settling wraps more securely around their ladies' shoulders. The officers had their mounts brought around as well. With a lot of laughter and some jostling, the ladies and children mounted the wagons, the gentlemen heaved themselves into their saddles, and Charlie handed Rebecca into her own little carriage. They set off for church, singing Christmas carols as they went.

As they pulled into the yard behind the small red church, Mrs. Williams was progressing regally across the walk to the side entrance, preparing to take her place at the small organ. She wore the white robes that were reserved for the Christmas season. The sight of 'her' churchyard full of Yankee officers in full dress uniform was almost more than she could bear. Her nose wrinkled in disdain and assumed a higher elevation.

Charlie handed Rebecca down from the carriage, while the other officers gallantly assisted the other ladies. They sorted themselves out into formal couples and proceeded to march into the church, looking very like a formal processional at a military wedding. The somber blues of the officers' tunics contrasted nicely with the more delicate colors of the ladies' full skirts.

Mrs. Williams' irritation could be heard in the vehemence of her playing. As was his habit, Reverend Williams stood at the door and greeted each worshipper as they entered the church.

The entire entourage spoke politely to the Reverend before filing in and taking seats. Rebecca sat down, settling Em next to her and supplying the child with a cracker or two that would keep her occupied for a few minutes. Rebecca and Mrs. Williams made eye contact, with Rebecca refusing to divert her eyes first. She was growing more and more irritated with Mrs. Williams, and she knew that now was the time to start standing her ground. Charlie would be returning here after the war, and Rebecca was going to make sure no one had the gall to say anything against him. Mrs. Williams finally looked away, mumbling something under her breath as she did. Rebecca just smiled.

Charlie leaned over and whispered to his fiery companion. "Did something just happen between you and Mrs. Williams? I felt a chill fall over the church for a moment, and the look on your face was —fascinating."

"Just defending my territory, darling."

"Do I want to know which particular piece of your territory you were defending?"

"All of it, love. I am just letting her know that enough is enough. I was embarrassed to death by her outburst last night."

"Her outburst was bad enough, but to be honest, I was more concerned about the effect of the stress on Miss Constance. She looked so pale and distressed last night. I am glad she decided to stay abed this morning. It is a shame Beulah is missing the service, but I do appreciate that she seems devoted to Miss Constance's care."

"Beulah and Constance have become fast friends. I am a little concerned about how Beulah will react should something happen to Constance. Elizabeth is very concerned about her ability to survive this birth, and we are preparing for the worst. I wish Elizabeth could stay to attend the delivery."

"Ah, the Reverend is about ready to start. We must continue this conversation later, dear. I, too, am concerned about Miss

Constance's health. But you know I have to balance that against the welfare of my men. Having Elizabeth with us to tend to our wounded in the field is critical. We will have to work something out."

Rebecca nodded, then resettled Em in her lap. She kissed the child's head as Em settled into her arms for the nap that would shortly overtake her while the good Reverend delivered his sermon to the more alert members of his congregation.

The Reverend's normally quiet voice rang out over the congregation: "Unto you is born this day in the city of David a Savior."

The church had been packed. Filing out of the church took time, as each person had to stop and say something to Reverend Williams. In the churchyard, the local folks gathered in a cluster, looking askance at the Union officers. Here, back once more, were the demons that had made their lives hell. But for the first time, they were in their church, contributing to the collection plate. Moreover, yesterday, many of the men from the winter camp had visited the townsfolk with various offerings, including straw dolls and small hand-carved wooden toys for the children, loads of wood ready for the fireplace or stove, and ham, cookies, breads, and other traditional Christmas treats to enhance their tables today. It was very confusing.

Sheridan looked over the crowd and made a decision. Charlie had been pushing him for supplies to help these folks. Hell, it was only a hundred and fifty people in total. And it was Christmas. He stepped into the open space between the cluster of folks from Redmond Stables and the winter camp and the local residents.

"Excuse me, ladies and gentlemen. May I have a moment of your time?"

The local residents looked at each other and then, by mutual unspoken consent decided not only would it be bad manners, but probably suicidal, to ignore the General, especially with so many of his men looking on. Slowly they all turned, giving him their attention, albeit a tad divided as they waited to see what his officers were doing.

"I know that General Redmond has been providing as much assistance as possible to you, and I would like to reaffirm his commitment. In addition, I will be putting together a load of basic supplies to be used to help get you back on your feet. I know about the need for foodstuffs, seed stocks, woolens, and such. However, if you would prepare your lists of the things you need, such as specific tools, I would be happy to include them in the shipment. I will be in the area for another two days, so if you will deliver your lists to Colonel McCauley here, we will attend to it for you. We do want to find ways to rebuild our national community once this war is over, and I hope that we have the opportunity to make a start with Culpeper." For Sheridan, that was a very long speech. He waited for reaction from the townspeople.

They talked among themselves for a few minutes, deciding that the man was indeed sincere. Several of the oldest men took the time to approach the General to shake his hand and offer their thanks.

As the men began hesitantly talking about tools, different crop options, and similar issues, Mrs. Cooper slid up beside Rebecca. "I wish you a very Merry Christmas, my dear. But where is Miss Constance? I was sure she would want to be here with her daughter."

"I am afraid Constance is not at all well. Her condition is not good, and Dr. Walker has ordered her to bed for the rest of her pregnancy."

"Oh, dear. I am so sorry. Does that mean you will be caring for the little one?" Em had awakened and was sleepily lying on Rebecca's shoulder, quietly sucking on her thumb.

"Charlie and I have discussed what would become of Em in the event of her mother's passing, and we will be keeping her with us if Constance has no objections. Em loves Charlie so, it would be a shame to separate them."

"I would say the little one loves you as well, my dear. I always thought you would make a wonderful mother." Mrs. Cooper looked over at Charlie, who was talking with several of the older farmers in the congregation. "On a somewhat different subject, have you talked to Charlie about your previous marriage?"

Rebecca glanced to Charlie and smiled, then returned her attention to Mrs. Cooper. "He knows that my previous marriage was not happy. But I have not told him of all of Mr. Gaines' faults. It is, after all, not Christian to speak unkindly of the dead."

"And what of his behavior toward you, my dear? Does he have any of the more... unpleasant attitudes Mr. Gaines had?"

Rebecca blushed and shook her head. "No, not at all. Charlie is kind and loving; I do not believe he has ever even raised his voice to me in anger."

"Well, that is well and good, but I do believe I will stand in the place of your dear mother and have a little chat with him." Mrs. Cooper looked at the newly minted General, who was currently chatting with her husband and looking rather embarrassed. Mrs. Cooper's eyebrow rose a bit. *I wonder what that is all about. I must remember to ask Mr. Cooper about it later.*

Mr. Cooper was, in fact, dealing with an uncomfortable Charlie. The question had been rather simple. Charlie wanted to know who had purchased Rebecca's mother's piano. If at all possible, he wanted to offer the owner a reasonable sum to regain the item so he could give it to Rebecca as a wedding present. However, there was a slight problem with the plan. Mrs. Williams had purchased the item in question, and getting her to give it up would be awkward at best.

"Please, Mr. Cooper. Perhaps you could act as an intermediary for me? I would, of course, be willing to replace her piano with a newer one, as well offer her some cash in consideration for her kindness."

"General, would it not be easier to buy Rebecca a new piano?"

"Of course, it would. But it would not have the same meaning for her as getting her mother's piano. I have learned that emotional attachment has more value for Miss Rebecca than monetary worth. Believe me, I would be much happier buying her a new one, but..." Charlie had a rather helpless look that told Cooper just how totally Rebecca had this man wrapped around her finger.

"Well, I suppose I could speak with Reverend Williams. Maybe he could convince his wife to give up the piano." The man scratched his jaw and smiled. "I really do not have any desire to deal with Mrs. Williams, either."

"Well, after last night's demonstration, I suspect she would be very amused at the prospect of having me at her mercy."

"That woman does seem to get pleasure from the most unusual things, I will grant you that. Tell you what I will do. I will suggest that I can get a new piano for them if they would like to use the old one in trade. As far as I am concerned no one need be the wiser."

"I would be very grateful for your assistance, Sir. I do want Miss Rebecca to have what she needs to be happy. And, Sir, I am very committed to coming back to this community and helping to rebuild after the war."

"And we are looking forward to it, General. It will be nice to have a happy young couple in our midst to remind us of what is important. I am sure you and Rebecca will have a household full of children once you get back."

Charlie flushed. Any reference to him fathering children with Rebecca put him in an awkward position. Thankfully, Mr. Cooper probably thought it was just a response to the implication of conjugal relations between them. Then a thought struck him. "By the way, Sir, do you know why Mr. Gaines left no heirs?"

"I do not know for sure. It is rumored, I am afraid from Gaines own lips, that Rebecca was unable to give him children. I suspect it was his own drinking that made it impossible. There was not a day I knew him when that man drew a sober breath."

"Well, Sir, even if Miss Rebecca cannot have children, I am sure we will end up with a house full. She opens our doors to every orphan who comes this way already."

Cooper chuckled, glancing at the woman in question, who at this very moment was attending to a grumpy Emily. "I do believe you are right. I suppose it does not matter how a family comes together, just as long as it does."

"Amen, Mr. Cooper. Amen."

The rest of Christmas Day was relaxing and uneventful. After dinner, small groups wandered to various parts of the house. Some were in the dining room, enjoying a quiet talk over coffee and brandy. Others were in the front parlor, playing charades. Jeremiah had wandered off to the encampment to go over the contents of his tackle box with Duncan. Em had been put to bed, after wishing her mother a quiet good night. Charlie planned to retreat to the sitting room upstairs with Rebecca, but before he could retire for the night, he needed to talk with Elizabeth about Montgomery's condition and to determine if Sheridan's plan to hold the court martial the next day was viable. He found the Doctor in the back parlor, quietly playing chess with Polk.

"Um, excuse me, Elizabeth, Richard. I need a word with you, Elizabeth, if you have a moment."

Richard rose to excuse himself. "No, Richard, stay. You know what this is about already."

Elizabeth settled back in her chair and laced her fingers together. "I assume it is time to deal with the issue of Montgomery."

"You are correct, and I am curious as to how you figured it out?" Charlie sat down on the settee and waited.

She sighed, "Well, I knew it was bound to come up, and that my opinion would be key to the whole affair."

"General Sheridan wants to hold a court martial while we have sufficient line officers here so that none of our staff will have to sit on the panel. In addition, since all of the witnesses are here, it is more appropriate than trying to convene at his headquarters later. He wants to know if Montgomery is sufficiently recovered to withstand the process. I suspect he will ask you if he is mentally able to undergo a trial as well."

"His physical condition has improved a great deal. However, his mental condition has not. He is angry and resentful."

Charlie smiled ruefully. "Well, I suppose that is an improvement over being angry, resentful, and suicidal."

"I am afraid he has decided that he will be hanged, so he does not have to give it any further thought. He is positive that you have some sort of personal vendetta against him."

"To be honest with you, I would rather see him sent home on a medical release with a recommendation that he get proper care for both his body and his mind. But I am afraid if he does go home, he may continue to vent his anger on people, and especially on women." Charlie stared bleakly into the fire. "The decision is out of my hands. General Sheridan will chair the panel. You know they will ask you for your recommendation as to the disposition of his case."

"Yes, I know. I am prepared to offer him my honest opinion as a physician, Charlie; that is all I can do."

"What is your opinion, Elizabeth?"

"He is both physically capable and mentally competent to stand trial. He understands what is going to happen. I cannot say I am happy about sending a man to the gallows after I worked so hard to save him, but he did bring this on himself and there is only so much I can do. I am a doctor, not a miracle worker."

Richard stood and moved to stand behind Elizabeth, gently patting her shoulder and offering what support he could.

"No, and I do not ask you to be one. I am just sorry we find ourselves in this situation in the first place." Charlie rose quietly. "I will leave you two to your game. Good night to you both."

He slowly climbed the stairs to Rebecca's sitting room, thinking of the strains that the next two days would present. As he came into the room, Rebecca was sitting before the fire, absentmindedly brushing her hair. "Good evening, Rebecca. You look lovely."

Rebecca turned and smiled at him, her smile quickly fading to a look of concern. "And you, my darling, look exhausted. Come in and sit by the fire. I will get you a brandy."

Charlie slumped onto the settee in front of the fire and merely nodded his thanks as she put a glass in his hand. He stared moodily into the fire.

She settled down next to him, placing her hand gently on his leg. "It is the situation with Montgomery that has you bothered." It was not a question; it was a statement.

"Yes, well, it is always hard to have a man under your command who has turned. Even though I was not in charge at The Wilderness, Wilson was, it is still hard. I am truly grateful I will not have to sit on the panel."

"Charlie, this is for the best. I am sorry this has happened to a man who, by all accounts, was a good officer; but I also get the feeling from things he has said that he is, and always has been, abusive. He needs to be stopped. Look at what he and his kind have done to Constance."

"How different is he from Mr. Gaines, dear?"

Rebecca looked away, staring into the fire. "In some ways, he is no different. Maybe that is why I feel no sympathy for him. But Mr. Gaines was acting within his rights as a husband, and Major Montgomery clearly was not."

Charlie looked at Rebecca for a long moment, then wrapped his arms around her. "I think I am beginning to understand. Perhaps it was just a matter of time before Montgomery's character became obvious to all of us, regardless of what happened to him."

"I believe that is probably true." She reclined into his arms, resting her head on his shoulder and gently running her hand over his suit, playing with the buttons. "Em is going to miss you and your buttons."

Charlie stroked Rebecca's back, just enjoying the sensation of holding the small woman for a moment. Finally, he asked, "And you, Ma'am. What will you miss?"

"My heart, for you are going to take it with you."

Charlie's breath caught in his chest. The intensity of the statement brought home to him, in a way that had never really penetrated before, just how totally his life and his future had changed. He held her closer. "I promise to return it to you in one piece, if it is at all possible."

"I expect you to return home to me, Charlie. As long as you are alive, that is all that matters to me."

Charlie closed his eyes for a moment, thinking over all the places he had been where coming back alive had been questionable. There was a reason why he was called "Lucky Charlie." Well, from now on, he was going to be "Careful Charlie." "Darling, I will come back. This is home. You are my life now."

"Will I be able to write you? Will you get the letters?"

"Yes, dear. There will be dispatch riders going up and down the rail line. I will make sure we have a mail stop here. I can make Culpeper a changing station and leave a small force here. I will write you as well."

She smiled and gave him a kiss on the cheek. "I would prefer you concentrate on coming home."

He nuzzled into her hair and murmured into her ear, "Letters from you will be an inspiration to end the war and come home as quickly as I can, my love."

"Then I shall write every day. I am sure Em will enjoy writing her Papa as well."

"And I will read the letters every night, and keep them under my pillow to be as close to you as I can."

She sighed, wishing there was some way the war would end before Charlie was due to leave, but she knew that was not very likely.

"Rebecca, dear, I do think the end will be fairly quick. Lee is besieged; he cannot hold out for too much longer. As it stands now, there is really only one path that has remained open for his supplies, and I am sure we will look to cut that off. You know they say an army moves on its stomach. If we cut the supply lines, they will have to surrender; and then we can start on the work of rebuilding from this horror."

She nodded, but remained silent. The realization that her Charlie was going away and might not come back was truly beginning to settle and weigh on her much like her brother's departure had. She prayed she would not receive that same word again. "Whatever happens, Charlie, just remember, I love you."

"You have managed to put much of the war out of your mind for a while, have you not, dear? So having the General and his staff here for Christmas rather brought that reality back home for you?" He could feel her nodding against his chest. "My love, I promise, I will be as careful as a man can be. I want to come home: to you, to your arms, to your love. I want to spend the rest of what I hope is a rather long life here with you."

CHAPTER 22

MONDAY, DECEMBER 26, 1864

The weather was gray and the sky lowering. It was a perfect day for the trial. Charlie rose early as was his habit, but did not go for his normal morning run. Instead, he took his time, carefully attending to his morning ritual. It would not do for the General to look anything less than perfect in his first formal military appearance. Rebecca and Jocko had carefully changed the insignia on all of his uniforms to reflect his new status. He wanted to do justice to the position he now held, as well as their loving efforts.

It was not a day he was looking forward to. Elizabeth had declared Montgomery competent to withstand the trail. Sheridan, in his usual way, was committed to moving forward without regard to the sensibilities of others. The day after Christmas was back to business as usual. And the most pressing bit of business for Sheridan was Montgomery's court martial. Once handled, Sheridan could get back to his own command.

As Charlie settled his coat and gave his cravat a final twitch,

Rebecca emerged from the bedroom, fussing over which dress to wear. While she had not said anything, it was obvious she was as nervous as a cat before a thunderstorm about testifying.

"Charlie, which do you prefer?" She offered two dresses for his inspection: one a medium blue, the other a dove gray.

"The dove gray, I think, dear. It speaks to your status as a widow; and, whether you like it or not, that does have an impact. Somehow, people find widows to be more believable."

"Oh, that is a lovely thought. Thank you, General." She placed the dress on the bed, then removed her robe with a long sigh. "I hate this."

He stepped behind her and gently embraced her, "I know you do. So do I, and for many of the same reasons. But look at what he did to Constance, and what he will probably do to others if he is allowed to go free. The alternatives are unacceptable, dear."

"Yes. I know. I will just be relieved when it is over and we can put it all behind us. Not just for ourselves, but for Constance especially."

"Do you think she will be in any condition to testify?"

"I do not think that would be wise, Charlie. She is so weak. We are already afraid of losing not only her, but possibly the child as well. I believe the strain would be too much."

"Well, we will have to ask Elizabeth. In this case, I believe the court would accept Elizabeth's testimony as to what Constance said. The rules of evidence for a military trial are different from those of a civilian trial. Alternatively, the panel may choose to go to her. I trust General Sheridan to be gentle."

"I would like to be with her, if General Sheridan will permit."

"And if Elizabeth will permit. She is as protective of Constance as a cat with new kittens."

"She is a good doctor and a wonderful friend. She knows Constance probably will not survive the birth, and she is doing everything she can to help her in the here and now."

Charlie, who had been buttoning up the back of Rebecca's dress while they spoke, stopped cold. "She is really not going to survive?

Should I try and leave Elizabeth with you and her when we are ordered back to the field? And what about Em?" Although they had discussed it before, and even committed to caring for Em if need be, Charlie had never really accepted the possibility that Constance would not survive.

Rebecca turned slowly and looked at him. "No, Charlie, it has been become more apparent every day she will not come through this birth. Constance and I have discussed what will become of Emily and the baby. As I have said before, she wants us to raise them. As our own."

Charlie looked deep into Rebecca's eyes, a bittersweet smile lighting his normally somber features. "Then, my dear, we shall raise them with all the love their mother would have given them herself."

"Of course we will. So think of this when you are away from home. Not only will there be a woman who loves you desperately, but also a daughter and possibly a son." She smiled and caressed his cheek. "Of course, it could be another daughter."

"Oh, my God, a house full of women. What will I do with myself?"

She laughed, and then hugged him. "Come home and love us."

Charlie had asked Beulah and Reg to clear the ballroom and set it up for the trial. There was a long table for the panel of judges set before the fireplace at the end of the hall. Two more tables were set facing them, with about ten feet of open space between them. A single chair was set to one side at a ninety degree angle to both tables, facing inward. Across from that, a small writing desk had been placed for the court clerk, closing the square. Behind the tables for the defense and prosecution, were several chairs for observers. The room was largely empty, giving the entire setting a stark and somber quality, which was further emphasized by the watery winter light.

Whitman and Samuelson carried Montgomery into the room in

an armchair and settled him behind the defense table. Colonel McCauley leaned over to speak to him. Montgomery very pointedly turned his head away, showing obvious indifference to McCauley and complete disdain for the proceedings.

Colonel Howard stood at the prosecution table, nervously flipping through his notes. Elizabeth and Rebecca sat together at the back of the room, while Charlie stood nearby talking quietly with several officers and enlisted men.

The side door opened and Sheridan, followed by Brigadier General Merritt and Colonel James, filed in. The officers and men in the room came to attention—all but Montgomery, who did not even bother to look at the officers who would decide his fate.

Sheridan, Merritt, and James took their places at the judges' table, and seated themselves. In a sonorous voice, the clerk announced, "Be seated. This court martial is convened to examine allegations that Major Harrison Montgomery, Commander, Company D, 13th Pennsylvania Cavalry, of Bucks County, Pennsylvania, did, on or about the eighth of July, 1864, aid, abet, encourage, permit, and observe without intervention, while several of his men did brutally force and outrage one Constance Adams, an innocent non-combatant and resident of the Commonwealth of Virginia. That he did himself participate in that heinous act, committing sodomy. That further, Major Montgomery did on more than one occasion, and acting either without orders or in direct contravention of orders, lead punitive raids against civilian non-combatants, abusing said civilians and removing supplies and other material goods without compensation."

Silence reigned in the room, then Sheridan asked Montgomery, "How say you to these charges?"

A longer silence settled as Montgomery refused to respond. Finally, McCauley spoke. "My client pleads not guilty, Sir."

Sheridan nodded to Colonel Howard. "Then, gentlemen, shall we begin? Colonel Howard, present your case."

Howard cleared his throat and spoke in a rather strained voice.

What he had to do was distasteful in the extreme. He was about to ask a group of women to discuss revolting behavior by an officer of the U.S. Army. Just thinking about it offended this devout Presbyterian; to have to prosecute it was disgusting.

"Sir, I call Dr. Elizabeth Walker."

Elizabeth rose and walked sedately to the witness chair. The clerk bustled over with a Bible in hand. "Do you swear to tell the truth, the whole truth, and nothing but the truth, so help you God?"

"Insofar as my Hippocratic oath and the sacred privilege between physician and patient allow, I do."

Howard stepped forward and began his questioning. "Dr. Walker, you treated Major Montgomery for head injuries. Would you describe, briefly, the nature of the injuries and any impact those injuries may have had on his ability to understand the process of this trial and to contribute to his own defense?"

"Major Montgomery received a trauma to the head as a result of being kicked by a horse. Upon my arrival, I performed a surgical procedure to repair the splintered skull and relieve the pressure to the brain. Over the course of the last few weeks, there has been marked improvement in the physical aspects of the Major's condition."

"Dr. Walker, during this time, you have spoken with your patient regularly. Have you found him to be lucid, aware, and logically normal in his communications?"

"I have tended to him every day. I have found marked improvement. He is alert and aware. I expect a full recovery of the physical body."

"Dr. Walker, you have emphasized the issues of his physical health. Would you care to comment on your observations of his mental health, remembering the definition of 'competent to stand trial' is the ability to understand the law and to differentiate between right and wrong?"

"He is competent. He understands the difference between the two."

Howard drew a large sigh of relief as he checked his papers again and prepared the next round of questions for the doctor. He really did not think a plea of insanity was reasonable for this situation, but feared Montgomery, when he realized a noose lay at the end of this process, would try and use it. "Dr. Walker, is it true Major Montgomery has made his point of view about Southern citizens clear, and that he has publicly stated that all Southern citizens should be punished for the results of this war?"

Elizabeth looked to the back of the room where Rebecca sat. They locked eyes, and Rebecca's sincere smile offered her friend as much silent courage as possible. "He has made such comments."

"To your knowledge, has he made specific comments about events in which he and his men may have participated that are contrary to the Military Code of Conduct toward civilian non-combatants?"

"Yes."

"Would you tell this court what specific statements you have heard Major Montgomery make that specified such actions?"

"I am sorry, Sir. To divulge these things would be in violation of doctor-patient confidentiality."

Howard took that in stride, having expected her answer. "Then, Doctor, can you tell me if Major Montgomery ever mentioned Mrs. Constance Adams to you in any context other than the fact that she was assisting in providing him nursing care while he was recovering from his injuries?"

"No, I cannot."

Howard took a breath. "Then, Doctor, let us turn to another subject. Have you had Mrs. Constance Adams under your medical care during the past weeks?"

"I have." Elizabeth sighed, and took a drink from the glass of water that had been provided for her.

"Could you describe for us the condition or conditions for which you have been treating Mrs. Adams, and the circumstances which led to her current condition?"

"Mrs. Adams is currently in the second stage of a very difficult pregnancy. I am sure you are versed in the circumstances that led to the condition."

"Since the charges here include forcible outrage and incitement, can you tell the Court if there is any physical damage or additional stress to her condition that can be attributed to or is the direct result of the event?"

"As you are probably aware, Sir, I was only able to start treating Mrs. Adams well after the point of conception. The physical trauma of such an occurrence would have been difficult to determine."

"Doctor, could you tell us what Mrs. Adams' current condition is? For example, in your opinion, is she well enough to testify before this court?"

"In my professional opinion, she most certainly is not. Her condition is not good. She is weak, barely able to sit up for meals. Subjecting her to this could very well kill her, as well as the child that she carries."

"Is that child the result of the events under consideration, Doctor?"

"Well, if you consider that her husband has been dead for a significant length of time, and that immaculate conception can, no doubt, be ruled out, I would have to believe that to be the most likely cause of her pregnancy."

General Sheridan interrupted. "Dr. Walker, if Mrs. Adams is not in any condition to come to this Court, would she be able to withstand some gentle questioning from the panel in her room?" He knew Elizabeth well; if she was getting acidic it meant that Howard was stepping very close to her personal sense of ethics and logic.

"Sir, it is my opinion that Mrs. Adams should not be brought into this matter at all. However, considering the nature and the gravity of the charges, if you really believe it is necessary, then you could question her for a few minutes. But I would request you allow Mrs. Gaines and me to be present as support for Mrs. Adams. She trusts us, and has come to rely on us."

"The panel will take your comments into consideration, Dr.

Walker, and will only resort to interviewing Mrs. Adams if we feel it is absolutely necessary." He turned to the prosecuting officer. "Colonel Howard, do you have any further questions for Dr. Walker?"

"No, Sir. Dr. Walker, thank you for your assistance."

Elizabeth waited quietly as McCauley whispered with his client and then looked frustrated when Montgomery refused to answer him. He then rose, and walked to stand in front of the waiting physician. "Good morning, Doctor. I would like to ask you some questions about Major Montgomery's mental condition, if I may. Is it true you have placed a suicide watch on the Major?"

"Yes. General Redmond and I believed that would be the best course of action."

"What specific events, acts, words, or attitudes did you observe that led you to take such extreme precautions?"

"Sir, to divulge specific information would be a violation of my oath. Suffice it to say, in my professional judgment; it was an appropriate preventative action."

"Would you say Major Montgomery was emotionally unstable? That perhaps he was showing signs of battlefield stress which led him to outbursts of anger, directed either at himself or others?"

"Major Montgomery feels a great burden after so much time in the field. The Wilderness Campaign left him emotionally wounded."

"Would you say he may have been so emotionally burdened by guilt and anger after that campaign that his sense of right and wrong was eroded?"

"No. He is aware of the difference between right and wrong. Good and evil."

"Would you say he understands that such an outrage and violence is wrong?"

Elizabeth sighed, feeling caught between a rock and a hard spot. "Sir, given Major Montgomery's attitude toward the fairer sex, I doubt he would believe it wrong under any circumstance."

Colonel McCauley cleared his throat, not having expected that response from the normally reserved Dr. Walker. It was definitely time to move on. "Thank you, Doctor, for your frank comments."

Elizabeth left the stand, walking regally back to her seat at the back of the room. Montgomery glanced at her as she passed, examining her as if she were a piece of carrion lying on the side of the road, his face twisted in a vicious glower.

Howard next called Trooper Abel Franklin, the man who had been on duty at Montgomery's door the day he confessed to Rebecca. After being sworn in, Howard asked Franklin a series of very direct questions about why he was on guard outside the door and what he had heard. Franklin answered honestly and directly. He was on guard because Major Montgomery had, at various times, threatened to kill Miss Rebecca, Miss Constance, General Redmond, or himself. The telling testimony came when Howard asked him what had happened on the morning of December eighteenth.

"Mrs. Gaines was sitting with the Major that morning, Sir. Major Montgomery became very abusive toward her. When I heard him raise his voice, I opened the door a crack to listen in and make sure she was not harmed."

"Trooper, when you opened the door, could you hear the two of them clearly?"

"Yes, Sir."

"What did you hear?"

"Well, first I heard the Major basically call Mrs. Gaines a whore. I thought that was pretty out of line, since she said she was engaged to the Colonel, 'scuze me, the General."

"Yes. Then what, Trooper?"

"He said a lot of pretty insulting things about the General. I thought Mrs. Gaines would get up and leave, or have a hissy on him, but she did not. She just kept listening. Finally, she snapped back at him."

"Snapped back at him?"

"Yes, Sir. She told him she understood he was a man who enjoyed watching women being violated. Then the Major really blew up at her. I remember exactly what he said."

"And that was?"

"He said, 'You cannot prove anything, you greedy little whore. It is my word as an officer and a gentleman against the word of that little lying, Bible quoting bitch.'"

Howard's Presbyterian soul was already offended, and he knew it was going to get worse. "Did he say anything else, Trooper?"

Franklin grew pale and thoroughly embarrassed. He stared at the floor and twisted his kepi in his hands. "Yes, Sir." In a strangled voice he went on. "He described what he wanted to do to Mrs. Gaines and told her she would like it just like Mrs. Adams had. He even told her that after three men had had their way with Mrs. Adams, he had committed sodomy on Mrs. Adams because the more natural way was too messy."

"What did Mrs. Gaines do then, Trooper?"

"I have to say, Sir, Mrs. Gaines did better than I would have right then. I would have simply hit him. She got him to say he had participated in the violation of Constance Adams. He told her that no one would believe her over him. But by then, both the Colonel and I had heard him."

"The Colonel was there?"

"Yes, Sir. The Colonel, um, General Redmond, you know? He had come up while they were talking, before Mrs. Gaines snapped at the Major. We both heard him."

"Thank you, Trooper. Your witness, Colonel McCauley."

McCauley looked at Montgomery for a moment, hoping for some shred of a lifeline to help him. Montgomery just smiled back at him, a smug, arrogant look.

McCauley turned away from Franklin and walked over to stand beside the clerk. He spoke in a reasonably low tone of voice, and further muffled his words by putting his hand over his mouth, trying to demonstrate that Franklin was not able to clearly hear the conversation between Rebecca and Montgomery through a partially closed door. "Trooper Franklin, is it possible you misheard any of the conversation?" The members of the panel strained to hear his words.

Franklin answered promptly. "No, Sir. I heard him quite clearly. They were not keeping their voices down, and I have always had pretty good hearing. I used to be able to find the squirrels' nests in my da's pecan grove by listening for their chattering."

"Thank you, Trooper." McCauley's shoulders slumped. Everything he could think of was failing.

Montgomery looked bored. McCauley was frustrated. He was honor bound to provide a reasonable defense, but without Montgomery's cooperation, and with the evidence against him building apace, he was unsure as to what course of action to follow next.

Howard called Charlie to the stand next. His testimony was almost exactly the same as Franklin's. It was obviously difficult for Charlie to present his testimony calmly, since hearing his fiancée called a whore and threatened with vicious outrage and violation was not an event that any gentleman could discuss calmly.

Finally, Howard called Rebecca.

"Mrs. Gaines, I know this must be very difficult for you. We shall make this as brief as possible. You have heard the testimony of Trooper Franklin and General Redmond. Do you have anything you would like to add?"

Rebecca twisted one of Charlie's handkerchiefs in her hands until she was sure she could feel the threads snapping. Finally, she looked up at the man before her. "He knew what he was doing."

"Do you mean he knew he was confessing to a heinous crime?"

"Yes. He knew what he was saying. He was deliberately trying to offend and insult me, by telling me what happened that night."

"The night he and his troops forced Mrs. Adams?"

"Yes."

"How do you know this, Mrs. Gaines?"

"He said, 'I dare you to attempt to prove any of it, slut. My word against yours, and my confession, as you call it, is pure hearsay that no court in the country would accept.'"

"Thank you, Mrs. Gaines. Your witness, Colonel McCauley."

McCauley knew when he was defeated. "No questions, thank you."

Sheridan looked at his fellow panel members. "We shall take a short break, then the counsels will have an opportunity to present their summations."

Howard stood. "Gentlemen of the panel, the prosecution waives any need for summation. I feel the testimony speaks for itself."

McCauley stood with him. "The defense, Sirs, throws itself on the mercy of the Court. Major Montgomery experienced extreme stress and anguish as a result of the devastation of battles such as The Wilderness. That terrible experience has warped this man's judgment and instilled an unreasoned anger and desire for revenge. Though it is a logical response to those experiences, it is unfortunate that his anger and pain have been so inappropriately expressed."

"Very well, then. The court will adjourn until after lunch, at which time we will render our decision."

Charlie escorted Rebecca and Elizabeth out of the door. Polk, waiting in the hall for them to emerge, took Elizabeth's arm. The two men escorted their respective ladies to the rear parlor, where a warm fire was burning and Beulah had tea and a light lunch already waiting for them.

Rebecca, still slightly shaken, allowed Charlie to help her to the davenport. She looked up at him, trying to hold back her tears. "Do you think they will want to talk with Constance?"

"No, dear. You and Franklin have done all that was needed about that. And Elizabeth made it clear he was not insane." Charlie gently put his arm around her shoulders and held her close. "You did wonderfully well, my brave girl."

"It certainly did not feel like it. I could feel him looking at me. I could not even meet his eyes. He is truly an evil man."

"He is, dear. You and Elizabeth stood up to him gallantly."

Richard had been standing behind Elizabeth, gently sheltering her in his arms as she warmed herself before the fire.

Elizabeth looked back at her own gentleman and whispered, "Did I do the right thing, Richard?"

He leaned over, holding her close and whispering in her ear, "Elizabeth, you did the only thing an honorable person could do. I, for one, am very proud of you for it."

"It is amazing how I know intellectually that it is the right thing, but still feel so horrible that it had to be done. I am a doctor; I am supposed to guard and preserve life, not make it possible to take it. Yet, I know a monster like that has to be stopped. He would only hurt other women."

"Think, Elizabeth. This is a man who enjoyed watching Constance being forced repeatedly, and then sodomized her. The man who will be responsible, by his acts, for taking Constance's life and changing Em's and the unborn baby's lives forever. Those children will be deprived of their mother's love because of Montgomery. How many other women and children would suffer the same fate if he were allowed to go free?"

"I know. I know it had to be done. It is just that, for me personally, it was a very bitter pill."

"I know, my lovely doctor. But I will remind you of what happens in the field. You have to make hard decisions—to treat those who have a chance of surviving and leave those who have none to their God. In this case, you have done the same thing—you have made a choice to protect the lives of women and children you will probably never meet."

There was a rap on the door. Lizbet pushed it open, holding Em's hand as she toddled into the room and directly to Charlie. "Papa." She managed to start the climb on her own, only to be assisted into Charlie's lap by Rebecca, who smiled and gave the girl a kiss.

Richard and Elizabeth turned at the sound of Em's happy cry. Elizabeth watched the little girl as she clung to these two people who had come into her life and given her love when things looked so bleak. "Yes, Richard. You are exactly right. My first priority is to protect them as much as I can."

Lunch was a subdued affair, with Em dominating the conversation. Somehow, even she managed to understand it was a serious day and kept her lunch mostly on her and her bib, rather than on Charlie's coat.

After giving Em to Lizbet for her nap, the four of them returned to the ballroom to wait for the panel's decision. Most of the officers filed in, and the troopers from Montgomery's company stood outside the windows, listening.

Sheridan, Merritt, and James filed into the room, settled themselves, and then waited for the room to settle down.

As president of the panel, Sheridan spoke. "It is the finding of the court that Major Harrison Montgomery is guilty as charged of the capital crime, by his own admission, as verified by an officer and an enlisted man in good standing in the U.S. Army, as well as by civilian witnesses. Before we pass sentence on you, Major Montgomery, do you have anything to say in your own defense?"

Montgomery looked up from the table. His eyes were filled with rage, hate, and anger. "In my defense? No. You would not listen to me. You have taken the word of the Southern sympathizer and his lackeys. You have heard the spewing of a whore who has lured him to her bed. Before you slip the noose around my neck, I will give you the names of the men who committed the crimes, and I expect you to hang them for failure to follow the orders of a senior officer." He paused and looked directly at Rebecca. "I told them to kill her. I told them to make sure it would never come back to haunt them. I suggested they cut her throat and the throat of the squalling, snot nosed brat across the room, crying for her mama." His gaze shifted to Charlie. "So, if you are going to hang one true Union soldier, make sure you get us all."

Phil Sheridan's face looked as though it was chiseled from stone. "Harrison Montgomery, for the capital crimes of forcibly violating a woman and threatening her with death, it is the judgment of this court that you be hanged by the neck until dead. May God have mercy on your soul."

He stood and walked toward the back of the room, then turned to Samuelson. "Get that vermin out of Mrs. Gaines' house. Schedule the hanging for tomorrow morning; and see to it that if he wants a minister, he gets one." Without saying another word, Sheridan walked out of the house and down to the pond, where he could be seen pacing and smoking cigar after cigar until the light of day faded away.

~

Tuesday, December 27, 1864

In the early morning, the cold was biting, even though the air was still. After listening to their former commander's virulent diatribe, the men of Company D had volunteered to build the gallows upon which Montgomery's life would end. By tacit agreement, they had elected to build it as far from the farm as possible, choosing a remote corner of the rail yard as their site. As the morning grew brighter, a small group of officers and troopers carried Montgomery to the scaffold. He had refused the ministrations of Reverend Williams, cursing that kind man as a 'damned rebel' and daring the devil to do his worst.

Charlie and Richard joined Sheridan and his entourage to serve as formal witnesses to the hanging. Sheridan personally stripped Montgomery of his insignia of office before the man mounted the steps to the platform. With a little assistance, Montgomery found a final reserve of strength and defiance, and walked on his own to his end. He turned to the hangman and said, "I should forgive you, but somehow I just cannot. You are no better than any of the rest of them, seduced by that damn Southern sympathizer to be soft on these vermin. So, do your worst; and I will see you all in Hell."

The hangman placed the hood over Montgomery's head, settled

the rope around his neck, tightly behind his left ear, made sure to bind his legs, and on Sheridan's signal, released the trap that dropped the man to his death. It was a clean death; his neck broke with the drop, his body twitched once and hung still. As the troopers of his own company cut him down, Sheridan and his escort turned and rode away.

Charlie turned to Richard as they watched the men settle the body into the waiting pine box. "God, what more will we have to pay before this war is over, my friend?"

"Charlie, it will end. And if we are lucky, we will find some kind of a life afterwards that will help erase this from our souls."

"Nothing will erase this from my soul. I just hope Rebecca and I can bring enough love into the world to balance it in the long run."

Charlie had spent the rest of the day processing all of the paperwork that resulted from General Sheridan's visit, thinking about the implications of that visit and his formal announcement of his intent to resign when the war was over. It was time for him to start putting his life in order. Even sooner, he would face battle again, and these inevitably final battles of the war would be bloody. The enemy was desperate, and desperate men were dangerous men. He knew he would have to do something to provide for and protect Rebecca in the event the Fates played the ultimate joke on him.

In other words, Charlie spent the afternoon brooding.

Rebecca watched him play with his dinner; he remained monosyllabic throughout the evening. Finally, she could not stand it anymore.

"What is bothering you, sitting like a statue and barely touching supper?"

"Why do you say anything is bothering me, dear?"

"Because you have not said more than two words in a row, you are keeping your eyes locked on your plate, and you are trying to hide your vegetables under your potatoes like young Jeremiah."

"I am sorry, love. I just have a number of things on my mind this evening. Let us adjourn to the back parlor and talk a little, dear."

She smiled as she sipped her coffee. "After you finish your dinner."

"I swear, Rebecca, you are beginning to sound like my old mammy." He softened the statement with a teasing grin.

"It is just the mother in me coming out. With all these children under foot, it was bound to happen. Now eat." She grinned and gave him a wink.

Charlie dutifully finished his meal in record time, then rose from the table. "Mrs. Gaines, will you join me in the parlor?"

"Of course, General Redmond." She stood, taking his hand and allowing him to escort her from the table.

As they left the room, Charlie turned to Sarah, who had come to clear the table. "Could you bring some tea into the back parlor for us, Sarah?"

"Why, yes, General Charlie. Right away."

Charlie escorted Rebecca in and settled her in her favorite chair. He then knelt in front of the fireplace, tending the fire and adding more wood.

She watched him. She sighed, knowing she was going to have to give him a gentle nudge, and if that failed, a swift kick. "Charlie?"

"Oh, yes, sorry, dear. I was just thinking." He fidgeted some more with the fire. "I need to go to Washington." The announcement was rather abrupt.

"Yes, I know. Why does this have you so concerned? It will only be for a few days, correct?"

"Yes, I will hurry, but I need to go and see General Meigs and deliver General Sheridan's message. I also need to see my attorney and my banker, and have you named my beneficiary for my pension."

Rebecca smiled and looked at her hands. "I wish...well...I

understand why you are doing it Charlie. I just wish we did not have to think of these things."

He went to her side and knelt down. He bowed his head and laid it in her lap. "I am afraid, dear. I am afraid the universe will play a huge, vicious joke on the two of us. I think, for the first time, I am afraid to die. And all of my errands in Washington are about taking care of you in the event that I do. Somehow, part of me thinks if I do everything I can to make sure you are taken care of if I do die, I can avert it somehow. And part of me is terrified because I need to do this to protect you."

"There is no joke waiting to be played, Charlie. Please, do not think like that. Just think of what you are doing as the things any husband would do to protect his wife and family. You will come home."

"My love, I would do anything to protect you and our home. I think that perhaps watching Montgomery's end today may have put me in a morbid mood."

"I am sure it did. The house has been rather subdued today. But, you, my dear Charlie, are going to come home when this war is all over. We will breed the best horseflesh in the state, and we shall raise a herd of children: little girls who will grow into fine women, and boys who will be kind and gentle like their father."

Charlie raised his head from her lap and looked into her eyes. "Are you sure, Rebecca? Are you really sure you want me as your husband? Are you willing to spend your life with someone who is fundamentally a fraud—a woman who lives and passes as a man? Are you willing to raise a family that is not of your own body? Those are all prices you must pay to spend your life with me. Are you willing to withstand the scandal if I am discovered?"

She ran her fingers through his hair. "First, you are not a fraud. You are kind, loving, and caring. There is nothing fraudulent about that. None of that matters to me; I fell in love with you. It is your heart and spirit I adore. The body makes no difference to me."

She caressed his face. "As for the children, why do you think one needs to be born of my body for me to love it? I hope you can see I love Em as much as if she were my own. That also does not matter."

She straightened and drew a deep breath. "And if you are discovered, well then, we will still stand together; and, if it must happen, we will move away from here and start anew." She smiled. "I hear the West is a fascinating place."

He could not help but chuckle at the tone of her voice. He looked at her and asked, "So you will marry me on the twenty-eighth?"

"Of course I will. You need not worry. I will be there."

"So, have you started planning the wedding? Is there anything you want me to do, or assist you with?" He mentally crossed his fingers—all he really wanted to do was to buy the rings, show up in his dress uniform, and settle down to a quiet life with his wife. He suspected that was not all he would be required to do.

"Well, actually, Grace and I have put together a small," she held the thumb and finger apart just a bit, "list of items we will require to make me a suitably lovely bride for my dashing General. If you could pick these things up while you are in Washington, it would be wonderful."

"Of course, dear. I would be happy to run whatever errands you need me to."

She smiled. "Good." She was not sure, but she thought she might have seen a brief flash of panic in his eyes. "So, tell me, my love, who will be at the wedding?"

Charlie's eyebrows rose. "Um, whomever you wish to invite. I suppose Richard and Elizabeth and Whitman and Samuelson, my senior officers, and your friends from town?" Charlie's voice rose to an unusual squeak. Guests were not on the list of things he was accustomed to defining.

"Charlie, this is our wedding. I want to make sure the people you care about are at the ceremony as well. What about friends in Washington? Surely there must be a few."

Charlie's forehead crumpled in concentration. "Well, I suppose

General Sheridan and perhaps McCauley might want to attend. Maybe General Grant as well; he probably would not attend, but would feel slighted if we did not invite him. I do have a few friends there. Some in the theater and a lady named Lizzie Armstrong, but somehow I suspect you would prefer she not attend."

Rebecca looked at him shrewdly, put two and two together, and came up with the name of the woman who had offered Charlie solace in the past. "Charlie, she is your friend. If you would like, please extend her an invitation. I am sure I would find her to be a delightful woman. Besides that, I do owe her a certain amount of thanks."

He looked at her with some curiosity. "You owe her thanks?"

"Yes, if it were not for her tender caring for you, we might not have found ourselves at this place."

Charlie had the grace to blush deeply. "Well, a certain amount of respect is due to one's teacher," he laughed. "And we have certainly both benefited, and will benefit even more as we grow closer."

"I know." She licked her lips, trying not to sound like a jealous wife to be. "So, while you are in Washington will you call on Mrs. Armstrong?"

"I believe I should. If nothing else, I think I owe her the courtesy of telling her about our marriage personally. Do you have a problem with that, dear? You know I am totally yours now. All that is, or will be, between Mrs. Armstrong and myself is friendship, rather like my friendship with Elizabeth." He had a slightly uneasy feeling about Rebecca's understanding of his friendship with Lizzie.

"No, of course not. You should see your friend. I was just curious."

"Rebecca? What are you thinking, dear?" He was rapidly growing uncomfortable.

"Oh, Charlie, I am not thinking anything. I was just wondering if you would see her." She smiled, trying to lighten the mood. "Maybe sow the last of your wild oats, before your oats become mine."

Charlie looked at Rebecca. For a second, his expression was that of a cornered rabbit. Then all of the implications hit him fully in the funny bone. He started laughing, a big, full belly laugh. In fact, he laughed so hard he slipped from his kneeling position and abruptly sat on the floor. Between guffaws, he managed to gasp out, "My... wild... oats... are... already... yours... and... yours... alone. I... am... just... waiting... for... your... permission... to ... sow... them."

Rebecca smiled and joined Charlie on the floor, slowly pushing him back until, with some amount of difficulty and fussing with her dress, she managed to straddle his waist and pin his wrists to the floor as she leaned over him. She was about to tease him further when the door opened and Elizabeth and Richard came in.

Without missing a beat, Elizabeth commented. "I find them doing the strangest things."

Richard nodded. "Indeed."

Rebecca looked over. "Good evening. Charlie and I were just discussing planting methods."

CHAPTER 23

SATURDAY, DECEMBER 31, 1864

Rebecca watched intently while Em toddled ahead of her as they made their way into the kitchen. She was pleased to see the child head directly to a small table and chair Duncan had fashioned for her. As soon as she was seated, Sarah gave her a cookie and a cup of fresh milk.

"Tank you, Sar." Em grinned so broadly that she showed two new molars that had almost completely come in.

"You are welcome, Miss Emily."

Rebecca could only smile at the child she was beginning to love as if she was her own. She had taken over as primary caretaker for her since Constance's condition had continued to deteriorate with each passing day. She was exceptionally proud at how well-mannered little Emily was becoming under their gentle care.

"Good morning, everyone." Rebecca immediately checked the stove and the dishes being prepared for the open house that would take place the next day. Reaching for a spoon to taste one of the pots, she found her hand smacked by Sarah.

"Not yet, Miss Rebecca, 'tis not ready." The cook smiled and just shook her head.

"Is everything going to be ready by tomorrow?"

Reg just shook his head at Rebecca's nervousness as he continued to unpack a crate of dishes that General Charlie had ordered down from Washington. "Of course it will, Miss Rebecca. Beulah, Tess, and the others are working on the house, and me and Sarah is getting everything else ready."

Taking a seat at the kitchen table, Rebecca smiled, then sighed, knowing she was being nervous for nothing. "I am sorry, Reg. It is just that this is the first time in many years that we have hosted a New Year's party. I want everything to be perfect. We need some relief after the unpleasantness of Major Montgomery's execution."

Sarah turned slowly and looked to her employer. "Miss Rebecca, they say there were some other men with him."

"Yes."

"And that General Redmond let them go from the Army."

"Yes, Sarah, but he did not know then what had happened."

"Yes, Ma'am, I know. But I am worried about them running around here. The folks over in the colored towns cain't protect themselves."

"I know. General Redmond has men keeping an eye out for them, but he thinks they are long gone from here."

"I sure do hope so."

"We all do."

~

Sunday, January 1, 1865

The group that made its way to church from Gaines Cove or, more correctly, Redmond Stables, that day was smaller than the previous Sunday. The visiting officers had left, and since Constance was having a very difficult day, both Elizabeth and Beulah had stayed behind to tend to her.

The congregation filed in quietly, but there was an underlying buzz of anticipation. Today was the first time since before the war there had been celebrations planned for the New Year. How the Yankee General would handle Southern hospitality was a matter of intense curiosity and anticipation.

Mrs. Williams had chosen music that was vaguely patriotic in tone, perhaps to remind the residents they were still Southerners and they were still at war. The Reverend ignored it completely. He mounted the steps to the pulpit and began his sermon.

"Our reading today is Ecclesiastes Chapter Three, verses one through eight.

'To every thing there is a season, and a time to every purpose under the heaven:

A time to be born, and a time to die; a time to plant, and a time to pluck up that which is planted;

A time to kill, and a time to heal; a time to break down, and a time to build up;

A time to weep, and a time to laugh; a time to mourn, and a time to dance;

A time to cast away stones, and a time to gather stones together;

A time to embrace, and a time to refrain from embracing;

A time to get, and a time to lose; a time to keep, and a time to cast away;

A time to rend, and a time to sew; a time to keep silence, and a time to speak;

A time to love, and a time to hate; a time of war, and a time of peace.'

"We have seen our time of death, our time of killing, our time when everything in our lives was broken down, and we were left with nothing but ashes. I do not believe there is a single person in this room who has not had their time of weeping and mourning.

"We have had our time of hating, our time of war.

"That time is coming to an end. We have had our enemies come among us and found them to be men of compassion, of honor, and kindness. It is true some of the enemies have not been able to let go of the past, to let go of the time for hate and war. For those poor souls, we offer our prayers and condolences.

"The year before us will be a time of great change. It is my prayer we find that it is a time to heal, a time to build up, a time to plant, a time to love, and a time of peace."

The sermon continued. Mrs. Williams sat at her keyboard with a look on her face that would have made sour pickles seem sweet. As the Reverend continued his message of peace and cooperation, one could only imagine the atmosphere in the Williams' home. Charlie speculated that it probably made the Battle of Vicksburg look pleasant in comparison.

Rebecca stood near the mantle in the large front parlor. She was gingerly holding a glass of wine in her hands and on the verge of seething. Charlie was standing in the center of the room surrounded by all the available young ladies of Culpeper.

Elizabeth wandered over, trying to hide the smile on her face as she sipped her own wine. "You may rupture something very important."

Reluctantly, Rebecca swung her eyes from Charlie to her friend. "Excuse me?"

"If the green-eyed monster grips you any tighter, your eyes will pop out."

"I have no idea what you are talking about."

"I am talking about the fact that your husband-to-be is standing there surrounded by all those young ladies of the community, and you do not like it much."

She nodded, ashamed of her feelings. "Yes, you are right."

"Rebecca, my dear friend, you need not worry about Charlie. He adores you. When you are away from him, all he talks about is you. I do believe he will see to your sainthood himself."

Rebecca chuckled and blushed. "I know he loves me. It is just that they are so...so..."

"Utterly charmed by the newly minted General?" She elbowed her friend. "Think how jealous they will be when you and Charlie are married. My dear, you will be the envy of them all."

Elizabeth watched as the blonde tried to do the proper thing and not gloat. It was obvious that she found it very difficult.

"Oh, enjoy it, Rebecca. It does not make you a sinner to be happy with the way your life is turning out. Especially since it came so close to falling apart."

"I do not want to seem too prideful, but you have to admit that if I were prone to it, Charlie would be a good reason."

"He would be the best reason. I think the good Lord will forgive you for feeling pride in the one you love."

As the two women chatted, Charlie broke away from his group of admirers and went over to the buffet where Jocko was standing in service. The two men whispered together for a moment, and Jocko nodded, then quietly left the room.

Charlie moved slowly across the room, stopping several times to chat briefly with some of the gentlemen in attendance, both from town and from among his own command. He kept looking over his shoulder, as if he expected something to happen.

As he drew near to Rebecca and Elizabeth, Jocko returned and nodded to him. A mixture of mischief and relief washed over Charlie's features as he turned to his bride-to-be. "I have a little surprise for you and the guests."

"A surprise? General, what are you..."

He smiled gently. "A surprise. Tell me, Mrs. Gaines, do you dance?"

She smiled back. "Why yes, General, I do."

"Ah, then the boys and I have done well. It happens we have several excellent musicians in the regiment who have consented to play for the guests today. They are ready, so, as our hostess, would you care to open the doors to the ball room and begin the proceedings?"

She took Charlie's arm. "We shall host the first dance of what I hope will be many dances at Redmond Stables," she paused and smiled, "together, Charlie."

Charlie stepped to the buffet and picked up a glass and spoon, tapping the crystal to get peoples' attention. "Ladies and gentlemen, Mrs. Gaines and the men of the 13th Pennsylvania have a treat for you." He nodded to Jocko, who threw open the doors to the ballroom. The room was decorated with evergreen and holly, and fires were burning brightly in the great fireplaces at either end. In the musicians' alcove, a small band, mostly violins, was playing softly. "Let us dance in the New Year."

Rebecca stepped forward and claimed her General. "Your dances are mine, General."

"My dear, I will have to do my duty to the matrons, but for you, the first and last dance." He nodded to the musicians and the strains of one of Mr. Strauss' scandalous waltzes were heard. "Mrs. Gaines, will you do me the honor?"

"Oh, indeed I will, General Redmond."

Charlie extended his left hand to her, and wrapped his right hand around her waist. Standing still for a moment, he waited to catch the beat of the music then led her into the whirling pleasure of that most shocking dance. "I love being able to hold you in public, my dear. And before this day is over, those who do not already know will know why."

"Oh, my dear, that sounds like you are planning something to set them on their ears." She glanced around the room to find all eyes were upon them. "Something other than this, I assume?"

"I plan to announce to them that you have done me the honor of consenting to be my wife, love, and that the wedding is set for the twenty-eighth."

"Yes, my dear, please do. But make sure someone is standing behind Mrs. Williams."

Charlie smiled an evil little smile. "I assume Reverend Williams will attend to his wife."

She moved just a shade closer and whispered, "My darling Charlie, you may assume too much."

"Then let her fall. The only woman I wish to attend to is you."

"I am very glad to hear that." She smiled sweetly at Mrs. Williams as Charlie guided her to the music. "I think she is ready to faint now. There goes my reputation," she teased, her hand moving up and down his arm.

After the initial surprise, Polk led Elizabeth out onto the dance floor. Mr. and Mrs. Cooper soon followed, and then Charlie's officers played the gallant to several of the younger women. Soon the room was swirling with men in dark suits and lovely women in gentle colors.

"You throw a wonderful party, General. We will be the talk of the county."

"We throw a wonderful party, darling." Charlie was relishing the feel of holding the smaller woman in his arms in front of everyone.

She took notice of the look. "Charlie Redmond, you are gloating," she smiled.

"Yes, Rebecca Gaines, I am gloating. I am holding the most beautiful woman in the world in my arms, I am dancing with her, and I am going to announce to the world she has consented to be mine for the rest of our lives. Of course I am gloating."

"Well, good. Then I will not feel guilty for doing it over you earlier."

He pulled back a bit so he could look into her eyes. "You were gloating?"

"Like the evil thing I am, yes I was."

"Well, darling, I wish I could give you more to gloat over." He smiled anyway. It was so wonderful to feel her possessive, proud love.

"Please Charlie. I am going to be married to the most charming, handsome man in the world. I have plenty to gloat over."

He grinned as the waltz came to an end. He bowed to her, as was appropriate for a gentleman after such an intimate dance, and escorted her over to the Reverend Williams and his wife, whispering as they walked, "You know, dear, we must play the proper host and hostess. So dance the quadrille with the Reverend, and I will see if I can further scandalize his wife."

"That will do it." She chuckled as she moved to the good Reverend. He smiled and escorted Rebecca back to the dance floor.

Mrs. Williams hesitated when Charlie offered her his hand. A quick glance told her everyone was watching and it would not do to snub him in front of nearly the entire town. "Thank you, General Redmond."

Charlie led her to the head of a group of younger dancers, primarily local girls dancing with Charlie's junior officers. "Gentleman, may we complete the square?" Shy nods and one "Yes, Sir, please, Sir" came back promptly. They squared up, and the dance began with the obligatory bow and curtsey. "Thank you for joining me, Mrs. Williams."

"One must be polite, General."

"Indeed, Ma'am, I have always found if one takes the time to come to know one's neighbors, frictions can often be reduced."

"General, right now I have no desire to know you. But if Rebecca intends to live this immoral life after the war, then I shall probably get used to you."

The steps of the dance took them apart for a few moments. When they returned, Charlie dropped his bomb. "Madam, as you know, I intend to make an honest woman of Mrs. Gaines, and very soon. I would be deeply appreciative if you would assist in preparing for our wedding on the twenty-eighth."

The minister's wife nearly stumbled when the words sank in. "The wedding? You have set a date?" She had not expected the Yankee to follow through on his promises to Rebecca. She had expected him to ride away to war in the spring and be gone for good. But with a firm date set, it seemed clear that the General would return to Culpeper. She was going to have to put up with this sorry excuse for a man for a long time to come. The thought repelled her.

"Of course, Mrs. Williams. Mrs. Gaines is a wonderful woman. Although a number of people already know of our plans, we will formally announce it tonight. I am, I do believe, the luckiest man on the face of the planet." Charlie fairly beamed with pride and anticipation—the perfect image of the eager bridegroom.

For the first time in her opinionated, small-minded life, Mrs. Williams was speechless. She could only shake her head.

Charlie looked at the thunderstruck woman with concern. "Mrs. Williams? Are you all right? Has the heat and exertion tired you?"

She nodded. "I rather think I would like to sit down."

Solicitously escorting Mrs. Williams to one of the chairs at the side of the room, Charlie signaled to one of the troopers who was serving the guests to bring some punch. "Ma'am, shall I call Dr. Walker?"

"No, General. I only need rest."

"Then, Ma'am, at least let me keep you company until you are feeling more yourself."

Rebecca and Reverend Williams noticed the small disruption created by Mrs. Williams' departure from the floor. They quietly left the dance floor so the minister could attend his wife. Rebecca smiled as she watched the haughty woman squirm at Charlie's proximity.

"Ah, Reverend Williams, I fear your wife has been overcome by the excitement of the afternoon. Mrs. Williams, I look forward to meeting with you to coordinate what I hope will be a small, but elegant affair."

The band started up a sprightly reel, and Rebecca tugged on Charlie's sleeve. "General, I believe this dance is mine."

Bowing politely to Mrs. Williams, Charlie smiled at Rebecca and led her to the floor.

"You are going to rot in the pits of hell for that, Charlie," she admonished playfully.

"No, dear, I am going to back our most vocal opponent in the community into a corner she simply will not be able to get out of."

"Oooh, what have you done?"

"I have asked her to assist in planning the wedding. As the minister's wife, she cannot decline; and as one of the sponsors of the wedding, she cannot continue to condemn me and retain her credibility."

"You expect me to work with that hateful woman to plan our wedding? Oh, Charlie, I will go fight the war and you can stay here for that."

"Darling, I assure you, you will never have to face her without me being present."

"One disparaging word out of her, Charlie, and I will not guarantee what will happen."

"Beloved, trust me. I have just backed her so far into a corner, that by the end of the evening she will be too busy saying 'I knew it all the time' to be any trouble to us."

Rebecca laughed. "I am marrying a very wicked man."

"You are, indeed. I would say, my dear, you and I are well matched."

And so the afternoon wore on, with dancing interspersed with singing. It was close to suppertime when the band struck up the waltz again.

"My love, dance with me."

"Of course. Now and forever."

The two danced as if there were no others on the dance floor, lost in the sensual joy of the dance, the flow of the music, and in one another's eyes. Charlie maneuvered them so at the end of the dance, they were standing at the head of the room before one of the great fireplaces.

After the music ended, the guests honored the band with a robust round of applause for their contribution to the day's festivities. Then Charlie's voice rang out over the assembled guests. "Ladies and gentlemen, it is suppertime, and we have prepared a buffet for you in the dining room. But before we adjourn, I have an announcement."

Rebecca smiled and looped her arms through Charlie's.

The room stilled; curiosity was a powerful motivation for focusing attention. Charlie signaled to the staff, who rapidly circulated glasses of champagne to all of the guests. Charlie waited patiently until each guest and trooper had a glass.

"Ladies and gentlemen, I offer you a toast this evening." He turned to face Rebecca, his heart in his eyes, his voice ringing with the sureness of total conviction and devotion. "To our gracious hostess and, as some of you know, after the twenty-eighth of next month, my most beautiful and beloved wife, Rebecca."

There was an instant of hesitation, and then the room resounded with one word. "Rebecca."

She turned, a bright smile on her face, as she once again clung to Charlie's arm and said, "Yes, General Redmond and I are to be married."

Charlie took her hand and bowed deeply, drawing her fingers to his lips. He looked into her eyes and smiled, silently mouthing the word, "Mine."

Her quiet response was simply, "Yours."

Charlie turned back to the assembly of guests, most of whom were applauding politely, some of whom were grinning broadly, and a few of whom were looking pole axed. "Ladies and gentlemen, let us adjourn to supper. And for this one night, forgive me my manners, but I would like to escort my bride-to-be."

As they made their way through the crowd toward the dining room, Rebecca walked slowly at Charlie's side. As they approached the door, Jocko's eyes met Rebecca's, and he gave her a little wink.

～

Monday, January 2, 1865

Rebecca sat in her parlor, making one list from the several that had been made by the ladies who were helping her with the wedding. She was pleased to see they were willing and even excited to be helping her. Most of them had gotten over their initial shock of seeing her with Charlie and were beginning to see them for what they truly were: a young couple in love. The demarcation between North and South was becoming very blurred for these ladies.

From her place at her desk, she looked out of the window. She could see Charlie and a couple of his troopers working with one of the horses that had received a nasty bruise during the competition. She watched as Charlie took the lead and put the beast through various paces to determine if and when it would limp on the injured leg.

A light knock at the door drew her attention away from the window. "Come in." She turned in her chair and was surprised to find Jocko standing in the doorway. "Sergeant Jackson, come in. What can I do for you?"

"Well, Ma'am, I think it is more a matter of what I can do for you. I understand you are making plans for the wedding. I thought you might like my assistance."

"That would be wonderful." She rose from her seat and poured him a cup of tea. "Please, come sit with me so we can talk."

Jocko looked a little uncomfortable as he sidled over to the chair and tucked his cap in his belt. "Thank you, Ma'am. I know you want to do this wedding right and all, and I thought maybe my knowing the military side of things would be helpful."

"Very helpful, Sergeant. It is important to me that Charlie has a wedding proper for both his standing in the Army and his future standing here in Culpeper. I want everything to be perfect." She placed his cup on the table in front of him, then retook her seat. "I would be grateful for your support."

Jocko took a sip of tea. "Good tea, Ma'am. Dark, like the stuff I had as a child." He cleared his throat. "Well, Ma'am, I am not sure what you want. Military weddings can be anything from very, very quiet and private to very formal. I think General C would prefer the more private end."

"Then that is what we shall give him. Perhaps you would be willing to work with Mrs. Cooper, as she is handling the details for the ceremony? I know I am having a devil of a time getting any information from Charlie about what he would like. I ask him a question and he says, 'Whatever pleases you, dear.' I swear to you, Sergeant, there are some days I want to choke him." Her chuckle with the statement made it very clear to Jocko it was a threat made with love and a goodly amount of frustration.

"Ah, as you may know, Ma'am, getting married was not something General C thought about very much, as he was not one who, ah, was on the list of available gentlemen, if you know what I mean. So, I think he may be a little stymied here. As a single gentleman, he has not had much experience with planning parties and such we always leave that to someone else."

"I am sure." She looked seriously at Charlie's friend and companion. "You do know that I love Charlie dearly?"

"I know he thinks you do. I know he is head over heels with you; and I know if you hurt him, I swear I do not know what I will have to do to keep him together."

She reached out and laid her hand over his. "Jocko, I promise you, I do love Charlie. I would never hurt him. I will spend the rest of my life caring for him and protecting him."

Jocko stood up and walked over to the window. Looking out, he could see Charlie and several other troopers working with another pair of injured horses. Charlie—the officer, the soldier and the man he knew—was in his element. But Jocko knew what lay underneath. He turned back to Rebecca. "And what about her—the woman? How do you feel about that, Mrs. Gaines?"

"I love her."

Jocko thought for a few minutes. "Well, so you say." He walked back over to the chair. "So, Ma'am, here is a list of the officers I think should attend, and a copy of the standard protocols for a small, second marriage to a man of Charlie's rank. I checked the protocol manual before I came."

She took the list and tucked it away. "Thank you." Then she looked at him with a look that only a frustrated Southern woman could muster. "You do not believe me, do you?"

Jocko looked the woman in the eye. "Ma'am, this has all been really quick. General C's been alone for a long time—in fact he thought he would always be alone and always be in the Army. Then you came along, and all of a sudden, he is ready to settle down, marry you and be a da to these bairns from who knows where. So I am wondering, when he comes back from the last battle, with his heart on his sleeve, will you be here? What if he is injured or maimed? Will you still want your beautiful boy?"

"Yes, I know it has been quick. But sometimes, when two people come together, there is just something that compels them to be with each other. My parents were that way. My father fell head over heels for my mother the first time he saw her, and courted her diligently for two years before she finally agreed to marry him. But my father always said that he knew from the moment he set his eyes upon her face, there was no other in this world for him."

Rebecca stood and looked out of the window at Charlie, who was gently petting and soothing the injured horse he was treating. "That is how I felt the very first time I saw him. I did not understand it at the time, but thinking back on my father's words, now I do. There is no other for me. And it is not just the image, Sergeant Jackson. It is very much the whole person that I love. Both sides of him."

She turned to face him. "I do not care how Charlie looks when he returns home. All that matters to me is that he does." She approached the Sergeant, standing over him to make perfectly sure he was clear on the next thing she was about to say. "I will not care if he is wounded. I will not care if he is maimed. I only care that he returns home alive."

Rebecca retook her seat. "I know you are one of Charlie's dearest friends, and I know you are only concerned for him. I value that, for Charlie needs his friends at his side. I had thought you and I were on our way to becoming friends, Sergeant Jackson, but if you do not believe in the sincerity of my feelings for him, then I cannot believe that is the case. I do appreciate your help with the wedding, and I will have Mrs. Cooper consult you about further plans." She sipped her tea. "Good day, Sir."

"Ah, Ma'am, I think I may have managed to join a clan I usually do not associate with. The Clan O'Blivious. You have my most profound apologies. I allowed my natural skepticism to overwhelm the evidence before me. And Charlie is going to have his hands full, I can see." With a sweeping bow, Jocko continued. "I do hope, Madam, that you and I can be more than friends—that we can be allies."

"I would like that very much, Sergeant. I do so want Charlie's friends to be my friends and find comfort in our home. Your apology is gratefully accepted, Sir. Thank you." She gestured back to his seat. "Now, please finish your tea while we figure out what kind of wedding to give our Charlie."

Jocko smiled as he took his seat. His General had found his match—a stubborn Southern woman with a high sense of honor and devotion. Well, perhaps he would take Charlie up on his offer of a position after the war.

~

Tuesday, January 3, 1865

A fine layer of frost lay over the ground, so the world glittered in the thin, clear early morning sunlight. Both men were squinting into the rising sun as Jocko drove Charlie to the train station.

Charlie rode with the engineer, fascinated with the intricacy of the great steam engine. Into the crisp morning, the black smoke filled with ashes and cinders from the burning wood of the engine left a trail of urgency that almost matched Charlie's need to finish his errands in the Capital and return to Rebecca. He was hoarding every moment with her; this trip was a necessity he was determined to complete as quickly as possible.

As the cab Charlie had hired at Union Station moved down Massachusetts Avenue in the direction of downtown Washington, the lamplighters were out doing their work. Charlie rode toward the hotel at which he always stayed, the venerable Willard, which was just a block away from the White House. He paid the cabbie then walked in.

"Ah, Colonel Redmond." The clerk at the counter registered the change in insignia. "Excuse me, General. Welcome. It has been many months. Congratulations on your promotion."

"Hello, Simpkins. Thank you. Do you have a room available?"

"Yes, Sir. Would you like some dinner while I have it prepared?"

"Something simple, I think. Perhaps just a plate in the tap room?"

"As you wish. I will have a bath drawn for you as well."

"Thank you, Simpkins."

"Would you like me to send around and inform Miss Lizzie you are in town?"

"Not tonight, Simpkins. I have another appointment this evening. I will see her myself tomorrow."

Charlie ate a simple dinner of roast mutton and greens, then took a quick bath to remove the dust and grit of the train from his hair and body.

As he finished dressing for the evening, a doorman knocked politely and handed him a message. The materials he had brought up to show General Montgomery C. Meigs, the Quartermaster General of the Army, had been delivered. The General asked Charlie to present himself at his home that evening at eight. Charlie smiled, although

"I am sorry, Redmond, but that is the best I can do right now. There just is not enough time in the day to do better, given that we have been draining the resources of this country for four years already. I wish you the best of luck."

Discouraged by what little Meigs could or would do to help with his particular problems, he was undecided as to whether the man was part of the problem himself. Charlie returned to his room at the Willard as the night watch cried midnight. Tomorrow morning would be long, dealing with the clerks in the Quartermaster's office.

Em had been grumpy all day. Her papa was not there to play with. Dinner was abysmal. If Charlie was not there to feed her, she did not want to eat. Bedtime was purgatory. All Em could do was sob and call for Papa.

Finally, she fell asleep. Rebecca kissed Em goodnight, pulling a blanket over the sleeping baby's shoulders. "Sleep well, little one. Papa will be home in a few days."

Rebecca stoked the fire in Em's room to keep it warmer through the night. Constance could no longer care for her child, having barely enough strength to eat the soup Beulah was constantly providing to the young woman. So Rebecca had moved her into her own room, with Tess sleeping with her to watch over her. While Lizbet had been providing a good bit of the care for Em up until now, with help from Tess, Rebecca needed Lizbet more than ever to prepare for the wedding. As a result, Tess had been promoted to full time nursery maid.

As Rebecca climbed into bed, her thoughts were a jumble, missing Charlie and knowing in her heart that Constance was not going to survive. She wanted to speak with the young woman, but was not sure how to broach the subject that was on her mind. It seemed more than rude to ask her if there was anything special she wanted for Em after she was gone. Rebecca felt almost like the angel of death, waiting for Constance to pass.

She rolled over and pulled Charlie's pillow into her arms, realizing that tomorrow she would have to speak with Constance. Things would simply have to be put in order; surely she would understand and appreciate her concern.

She rolled over again and stared into the fireplace, thinking about all the things that had to be accomplished before Charlie left for the spring campaign. The most important thing, of course, was their wedding, which was coming closer every day. Rebecca was terrified they would not be able to provide a wedding worthy of Charlie and his position.

The ladies of the community were very reassuring, and quite good about letting Rebecca fret. They actually found her quite amusing. She, on the other hand, was becoming the epitome of the nervous bride-to-be.

She had been nervous on the day of her wedding to Gaines, but for entirely different reasons. Her nervousness with Gaines had been generated by fear. With Charlie, it was because of the love she felt. She decided she definitely preferred the feelings evoked by marrying Charlie.

When she drifted into sleep, it was restless; she was continually searching for him. His absence was having a severe impact on her ability to sleep. Then the dream started: Charlie's lips tenderly kissing her neck. She groaned and threw the covers off to try and cool her body, which was quickly becoming overheated.

CHAPTER 24

WEDNESDAY, JANUARY 4, 1865

Charlie's first stop on that cold morning was to meet with his attorney and financial manager, Jerome Lord. There, he ordered a new will drawn up with Rebecca as primary beneficiary and a trust fund to be established for her. Then he headed off to the bank to add Rebecca to his accounts. He was surprised, and quite pleased, to discover he was a more wealthy man than he had thought. The balance was several hundred thousand dollars, due to some astute investments his lawyer had made in basic supplies such as woolens and ammunitions at the beginning of the war. On every payday for almost twenty years, he had placed the bulk of his paycheck in the hands of Jerome's investment and estate planners, and they had done a fine job for him. For a moment, he wondered if his investments had been in the shoddy products he had been delivered at times. He made a mental note to ask Jerome about that the next time they met. While he had not made the incredible fortunes that men like Cook, Gould,

Rockefeller, and Carnegie had from wartime investments, he was, by all social conventions and measures, a very wealthy man.

From there, he went to the office of the Paymaster of the Army. He spent a very long time working with the Army's clerical staff, arranging for Rebecca to receive his pension in the event of his untimely demise, as the terms of the Army benefits contract stated.

Having completed his legal tasks, he set off to the haberdashery on G Street, with Rebecca's list clutched in his hand. Walking into the store and looking around was an intimidating experience for the usually self-confident General. It was a world that was very definitely feminine, filled with bolts of fabric in all weights, materials, and colors, with great racks of buttons, pre-made bows, rolls of lace, threads of more colors than any rainbow ever contained. There were forms that could be adjusted to simulate the exact body structure of a woman. All of this was flanked with acres of hat forms, feathers, ribbons, and things for which he simply could not identify a purpose.

He looked at the list in his hand and at the bewildering array in front of him, and realized he needed help... lots of help.

He turned around and marched out of the building. The jeweler would be much easier. Rounding the corner, he went into the discreet and elegant shop a few doors down from the haberdasher. The shop owner looked at the dapper General and recognized a gentleman of taste. The two men talked quietly, and then he looked at some stones and settings. In less than thirty minutes, they had reached a satisfactory agreement. Charlie arranged to return the following afternoon to pick up three rings—two for Rebecca and one for himself.

He took himself back to the Willard for a glass of beer in the lobby. It had become a tradition in town that all gentlemen of substance met in that large lobby at around four o'clock every afternoon for a glass of beer. Mr. Lincoln walked over from the White House, along with his command officers and advisors. Anyone who wanted to see the President made a point of being there to join him. Charlie wanted to have a final word with the Quartermaster General, and meeting at the Willard during the afternoon gentlemen's constitutional was much easier than trying to get another appointment. Unfortunately, General Meigs did not show up. Charlie politely saluted his Commander-In-Chief, who had a couple of kind words and congratulations on his promotion for him. He finished his beer, then went upstairs to don eveningwear. He had a mission—to acquire knowledgeable feminine support when he went back to the haberdashery on G Street the next day.

His evening would be spent convincing Lizzie to help.

Pausing with the breakfast tray outside the door of Constance's room, Rebecca decided she would see how the young woman was feeling before bringing up the unpleasant business at hand.

Entering quietly, so as not to disturb her if she was resting, she was surprised to see her sitting up in a chair looking out of the window.

"Good morning, dear. It is good to see you up and about."

"Good morning, Rebecca. It is a lovely morning, is it not? I think the view from your front windows, out over the fields, with the mountains in the mist, is one of the most peaceful sights I have ever seen."

There was a strange quality to Constance's visage. She was wan and frail, except for the swelling of her belly, but there was clarity and a peace Rebecca had never seen on anyone's face before.

"Yes, I love it here. It is a beautiful place." She set the tray on the small table, then moved the table in front of the young woman. "I am fortunate that I will be able to remain here, when so many others have lost so much."

"But you have chosen to share it with us, and for that I am very grateful. You have given me more than I can ever express adequate thanks for. You have given me peace at a time when I thought I would never experience it again. And you have given me a vision for my future and my children's future with which I am very happy."

"I am glad. You know you are welcome to remain here for as long as you like. Charlie and I have fallen in love with Em, and we would miss her terribly."

"I am glad that you have. For I am thinking that the reward of bringing this little one into the world," she patted her belly, "will be for me to rejoin my darling Henry. If God does grant me that dearest gift, I hope you and the General will raise my children to be loving, devout, and honorable people."

"I know you are not feeling well, but there is always hope."

Constance looked at Rebecca and smiled gently. "My dear, you really do not understand. Without Henry, my life is a torment of pain and aching loss. This child is just a small part of that. More than anything, I am without the other half of my soul. My hope, my greatest wish is for me to be with Henry again. With you and Charlie to look after my children, I can go to him with no regrets, for I know they will have a far better life than I could ever give them. They will be loved, cared for, and raised as your own. So, yes, I have hope. I have hope that this pain, this empty aching that plagues me day and night, will be eased."

Rebecca fought hard not to cry. She blinked away the tears that filled her eyes and took Constance's hand. "I promise you, with my heart and soul, that if you should join your dear Henry, Charlie and I shall give the children the best upbringing possible. But I have a request of you."

"What is that, dear Rebecca?"

"I would ask you to write a letter to each of the children, telling them of yourself and of Henry. Then, when they are older and the time is right, I will see to it they are given the letters. While Charlie and I will love and raise them as our own, I believe it will be important for them to know they had parents who loved and cared for them."

"Of course, and Rebecca, you and Charlie will be their parents as much as I ever was. For this little one, I believe you will be far more of a parent than I ever could be, even should I survive. I would request that if the price of this child coming into the world is that I pass on, you raise him or her as your own, as if the child were born of your body, not mine."

"As you wish. I promise."

"Rebecca, you are not understanding, are you?"

She shook her head. "Apparently not."

"Think about how you feel with Charlie. What if Charlie was never coming back? How would you feel?"

"I have been trying not to think of that very thing lately. I would be devastated."

"Think of what I have lost, dear: my beloved husband, the other half of my soul; my home; my family. Think of how you would feel if Charlie were killed. All I have left is Em and the child conceived of my rapists. The child will come into the world, and I will pass out of it. As far as I can tell, God decided to keep me around for a while so the children would have the home and family and love they deserved. Otherwise, I should have died the night that Montgomery and his men visited. So know, as I know, Charlie will survive. He is meant to be a father to these children."

Those words brought an end to Rebecca's control. Tears flowed from her eyes as she stood and gave Constance a gentle hug. "We will love them and raise them as you and Henry would have. We will give them a good life."

Jocko whistled as he rode up to the little house on the edge of the village of Alanthus. He was looking forward to calling on the lovely Esther White. After that first visit with Charlie when she had approached him to ask for help, he had called on her a number of times. In fact, he visited her whenever he could get a day off, which lately had not been very often. If he left just after morning chores, he made it to her house by late morning, could spend time and have lunch and tea, then return to Redmond Stables in good time. He was looking forward to lunch today, as she was a dedicated and skilled cook.

There was a thin trail of smoke coming from one of the two chimneys in her small cottage. In this weather, she should have had both fireplaces going. Jocko looked around, concerned that perhaps she was conserving firewood since he had not checked her woodshed in several days. As he rode by, he looked. There was plenty of wood in the shed.

He got to the door and tethered his mount to the fence railing. Usually, by now she would be at the door to greet him. He hurried to the door and knocked. A faint voice answered him.

She sat huddled beside the single fire, staring listlessly into the flickering flames. She had been beaten. Her hands shook. Her eyes were dull with pain and shame. Her clothing was ripped. To Jocko's war hardened eyes, it was obvious: she had been violated.

His first reaction was anger, which he quickly swallowed. She needed his gentleness now, not his anger.

"Esther, dear, it is Jocko."

"Go away." She did not turn to look at him. "I cannot see you anymore."

"Esther. Who did this to you?"

"What do you mean?"

"Esther, who beat you?" He took a deep breath and asked the obvious question. "Who did this to you?"

She laughed without humor. "One of the men who came out here to fill our woodsheds. Davison, I think his name was. He had two friends. This is what I get for letting you Yankees take care of me. They said they came back to collect for the work they had done."

"Davison." Jocko clenched his fists. The name fell into the void between them. "Esther, General Redmond expelled him from the Army about a month ago and sent him home. He is no longer a soldier. We thought he had left the area. All we can do now is to find him, arrest him, and deal with him. But first, my dear, I need to get you to a doctor."

"No. Leave me."

"Esther, I cannot leave you. I love you." Jocko spoke the words without thinking. He had never said them to any woman, save his mother, in his life. Yet, he knew as he heard them leave his mouth that they were true. "Let me take you to Dr. Walker. She will help, I promise."

Esther White nodded numbly. She moved like a puppet as he scurried around collecting a change of clothes and some other odds and ends, banked the fire, and then wrapped her in a warm quilt and carried her outside. Gently he lifted her up into the saddle and pulled himself up behind her. Holding her battered body in his arms, he set out for what he was beginning to think of as home.

Charlie walked up the steps to Lizzie Armstrong's Capitol Hill mansion at the socially unacceptable hour of seven in the evening— too early for dinner, too late for tea. He hoped to catch her before the evening's festivities started and convince her to assist him in braving the unknown world of feminine finery. Tucking his hat under his arm, he knocked on the door.

A very proper butler responded with a superior look on his face. No one who was anyone would knock on the door this early.

"Good evening, Sir. Whom may I say is calling?"

"Good evening. Would you please tell Mrs. Armstrong that Charlie Redmond would appreciate a moment of her time?"

The butler left Charlie waiting in the hall instead of showing him to a parlor.

Lizzie came down the steps, not even trying to hide the smile on her face at the appearance of her favorite companion. "General Redmond, you dear man." She took the last two steps to the landing and threw her arms around his neck, bestowing on him a passionate kiss. "I heard of your promotion. Congratulations."

"Uh..." Charlie was captured in the woman's arms, struggling gently to disengage her embrace. "Lizzie, I need your help, and you and I really need to talk. I have some news..."

"Oh, I am sure you do. It has been months, Charlie. Come on upstairs, we can talk up there."

"Can we go to your parlor?"

She chuckled and took his arm. "The parlor? A bit public for your usual tastes."

"Lizzie, dear friend, perhaps you had better hear my news before we go any further."

The woman sighed and smiled. She knew her General was an odd bird at times. Drawing him closer to her side, she guided him to the parlor as requested. "All right, Charlie, what is your news? Let me guess, you have decided after the war to come back here, sweep me off my feet, and take me away from all this."

He had the grace to blush. "Actually, Lizzie, I have met someone."

"Oh." She tried to mask her disappointment. Over the years, as she had come to know him, she had come to care for him very much, if not love him more than a little. "I see. Congratulations."

"I wanted to tell you personally, dear friend, because if you had not taken me in hand, I would never have had the courage to find my mate. I owe you a greater debt than I can ever repay."

"Well, I am happy for you, General." She took a seat on the davenport and tried to give him a sincere smile. "She is a very lucky lady."

Charlie looked at Lizzie. He knew that something was wrong, but had no idea what it was. "So, my dear lady, something seems to be bothering you. Can I help?"

"No, Charlie. I must admit this is a bit of a surprise." She patted the sofa. "Come, sit, and tell me of your lady." She got up and moved to a small brandy cabinet. "Your usual?"

"Yes, thank you. Her name is Rebecca, and she has a horse farm down in Culpeper. She is the most delightfully spirited woman I have ever met: courageous, strong, sure of herself—and so kind and gentle."

Lizzie poured the drink, trying to gain control of her emotions. It would not do for a woman in her position to show concern over this. Picking up two glasses, she settled back down next to Charlie, handing him one of the glasses. "Well, now, she sounds like she has completely captured your heart."

"She has, Lizzie, she has." He paused. "She knows, you know. She wants... me."

The woman smiled and took Charlie's hand. "I am glad, dear Charlie, truly glad. I am sure she is a special lady. You know, though, if you ever find yourself wanting, I will always be here for you."

Something in Lizzie's voice caught his attention. "Lizzie?" He looked into her eyes. "What is wrong, Lizzie?"

She looked away for a moment, then looked back. "I suppose now is as good a time as any to confess. I have always been just a little in love with you, Charlie. I know a woman such as myself could never be a proper wife to someone of your standing. But there were nights, after you had been here, that I would lie awake and wonder about you and harbor just a little bit of a dream."

"Why, Lizzie? Why did you stay quiet?"

"Charlie, look at what I am. I could never have gotten past this. I am a lovely distraction, a convenience. I am not the type of woman a man would make his wife."

"I am not the type of man a typical woman would take as her husband. We could have talked about it. I am truly sorry."

"You had no way of knowing. But you have found someone, and I am happy for you."

"Thank you, my dear. You know if there is anything you ever need, you have only to call on me."

"Oh no, Charlie. It would not do for me to come into contact with this lady of yours. I doubt she would appreciate me as much as you do."

"Rebecca would understand my giving assistance to anyone who is my friend. I have told her a little about you, you know."

"Oh, Charles Redmond, you have not!"

"She asked me what I had done for companionship. I told her. I also told her how kind and what a good friend you are."

"Oh lovely. You know as well as I do that gentlemen do not speak of me to wives and sweethearts. I cannot believe you did that."

"She asked and I answered honestly. That is what our relationship is built on—our ability to be truly honest with one another."

"That is a very interesting relationship." She smiled and sipped her brandy.

"Lizzie, you know what I am. How can I be anything other than totally honest and still hope to have a relationship that will last?"

"This is true. So she knows? I did not think you let most people know your secret, Charlie. I thought I was one of only a handful."

"You are, my dear. But I think that if one is going to have a relationship that works for life, honesty is important. She knew the day she met me."

Lizzie chuckled. "She is clearly a very perceptive woman as well. It took me what, a month before you told me? So tell me, what are your plans?"

"I want to marry her before I go back into battle. That is actually one of the reasons why I called on you. I need your help."

"My help? How could I possibly help you?" She smiled and raised her brows. "A tutoring session for the wedding night, maybe?" She winked and squeezed his thigh, letting her finger track gently up and down it, as she knew he liked.

He quickly, quietly captured her hand with his own, stilling those distracting strokes. "I was actually hoping for something more prosaic. I have a list of things that she wants me to get for the wedding, and I do not even begin to understand it. I went to the

the smile did not travel all the way to his eyes. Perhaps he would finally get to the bottom of this problem.

He checked his appearance. He needed to be Sheridan's perfect Regimental Commander tonight. With the letter from Sheridan tucked carefully into his breast pocket, he set out. It was unusual for Charlie not to have met a career officer like Meigs before, but then, Meigs had been a desk officer or an engineer for his entire career, while Charlie had been a field officer. While most of the men Charlie knew, himself included, had at some point drawn administrative duty, the idea of doing it all the time made Charlie uncomfortable. He liked to be out and about too much to be stuck at a desk all day.

He arrived at Meig's door exactly at eight o'clock. A well-mannered young captain met him at the door and escorted him into Meig's study. It was nothing like Charlie had expected. The furnishings were good, but worn. There were ledgers and files carefully stacked on every available flat surface. As for the man himself, Charlie had expected someone with money, power, and a number of lackeys. Instead, he found a lean man with ink stained fingers, mediocre brandy, and a nervous habit of riffling through piles of papers as he talked.

The two men talked at length. The problems were clear, but there was little either of them could do about them. With all of the money flowing to purchase the basics needed to run an army, it was easy for the purchasers in the field to make a little extra here and there by substituting lesser quality items for the goods ordered. And all those 'littles' added up to an irresistible temptation for many of the men in Meigs' command. In addition, there were too few people in the Quartermaster's office, too many people in the field, and too many supplies needed for one man to be able to control everything. Meigs was fully aware of the problems; he had not found a way to fix them.

Meigs had some suggestions for Charlie, and prepared a number of notes for him to deliver the next day to the clerks and purchasing agents who provisioned his forces.

haberdasher's on G Street today and found I needed to make a strategic withdrawal and get myself some reinforcements. I was hoping you would be my guide."

She stifled a laugh and took his hand. "Yes, of course, my dear man, I would be very happy to help you with anything you need." She moved closer and placed a kiss on his cheek before whispering in his ear, "Anything."

"Ah, well, then, shall I call for you tomorrow morning?"

"If I cannot convince you to stay the night. Really, Charlie, you are not married yet. And even then, you know most of my customers have wives at home."

Charlie smiled gently. "I know, Lizzie. Believe me, I do appreciate the offer. But I have promised her my heart, my soul, my honor, and my body. And as much of a temptation as you offer, I know you would not have me break my oath."

"Of course not. You are the most honorable gentleman I have ever met. I would ask you to do nothing to compromise that."

"I shall not. Then, dear, I know your livelihood depends on your ability to be a wonderful hostess, so I will not take you away from that tonight. Shall I call at noon tomorrow?"

"That would be fine, Charlie." She took his hand and stroked it over her cheek, her eyes closing slowly. "I am going to miss you."

He cupped her face in his hand and then leaned in to place one very tender kiss on her lips. "You will always hold a very special place in my heart, dear Lizzie."

"And you in mine, Charlie. If she ever hurts you, I shall take her to task over it."

"Thank you, dear, but I think she is, if anything, even more protective of me than you are."

"Good." She smiled. "Then she is certainly the right woman for you."

"She is. Now you, dear, need to finish getting ready for your evening. And I must go off and be polite to the political branch of the Army."

Lizzie stood and walked him to the door. She held his arm and gave him serious consideration. "I think I shall have to find you a very special wedding gift, General Redmond. One that both you and your new wife can enjoy."

"Of course, we would both be honored by anything you gave us. Until tomorrow?"

She laughed. "Tomorrow. Good night, Charlie."

He walked through the chilly night, deep in thought. *Lizzie had fantasies of a life together? But Lizzie could have any man she wanted—and often did. Why me? She knows what I am, and still she had fantasies? Oh my.*

~

Thursday, January 5, 1865

Washington, which was usually marred with the soot from thousands of chimneys and mud and droppings from hundreds of horses and carriages, looked bright and sparkling with the morning frost. It was a stark contrast to the dark, cramped, lamp-lit offices of the Quartermaster's staff.

Charlie spent most of the morning at the War Office, discussing provisioning of the troops for the coming spring campaign. He worked his way patiently through a veritable battalion of clerks until he finally found himself across the desk from an old colleague from West Point. Together, they bemoaned the dishonesty of military suppliers, but no real resolution to the boot problem was found. Finally, he took his leave and strolled up to Capitol Hill and Lizzie's quietly elegant home.

A knock on the door brought the same stiffly formal butler as on the previous day, but a much warmer welcome. Lizzie was waiting for him in the private parlor, wearing a deceptively simple day dress, with a fur-collared overcoat waiting on the chair.

"Good afternoon, Lizzie. I cannot thank you enough for your

assistance. I brought the shopping list Rebecca gave me." He looked a little embarrassed.

She rose from the chair and smiled at her friend. "It is my pleasure, Charlie. Anything I can do to help."

"Then, Ma'am, shall we be on our way? I asked your butler to hail us a hackney as I came in." He held her coat for her.

Slipping into her coat, she touched Charlie's hand. "Now, you must tell me all about your dear Rebecca."

"What would you like to know, my friend?"

"Anything that will help me to help you." She took his arm as they walked toward the door.

"Well, she is a small woman, about so tall." Placing his hand level with the line of his chin, he indicated her height. "Very slender, with a lovely, delicate figure. It is deceptive; she looks fragile, but she is an outstanding horsewoman with enormous stamina. She has long, slender hands and feet; I think they are elegant. Her hair is ash blonde with a touch of gold in it. Her eyes are a mossy green and change color with her mood—sometimes clear like early spring buds, sometimes darker like the color of pines in the late afternoon. There are little flecks of amber in them, as well. Oh, and she has a strong chin that sometimes juts out when she is being determined."

Lizzie laughed at her friend's description. "Is there anything you have not noticed, Charlie?"

He had the grace to blush. "Probably. But I cannot for the life of me think what it might be. I even know where she has a couple of scars from chickenpox."

"Really?" She moved closer and whispered. "Where?"

He laughed, as his blush grew deeper. "One on her cheek near the corner of her mouth, and one on her belly next to her navel."

"My, my, Charlie. You do know the lady well."

The blush spread and deepened still further. "Well, not as well as I would wish, to be sure, but yes."

They climbed into the cab, and Lizzie settled herself. "Tell me, are you two intimate?"

A long sigh escaped from deep in his chest. "That is a relative question, my dear friend. Have we played with intimacy? Yes. Have we claimed one another completely? No, not yet. She was married before, to a man who used and abused her; so, in many ways, she is just learning about intimacy. We move slowly, as I want her to find pleasure and comfort in the physical aspect of our relationship."

"Well, I will tell you now, Charles Redmond, that in your arms she will find nothing but tenderness. You were the most tender lover I have ever had."

"I do hope so, Lizzie. There are moments when I do not know if I can maintain that tenderness, or even my most basic control. I confess, sometimes wanting her seems to burn through me. But watching her grow and blossom under my hands and my patience is a wonderful thing."

"Hmm. I am sure. You have made headway with her, I take it."

"I think so." Charlie paused for a moment. "Lizzie, thank you. If this is uncomfortable for you, I will understand, but I really have no one else that I can talk with about it."

"Charlie, you should know that speaking about matters of intimacy and love is not uncomfortable for me. I will help you in any way I can. I only want you to be happy, my friend."

"Thank you. And thank you for braving the wilds of the fabric merchants. I was totally overwhelmed when I walked in there yesterday."

"It can be very overwhelming. Tell me, what color dress does Rebecca want?"

"Well, the list of things she asked me to get should cover that."

Lizzie continued to chuckle as she looked at the list. "Nothing here is all that unusual, Charlie. Fabric, buttons, hooks, some lace..." She looked at him and smiled. "I think you are just a nervous groom."

"You are very right about that. I never believed I would meet someone I would want to settle down with, let alone someone who would actually want me."

"Life is full of surprises, Charlie, but I never doubted for one moment that one day you would find someone."

A bittersweet half smile illuminated Charlie's face for a moment. "You know what I am, Lizzie. What were the chances of finding someone who could deal with that in a spouse?"

"Dear Charlie, I hate to break this to you, but your situation is not all that uncommon. Granted, it is not spoken of, but there are many women such as you."

"Who disguise themselves as men and pass within the community? Or women who seek the company of other women?"

She patted his hand. "Both. I have another client."

Charlie looked at Lizzie with a stunned expression. "Another client? Like me?" A quizzical expression passed over his face. "Is he here in town? Do you think he would ever be interested in meeting? Just to chat, you know." The idea of another like himself fascinated Charlie.

"Yes, Charlie, here in town, just like you."

"I cannot help but wonder what circumstances drove him to the same place I am in."

"He simply is, Charlie. Nothing forced him to live this way. It is how he is comfortable."

A confused look passed over Charlie's face. The idea that anyone would choose to live the life of the other gender, without being forced into it by circumstances, was a new one for him. "You mean he just wants to live as a man?"

"That is what I mean, Charlie. It is how he is most comfortable. He feels like he was born in the wrong body."

Charlie thought about that for a few moments. Then he realized he would have to spend some quiet time considering it further. He knew Lizzie would never reveal the identity of this individual. After a bit of silent consideration, he changed the subject. "So, tell me, how has your business been?"

"Remarkably robust, considering the national circumstances. I think as things wind down, more and more men are seeking a brief respite from the stresses of this war. The politics here in town are getting more vicious, as so many wish to punish the South for all of the pain of the past years, while Mr. Lincoln and his associates want to try and reconstruct the Union as quickly as possible."

"Believe me, I have the same problems in the field."

"We did have a small problem with one of the girls. She got pregnant, and was trying to coerce one of our customers into paying for her upkeep and the child's. I let her go."

"A shame, truly. You always tell your girls to take care to avoid that, and I know you told me that you buy more sheep skins than anyone else in town. But I imagine that a desperate woman will do many things."

"I do not think Alison Hobart is desperate. I think she is avaricious and careless. I wish her good riddance."

"Alison...Alison...Did I meet her?"

"You may have, at one of our parties last spring. I honestly do not remember."

"Ah, well. I trust you are happy with your staff now?"

"Yes, quite. The girls are all discreet, and they all understand they will do better in the long run if they take my advice. Most of them have nice nest eggs put away for their later lives. I do try, you know."

"Yes, my dear, I know."

"I would like to have another one of my little parties. Will you be in town for a while?"

"I must return to Culpeper tomorrow. I leave at first dawn. Unless you can arrange it for this evening, perhaps we can join you on my next visit to town?"

"Whatever your pleasure, Charlie. Now, shall we go and shop for Rebecca and try to calm your bridegroom nerves just a bit?"

"Yes, please. And if you do not mind, we will also need to stop in at the jeweler's this afternoon to collect a couple of things."

"I am completely at your disposal for the entire day."

"Then, my dear, as long as the list in your hand is filled without emptying my entire bank account, you are free to do whatever is necessary to meet Rebecca's needs and get me back on the road tomorrow morning."

"I am sure we will do fine. The things on this list are fairly simple and straightforward."

"Oh, well, for you, perhaps. Then afterwards, to the jeweler's, and then to the wine merchant, after which I will gladly buy you the most elegant tea the Willard has to offer."

"Lovely payment, my dear man. And when we return to the house, remind me that I have a little gift for you." She tried to hide her smile, but failed.

"Ahhhh. Should I be concerned? I know that little smirk of yours. You have something... one might consider either very private or personal."

"Both."

Charlie groaned. "Lizzie, sometimes you do test my sense of propriety to its limits."

She laughed loudly as she walked with him to the store. "And that, my dear Charlie, is why you enjoy my company so."

"As ever, Ma'am. As ever."

"Trust me, I do believe you and your new bride will enjoy this."

A clerk hurried over to greet the always generous Mrs. Armstrong. She was a regular customer, and one of the few in these stressful times who paid her rather large tab consistently. In a flurry of commands, with clerks bringing samples of materials, laces, threads, buttons and other objects which Charlie did not recognize, Lizzie picked out a large number of items. They accumulated on the counter and still she ordered more. Charlie wisely found a chair in a quiet corner and waited until it was time to pay the bill.

Finally, she was done. Charlie looked at the welter of items on the counter, dominated by several bolts of rich green velvet and blue and ivory silk, not to mention large quantities of a delicate ivory lace. He quickly gave orders for express shipping everything on the supply train that was scheduled for the next day and asked for the accounting. When the bill was presented a few moments later, he did manage not to stutter, and paled only slightly. Manfully, he wrote out the check and laid it on the counter, including a tidy sum for packing and ensuring the goods were delivered to the military supply train on time.

"Well, oh-mistress-of-the-art-of-shopping, shall we stop by the jeweler's?"

Lizzie patted his hand as she took his arm. "Marriage is not cheap Charlie. I assume we are going to pick up rings? Should I take smelling salts with us?"

"No, I have already paid the piper for these. That was yesterday's attack of vapors. I confess, I adjourned to the Willard for a good, tall beer afterwards."

"I am sure you did. Tell me, where are you planning on going for the honeymoon?"

"Honeymoon?"

She laughed again. "Yes, the honeymoon. You know, the trip most newly married couples take after the wedding."

"Ummm. I cannot leave my command. And we have so little time until the spring campaign begins. I thought we would just spend the time together at home. Then after the war, we can take a nice long trip together. Perhaps I will take her to Europe. I can afford that, I think."

"I will tell you what, Charlie. If you can convince Phil Sheridan to give you a few days leave after the wedding, you bring Rebecca to Washington, and I will cover your bill at the Willard."

"I could not accept that from you, dear Lizzie. But I do believe it would be a good idea to have at least a short amount of time for just the two of us. And it would give me the opportunity to introduce Rebecca to a few people. I believe she will want to meet you, my friend."

"Charlie, I am sure Rebecca will have far more important things to do than meet with the likes of me. But you will accept this. It will be my wedding gift to you. You deserve it. So, you bring your new bride to Washington and romance her."

"I will bring her. And I know she will want to meet you, dear. Are you sure you will not join us for the ceremony?"

"I am quite sure, for two reasons: one, your wife would not want a common whore at her wedding. And two, I can deal with you not being mine anymore, but I do not think I could watch it happen."

Charlie drew her to halt on the sidewalk in front of the jeweler's. "First, you are not a common whore. You are one of the most gracious, generous women I know; and I am proud to call you my friend. As to the second, I am sorry, Lizzie, that I am not for you. You will always have my friendship, my loyalty, and my trust. If you ever have need of anything—anything—you have but to ask."

"Thank you, Charlie. You mean the world to me as well. You know my door is always open to you and yours." She took his arm. "Now, show me these lovely rings you have chosen."

The two of them entered the shop. The jeweler, like the haberdasher, knew the generous Mrs. Armstrong well. He was startled to see her arm-in-arm with the very formal and proper General Redmond. A slight flush rose to the man's cheeks. "General Redmond, Mrs. Armstrong, welcome. General, I have your order ready. I do hope Mrs. Armstrong approves."

"Oh, I only wish, my good man. But I am only the gallant General's assistant today. His lovely bride awaits him in Culpeper."

The clerk looked at the General, who was smiling benignly, and reappraised the man. Clearly, his presentation was as formal and proper as one might wish, but to have the social grace and impudence to call upon the most notorious madam in town to assist in purchasing his wedding rings and his bride's engagement ring was downright stunning. Hastily, he presented the three bands, two plain and one bearing a beautiful square cut emerald surrounded by diamonds, to the obviously discerning audience.

"Oh, Charlie," she gasped. "They are beautiful. I am sure Rebecca will be very pleased."

"I do hope so. The emerald seemed so appropriate for her. It matches her eyes."

"Oh, you are smitten. Tell me, if she asked you for the moon, would you pull it down for her?"

"If it were in my power to do so, yes." His answer was stated simply and with total conviction.

"And I am sure she would do the same for you."

"I would not ask her to." *All I want from her is whatever love she chooses to give me. No more, no less.*

"From what you tell me, you would not need to ask. I think she would face the fires of hell for you."

"I think she may be already. You see, there are these women in town she calls the "biddy brigade." They are not exactly pleased with her choosing to marry a Yankee. Excuse me. A damned Yankee."

"She is not marrying a Yankee, she is marrying a wonderful person who adores her, and years after this conflict is over, that is all that will matter."

"Actually, Ma'am, she is not marrying a Yankee at all. I am from Charleston, remember?"

"Indeed you are, Sir. Indeed you are." She watched as Charlie tucked the ring boxes in his pocket. "Now, may I suggest that we have that tea?"

"I need to make a brief stop at the wine shop, which is on the way, and then tea, I promise."

"Wonderful."

They strolled up E Street toward 15th and the small vintner's shop that was located on the way to the Willard. A quick stop, whereupon Charlie ordered several casks of brandy, some small casks of rum for his men, and several cases of champagne and other wines for the wedding.

They entered the Willard arm-in-arm, and Charlie commandeered the most desirable table in the lovely garden room for the two of them to partake of a formal tea.

"You know, you are taking a terrible risk?"

"How so, my dear?"

"A lot of these men know you. To be seen with me, on what is essentially the eve of your wedding. What if Rebecca finds out?"

"I told her I would be seeing you on this trip. She felt it was a good thing for me to inform you of our plans personally, and asked me if I would invite you to the wedding."

"You are going straight to hell for telling such lies, Charles Redmond."

"Why would I lie about such a thing?" He was genuinely confused. He had been honest with Rebecca, who knew that Lizzie was a good friend. Why would Lizzie think otherwise?

"Propriety, my dear friend, does not allow for such things. You and I both know that."

"Propriety is not a particularly vital part of my relationship with Rebecca." Charlie's tone was wry.

Lizzie sat back in her chair and smiled at her friend. "So it would seem. You two are going to turn Culpeper on its head, I think."

The smile turned to a grin. "I think we already have."

"And you are enjoying every moment of it," she teased, giving his hand a squeeze. "Are you not? Tell me, what have you done?"

Charlie launched into an animated depiction of the efforts to begin an orderly transition from wartime to peacetime relations with the citizens of Culpeper County. Of course, Mrs. Williams and her harridan ways were key elements of his narrative. He spoke of many things, none of them relevant to the military actions of his regiment. Finally, he told her of the refugees and the problems they faced. Little Emily played a prominent role in his story.

"So, not only a wife, but a surrogate daughter as well?"

"Poor child lost her father. Evidently, I look somewhat like him, so she has attached herself to me. Her mother is just grateful she no longer cries for her papa." He paused for a moment. "Her mother is not doing well. Elizabeth Walker believes she will not survive her current pregnancy, so I may indeed end up with a daughter."

"Hmm. I will wager when you return home, you will find she has been crying for you. I am sure everyone will be relieved." She sipped her tea and gave Charlie a look he instantly knew was trouble. "So would you like some instruction for the item I intend to send home with you?"

"Ah, I suspect that I would need to know just what you were sending home with me, Ma'am, before I could answer that question."

"Well, now, I think you and Rebecca will find a use for the item." She grinned. "In the privacy of your bedroom."

"Ah, Lizzie, could we have this discussion somewhere less... public?"

Now she was really laughing. "Oh Charlie, you are a sweet man. I love the way your ears turn red."

He took a deep, calming breath. "Yes, well, I am told the color compliments my eyes rather nicely."

"Yes, it does." She reached out and stroked gently just around his eyes. "I shall miss them."

Abruptly, Charlie wiped his mouth with his napkin. "Are you ready to leave, my dear?"

"Of course."

Each time Charlie was confronted with Lizzie's real affection and the wistful regret that surfaced, he felt a bittersweet combination of regret and guilt coupled with fondness. No, she was not the love of his life, but she had been one of the few true friends he had ever had. And she was the only lover he had ever had, one who had gently and very tenderly taught him to be comfortable with his body and with the act of love.

He escorted her to the cabstand and gently handed her into the hackney, climbing in after her. For a long time, he was silent as they rode back toward her home. Yet he held her hand in the crook of his arm, with his own larger hand over it.

"Charlie, what is wrong?"

"I have just been thinking on all of the things you have meant to me in my life, all of the gifts you have given me. I want you to know, you will never lose my friendship. True friends are far too rare and precious to ever walk away from."

"I know that, dear friend. You have given just as much to me as I have given you, Charlie. I was with you because I wanted to be with you. Think about it. Did I ever take any money from you?"

"No, you never did. And I have always known it was because you and I were friends. No, we were more than that. We were lovers. I do not know if you have had other lovers, but I do know I will always cherish the memories of our times together and the gifts you gave me, the things you taught me." He raised her hand to his lips and caressed the backs of her fingers very gently.

"There were no others in my life I cared for as I care for you, Charlie. I am so happy you have found your happiness with Rebecca."

The cab stopped before Lizzie's house. Charlie helped her out and flipped the driver a coin, then escorted her into the house. By silent consent, they went to the small parlor that was her private place. Just as silently, Charlie took her in his arms and just held her tenderly for a long time.

"I love you, Charlie. Be happy." She pulled back to look at him, and smiled. "And now..." She crossed the room to fetch a box, which she handed him. She winked as she placed the box in his hands. "This should help."

Charlie carefully opened the box. There, lying on a bed of dark red satin, was a blunt ended cylinder covered in the finest leather. Fine leather straps were attached to the base and coiled in the box alongside the object. Here was the prosthesis Charlie had offered to find for Rebecca when she had told him that all she needed was him.

Charlie's ears turned a fascinating shade of red.

"There they go again," she teased. "Think you can figure out how to use it? Or would you like a demonstration?"

"Ah, it is, ah, umm... Oh, Lord. How do you describe one of these things?"

"Interesting?" She did enjoy teasing him.

"It is a...handsome version. I'm sure that Rebecca and I will enjoy it, though I must confess, it is a somewhat unusual wedding gift."

"Use it in good health, Charlie."

He laughed, a full, open laugh. "My dear, I am sure it is not just my health that will benefit."

"I think you can handle it." She grinned and handed him the box. "In fact, I am sure of it."

He grinned and accepted the box from her. "I am sure both of us will appreciate this gift to the fullest measure."

"It seems your nickname is holding true, Lucky Charlie." She gave him one last hug. "Be safe on your way home."

"I will, my dear. And expect to see the two of us at the beginning of February."

"I will look forward to it."

~

Rebecca was mending a pair of Charlie's trousers, which he had ripped while helping a few of his men repair a fence that had been damaged by a high wind. She watched from the window, knowing full well Charlie was not due back for a few days, but wishing him home just the same.

Their time together was so limited; she hated the fact that he had to make this trip. And he had looked so befuddled when she had given him the list of things the ladies had insisted they would need for the wedding.

She sipped her tea, carefully checking the stitching in her repair. The door to the parlor opened, and Elizabeth stepped in looking tired and frazzled. Wordlessly, she took the teapot in hand, poured a cup, and took a seat next to the fire.

"Difficult day, Doctor?"

"Very. Nothing seemed to go right. I believe I would have been more useful if I had remained in bed today. I do swear some days I am not sure if Charlie commands men or ten-year-old boys. I have treated so many sprains and scrapes caused by their acting like children, I am ready to have Richard take them to the woodshed with a strap.”

Rebecca chuckled as she nipped through the thread with her teeth, then held the trousers for Elizabeth to see. “Charlie is no better. I have sewn up a dozen tears in his trousers and tunics. There are times when he is nothing more than a large boy himself.”

“I thought Jocko took care of his wardrobe.”

“Yes, well, I have taken to dealing with the domestic issues of caring for Charlie. I do believe Jocko is glad to be rid of the more tiresome chores. It gives him some additional time to spend with the Widow White.”

“Oh, so we have another local romance on our hands? Did Jocko take a page from his master’s book?”

Rebecca laughed as she folded the trousers and set aside. “I believe so. Seems to be a lot of it going around at the moment.” She looked directly at her friend and raised her eyebrows. “Correct?”

“Are you suggesting Richard and I...” Elizabeth had the grace to blush as she looked away with a wistful smile on her face.

“Elizabeth,” she poured another cup of tea, “would I suggest such a thing?”

“You would, you crazed woman. I was afraid you and Charlie were going to declare a new profession for yourselves on Christmas Eve, with that sprig of mistletoe he was so proud of.”

“Oh, Charlie is the matchmaker in the family. Did it work?”

Elizabeth’s blush deepened. “I suppose that would depend on your definition of ‘work,’ my dear. If you are asking whether Richard and I are exploring a more meaningful relationship, the answer is yes. If you are asking whether I have altered my level of personal experience in terms of the more physical aspects of an intimate relationship, the answer is no. I suppose I will have to continue to depend on my textbooks and listening to you for a while yet.” Elizabeth gave her a very wicked grin.

Rebecca laughed, nearly losing her tea. “And you call me crazed.” She paused, wiping the edge of her mouth with a napkin. “My dear,

Charlie and Richard would just die if they knew the things we talked about when they are not around."

Elizabeth's tone was tinged with resignation. "Richard would probably love it. He is such a salacious old wretch."

"Good for Richard. Charlie on the other hand is very shy about these subjects, which is understandable, given the situation. If he had any idea I talked to even you about these things, he would find the nearest rock to crawl under."

"Fortunately for you, he does not seem to suffer from the same hesitation or shyness with you." Elizabeth thought for a moment. "You know, I suspect it is not that he is shy about intimacy, but rather he is in the habit of privacy to keep his secret safe. Once he knows it is, I believe he is quite open and forthcoming. I do know he and Whitman talk about things regularly. A sort of odd masculine friendship, there."

"That is an understatement. I am glad there is someone he is comfortable talking with."

"Rebecca, Charlie has few friends, but those he does have he is very open with. I am proud to count myself one of them, actually. Oh, and he did tell me about your little...problem that first night he went drinking with Whitman."

"Seems you are the Mother Confessor for the Redmond family." Rebecca smiled into her teacup. "How was I supposed to know everything was all right?"

"My dear, how was Charlie supposed to know you were not asleep?" Elizabeth grinned, and then added, "Well, with you two, I certainly have added to my own education. Some of the drawings in my medical books make far more sense after having talked with the two of you." Elizabeth could no longer stifle the giggles that had been threatening for a while.

"Thank you so very much, Doctor. It is nice to know we are a part of your continuing education." Rebecca poured Elizabeth more tea.

"My pleasure, I assure you. And I am very appreciative of the trust you both have given me."

"Of course, you are one of Charlie's dearest friends." She looked out the window as a blue uniform rode by. She simply could not help herself. "I will be very glad when he comes home."

"I am sure you will, dear. I rather suspect he will be very glad to get home. And Rebecca, I hope you know I am your friend also."

"I do know, dear Elizabeth." Rebecca sighed quietly, then gave her friend a very serious look. "He is going to see his friend Mrs. Armstrong while he is there."

"Oh, did he say so? I would imagine he would want to personally tell her of his impending marriage to you. They were reputed to be rather...close... and Charlie is nothing if not a gentleman."

"Yes, he mentioned it before he left. And yes, they are very, very close."

"Rebecca, dear, I hope you are not worried about him seeing her. I know Charlie. He is devoted to you."

"Oh, I am sure of that, but, well, they do have a relationship. He is very fond of her. We are not married yet so I really could not protest if he did pay her a social call."

"Rebecca, you are not suggesting...?"

"Well, I hope not, but I suppose anything is possible. I have heard the men talk of Mrs. Armstrong. I know she is an attractive woman and she is probably more, shall we say, adept at giving Charlie what he needs."

"Rebecca Gaines, you put that idea right out of your head. Charlie has pledged himself to you. I would imagine the only thing that will go on between them is an honest conversation in which he tells her he is no longer available." Elizabeth had a bemused look on her face. "Besides, he is so charming when he wants to be, he will probably enlist her assistance with the shopping; one cannot accuse General Redmond of being particularly skilled in selecting ribbon, lace, fabric, and threads."

"He did look like a startled rabbit when I gave him the list."

Rebecca smiled at her friend. "Please believe me, Elizabeth, when I tell you that even if Charlie does spend time with Mrs. Armstrong, I love him and I will not hold it against him. For all intents and purposes, Charlie is a man; and that is what men do."

"No, my dear, you are wrong there. In this matter, in matters of the heart, of love and commitment, Charlie is still, and always will be, a woman. And for our Charlie, there is now only one person who has access to his body—the one who holds his heart and soul."

"Thank you."

"You are still worried, are you not, my dear?"

"I am afraid I have many ghosts in my own past that make me uncomfortable at times."

"Well, dear, if I were you, I would simply ask Charlie when he comes back. I am sure he will tell you the truth."

Rebecca chuckled. "There are some things I would rather not know."

Elizabeth looked at her friend and then started laughing. "You really do not want to give the boy an inch of slack, do you? You worry he may sleep with her, and it will always shadow you. But you will not ask him, and I suspect, in your heart, even if he swore on a stack of Bibles that he had not dallied with her, you would always have doubts."

"And in the words of my mother, who was by the way, a very wise woman: 'When it comes to the ways of gentlemen, which you do not understand, ignorance is bliss.'"

"Perhaps, my dear, but for you to always doubt him, even a little, will put a burden on your relationship that is probably not a good thing."

"Elizabeth, I do not doubt Charlie; I know he loves me. I know he wants to come here and make a life together. I certainly will not let his relationship with Mrs. Armstrong come between us. Regardless of what that relationship may be now or in the future."

Elizabeth raised her eyebrows. She clearly knew Charlie and his sense of honor better than Rebecca did. "I think this is important.

Given who Charlie is, there is no possibility he will allow anything other than friendship to continue with Lizzie Armstrong. She will, no doubt, have the same status with which I am honored—close personal friend. Unfortunately, trying to convince you of this truth about our mutual friend is beyond me today." With a frustrated laugh, Elizabeth went on. "Drat. Why should I expect to be able to alleviate your concerns? I have been unsuccessful at everything else today."

"Elizabeth, you are a good friend my dear, but there are just some things beyond your help. My personal insecurities are among them."

The two women sat in silence, each drinking their tea and ruminating on the frustrations of the day. A somber quiet filled the room, broken only when young Em came galloping into the room crying, "Mama 'Becca. Mama 'Becca. See Em's new clothes. Look, Mama 'Becca." Lizbet had made the little girl's doll a new outfit from scraps. The two women became occupied with praising the child and her doll, and the worries of the afternoon slid into the background.

Charlie left Lizzie's with a light heart and a vision of a loving future in his head. It was late afternoon, that hazy time between day and night. He walked back toward the Willard, past the homes and boarding houses that had grown up around the Capitol building, across the Mall that would remain pristine and green in the center of this growing city, past the small shops that had sprung up along Constitution Avenue. As he strolled, he glanced in the windows of those shops, on the odd chance that the perfect gift for Rebecca would present itself, some memento to ease the loneliness of this trip and the coming spring campaign.

Instead, he found something entirely unexpected. There in the window was a doll. A wonderful doll. A doll with green eyes and hair the color of red gold. The perfect doll for Em. He looked at the time and realized it was a bit late for most merchants. Trying the door, he was disappointed; it was locked. But that doll was perfect for little Em. And the child had so little to call her own. He tapped on the door.

A wizened, gray-haired man wearing shirt, vest, and a leather apron shuffled to the door and opened it. "I am sorry, Sir, I have closed for the evening. I was just cleaning up when you knocked. Could you come back tomorrow?"

"I do appreciate your answering my knock then, Sir. I am afraid I am leaving on a train tomorrow. The doll in the window is perfect for a little girl I know. She has very little; the war has taken most of the comforts of home and family from her. Could I just purchase the doll? Please?"

The old merchant looked at the man standing before him—a General, obviously a man of means from the quality of the material in his cloak. A man who would take the time to try and obtain a doll for a war refugee. Well, if the General could take the time, so could he. "Yes, Sir, I think I can do that. Come in, and I will wrap it for you. I must confess, it is a rather expensive doll."

"That does not matter. It is a perfect doll for little Em."

With his pocket lighter by a ten-dollar gold piece and his arm full of a carefully wrapped package, Charlie returned to the Willard. There he took a simple meal, and went to bed early, where he tossed for most of the night, missing Rebecca's tender touch.

CHAPTER 25

FRIDAY, JANUARY 6, 1865

Early the next morning, after having booked the finest suite at the Willard for the end of January and the early part of February, Charlie hurried to his last meetings at the War Department. As the meeting dragged on, he found himself looking at this watch every ten minutes, eager to excuse himself so he could start the journey home. Finally, after a tedious luncheon with a delegation of military supply vendors, he escaped.

He hailed a hackney cab to the train station and headed home. Most of his purchases had been sent over earlier that day by the staff of the Willard and were already loaded in the express carriage of the train. The gift from Lizzie was carefully tucked in his personal bag, as was the doll for Em. The papers from the attorney and the bank, along with the three precious rings, were stowed in the inside breast pocket of his coat.

At his urging, the engineer made record time returning to Culpeper. Even so, night was falling before they pulled into the station, where Duncan was waiting patiently with a dray for the goods. Duncan had also brought Black Jack, who was not so patient. But with Jack there, the General could go home without having to wait for the baggage to be loaded and the mules to plod down the road.

~

Beulah entered the parlor with a smile. "Miss Rebecca?"

"Yes?"

"Reg just stopped by to say that General Redmond is on his way home. He should be coming down the road any time now."

"Wonderful!" Rebecca practically jumped from her chair, grabbing her shawl against the evening chill, and made her way to the front door. Pulling it open, she took her place on the porch and waited for Charlie, like a good wife-to-be should. When at last she saw him emerge from the evening shadows, a huge smile broke across her face and she waved at him.

Smiling, he threw himself off Jack's back, and tossed the reins to Reg, who had come running around the house as soon as he had heard the hoof beats. "Reg, take my bag up to the bedroom and make sure Jack gets special treatment. He had to wait for much too long, according to him. Duncan should be coming along shortly with a cart full of things for Miss Rebecca, so hurry back to help him unload." He turned to Rebecca almost shyly, and said, "Hello, dear one. I have missed you."

She put her arms around his neck, her heart hammering in her ears as she kissed him on the cheek. "And I have missed you," she whispered in his ear, "and if I do not get you inside, your stock with the men as a lady's man will triple in value."

"Darling, I am filthy. Every inch of my body is coated with half of the dust and soot from the rail bed between here and Washington."

She refused to let go of his arm as they walked inside. "Then I shall take you upstairs and wash every inch of your body."

Trying to contain the heat between them, at least until they could be alone, Charlie asked, "Do you know why Duncan rather than Jocko brought the wagon and Jack to meet me?"

Rebecca weighed her words carefully. Not willing to relinquish Charlie to his sense of duty, she told him the bare truth of the situation. "Jocko brought a sick woman in to Elizabeth the night before last, and then Richard sent him on an errand. I have not seen any of the three of them since." She was stroking his arm through his coat, clinging closely to his body.

Charlie's heart rate went up several notches at her possessiveness, and all thought of Jocko disappeared. His time with Lizzie had certainly set his hormones to running free, and now this passionate reception from Rebecca was pushing his desire higher and higher. "Come into the back parlor, dearest, while Reg settles my things in our room." Alone, he wanted her alone, and until he heard Reg's feet pounding down the stairs from depositing his bag upstairs, the back parlor was the best he could do.

"Of course." She smiled like the cat with the canary as they walked to the back parlor. Rebecca let Charlie go in first, then she closed the doors, threw her arms around him, and kissed him with all the pent up passion she felt.

He welcomed her kiss, holding her close and tight against his body, reveling in the feel of her solid, lithe frame against his own and the heat of her lips on his. Their tongues teased and caressed one another, exploring, tasting, savoring. He broke the kiss to ease her into her chair, kneeling beside her to lavish caresses on her neck and shoulders.

She moaned, allowing him to explore as she tugged on the buttons of his coat. "I missed you, Charlie." She began undoing the buttons as fast as she could.

"Love you so." Her hands on his body, the urgency of her touch was driving him insane. He heard Reg's steps on the back stairs. Their room was empty. "Upstairs. Now. Please," he begged.

"Oh, yes," she managed to gasp out even as they continued to kiss while she struggled out of the chair. It was as if they had been apart for months and not just for a few days. She had never missed someone so much in her entire life; she wanted nothing so much as to go upstairs and really make love with him. Her mind considered for the briefest of moments that if it did not happen, she might die. "I want you, Charlie."

Her words seared through him like lightning. He could not talk. He grabbed her hand in his and pulled her through the door. The two of them rushed up the stairs, breathless and laughing at the same time. His coat, weskit, and tie came off as they passed through the sitting room. By the time they reached the bedroom, he was standing in boots, breeches and shirt. His eyes were flashing silver with his need. The chances of Rebecca's dress surviving the evening were slim.

She reached up and began unbuttoning his shirt. "I have no intention of stopping tonight, Charlie. I have missed you so much." She leaned in and kissed him again as she unbuttoned his shirt and pulled it from his breeches.

"Wait. Wait a minute. Let me get out of these boots." He jammed his heel in the jack and yanked his foot out of the boot, then repeated the process with the other foot. He turned back to her. "Turn around."

She smiled and turned her back to him. Her stomach was fluttering wildly and her hands were trembling with desire and arousal. "Hurry, Charlie."

His fingers refused to manage the small buttons that went up the back of her dress. With a muffled groan of frustration, he finally slid his hand under the material and popped every button off the dress in a sweeping stroke.

She laughed at his unusual method of undoing her dress when she heard the buttons clatter to the floor, then turned around to face him. Their eyes locked as she pulled the dress off her arms and pushed it to the floor. Clad only in her chemise, she turned her back again. "I think you can manage these buttons. They are a bit bigger."

With a little fumbling and an uncounted number of kisses on her shoulders and lovely neck, he managed to unbutton the chemise. By the time he was finished, he was panting; and the need to feel her in his arms was overwhelming. Charlie spun her and lifted her, carrying her to the bed, where he laid her down and immediately covered her with his own partially clad body.

"Oh, Charlie," she moaned, arching into him. "I am yours. I will be anything you want or need me to be." She wrapped her arms around his shoulders and pressed her body as hard against his as she could.

Charlie's heart was pounding. "I just need you to be you, darling. My love. My heart. My home. Mine." Each word was punctuated with lavish kisses to her throat, the hollow formed by her collarbone, and the valley between her breasts.

It was, no doubt, the long loud moan coming from Rebecca's throat and the sensation of her nails on Charlie's shoulders that kept either of them from hearing the door to their bedroom creak open.

"Papa?" a little voice called.

A small voice saying "papa" was not what Charlie expected to hear from Rebecca. Slowly, it penetrated his befogged mind that Emily was there and was calling for him. Reluctantly, he raised his head. He did not shift his body, as it was currently the only thing covering Rebecca's completely nude form. He looked into Rebecca's eyes, confused and clearly frustrated. "Emily is here," he announced, stating the obvious.

Rebecca managed to keep from cursing in frustration as she tried valiantly to reclaim her breath. "I heard. We need to send her on her way, Charles Redmond."

Charlie nodded agreement. Moving carefully, he pulled the covers over Rebecca's oh-so-tempting body as she helped re-button his shirt.

Charlie turned to the small child. Gently, he asked, "Emily, what are you doing here? It is past your bed time, little one."

She smiled as her little feet carried her across the room, and, giggling, she flung herself at the bed. "Em miss Papa."

Charlie caught the small, squirming bundle of energy and held her close. "I am here now, little one. Here, you have your hug and bedtime kiss." He matched his actions to his words. "Now, Em, it is past your bedtime, so I am going to take you back to bed. Tomorrow we will play together."

"Papa. Em stay Papa."

"Not tonight, little one. Tonight, Em stays in her own bed with dolly Em." He carried the small girl towards the door on his way to depositing her in her own room and, he hoped, quickly tucking her into bed. Rebecca, his beautiful Rebecca, waited.

As he stepped out of the room, he heard a long groan from the bedroom. "Hurry back, Charlie," was the whimper that followed.

"I will, darling 'Becca." Unfortunately, now that Charlie had returned, Em was back in her old room next to Constance's, which he needed to pass through to put the child back to bed. Charlie strode down the hall to Constance's room and tapped on the door. All the while, Em clung to him like a very determined little leech.

Constance had been dozing; the knock startled her. "Come in," she called, pulling the covers a little higher around her neck. As Charlie entered, carrying the small human remora, a look of shock registered on her face. "Em! How did you..." She stopped when she noticed the General's state of partial undress and the flushed look to his skin. "Oh, General, I am so sorry." She reached for the baby. "Emily, you come to Mama right now."

"It is all right, Constance. You need not get up. I can put her back to bed." Putting action to words, he strode across the room to the half open door into Em's room and laid the small child in her bed. He gave Em a quick hug and a kiss on the forehead. "Good night, Em. You be a good girl. Tomorrow, you and I will play together for a time before supper." Charlie pried Em's death grip from around his neck. "Good night, little one." He headed back out through her mother's room.

"Sorry to disturb you, Constance."

"Of course, General, I am really very sorry she got past me. Please have a good evening."

A small voice was heard from the other room. "Em miss Papa," the child cried again, trying to get his sympathy.

"There is nothing to be sorry for, Constance. And I appreciate your understanding." He called to the little girl again, "Bedtime, little one. You be good, or tomorrow's play time might be tomorrow's lesson in manners time."

"Yes, Papa. Em love."

"Papa loves you, too, Em. Good night, little one. Good night, Constance."

The brief interlude with Emily had given Charlie a chance to get a grip on his emotions, at least enough to slow down and give Rebecca the experience she deserved. He re-entered their room with every intention of going slowly and showing Rebecca just how good their loving one another could feel.

Rebecca had taken the time to turn down the bed properly and climb under the covers. That is where he found her. Lying in bed, facing the door, with the sheet modestly pulled over her body. "I assume you got her to bed?"

"I did. And how would you like to get me to bed, darling girl?"

"I would like that." She sat up, allowing the sheet to pool at her waist. "I would like that very much. Come to bed."

Charlie just stood for a moment, entranced by the vision that Rebecca offered him. Then slowly, he removed his own clothing, offering his transformation from male to female as a gift to her.

Rebecca smiled and held out her hand. "Mine."

Charlie walked to her slowly, almost dancing, soft and sensuous. The tempo of their intimacy had changed, from feverish urgency to a slower, pulsing pace that seemed to Charlie to be as true as the beat of her heart.

Rebecca hummed in pure pleasure when Charlie settled into bed with her. This was their first total contact of skin on skin, and Rebecca's temperature skyrocketed when she felt the smoothness of

Charlie's skin against her own. She wrapped her arms around the tall woman and whispered, "I love you."

The heat of Rebecca's body against her own sent shivers of want racing through Charlie. "Oh, dear God, I love you, Rebecca," she breathed, as she submerged her face in Rebecca's soft hair. Their bodies fit together perfectly. Very softly, Charlie began caressing Rebecca with her fingertips.

Rebecca pushed closer to Charlie. Taking her by the wrist, she guided her hand between their bodies. "Touch me, Charlie," she begged, all the while placing soft kisses on her lover's shoulder.

That request, coupled with the intense intimacy of their connection overtook Charlie's senses. Every intention of slow, tender exploration melted away, dispelled by the obvious urgency in the small frame beneath hers. "I want it to be right." She caressed Rebecca firmly. "I want to take it slow and gentle. I need you."

"I need you, too. I want you," she said in a husky voice. Rebecca took the initiative. "Love me. Please." She licked her lips before they sought out Charlie's in another smoldering kiss.

Charlie may have wanted to take it slowly, but Rebecca's need was urgent.

After what seemed like forever and an instant, Rebecca's body relaxed and fell back into the mattress. She did not let go of Charlie, however, and brought her with her, so her lover was lying right on top of her. She sighed her pleasure and kissed Charlie's ear. "Love you." She drew a deep breath through clenched teeth when one final tremor ran through her body. "I am so glad you are home."

Charlie was holding most of her weight on one arm. One very shaky arm.

"My home. My heart. My love."

A tear trickled down and fell on Rebecca's shoulder.

"Charlie? Darling? Have I done something wrong?"

"Oh, no, beloved. You have done something very right. I am home. In your arms, I am home. In your touch, I am home. For the first time in my life, in your love, I am no longer alone. I love you so much."

"I love you, too, Charlie. You are what I have been wanting all my life." She squirmed under her. "Now put your arms around me and keep me safe and warm for the rest of the night."

Charlie shifted her body and wrapped herself around the smaller woman. They pulled the covers up over themselves. Entwined, Charlie laid her head beside her love's. "I am not sure which one of us keeps the other safe and warm, love. I adore you." Long minutes were spent in quiet cuddling, and simple words of love and acceptance. For all of the strength that Charlie brought to the relationship, in the face of Rebecca's love and passion, she was reduced to a simple, childlike wonder.

"All that matters is that we are here, together." Rebecca rolled over to face her lover. "And now that I have said hello, how was your trip?" she giggled, curling into Charlie's body.

"My trip was very successful, darling. All of the things that you ordered I brought with me on today's supply train. I called on Lizzie Armstrong, and she assisted me with the adventure at the haberdasher's."

"How is Mrs. Armstrong, Charlie? Well, I hope. I am glad you had assistance. I wondered if you would feel somewhat befuddled by that shopping."

"She also gave us a rather personal wedding gift. I hope you like her. She does not expect you will be willing even to meet her."

Rebecca drew back and looked at Charlie. "A gift? What kind of gift? I would love to meet her. She is your friend and important to you. I will admit to a certain amount of jealously at first, but I am well over it."

Charlie neatly avoided the issue of the gift. "Thank you, love. I felt sure that you would, but she is rather notorious and I was concerned you would find her beneath you."

"Never. She is your friend and I would like her to be my friend and know our home is always open to her."

Charlie pulled Rebecca closer and kissed the top of her head. "Can you imagine what a visit from my dear friend Lizzie would do to Mrs. Williams? The poor woman would faint dead away."

"Oh then, Charlie, we must have her down as soon as possible."

Charlie chuckled, hugging Rebecca tighter and getting comfortable for the irresistible call of sleep.

~

Rebecca awoke the moment that Charlie stirred in the morning. She hummed as she rolled over and opened her eyes to see him shrugging into his robe.

"I suppose it is back to work as usual?" she questioned, even as she ran her hand over the covers, silently inviting him back.

"Well, darling, I have been gone for most of a week. I rather think that Richard would appreciate me showing up and relieving him of the hard part." He smiled. "The decisions."

Charlie walked around to Rebecca's side of the bed and stroked the soft skin of her shoulder where it peeked out from under the covers. "On the other hand, after a day of travel, I might be forgiven for sleeping in a little."

Rebecca drew a deep breath and closed her eyes in frustration as she remembered something very important. "Oh no! Charlie, we do need to get up, and you need to find Richard, Elizabeth, and Jocko. We had an "incident" while you were gone."

Charlie stopped. The tone of Rebecca's voice told him clearly he was not going to like what he was about to hear. "Would you care to tell me the basics? Prepare me for what I will have to face?"

She pulled herself up and gestured for Charlie to hand her the robe from the foot of the bed. Once she had slipped into it, she sat up and took his hand. "While you were gone, Jocko went to see Mrs. White. When he arrived, he found her beaten and..." She paused, lowering her eyes then lifting them again. "Davison and his men. They forced her."

Charlie rolled his head back and stared at the ceiling for a moment. He drew a deep breath. "Damn. How is Mrs. White?"

"When she first got here she was bitter, hurt, angry, and scared. But under Elizabeth's tender ministrations and Jocko's constant attentions, she will be fine. I am going to let her stay here with us. I am taking in another stray, my dear, but she should not be alone, and she will be a delightful addition to the household."

Charlie drew another deep breath and blew it out through pursed cheeks. "She is certainly welcome, and I am sure Jocko will be pleased to have her here. Do we have enough room for her?"

"This is a big house, Charlie. For now, we will put her in the room we used for Major Montgomery. Once you and Elizabeth leave, I will rearrange the bedrooms; but we are fine for now."

"Has Richard found Davison and his men?"

"I know he has patrols out looking for them, but you will have to ask him for the details."

Charlie ran his hands through his hair. This was not the kind of thing one enjoyed coming back to. Outraged civilians would blame the Army, and there would be the very sensitive issue of jurisdiction to deal with when the men were captured. "Darling, why did you not tell me this last night?"

"I am sorry. I should have let you tend to this last night when you returned, but I was so happy to see you and there was nothing you could do past what Richard was already doing." She looked down at the rumpled sheets. "I did not tell you last night for the most selfish of reasons: I needed you. I truly am sorry if this has caused a problem."

"Darling, I would not trade last night for anything. If necessary, I will happily respond to any suggestion I was derelict in my duty by pointing out that my duty to my betrothed and family comes before my duty to country."

Rebecca's brow rose as she considered him. This was certainly a change in priorities for the officer. He had always made it quite clear that his duty to the Army was the most important thing. She smiled and caressed his cheek. "I am delighted to hear that. Let us get on with our day, Charlie. You have this issue to deal with, and I have a feeling that in very short order, Little Em will be tearing down the walls to find her Papa."

Charlie kissed Rebecca's forehead. "Yes, dear. Why do I suspect that one of the things you are going to have to do when you rearrange the rooms is to set up a nursery?"

"It is already being seen to. Duncan and some of the other men have fashioned furniture, the ladies are making blankets, and a few have been making clothes. At a later time, when you are in need of a good laugh, I will show you my attempt at booties."

"You have been crocheting? My, how domestic of you." Charlie smiled at the homey exchange, but a part of his mind was already elsewhere: considering the implications of a band of former Federal soldiers raping and stealing their way across Northern Virginia.

"Do not worry, Charlie; I would not. I am afraid I shall give it up as well. Unless Jack needs socks for the spring campaign."

"Well, dear, as much as I would love to stay with you this morning, duty calls."

Charlie went through his morning routine quickly, as he needed to get to Richard as soon as possible and find out the status of the situation with Mrs. White and Davison. He pulled on his simplest uniform and headed out to the Officers' Mess. There he found Richard savoring the first cup of coffee of the day.

"Good morning, Richard. I hear we have a major problem to deal with."

"You could say that, oh fearless leader."

"So, have we caught them yet?"

"If we had, we would not have the problem, Charlie. I have had details out around the clock since Jocko brought Mrs. White back. There are indications they are still in the area, but they are well-trained soldiers; they know how not to be found."

"Have you wired the other commands to tell them to be on the lookout?"

Richard tried not to look annoyed. He failed. "Yes, Father."

Charlie looked at Richard. "Doing it again, am I? I am sorry, my friend. Have you gone so far as to initiate a door-to-door sweep? And, no, I am not asking because I doubt you, I just want to know what has and has not been done. You, my friend, are not the one who has to go talk to Mayor Frazier."

"It is all right, Charlie. This whole mess has us all on edge. The men are bound and determined to find these devils. Our troops have actually come to respect these citizens, and they are hopping mad over this. I have had men out standing sentry in all the communities. They started house-to-house yesterday. And I have already had to deal not only with Mayor Frazier, but also the Reverend and Mrs. Williams. Charlie, are you sure you want to come back here after the war? Would it not be easier to move Rebecca and the children to, say, Paris?"

"Oh, shall I assume the ever gracious and gentle Mrs. Williams presented a certain challenge for even your charm?"

"Charlie, I would rather face Lee and his entire army while under the command of George Custer, than spend even one more day with that woman."

"Do I want to know, or are you going to let me walk into the lions' den unprepared?"

"It is Mrs. Williams, Charlie, at her most indignantly righteous. I am sure you can just imagine what you are in for."

Charlie rolled his eyes. "Wonderful. I have an already touchy situation, three rapists or worse, and Mrs. Williams. I will offer you a deal; you take Mrs. Williams, and I will handle all the rest of the problems."

Richard threw his head back in hearty laughter before he slapped his friend on the back. "Oh no, my friend. This is your community now; you should be the one to deal with it. I will be more than happy to wrap the nooses for when we find them; hell, I will even build the gallows, but I will not deal with that termagant again."

Charlie sighed a heartfelt, long suffering sigh. He placed one hand over his heart. "I could order you to, but if I must, I must. The things a man must brave in the name of duty."

Richard grinned at his friend's histrionics.

"So, Richard. What say you come up to the house and have breakfast with me? You can fill me in on the more mundane happenings this week. That is, if you can manage to drag your eyes away from Elizabeth."

Richard stood and tossed away the dregs of the coffee in his cup. "Like you will be listening to me. You do not notice anything when Rebecca is in the room."

Charlie laughed. "Well, I suppose we are even, then." He smiled slyly. "Of course, there is another female who can distract both of us from our ladies. And she will probably be at breakfast."

"Oh yes, in your absence I became 'Unc Wichawd.' Jocko was just as good about cleaning my coats as he is of cleaning yours."

"Oh, so you have found creamed wheat to be as beneficial to your woolens as I have? I am particularly impressed with how it makes the brass shine."

"I am not sure whether it is the wheat, or the copious amounts of Emily drool."

The two men were strolling toward the house as they chatted. A small figure burst from the winter kitchen door, her leading strings trailing behind her and Beulah's younger sister running after the little imp. "Papa!"

A small human rocket launched itself at Charlie, fully relying on the man's ability to catch her and keep her safe.

"You have been practicing." Richard chuckled as he watched Charlie hoist the girl into his arms. "I dropped her three times last week."

"Hello, little one. Were you good while I was gone?"

"Yes, Papa. Em good." She smiled, showing him the teeth, which were becoming more prominent every day, and then hugged him tight around his neck. "Em miss Papa."

"And Papa missed Em, too. Were you good for Uncle Richard?"

Charlie gave his friend an evil grin over the black mop tucked into his shoulder.

"Yes. Mama 'Becca spank Em."

"Oh. Were you naughty? I think that Mama 'Becca only spanks when little girls have been very naughty indeed."

"I am afraid Emily gave Rebecca quite a scare. She decided it would be fun to play a game of hide and seek with Rebecca, and would not come when we were all looking for her. Rebecca was beside herself with worry. Almost an hour after we started looking, we found her hidden behind the curtains in the parlor."

"Em, did you hide from Mama 'Becca?"

"Yes, Papa." Her eyes dropped and her lip poked right out; it was obvious she was seeking his forgiveness.

"Little one, hiding from me or Mama 'Becca or your mother or Dr. Walker or Tess is particularly bad. We are the people who take care of you, and if you hide from us, we get very, very worried. So, do you want to tell me why you hid?"

She lay against his shoulder. "Pwaying."

"Well, little one, there are lots of ways to play. That was not a good one. So you are not going to do it any more, are you?"

"No, Papa. Mama 'Becca spank Em."

"And if Em does it again, either Mama 'Becca or Papa will spank Em again." Charlie kissed the little girl's forehead. "Now, how about some breakfast?"

Tess looked at the General gratefully as he waved her off from the energetic child. She went back to the kitchen, where she would actually get a few minutes of sitting quietly, eating breakfast, and gossiping with Sarah before she had to chase the little imp around again.

They strolled up the back stairs and entered the breakfast room from the veranda. Elizabeth and Rebecca were already there, waiting for them. More importantly, from Richard's point of view, the coffee pot was already there.

"So, Charlie, how was your experience of shopping in

Washington?" Elizabeth had a wicked grin on her face, knowing full well how much he enjoyed that chore.

He raised a defiant eyebrow at her. "Quite successful, thank you very much. I believe the supplies were unloaded yesterday evening and are in the storage rooms downstairs."

Rebecca turned to Elizabeth and gave her a slight grin. "Yes, Charlie got all the assistance he needed from Mrs. Armstrong."

Richard snorted into his coffee. "Lizzie Armstrong, Charlie? Well, I must say, if you needed to find a professional shopper to assist you, you could not have done better."

Charlie just smiled.

"As long as those were the only professional services she offered," Rebecca mumbled from behind her coffee cup.

Richard gulped the mouthful of coffee and scalded his throat, which set off a coughing fit. Still, it was better than spraying coffee all over the table.

Charlie calmly responded to his fiancée's comment. "My dear, what services she may or may not have offered are moot. I am yours, and only yours. She did send us a wedding present."

"I know that, Charlie. I was just making an observation."

"I got a present for you, my dear, and one for young Em." Em, who was happily sitting on her Papa's knee eating her morning cereal, heard her name and the word "present," and immediately perked up.

"Fow Em?" She grabbed his coat and met him nose to nose. "Em good, Papa."

"Yes, for Em. After you finish your breakfast. And you must eat all of it, little one."

"Mmmm..." Em made quite the show of going back to her cereal and shoveling it into her mouth.

Just then, there was a clattering in the front hall. Reg came into the room, followed immediately by Captain Maguire of Company G. The youngest of Charlie's company commanders was covered in dried mud and road dust. His eyes were bloodshot, and it was obvious he was suffering from lack of sleep.

Blushing to the roots of his hair, he snapped to attention, realizing he had barged into the family's breakfast. "Captain Maguire reporting, Sir."

"At ease, Captain. You look like you could use a cup of coffee. Pull up a chair and tell me what has you in such a rush." Rebecca signaled Reg to get the captain a cup.

"Thank you, Sir." The young man took a seat, turning earnest eyes on his commander. "We caught them, Sir."

Charlie sighed. He was silent for a moment, and then asked, "Did you obtain any evidence of other crimes?"

"Well, Sir, we found several things a man would not normally have on his person in their possession. Ladies' jewelry and things of that nature, not much, but a few things. Sir, we caught them just outside Culpeper. Seems they heard you had gone to the capital, and they were comin' back," he paused and looked around, his message clear. "Here, Sir."

"What kind of shape are they in?"

He exhaled. "Well, Sir, you can imagine. They are dirty and hungry, but they were fightin' with my men, Sir."

"I believe you have Davison's cousin in your company. How did he behave?"

"Well, Sir, he, well, he beat the tar out of Davison before we could pull him off."

"Hummmm. Well, I suppose that is an indication that we have done our job in inspiring the men to want to work as a team, with a common sense of honor." Richard snorted in the background. "Have Samuelson look them over and patch them up. Where are you holding them?"

"We have them locked up nice and tight in the overseer's cottage. And there are men posted all around the building, Sir, with orders to shoot them on sight if they get out."

"I take it that there is little sympathy for them in the ranks?"

"None at all, Sir. 'Twas bad enough what they did to Mrs. Adams, but when they had the chance to leave and then stayed, and hurt that nice Mrs. White, well, Sir, that was about the end of the line for most of the men, Sir. A lot of us had done chores for Mrs. White and her townsfolk, and they did not deserve this. I doubt you will find a man willing to stand up for them, Sir."

Charlie nodded his appreciation to young Maguire. "Well, George, you look like a man who needs some sleep. Turn your responsibilities over to one of the other companies. Then you and your men turn in. We will be handing these three over to the civilian authorities. They are no longer soldiers, and they will have to be charged by the local civilian government."

"Yes, Sir, right away." The young man stood and smiled at Rebecca. "Thank you for the hot coffee, Ma'am."

With a crisp salute he left the room, which remained quiet as everyone considered the new problems that had just arisen. Finally there was a small voice.

"Papa?"

"Yes, Em?"

She put her spoon down and looked at him very seriously. "Papa get da bad man?"

"No, honey. Captain Maguire got the bad men. Papa has to go and figure out what to do to punish them."

She climbed up into his lap and placed her hands on his cheeks. "Papa spank da bad man."

"No, honey. Papa will have to do something else. These men were too bad to just spank them."

Em settled herself back on his knee and picked up her spoon, her little brows coming together as she considered it. "Bewy bad man," she mumbled around another spoonful of cereal.

Richard and Charlie, preoccupied with the fact that Davison and his men had been captured, hurriedly finished breakfast, and departed to interview the criminals. This left Rebecca with a very distressed little girl.

"Mama 'Becca, Em good. Papa fowgot pwesents." Em's face was a portrait of confused disappointment.

"Oh, sweetheart, Papa is very busy. He will give you your present later, I promise. How about this? Shall we go see what Papa brought back for the wedding?"

"Pwesents for wedding?"

Rebecca laughed and picked up the little girl. "Yes, in a sense. These are the things Mama 'Becca needs to have a proper wedding to Papa." Rebecca turned to Elizabeth. "Would you care to join us?"

The little girl settled happily in Rebecca's arms. She was growing like a weed with the good food Sarah had been feeding her. Soon she would be too heavy for Rebecca to pick up easily and carry around. "Mama 'Becca? What is wedding?"

"Good question. I do wish I had an answer you would understand." She gave it further thought as she continued down the hall. "It is a party, Em."

"Good. Em likes pawties."

Elizabeth chuckled as the two women proceeded to the back parlor to examine Charlie's acquisitions. Entering the room, they were confronted by a sizable pile of bundles, bags and boxes, all heaped haphazardly in the middle of the room. Rebecca immediately went to the bell pull and summoned Lizbet, Tess, and Reg.

"It appears as if absolutely everything that Charlie brought back was just piled here. I do believe I will need at least one pot of tea to get through this Herculean task." Elizabeth's eyes were sparkling with laughter.

Rebecca was a bit overwhelmed. "It is not funny, Elizabeth," she chastised playfully as she placed Em on the floor and continued to stare at the pile. "You would think he could have labeled things a little better."

"My dear, this is Charlie – the man who never shops. I think he has had Jocko do all of his shopping, except for the fittings of his clothes and boots, for years. We are fortunate he managed to get everything on your list, dear." Elizabeth was poking at the pile, shifting bags, and examining boxes. "It will get much better once we get the cases of wine and kegs of brandy out of here."

Rebecca looked closer at the pile. "Good Lord, is Charlie planning on getting the entire county drunk?"

"Well, there is the gentlemen's bachelor party the night before the wedding." Elizabeth smirked.

Rebecca stood up, giving Elizabeth a very serious look. "Oh, I had forgotten about that. Do you think Charlie will have such a thing?"

"I think Richard will probably insist. That man will take any opportunity to celebrate, and if he can do it at Charlie's expense, well, so much the better, according to him."

"As long as Charlie is in proper condition for the wedding the next day, because if he is not I will take it out of Richard's hide myself."

"My dear, please leave me some of that hide." Elizabeth continued to poke among the packages. "By the way, I believe Mrs. Carter said something about being a seamstress. Perhaps we should ask her to join us?"

Just then, Lizbet, Tess, and Reg appeared at the door, Lizbet in the lead. "You rang for us, Miss Rebecca?" Tess immediately took charge of the youngster, who had disembarked from Rebecca's arms and was using the mound of merchandise to play a small version of King of the Mountain. Reg, who had already hauled all of this stuff up from the storeroom, was fully aware of how much was piled in the middle of the floor, and fearing that he was about to be told to put most of the heavier stuff away, was trying to make himself invisible.

"Yes, we must sort through these things and determine what needs to be put away." Rebecca looked at the man standing quietly in the corner by the door. "Reg, I am sure you will see to that right away."

"Yes'm." Reg rolled his eyes as Rebecca turned away. He had hauled most of this stuff into the parlor from the storeroom this morning, and into the storeroom from the wagon last night. Now he would have to haul it again. He already ached.

"Tess, could you go find Mrs. Carter and ask her to join us? You can leave Em here with us." She turned to Elizabeth. "Thank you for reminding me. Mrs. Carter offered to assist in preparing for the wedding, as did several of the other women."

"And, Lizbet, you know I will depend on you heavily in the coming weeks. So, please, consider yourself part of the wedding party. Dr. Walker needs some tea to get through this; perhaps you will bring enough for all of us – and Lizbet, bring cups for you, Tess, and Reg."

Elizabeth looked at her friend. "Good thing Mrs. Williams is not part of this little wedding party. She would faint if she knew you let your servants drink tea with you."

"Remind me to tell her the next time I see her."

Elizabeth snorted as she picked up a package that was clearly a bolt of cloth and handed it to Rebecca. "I think you may want to look at this."

Rebecca opened the package and smiled at the contents. It was beautiful, ivory, semi-sheer voile that would be the outer shell of her wedding gown. "It is stunning."

"Yes, dear, it is. What are you planning, if I may ask?"

"Mrs. Cooper had a lovely picture of a dress I thought would be appropriate. Mrs. Carter agreed, and said that she could make it for me fairly quickly. It has a simple underskirt of palest blue satin with a voile overskirt that is gathered to the waist over one hip. The bodice is more of the blue satin with ivory lace, with a scooped, off-the-shoulder neckline. There are lace rosettes around the skirt. Simple, elegant, and I love it."

Mrs. Carter entered as Elizabeth was describing the dress. "Ah, Mrs. Gaines. I see the supplies have come. Let us get them sorted out, and we can begin cutting the pattern today."

Silently, Reg trudged in and out of the room, carrying cases of wine and kegs of brandy back downstairs to the cellar.

~

Jocko knocked gently on the door of Esther White's room. A soft voice bade him enter. "Good morning, Esther. Are you feeling any better, dear lady?"

"Good morning, John. Yes, I am. Thank you. Please come join me." She patted a place next to her on the small davenport.

"I, um, I wanted to check and see if Dr. Walker had taken care of you, if there were any problems." Jocko was nervous. What he really wanted to tell her was that Davison had been captured, but did not quite know how to do it.

"Yes. Dr. Walker and Mrs. Gaines have been very kind to me. I am feeling much better. I do believe I will make a full recovery." She paused, glancing down at her hands. "John, I am so sorry for the way I spoke to you when you first found me."

"Esther, dear lady, I am surprised you will talk to anyone wearing this uniform after what those fiends did to you. I am just grateful you let me help you and bring you here."

"John, I learned a very long time ago that there are good men and there are evil men. The clothes do not make the man; it is what is in your heart. You are a good man, they are evil."

"Thank you, Esther. I am honored to know you think me a good man. I fear there are more people in the world who think I am more of a rake than a saint."

"Yes, well, I would imagine that would be my rather vocal Southern cousins. Would you think me odd if I told you I never supported this war? I knew it would be a foolhardy venture. I am proud to be Southern, John, but I never believed we could win a war with the Federals. If our way of life has been destroyed, we destroyed it ourselves."

"Ah, I appreciate your perspective on this war, but I am afraid I was referring more to my own personal life. I have, um, been known to, ah, avail myself of, er, the company of ladies of less than sterling reputation in the past. I have also been told I have the Irish predilection for a bit of the jug."

"I have never known an Irishman that was not a rascal, John Jackson. You are a perfectly charming gentleman, and you know it."

"Well, Ma'am, if you can stand having the support of a known rascal, I would be honored to stand as your support. And when this whole thing is over, perhaps..." Jocko stopped for a moment, then looked at the floor.

"You see, Esther, I think you are going to need someone to stand for you. Our troops captured Davison and two other men last night. The General said he plans to turn them over for civilian justice, but either way, you will be asked to testify."

"Will they be hanged?" she asked, with very little emotion.

"If I have anything to say about it. I know that General Redmond does not have any compunction about hanging rapists, but it remains to be seen what Mayor Frazier chooses to do."

"Frazier does not have the backbone to make a decision like that. I can say that, as I have known him all my life. He and Mr. White used to go rabbit hunting together. Horace is a good hearted man, but he is not a strong leader."

"Well, I suspect that whatever happens, General Redmond will play a major role. And he does have the backbone."

"You are very fond of your General, very loyal to him. What has he done to deserve such fierce loyalty?"

"He saved my life, and then he gave me a place in the world." The stark simplicity of Jocko's statement spoke volumes about the relationship between the two men.

"I can tell you the people in the area are torn between calling him friend and hating him just because he is a Yankee officer. They realize he has done more than they ever expected, but their damn foolish pride will not let them thank him." She sighed and looked to her friend. "I would be grateful for your support through this John. Thank you."

"You know, Esther, I have seen women after they had been violated, and most of them were far more emotional than you are. I am worried about you, sweet lady. Holding in the anger and the pain are not good for you."

"I am past all that, dear man. I am old enough to know it will not make anything different. What happened, happened. I did nothing to encourage it, but I most certainly cannot change it."

"Well, Ma'am, I believe you can expect a visit from the General soon. If you would like, I will be here with you when he calls."

"Yes, I think I would like that very much. Thank you."

"Now, Ma'am, to pass the time, would you like to play a little two-handed whist, or perhaps some checkers or chess?"

"I would be careful if I were you, Sergeant. Before my husband died, when he could no longer get out of his sickbed, we played checkers all day. I am quite good." She smiled as Jocko brought the game table closer to her seat.

Jocko set the checkerboard down on the small table and pulled out the box of markers. They were setting them in place when they heard the crack of gunshots ring out. Jocko leapt up, knocking the table over, and raced through the door.

Charlie and Richard had gone to Charlie's office to review the reports of the arresting officers. Charlie then prepared articles of arrest, defining the formal charges and remanding the three men to the civilian authorities. Finally, he prepared copies of the documents, along with a letter to Frazier, and sent them off with a trooper to be delivered to the Mayor post haste.

He then stopped upstairs to check on Rebecca and the ladies. As he entered the small back parlor, he was confronted with most of the women in the house, all sorting through the material, lace, and notions he had brought, sketching details of design, or sipping tea. The din was overwhelming, and he hastily kissed Rebecca, tousled Em's hair and started backing out of what had become a totally feminine domain. The sound of gunfire penetrated even that cacophony. He bolted from the room.

Captain Peter Dewees, the new commander of Company D, had accepted responsibility for the prisoners from Captain Maguire with a certain level of pride. All three men had been members of his company, all three had been special cronies of the late and, to be truthful, unlamented, Major Montgomery, and all three were an embarrassment to his company. That Colonel Polk saw fit to allow his company to mount the guard was an honor, one that he believed they had earned by winning the gymkhana.

Dewees strode into the small stone building. The three men were standing in irons, looking decidedly the worse for wear. Maguire had said they had resisted arrest; from the looks of them, the men of Company G had not been gentle in their efforts to subdue them.

"Shamus Davison, Otis Dumpire, and Edward Osborn, you are charged with the crimes of violation of an innocent woman, theft, and assault on a civilian. Because you have broken the terms of your dismissal, you are also charged with failure to obey a commanding officer and dereliction of duty. On the charges of violation of an innocent woman, theft, and assault, you are to be remanded to civilian authorities, as is appropriate because of your discharge from the Army. Only after the civilian authorities have pursued their charges will you then be tried on the military charges. Consider well, men. Mr. Samuelson will be along shortly to tend to your injuries."

Young Lieutenant Swallow led the detail assigned to guard duty, supported by Raiford, the new color bearer. Raiford and the other guards unshackled the men, one at a time, and marched them into the empty storage room at the back of the overseer's office. A few minutes later, Samuelson arrived. Raiford volunteered to go in with him.

When the door opened, the prisoners exploded out of their makeshift jail. One stiff-armed Samuelson, who fell unconscious. Another grappled with Raiford for his carbine. The third went for Swallow, who reacted as he had been trained. He fired his pistol, one clean shot to the heart. Raiford's carbine went off at almost the same time, blasting up through the jaw and brain of his assailant. The third man ran; Dewees dropped him with two shots in the back.

Dewees checked on Samuelson and the other men. Apart from the obvious fact that the medic had been knocked out, the men were unharmed, if somewhat shaken. All three miscreants were dead. Dewees was just ordering a detail to handle the bodies as Charlie, Richard, and Jocko roared around the corner, the two officers with side arms drawn. They drew up short as soon as they saw the three bodies on the ground.

"Captain Dewees reporting, Sir. The prisoners attempted to escape, assaulting several of our men. As is standard procedure, we responded with force. I am sorry, Sir, that we were unable to bring them to trial, but to be honest, I am just as glad it ended this way. Good riddance to bad trash."

Charlie looked at the bodies crumpled in the mud, then at the faces of the men around him. These were the same men who had marched, slept, eaten, and fought side by side with those lying in the mud. There was not a single face that showed any grief for the loss of a comrade. Perhaps justice had been done.

Charlie and Jocko walked back to the house, leaving Richard to oversee the burial detail, handle the paper work, and dispatch a messenger to Mayor Frazier. It was time for Charlie to meet with Mrs. White and carry the news that she would not have to undergo the strain of a trial.

They mounted the back stairs and walked down the hall to her room. Just as they knocked on Mrs. White's door, the door to Constance's room burst open and a small tornado with black hair burst out. Having been extremely good during her morning visit with her mother, she was full of energy and ready to play.

"Papa!" Em ran over and threw herself at him, wrapping around his legs and trying to climb him like a tree.

Esther White had been up and pacing when the knock came on her door. Like everyone else in the house, she had heard the gunshots. She opened the door to the highly amusing vision of a tall, slender, black-haired officer being climbed by a small, eager black-haired monkey child. It was a vision so far from what she had expected she could not help but burst out laughing.

While she laughed, Charlie settled Em in the crook of his left arm and admonished her, "Be good, now. Papa has to talk to the nice lady."

Em curled into Charlie's shoulder and watched the woman as her Papa walked into the room.

"You are this child's father, General? How is that possible?"

"No, Mrs. White, I am not. I simply resemble her father. Her mother is unwell and is advanced in another pregnancy, so Em has rather attached herself to Rebecca and me. Welcome to our home, although I would have wished it to be under much more pleasant circumstances." Charlie was obviously comfortable in the role of father to the little imp who was peeking at Mrs. White through her fingers, flirting and smiling.

"Thank you. It was very kind of Miss Rebecca to take me in." The older woman reached out and ran her fingers through Em's bangs. "Something has happened? I heard the shots. Was anyone hurt?"

"I must inform you that the prisoners attempted to escape and were killed in the ensuing ruckus. Perhaps the good news, Ma'am, is that you will not have to undergo the ordeal of a trial."

She lowered her eyes and said a quiet prayer; then she looked back to Charlie. "Thank you, General. I am grateful for your assistance and your honesty."

"Mrs. White, I do understand this is a difficult time for you. You are welcome to stay here for as long as you wish. In fact, if you are up to it, I suspect that Mrs. Gaines would enjoy the additional company. It seems the house has been taken over by women in a wedding planning frenzy."

"Oh yes. John had mentioned that during one of his visits. Congratulations, General."

Charlie's eyebrow rose. The last time anyone had called Jocko "John" was when he renewed his induction oath. "Yes, thank you, Ma'am."

"You mentioned the child's mother is expecting and unwell? I am a midwife; perhaps I could be of some assistance."

"I suspect so. Mrs. Adams has been under Dr. Walker's care, but unfortunately, she is not due until after I believe we will be ordered back to the field. Dr. Walker will be with our support staff then. Perhaps you can discuss it with Dr. Walker and Mrs. Adams after you have had a chance to recover yourself."

Mrs. White smiled and nodded agreement. "Perhaps I shall, General."

Just then, Em tugged on Charlie's lapel. "Papa?"

"Yes, Em?"

"Em good. Papa give pwesent now?"

Charlie flushed. In the fracas surrounding the arrest of Davison and his henchmen, he had totally forgotten about the doll he had bought her in Washington. "Yes, little one. You have been very good." He turned to Mrs. White. "Ma'am, I believe our young lady has demanded some attention from her Papa. So, if I may excuse myself?"

Esther White nodded, and Charlie excused himself with a small bow. She watched as the tall man carried the daughter of his heart off to his room and the promised gift.

~

The day had been a long one, stressful in different ways for all members of the household. Most significantly, it had been a day where Charlie had had no time alone with Rebecca. Other than the period when all had wondered over the fate of Davison and his men, the women had been occupied with wedding plans. As a result, the small ring box in his breast pocket was burning a hole in his chest.

By dinner, everyone was tired; and by mutual agreement, all withdrew for some quiet time in their rooms and an early bedtime. Charlie slipped up to their sitting room ahead of Rebecca, with a bottle of champagne and two glasses in hand. He built up the fire and dimmed the lamps. He was ready.

He joined Rebecca in the hall, and they both went to tuck young Em into bed for the night. Then, with a gallant bow, he swept open the door to Rebecca's personal bower.

Rebecca smiled at him as she looked into the room before entering. "What has gotten into you tonight, Charlie?"

"I not only bought Em a present, I also got a couple of things for you, dear, and I wanted to give them to you."

She looked at him very carefully. He was in a rare playful mood, and she found she rather enjoyed this side of her normally reserved General. "Is that so? And what, may I ask, have you found?"

"Well, there is the mundane. I went to my bank, put my accounts in both of our names, and opened a fund for you. Here, my love. It is the paperwork. I think you will find you are a rather wealthy woman in your own right. Consider it my engagement present." With a flourish, he laid the paperwork on the small table beside her. The top page noted Rebecca's personal account of fifty thousand dollars. She riffled through the other papers, seeing the total sum in their joint accounts that made her eyes widen. The last documents were Charlie's will and his military pension.

She turned to him, not knowing what to say. "I...Charlie, it is too much."

He took her in his arms. "No, dear. It is just a fraction of what I wish I could give you. To me, you are worth more than all the money in the world. While I am gone, you will have a great many issues to deal with. This gives you the financial freedom to do so. In just a few weeks, I will stand up and pledge, 'And with all my worldly goods I thee endow.' I just got a head start on it."

She smiled and kissed him. "Thank you, Charlie," she sighed, and laid her head on his shoulder. "Are you as nervous as I am?"

"About marrying you, or about the wedding?"

"Both?"

He laughed and settled on the davenport in front of the fire with her in his lap. "I am always nervous about public events and ceremonies. I worry about falling over my sword; I worry my jacket will get tucked into my trousers; I worry I will say or do something stupid; I worry I will give myself away. But as to marrying you…" He stopped and tenderly kissed her under the curve of her jaw, his lips whispering just below her ear, "As for marrying you, it is the best thing I have ever done and will ever do. I am joyous, excited, can barely wait, but no, I am not nervous about it." He slipped his hand inside his jacket. She had felt an odd little lump under her shoulder where it rested against his coat. They adjusted their position as he pulled out the small box. "I thought you needed something of your own, so I got you these. One is for now; the other two are for later."

Rebecca looked at the rings in his hand. "Charlie, they are beautiful."

He extracted one ring. It was an emerald, cut in a fine square and surrounded by a rosette of diamonds, all mounted in white gold. In the firelight, the stones flashed and sparkled. "Give me your hand, my love."

Rebecca tried to stop her hand from shaking as she presented it, but was not as successful as she would have liked. All she could do was give him an embarrassed little smile.

He carefully slipped the small garnet ring she had been wearing off her left hand ring finger. He then just as carefully placed the emerald at the tip of her finger and asked again, "Rebecca Gaines, will you marry me? All of me: the man and the woman? Will you let me love you for the rest of our lives, and share with you all that I have and all that I am? Will you raise our children with me, and build a life together filled with love and laughter?"

Words were far beyond Rebecca's reach at that very moment, and all she could do was nod and try to hold back the happy tears that threatened to escape. Finally she drew a deep breath and managed to whisper, "Yes."

Charlie slipped the ring on her finger. It settled firmly, as if it were a part of her hand. Then he gathered her close in his arms and they sat, holding one another, until the need for sleep overtook them.

FRIDAY, JANUARY 27, 1865

Mr. Cooper drove the big wagon behind the house and removed the tarp to show Charlie the lovely rosewood spinet piano in the back. Mrs. Cooper sat up on the box, waiting for the men to figure out how to move the heavy instrument.

It was unusual for Mr. Cooper to deliver anything personally; it was far more unusual for Mrs. Cooper to accompany him, but today she wanted to have a word with the General, and then assist Rebecca in the preparations for the wedding.

Charlie, Jocko, and Duncan, sweating in the cool air, carefully moved the piano and matching stool off the wagon and into the house. They stashed it in the musicians' alcove in the ballroom, from which they could move it into the front parlor quickly and relatively painlessly on the morning of the wedding.

Charlie then invited the Coopers to join him in his office for a cup of tea. Mr. Cooper declined, citing the need to return to his store. Mrs. Cooper accepted, after Charlie assured her one of his men would be happy to drive her home later.

"Mrs. Cooper, I do appreciate what you and your husband have done to get Rebecca's wedding present. I am sure that dealing with Mrs. Williams on my behalf was...challenging."

"Well, I am certain that Mrs. Williams would not have been so accommodating if she had known Mr. Cooper's plans. I am sure she will be irritated when she finds out." She sipped her tea then said, "General, I am glad we have this few minutes together. There are a few things I wanted to discuss with you privately."

"Of course, Ma'am, anything I can do to be of assistance to you or Mr. Cooper."

"Rebecca's mother was my closest friend. We were almost like sisters, and I have always held Rebecca in a very special place in my heart. So, with her mother gone, there is no one but me to speak with you as a mother would. I hope you do not take offense at the presumption."

Charlie smiled, then he sat up very straight in his chair, understanding what was about to happen. "No, of course not, Ma'am."

Mrs. Cooper paused for a moment and then began with a simple question. "What has Rebecca told you about her first marriage?"

"She has told me bits and pieces of her marriage to Mr. Gaines. Enough for me to surmise that she was treated very badly."

"She was treated very badly indeed. I personally believe he beat her, although she has never said anything directly."

Charlie nodded. "Yes, he did. She has confided that to me."

"I also believe he abused her... conjugally."

He swallowed hard, nodding, trying not to tear up at the thought. "I know from what she has said that he did. However, I am not sure Rebecca sees it for what it was."

Mrs. Cooper looked at him questioningly. "What do you mean, General?"

"I think Gaines had convinced her it was her duty and his right.

She knew he was wrong and he was hurting her, but I do not believe she equates it with what happen to Mrs. Adams, because Gaines was her lawful husband."

Mrs. Cooper looked at the man before her with some surprise. She knew the General was a sensitive man, but this perceptiveness was more than she had thought any man capable of. "Well, Sir, you seem to have a good grasp of what she has been through. In addition to being violent and controlling, he was unfaithful, and unfaithful in ways that were very insulting. Rebecca tolerated it in silence, but I could see how much it pained her."

"I hope you know I would never insult her in that way."

"General, may I be perfectly blunt with you?"

"Of course you may."

"I have never known a gentleman who did not stray at some point in his marriage. I just ask that you be discreet about it. Furthermore, Sir, if you ever hurt her like Gaines did, I will personally see to it that you are called to task. She is a sweet woman; she does not deserve that kind of treatment."

Charlie nodded. "I would hope so. I can see how much you care for her, and I am pleased she will have you to rely on when I am called back to service. But rest assured, when I return home I will be faithful to Rebecca as no man has ever been faithful to any woman before."

"I hope so, General, I truly hope so. I assume you have also heard the rumors that Rebecca is...unable to bear children?"

"Yes, but that does not concern me. As you know, Rebecca has decided to take in every waif that passes through Culpeper, and..." Charlie shifted, knowing now was the perfect time to fix this particular problem before more rumors got started. "You see, Ma'am, I was injured. I am afraid I cannot father children."

"Oh my, Sir. That is most unfortunate. If it is not too personal, may I ask how extensive the injury was? I mean, I know Rebecca is a passionate woman, and I..." She trailed off, embarrassed to ask the question that was floating just out of reach, past the boundary of her Southern propriety.

He blushed and ducked his head, eye contact was beyond him. "I assure you. I am capable of satisfying Miss Rebecca, just not fathering children."

Mrs. Cooper blushed, a rather becoming color on the older woman, and smiled. "I am sure you will extend yourself to the limits of your capabilities, Sir. I just do not want to see Rebecca hurt again."

Charlie could not help but smile. He gave Mrs. Cooper a little wink. "I give you my word, Ma'am, I will not hurt her."

Charlie escorted Mrs. Cooper upstairs. Entering the back parlor, he announced, "Darling, look who has come to help you through the day." Rebecca looked at Charlie and Mrs. Cooper with an odd lack of comprehension.

"What?"

"Honey, Mrs. Cooper has come to help you today." Rebecca was wandering around the room, aimlessly toying with the flowers, the carefully sorted dishes for the following day, the ribbons for the ballroom, and various other items that were carefully staged in the parlor for deployment the following morning. She rather reminded Charlie of a lost lamb, milling around looking for its ewe. He looked at Mrs. Cooper. "Perhaps, Ma'am, I should send a messenger to your husband asking him to join us here for the evening."

"Ah, yes, I suspect you are right. She looks a little... disoriented. Mr. Cooper and I can take her to our home to dress for the wedding in the morning. Thank you, General."

Rebecca looked up from a flower arrangement. "Hello, Charlie."

"Hello, darling." He went to her and gave her a soft hug and a kiss on the forehead. "Mrs. Cooper is here to see you, dear."

Rebecca looked from Charlie to the woman across the room.

"Hello, Grace." She looked back to Charlie. "We are getting married tomorrow."

"Yes, dearest, we are getting married tomorrow. At least, we are if you still want to." Charlie looked over at Mrs. Cooper, a silent plea in his eyes. He was starting to panic. Had the stress finally gotten to her? Had his beautiful, strong lady finally snapped? "Darling, are you all right? You seem so...distracted."

She looked at him, not fully understanding what he was saying, but understanding the look of concern on his face. "I am fine...really."

He was at a loss. She seemed totally removed from him, from the events going on around her, from the bustle of the day. "Are you sure, darling? I do not want our wedding to put you back in bed, as you were before Christmas."

"General, I think you will find that your bride is merely suffering from a severe case of nerves." Mrs. Cooper joined them and placed her arm around Rebecca's shoulder. "She will be fine. I will take care of her, and she will be at the church in the morning. You need not worry. Everything is fine."

"Perhaps I should take her up to her room? Maybe a nap and some quiet time together?"

Mrs. Cooper smiled. "General Redmond, I realize that over the last few months, you and Rebecca have had a rather unique situation as far as sleeping arrangements are concerned. But for today and tonight, I think it would be best if you made arrangements to sleep elsewhere." She gave him a protective and motherly smile.

He looked at her with his mouth hanging open. It had never occurred to him that he would have to observe that particular tradition. He and Rebecca had slept together every night since he had come to Culpeper, except for the few days he had spent in Washington. Spending the night on the chesterfield in his office was not exactly what he had planned for the night before the wedding. He had had visions of cuddling and wooing his lady. They evaporated with a snap before Mrs. Cooper's gentle but firm presence. To make matters worse, he had just invited her to spend the night, so she was there to enforce this token gesture to propriety.

"So, I assure you that Rebecca will be fine, General. Perhaps you should go enjoy your last night as a bachelor with a few of your men. If you are of a mind, I am sure Mr. Cooper would like to celebrate with you."

Meekly, Charlie acceded to her instructions. "Yes, Ma'am. I will see you at dinner, and will send a messenger now to inform your husband of your presence here tonight."

"Thank you, General."

Banished from the main part of the house, Charlie wandered down to his office. He summoned Duncan and asked him to send a messenger to Mr. Cooper. Then he walked through the stables to see Jack, who was far more interested in Shannon. He made a note to have Tarent mate them, as it was clear Shannon was coming into season. He then wandered through the camp, which was eerily quiet and seemingly deserted. Finally, he went back to the house and up to Em's room. Tess was keeping her in her room, playing with her quietly to keep her out of the way of the final day's preparations. Charlie sat on the floor, playing blocks with her, until it was time for supper.

That was not much better. Samantha Carter was running the house for the day, and had rustled up some cold ham and a pot of soup for supper. It was simple; it was easy for everyone to take what they wanted; and it meant Sarah could focus on the wedding banquet. Charlie fed Em and gave her to Tess for her bath, then wandered back to pick up something for himself. He was really hoping to see Rebecca.

Mrs. Cooper flashed into the morning room, gathering two plates. "How is Rebecca, Mrs. Cooper? Is she coming down for dinner?"

"No, General, she is resting in her room. I told you to go out with the other gentlemen. Now git."

Richard strolled up, overhearing Mrs. Cooper's side of the conversation. "Come on, Charlie. The boys and I will keep you occupied for the evening. You need to escape from this hive of feminine activity."

Having no other options available, Charlie followed Richard.

Richard nudged his friend. "Buck up, Charlie, it is only one night."

"That is fine for you to say, but..." Charlie could hear himself. "God, I am whining. Get me out of here."

"With pleasure."

Richard threw Charlie's greatcoat at him. "Come with me to the Officers' Mess. Surely we can find something to do down there."

As the two men strolled down to the encampment, they chatted about the order of tomorrow's events. The wedding was scheduled for three in the afternoon; then the guests were coming back to Redmond Stables for a festive banquet. Charlie and Rebecca would spend their first night as a married couple in their own bed, leaving on Monday for a week in Washington.

They arrived at the Officers' Mess to find the timbered tent alive with voices. Richard threw the door open and literally pushed Charlie through it.

There were more men in the tent than usual, and some of them were civilians. All of Charlie's senior officers were present, as well as Cooper and Frazier and a couple of other local men of Charlie's acquaintance. But there were also several unexpected gentlemen present. Sheridan, McCauley, and Merritt were over by a large punch bowl where Duncan presided. In the corner with Mayor Frazier sat a stubby man with three stars on his shoulders and a cloud of cigar smoke above his head. Charlie was overwhelmed.

It may have been his bachelor party, but Charlie's training took over spontaneously. He snapped to attention and saluted. "General Grant, Sir."

"Take the stick out of your arse, Redmond. This is your party." Grant grinned and went back to his conversation with Frazier, who he had met and befriended when he had used Culpeper as his own base of operations the previous spring.

Whitman handed Charlie a mug. He immediately took a large mouthful and nearly choked. He had expected coffee, perhaps laced with brandy. What he got was hot rum punch, and by the intensity, one made mostly of rum with only a nod to the other traditional ingredients.

The officers stood in response to Richard tapping on his mug. "Gentlemen, I give you our beloved friend and commander, General Charles H. Redmond. Charlie Redmond, the model soldier, 'til green eyes smiled and made his blood smolder. Now Charlie's a groom, Rebecca's in charge and together, we pray, they shall grow older. To Charlie and Rebecca."

The men duly drank the toast then pummeled Richard for his atrocious poetry.

The officers brought out their gift to Charlie, with Swallow, the senior officer of the company commanders, presenting it. "General, as much as we regret it, we understand that you intend to return to civilian life when this war is concluded. Therefore, we have decided that you need to learn to ride in something other than a cavalry saddle. So we got this for you." He unveiled a beautifully tooled hunt saddle that had the distinctive mark of Crosby Leatherworks. Charlie ran his hand over the butter soft leather. Young Dewees spoke up. "We tried it on Jack, Sir. Fits him like a glove." Charlie was deeply touched; he went to each man in his command with a word of appreciation.

Richard's toast had opened the door to a round of raucous toasts and jokes. The tale of Rebecca and Charlie in the stable, which had made the rounds of the camp very quickly, was resurrected and speculated upon. Charlie spent much of the evening blushing, but as his consumption of the rum punch continued, the blushes turned to the flushed face of a man who had had a little too much to drink.

As the midnight guard changed, General Grant decided it was time for this little party to break up, or risk the groom being useless the following day. He stood and cleared his throat. Of course, General Grant had helped himself liberally to Charlie's supply of brandy, and his words were none too clear; nor was he particularly steady on his feet. "Gen'lmen, 's been a fine evenin', but 'tis time to bid our grushing bloom—uh—blushing groom, good night." Grant stumbled over towards Charlie, where he promptly flopped on Charlie's shoulder. "Bed time, boys." Laughing, Sheridan and Merritt relieved Charlie of the unexpected burden of their commander.

Charlie pulled on his greatcoat and headed out the door, escorted by Richard. They trudged through the cold up to the house, where Charlie let himself in the front door. Richard, unexpectedly, followed him in. "What are you doing, Richard? I am perf'ly fine. I can find my own bed, thank you."

"Oh, really, General 'Totally In Control'? Then why are you headed upstairs?"

"Because that is where my bed is, of course."

"Not tonight, my friend. Tonight you sleep in your office."

"I have to go to Rebecca."

"Not tonight, laddio. Tonight you sleep alone. Jocko and I will collect you in the morning."

Richard steered Charlie down the back stairs to his office. Jocko had thoughtfully laid out blankets and a pillow on the old chesterfield sofa, pulled it in front of the fire, and banked a slow burning fire in the fireplace. Richard relieved Charlie of his overcoat and uniform coat, then pushed his friend into the sofa, and pulled his boots off.

Charlie realized that Richard was planning to put him into bed. His innate sense of survival helped him to pull himself together.

"Thanks, Richard, but I can handle the rest myself. I believe you also have a role to play tomorrow, old friend. So off to bed with you as well."

"If you are sure, Charlie." Richard grinned evilly. "Sleep well, because I am sure that you will need all your energies for tomorrow."

Charlie woke at dawn, as was his habit. A watery stream of sunlight was coming through the cracks in the curtains, hitting him right in the eyes. This was unfortunate, as he had more than a slight hangover. He struggled out of his covers, buttoned his rumpled, slept-in shirt, and half tucked it back into his trousers. In his stocking feet, he padded out into the hall and over to the winter kitchen, praying to all the gods there were that Sarah had a pot of coffee going.

Sarah and several other servants were bustling around the kitchen. Reg was setting up the clockwork spit that would rotate for several hours without being tended. Charlie stood in the door for several minutes watching them before anyone noticed his presence.

"La, General Charlie. What are you doing in the kitchen this early?" Sarah had turned and saw him standing there. She grabbed a mug and drew a cup of coffee from the urn she had set on the warming stove. "Well, Sir, are you going to just stand there, or come in and have your coffee?"

As she drew closer, she took in Charlie's disheveled appearance and the bloodshot look of his eyes. "Ah, I see. Had a good time last night, did you, Sir?"

Charlie nodded dumbly and took the coffee mug from her. He cradled it to his chest, willing it to cool enough for him to drink.

"You got a bit of a head there, Sir?"

He nodded carefully once again. Right now, any movement hurt.

"Well, Sir, come and sit at the table and I will fix you right up.

You know, my old master had a taste for the grape, and he swore by my cure. Or perhaps he swore at my cure. Whichever, it works."

Sarah continued to chat and bustle around as she prepared a concoction for Charlie's head. She broke two eggs into a tall glass, added some Worcestershire sauce, a touch of bottled hell, which was her own distillation of hot peppers, some sassafras root, some ground willow bark, some benne oil, and a shot of cooking brandy. She vigorously shook the miserable concoction, so that it was a viscous, brown mess and set it in front of Charlie. "Drink it down. I know it looks horrible, but it does the trick, General C."

The General looked at the mixture in the glass and almost lost whatever was in his stomach. However, he manfully closed his eyes, screwed up his face, and gulped down the contents of the glass. As soon as it was down, he grabbed for his coffee cup. He needed something, anything to wash that filthy taste out of his mouth.

Sarah set a glass of water in front of him. "Here. You need more fluid. Give it half an hour, and you will be right as rain."

He dutifully drank the water and thanked Sarah. He made a mental note to himself never to get drunk again if this was the only cure.

Charlie was feeling somewhat better an hour later when a small form, one who had recently learned how to turn a doorknob, burst into his office, wearing her night dress and dragging her doll behind her.

"Papa. Morning, Papa. Tess say you have bweakfas' here, so Em come hewe."

"Well, good morning, little one. I see that at least one of the women in this house remembered me." Charlie scooped the little girl up and set her on his lap. "So, how are you this morning?

"Em good. See Papa. Web say Em good." Em held up the doll that Charlie had brought her from Washington, who she had, after serious thought, named Reb, after Rebecca because she thought the doll looked like Mama 'Becca. Unfortunately, Em had not yet mastered the "r" sound.

"Papa, Em hungy."

"Let me go get us some breakfast, little one."

Charlie set the child on the sofa, admonishing her to not touch anything on Papa's desk and wandered over to the kitchen for a couple of bowls of hot cereal. Sarah ladled up two bowls of cornmeal mush and drizzled honey on them.

"Gen'l Charlie?" Reg came in lugging hot water buckets, having just finished filling Rebecca's bath.

"Yes, Reg?"

"When do you want your bath drawn? And do you want it in your office?"

"Well, I suppose it depends on when Miss Rebecca is leaving. I think I will bathe just after she leaves upstairs, if you can manage it."

"Yes, Sir. The washing room or your room?"

"My room, I think. That will leave the wash room open for other folks."

"Yes, Sir."

Charlie returned to his office, where he and Em had a quiet breakfast together. Tess came looking for the little girl shortly after she had finished eating. "General Charlie, I have been looking all over the house for this little imp. I went to her room to get her for breakfast, and she was gone."

Em looked abashed. She had gotten herself up and gone to her Papa. Tess would have fussed over her and made her put on clothes before she got her breakfast. Papa let her eat in her nightgown.

Jocko appeared shortly after Tess had swept Em away to bathe and dress the little scamp. Keeping the child clean until the wedding was going to be a challenge—she was having one of her playful days, when very little would stop her from doing what she wanted. Charlie had heard friends who had young children talk about the demands of a two year old being terrifying. Em was giving new meaning to that concept.

"Good morning, Charlie. I hear you needed Sarah's cure this morning."

He grunted and nodded. Sarah's cure was not high on his list of popular conversation topics for the day.

"Miss Rebecca left for Mrs. Cooper's house a few minutes ago."

He perked up immediately at the mention of her name. "How did she look? Was she rested? I was worried about her yesterday, she looked so...lost."

Jocko chuckled, "Yes, Charlie, she is fine. Very happy, almost giddy this morning as they packed up her dress and other things. She had a delightful blush on her cheeks."

Charlie sighed, relieved past words. He had a secret fear that she would decide that marrying a woman who passed as a man was just not what she wanted to do with her life and would leave him at the altar.

"So, now that she has gone to get ready, I can tend to my toilet?"

"You can. And I would suggest to you that you spend the morning lounging around in your most comfortable clothing."

"Oh? Why is that, oh seer of wedding days?"

"Because at about one o'clock, I will be coming over here to stuff you into your most formal dress uniform."

Charlie smiled. The formal dress uniform was one of those outfits that required him to wear his more unusual undergarments. "I see. Good thing I have been running lately?"

"Indeed. It is also a good thing that we have a large canister of talc to get you into those trousers."

Rebecca, Samantha, and Grace sat in the small kitchen of the house sipping tea while Rebecca tried to eat a few pieces of sweet bread to settle her stomach. Elizabeth came into the kitchen with a huge smile on her face.

"And how is our blushing bride this morning?"

"Nervous. Elizabeth you are a doctor, can you not give me something for my stomach? I am afraid I shall be sick before the day is over."

"I have two prescriptions for you. The first is this little vial—a simple tonic with raspberry and mint to settle your stomach without making you feel fuzzy. The second is for you to close your eyes and think of Charlie, of the look on his face as you walk down the aisle."

Rebecca could only smile like a schoolgirl. When she had done what Elizabeth suggested, she opened her eyes and looked to her friend. "Now is he not just the most handsome thing?"

Samantha and Grace started laughing, as Elizabeth commented wryly, "Well, dear, I suspect that depends on your taste in gentlemen. I do have to admit, Charlie is a handsome man."

"Yes, he is." She scratched her forehead as she tried to ease the headache coming on. "Why am I so blasted nervous? It is not like I have not done this before."

Grace leaned forward and patted her hand. "Perhaps, dear, that is exactly why you are so nervous. But you have to keep remembering the General is not Mr. Gaines; you chose the General."

"True. I suppose this is what a bride is supposed to feel on her wedding day."

Samantha looked askance. "I am not sure what a bride is supposed to feel. I was fortunate enough to have a husband I knew and loved before we married, so I remember feeling excited and joyous. But your first marriage was to a man you not only did not know well, but one you did not even like. I certainly understand why you may be feeling nervous. Just keep thinking about your Charlie. Put those old memories aside, and know that you will look back on this day as one of the best in your life."

"I remember on the day I married the first time, I spent most of the morning in tears. I was frightened and I wished for a way out.

But today I am just wishing for the day to go quickly so I can be with him." She looked to Elizabeth. "Have you seen him the morning? How is he?"

Elizabeth smiled. "I have seen neither him nor Richard. Perhaps Mrs. Cooper could enlighten us. I understand Mr. Cooper was in attendance last night."

Mrs. Cooper grinned evilly. "I do not know the details. All I know is, I came in this morning to find Mr. Cooper sound asleep in the pantry where we store the dry goods. I am not sure how he got there, I am not even sure I want to know how he got there. From the mumbling he was doing on his way upstairs, there was some mention of hot rum punch, a new saddle, and General Redmond's men dancing with a horse. I am still not sure I understand that."

Rebecca could not help but chuckle. "Dancing with a horse?"

"Well," drawled Elizabeth, "you know how cavalry men are about their horses."

Samantha chimed in. "I heard the servants saying something about Grant and brooms."

Rebecca just looked to Samantha and then to Elizabeth. "Grant? Brooms? What in the name of God did they do last night?"

Lizbet walked in at that moment. "Miss Rebecca? Time to do your hair. And I believe the menfolk had some kind of party last night. Gen'l Charlie needed Sarah's cure this morning."

"Oh Lord," Rebecca rolled her eyes. "I will be lucky if Charlie makes it to the church."

"Oh, I think that he would make it to the church if he were on his deathbed, dear. I have never seen that man so determined." Elizabeth smiled. The changes her old friend had undergone in the past months were astounding. They were all for the better, and all because of this diminutive blonde.

"I suppose it was Richard's idea to get my husband-to-be drunk? Richard is a bad influence on Charlie," Rebecca teased, realizing she was starting to feel much better.

"Well, as I heard it, it was everybody's idea to get your husband-to-be drunk." Grace Cooper grinned. "I sent him off to play yesterday, and I understand that both General Sheridan and General Grant came down on the supply train last night to assist in the festivities."

The ladies watched as all the blood drained from Rebecca's face. "General Grant? Is here?" That was all she managed to get out before she promptly fainted.

A few burnt feathers, a sniff of salts, and Rebecca rejoined the ladies. Lizbet took charge in her quiet way. "Miss Rebecca, I really need to start on your hair now."

Charlie finished dressing. His uniform was immaculate; the buckskin breeches were spotless, his boots gleamed, the cutaway tails of his dress coat were so thoroughly brushed that they looked more like beaver than wool. The brass on his jacket sparkled and the new fringed shoulder boards set off his new stars beautifully.

He walked out of the house to mount Jack, who had also been brushed until he glowed. Somehow, the big horse knew this was an important event, a time to be sedate and showy. He flicked his feet out with every step, prancing as if he were one of the dancing Lipizzaner horses from Europe.

Richard was waiting with the rest of Charlie's staff, dressed in their best uniforms, all spit and polish, to escort their commander to the church. Duncan, Raiford, and Jocko rode attendance, as well as Tarent and MacFarlane, who would tend the horses.

They rode on the grass to keep their immaculate clothing dust free, and proceeded to the church in good order.

They arrived at the church about forty-five minutes before three; plenty of time for Jocko to brush any last minute specks of dust from the uniforms and make sure each man's appearance was perfect. As the guests began arriving, the officers adjourned to serve as ushers. Charlie paced—non-stop—back and forth. Richard watched him with a bemused smile. Every five minutes, he would stop to ask Richard if he had the rings. Richard would fish in his vest pocket, pulled them out, show them to Charlie, and put them back. Charlie would go back to pacing.

They heard a small commotion and Sheridan came in to tell Charlie it was time to get ready; Rebecca had arrived.

Charlie turned to Richard. "Am I ready for..." There was clear panic in his eyes.

Richard grinned and took his friend by the arms. "Breathe, Charlie. You have been sleeping with her for months. She is not going to turn into a gorgon just because you say "I do." You love her; she loves you; the rest is just not important."

Sheridan looked at his very nervous officer. "Charlie?" The younger man looked wide-eyed and ready to either faint or bolt. "Remember, never lock your knees." Sheridan's practical advice brought a grin. Locked knees were an invitation to keel over when you had to stand for too long.

Charlie nodded, squared his shoulders, and walked to the back of the church. He strode confidently to the altar and took his position, with Richard at his shoulder. Both turned to look back toward the door. Mrs. Williams, her face drawn in a perfectly neutral mask after spending the morning helping to decorate the church, started the first chords of the bride's processional.

Rebecca tried not to show the nervousness she felt. She looked to Elizabeth. "Tell me again how everything is going to be fine."

Elizabeth stood so that only Rebecca could hear her, whispering in her ear. "You love her. She completes you. You need him. He will stand by you through anything. What could be bad about this?"

Rebecca nearly choked as she tried not to laugh. She looked to her friend with wide, amused eyes. "That was not nice."

"No, but it did get you out of your panic. Now, are you ready to go and marry your dashing General Redmond?"

Rebecca took a deep, calming breath and nodded as Mr. Cooper moved next to her and offered his arm. "You are beautiful, my dear."

Grace and Samantha slipped into the church and took their seats in the bride's family pew. Their entry was Mrs. William's cue. The first strains of the processional rang out as Rebecca and Mr. Cooper walked to the door, with Elizabeth following behind. They stepped slowly up the aisle, the very image of dignity.

Richard whispered to Charlie, "Close your mouth. You are gaping."

Rebecca could feel the tears welling in her eyes as she saw Charlie for the first time in his dress uniform. He had never looked more dignified and perfect than he did at that moment.

As she approached the altar, his eyes locked with hers. For Charlie, there was no one else in the world but Rebecca.

Reverend Williams cleared his throat to get their attention. They may have been besotted with one another, but this was a wedding, and he needed them to say the vows.

When they finally realized they were supposed to look at the minister and not at one another, the Reverend began. After a brief welcome, Williams pointed out that Rebecca and Charlie represented the possibilities for peace, for resolution of the discord that had taken so much from them, and the triumph of the power of love, even in times of great strife. Then the simple, beautiful words of the wedding service flowed from him.

"Dearly beloved, we are gathered together here in the sight of God, and in the face of this company, to join together this man and this woman in holy matrimony, which is an honorable estate, instituted of God, signifying unto us the mystical union that is betwixt Christ and his church: which holy estate Christ adorned and beautified with his presence and the first miracle that he wrought in Cana of Galilee, and is commended of Saint Paul to be honorable among all men: and therefore is not by any to be entered into unadvisedly or lightly; but reverently, discreetly, advisedly, soberly, and in the fear of God. Into this holy estate these two persons present come now to be joined. If any man can show just cause, why they may not lawfully be joined together, let him now speak, or else hereafter forever hold his peace."

Reverend Williams waited the long pause that traditionally was allowed for anyone who wished to object to speak up. Charlie felt a bead of sweat slide down his temple; his ingrained fear of disclosure once more raised its head and the little voice taunted him. *What if someone comes forward and tells them what you really are. It would serve you right.*

Rebecca looked into his eyes, trying to put all of her love and faith in him and in them into her expression. *All is well my love. We are going to be together forever.* She took a deep breath and focused on the silence around them. *If Mrs. Williams opens her mouth, I will slap her silly.*

But no one objected, and Reverend Williams continued.

"I require and charge you both, as ye will answer at the dreadful day of judgment when the secrets of all hearts shall be disclosed, that if either of you know any impediment, why ye may not be lawfully joined together in matrimony, ye do now confess it. For be ye well assured, that if any persons are joined together other than as God's word doth allow, their marriage is not lawful."

If he knew, he would end this. If any of them knew, they would end it. You are no man, Charlie, and the church does not sanction marriage between two women. Charlie stood silent, defiant to his little voice and proud. In all ways, for most of his life, Charlie had been a man. He loved Rebecca as a man loves a woman.

Rebecca smiled at him, trying to reassure him with the devotion in her eyes.

"Charles, wilt thou have this woman to thy wedded wife, to live together after God's ordinance in the holy estate of matrimony? Wilt thou love her, comfort her, honor, and keep her in sickness and in health; and, forsaking all others, keep thee only unto her, so long as ye both shall live?"

Charlie swallowed hard, then answered clearly, "I will."

"Rebecca, wilt thou have this man to thy wedded husband, to

live together after God's ordinance in the holy estate of matrimony? Wilt thou love him, comfort him, honor, obey and keep him in sickness and in health; and, forsaking all others, keep thee only unto him, so long as ye both shall live?"

Rebecca nodded. The slight giggles from the front row made her realize she needed to speak her answer. "I will," she managed to get out quietly.

"Who giveth this woman to be married to this man?"

Mr. Cooper stepped up and declared clearly, "In the name of her dear, departed father, I do." With that, Mr. Cooper took Rebecca's right hand and lifted it.

Reverend Williams took her hand from Mr. Cooper and laid it in Charlie's right hand, laying his own hand over their joined fingers in blessing. He turned to Charlie and said, "Repeat after me.

"I, Charles, take thee Rebecca, to be my wedded wife and with all my worldly goods do thee endow, to have and to hold from this day forward, for better for worse, for richer for poorer, in sickness and in health, to love and to cherish, 'til death us do part, according to God's holy ordinance; and thereto I plight thee my troth." Charlie declared his oath in firm, ringing tones.

Charlie loosened his grip on Rebecca's hand; she then cradled his large hand in her own for her vows.

"I, Rebecca, take thee Charles, to be my wedded husband and with all my worldly goods do thee endow, to have and to hold from this day forward, for better for worse, for richer for poorer, in sickness and in health, to love and to cherish, 'til death us do part, according to God's holy ordinance; and thereto I give thee my troth." With each phrase, Rebecca's voice grew stronger and clearer, until her last line rang through the church.

Reverend Williams then asked, "Where are the rings?" as he looked expectantly at Richard. Richard fumbled slightly as he drew the two rings from his vest pocket and laid Rebecca's gently in the center of the prayer book that the Reverend was holding. The Reverend blessed the ring, saying, "Bless, O Lord, this ring, that he who gives it and she who wears it may abide in thy peace, and continue in thy favor, unto their life's end; through Jesus Christ our Lord. Amen." He turned to Charlie and said, "Take this ring and place it on Rebecca's finger, saying the following words: 'With this ring I thee wed: in the name of the Father, and of the Son, and of the Holy Ghost. Amen.'"

Charlie took the ring and very gently placed it on Rebecca's hand. With this action, he was claiming Rebecca as his very own. His voice was husky with emotion as he declared his vow to her.

Richard offered the second ring, an action that was not common but gaining more acceptance in recent years. Reverend Williams blessed the ring for Charlie.

Rebecca took the ring with a very shaky hand, afraid for a brief second she would drop it. She licked her lips as she slid the ring on Charlie's finger and repeated the words she barely heard. She was far too busy smiling at Charlie.

Reverend Williams' voice broke into the moment. "Let us pray."

The entire congregation stood and repeated the Lord's Prayer; all except Charlie and Rebecca, who were too busy looking at one another to be aware of what anyone else was doing.

Reverend Williams added the benediction for married couples. "O Eternal God, creator and preserver of all mankind, giver of all spiritual grace, the author of everlasting life; send thy blessings upon these thy servants, Charles and Rebecca, whom we bless in thy name; that they, living faithfully together, may surely perform and keep the vow and covenant betwixt them made, whereof these rings given and received are a token and pledge, and may ever remain in perfect love and peace together, and live according to thy laws; through Jesus Christ our Lord. Amen."

He joined their right hands together again and said, "Those whom God hath joined together, let no man put asunder."

Charlie felt a great weight lift from his soul. The wedding was over; no matter what, Rebecca was his wife.

Rebecca could not help herself as she let the tears slip down her cheeks, she was so happy to finally be Charlie's wife.

The Reverend continued: "For as much as Charles and Rebecca have consented together in holy wedlock, and have witnessed the same before God and this company, and thereto have given and pledged their troth, each to the other, and have declared the same by giving and receiving rings, and by joining hands; I pronounce that they are man and wife, in the name of the Father, and of the Son, and of the Holy Ghost. Amen."

The two of them knelt for the final blessing.

"God the Father, God the Son, God the Holy Ghost, bless, preserve, and keep you; the Lord mercifully with his favor look upon you, and fill you with all spiritual benediction and grace; that ye may so live together in this life, that in the world to come ye may have life everlasting. Amen.

"By the powers vested in me by the Commonwealth of Virginia, I declare you man and wife. Charles, you may kiss the bride."

Charlie took her in his arms and slowly, reverently lowered his lips to hers. It was a kiss like a symphony; it began slowly and tenderly and ended with all of the reverence and love Charlie knew how to express.

Before Rebecca could think clearly enough to breathe, a tiny familiar voice rang through the church, "Papa!"

Elizabeth lunged to stop the little imp who had managed to escape from Tess and was making a very determined beeline for her Papa's legs. She failed.

Charlie had no choice but to tear his attention from Rebecca in order to catch the little girl who was flinging herself at him with abandon. Rebecca could only smile as Charlie scooped her up; she took his arm as the three of them turned to face the assembled guests.

Reverend Williams could not resist the impulse, "Ladies and gentlemen! May I present General and Mrs. Redmond—and Emily." The applause was mixed with laughter as the congregation greeted the new couple and the child whom all knew would soon be legally theirs.

The kitchen was a scene of organized chaos. Sarah had recruited several of her family members to assist in the cooking. Reg had taken charge of the wine room. Duncan had organized a group of volunteers to act as servers. The wedding party was due any minute, and Duncan and Reg were organizing glasses and bottles of champagne to greet them.

The guests started arriving, pulling their carriages, wagons, traps, and mounts into the front yard, where men under Tarent's supervision took charge of them. They then assembled on the front portico, waiting for Charlie and Rebecca to arrive before they entered the house.

Finally, Shannon came prancing into the yard, drawing Rebecca's small trap, which was decked in blue and ivory ribbons. Charlie was driving; Rebecca was holding young Em. All three were smiling and laughing, evidently at something Em had said.

Charlie drew the small carriage to the front door. He took young Em and handed her down to a waiting Tess, then got down himself. He walked around and gently lifted Rebecca from the carriage. Instead of putting her down, he simply walked to the front door and carried her over the stoop, to the applause of the guests crowding into the house behind them.

When Charlie finally settled Rebecca back on her own feet, she wrapped her arms around his neck and kissed him on the cheek. "Welcome home, General Redmond."

"Welcome home to you, Mrs. Redmond. Shall we stand here and cuddle, or shall we greet our guests?"

She sighed. "I would rather cuddle, but I suppose we should be civilized and greet our guests."

"I could just sweep you off your feet and carry you upstairs. We could leave Richard and Elizabeth to cope with the rest of it."

She laughed and whispered in his ear, "I dare you."

Charlie made as if to lift her back into his arms. "You know better than to dare me, darling. And I missed you so much last night."

"Well, are you going to stand here and talk about it all day?"

Charlie, in quite a mood himself, decided that this teasing was too tempting, and, sweeping her up in his arms, he started moving determinedly toward the stairs. As he passed Richard, he whispered, "Handle the guests for me for a while, will you?"

"Oh. And... what should I..." He stopped and shook his head. "Never mind, I will think of something."

As Charlie carried Rebecca up the stairs, the assembled guests broke out into gales of laughter. Richard stepped to the foot of the stairs. "It seems our hosts have urgent...affairs to tend to, so until their return, please enjoy yourselves."

Duncan and his group of volunteers had been standing at the door, handing out glasses of champagne as the guests filed in. When Charlie reached the top of the stairs and stopped for a moment to put Rebecca down on her feet, Richard raised a glass. "To the Redmonds." The entire company joined him, still laughing.

Charlie, a little breathless, just grinned and tossed a casual salute.

Rebecca gave an embarrassed little wave and took her husband's arm. "You are a bad man, Charlie Redmond," she teased as they walked down the hall.

He opened the door to their rooms and ushered her in. "I am being no worse than usual, dear. And I do have experience as your lady's maid. I thought you might like to change into something more comfortable. I seem to remember some lovely green velvet that I suspect is no longer a bolt of fabric. I also thought you might like this." He stepped up and took her in his arms, laying her back a bit and kissing her thoroughly.

When Charlie let her up, she took a deep breath, a rather silly smile etched on her face. "Yes, yes, I suppose I could change." She breathed deeply again, trying to calm her racing pulse.

He began undoing the many little buttons on the back of her

bodice. "Of course, we could take a little rest before we go down to our guests. Just a few minutes together, on that nice, soft bed?"

"Charlie, if we lie down on that bed, we will not get back up before tomorrow. Now, do you want to have to explain this to all our guests, who I might remind you include Generals Sheridan and Grant?"

Charlie sighed a large, dejected sigh. "No, I suppose you are right." As he continued to undo the various buttons and ties of her dress, he peppered her shoulders with little kisses. "I just... I just want ..."

Rebecca shivered and moaned quietly as her knees went weak and her stomach dropped. "Charlie...be good."

"Oh, all right, my dear, as long as you promise that I do not have to be good tonight."

"I do not expect that either one of us will be good tonight."

Charlie grinned at that comment, then set to work helping Rebecca remove her wedding dress and don a more comfortable party dress. The sooner they got back to the guests, the sooner they could bid them good night.

The guests were cheerfully drinking Charlie's champagne and munching on little delicacies that were being handed around by the troopers turned waiters. Most were happy and amused by the antics of their hosts, willing to wait until Charlie and Rebecca returned before they began the serious celebrating. A small cluster of ladies, centered on Mrs. Williams, were busy noting every flaw, every occurrence that strayed from Southern tradition, every ineptitude of the troopers as waiters. The lovely Misses Reynolds and Simms were part of the crowd. It rankled that Rebecca Gaines had captured such an eligible bachelor, particularly since she had already proven she could not give the distinguished General any heirs.

Elizabeth stood quietly listening to them carry on until she simply could not take it any longer. She finally stepped into the middle of the group, turning slowly and managing to give each one of them a pointed look. "All right. I have had quite enough. From the moment I met all of you, all you have done is continually harp on Rebecca and Charlie. You do not like the fact that they have found each other in this disturbing time, and you are miffed that Charlie would rather have an educated and talented lady on his arm than whiney young girls who have no clue what it means to be a woman. And you," she turned to Mrs. Williams, "you hateful, spiteful creature. If you are so taken aback by all of this, then why do you not ride your high horse right out of here? These two people are my dear friends. They are kind, loving, charitable, good Christians. I will not brook anymore of your sniping on what should be the happiest day of their lives."

As Elizabeth took the hen fest to task, Richard watched with raised eyebrows, pursing his lips to keep from grinning outright. *My, my, she is a feisty one. If only she could see her way...* Richard shook his head slightly. He had not found the same courage that Charlie had. Perhaps before they left for the spring, he would ask her. Smoothly, he inserted himself at Elizabeth's elbow. "Excuse me, my dear, but General Sheridan is asking for you."

Elizabeth looked at Richard and started to argue, but she could see by the look in his eyes that she should just be quiet and leave gracefully. "Yes, Richard, of course."

She looked back at the women she had just scolded. Mrs. Williams was an interesting shade of red, while some of the younger women had the grace to look abashed. "Excuse me, ladies, but duty calls." The acid behind the words was unmistakable.

Richard, in the interest of veracity, escorted Elizabeth over to the corner where Sheridan and Grant were chatting; the Generals had watched the little contretemps with interested amusement. Grant spoke up first. "Ah, Doctor Walker, lovely day, lovely wedding. By the way, in the future, may I call on you to admonish my troops when they get out of hand?"

At that point Elizabeth had the good grace to blush.

"Oh, no, General. You cannot have her. She is my secret weapon in keeping my troops motivated in the field—and not just because of her lovely appearance or her skill as a physician." Phil Sheridan was grinning ear to ear. "By the way, Polk, when are you going to step up to the line with the good doctor?"

Richard choked on the champagne he had taken into his mouth before Sheridan had posed that question. Elizabeth managed to give him a gentle pat on the back. "Actually, Philip, I am not sure Richard is the marrying type. I think he is married to the Army."

Richard blushed, a rare sight on his usually relaxed and self-confident visage. "I am not sure of that, Sir, but I suspect that Dr. Walker is married to her profession." In that moment, Richard found a certain courage, as he turned to Elizabeth. "Nevertheless, I would be overjoyed to join you in supporting that commitment, if you will have me."

Elizabeth did not have an opportunity to answer before several things happened at once. Richard realized what he said, and looked as if he wanted to bolt. General Grant, completely amused by the junior officer's inopportune proposal, allowed himself a loud laugh. Rebecca and Charlie entered the room, drawing all the attention to them; and Em piped up for her Papa.

Sheridan leaned forward and whispered in Richard's ear, "You know I will hold you to that, even if she does not." Richard gulped and nodded.

Rebecca and Charlie stopped halfway down the stairs, as the guests turned and again applauded the newlyweds. Rebecca, in her blue and ivory wedding dress, had been radiant. In the green velvet and lace ball gown, she was absolutely alluring. The look on Charlie's face, a mixture of pride and joy, was an image that burned itself into everyone's memory. The moment was broken by a small voice piping, "Papa, Mama 'Becca, Em hungry."

Charlie caught Duncan's eye and nodded. As the doors to the dining room were thrown open, he announced, "Ladies and gentlemen, dinner is ready. Please, join us." He scooped Em up in his arms and escorted Rebecca into the room, followed by Richard and Elizabeth as their best man and maid of honor. The other guests filed in as well. Between tables in the dining room and the large reception hall, there was seating for all sixty plus guests.

The flurry of formal actions gave Elizabeth a moment to regain her composure, as well as a bit of privacy with Richard in the midst of the crowd. "Did you mean what you said?"

"Umm...well..." He straightened up, took her hands in his, and bestowed his best and brightest smile on her. "Absolutely, my dear. Absolutely. Whenever you are ready and are willing to have me."

Elizabeth bit her lip. Richard was always charming and courtly. She had come to rely on his steady presence and support more than she liked to admit. But intensely personal emotions were something Richard had trouble expressing. *Do I love him? Yes, I think I do. Will I marry him? I think we will need to talk about that.* She smiled tenderly, knowing full well what that proposal had cost her friend. "Thank you, Richard. Can we discuss this in a more private setting?"

"Of course, my dear. Whenever you are ready."

With that, they were seated; and the meal that Sarah and her aides had labored over for so long was served. It was a jovial meal, laced with laughter, good food, good wine, and more than a little teasing. In the midst of so many people, Em glued herself to Charlie and would not let go, so he found himself with his hands full indeed. Two women to attend to, two women who loved him, each in their own way. Much of the teasing he got that day was about starting his family early.

With stomachs replete, Charlie invited the guests to join them in the ballroom, where the musicians of the regiment had formed their band, this time with a piano player to round out their melodies. Charlie had planned to let the strains of the piano playing the first dance, a waltz, announce his wedding gift to Rebecca. The two took their place at the center of the ballroom, waiting for the first notes.

Rebecca looked at Charlie as the music started, then turned her head to make sure of what she was hearing. When she saw the piano, tears formed in her eyes as she looked back to her husband. "How did you find it?"

"Mr. Cooper had kept track of it, and we managed to get it back."

At the same time, Mrs. Williams heard the notes from the spinet. Again, her face reddened. Under her breath she muttered, "Why, Edward Cooper, you will pay for this."

Rebecca caressed Charlie's cheek and bestowed upon him a very sincere and intimate kiss, not caring that everyone they knew was surrounding them. "Thank you," she whispered as she gazed at him again. "I love you, Charlie."

"I love you, Rebecca. Now, dance with me, wife, or I will have to embarrass you in front of all of these people." Charlie was already eager for Rebecca's touch. Her kisses just made waiting that much more difficult. He was feeling rather like a cat in heat.

"As you wish, husband." And with that, she let him lead her around the dance floor.

The second dance began with Mr. Cooper, representing Rebecca's father, and Mrs. Cooper, in place of her mother, dancing with Rebecca and Charlie, respectively. As their dance progressed, the officers and gentlemen of the community solicited the hands of the various ladies present. Richard found himself holding Elizabeth in his arms, a pleasure he always anticipated. Mrs. Williams was stiffly dancing with her husband, who proceeded to use the intimacy of the dance to scold his wife.

"Now you listen to me, Margaret Williams, it is time for you to stop being cruel to General and Mrs. Redmond. They are good people, they have done much for this community, and people are talking about how you are acting towards them. It is shameful. And from this moment on it will stop."

"James, it is impossible. How can you expect me to welcome this... Yankee riffraff into our community? He represents everything our glorious sons of the South have fought against. He and those like him have destroyed our Virginian culture, our lands, our youth, and our future. How dare you ask me to accept him and his like?"

"I am not asking you, Mrs. Williams, I am telling you. As your minister and your husband, I expect you to listen to me and stop this nonsense."

It was unheard of for the Reverend James Williams to command his wife, and she did not take it well. How dare he do such a thing to her, embarrass her publicly, and demand she accept the interloper? She was so angry with Rebecca for accepting this—enemy—into their community, and with her husband for ordering her around as he had never done before, that she was sputtering. "James —"

"Margaret, there is no room for argument here. You will cease your public condemnation of Charlie and Rebecca. You may feel how you will in private, because I cannot change that, but I am demanding that you stop speaking out against them in the community."

The intractability of the Reverend's dictum finally penetrated Mrs. Williams' stubborn skull. She had crossed the line one too many times, and her husband had more backbone than she thought. "Yes, husband."

The dancing continued until it was time for the cake and the toasts. Charlie had been anticipating this moment eagerly, as it signaled the time when he could take Rebecca off to their room. Richard had been dreading it, for it was up to him to deliver the first toast.

Duncan and Raiford carried in the wedding cake, while other troopers served more champagne. Charlie and Rebecca stepped behind the cake, while Richard stood before them with a raised glass.

Richard grinned. Charlie looked concerned, having a vague memory of the toast at his party the previous night. "Today," Richard began slowly, looking at Charlie, "I lost my position as the first person my best friend turns to when things are difficult. He has found a lovely lady with whom he will spend his life, and I am exceptionally happy for him. I hope that Miss Rebecca finds him to be not only a wonderful husband, but also the best friend she has ever had. To Charlie and Rebecca Redmond, may they only know happiness for a very long time to come."

"Charlie and Rebecca!" rang through the room as the guests joined Richard in his good wishes.

General Grant stepped forward. A normally retiring, soft-spoken man, those at the farthest corners of the ballroom had to strain to hear him.

"Just about eighteen years ago, when I was a second lieutenant serving in Mexico under Zachary Taylor, I had the honor of serving with a young captain from Virginia, Robert Lee, though under separate commands. During the horrors of the Battle of Buena Vista, Captain Lee and I had observed the valor and skill of a young recruit who rose to command with a field promotion to second lieutenant. Both of us endorsed this young man to our commanders as true officer material. Over the years, we watched Charlie Redmond rise through the ranks, always the model of a soldier and a gentleman. I, for one, never thought he would find a place in the world outside of the Army. It gives me great joy to be here at his wedding. I am just sorry my wife could not join us in wishing you, Charlie and Rebecca, all of the best. We will be sorry to lose you from the Army when this war is over, but I can tell you folks of Culpeper, and I think Charlie's old friend General Lee would agree, you are getting one of the Army's best."

To hear Grant, who to Mrs. Williams was the devil incarnate, speak of that man's friendship with the hallowed General Lee was incredible. The woman was overwhelmed: first, her husband had chastised her publicly, and now she discovered that the abominable Redmond was a friend of General Lee. It was too much. She fainted dead away, creating quite a stir in the room.

Charlie looked over at the woman with a raised eyebrow. "Looks like she finally exceeded her limit."

CHAPTER 27

SATURDAY, JANUARY 28, 1865

Much to Charlie's relief, Tess took Em up to bed before the dancing began. The party progressed with much gaiety and no more major scenes. Mrs. Williams spent the last part of the evening reclining in one of the small sitting rooms, supported by an elderly cousin. Richard had been hard pressed to relieve Elizabeth of her vial of pepper oil and replace it with smelling salts when reviving the offensive woman. Reverend Williams remained downstairs for the rest of the toasts and the cake. Following tradition, Rebecca tossed her bouquet from the top of the stairs. Her aim had been good; Elizabeth was hit squarely in the chest.

With that traditional closing to the wedding party, the local guests left in varying degrees of sobriety. Finally, Charlie and Rebecca escaped the wedding party. Charlie stood regarding his bride, who was still flushed with the excitement of the last few minutes of the evening.

"You know, darling, marriage seems to be bringing out the imp in you. You certainly managed to embarrass our dear friend the doctor this evening. Did you know that Richard asked her to marry him tonight?"

"Elizabeth made a comment about it. She is very nervous."

"You think she is nervous? Richard may have left bruises on my arm from hammering on it as he told me. It was actually funny. He kept saying, 'My God, Charlie, do you know what I have done? I really did it—right in front of Sheridan and Grant. If I do not follow through, Sheridan will have my ass for breakfast, I think.' The babble level was amazing."

"Oh yes. Elizabeth certainly did not expect him to propose tonight." Rebecca made small talk as she prepared for bed. She turned to him, offering him the buttons of her dress. "Would you, please?"

His hands were shaking. They had slept together every night for several months. They had made love frequently after his return from Washington and that first fantastic night. But tonight was different. Tonight he was going to claim her as his own, his wife, his love, his future. Carefully, he began unbuttoning her bodice. The soft skin at the back of her neck was too tempting; he leaned down and tenderly kissed her shoulder.

"Charlie, if you finish the buttons, I can get out of this dress," she reminded him, even as her hand went back and caressed his cheek.

He tore himself from the tender skin and turned more of his attention to her dress. This night of all nights, he was enjoying being her lady's maid. He had had more than enough of waiting, of being with other people. He just wanted to be with her. The bodice came off, and Charlie untied the laces of her full skirts, letting them pool at her feet. She stood before him, wearing her pantaloons, chemise, and jewelry. He turned her to face him. "You are beautiful, my wife."

She reached out for the buttons of his vest. "And you are overdressed."

"That can be remedied. Which side of me do you want tonight, darling? The man or the woman?"

"I just want you, Charlie, all of you. Tonight is our night to explore and learn."

Charlie shed his sword belt and sash, then his coat and then unbuttoned his vest. Slowly, teasingly, as if he were performing a dance, he eased his cravat off and began unbuttoning his shirt. Soon he was standing before her in boots, breeches, and open shirt, with the bindings showing through the placket. It was a halfway point in his mind, presenting Rebecca with both the male and female aspects of who he was.

Rebecca approached slowly. She pulled Charlie's shirt from his trousers and slipped it from his shoulders. As the shirt dropped to the floor, Rebecca wrapped her arms around Charlie and started working the bindings free. "I love you, my handsome gentleman." When the bindings fell the way of the shirt, she continued, "and I adore you, my beautiful woman." She then began working the clasp on the trousers, all the time leaving soft kisses on Charlie's shoulders and collarbone.

Charlie ran her hands under Rebecca's chemise and slowly slid it up her body. Rebecca briefly broke off her attentions to her to let her lift it over her head.

Rebecca smiled at her. "I think we should go to bed." She slowly stepped out of her shoes as her hands went to her hair, removing a few pins and letting it drop around her shoulders. She turned her back on Charlie, removed her necklace and then, very languorously, she pushed her pantaloons to the floor, making sure to bend over slowly as she did so.

Charlie stopped breathing. This beautiful woman wanted her, desired her, and was clearly seducing her, offering Charlie everything she had ever dreamed of. Softly, Charlie caressed Rebecca's back, running her fingertips down the strong muscles on either side of her spine, over the firm globes and down the backs of her thighs, as if reading her own future with the touch.

Rebecca turned around, smiling shyly, holding her hands in a position of false modesty. After all, they had already made love several times, and she was not sure there was anything left undone between them. But she wanted to give Charlie the image of the nervous bride.

Charlie tipped her wife's face up to look into her eyes, and tenderly kissed her. Slowly, thoroughly, she made it clear to Rebecca that this night was going to be devoted to sensual love. As the kiss continued, Charlie's hands slid back and tangled in Rebecca's long, blonde locks. They were both breathing hard when the kiss ended. Charlie swept Rebecca up in her arms and carried her to the bed, laying her down on the soft cotton sheets, then stepping away to finish undressing herself. As she pulled her boots and breeches off, she wondered how Rebecca would respond to what she had planned for the evening.

Rebecca was presenting the image of a nervous bride, but Charlie really was one. Rebecca had asked for both the man and the woman. Earlier in the day, Charlie had taken Lizzie's gift, and cleaned and oiled the leather. It was in the drawer of the bedside table, ready for use.

"Charlie, come to bed. Come to me. Please."

Charlie turned, and walked toward the bed. Her movements were feline; her eyes were hooded with desire. As she slid into bed beside Rebecca, she whispered, "I love you, my darling wife."

"And I love you," she paused and grinned, "wife."

"Wife?" Charlie pulled back to look into Rebecca's laughing eyes. "You really do like it that under all the trappings, I am a woman?"

"Yes." She traced her fingers slowly, gently over Charlie's arm. "I love it. With you, here, like this, there is only love and tenderness. It is wonderful, something I have never experienced before. You gave me this gift, Charlie. There is no way I could love or trust another man. Not after what Gaines did to me. You, my love, are perfect, everything I need and desire."

Charlie propped herself over Rebecca, looking deep into her eyes to gauge the truth of what she had just heard. There in Rebecca's eyes, she found nothing but honesty and love. It was a blessing. Then Rebecca twined her hands behind Charlie's neck and pulled her down into another heated kiss.

~

Sunday, January 29, 1865

Rebecca rolled over and curled into Charlie's body. She hummed, still delightfully sated from the previous evening. She smiled as her hand rubbed over Charlie's stomach and up her chest. "Good morning, my love."

Charlie stretched like a big, happy cat and literally purred before she found her voice. "Good morning, darling wife."

She continued to run her hand over Charlie's warm skin. "So, would we be horrible people if we did not attend services today?"

"Probably. Likely Mrs. Williams would say things like 'Oh, Lord, he has taken her away to have his evil Yankee way with her. Poor Rebecca. I always said she should stay away from that damned Yankee.'"

Rebecca burst out laughing so hard the bed actually shook. "Oh, if she only knew the truth, she would explode on the spot." Then she rolled over and covered Charlie's body with her own. "I am very fond of your evil Yankee ways."

Charlie stroked her hands down Rebecca's bare back and bottom. "And I love your sultry Southern ways, my love." She raised her head and nipped at Rebecca's shoulder.

"Hmmm." Rebecca's body was responding to Charlie's touch in the most carnal of ways and she knew if she did not get up soon, they would indeed miss services. "All right, Charlie, I am going to be good and get up now."

Charlie drew in a deep breath and sighed. "Yes, I suppose. We should be good. We should be appropriate. We should take Em to church." As she spoke, she continued to stroke Rebecca's back, and then reached farther down to cup her bottom in both hands and pulled her close.

"Oooo bad, Charlie!" Rebecca giggled like a schoolgirl and got up from the bed. "Now be good!"

"Oh, all right. I will be. Shortly." She captured Rebecca by the back of the head and pulled her down for a resounding kiss.

Rebecca let herself get lost in that wonderful kiss and was almost ready to get back into bed and say to the devil with the services, when her conscience got the better of her. "Oh, Charlie, please be good and get up. Please?"

An insistent tapping at the door, accompanied by an obvious effort to turn the latch, over which Charlie had looped the stop, interrupted their conversation. "Well, it seems that the outside world wants in, so I suppose we must rejoin civilization."

"Papa." The tapping grew more like pounding. "Papa." The doorknob rattled, accompanied by an outright, very insistent wail, "Papa!"

Charlie and Rebecca looked at one another, resignation mixed with humor on both of their faces. Rebecca capitulated first. "Yes, I suppose we must."

Rebecca tossed her sleeping gown and her robe on and went to the door, waiting with her hand on the knob until Charlie was properly presentable in full "Papa" mode. When she opened the door, Em stood there, looking at her for a moment.

"Mow'in' Mama 'Becca." The child stretched her arms out for a hug, which Rebecca was more than happy to give her.

"Good morning, Miss Emily." Charlie and Rebecca had been teaching Em her basic manners and the child beamed when Rebecca rewarded her efforts with a smile and a formal greeting.

"Papa?"

Rebecca pointed at Charlie who was now sitting on the bed putting on his slippers. "Your Papa is there."

Em smiled and ran into the room, straight to Charlie.

"Good morning, imp." He picked the child up and gave her a bear hug, a kiss, and a tickle. "So, what are you doing here in your nightgown? Have you gotten away from Tess again?"

The question was answered not by Em, but by Tess, who stopped in front of the door and placed her hands on her hips. "There you are, Miss Emily. Now come to Tess and let us get you dressed."

"Go on, little one. It is church day, and you must look your best. You know, when you look pretty and are a good girl, people think that Mama, Mama 'Becca and I are being good parents to you."

"Yes, Papa." Little Emily was learning very quickly that when Papa and Mama 'Becca told her something was to be done; it was best to be a good girl and do it. She slid off his lap and went to Tess. She took the hand Tess stretched out to her and, flashing a big grin over her shoulder to her Papa and Mama 'Becca, trudged off to do their bidding.

With Tess off to tend to Emily's morning toilet, Charlie and Rebecca turned to their own morning rituals. Somehow, they managed to get in one another's way under the guise of "helping," so they were both very late in getting down for breakfast. Elizabeth, Richard, Samantha, Jeremiah, and Em were waiting for them. "So," Elizabeth drawled, "did you sleep well?"

Rebecca blushed and said the first thing that came to mind. "Eventually."

The adults at the table burst into laughter, while Jeremiah tried to figure out what they were laughing about and joined in a moment later. He did not know why, but it was a grown-up thing to do, so he did.

Rebecca and Charlie ate a hasty breakfast, and then joined the others for the short trip to church. They arrived just as Reverend Williams was preparing to enter and begin the service, so they hurriedly made their way to their pew and settled in.

The service went by in a haze for Charlie and Rebecca. They were too busy trying not to grin like idiots. Their restless desire to return home conveyed itself to Em, who spent most of the service trying to decipher the hymnbook, page by upside down page.

As usual, when the Reverend was finished with the service, he moved to the door to greet each member of the congregation as they filed out. This day, he chose to escort his wife to the door with him, having Miss Simms take over the small organ to play the recessional.

Rebecca held Em close to her as she and Charlie made their way to the door. She watched with some amount of amused satisfaction as Reverend Williams gave his wife a gentle nudge in the ribs to speak with Charlie.

She tried not to hiss as she grudgingly offered, "Good morning, General."

"Good morning to you, Mrs. Williams. Is it not a lovely morning, dear lady?"

Rebecca had to bite her lip to keep from laughing as Charlie did everything he could to add to the woman's misery.

"Yes, a beautiful morning. Spring will be here soon." Unspoken, Mrs. Williams obviously added *and you will be gone, at least for a while.*

"Yes, indeed. I am so looking forward to returning and making Redmond Stables a fine horse farm. General Grant does not believe the spring campaign will last very long, so I should be home before you even know I am gone."

Rebecca looked to the Reverend, who himself was hiding a grin behind his hand.

After services, Sarah fixed a simple lunch, which Rebecca, Charlie, and Em intended to share with Constance. Elizabeth assured them that Constance was feeling well enough for visitors, and would no doubt enjoy the company.

Charlie, knocked on the door softly, just in case the woman was resting, but pushed it open the moment she called for them to enter.

Em was being very good; she walked to her mama's bed and waited. Charlie entered after Rebecca, who placed the tray on the table near the window.

"Congratulations, General. I understand from Dr. Walker the wedding was a complete success."

He smiled shyly. "I certainly thought it was a success, and I think Rebecca did. It remains to be seen how others feel about it. I understand Richard asked for Elizabeth's hand, although in a rather...unconventional way. We shall see what Elizabeth does about it."

"Mmm, it seems that love is in the air. I am very happy for all of you." She looked down to her daughter. "Did you go to church today, Emily?"

"Yes, Mama. Why go church?"

"We go to church because we are good Christians and we want to hear the message of the Lord our God."

"Who is Lowd?"

Constance smiled and ran her fingers through her daughter's hair. "The Lord is our King and Savior, Emily."

Emily thought about that. She had heard the word king and thought that kings were important people, but savior was totally beyond her.

Charlie looked at Rebecca and Constance. "Our little one is growing like a weed—and so is her vocabulary. I swear, I believe that in the last few weeks, she has used the word "why" more than all of the words she has ever spoken before."

Constance smiled and gratefully took a cup of tea from Rebecca when it was offered. "General Redmond, I have a very serious request to make of you, Sir."

"Whatever I can do, I will certainly try." He looked to Rebecca. "I think I speak for both of us in that."

"I wish to draft a formal document, giving you and Rebecca guardianship of Emily." She placed her hand on her very swollen midsection. "And this child, if it survives. I would also like for you to give them both your name, make them truly a part of your family."

Charlie looked helplessly at Rebecca. He had been hoping that, with the help of Elizabeth, and now Mrs. White, Constance would survive her pregnancy.

Constance took his silence as a possible refusal. "Unless, Sir, you would prefer not to." Her eyes were downcast. "I am sure there is some place that would shelter them. I have no living relatives, but..."

Charlie panicked. "No, no, not at all. We love Em, and would be honored to raise both her and her brother or sister as our own. Would we not, Rebecca?" He looked at her desperately. "It is just that I have hope you will survive this confinement to stay with us and raise your children. You must know both you and your children are welcome here for as long as you wish. I think of you as part of my family already, so, please do not imagine you are imposing on us. Little Em is truly the daughter of my heart."

Constance reached out and took Charlie's hand. "Thank you. And know that I have come to terms with what will happen when this child arrives. I will rejoin my Henry, and I will leave two beautiful children for two parents who will love them as if they were their own. I am quite content to go to my Lord's side and reside in peace and grace, General."

Charlie bowed his head over Constance's hand for a moment. When he looked up again, there was a look of gentle compassion on his face. "I will need to get some information about you and Emily so that I can have my attorney draw up the papers while Rebecca and I are in Washington."

"Anything you require, General. I will give you all the information I can. What I cannot remember, you will find recorded in the family Bible on the table." She gestured weakly to the book across the room.

"Perhaps I can start with the Bible and then ask you anything else I need to know, dear lady. You look tired."

"I am a little, Sir." She gave his hand as much of a squeeze as she could manage. "Thank you. Thank you for everything."

Charlie gathered the Bible and Em, while Rebecca helped the failing woman settle more comfortably. "Come along, imp. Tess is waiting with your blocks."

Constance watched Charlie go out with her daughter, then she turned tired eyes on Rebecca. "That is a person with a truly good soul."

"I think so, too. You must know, Charlie loves Em as if she were his own. And he and I will raise her to be a good Christian woman."

"I am sure of that Rebecca. I am very sure of that."

Charlie walked into the back parlor later that afternoon, holding Constance's Bible. "Rebecca, do you know what?"

She looked up from another failing attempt at making something for the baby. "I know a great many things, General Redmond. What would you like to know?" she teased as he sat down next to her.

"Actually, I will wager you do not know this. We have a birthday coming up in this family."

Rebecca laughed and set the sewing aside. "You know, it does occur to me I do not know when your birthday is."

"My birthday? It is in September. The thirtieth. But I was referring to another birthday. Em will be two in a couple of weeks. By the way, when is yours?"

She chuckled as she sipped her tea. "If I do not tell you, do you suppose I will not get any older but will remain the young woman you married?"

Charlie knelt beside her. "Rebecca, darling wife, you will always be the most beautiful woman I know—young, fresh, and at the peak of your womanhood. So, age does not matter. Our love is what matters. Now, when is your birthday? You may as well tell me, as you know I will find out one way or another."

"All right, you demanding thing, you." She winked and took his hand. "My birthday is in April, the twenty-second. So, when is Em's birthday?"

"February seventeenth. Shall we have a little party for her when we return from Washington?"

"I think that would be lovely. Oh, by the way, when are you going to break our leaving to her?"

"I thought we would tell her after supper."

"Such a brave and well decorated soldier in President Lincoln's Army," she considered, "and yet you are a coward when it comes to your daughter, putting it off until the very last minute and then demanding that I participate."

"I most certainly am not a coward when it comes to Em. I just want to make sure that she knows that both of us are her parents, just as much as Constance is. Rebecca, really, the child loves and depends on you as much as she does me."

"I know, but I am trying hard not to interfere with what time she has left with her mother. There will be plenty of time for me to be Mama 'Becca, later."

"I understand, but you need not deny how important you have become to her, dear; she adores you. And since we are both leaving, I think we both need to tell her. Anyway, you know what she will say."

"No, what will she say?"

Charlie rolled his eyes. "Why?"

It was that quiet period after dinner, when Em had grown accustomed to spending time with Charlie and Rebecca. They would read her stories, draw pictures, play cat in the cradle or blocks, and prepare her for bed. Tonight they were going to talk, something they also often did. Charlie took her on his lap, with Rebecca sitting beside them.

"Well, my imp, how was your day?"

"Good." She settled down in the crook of his arm, getting quite comfortable.

"What did you learn today?"

She looked at him with large blue eyes and simply stuck her thumb in her mouth, while curling tighter into his arms.

"Oh, is my little why-bird tired?"

"Yes, Papa." Em nodded, and nuzzled into Charlie's shoulder.

"Well, little one, you will have plenty of time to rest up. Mama 'Becca and I have to go to Washington tomorrow, so Uncle Richard and Aunt Elizabeth will be looking after you, as well as your mama and Tess. We will be gone for seven days. Can you be a big girl while we are gone?"

She looked to Rebecca, then back to her Papa. "No."

"Will you at least be a good girl while we are gone?"

Her arms went around Charlie's neck as if holding on tight would prevent him from leaving her again. "Papa no go." Her brows came together as tears started forming in her eyes. "Pwease."

Charlie looked at Rebecca, seeking her assistance.

"Emily," Rebecca's voice was firm, yet soft as only a mother could be. "Your Papa and I are going to take a trip, but we will be back. You know that when Papa takes a trip, he comes home soon. Remember the last time he took a trip?"

"Yes." She thought for a minute. "Bwought Web home."

"Yes, Papa brought you Reb. Now you know it is all right for Papa to take a trip because he will come home. We are going to take a trip together so Mama 'Becca can meet some of Papa's friends, but we will be back. And you must be good for Uncle Richard and Aunt Elizabeth."

She sat and pouted. "Pwease no go."

"We will miss you, Em, but we are going. And you will be a big, good girl, and make us proud of you."

"Yes, Mama 'Becca."

Charlie carried a very dejected, quiet little girl up to bed that night. When he kissed her good night, she held tight. "Pwomise come back?"

"I promise, Em. We will be back in a few days."

CHAPTER 28

MONDAY, JANUARY 30, 1865

It was a gray, foggy morning as Rebecca and Charlie boarded the train for Washington but to Rebecca, it was as if it were the most glorious spring day, with the sun shining and the azaleas in bloom. She was on her honeymoon with Charlie. They would have an entire week together, with no demands of duty. General Grant had done them a favor, sending his personal railcar down with the Saturday supply train to serve as the first locale of their honeymoon.

Charlie ruefully regarded the luggage rack at the back of the car. *One week and we have a trunk, two cases and three hatboxes. Oh—and my satchel. I suppose that traveling light is not in her plans for our future.* He heaved a sigh and decided that a simple hack would not be sufficient to convey them from the train station; he would need to hire a carriage.

Rebecca was so excited she could hardly contain herself. "Oh, Charlie, look. There are little holders for the teacups so they will not spill, and a spirit lamp to heat water. Oh, these chairs are so comfortable. General Grant is so sweet to lend us his car. He must think very highly of you to give us such a lovely gift."

He smiled, knowing there was no stopping her. Using a response he somehow suspected was going to constitute a major part of his vocabulary from then on, he said, "Yes, dear."

Rebecca found the passing landscape to be fascinating. The train chugged through towns and fields that had seen thousands of soldiers move through them, but it also traveled through towns and past plantations that had played key roles in previous conflicts. It mirrored part of the path that Dolly Madison had taken when she escaped from the British in the War of 1812, saving some of the greatest treasures of the new country.

Charlie found he enjoyed pointing out these sites to Rebecca, as they shared an interest in history. When they arrived in Washington late in the afternoon, they were both relaxed and very happy.

He hailed a carriage at the station, and with the porter's help, loaded their luggage for the short trip to the Willard, where they were met by Simpkins. Charlie had been going to the Willard since he was first promoted to captain; and Simpkins viewed him as one of the Willard's best clients—always quiet, generous, and undemanding. Having anticipated their arrival, he had personally overseen preparation of his best suite for the General and his new wife.

He escorted the couple upstairs to the lovely set of rooms. There was a sitting room that looked out toward 15th Street and the gardens at the foot of the newly constructed Treasury building. The adjoining bedroom was spacious, with a huge four-posted bed, a fine fireplace with a marble mantle, and lovely green and ivory furnishings. Rebecca was charmed.

"Oh Charlie, it is beautiful."

"Rebecca, it is exactly what you deserve. A beautiful setting for a beautiful woman."

"You are going to spoil me, Charles Redmond."

"That is exactly what I would like to do, darling."

A knock on the door disturbed them. Charlie opened it, and a smiling servant wheeled in a cart bearing a lovely teapot, fresh flowers, little cakes, and an assortment of cookies. "Compliments of the house, Sir. Congratulations to both of you. Your dinner will be ready and served in the garden room downstairs at eight. There is hot water in the reservoir in the bathing room, if you wish to wash up." The maid bobbed a curtsey and backed out of the room. Just as she was about to leave, she added, "Oh, and Ma'am, if you need help dressing or with your hair, just ring and I will be happy to assist you."

Rebecca could only smile as Charlie closed the door. "Oh yes, I am going to get spoiled, General Redmond."

"Yes, Ma'am. If I have anything to say about it, you certainly are."

They had just managed to wash their faces and hands, and settle down for a nice late afternoon tea when there was another knock on the door.

Charlie's response was muffled by the piece of lemon chess he had just stuffed in his mouth. "Come."

"Sorry to disturb you, Sir, but there are a number of notes for you and Mrs. Redmond." The maid set a silver salver heaped with small envelopes on the table between Charlie and Rebecca and excused herself with, "If you wish to reply, there is paper in the writing table; and you have only to ring for a messenger."

Rebecca looked at the pile of envelopes. "What is this, dear?"

"I would assume they are invitations from various folks in town."

"That much is obvious, but I did not realize that we would attract so much attention. I thought it was going to be a quiet week with just the two of us."

"It is your choice, my love. I do have tickets for a play at Ford's on Thursday. Mr. Junius Booth is doing *King Lear*. And I suspect that Mrs. Grant will want you to join her for tea. As for the rest, I am as surprised as you."

She looked at the pile in total amazement. "What about Mrs. Armstrong? Will we be calling on her?"

"I made no arrangements, as, to be honest, I was not sure how you felt about really meeting her."

"You know I want to meet her, Charlie, very much. Is there some reason you do not wish us to meet?"

He had the grace to look abashed. "Well, there is the issue of you meeting with a well-known Washington courtesan. I was not sure whether you really wanted to, or if were just being polite."

Rebecca chuckled and took Charlie's hand. "Think about it, my love. What, exactly, about our relationship is normal? There is no reason on the face of the earth that I should not want to meet Mrs. Armstrong. Considering our situation, I would think that we should disregard what most people consider the social norm."

He laughed. "I knew there was a reason why I love you so much, darling." He kissed her hands, and then continued, "Shall I invite her to join us for a private luncheon? Or would you prefer to do the inviting? I think she might appreciate the invitation coming from you."

"I would be very happy to invite her."

"Then, let us go through the rest of these invitations and plan our week, shall we?" He smiled and started opening envelopes. A number of them were the rather expected invitations from various social butterflies, an unavoidable part of the atmosphere of Washington. But a few were certainly worth responding to, and a smaller number were politically mandatory.

The invitation from General and Mrs. Grant were graciously accepted, as was Rebecca's invitation from Mrs. Lincoln to take tea at the White House. They considered and agreed that, politically, they could not refuse the invitations from Mr. and Mrs. Seward, nor could they turn down General McClellan. Perhaps the most fascinating invitation was from Mr. Jay Cooke, the Philadelphia financier. All of these engagements still left them time to attend the play and a concert by the Marine Corps Band, and to do some touring and shopping. Charlie and Rebecca quickly wrote their acceptances and politely declined the other invitations.

"With that piece of business out of the way, would you like a bath before we have dinner? Even though the General's car was very nice, I, for one, am lightly coated with ash from the engine."

"I think that would be wonderful and I would very much like a nap as well."

"Well, darling, there is a huge bathtub and hot water waiting for you."

"So there is. Now should I call for the maid, or would you prefer to help me out of my traveling clothes?"

Charlie slid his arms around her waist and kissed her shoulder. "You should know by now that I adore serving as your lady's maid. Would you like me to wash your back as well?"

She lifted a brow at him. "Hmmm...maybe, darling. Would you consider washing my front, too?" She looked past Charlie into the bathing room. "Do you think the tub can hold us both?"

He looked at the tub, then at his wife, then back at the tub and down at himself, as if considering a serious engineering problem. "I do believe it will hold both of us, if we are willing to be extremely friendly."

"I do not believe that is an issue with us." She grabbed Charlie's cravat. "Come, husband."

Grinning, Charlie joined her in the bedroom, where he disrobed his wife with all of the finesse of a skilled maid, ran the bath, and much more hastily shed his uniform. Charlie slid into the huge, claw-footed tub behind Rebecca and drew her back to rest comfortably in her arms. The hot water, the smell of Rebecca's hair—all of it was more than Charlie had ever thought she would have.

"Do you know, Mrs. Redmond, that I love you? I love everything about you. And I love it that you love me. All of me."

Rebecca ran her hands up and down Charlie's outer thighs. "All of you, every inch of you."

The Willard staff extended themselves to provide Charlie and Rebecca with a lovely dinner. The Garden Room was quiet and discreet. Each table was in its own quiet alcove, screened from the other guests by plants and trellises. A fine meal, with a good brandy afterwards, and the two retired to their room to explore the attributes of the bed.

~

Tuesday, January 31, 1865

They slept in, a luxury in which Charlie rarely indulged, then rose and strolled about the gardens and streets of the neighborhood. Rebecca was particularly enthralled with the construction that had begun on the planned monument to President Washington. The great obelisk was not yet completed, and the war effort had suspended work indefinitely, but it was still clear it would tower over all other buildings in the capital city.

Charlie had reserved a small carriage for them from the Willard's livery stable, so they were able to tour about comfortably, looking at the various sites in the city. As they rode down the dirt track toward Georgetown and General Meigs' home, Rebecca marveled over how much progress had been made towards turning Washington into a real city in the seventy years since its founding.

"I am surprised that you do not want to return here, Charlie. It seems to me that someone with your record and standing in the service would have many opportunities here in Washington after the war."

"I am sure I would have. Do you think you would prefer to live here, dear? I had not thought of it, but if you wish..."

"I want what is best for you. I love the farm, and I think we could have the best horse-breeding program in the state. But we must do what is best for you."

"My dear, we must do what is best for us—and for our children. If living here in Washington appeals to you, I am willing to discuss it. But I am tired of the politics and the infighting. I would be perfectly happy on the farm."

"Then let us agree to this: we will keep the farm and remain there, but if opportunities should arise for you here, then we shall discuss it again."

"That seems perfectly reasonable to me, dear. And there is always the prospect of bringing more advantages to Culpeper. There are so many things that we need to rebuild the infrastructure of the town—a bank, more rail traffic."

"This is true. We will take things as they come. One day at a time."

"For now, love, we have arrived." Charlie pulled the buggy to a stop in front of a typical townhouse. Georgetown was the last port on the Potomac River before it became too rocky for large boats to navigate it, a vital and bustling town for the past hundred and fifty years. Charlie helped Rebecca to the street, handing the reins to a post boy who had been waiting for them.

They walked to the front door, where they were met by the young captain who served as Meigs' aide, and escorted to a lovely formal parlor overlooking the garden at the back of the house. Mrs. Meigs apologized for not rising to greet them, as her rheumatism was plaguing her in the chill, damp weather. The General abducted Charlie to discuss a business matter for a few minutes.

"I declare, it is always damp here. In the winter, chill and damp; in the summer, hot and humid, but always damp. Be thankful, Mrs. Redmond, that you live in the foothills, where you are not plagued as we are in the city."

Rebecca smiled politely. "Of course, Mrs. Meigs. Perhaps after the war, you and General Meigs would be our guest at Redmond Stables."

"That would be delightful. I have heard that the country around Culpeper is beautiful. Tell me, can you see the mountains from your home?"

"Oh yes, very clearly. Our land is actually backed up against the mountains."

"That must be lovely. Being in the military, we have had to move about so often that I have had no real hope of establishing a family home like that. Why, I believe this house in Georgetown is the closest to a home we have ever had."

"I can only imagine. Redmond and I were just discussing if we should consider moving to Washington. But since he is leaving the Army after the war, we have decided to remain in Culpeper for the time being."

"So, General Redmond is leaving the Army. I do indeed envy you. I believe that General Meigs will be in the service until the day he dies."

"Yes, he has decided to retire. He will be at his twenty-year mark soon, and does not want to go west. We are going to start a horse-breeding program."

"Oh, how lovely. But do you really think that the folks in Culpeper will accept having a Yankee general in their midst?"

Rebecca chuckled. "They are divided in their opinions. But I am sure that, in time, General Redmond will overcome his detractors."

"Well, I do wish you good luck. Here in Washington, we have the reverse situation. Staunch supporters of the Union who are Southerners often receive less than charitable treatment. Why, even Mrs. Lincoln has had to suffer at the hands of the more rabid Northerners."

"I am sure. These times have been very difficult on everyone. I do hope it is over soon."

"Well, I cannot say for sure, but many of the conversations I have heard suggest that the Confederacy cannot stand for much longer. I know that we all, North and South, have paid a dreadful price for this war. But there are so many who want to somehow punish the Southern states for their personal pain, that I cannot help but fear that even when the battles are over, we will not have seen the last of reprehensible behaviors."

"I must admit that I have a very personal interest in seeing this end soon. I wish for my husband to come home, so we can begin our life together. It may seem selfish, but I cannot help it."

"For your sake, my dear, I hope that General Redmond can

return to you. So many women have lost their husbands, their fathers, their sons." Mrs. Meigs could not help the tears that came to her eyes; her son had been killed just a few months earlier.

~

Riding back to the hotel that afternoon, Rebecca could not help but brood over the possibility of losing Charlie in the war. She clung to his arm tightly, but would not tell him why she was so distressed. Finally, in their room preparing for a quiet dinner beside the fire, he forced the issue.

"Rebecca, darling. You and I have been married for less than three days, yet you are acting like a woman in mourning." He swallowed hard, not wanting to hear the potential answer to his question. "Have you found that being married to me is not what you want?"

"Of course not. I love you and want to spend the rest of my life with you. I just know that our time together is getting short, and I cannot help but feel helpless because there will be nothing I can do but watch you ride away. And from what I have heard, the last days of this war are going to be vicious and deadly. I am worried for you."

"Do not worry too much, darling. I have managed to come through some of the worst of two wars with only minor injuries. I cannot believe my luck will change now." He lifted her hand and tenderly kissed her palm. "For luck, darling. On a different topic, dear, are you ready to meet Lizzie tomorrow?"

"Yes. I am quite looking forward to it. I hope that we will become friends."

Charlie just smiled, a somewhat forced smile, and served Rebecca some sliced beef. *Oh, my God, what will happen to me when those two get together?*

"You are nervous about this," she hazarded as she poured Charlie a glass of wine.

He thought about it for a moment and then agreed. "Yes. There are three women in the world who actually know me pretty well. You. Elizabeth. And Lizzie. You and Elizabeth with your heads together are dangerous enough without adding Lizzie. Among the three of you, I suspect you will identify every single flaw and weakness I have. Fortunately, I also have enough faith in your love for me to know I will be more the object of teasing than of hurtfulness."

"I am not interested in finding your flaws, Charlie. I just want to know your friends. I want to know the people you trust enough to share your true life with."

Charlie knew when it was time to surrender and tuck his insecurities back in the little black pit where they belonged. "Yes, dear." *Hmmmm. There was that phrase again.*

~

Wednesday, February 1, 1865

Elizabeth Armstrong had dressed in a modest gray walking dress and a veiled hat, and her hair was up when she walked into the Willard that day. This was not the flamboyant hostess and confidante of the Washington powerful, but instead a quiet, discreet woman on her way to lunch privately with friends.

She knocked at the door to Charlie and Rebecca's suite, where she was immediately greeted by both of her hosts. As Charlie took her wraps and hat, Rebecca looked her ex-competitor over carefully.

"Hello, Mrs. Armstrong, it is so nice finally to meet you."

"Good afternoon, Mrs. Redmond. I am very grateful that you have invited me."

Charlie looked at the two of them, a little stunned. He had never seen Lizzie dressed so conservatively. Nor had he ever seen her so...reserved.

"Please, come in and sit. I have been looking forward to meeting you. Charlie has told me so much about you."

"Thank you, Ma'am. When he was here last month, he told me a little of you, as well. You seem to have given him something very special."

Rebecca led her guest to the davenport. "Well, I hope so, but I have not given Charlie anything he has not given me."

Lizzie spent a moment settling herself on the davenport. She looked at the room, at the warm fire in the hearth, in fact, everywhere except at Charlie or Rebecca. In a small voice, she said, "I envy you."

Rebecca looked to Charlie, feeling very lost and encouraging him to say something to the woman.

Charlie cleared his throat, groping for something neutral to say. "Um. Thank you so much for your wedding gift." He realized what he had just thanked her for and turned a truly startling shade of red.

Rebecca realized their encounter was not going to get any better as long as Charlie was there to insert his boot into his mouth. "Darling," she smiled, trying to force the blush from her own face, "there is a matter to be taken up with your lawyer; now might be a good time to do so."

Charlie looked at her gratefully. Escaping was the best idea he had heard in a while. "Why, yes, dear, I do need to drop in on him. Let me just get the papers and my coat, and I will leave you two ladies to have a nice chat. Do not worry about lunch for me; I will grab something with my attorney." With that, Charlie bustled about for a moment, put some papers in his coat pocket, threw his greatcoat over his arm, and bolted from the room.

Rebecca watched him go and smiled. Turning back to Lizzie, she sighed. "He is very good at the tactical retreat."

Lizzie laughed. "You know, I do not think I have ever seen the man so flustered."

"He tends to get that way when he feels overwhelmed by the fairer sex, and I believe that you and I in the same room was more than he could handle."

"So we have overwhelmed him. Hmmm. The great "Lucky Charlie" abashed by his own gender. It does have a certain...irony."

Lizzie fussed for a moment, and then changed the subject. "I hope you did not find my wedding present to be too...presumptuous."

"No, actually, I found it very intriguing. Thank you. So tell me Mrs. Armstrong, why do you seem so nervous? I promise you I mean you no harm," Rebecca teased as she poured two cups of tea.

Lizzie drew in a deep breath. "Mrs. Redmond, a woman such as I am is not proper company for a lady like you. If the people you meet socially knew you had me as a guest in your rooms, they would shun you in a heartbeat."

At that, Rebecca laughed heartily, eventually regaining control of herself and offering Lizzie a pat on the arm. "My dear Mrs. Armstrong, the last thing in this world I am concerned with is what other people think. You are a friend of Charlie's, and I wanted to meet you in hopes that we also could become friends."

Lizzie blushed at Rebecca's outburst. Charlie's new wife clearly regarded social mores as annoyances, which was a refreshing difference in attitude from Lizzie's experience. "Ma'am, you do not understand. If I happen to meet one of the "proper" ladies of this town at the haberdashery or the tearoom, they will cut me dead. I would not like that to happen to you."

"Mrs. Armstrong, I honestly do not care what people think. You are an important person in Charlie's life, a person who cares for him and a person for whom he cares. Your friendship is far more important than what people I do not know may think, or even, for that matter, what people I do know may think, because to be perfectly honest I do not like most of them anyhow."

Lizzie looked at Rebecca with astonishment. Ladies of her acquaintance were simply not so outspoken. Slowly, astonishment turned to amusement. "My, my, Charlie has indeed found his match in you, Ma'am," she grinned.

"I hope so. So, now, let us put all this talk of propriety away and enjoy ourselves."

Lizzie took a sip of tea and looked over at the table with their luncheon set out, waiting for them. "I will, if you promise not to let that lovely luncheon get cold."

"Very well. Shall we?" Rebecca moved to the table, gesturing for Lizzie to join her. Once the woman was seated, Rebecca picked up the conversation. "Tell me, when did you meet Charlie?"

"He and I met back when he was newly made a captain and was assigned to work here in Washington for the first time. I was just a young thing, working for one of the more discreet madams in town. She knew I could; handle Charlie and his particular needs. In fact, he helped me go into business on my own, a kindness for which I am very grateful. Over the years, we have renewed our acquaintance whenever he was in town. We spent a lot of time together during his time here in '59 after his promotion to Lieutenant Colonel. He has always been more of a friend than a client."

"I could tell that. He speaks of you as if you are one of his dearest and most trusted friends. You must know it is very hard for him to allow anyone to get to close. Even Colonel Polk, who has been Charlie's friend for many years, does not know. As far as I know, there are only five of us who know his secret."

"So how did you figure it out? More significantly, how did you feel about it when you did realize what he is?"

"I noticed the first time I met him. He had been wounded in the shoulder. When I cleaned the wound, I noticed the bindings under his shirt. As to how I felt, to be honest, I was both terribly confused and amazed. Amazed he had been able to hide so well for so long. When I realized I was developing feelings for him, I fought them for the longest time." She smiled at Lizzie. "Then I realized it was just useless to fight something so powerful."

"It must have been very perplexing for you. I doubt you had ever met anyone like him before."

"Not that I was aware of, that is for certain. But I fell in love with Charlie, not his body. She is an amazing woman, and quite the gallant gentleman."

A wistful look came over Lizzie's features as she looked away from Rebecca. "Yes, she is amazing and he is infinitely gallant."

"You love him." It was not a question.

Lizzie took a deep breath. "Of course I do. He is one of my dearest friends."

Rebecca smiled. "That is not what I meant. You would have gone away with him and lived as his wife."

A long silence ensued, while Lizzie simply sat there with her eyes closed, twisting her napkin into an unrecognizable wad. Finally, she responded. "No, I would not have, for Charlie never asked me and, to be honest, never loved me that way. I was his friend, his mentor, and the place he went when the pain of being alone became too great. I was never the dream he reached for, as you are."

"Mrs. Armstrong, I think I know Charlie well enough to say that had you made your feelings known, it might very well have been you. I can say with a great deal of sincerity that he loves you. Very much."

"He loves me as a friend. But he is not, nor has he ever been, **in** love with me. There is an enormous difference between what he feels for you and what he feels for me. I envy you. I wish it had been me that he saw his future in, but it was not. Perhaps it is because of the decisions I have made in my life; perhaps it was just not meant to be. But, my dear lady, I do love him enough to wish you both well."

"Mrs. Armstrong, that means so very much to me; thank you. And I will say, to you and to Charlie, that if he finds himself in a place where he needs someone by his side again, he would be well served to be with you."

Lizzie stood and walked to the window, looking down on the bustling street. "Mrs. Redmond, you are a young woman, younger than I. I do not expect he will be alone again. For that, I am very glad."

"Still, I am resolute in that idea, Mrs. Armstrong; and, please, if we are ever to become friends, you must call me Rebecca."

"My friends call me Lizzie, Rebecca."

"Good." She smiled and quietly gestured for Lizzie to sit down

smiled from behind her teacup. "It does seem that we have had the same experiences with him. Apparently I am doing it right."

"So it would seem. I have noticed that Charlie seems to prefer external stimulation to penetration."

"To be honest, I have never tried. When we are like, that, she guides me, and I do what she asks." Rebecca considered the comment. "Interesting that I had not thought of that, or even noticed."

"Perhaps you might want to...experiment a bit to discover what our oh-so-reserved gentleman prefers."

"I suppose I should." She bit her lip, trying to hide the smile caused by the simple imagery. "I wonder how it will go over."

Lizzie looked into Rebecca's blushing face. "Of course, dear, Charlie may allow you to do things to that would not be accepted from me or anyone else."

"Hmm, there is some truth to that, I suppose; but he has known you for so much longer."

"It does not matter, dear. Your relationship with him is far different from what mine ever was. He lets you into his soul as well as his heart. I suspect that he is less reticent with you than he was with me."

The blonde blushed again and nodded. "Indeed. That may be true. Thank you, Lizzie, for everything. So tell me, will you come to Culpeper and pay us a visit when Charlie is home?"

"My dear, if there is a social problem with you and me being together here in Washington, what kind of scandal would it create in Culpeper if I were to visit? I suspect my name is rather well known in certain circles."

"Well, I am not sure who of the remaining citizens in Culpeper might know of you, but I simply do not care. Please know that our home is open to you anytime you choose to visit."

Lizzie looked a little wistful. "Perhaps sometime in the future. For now, I think the two of you need time to settle in to your relationship. And I need some time to accept that what I will see is something I cannot have."

"Lizzie, after my first husband died, I was sure the war would be the end of me. I had accepted the fact I would be alone for the rest of my life, or possibly dead. Not many men are interested in marrying a woman who has been married once and, by all accounts of local gossip, was a horrible wife. Then Charlie came into my life, giving me hope again. You should not give up. Your time will come."

"I hope so. Sometimes I think I should take my earnings and go somewhere far from here, living life as a quiet widow who does charitable works through the local church and supports a community lending library."

Just then, Charlie stuck his head through the door. His hair was tousled by the wind, his cheeks and nose reddened with the cold. "Is it safe to come in, yet?"

Rebecca and Lizzie looked at each other and burst out laughing. Charlie, wise man that he was, retreated back downstairs to have a hot coffee and brandy in the Willard's smoking lounge.

Since Charlie and Rebecca's departure, Em had vacillated between being demanding and cranky, and being sullen and cranky. Mostly, she had been cranky. This afternoon, Elizabeth was sitting with her in the rear parlor, playing with her blocks, trying to quiet her before Tess came to put her down for her nap.

The little girl threw one of her blocks, causing it to bounce and just miss the fireplace.

"Em, did you see where your block almost went?"

"No care. Em mad!" The little girl turned her back on the doctor and then proceeded to fall to the floor in a crying fit.

Elizabeth gave the wailing child a jaundiced look. "So, do you think if you do that enough, I will magically get them back here before Monday night?"

Em, unaffected by the doctor's attempt at humor, just kept crying. "Why Papa leave?"

"Because Papa and Mama 'Becca needed to go to Washington for a week." Elizabeth refused to talk down to the child. She knew that Em was smart, and that she knew exactly what she was saying.

"Why?"

"Because they did."

Em sat up and sniffed. "Papa come home?"

"Papa will be home on Monday night."

Em wiped her eyes, then blew a bubble from her rather runny nose. "Want Papa."

Elizabeth pulled an already soggy handkerchief from her pocket. "Here. Blow. Papa will be home on Monday night."

Richard wandered into the room just in time to see Elizabeth wiping Em's face. "Did I miss the two o'clock tantrum?"

"Yes, lucky for you. You can have the supper one." Elizabeth looked up at him. "And once more, we can see just how far around her finger she has managed to wrap Unca Wichad."

"Ooo, are we in a mood today, my dear? Does playing the surrogate mother not appeal to you?"

"Actually, the mothering part suits me nicely, thank you. It is the fact that neither of us can fill General Redmond's boots that I find stressful."

"Yes, she is quite attached to him. Can you imagine what Rebecca will have to deal with when we leave for the spring campaign?" Richard sat down on the floor and opened his arms, and Em crawled right into them.

"Unca Wichawd. Make Papa come home," the baby begged as she clutched his lapel.

"Emily, your Aunt Elizabeth and I do not have the power to make Papa come home. He and Mama 'Becca will be back in five days. Now would you like to help Uncle Richard keep track of the days until they come home?"

"Em help?"

"Absolutely." Richard rooted around in his pocket until he pulled out five pennies. "There is a penny here for every day that Papa will be gone. Now if you are good and do not cry for Papa anymore, every night before bed, Uncle Richard will give you a penny."

"Pennies pwetty."

Elizabeth chuckled while she watched Richard basically bribing the child.

"Yes, they are very pretty; and they can be all yours if you are good until Papa comes home."

Elizabeth intervened. "Emily, do you know how many pennies Uncle Richard has there?"

She looked at his hand and then to Elizabeth before shaking her head.

"How many fingers do you have on your hand, little one?"

She looked to her hand. Her brows came together and she guessed. "Fouw."

"Shall we count them?"

Em nodded, distracted from her tantrum by the pennies and the attention she was getting.

Elizabeth held up her index finger. "One"

"One." Em grinned and held up another. "Twu."

"That is right." Elizabeth's next finger went up, and she waited to see if the little girl could respond.

"Twee."

"Very good, Em. I will have to tell your Papa and Mama 'Becca what a smart little girl you are." The next finger went up.

"Fouw." She looked to Richard for his approval, which he gave with a nod.

Elizabeth held up her thumb. "How many is this, Em?"

"One."

"And how many total fingers do I have?"

Em considered the question and then shrugged.

Elizabeth counted off her fingers. "One, two, three, four, five."

"Fwive?" She looked to the coins in Richard's hand. "Fwive?"

"Very good, Em. Mama 'Becca and Papa will be back in five days."

"Em have penny?" She gave her best smile to her Uncle Richard.

"Em can have her penny at bedtime, if she is a good girl."

Just then Tess walked in and took Em up for her nap.

"So, apart from Em acting like a two year old, how is your day going?"

"Interesting. Constance is slowly failing, so that is a worry; and Em has been atrociously demanding, but other than that, I have had some time to think. And I think I want to talk to you a little, Sir, if you are willing?"

"Of course. I am yours to command," he said with a grin as he lifted himself off the floor and onto the settee with her.

Suddenly, the normally acerbic Elizabeth was rather vulnerable. "Ah. Is that true, Richard?"

"It is, my lovely lady. Very true."

"What you said Saturday? Did you mean it?"

"I meant every badly stuttered word." He smiled shyly. "I do believe seeing Charlie and Rebecca together finally made me realize what it is I have been missing: you."

Elizabeth stared at her feet. They had been friends for a long time. She had come to rely on Richard's quiet strength, his humor, and his unfailing presence. Was she in love with him? She was not sure. Could she imagine her life without him? No. "So, are you asking for permission to court me officially, after the war is over?"

"Well, I think it is about time we made it official. We have been keeping company for some time now."

Elizabeth, even though still a little confused, recognized that Richard was busy being Richard. Once again, his ability to evade serious emotions was impressive. "Ah, I understand. You are asking me to consider whether I am willing to have you ask me to think about whether I should marry you or not." She could not help it; she was overcome with giggles.

"Ah, no, my dear doctor. I am not being politic, nor am I waffling. I am specifically asking you. I would be delighted if you would accept my proposal of marriage, although I must admit I am a little concerned that the concept causes you to laugh."

Elizabeth caught her breath. The giggles stopped abruptly, and she looked him in the eye. "Are you serious, Richard? Do you really want to be married to me, even though I am a doctor? You do not want to make me give up my career?"

"Yes, I want to be married to you, and no, I would not ask you to give up your career. Elizabeth, you are doing important work. I would not dare ask you to relinquish it for fear that the Good Lord would strike me down for trying to clip the wings of an angel on earth."

Elizabeth looked at Richard, blinking like an owl when a bright light is shone on it at night. "You mean it?" She regarded him with a certain sense of wonder and realized that no, she could not envision her life without him when he nodded the affirmative. "Yes."

Now it was Richard's turn to be breathless. "Yes? Yes, you will marry me?"

"Yes."

He sat there for a moment with his head bobbing up and down like a cork in a choppy stream. *Yes. She said yes. Yes is the best word I have ever heard.* Then he smiled and took her in his arms. "I love you, Elizabeth Walker."

Elizabeth simply melted into his arms. "Me, too, Richard."

Charlie watched the lobby from his place in the smoking lounge, waiting for Lizzie to leave before he went back to his rooms and Rebecca. Somehow, the two women together just plain scared the bejezus out of him. But he did have to get back to the room sooner or later, as he needed to get cleaned up for dinner with the Grants, an event that called for full evening dress. Finally, he saw Lizzie stroll out to the cabstand. He hastily finished his coffee, stubbed out his cigar, and scurried upstairs.

He walked into the room to find the maid assisting Rebecca with undressing and bathing, preparing for the first formal evening they would spend in Washington society.

"Hello, darling. I see you thought it safe to return." She sent the maid out with a gesture, then returned her attention to Charlie. "We were good, I promise."

"Not from the little bit I heard. How did you really get along?"

"We got along very well. I like her very much, and I think we are on our way to becoming friends."

"I am glad, in an odd sort of way. I know Lizzie lives outside of the bounds of propriety, but I have found her to be a strong, honorable woman."

"She is indeed...a very sweet woman. I would be proud to call her my friend. I mean, if I can marry a Yankee officer, then nothing is off limits for me, is it?"

Charlie looked at her and rubbed his hands over his cheeks. "I suppose not."

He started getting undressed, pulling off his boots, and unbuttoning his coat and weskit. As he did so, he pulled the papers from the lawyer out of his pocket. "I did see the attorney. Here are the adoption papers. They only have to be signed and notarized."

"Charlie, is something wrong?" Rebecca slipped on her robe and sat down next to him, gently taking his hand. "Have I upset you?"

"No, darling, not at all. It just hit me that you and I are officially about to have a family, that I have a responsibility that goes far beyond anything I ever anticipated having, and that I love you madly."

"Just remember when Em is hanging off your trouser leg and another baby is spitting up lunch on your best coat," she winked, "you asked for this."

"Perhaps I should ask General Sheridan to get me that bib."

"I am sure he would be happy to do so. Or transfer you to one of those Western forts" She sighed and squeezed his hand. "I only want you to be happy, Charlie."

He dropped his cravat on the foot of the bed and walked over to sweep Rebecca up in his arms. "I, my love, am the happiest human being on the face of the planet. Now, shall I wear my uniform or civilian attire to General Grant's this evening?"

"Oh, I think it is best to wear your uniform for dinner at the General's home."

Later, after much cuddling and teasing, the two were ready to set out for their engagement. Rebecca was elegant in her green velvet evening dress; Charlie was, as usual, immaculate in his uniform. As he handed her into the carriage, he asked, "Are you ready to go and act the proper General's wife?"

"I am ready to go in and try." She was very nervous, as could be heard in her voice and seen in the gentle shaking of her hands.

"Well, darling, if you had to choose an easy first time, it would be at General Grant's. He is rather shy and soft spoken. His wife is a very gentle lady. Neither of them stands on formality."

"Thank the Lord for small favors."

The rest of the events planned for the week went as planned. On Wednesday evening, the Redmonds dined with the Grants and a few old time career officers and their wives. In many ways, it was an enlightening evening for Rebecca. Conversation during dinner turned to politics, as was expected. There were clearly mixed feelings about President Lincoln's policy of lenient reconstruction. Rebecca was saddened by the harshness of some of the opinions, which seemed to be in inverse proportion to the amount of time those expressing them had spent in the field against the Southern troops.

After dinner, the gentlemen retired for cigars and brandies, while the ladies gathered in the parlor for tea and gossip. On discovering that Rebecca had just joined the ranks of Army wives, the ladies had abundant advice on how to survive the rigors of travel, on trying to establish a home in a new location every few years, on the politics of being an Army wife. While fascinated, Rebecca quietly and, to be honest, smugly thought, *I will not have to endure these problems, for my Charlie will just come home to me when this is over.*

The next day brought a languid morning where Charlie and Rebecca stayed abed and explored the joys of being a married couple. Finally, they rose and dressed for tea with the Sewards. Rebecca found Mrs. Seward utterly charming, but Secretary Seward reminded her of some great snake: coiled, watching, and waiting to strike. She noticed that Charlie was far more guarded with the great man than she had ever seen him.

The evening was far more pleasant. Rebecca had never been to a real theater; she had seen only a few performances that had been presented by traveling players in Culpeper. The opulent setting of Ford's Theater and the power of one of the leading Shakespearean actors of the day were fascinating. Mr. Junius Booth was an older man with a most powerful presence and voice. At his peak, he had perfected his interpretation of Hamlet. Most people said that his son Edwin had already surpassed him, but Rebecca and Charlie both found his King Lear to be entrancing.

Rebecca was a bit nervous as they rode home. Tomorrow, she was invited to tea with Mrs. Lincoln, and without Charlie's presence for support.

"Dear heart, Mrs. Lincoln is just a woman, like any other. And, I suspect, a rather lonely one. She has taken a great deal of abuse because of her Southern roots and her spendthrift ways. Of course, there is also the fact that she has not been quite right since the death of her son."

"Well, Charlie, you cannot blame me. I mean I am going to the White House, the home of the Federal President and his wife. I am a Southerner. I cannot help but be nervous."

"It is no different than going to tea with Mrs. Grant. Just be yourself, dear, and be kind to a lady who is in a very difficult situation."

"Of course I will." Rebecca chuckled and squeezed Charlie's hand. "Can you imagine what the biddies will have to say when they find out I had tea with Mrs. Lincoln. My reputation will be beyond repair."

"Darling, you married me. Your reputation is already beyond repair."

"I assure you that this will put the final nail in the coffin." She leaned over and gave him a kiss on the cheek before whispering in his ear. "Not that I care."

As it turned out, the afternoon with Mrs. Lincoln was very pleasant. The lady was pleased to have another Southerner to talk with—and very informative about the politics that Rebecca would face that evening at the formal dinner with the McClellans.

Saturday, February 4, 1865

Rebecca had been very kind to Charlie; she had not demanded that he take her shopping every day. They had agreed Saturday would be their day to shop, as their only plans for the day were to attend a small concert in the evening. Charlie tucked his wallet in his pocket, pulled on his most comfortable walking shoes, and girded himself to endure with a smile that which he considered torture.

Rebecca entered from the bathing room wearing the light blue walking dress of which Charlie was so fond. "Am I presentable for the masses?"

"Entirely, my dear. I believe I may have to carry a walking stick just to keep the local bucks away from you."

She laughed as she ran a hand over his chest. "Much like the one I will need to keep the ladies away from you."

"Shall we, my dear?" *The sooner we get this started, the sooner it will be finished, I hope.*

"Of course. Oh, while we are out I would very much like to buy Reverend Williams a gift. He has been so kind and supportive. I would like to thank him properly."

"What would you like to get him, dear?"

"I think a new Bible. The one he has is old and worn. I noticed during services last Sunday that the pages were starting to come loose."

"Ah, a lovely gift. There is a very nice bookstore just around the corner from the haberdashery."

"Wonderful. Then I am at your disposal, dear husband. Please take me and show me your city."

They strolled up 14th Street to G Street and turned east toward the Capitol. While many of the streets were cobbled, some of the smaller cross streets were still dirt and mud. Fortunately, there were raised boardwalks all through the city to help ladies protect their long dresses. One block over, they found a lovely bookstore, with a large selection of religious works.

Rebecca spent quite a while trying to choose just the right Bible for the good reverend. All the while, Charlie leaned against a wall and tried to look like he was paying attention.

She finally settled on a beautiful leather bound volume that, the clerk informed her, could be embossed with Reverend Williams's initials. She presented the book to Charlie.

"What do you think of this one?"

"Hummm. Nice leather."

Rebecca looked around to make sure no one could hear her, but she needed to find out if he was actually paying attention. "Charlie, I think we should go back to the hotel room and you should let me strip off all your clothes and have my way with you."

"Whatever you want, dear."

"Charles Redmond! I swear!" She turned on her heel and went back to the clerk. "This one will do nicely. Thank you."

Charlie looked around, a little bewildered. He had found a copy of Xenophon's *The Thousand,* and was enthralled by the new translation. Rebecca was standing at the counter and, by the look on her face, she was not happy. Perhaps the Bible she had chosen was more expensive than she had expected.

Rebecca returned to him and tugged on his shoulder. "Perhaps, my dear, we should go to a tack, leather or gun shop, some place you might find more appealing." As she said this, she handed him the package, which he was expected to dutifully carry.

"No, dear, of course not. This is your shopping trip, so we will go where you want."

At this point she could not be mad at him any longer. She realized that he was a fish out of water, and that he really was trying. "All right, Charlie. Perhaps a bite of lunch somewhere?"

"Certainly. I think there is a little tea room over on 11th that you would like." Manfully, he escorted her out of the bookstore and two blocks down the street, carrying the heavy Bible under his arm. As they walked, he talked about how construction was progressing on new office buildings and especially on the Archives, which was being designed specifically to house the Constitution and Declaration of Independence.

"That big building for those two documents?"

He laughed heartily. "Those two documents and all of the ensuing paperwork that goes into running the country those documents created, my dear."

Rebecca blushed, realizing that she sounded like a simpleton. "I guess you can take the woman out of the country, but not the country out of the woman. That had to be one of the most idiotic questions that has ever passed my lips."

"No, darling, not at all. I think very few people ever think about how much paper has to be created and stored to run a country."

"You are very kind, my darling." she chuckled, as they continued down the street.

The rest of the day was spent going from store to store, acquiring all of those things Rebecca had done without for so many years as the war had inexorably narrowed her purchases to the basics necessitates for staying alive. It was heaven for her, hell for him, and rough on his checkbook. Charlie stopped at his favorite wine shop and sent a profuse thank you note attached to a case of outstanding brandy to General Grant for the use of his train car. Without it, Charlie would have been hard pressed to transport all of his wife's purchases home.

That evening, they attended a concert put on by the Marine Corps Band. On the carriage ride to the Marine Barracks east of the Capitol building, Charlie told her how the band had come into existence. The ensemble was really a small orchestra. Called "The President's Own," it was a Washington institution, providing music for the people of the city since John Adams first took up residence in the White House. They held a concert every Saturday evening in Lafayette Park, across from the White House, and on Sunday afternoons and Wednesday evenings on the grounds of the Marine Barracks. It was a lovely time.

Sunday was a quiet day. They rose and attended services at St. John's church, diagonally across the park from the White House. Mr. and Mrs. Lincoln quietly joined the congregation, taking their seat in pew 54, as had every president since Mr. and Mrs. Monroe. The service was a gentle plea for peace and reconciliation, with the text based on the prodigal son. Mrs. Lincoln politely greeted Rebecca and Charlie after the service, introducing them to her husband. The President smiled gently, remembering Charlie from their brief meeting at the Willard. Having been told many times by Sheridan and Grant what an asset the man was to the Federal cause, he gave Rebecca a polite kiss on cheek, congratulating her on her marriage to one of the Army's finest officers.

That evening was most entertaining. Mr. Jay Cooke, the well-known financier, was visiting from his home in Philadelphia and staying at the Willard. Charlie and Mr. Cook had run into one another earlier in the week, and Mr. Cooke reaffirmed his invitation to Charlie and Rebecca to join him for dinner.

He was a charming and gracious host, and Rebecca enjoyed the evening enormously. After dinner, the gentlemen excused themselves briefly to discuss business. Charlie was very contemplative that night. When Rebecca tried to pry information out of him, he was not particularly forthcoming. "Thinking about the future, honey. Thinking about the future." Rebecca resolved to ferret it out of him in the not too far distant future.

But for now, they needed to pack and get some sleep. The train for home was to leave early the following morning.

CHAPTER 29

Sunday, February 5, 1865

Rebecca settled into bed, while Charlie finished in the bathing room. She let her mind wonder at the possibilities for the evening, knowing full well that Charlie would not turn away her attentions. The blonde had decided that perhaps tonight was the night when the tables would be turned. She would place a foot in what had been Charlie's world, while inviting Charlie into her own.

She tapped her fingers against the covers as she stared at the door, behind which he was still ensconced, doing God only knew what. "Charlie? Are you all right?"

"Yes, dear. I was just, um, brushing my teeth." Charlie had taken special care, cleaning every nook and cranny of his body, brushing his hair until it gleamed. It was the last night of their honeymoon, and he wanted to make it memorable.

Rebecca watched as Charlie dropped the robe she was wearing, revealing the trueness of their situation to Rebecca's eyes, and got into bed. The blonde smiled and gave the evening an unexpected start when she opened her own arms, inviting Charlie there.

Charlie settled into her arms—a little awkward, a little surprised, but very pleased. Being held was something that Charlie had seldom experienced since she was a small child.

"Comfortable?" Rebecca asked as she traced her fingers over her partner's arm.

Charlie burrowed her head into the hollow of Rebecca's shoulder and purred like a big, happy cat. "Incredibly. This feels so good. I think I understand why you like it so much."

"It is my favorite place, Charlie. Safe in your arms." She paused and let her hand slip under Charlie's arm to caress her side. "Are you ah, tired?"

Charlie's voice dropped an octave as she stroked the soft skin over Rebecca's ribs. "No, darling. Being with you always excites me." Charlie gently kissed the warm skin under her cheek.

"Oh, yes, well..." Rebecca was breathless with Charlie's touch. Then she remembered she was the one who was supposed to be doing the seducing. She placed her fingers under Charlie's chin and lifted her face, and then she kissed her. Kissed her with all the passion she felt for her lover.

Charlie stiffened for a moment. In her entire life, even when she was first learning about the love that was possible between two women, she had never been anything other than the aggressor, the initiator. Rebecca taking the lead in their lovemaking was startling. Charlie felt overwhelmingly vulnerable. But then the tenderness mixed with passion that was so uniquely part of Rebecca's love broke through Charlie's defenses. She surrendered to her partner's kiss and touch.

Rebecca pulled back from the kiss and looked into Charlie's eyes; having felt her stiffen, she was concerned. "Are you all right?"

Charlie looked straight into her eyes. "I am very all right. And I am very yours."

Rebecca cleared her throat nervously. "I am glad to hear that,

Charlie. If it is all right with you, I would like to experiment a little tonight."

"Whatever you want, however you want me, is always all right with me, darling. I am yours tonight, as always."

Rebecca kissed Charlie again. In a very serious voice, she asked, "Whatever I want?"

Charlie took a deep breath. Rebecca was asking for something Charlie had never surrendered to anyone. She thought about it for a moment, then smiled. "Anything at all, darling."

Monday, February 6, 1865

Charlie wired ahead to inform Jocko that the little trap was not sufficient to carry home their baggage. They arrived at the station late in the afternoon, and Jocko and several troopers worked furiously for a few minutes to unload the luggage, including the extensive purchases Rebecca had made in her one day shopping frenzy.

As they rode home in the big supply wagon, Charlie looked at Rebecca. "Darling, I have to say, spending a week in Washington with just the two of us and few duties to attend to was lovely, but I think I like the fact that we are coming home."

"Yes, I loved the trip. My first time out of Virginia, but this is my home." She took his hand. "Our home, and I am glad to be back."

As they rounded the curve of the carriageway to the house, Charlie spotted a forlorn little figure sitting slumped on the portico steps. As the sounds of the team reached the house, the little black-haired head popped up and a small body propelled itself like a missile at the moving carriage. "Papa!"

All Charlie could see was Em running toward the horses. He jumped from the carriage and, with long strides, caught the child up before she and the horses intersected. "Emily. You know better than to run at horses like that!" Charlie, like most parents, reacted in fear first and then anger that his little one had done something so dangerous.

All Em knew was that her Papa was home, and he was definitely not happy with her. The tears started like a spring that had been plugged and was suddenly cleared. "Em sorry. Papa!" she whimpered through the flood of tears.

Jocko drew the wagon to a halt, and Rebecca joined the wailing child and shaky father.

Rebecca rubbed Charlie's back to soothe him as she carefully looked Em over. "Charlie, she is fine. I think you scared her more than the horses did."

Charlie settled the little girl more securely on his hip. "I am sorry, Em. You scared Papa. The horses are big, and they could have hurt you if you had surprised them. They could not have stopped if you had run in front of them."

She wrapped her arms around his neck. "Miss Papa."

"Papa and Mama 'Becca missed you, too, imp."

She pulled back and grabbed his cheeks, as was becoming her habit. "Papa not leave 'gain."

"Little one, Papa has to work, and has to leave sometimes, but Papa is home for a while."

At the thought of her Papa leaving again Em decided to go into a full blown pout and reached for Rebecca. "Mama 'Becca."

Rebecca took the child in her arms and grinned at Charlie. "Let us go inside. It is far too cold out here for her."

They walked in to a scene of minor mayhem. Jocko and Reg were trying to unload the wagon, simultaneously directing several troopers in various, usually contradictory directions. The three escaped to the back parlor, where a nice fire was already lit and a small kettle was simmering on the hob, with the teapot waiting to be filled.

"So, imp, were you good for Aunt Elizabeth and Uncle Richard while we were gone?"

"Yes, Papa, Em good. Get penny fwom Unc Wichawd."

"Oh. Just one?"

"No. Penny." She held up her hand stretching her fingers as far apart as they would go. "Many."

"How many pennies did you get?"

Rebecca chuckled as she poured them both a cup of tea. "Charlie, Charlie, Charlie, she is trying to tell you how many pennies Richard gave her."

"Oh." He grinned at her. Learning to be a commander was much easier than learning how to be a papa. "So Uncle Richard gave you this many pennies." He held up his own hand with all five fingers spread."

"Yes. Em not cry, Unc Wichad give penny."

Charlie looked at Rebecca. "Seems that Richard learned the advantages of bribery, too." Then he turned back to his daughter. "So, Em, how many pennies?"

She looked to her hand and then to her papa. She gave a soft sigh. "Fibe."

"Very good, Em. I am proud that you are learning to count."

Rebecca settled down on the couch and took Em from Charlie, cuddling her into the crook of her arm and kissing her on the top of the head. "I missed you, my little darling."

"Em miss Mama 'Becca."

Charlie stood and looked at his beautiful wife and their very lively daughter, cuddling, laughing, with Em plastering soggy baby kisses on Rebecca's face. At that moment, he felt a peace he had never known before. The idyllic moment was broken as Elizabeth stormed into the room.

"Thank God, you are back. I swear this child has driven me to distraction with moping and wailing and sulking and wanting her Mama 'Becca and Papa. I gave up today. She was plastered to the window in the hall at dawn. She nearly ran down the first person that opened the front door so she could go sit on the porch and wait." Elizabeth's description and the angelic little girl in Rebecca's arms somehow did not match.

It was probably not the wisest move Charles Redmond ever made; he burst out laughing at his flustered friend.

"Ignore him, Elizabeth." Rebecca turned mischievous eyes on Charlie. "He has just not been himself since last evening."

Charlie had the grace to blush a charming shade of red, starting with his ears, as usual, and working its way across his face. He rather gracelessly changed the subject. "So, Elizabeth, how are you and Richard?"

"Engaged."

"Ah, good, good...Engaged? He really meant it?"

"He did, indeed. We managed to get the confusion cleared up while you were off lollygagging in Washington."

Charlie stood with his mouth gaping. He looked back and forth from Elizabeth to Rebecca. The very thought of being in this household while another wedding was being planned put the fear of God in him. Eventually, he managed to stammer out, "Ah... congratulations. You will, of course, be married here?"

"I am not sure where we will be married, Charlie. We have both agreed it would be best to wait until after the spring campaign."

"Well, we must celebrate. Is Richard joining us for dinner?"

Elizabeth laughed, "Actually, my clumsy fiancé is in his tent resting. He wrenched his ankle this morning. It is nothing serious, but he will be off of it for a day or two."

Rebecca stood and gave Elizabeth as much of a hug as she could with Em in her arms. "Congratulations, Elizabeth. If you and Richard would like to come back here for your wedding, please know you are welcome."

"You know, Rebecca, now that we have the guest population under control, do you think we could find a room here in the house for Richard?"

The blonde grinned. "Oh, I do not know, Charlie. Do you think it would be safe to let them be under the same roof? I am not sure we can chaperone them all the time."

Charlie grinned back. "Well, perhaps they would like as much chaperonage as you and I had."

"Hmm. This is true." She turned green eyes on Elizabeth. "What do you think? Can we trust you and Richard not to corrupt the moral fiber of Culpeper if we let him stay in the house?"

Elizabeth raised her eyebrow. "Considering what you two have done to the normal standards of propriety, I have no doubt that we will be able to conduct ourselves appropriately."

"Well, make sure that you at least live up to our standard," Rebecca teased, then rang the bell for Reg.

When the butler appeared, she gave instructions that a room should be prepared for Colonel Polk.

"So, do we need to organize a team to transport Himself up to the house?" Charlie asked with a chuckle.

"I think he could use a hand or two. Perhaps Jocko and Duncan could help him."

Charlie caught Reg in the hall, and instructed that Jocko, who was just finishing with unloading the wagon, be asked to step in for a moment.

After a few minutes, Jocko came into the room and bowed very deeply at the waist. "Oh yes, Your Majesty, what can your lowly serf be doing for ya now?"

"Thank you, Sergeant Jackson. Your impression of a Russian is outstanding. How is Mrs. White? And, so you know, I invited you in to help us congratulate Doctor Walker, and to ask if you will perform a mission of mercy."

"Mrs. White is fine." He turned to Elizabeth. "I am not sure what I am congratulating you for, but well done, whatever is it. And, who needs rescuing now?"

Charlie broke out in gales of laughter. "I am glad, and look forward to seeing her. Do you think she would join us for dinner? Doctor Walker is engaged to Colonel Polk. And Colonel Polk, with his twisted ankle, needs a hand in moving over to his new room here in the main house. Oh, and Jocko, will you join us for dinner as well?"

Jocko smiled when he realized he was being a complete ass. "Yes, Sir, thank you, Sir." He nodded to Rebecca. "Thank you, Ma'am. I will take care of everything, General."

Charlie and Rebecca, carrying Em with them, excused themselves to go upstairs and freshen up. Jocko and Elizabeth set off to collect Richard and get him settled in the house. All in all, the evening promised to be amusing.

Charlie carried Em upstairs and handed her over to Tess. He had a very tired, much happier little one in his arms than the household had evidently seen for the past week. As he emerged back into the hall, he took a deep breath, preparing himself for what he feared would be at best a bittersweet meeting. He patted his coat pocket to make sure that the papers were all there, then knocked lightly on Constance's door.

As he stepped into the room, he had to discipline himself tightly. In the week they had been gone, it was obvious that Constance's condition had worsened. She was pale and languid; only her eyes remained truly vital. Her Bible was open at her side and the room was decidedly warm from the carefully tended fire in the hearth.

"Good afternoon, Miss Constance. I hope I am not disturbing you."

"Not at all, General, please come in."

Charlie entered and walked to stand beside the window. It was cooler there. "So how have you been doing while we were gone? I hope that things have not been too great a strain on you, Ma'am."

"I have been as can be expected, Sir. Not much use to anyone except my little one here." She slowly rubbed her belly.

"You are doing the most miraculous thing that any woman can do, Ma'am. You are creating a new life. I believe that is of use to the whole world. And to bring new life into the world as it is now—well, to me, that is an act of incredible courage." He smiled at her, a tender smile. This woman was as valiant as any man in his regiment. But trying to tell her that was useless. She was bringing a life into the world, something Charlie would never be able to do. He was perfectly well aware of the price that Constance was willing to pay.

She gave the edge of the bed a gentle pat. "Come here, General."

Charlie sat rather gingerly on the very edge of Constance's bed. For a moment, he fidgeted with his hands, not quite sure where to put them, then settled on folding them on one knee, using them to brace himself in a rather uncomfortable position.

Without a word said between them, but looking him directly in the eyes, Constance took Charlie's hand and placed it on her stomach. "Do you feel that?"

Charlie's eyes widened, first from the mere fact of the touch, which was unheard of in his world. Women in the advanced stages of pregnancy were not even seen socially, let alone touched so intimately by a man other than their husband or physician. But then he felt what she meant him to, the movements of what felt like a very robust child, battering at his or her mother, eager to be out in the world. A look of pure wonder filled Charlie's face. "Is that...?"

"That is life, General. The life of your son or daughter."

Tears instantly filled his eyes. He took Constance's hand in his own and raised it reverently to his lips. "You give me a gift for which I can never even begin to express my gratitude. I pray daily for your survival, dear lady. Please know that should you survive this birth, you have a home and my protection for the rest of my life."

"That is a very kind offer, but all I ask is that my children have a home and a family to love and care for them."

Charlie laid his right hand on the Bible that was still lying on the covers beside Constance. "Ma'am, I swear on all that I hold holy and sacred, I will love them, care for them, and raise them as I would children of my body. Em is already the daughter of my heart; this child," he reverently placed his hand on her belly, "I think, will be my firstborn son."

Constance could not help but smile. "Then I hope, for you, it is a boy. A fine son and heir for you and Rebecca."

Charlie looked very serious. "And if it is a girl, can we name her Constance? For you must know, whether it is a boy or a girl, this child will be greatly loved."

"I would be honored, and yes, I do know that. But tell me, General, if it is a boy, what will you name him?"

Charlie could see in her eyes she was teasing him. "I have always thought Charles to be a fine name. However, I suspect that Rebecca may have some thoughts on the subject."

"So it is. Tell me, General, what has brought you to my bedside?"

"You asked me to handle all of the appropriate legal issues so that adoption of these children would be very clear. I have done so. For Emily, all we need do is fill in her date and county of birth, have you sign it, and have it witnessed. For this little one," he gestured at her distended belly, "we will have to fill in the name, date of birth and county, when the time comes."

Charlie laid the two documents at her side, then rose and retreated to the window. Looking out, he continued in a quiet, determined voice. "I want you to look over the papers before you sign them. There is a third document I want you to examine as well." He pulled the papers from his pocket. He had set up a trust fund in Constance's name, which would automatically be split between the two children in the event of her death. "I wanted you to know that you, and they, would be taken care of financially, regardless of what may happen to me in the upcoming campaign."

"General, that really is too much. I am sure you will be fine. However, if something were to come to pass, I am certain Rebecca would still stand with the children."

"I know she will. But if you survive, you will not be dependent on her or anyone. And if you do not, you can rest assured that they have their own means, regardless of what may happen here. I just wanted to be...thorough and let you know how serious my commitment to them is."

"You are indeed a kind man. Thank you for your generosity."

Constance looked at the papers beside her, and then at the fidgeting man at the window. "General, I have faith in your honor and the completeness of these documents. Will you go and find witnesses so that we can finish this now?"

He nodded and stepped to the bell pull, summoning Tess. He asked her to fetch Dr. Walker and Sergeant Jackson. As they waited for those two old and trusted friends to join them, they sat together in silent companionship; all that needed to be said had been. When Elizabeth and Jocko entered the room, Charlie quietly explained what he needed from them.

"We will be glad to help you, Charlie." Elizabeth sat on the bed and took Constance's hand. "And you are sure? You trust Charlie and Rebecca to raise these children?"

Constance smiled, her face lighting so, that for a moment she looked almost healthy. "I cannot think of two people who deserve children more than the General and Rebecca. And besides, we could not pry Em away from the General if we had to. Now, let us get the legalities out of the way."

Charlie laid the papers out while Elizabeth helped Constance sit up in her bed and positioned a lapboard across her knees. The signing of the adoption papers went quickly. The final document, the trust fund, brought raised eyebrows from both Elizabeth and Jocko.

"Hmmm, Gen'l C. You are bound and determined to cover all bases. Would you consider adopting me?"

Dinner had been comfortable but slightly subdued after the signing of the adoption papers. Constance's confinement and probable death hung like a cloud over what was otherwise a festive occasion.

As the meal finished, Jocko and Mrs. White excused themselves. With a bit of teasing and smirking on the part of the other folks at the table, they made a laughing exit from the dining room. Courting couples were always fair game for teasing.

Charlie assisted Richard from the table and, limping heavily, into the back parlor. A small game table was set before the fireplace, and the four of them sat down for an evening of cards and gossip. As Charlie shuffled, Elizabeth started quizzing Rebecca on what they had done and whom they had seen in Washington.

"Well, my friend, I do not think there was a fashionable home in Washington we did not call on. I even had the good fortune to take tea with Mrs. Lincoln at the White House."

"Tea with Mrs. Lincoln? I have heard many things of her. So tell me, what is she really like?"

"Oh, she was absolutely charming. I think, perhaps, she is very lonely. There is so much animosity toward Southerners in Washington nowadays, and she is still obviously one. I hear tell that many people do not understand how important it is to maintain appearances at the White House, and do not appreciate what she has done to refurbish the place."

Charlie and Richard sat quietly, neatly arranging their cards and pretending to be part of the furniture.

"I have heard that she has mediums in and out of the White House regularly to try and contact her dead son. She seems to have a reputation as a rather strange bird."

"I think the loss of her son, coupled with all of the horror of this war, has left her with a great sadness and a longing for something she cannot articulate."

"Before I arrived here, I took dinner with a friend of mine who is an aide in the White House. He said there was rumor of a dream that President Lincoln has been having regularly for the last few months, and it may also have something to do with her mood."

"Yes, she mentioned it, and I think it weighs heavily on her heart. Mr. Lincoln does not expect to survive his tenure. I pray sincerely he does, for if he dies, the South haters will gain control, and I fear the aftermath will be very hard."

Charlie and Richard continued their silence. Both were aware, far more so than Rebecca and Elizabeth, just how deeply the desire for revenge ran in some of the Northern politicians.

"I do believe," Rebecca patted Charlie's hand, "that my dear husband was a little stunned when we went shopping."

Charlie had the grace to hang his head a bit. "Well, uh, it was a bit, uh, extensive." He looked intently at his cards. "Will you open the bidding, dear?"

Rebecca sighed and for the first time looked at her cards. After a moment of arranging them, she made her bid, then looked to Charlie. "Yes, dear."

For a few moments, the four of them concentrated on their cards. Charlie then commented, "You know, we did have dinner with Jay Cooke."

Richard's eyes left Elizabeth for a moment. "The banker?"

"Yes. He and I discussed what the business world would be like down here after the war is over. I think Culpeper will be in need of a fair bit of support to recover, so we are beginning to explore the idea of opening a bank here when I get back."

Rebecca's eyes widened. "A bank? Charlie, that is wonderful."

"Well, dear, we are still at the talking stage. Nothing specific has been set down yet, and I did not want to get your hopes up."

"It certainly does not matter to me. We will be busy enough with the farm, but if the opportunity arises for you, it would be tremendous."

"Oh, I do not think I will have the day to day running of it, if it comes about at all. I really do not have the skills for it. But several of our men were clerks and such before the war, and perhaps one of them will be willing to move here and help us out."

Rebecca nodded and laid a card on the trick. She could tell Charlie was excited. "You would make a wonderful banker. Perhaps Elizabeth will come back and open a hospital. And Sergeant Jackson could come in and run the local tavern," she teased, as she watched Richard try to decide which card to play.

Charlie and Richard both laughed. The idea of Jocko as a tavern keeper was most amusing. Richard, in particular, had a history of attempting to drink Jocko under the table—and failing miserably. "My dear, if Jocko were the tavern keeper, he would likely drink all his profits and then some. That man has the original hollow leg." Richard thought for a moment. "On the other hand, if he ran out of rum, all he would need to do is tap into his own arm, for with all he has consumed over the years, I suspect he has it running in his veins instead of blood." Richard laid down his card and surrendered the trick to the ladies.

~

Friday, February 17, 1865

All through the day, Sarah had been cooking. A birthday—the first birthday that sweet little girl could really celebrate—was an important event. Sarah was busy fixing everything the little one liked for dinner and baking a lovely spice cake, decorated with whipped cream frosting. Gen'l Charlie had brought home some fine sugar instead of the heavy brown stuff they got if they were lucky. Sarah was in her element.

At the same time, Tess had a very excited little girl to contend with. All she could think of was the party that had been promised to her. It was not obvious that Em understood what a birthday was, but she certainly understood the idea of a party. And she wanted it to start immediately.

Charlie came in from his daily rounds and went upstairs to change into his oldest coat. As surely as the sun rose and set, he knew he would be wearing birthday cake before the day was complete.

Rebecca entered their room and slid up behind him, wrapping her arms around his waist and laying her head on his back. "I love you, Charlotte Redmond."

Charlie stopped breathing. No one had called her Charlotte in twenty years. As far as she could remember, no one had said "I love you" to Charlotte since her mother, that blurry figure in the recesses of her early childhood memories. He managed to find his voice. "I love you, Rebecca Redmond."

She drew in a deep satisfied breath and patted his back. "But now, my dashing husband, you have a little girl who is chomping at the bit for her "pawty" to begin, and I think we should get downstairs before she has a full blown conniption."

Charlie laughed, settled his coat, and offered Rebecca his arm. "Well, Madam, shall we?"

Arm in arm, they went to the nursery and collected Em and Tess. "Well, little one, it is time. First, we will visit your mama, so you must be very good and gentle."

"Yes, Papa. I be good."

They entered Constance's room quietly. The fragile woman was waiting for them and beckoned Em to her with open arms. "How is my big girl today?"

"Mama, I am good. Papa say."

Charlie and Constance smiled at one another over the shining black head currently cuddled onto Constance's shoulder. "So, Emily, what are you going to do now that you are two and a big girl?"

"Unc Wichawd make me count." She held up her hand. "Dis many."

Constance laughed, an act that unfortunately set off a coughing fit. Rebecca lifted the little girl from her arms, while Charlie braced her through the episode. Finally, she regained her breath. "Well, little one, I wish I could come downstairs with you, but I am afraid I have to stay here in my bed. You have a lovely birthday, my darling girl."

"Yes, Mama. I love you."

The little girl was very quiet and solemn as Rebecca carried her downstairs. "Mama bewy sick."

"Yes, sweetheart, she is."

"Mama go be with other papa?"

Rebecca looked at the child, for the first time realizing how much this little girl really understood. "Yes, your Papa Henry and God."

Em thought for a few minutes. "You be my weal mama then?"

"If you would like. Yes, I will be your mama."

"Good. Mama be happy, Em be happy with you. Pawty now?"

Rebecca chuckled and hugged her little girl. "As soon as papa comes down from tending to your mama."

Rebecca, burdened with the weight of the rapidly growing child, had walked down the stairs slowly. Charlie, having settled Constance, hurried behind them.

Together the three of them entered the main dining room. Elizabeth and Richard were waiting, along with Samantha Carter and Jeremiah, Jocko and Mrs. White, and even Duncan. He had recently been elevated to the rank of sergeant and was looking a little uncomfortable. It was unclear if it was because of the new stripes on his tunic or the basket he held awkwardly in his hands.

Charlie relieved Rebecca of Em and announced for the room. "Ladies and gentlemen, may I present the birthday girl, Miss Emily Adams Redmond."

Applause broke out as Charlie set the little girl down on her own two feet. "Your curtsy, if you please, Miss Emily."

Emily looked up to him and ran her tongue between her lips. They had secretly been practicing this every morning during breakfast, and she knew what she was supposed to do. Very carefully, she held the hem of her skirt and executed her curtsy.

Charlie beamed. His little girl was starting to grow up. If he were very lucky, he would see that curtsy many more times.

Elizabeth called the child to her. "Emily, you are two now, and two year olds are starting to grow up. So tell us, which do you want first—your dinner or your presents?"

Emily looked at every face in the room, all of which were desperate to hide grins. She looked to her papa and sighed, her shoulders slumping a little. "Dinnew."

Rebecca was also beaming. Her little girl could think about

others, something that was very important, in her opinion. "Well, little one, I think that perhaps our guests could wait for their dinner while you open one present." Just then, a suspicious little yip was heard from the basket Duncan was holding.

Rebecca turned her head very slowly in Duncan's direction. "Is there something you want to tell us about your basket, Sergeant Nailer?"

"Um, yes, M-m-ma'am. Miss Em, the b-boys found this little g-girl, and we thought you wo-would l-like her." The yipping had grown louder, and just then a small head, white with black and brown markings, popped up out of the basket. "'Tis a terrier, M-ma'am. A Jack Russell b-bitch."

Em clapped her hands together and looked to Rebecca for permission. When it was granted with a slight nod, Em joyfully ran across the room to Duncan and her new puppy.

Charlie looked on as Emily clasped the squirming puppy to her chest. "Upstaged by my own men—again!"

Monday, February 20, 1865

The weekend had been unremarkable in most ways, other than the challenges presented by trying to house break a puppy and teach a two year old what was and was not appropriate behavior with said animal. Charlie woke early, as per normal, and took a morning run in a fine, cold misty rain. Winter was not quite ready to release its hold.

He returned to the house, cleaned up, and settled into his office to read the normal dispatches. There on top of the pile of documents that were a normal part of his life was a telegram.

A sense of dread clutched at his stomach. Telegrams usually meant bad news. He sat for a good five minutes with the envelope in his hand, hesitating to open it, knowing what was probably in it.

Finally, he read the dreaded but not unexpected words.

Prepare to mobilize stop

Troops to be field ready within seven days stop Sheridan

The flimsy yellow paper drifted from Charlie's numb fingers. It was time. He sat there in a stupor, for how long, he had no idea. Then the door opened and Rebecca came in with the mid-morning tea.

She stopped as soon as she saw the look on his face; approaching him slowly, she placed the tray on the desk. "It is bad news."

Silently, he picked up the telegraph and handed it to her.

Her hands were trembling as she took the paper from him, tears forming in her eyes before she had even read the first line.

CHAPTER 30

MONDAY, FEBRUARY 20, 1865

Rebecca and Charlie finally shook themselves and set about the immediate tasks before them. Rebecca left to consult with Reg, Beulah, and Sarah. She had to see to her household, making sure she had the supplies, medicines, and equipment she would need once the men and the facilities they provided were gone. She knew Charlie would be leaving a contingent of men behind in Culpeper. Some of the men remaining were mustering out because their terms were completed and they had chosen to make Culpeper their home. Others would be left behind to man a key communications center on the always-vital rail line. Housing would have to be found for the new residents, as well as quarters for the small detachment remaining behind.

Meanwhile, Charlie sat at his desk and started drafting orders for his men. The daily lunch meeting of officers would be interesting, to say the least, as he would be asking one of the company commanders to volunteer to stay behind.

He walked into the Officers' Mess tent and took his place at the head of the table. As usual, the officers were chatting amongst themselves as troopers served lunch under Jamison's watchful eye. When Charlie joined them for lunch, he usually sat, was served and ate with them, then carried on whatever discussion he wanted to have after the meal was over. Today was different. He stood silently at his place at the long table until he had the attention of every man there.

"Gentlemen, we have received orders. We are to be ready to march within one week."

A rumble of sound went around the table, some grumbling, and some eager to be back in the field. Young Avery of Company I spoke up first. "General, do you know where we are bound?"

"No, not yet. I do know we will be heading south, but beyond that, no. General Sheridan always keeps his plans close to his vest. So, we go where we are told, when we are told—as usual." Charlie stopped for a minute. "However, one company is not going to be joining us. We have been ordered to leave a detachment here in Culpeper to guard the railhead from marauders and maintain communications. It is inevitable there will be a number of deserters —we are already starting to see it happen—and we will need guards here to maintain civil order as they start to return to their homes, or what is left of them. They will be hungry, probably angry and desperate. It will not be easy service."

Dewees of Company D, eager to prove his company's loyalty after the problems with Montgomery, spoke up first. "But, Sir, if one company is left behind, they will not be there to participate in the glorious finale."

Charlie raised his eyebrow at Dewees. "Captain, I hardly think the finale, as you call it, will be 'glorious'. General Grant has held General Lee's forces pinned in Richmond and Petersburg for over two months. We know the siege has been at least partially effective, as we continue to cut their supply lines. Going against men who are half starved, short on clothing, supplies, food, and ammunition is hardly glorious. It is simply the inevitable end to this miserable war. Be at ease, Captain Dewees. Your company won the right to stand as vanguard at the gymkhana. I will not rescind that status now. But put out of your mind that the coming battles will be glorious. They will be anything but.

"Gentlemen, it is my thought we will want to cull a company from among all of your men—choosing those men who are technically fit for light duty, but whose injuries have not completely healed or have left them with some limitations. In addition, I would like to cull out those men whose terms of service have expired, muster them out if they wish and provide them with the means either to return home or settle here in the Culpeper area." A buzz went around the room. A number of the men from the original Pennsylvania troops were still feeling the effects of their injuries, but not one of them was ready to voluntarily excuse themselves from these last days of the war.

"I will need a volunteer to remain behind and command our communications detachment." Charlie waited a moment. No one jumped up to volunteer. "Then discuss it amongst yourselves. If no one volunteers, we will draw straws tomorrow at lunch." He turned to Captain Dewees. "You, Sir, because of the special circumstances with Company D, will be excluded from the draw, if you wish." The other company commanders nodded their heads in agreement.

"Until then, I expect each of you to initiate immediate mobilization efforts. Tear down any temporary structures, clean up any areas, fill the latrines, et cetera. Colonel Polk and I will develop any special orders as we progress. For now, start your men getting their own equipment in order."

Charlie then sat down and ate, while fielding a wide variety of questions as the conversation turned on the massive logistics of remobilizing the regiment.

After lunch, Polk and Charlie retired to his office to write the detailed mobilization orders. All afternoon, a constant stream of officers and key men filed in and out, as plans for supplies, foodstuffs, horse management, and equipment transportation were discussed and finalized.

Elizabeth, accompanied by Samuelson and Whitman, was one of the last staff members to be consulted. Charlie was concerned they would end up trying to fight a series of running skirmishes, rather than fixed battles. Designing a way to treat injured men when the regiment was on the move was a major challenge. They worked through dinner, which was brought in on trays, to find a way that, while not exactly satisfactory, was at least viable.

Charlie dragged himself to bed that night exhausted. The lamps were dimmed, no candles were lit, and the house was silent. It seemed everyone else had finally fallen into bed; sleep called him like a siren.

He quietly entered Rebecca's private sitting room and stripped his clothes, hoping to grab his nightshirt and slip quietly into bed and her sleeping warmth.

He found Rebecca waiting for him in bed, holding his pillow to her chest, crying quietly.

"Darling, what is it? Why did you wait up for me? It is so late, my love, and you need your sleep."

"I cannot sleep. I am too worried about your leaving and what will happen then."

"Darling, please, do not do this to yourself. I am leaving men here to take care of the place and to help Mayor Frazier keep order in town in case deserters start coming through. I will take the utmost care of myself. The war cannot last much longer. As things are going, I will be home before you know it, a month or two at the most, if General Grant's siege works as expected." Charlie took her in his arms and gently soothed her back and shoulders as they spoke.

"I am your wife and I love you. How can you ask me not to

worry?" Rebecca smiled, gently running her hand over his chest. "I only want you home."

He nuzzled her hair. "Can I tell you a secret?"

"Of course you can. You can tell me anything. I hope you know that."

"I really wish I could stay behind and send Richard off to the front. I am so tired of war, and want so much to begin our life here together properly." He sighed, "Unfortunately, I believe I have to complete my commitment to the Union and the Army. It is very hard for me to leave you, darling—but you are a powerful incentive to come back as quickly as I can."

"I know, but it still does not keep me from worrying about you. For the first time in my life, I have found love, and I do not want it to end. I realize you have commitments, but that does not make the fear and the pain of your departure any less."

"Nor does it make my task any easier, when my leaving is the last thing either of us wants. But I must, dear. Please understand why." Charlie laid his head on her shoulder and softly kissed her neck, offering comfort and taking it at the same time.

"I do understand, I truly do. I just cannot help but feel my heart is breaking for fear I will lose you. The only person I have ever loved passionately, the way I love you. Sometimes I think this is all so new to you, that you do not understand what will happen to my heart if you are killed." She paused, curling closer to him. "It will die with you, Charlie."

Charlie froze. The image in his mind of her life without him overlaid the image of his without her, and he knew the truth of what she said. "Then I suppose I just cannot let myself get killed. We have a daughter and another child on the way who just would not understand if their mother's heart died before its time."

"No, you had better not. I want you home; Em wants you home; and by the time you return there will be a new life for you to meet." She sighed and closed her eyes. "But do not be angry with me for doing what my heart tells me to do, which is worry."

"I cannot control that anyway, my love. I have learned I have as much ability to change the way you feel as I do to control the weather, so I shall not try. But," Charlie nibbled on her earlobe, "I can try and distract you for a bit."

"Charlie, stop." She pulled back and tried to make him understand. "Not everything can be made better by making love, and right now I need you to hold me more than I need to make love."

Charlie was immediately contrite. He pulled back, shifted, and took her in his arms, her head lying on his chest. She could not see the bleak look in his eyes. His fears and worries were just as great as hers, if not greater, as he knew what risks he was facing. Desperate men made dangerous enemies. Charlie's demon just laughed.

Tuesday, February 21, 1865

Charlie had just finished his morning run and was having his first cup of coffee when he heard a light tap on his office door. Whoever was knocking this early must have something important to say—and private. "Come."

"Major Timothy Byrnes, Commander, Company F, requests permission to speak freely, Sir."

"Have a seat, Byrnes. Since when have you had to stand on formality with me?"

Byrnes grinned ruefully, then unconsciously rubbed his thigh. Since he had taken a Minié ball in his leg the previous summer, he had developed the nervous habit. "Well, Sir, I think anyone actually volunteering to remain behind may be faced with a problem. These boys have a certain... enthusiasm for seeing an end to the war and getting home. I think a lot of them can taste it, if you know what I mean? If a man volunteers, he might be seen as a slacker—or even a coward."

Charlie shook his head and snorted. "I have been at war for so long and wanted to have peace so badly, I honestly never thought of that. I knew Dewees was eager, but given the problems we had earlier, it is understandable."

Byrnes raised his eyebrow. "Aye, he is a bit, Sir. I think he has the makings of a good commander, but under Monty he had very little opportunity to develop. Keep an eye on him, he may do something rash out there in the vanguard."

Charlie nodded. "However, I suspect you did not come here to talk about Company D's young commander. How can I help you?"

"Well, Sir, I think I might just want to stay behind. I have a good second who is entirely ready to take command and, to be honest, this leg is just plain bothering me. I have met some of the folks in town and seem to get on well with them. And I have the right experience. I was the local sheriff in Bucks County before the war began."

"So you would like me to arrange it so the men do not know you have volunteered, but you are actually volunteering?"

"That is about the sum of it, Sir. I think I could do a good job. And, um, Sir?"

"Yes, Byrnes?"

"I will make sure Mrs. Redmond's letters get through to you in the priority dispatch bags." Byrnes grinned at the General. It was not strictly by the book, in fact, it was specifically forbidden to put civilian correspondence into the priority military dispatches, but Byrnes was one of those who thought Rebecca was a good influence on the spit and polish officer.

Charlie called a meeting of all his officers that morning. The announcement was simple. "I recognize that every man of you, as well as every man you command, is dedicated to ending this conflict. Being asked to remain behind is a hardship, one that is necessary, but even so, a hardship. I thought long and hard last night, and reviewed the records and condition of every man in this regiment. My decision has been made strictly on the records of the individuals, their enlistment status, and their physical condition. Major Byrnes will lead the garrison here. He has been selected because of his civilian experience and because he has not fully recovered from the injuries he sustained last summer. Here are two lists. One is of men who will be assigned to the garrison in Culpeper. The other is the list of men who will be mustered out because the term of their enlistment has expired. Quartermaster, please handle the muster out pay and arrange for transportation for any who wish to return home. Major Byrnes, please take command of your garrison."

A roar of comments greeted his announcement. Charlie just smiled and sorted through all of the questions. One more thing had been accomplished—a safe garrison for Culpeper and his growing family.

~

Wednesday, February 22, 1865

Rebecca watched from the back porch as the men continued their task of dismantling the camp. She pulled her cloak tighter over her shoulders to ward off the evening chill.

Charlie had been dreadfully busy since the orders to get ready to move had come down. He was up and out even earlier than usual, and in much later than normal. Rebecca hated every moment of it. She held her tongue; however, knowing this was just as hard if not harder on him. Not only was he leaving home, but he was about to lead his men into what they believed would be the worst of the battles.

She tried to remain cheerful, but with every moment she felt slipping through her fingers, her mood turned darker. She continued to watch as more tents were struck down and the men worked to roll and secure them.

In the distance she could see Charlie on Jack, riding through the camp giving orders and ensuring that everything was done properly. She resisted the urge to call to him and ask him to come in. She again. "Now, I have a few questions, and you may feel free to be horribly mortified that I would even inquire about such things, and choose not to answer."

Lizzie shook off her own melancholy and sat back down. Lifting her fork, she paused before tasting the delicate omelet that was part of lunch. "I am beginning to suspect that there is nothing you will not explore if it suits you, my dear."

"This is true. I have learned that it does not pay to pretend that certain subjects are off limits or too delicate to talk about. So, bluntly, my question is about sex."

Lizzie snorted. She had rather suspected, given the introduction that her professional skills were about to be called upon. "Yes, my dear? You choose to question a professional about her area of expertise. That seems a wise course of action." Lizzie could not help but grin at her own saucy response.

"Well, I do not seem to have any problems satisfying Charlie; he is very responsive to my touch. I was just wondering if he has any particular needs that I would be better off knowing about. Since you have always been the one to meet those needs, I just thought you would be the one to ask."

Lizzie started laughing. "So, this conversation is so that one lover can hand him off to the other?" The image was priceless. Lizzie could not stop laughing.

"I do believe that sums up the gist of this conversation, yes." Rebecca could not help but smile. "Actually," she began to blush, "did you ever notice the little squeak Charlie makes when…"

"Yes. A most ungentlemanly little squeak. And entirely gratifying, I would say."

"So it would seem. The first time it happened, I thought I had done something very wrong."

"Oh, no, that is a symptom of something being very right. I have also noticed that she sometimes forgets to breathe."

"Oh yes, quite often. Then there is the resounding gasp." She finally had some idea of what it was like to be the wife of a military officer. In a way, she did envy the others, because they tended to travel with their husbands and she would not be able to do so.

She turned and went back into the house to find Em and Tess there to greet her. She knelt down and hugged the child, holding her close and envisioning her future with Charlie, raising his little "imp." "And how is my little darling tonight?"

"Hungwy."

"I was going to give her a little bread and honey before bed, Miss Rebecca."

Rebecca smiled at the nanny who adored Em and catered to her every whim. "Thank you, Tess, but I will take care of her. You can take the rest of the evening off."

"Thank you, Miss Rebecca." Tess gave a quick nod and left the room.

Rebecca and Em continued to the kitchen where Em was placed in her own chair, after which Rebecca busied herself with fixing the child an early evening snack. She settled down at the table with Em to drink a cup of tea while the child tried her best to devour a piece of bread covered in honey.

"I hope your Papa does not come in while you are a gooey mess; he will never forgive me." She sipped her tea. "Of course, with the smell of horses and sweat clinging to him, he may not notice." Rebecca sighed while she watched Em cram her mouth full of the sweet concoction.

Elizabeth entered quietly to join them. "You make a wonderful mother, Rebecca. She has flowered under your care, you know."

"Well, considering the situation, she does seem to be very happy. I am glad to be a part of that, but I am concerned about what will happen when you-know-who has to l-e-a-v-e." They had taken to spelling the word around Em, because saying it out loud sent her into crying fits.

"To be perfectly honest, I am almost more concerned over how she will handle it when Constance..." Elizabeth looked at Rebecca with a helpless shrug, unable to keep the sadness from her eyes.

Rebecca rose and poured her friend a cup of tea, placing it on the table as a silent request for her to sit. Then she retook her seat. "You know, she seems to understand. She knows her mother is going to go away, and she seems to have accepted it."

"I do not envy your position here when we move on, dear. It will not be easy. I have spoken with Mrs. White and she understands what needs to be done, but still it will be very hard."

Rebecca nodded, trying to keep tears from her eyes. "I am doing my best to..." She shook her head and reached out for Elizabeth's hand. "Thank you. Thank you for everything. I feel I have gained more than a friend; I feel as though I have gained a sister."

Elizabeth looked out of the window to the rolling meadowlands, the little pond, and the shadows of the mountains to the west and sighed. For once, she spoke her heart, a rare thing for this stoic woman. "I know I have found a sister in you, my dear—and somehow, perhaps even a home, something I have not had for a long time. I will miss you deeply."

"Then know you have a place here anytime you desire it. I would be delighted if you chose to come back here after the war." Rebecca tried to lighten the mood with an evil little grin. "We can work together to make Mrs. Williams as uncomfortable as possible. I will teach you the fine art of maliciously taunting unsuspecting bigots."

Elizabeth broke out into raucous laughter. "Just for that, I might have to find a colored assistant and make her really uncomfortable." She hesitated for a moment. "Did you really mean it when you said I could be married in your house?"

"Of course I did, my dear. However, I think Charlie will run to the hills. Being around women planning a wedding is too much for him, I think. I would be delighted if you and Richard were married here."

"Then, this is not a permanent farewell, dear. I promise I will be back, and I will bring both of those two recalcitrant fellows with me."

"You know, I am worried for all of you, but with your promise, some of my concern is lessened. Thank you."

~

Rebecca was tucking Em in, and making sure the pup was also nested in the pile of blankets by the fire. Em rolled over in her bed and watched as Rebecca checked the fire. "Mama?"

The call surprised Rebecca, simply by the fact it did not have "'Becca" attached to it. She turned, moving next to Em's bed and sitting on the floor so she could be eye to eye with the girl. "Yes, my little darling?"

"Papa?"

"Oh, Papa is working." She brushed her fingers through Em's dark hair once again marveling at the fact that it was the same color and texture as Charlie's.

"Papa leaving?"

"Yes, Papa must go away for a while, but he will come home. He has promised us."

A little chin quivered.

"Oh, sweetheart. Would you like Papa to promise you, too?"

"Pwease."

"All right, you wait here and I will go get Papa. We will be right back."

Rebecca decided it was time to have Charlie come in. His men were grown and quite independent of him, but his daughter needed him.

As she stepped out on the back porch to try and find him, she saw him coming up the steps. "Just the Papa I need to see."

He bent and softly kissed Rebecca's cheek. "Yes, darling? So what does Mama require of Papa?"

"It is not so much what Mama requires, as what Emily needs."

He put his arm around her shoulder as the two walked into the house and up the stairs. "What does the little one need, love? You know I will do whatever I can."

"She wants you to promise her you will come home."

"I will promise to do everything in my power to come home as quickly as I can."

"Then let us go so you can do that, or she will not sleep tonight."

They went upstairs to Em's room. When they opened the door, they caught a glimpse of a tiny body running across the room to jump into bed. There was one very confused puppy by the fireplace.

Charlie looked from the puppy to the little girl. "Hmmm. Seems somebody was out of bed when she was not supposed to be. Were you cuddling your puppy, little one?"

Em looked to the puppy, then cast her eyes down, nodding guiltily. She knew the dog was not supposed to be in the bed with her.

Charlie walked over and sat on the side of the bed, taking the child in his arms. "Well, little one, if you need cuddles, you have only to ask me or Mama."

Em settled immediately into his arms, "Papa leave?"

"Yes, honey, Papa has to work, and my work makes me leave sometimes. But I will come back, I promise."

The little girl sighed, cuddling closer. "Miss Papa."

Charlie held her very close. "And Papa misses you when I go away, too. But you have Mama and your puppy and friends like Jeremiah and Tess to keep you company when I am gone."

"Yes, Papa." She said it, but it was clear she did not mean it.

"And I will write Mama all the time, and I promise each letter will have a message for you."

"Yes, Papa." She curled even deeper and yawned. Clearly Charlie held one very tired little girl in his arms.

"Ready for sleep, little one?"

She only nodded, taking a death grip on his tunic.

"Then into bed with you. You need to let go of Papa's coat."

She yawned again, her eyes falling shut, but her grip remaining tight.

Charlie looked at Rebecca, beseeching her help with his expression. As he had been talking with Em, the little puppy had crawled out of her bedding by the fire and was now lying over Charlie's boots. He was well and truly pinned.

Rebecca lifted the puppy to the bed and placed it next to Em's spot then untangled the now nearly asleep girl from her Papa. She placed both child and puppy under the covers, leaning over to kiss Em on the forehead.

Charlie rose, leaned over and emulated Rebecca, then stepped back and put his arm around his wife as the two of them just watched their little girl and her puppy for a few moments.

Charlie walked through camp, proud of the work that his men had accomplished. He made his way to the stables where he found Tarent cleaning the hooves of one of the auxiliary mounts. Charlie leaned against the stall and watched the man working with the great ease that came with tremendous skill.

"Sergeant," Charlie called, when he could see the man was finished with the hoof he was working on.

"Aye, General. What can I be doing for you today?" The older man did not even bother to straighten before throwing a tired salute.

"I want to talk to you about the spring campaign. It is not going to be easy."

Tarent sighed and shrugged his shoulders. Charlie could hear the crackling of arthritic joints from several feet away. "Aye, I do not expect it will be. I have been training my boys hard; the horses are going to need the best tending."

"So they are, but I am more concerned about you. I mean no disrespect, but you are not a young man anymore."

"Ah, no, I am not, to be sure. But who but the Army is going to take a broken down old farrier?"

"Well, actually, I am prepared to offer you the position of barn manager here at Redmond Stables." Charlie looked at his mud caked boots and then back to his friend. "But it means you will have to muster out and stay behind to help Miss Rebecca get the place running."

Tarent looked at the shoe in his hand, carefully removing the old nails from it and stashing them in a pocket before he looked back at Charlie. "Muster out of the Army, eh. Well, Lord knows, I have done my time and more. I passed my thirty year mark last month."

"I know. Miss Rebecca and I think you would be perfect. I trust you not only to look after the farm, but her as well. It is not going to be easy on her when I leave." He leaned on the stall door. "I have already found her crying twice, and I am at my wits' end. By asking a few of my most trusted friends to muster out, I hope she will find some comfort while I am gone."

"Well, since you put it that way, General, how can I refuse? Do I get the cottage that goes with the farrier's job?"

"Complete with all the holes in the roof." Charlie offered his hand, "Thank you, Tarent."

Tarent took Charlie's hand in a strong grip. "My pleasure, Sir. Oh, and in all the fixing up around here this winter, I had the boys put a new roof on it. Fireplace draws well, too." A laconic grin, and the old man was off to his forge.

Charlie spent the rest of the day talking to various men about the same option; of the twenty he asked, seventeen took him up on his offer. As he scraped the mud from his boots before going into the house, he wished someone would ask him to muster out.

He removed his boots in the kitchen so as not to track the remaining mud through the house. Pulling on a pair of carpet slippers kept by the back door, he set off for his office to finish some paperwork before beginning the task of packing.

~

Around midnight, the door to his office opened and he looked up to find Rebecca standing there.

"Charlie?"

"Come in, darling. I am so sorry; it must be late. I lost track of time." She was in her nightdress and a robe. From the look of her eyes, she had been crying again. He rose from his desk, which was piled with various stacks of paper, and hurried over to take her in his arms.

"I...I want to give you something." She took his hand and laid her father's watch in his palm. "Father always said this watch brought him luck. He was wearing it the day he met Mother. I want you to take it with you."

Charlie gingerly took the heavy gold watch. "Dear heart, this is the only thing you have left of your father. Are you sure you want me to take it into battle with me?"

"I want you to take it into battle, then bring it home with you."

"Then I will use it to count the hours until I return to you, dearest." He settled the watch into his vest pocket, then lifted Rebecca up in his arms and carried her over to the settee before the fire. He sat down with her still in his arms and held her close. "I love you, Rebecca Redmond."

Rebecca could not answer, or tears would start again. She curled her hand against his chest and rested her head on his shoulder as they watched the flames.

~

Thursday, February 23, 1865

Duncan had thought his position as the General's personal aide, won at the Christmas gymkhana, was an honorary one. In the past four days, since the mobilization orders had been received, he had discovered it was far from honorary. It was, in fact, a massive task to be the General's personal errand boy. General Charlie was keeping hellish hours, therefore so was Duncan.

There were really only a couple of people the shy young sergeant wanted to bid goodbye before they went back on the road. One was Miss Rebecca, but he did not think he could find the courage to go seek out the General's lovely and very kind wife. The other was young Jeremiah. They had spent many hours together fishing and getting to know one another. Jeremiah did not tease him about his stutter and found the various skills he did have to be fascinating. He had an old whittling knife he wanted to give the boy as a keepsake. Perhaps he would remember his Yankee friend kindly.

Finally, he asked the General if he could have a couple of hours to take care of personal business. Charlie looked up absentmindedly and nodded casual permission. Duncan found Jeremiah sitting up in the hayloft of the stone barn, where he could watch all of the activity without being in anyone's way.

"Hey, Jeremiah, you got a few m-mi-minutes?" Duncan had to shout to be heard over the hubbub in the nearby stables.

"Sure," The boy smiled and dropped from the loft to stand before his friend.

"Walk d-down to the c-creek? I wa-wa-want to visit the t-trout hole one more t-time."

"Sure! Wish we had time to drop a line."

"Me, too, l-lad. But when we are g-gone, you w-will have to do it yourself. G-g-got to keep m-making your co-con-contribution to the t-table."

"I will, I promise. Still gonna be folks to feed."

"You make your ma p-pr-proud of you, young Mister C-carter. You h-help them out when we are g-gone, you h-hear? And if I h-hear you are being stuffy, why I wi-wll just have to c-co-come back and whup you."

"I promise, Duncan." The boy stopped, and looked down at his feet before taking a deep breath and looking back at his friend. "I hope you come back."

Duncan laid his hand on the boy's shoulder. "I hope I c-come b-back, too." They walked together in silence for a few steps. "D-d-do you th-think your ma would like me to c-co-come b-back, too?"

Jeremiah stared at Duncan for a moment, then shrugged. "I suppose."

Duncan nodded his head and continued walking. They got to the fishing hole in companionable silence. "They are f-fe-feeding t-today. The flies are st-st-starting to ha-ha-hatch. You want to j-just throw a l-line out?"

"No line."

"Got one r-ri-right h-here." Duncan pulled a spool of line and a hook from his belt pouch.

"Duncan, we got no pole."

Duncan pulled the whittling knife from his pocket. "I figger you ca-can t-trim one with this." He handed it to Jeremiah. "K-ke-keep it. It w-was my D-da's, and I would l-like you to h-ha-have it."

Jeremiah looked at the knife in his hand and a large lump formed in his throat. "Dunc, I...Ma would skin me if I took your da's knife. You should save this for your son."

"W-well, you know, I d-do not have a so-son. B-but I do have you, l-lad, and I know my D-da would be p-pr-proud to have s-such a fine young m-man have his knife. K-k-keep it for m-me. If you still w-want to, you c-can r-re-return it when I c-co-come b-back." *And when I come back, if I come back, maybe Miss Samantha would not mind if I came calling.*

"I promise to keep it safe, and good and sharp until you come back for it, Duncan."

"You d-do that, l-lad. Now, see if you c-can pu-pull in a f-fish or two for d-dinner. I have to get b-ba-back to the G-general." *Yes, indeed, my da would be proud of a son like Jeremiah.*

～

Saturday, February 25, 1865

Jocko was pawing through Charlie's wardrobe, pulling out those articles of clothing he would need on the campaign, and leaving those items that were more appropriate to social events. Field uniforms, the tight breeches and tunics he wore to work in, extra socks, and underthings that were comfortable, warm, and hid his gender were all being tightly packed. Jocko wanted to travel light. Charlie's clothes were one of his primary responsibilities, both because that is what a batman did and because, in Charlie's case, image was especially critical.

As he packed the well-worn leather satchels, Rebecca entered the room. "Good afternoon, Miss Rebecca." Jocko acknowledged her and continued on with his work.

"Good afternoon, Jocko. Packing his things I see."

"Not everything, Ma'am. This is his home now. Just the things he will need on the campaign."

She smiled. "Thank you." She took a seat on the bed and watched as he continued. "You know, Charlie is not the only one I am going to miss."

"Yes, Ma'am. You and Dr. Walker have gotten to be quite close, I believe."

She chuckled, "Yes, I shall miss Elizabeth, but she is not the subject of this conversation."

"Oh, Ma'am?" Jocko was busy being the very appropriate sergeant and batman. Why, if he admitted to being attached to anyone, he might just have to settle down. Mrs. White had already done more than enough of making him suspect he was fated to do so after the war was over.

"Yes, Jocko. I shall miss you very much, too. If I were you, I would be a little more careful about teasing Charlie about the clan O'Blivious."

"No, Ma'am, I am not normally a member of that illustrious family, but there are times when it is far more comfortable to pretend to be." He looked at her and grinned, "Anyway, if Mrs. White has her way, I will be back."

"I think if my husband has his way, you will be back. He seems to have plans for the reconstruction of Culpeper, and I believe you are key to those plans."

"Then, Ma'am, I suppose between you, Gen'l C and Mrs. White, I have no other options available, unless I choose to fling myself in front of some rebel sword." He pantomimed careful thought, grinning like a monkey. "No, no options there. I suppose I will be back."

"I am delighted to hear it. Please make sure to bring my husband with you."

"I shall do my best, Ma'am, but you know Gen'l Charlie. Once he gets his mind set on something, there is very little that will turn him. Now that you mention it, I believe his objective is to come back."

Charlie had a quiet word with Sarah that afternoon, asking her to prepare a special dinner for Miss Rebecca, and serve it in the little parlor that was her favorite room—a quiet dinner for just the two of them. Some early daffodils had snuck their heads up in some of the more sheltered areas of the farm; Charlie had picked them, and a bowl of sunshine yellow flowers graced the mantle.

Charlie escorted Rebecca into the room, where their dinner was already laid out and covered to keep it warm. "My darling, I hope you like this. I wanted some time for just the two of us tonight."

"Of course, this is perfect, Charlie."

He lifted a bottle of champagne from the cooler and opened it. "I saved this from our wedding for a special night together. There is another in the cellar for when I return, my love."

She smiled, managing to hold back the tears that seemed to be living in her eyes these days, and she took the offered glass. "You think of everything."

"I try, my dear wife. As I think I told you, I believe if I plan for every contingency, even the worst, then I can usually avoid it. This is just my way of trying to show you I am doing everything possible to come home soon."

"I know you are. I know you want that as much as I do." She settled at the table. "You know how you have spent all your life learning to be a man?"

Charlie was confused. What his assumed role had to do with this evening and the upcoming separation was beyond him. "Yes, love?"

"Well, I spent my entire life learning to be a woman, a woman who is taught to worry and fret and who is left behind to pray everything will be all right. We are expected to tend home and hearth, and raise children. You have given me so much more. You have made me feel like your partner, your equal. I feel, with you, I can do anything. I am not limited to the traditional roles. If I lose you, I lose that. I cannot stand the thought of being without you, and I am terrified of being 'put back in my place.' So you see, Charlie, you not only own my heart, but you have given me more than any man ever could, and I want you home so we can continue to grow and discover what is available to us." She smiled. "Who knows, maybe I will take up medicine as Elizabeth has."

"Then, my love, for your future, our children's future, and my own, I clearly must return. In leaving, I leave you my heart and soul. I hope you know that." He took a sip of his champagne. "I also hope you know I have left you sufficiently financially secure so you and the children will never have to worry about subjecting yourselves to someone else's control. There is enough money there for you to go to medical school if you wish, and for both children to be well educated."

She smiled and sipped her champagne. "Yes, which is what I expect of you. I could not care less about money, Charlie. Nothing matters without you."

He lifted the champagne glass out of her hand and took her in his arms. "Then, dear heart, I will come back. I am only half alive without you; so I will do my utmost to return as quickly as I can. I love you." He was a little lost. She talked about what he provided in her life. Yet the explanation of how he had tried to ensure freedom for her was brushed aside. But he did understand one thing. He needed her and, somehow, she needed him. It was all that mattered to him at this point. If he could get through the coming months, maybe he would come to understand the rest of what she was trying to tell him.

~

Monday, February 27, 1865

The orders to mobilize arrived via telegraph. At first light on Tuesday, the 13th Pennsylvania Cavalry was to break camp and head for Rockfish Gap, the central passage from Virginia's breadbasket in the Shenandoah Valley to the east.

That evening, Charlie hosted a farewell dinner with all of his company officers and the leading families of the community. It was a critical meeting, for that evening, Major Byrnes, formerly commander of Company F, was officially taking charge of the military-civilian liaison for Culpeper County. Byrnes and Mayor Frazier found they had several things in common, not the least of which was a love of chess. The two men had spent a number of hours together over the past several days, and not all of the time was spent planning for the upcoming changes.

Rebecca was there in the role of hostess—her first adventure as a true field officer's wife, and hopefully her last. Reverend Williams insisted on attending so he might bless the troops, a concept that mortally offended his wife. The Coopers and several others joined the rather subdued dinner.

The dinner progressed with minimal stress. Mrs. Williams only snarled a few times, until it came time for Reverend Williams to offer the benediction. Mrs. Williams refused to look at her husband during his blessing. Instead she locked eyes with Rebecca, and they both remained that way until Charlie took Rebecca's hand and whispered in her ear, "Down, girl."

She just smiled at Charlie and sighed, "Yes, dear."

"Just think, darling, what her future holds in store for her. Why, I can just imagine what inventive punishments the devil has available for those like her. Do you think that using her tongue to strop razors would be a good start?"

"That is almost too good for her. I personally hope every Yankee who needs a home will decide to settle in Culpeper."

"Do you think we could redo her living room with Yankee carpetbags? Sort of a patchwork effect?"

"I do believe it is the least we could do." She smiled and took his hand.

Charlie tightened his grip on her hand. "By the way, the quilt from the ladies is lovely. What a thoughtful gift. I am quite sure you had a hand in it."

"Actually, I did not. I knew they were planning something for you, but I had no idea what. It was very sweet of them to give you something to make sure you stay warm."

"My love, I will never be completely warm until I am back with you." At that point, the polite conversation and thanks that had followed the minister's words trailed off, and Charlie and Rebecca were called upon to bid their guests good night. Charlie patiently stood as all of the Culpeper residents save one wished him farewell.

Finally, the last guest left. Charlie turned to Rebecca. "I have been both dreading and anticipating this moment. I hate saying goodbye to you, but the only thing I could think of all evening was being alone with you."

"Then I suggest we go to our room, so we can be alone."

"After you, Mrs. Redmond." Charlie escorted her up the stairs with all due formality.

~

Charlie held Rebecca close in her arms, their hearts pounding in rhythm with one another's, their bodies damp, boneless, and sated. All Charlie could do was murmur over and over, "My love, my love."

Rebecca shifted, getting as close to Charlie as she could. "I love you, Charlie. So very much."

"I love you, Rebecca. You are my heart, my reason for living."

"I doubt I will sleep tonight. I want to spend every moment we have…" She stopped and buried her nose in Charlie's neck. "I want to remember everything."

Charlie smiled. She knew exactly what Rebecca meant. "Ah, darling. I believe I have memorized every single mole, freckle, and dimple on your body. The smell of your soap; the color of your hair in the sun, in firelight, in moonlight; the texture of your lips; the skin at the hollow of your throat. I hold you in my memory. Each smile and laugh and kiss is a jewel I can hold in my heart."

Tuesday, February 28, 1865

Dawn brought sleet and freezing rain. The men, grumbling, pulled themselves out of their warm cots and efficiently packed up their last few personal belongings. Rebecca woke to the clash and call of men pulling down tents and loading wagons with poles and rolls of canvas.

A small head poked up over the edge of the bed, "Mama? Papa? Cuddles?"

Rebecca smiled and moved to lift Em into bed with her. "Good morning, my little darling. I will be happy to give you cuddles, but Papa is already up and out with the soldiers."

Em's face fell, "No Papa? He pwomised."

"Emily, listen very carefully to Mama. Today, Papa has to leave, and it is very important that we are strong for him and make him proud of us. Papa does not want to leave, but he must. So we must be strong, big girls."

The little girl shook her head sadly, "Em little."

"Emily, you are a big girl of two now, and Papa needs us to support him. He does not want to go away, but he has orders. He will be coming home soon. So this morning, when it is time to say goodbye, we have to make Papa proud."

"Yes, Mama. Em be good." The toddler sucked on her finger for a minute, then looked back up at Rebecca, "Mama cuddles?"

By eight o'clock the sleet had settled into a steady, freezing rain. Charlie was huddled in his greatcoat, his oilskin slouch hat on his head, a warm woolen muffler wrapped around his neck. An entire regiment of rather grumpy men was ready to move on his orders within the half hour. He left the final bits and pieces of preparation to the company commanders, and rode back to the house for a private farewell.

Rebecca was in the parlor, waiting. Em was dressed in her best dress and sitting like a little lady on the davenport.

Charlie stepped in and stopped at the door, surveying the scene before him. Somehow the two of them managed to capture the grace and elegance of the time before the war, until he looked into their eyes. Rebecca was fighting to keep the tears from falling. Em was crying quiet, heartbroken sobs. Charlie stepped farther into the room then opened his arms.

Em immediately squirmed off the davenport and flew into his arms. "Papa!"

Charlie swept the child up into his arms and held her close. "My little girl. Will you be good while I am gone and help Mama 'Becca? I will be home just as soon as I possibly can. I love you, Em."

"Yes, Papa." The child began to wail, "Love Papa."

Charlie dug in his pocket and pulled out a handkerchief. Jocko had known he would need it and had conveniently stashed a spare in his greatcoat pocket. "Now, no crying. I will be home as soon as I can. I love you, little one."

Rebecca stepped forward and took Em into her arms, then stepped into the circle of Charlie's arms. "I love you. Come home soon."

He wrapped his arms around them both. "God willing, my darlings, God willing, I will be back as soon as I can."

CHAPTER 31

Tuesday, February 28, 1865

The day had been hard and long. Since they had wintered in Culpeper, no one in the entire regiment was used to being in the saddle all day. The cold rain and sleet, and the mud that mired horses' feet and wagon wheels, just contributed to the misery. At the end of the day, after seeing to all of the myriad niggling issues that were part of making camp, Charlie finally sat down in his tent. An oil lamp, hung haphazardly on the center pole, provided a flickering light. Jocko had unrolled his bedroll on the folding cot. There, in the middle of the bedroll, was an envelope addressed to Charlie in very familiar script.

Monday, February 27, 1865

Dearest Husband,

I am writing this letter even as I watch you slumber just a few feet away. Right now, at this very moment it does not seem as if there is anything that can hurt us. However, I know that in just a few short days that will change.

I can still feel your touch from our lovemaking tonight. I savor it, Dearest, and will let the memory wash over me to keep me warm and safe when you are far from home.

You know I will worry, but I will try not to do it every moment of every day. I do not know how to express the abundance of emotions that I am feeling.

I am scared, of course, but there is also a great deal of pride for you. That you would see this through so gallantly and stand fast until the end, yes I am very proud of you.

I believe the thing that concerns me the most is that we have no way of knowing how long you will be away. Will it be a few weeks or many months?

Just know, in your heart, that however long it must be, I will be here, waiting and praying.

I love you Charlie, please know that. I love you, all of you, and I want you to come home.

Eternally yours,

Rebecca

Charlie immediately sat down and, balancing his lapboard across his knees, wrote his response, trying with only marginal success to keep the ache of missing Rebecca from his letter.

Tuesday, February 28, 1865

Dearest Wife,

Oh, how joyously I write the above words. Wife. I never thought I would have a partner in all of the love and joys, trials and sorrows, challenges, defeats and victories of life. Then you came into my life and changed it in more ways than I will ever be able to express to you.

Finding your letter in my bedroll was such a gift. It is as if a little bit of you is here with me, and I have placed your letter next to my heart.

This first day of travel has been about as miserable as any I can remember. The complaints from the men are legion! I doubt there is a single dry anything in this camp, yet there is a strange energy among the men. I think that, like me, they feel the end is in sight, for better or worse. At this point, any ending will be greeted with thanksgiving.

We travel south, along the rail lines until we can turn west. It is no secret that General Grant has General Lee's forces surrounded with a three-pronged pincer. I believe the way the war ends will hinge on the supply lines—as General Meigs so aptly reminded me, an army moves on its belly, and the siege of Richmond and Petersburg has seriously limited the South's ability to feed its troops.

My loyal cavalrymen are less than thrilled at the idea of guarding rail lines. The more glory-hungry boys want to be part of great cavalry charges. I am perfectly happy to be on this duty, though, as the risks are fewer, and I hate having to write the sorrowful letters to the bereaved families those glorious, foolhardy charges tend to engender.

So rest easy, my love. We are up to our hocks in mud, but are basically on reasonably safe ground in terms of how we are being deployed.

My love and kisses to our little imp. Please write and let me know each wonderful thing little Em learns. I know this is a time when she will grow up quickly. I am sorry I will not be there to see her in the coming weeks. Has she settled on a name for the little monster called a dog that Duncan and the boys gave her?

All my love, my heart and soul, to you, my dear. I will dream of your head on my shoulder tonight and every night until I am back beside you.

Your Charlie

Thursday, March 2, 1865

Charlie's regiment moved with great urgency. Sheridan was determined to prevent Early's troops from crossing over Rockfish Gap and supplying Lee's beleaguered forces. Charlie's orders were to defend Rockfish Gap at all costs. As his forces arrived at the eastern end of that easy passage over the Blue Ridge Mountains, couriers and telegrams started arriving, reporting that Custer had successfully engaged Early. Instead of riding into battle, Charlie's troops spent a very tense day scanning for escaping rebel soldiers. When Charlie returned to his quarters that night, a letter from home was waiting in his non-urgent dispatch case.

Wednesday, March 1, 1865

Dearest Charlie,

Things progress here as you might expect. A few of the men that you mustered out have decided to stay on and help me get the crops sown, and we are currently deciding what would best be put where, when the time comes.

I must say that I am surprised they come to me for my thoughts. They seem to understand I am, until your return my darling, the head of this household. Of course, I do believe that Tarent keeps them in line as well.

Em misses you terribly and I have had my hands full trying to make her understand that you will be home. It is not unusual for me to find her plastered to the window in the front parlor. We try to keep her occupied, but she is easily distracted when her thoughts return to her Papa.

Constance is not improving at all, but at this moment she is still holding her own. The baby certainly seems healthy enough, as it moves around almost continuously.

I went into town the other day for a few supplies. It had been raining as if the good Lord was bringing another flood. To this end the roads were a complete mess, filled with water and mud. As I was going into the mercantile, Mr. Cooper was getting a shipment of supplies. (He said to thank you for assisting him in that endeavor as well.) Two very sturdy young men were unloading a crate from the wagon when it slipped and splashed down in a large mud puddle. Guess who was standing near the puddle? I swear, Charlie; it was all I could do to keep from laughing out loud. I have never seen Mrs. Williams turn that particular shade of blue. It was truly amazing.

I miss you so and the place seems empty without you and your troops around.

Please give my best to Richard and the others and give Elizabeth a hug for me, as I miss her like a sister.

Eternally yours,

Rebecca

He immediately sat down and composed a response. These letters were a lifeline to him, he had discovered.

Thursday, March 2, 1865

Darling Wife,

The rain, sleet, and mud continue here, as well. I begin to believe that all wars are fought against the weather, as well as against the enemy, whoever they may be. I am sure Mrs. Williams managed to inform the clumsy young man of every failing he had ever had. Ah, the sweet wine of charity does not run in that woman's veins, does it?

We reached Charlottesville with no major problems other than a couple of mired wagons. The men unloaded everything, and with horses pulling and men pushing, we managed to free them from the mud. Then, of course we had to reload them until the next muddy bottom trapped the wheels again.

Upon reaching Charlottesville, we turned west, toward Rockfish

Gap. Before we could join with the rest of Sheridan's forces over in the Shenandoah Valley, his troops encountered the remnants of Early's forces. Custer's cavalry surprised them in the early morning in Waynesboro. It was a rout. We took up guard positions on the eastern side of the Gap, but very few of Early's forces got through. Most of the Confederate forces surrendered—I have heard as many as fifteen hundred men. General Early and only a handful of men escaped. I suspect most of them headed south, down the Valley toward Lynchburg.

We are to wait here until General Sheridan's forces manage to get across the Gap, then we head east to join the western flank of General Grant's forces.

I am sorry that the little imp is being such a bother. Tell her that Papa says she has to pay attention to her lessons, that I love her and am proud of her.

I pray daily that Constance can find the health she deserves, but if not, that she goes to her Henry with a full heart and a clear conscience. I know you and I will be the parents to her children she hopes we will be.

I love you, darling, and miss you and little Em more than I can tell you. Please keep me advised as to Constance's condition. She looked so pale and fragile when I left.

All my love, my heart, and soul to you.

Your Charlie

Eventually, all of Sheridan's forces made it across the Gap. There was much milling about and confusion as the troops reorganized, so Charlie had no time to write. Each night before he went to sleep, he pulled his little packet, carefully tied with one of Rebecca's blue ribbons, from his pocket, and read each letter in sequence. Some men prayed every night. Others drank. Charlie read his letters.

Elizabeth, who had been swamped with managing the complexities of mobile medical services, finally found a few minutes to herself on Saturday evening. She found Charlie sitting there, just holding his little package of letters between his hands and looking wistfully into the night sky. "You miss her?"

"You have to ask? I left my heart and soul back there, my friend. I can only pray that the rest of me can rejoin it when this is over."

"You will, you will. Why else do you think they call you Lucky Charlie?"

~

Monday, March 6, 1865

The camp was packed and would move out at first light. Their objective was the great locks on the James River at Goochland Courthouse, which would cut yet another supply route to Lee's forces. Without those locks, the Southern forces could not get boats or barges down river to provision the troops at Petersburg. It was an engineering problem, not a battle they were facing. The cavalry would be used to guard against raiders and give the engineers time to complete their task. Rebecca's letter was a welcome break from very routine action.

Saturday, March 4, 1865

Dearest Charlie,

I am sorry to hear the weather is causing so many problems for you. I wish this campaign could be an easy one. Or at least, I wish I were there to help.

I spoke with a lady the other day who is looking to possibly start a school here when the conflict has passed. She told me there are such things as "camp wives" and she was one until her husband was killed at Antietam. You are very lucky I did not know that, or ...

I love you and miss you so much.

It was lovely to speak with her as she knew Andrew and had spoken with him just a day before his death. She said he was a delightful and charming young man who spoke proudly of Culpeper and his sister. That is why she has decided to come here.

Em has finally named the puppy Papa. Sounds like our Em does it not? She is not crying as much now. Every night at prayers she remembers you, her mama, the puppy, and me, in that order.

I hope the weather clears for you soon and I hope you continue to draw the less dangerous duty. I cannot help it, my love. I want you home, safe and sound.

My love to Richard and the boys and a hug for Elizabeth.

Eternally yours,

Rebecca

~

Monday, March 6, 1865

Darling Wife,

Elizabeth and Richard stopped by my tent last night, so I had no opportunity to answer your letter as soon as I received it, as is my usual pattern. I conveyed your message to them, as well as tales of young Em and "Papa."

I am not sure I am particularly happy about having the dog named after me, although perhaps the little bitch is more aptly named than Em knows. But if it keeps her from grieving at the window, I will suffer the animal to carry my moniker.

We move out this morning, headed east and south to block as many supply routes as possible. I will continue this letter when I have a moment.

. . .

Charlie hastily tucked the unfinished note into his traveling secretary, stuffed the leather folder into his saddlebag, and mounted up. Finally, the rain had stopped, the only blessing in an otherwise miserable campaign.

~

Tuesday, March 7, 1865

Rebecca and Em were on the floor playing with a new carved horse Charlie had sent along with his last letter. Duncan had taken some spare time to whittle it, and the proud papa sent it along as soon as it was ready.

Em held the toy up for inspection. "Papa sent?"

"Yes, sweetheart, Papa sent you this toy."

"Miss Papa." She put the toy down on the floor gently, making it run across the floor in small movements. "Papa come home?"

"Papa will be home just as soon as he can. I promise."

The door opened into the parlor and Beulah entered. "Miss Rebecca?"

"Yes?"

"Ma'am, uh, there is a woman here, wanting to speak with General Charlie."

"I will tend to it. Can you take Em up for her nap?"

"Of course."

Rebecca got up from the floor, leaving Em in the care of the maid. She walked to the entry where she found a young woman with a carpetbag at her feet and a baby bundled in her arms. "May I help you?"

"Good afternoon, Ma'am. I am looking for General Charles Redmond. I was told he had headquartered here."

"I am sorry. General Redmond and his men left a few days ago. I am his wife. How can I help you?"

"His wife! How could he?"

"It was only a matter of getting the minister to officiate. Now, would you mind telling me why you are calling after my husband?"

The woman started crying. "But, but he promised...He told me that he would take care of me and our child...Oh, how could he." She dissolved into loud wailing.

"Excuse me?" Rebecca tried to bite back a grin. She knew she was going to have to get to the bottom of this.

"Look. Look at this child. The hair, the eyes. This is Charlie's child. And I was to be his wife. And now, nothing, nowhere to go, no home..." The wailing got louder.

Rebecca managed to remove the infant from the woman. She had to admit it was a handsome child and, if Charlie had been capable of procreation, it could have been his. "Let us go to the parlor and discuss this, shall we?"

As they walked toward the back parlor, the woman began a diatribe. "I cannot believe he has done this to us. He promised me. He told me he would take me away from the place I was in and give me a good life, care for our children, and build a home after the war. Then he just goes and throws it all away for you and, I suppose, for this place."

Rebecca settled down on the davenport, carefully looking over the child, who was not more than a month old. Its bright eyes tracked her every movement. "Is it a boy or a girl?"

"It is a boy, Ma'am. I call him Charlie."

"I see, and you say my husband is his father? Where did this take place? I mean, he is my husband. I have a right to know."

"We met in Washington, at the home of a mutual friend. We saw one another frequently for over a month while he was there. Then when he was sent back into the field, I found that I could no longer stay with my friends in the city."

Rebecca looked at the woman and tried not to laugh in her face. "And you have come here because..." She left the rest of the question to be answered by her visitor.

"I have come here to find Charlie and to claim my rights and the rights of my child. He owes us. He owes his son a future, and his son's mother a home."

Rebecca sighed. "Well, I will tell you what I know for a fact, Miss...?"

"My name is Hobart, Alison Hobart."

"Well, Miss Hobart, I will share with you that I know that Charles Redmond is not the father of this child. Now would you like to tell me why you have decided to lay the blame at his feet?"

"Mrs. Redmond, your husband is indeed the father of this child. Look at his hair, his eyes, and tell me if you do not see your husband's features there."

"While this child does resemble General Redmond, it is but a newborn, and newborns often look like many people. There is a little girl in this house right now who most certainly is not General Redmond's daughter, but to look at her you would never know that. My husband is blessed with classical features. Now, please tell me why you want to blame my husband for this?"

"Because your husband is an honorable man, who I am sure will care for his child and his child's mother."

"Yes, you are correct. He is an honorable man, and I think it is terribly dishonorable of you to try and blame him for something he had nothing to do with. So, did you work for Mrs. Armstrong? Is that how you came to have this child?"

The woman's self-righteous facade crumbled. "How...how do you know about Mrs. Armstrong?"

"Charlie told me about her. You see, Miss Hobart, my husband and I have no secrets from each other. By the way, I know for a fact that Charlie was never intimate with any of Mrs. Armstrong's employees; that he only consorted with Mrs. Armstrong herself. So, do you want to tell me the real story?"

The woman started crying quiet tears of despair. "I got pregnant by one of my customers. Mrs. Armstrong let me go and I had nowhere to turn. I met General Redmond while I was at Mrs.

Armstrong's and knew he was a kind, generous man. I hoped he would…not remember, or take pity on us."

Rebecca looked down at the child who now had a tight grip on her finger. *A son for Charlie.* She looked up with an icy smile. "Miss Hobart, is it your child for whom you are truly concerned?"

"Yes, Ma'am. I know I can fend for myself, one way or another. There is always a place for a woman if she is willing. But a woman with a baby is more than most men will take on. He is a good baby, never fussy. I just want him to have a good life, a better chance than I had." The saccharine quality of her words, coupled with her inability to look Rebecca in the eye, told a very different story.

"Then I will make you an offer which I think is more than fair."

"What kind of offer, Ma'am?" The tears had dried and the woman had a predatory look.

"I will give you a sum that will allow you to travel to get a new start; New York or Philadelphia, perhaps. You will leave this child with me. When General Redmond returns home, we will raise it as our own. You will never come back here. You will never make yourself known to this child."

Miss Hobart looked away, but not before Rebecca could see her calculating how much she could demand. Alison Hobart mumbled, "Easy touch." She then turned back to Rebecca. "How much will you give me?"

"I thought as much." Rebecca stood and rang for Beulah, who was listening outside the door.

"Yes, Miss Rebecca?"

"Beulah, take this little one and see to it that he is bathed and properly dressed, and if he is in need of a meal, ask Ginny to take care of him."

"Yes, Miss Rebecca, right away." Beulah lifted the little one into her arms, talking to him all the way out of the room.

Rebecca closed the doors and then took a seat at her desk. "So, who is the father and would he have any interest in the whereabouts of his son?"

"His father is a damned Southern sympathizer who will never darken either your or my door. He is of no concern to you."

Rebecca raised her eyebrow at the sneering comment on Southerners, but removed the checkbook Charlie had left with her before he departed from the desk. She dipped her pen into the inkwell and sighed. "How much do you want?"

Now that she was sure a transaction was in the offing, Alison Hobart no longer bothered to hide her contempt or her avarice. "So, if I can ask, what makes a lady like you willing to buy a child just because it looks like your husband? Why do you not just have your own? Or are you too much of a prig to bed a man like the General?"

"I am merely trying to give this child a decent life so he will not have to grow up on the street, stealing to keep you satisfied. How much?"

"Oh, I think there is something more here, Ma'am. I think we shall make this trip worth my time and energy. How does a thousand dollars sound to you? For just a thousand dollars, you get the heir that you evidently do not want to give the good General yourself." She laid some paper on the table. "See, I have already drawn up the paperwork. All that remains is for you to sign the check."

Rebecca bit her lip and fought the urge to throw the whore out on her ear. She very carefully wrote the draft, removed it from the book, and stood, holding it out, "This is all you get. It is my best guess that two hundred dollars will get you out of Virginia. Now get out of my house."

"Two hundred dollars. You cheap…Give me back my son. He is surely worth more than that." She went to snatch up the paper giving Rebecca legal custody of the child, but Rebecca was too quick for her.

"Yes, I agree he is worth far more than money, and in time he will have all that he requires to grow up as a fine young gentleman. But it is clear that all he is to you is a burden and a possible source of income. Now take this, and get out of my house, off my property, and far away from Culpeper."

"You could at least make it five hundred—that would give me plenty of money to set up in New York, and I would never bother you from there."

Rebecca took a deep breath, walked to the young woman, pressed the draft into her hand, and then escorted her to the door. She placed the carpetbag in the woman's hand and opened the door. "Will you leave, or will I have to toss you out bodily? I am very capable of it and if I find I am not, I have a staff who would be more than willing to help."

"You will regret this, Mrs. High and Mighty Redmond. I promise. You will regret this."

"Madam, I have survived a war. I have many things I regret. I am sure this will not keep me awake at night."

After the woman had left, Rebecca closed the door and leaned against it. When she looked up, she saw Tess, Beulah, and Sarah standing at the end of the hall looking at her. "What?"

"Did ya toss her out, Miss Rebecca?" Tess asked from the corner.

"I did." She sighed and stared down the hall toward the women. "Not very Christian of me, was it?"

Beulah met her employer half way down the hall. "We was about to go get Reg and have him come help you."

"Where is the baby?"

"In the kitchen with Ginny."

"Well, let us go meet my son, shall we?"

Rebecca sat in her bedroom, holding the baby close to her. Ginny had just finished with his feeding and Rebecca wanted to be Mama now. Em sat at her feet, peeking up to look at the squirming bundle.

"Baby?"

"Yes, sweetheart, this is your brother." She brushed her fingers through Em's hair, wondering if she would be able to get the child to sit still for a trim. "He needs a name. What shall we name this young man?"

"Baby."

Rebecca chuckled. "Well, he will not be a baby forever, and he will need a name like you have."

"Em."

"Yes, your name is Em. I do not think your brother would take well to that name, and it would get very confusing."

"Papa."

Rebecca smiled. "Should we name this baby after Papa?"

"Yes."

"All right then." She looked at her son, who was now sleeping peacefully in her arms. "Charles Huger Redmond the Second it is." She looked back to Em. "I think your Papa will be very pleased."

Rebecca settled down at her desk once again. She drew several sheets of paper from the drawer and prepared to write two letters. She glanced over at Charlie, sleeping peacefully in a cradle near the fireplace. Em was content there as well, laying on a thick blanket and playing with her dolls.

Rebecca dipped the nib and gave careful consideration to how to begin the letter to Charlie Sr.

Tuesday, March 7, 1865

Dearest Charlie,

Congratulations! You have a son. Not the one you are thinking of, of that I am sure.

Yesterday, a young woman who had formerly been in the employ of Mrs. Armstrong came knocking on our door.

Her name was Alison Hobart, and she had a rather fascinating story about how you fathered her son. You truly are an amazing man, Charlie Redmond.

Of course, it became quite clear she was only after money. I gave her two hundred dollars, and relieved her of the baby boy, who is not more than a month old.

She did not care for the child, Charlie; she was only looking for a tidy sum. I certainly did not give her what she demanded, but I gave her enough to send her on her way.

So, last night, Miss Emily and I were discussing the new addition to our family and decided his name should be Charles Huger Redmond II. I do hope you approve.

He is an adorable little boy, and appears to be very healthy, with a demanding appetite. He does keep Ginny quite busy.

We miss you so, my love. I hope you are well and staying dry and warm. Everything here is progressing as expected. Tarent and MacFarlane have taken to getting the farm up and running as soon as possible , and have even hired several of the young Negro boys to help them build or repair anything that looks even slightly in need of work.

Shannon is doing very well; she does so enjoy running and kicking up her heels. She is actually quite playful and will run the fence when she sees Em and me coming for a visit to give her a special treat of carrots. I do think she misses Jack, though. Sometimes I see the same look in her eyes that I see in my own when I look in the mirror.

Emily is trying very hard to understand that Papa is gone, but will be home as soon as he can. She asks for you every night and always remembers you during prayers.

Please take care, my darling. We wait for your return.

Your loving wife,

Rebecca

. . .

She laid Charlie's letter to the side to let the ink dry. Then she set pen to paper for yet another letter.

Tuesday, March 7, 1865

Dear Mrs. Armstrong,

I am sure I am the last person from whom you ever expected to receive correspondence. However, because you are a dear friend of Charlie's, I believe you should be aware of a situation that has arisen.

First, let me reassure you that, as far as I know, Charlie is fine. I have not received any word of the opposite, so I must believe he is well.

The reason I am writing you now is to tell you of a visit I had from a woman who claims to have been in your employ. Her name is Alison Hobart. She arrived on my doorstep yesterday with a newly born baby son, who, to my private amusement, she tried to credit to Charlie.

I gave her funds, relieved her of the baby, and sent her on her way. I believe you need to know what this woman is trying to do. She specifically mentioned she remembered Charlie from his visits to your establishment.

I will admit to you, a certain amount of pleasure when I could confront her with the truth that Charlie had only ever come to visit you and I knew of his relationship with you. You have never seen a woman go so pale so quickly.

I have given the child Charlie's name. I will wait for a proper christening until after Charlie comes home.

I do hope that once the conflict is over and it is again safe to travel, you will come and spend some time at our home and meet our growing family.

Please, Mrs. Armstrong, be very careful about this young woman. I would certainly hate for her to cause you trouble.

Regards,
Rebecca Redmond

~

Friday, March 10, 1865

Charlie dismounted from Jack and handed Jocko the reins, his gauntlets, and his canteen. "God, Jocko. I think I am getting too old for this."

"Well, Gen'l C, I have something to cheer you a bit and put that youthful bounce back into your step. A special courier came with another letter from Miss Rebecca."

"I feel a bit guilty. With these last days of hard riding, I have not had time to finish the letter I started before we left Crozet."

"Well, Sir, we are to settle here for a couple of days before we go on toward Goochland Courthouse, while the infantry catches up. I suspect you will have plenty of time now."

"Good. I can use the break from being all day in the saddle. Are we setting up the Officers' Mess tent?"

"Yes, Sir. Jamison's boys are already working on it."

"Good—send word that I will expect the officers to dine together."

"Oh, and Major M'Cabe's boys found a herd of goats wandering untended."

"Goats? And what did the boys from Company E do?"

"I understand they tried to find the owners, but from what the locals say, the goats have been wandering for a while. Seems their owners fell to the grippe last winter. So Jamison's boys dressed them out and roasted them."

"Ah, good. Fresh meat will do wonders for morale—especially after all the rain and mud we have had to endure."

Charlie was fingering the rather thick letter that Jocko had brought him, obviously wanting to read it in the privacy of his own tent, but too courteous to send Jocko away. Jocko, knowing his boss very well, excused himself.

He settled into his camp chair and lovingly opened his letter. He read the first line and nearly dropped the paper. He read it again, and just sat there with his jaw hanging open. "A son? I have a son?" It came out of him as a reverent whisper. Then it dawned on him that if he had a son, it probably meant that Constance had passed on. With trembling hands, he carefully read the whole letter through. Finally it sank in. He had a son, and not at the price of Constance's life.

"Jocko!" He waited about fifteen seconds. Then he bellowed. "Jocko!"

Jocko came running. The Boss never yelled like that. As the batman burst through the tent flap, Charlie grabbed him by the shoulders. "I have a son. A son! Break out a keg of my best brandy; we will toast Charlie the Second at dinner tonight!"

The General announced his good news to his officers amid great good cheer and mirth. The men all knew that Charlie was rapidly acquiring a family through adoption, but, except for Jocko and Elizabeth, all present believed that Charlie was celebrating the birth of an illegitimate child Rebecca was generous enough to adopt as her own.

Late that night, he continued his letter to Rebecca.

Friday, March 10, 1865

Darling wife,

I continue my letter begun several days ago still reeling from your news. A son. My namesake. I do hope he is a healthy, hale little fellow.

We celebrated this evening. For the first time in several days, we are settling down in a real camp, where we will stay for a while. So we actually have tents, other than our sleep tents that are quickly raised, and time for a decent meal. M'Cabe's men found some goats, which Jamison roasted, so we had fresh meat and good brandy to toast my son.

I must confess, I have absolutely no memory of Miss Hobart. I suppose I met her at Lizzie's, but then she had many attractive young women in her employ over the time I have known her. I think you handled the situation artfully, dear heart.

I am also sure you are handling the farm well. Tarent is a good man, and I am glad you and he have formed an effective alliance. I know, from all of the talks we have had, you know more about the running of an efficient stud farm than I do. I have full faith in your ability to do what needs to be done, and in Tarent to ensure it is done correctly.

By the by, dear, is Shannon showing signs of being in foal? I would love to see what she and Jack produce. I believe any foal of theirs will either be ugly and mean tempered or absolutely elegant and sweet. Of course, it could be elegant and mean or ugly and sweet as honey.

We are headed east, and have lain over for a bit to allow the infantry to catch up. This gives me some time just to sit and relax. I picked up some very nice fine cotton yarn in the supply depot in Charlottesville, and have taken to knitting booties. Believe it or not, I learned how to knit from a grizzled old sergeant who swore that every soldier should know how so he could take care of his socks and keep his feet healthy. I have been knitting my own socks for years, and find baby booties are an easy adaptation. Perhaps you can surrender and stay with crocheting caps and blankets, dear.

I think I will turn in now, and send this to you in the morning pouch. I fear I have had a bit of my own medicine—but it was a good brandy and a wonderful reason to celebrate.

All my love, my heart and soul to you.
Your Charlie

Wednesday, March 15, 1865

With eager fingers, Charlie tore open the seal on Rebecca's next letter. They had been sitting in camp, doing what soldiers did best—hurrying up and waiting. He was aching to be home, to be with Rebecca, to meet his new son. These letters were the closest things he had.

Monday, March 13, 1865

Dearest Charlie,

Rest assured your son, is quite the healthy little fellow, with lungs that would make your best drill sergeant proud. When little Charlie needs something, he is not the least bit shy about letting us know.

Em is quite proud of her little brother and bestows him with kisses at every opportunity. She is also doing very well with Papa now. The pup follows her everywhere and even sleeps at the foot of her bed.

I am glad you are having some time to rest. I am sure it is difficult moving so much. The weather here has been reasonable, and I hope it is the same for you.

Shannon does appear to be in foal. I have faith we will have a foal that is as beautiful as his father and mother and very sweet, like my Shannon, and not so full of devilry, like your Jack.

Reverend Williams and I discussed the christening of Charlie Junior and we decided it would be all right to wait for the birth of the next baby and your return home. Also, more of my fight to drive Mrs. Williams insane, I asked Reverend Williams if we could take the Gaines name off our pew and replace it with Redmond, and he said he certainly did not see a problem with it. I thought for sure she would pass out. Unfortunately, she did not.

I am sorry to report that the next time I write, there will probably be both good and bad news. I am sure I will be telling you of our next child, and of Constance's passing. I have arranged for her to have a plot in the church cemetery.

Be well and be safe my love. Wishing you home.

Eternally yours,

Rebecca

Charlie read Rebecca's missive eagerly, until he got to the bittersweet news of Constance's condition. He folded his letters and went in search of Elizabeth. He tapped on her tent flap and waited.

"Come in."

"Good evening, Elizabeth. Do you have a few minutes?"

"Of course, Charlie. I am just making some tea from my hidden supply. Would you join me?"

He nodded as he settled himself on a heavy case in the corner of her tent. The silence continued as Elizabeth prepared the tea and handed him a mug of steaming fluid.

"So, what has you so moody? Orders you are not happy with?"

He shook his head. "Rebecca wrote about Constance." He sat there slumped over his tea. The doctor waited for him to continue. Finally, he spoke. "Why does she have to die, Elizabeth?"

"Because she became pregnant at a time when her body was not healthy enough to sustain both her and the baby."

"Yes, but why? Why did Montgomery go all vicious? Why did we do this to ourselves? Why are we doing everything we can to keep food from men who are probably starving?"

"Because," she took a seat next to him and took his hand, "that is the nature of war, Charlie. You know that. Good men lose their minds, and soldiers do what they must to end the conflict."

He shook his head. "It is just so senseless. That a lovely and loving woman like Constance should give her life because of the stupidity of men who would not or could not find a rational, civilized solution. So we have brother fighting brother, women and children dying, men left with nothing but rags and rage. I cannot do it any more, Elizabeth. I just cannot." He buried his head in his hands. In a small, choked voice he cried into the night, "I just want to go home."

She sat there for a moment, then leaned over and put her arms around him. "You will very soon, Charlie. Very soon. Now tell me, do you have another son or daughter?"

"I may by now. Rebecca's last letter came tonight. She says it will be soon."

"Then, when you go back to your tent, do not mourn for Constance who is going to her Lord quite willingly. Be happy for your wife and the three little ones who wait for their Papa's return."

~

Friday, March 17, 1865

Two days after his conversation with Elizabeth, a letter from Rebecca came by special courier. Without opening it, Charlie knew what it said.

Thursday, March 16, 1865

Dearest Charlie,

Constance has passed. The birth was difficult, but she survived long enough to see her son. A fine baby boy, a bit small, but healthy.

I have named him Andrew Richard, after my brother and your best friend.

We laid Constance to rest with a small sermon. Mrs. Williams was nearly beside herself when I told Beulah it was all right for her to attend. She and Constance had become very close, and I was not going to refuse her the right to say a proper goodbye.

So now, my darling, we have three beautiful children, a daughter who loves her Papa and misses him terribly, and two fine sons who are keeping the entire house very busy. It is still early to know, but I do believe that Andrew is going to have blond hair.

Tarent is thinking of attending an auction in a few weeks to pick up some new horses. He says he knows this particular fellow, and trusts him to sell us good stock. Would it be all right for me to release him some funds for traveling and purchase?

Emily wants me to tell you that she sends you hugs and kisses and you should do the same, with a toy as well. I tried to tell her you probably were not somewhere that you could get a toy, but if any of the boys have time and are interested in doing a little carving, she would be delighted.

Hugs to Richard and Elizabeth.

Waiting as patiently as I am able for your return.

Eternally yours.

Rebecca

CHAPTER 32

FRIDAY, MARCH 17, 1865

Charlie walked to the Officers' Mess that night with very mixed emotions; saddened by the loss of a woman who in her quiet way had become a dear friend, and joyous at the birth of his second son. In addition, he had received orders to march. The James River Locks had to be taken and dismantled before the end of the month.

The officers received the news of Constance's death with quiet sympathy. Most had only met her briefly, or not at all, but all of them had come to know the energetic toddler who called their commander Papa. Another son was cause for a round of toasts, this time sponsored by Richard, who could not resist the impulse to tease Charlie a bit about his rapidly growing family, particularly since the latest one, Andrew Richard, carried his name.

But of greatest concern that night, was the need to mobilize rapidly. The James River was a vital link for Lee's forces. While there were no large deployments of Southern troops, they knew they faced days of extreme vigilance and probable skirmishing with small bands of raiders along the way. It would be a hard march.

Charlie's letter to Rebecca that night was short.

Friday, March 17, 1865

Darling Wife,

I am grieved past words that we have lost our dear friend Constance. I am glad that Beulah attended the service with you, and the devil take Mrs. Williams and her bigoted sensibilities. How is our little girl doing? More to the point, how are you doing, darling? A newborn, a six week old sprat, and a grieving toddler are more than any one person should have to handle. I wish I were there with you, beloved. I miss you more than I can tell you.

When it comes to horseflesh, I trust Tarent more than any other man. Give him whatever he needs; he will serve us well.

We mobilize tomorrow, so I must make this short. I adore you, my beloved and miss you with every fiber of my being.

All my love, my heart and soul to you.

Your Charlie

~

Saturday, March 18, 1865

The ride to the James River Locks was hard, not because of the terrain, which was rolling hills, fields, and old woodlands, but because the cavalry troopers were assigned to ride constant patrol and surveillance. They covered the same territory over and over, watching for attackers and potential saboteurs attempting to infiltrate the lines. It was grueling work, tedious, and, above all, dangerous. In the four days it took to reach the river, every company under Charlie's command had encountered rebel forces, with running skirmishes being the order of the day. While no one was killed, there were a number of injuries—most minor, a few serious.

Elizabeth had her hands full. She could not afford to stop and set up a field hospital, so men were treated in wagons as they moved forward. The weather had cleared; it was warm, and with the sun beating down on the canvas used to shield the injured, the interior of the wagons was stifling.

Charlie, his hair plastered to his head with sweat, pulled Jack up to the moving mess tent for a quick lunch and some desperately needed water. He was hailed by Elizabeth.

He rode up to the wagon, and then paced alongside it. He took off his hat and bowed to Elizabeth from the saddle. "Dr. Walker, how can I help you?"

"You can help me by finding a place to stop so I can treat these men properly," she growled as she ripped another bandage, then wiped the sweat from her brow with the back of her sleeve.

"You know General Sheridan has ordered us to make all possible speed. I fear I cannot stop until we reach the river, Doctor. I am sorry."

"Charlie, I cannot care for these men with the ruts in the road and the swaying of the wagon. Some of these men need stitches. I cannot do it under these conditions."

He heaved a deep sigh, then thought for a minute. "If I had your wagons ride toward the front of the line, until you find a place to pull off that is defensible, you could have about an hour or so before you would have to move again. Would that help?"

"I can make do with that. I just need some time to tend to the worst of this."

"All right, let me see to it." Instead of stopping for lunch and a drink, Charlie was off again, this time looking for young Captain Avery of Company I, whom he had just relieved from outrider service.

The days went on with running skirmishes until they reached the locks. The 13th held the northwestern perimeter, as Sheridan's engineers destroyed the locks and made the upper James River impassible.

~

Sunday, March 26, 1865

As the locks fell, the weather, which had been beautiful, changed again. A cold wind with rain blew in from the north; that meant mud. Winter was having her last, brief say.

The roads were muddy and slick as they moved out, south toward Cumberland County. The next goal was to reach the final rail line from Petersburg and Richmond to Lynchburg and the southern end of the Shenandoah Valley. The valley had been the breadbasket of the South; if they could cut the final supply line, the end was in sight. Charlie and his men were tired. It showed in the way they moved, in the strain on their faces. It showed in the tired arc of the horses' necks.

It only took a moment. Charlie was distracted; Jack was tired. The horse stepped wrong and caught his shoe on a hidden stone buried in the mud. It ripped the nails out of his hoof and the shoe off his foot. As Jack struggled to regain his balance, he strained the hock. Jack was dead lame.

Cursing a blue streak, he changed out horses for one of the reserves and they rode south, advancing a few miles a day until they reached the junction of Amelia, Prince Edward, and Nottoway Counties.

~

Wednesday, April 5, 1865
April 5, 1865

. . .

Dearest Rebecca,

There is a special quality on the eve of battle. It is a breathless waiting, a stillness that, no matter how I try, I will never be able to describe. In many ways, it is like the stillness of the early morning before the sun rises, when false dawn lights the sky with a silvery gray and one does not know what the day will truly bring.

Richmond has fallen. The Confederate Army is in retreat. I pray the battle will be easy, that these men will see reason and know it is time to concede gracefully. I fear they will fight like cornered dogs.

I know no more than this. I love you with all my heart and soul. I love our children, though I have only met one of them. I long to be home, with you and them, in a world where war is no more. I pray to God above that I may be allowed to realize my dream, that my men and I will survive these last, terrible days.

I love you.

Charlie

~

Thursday, April 6, 1865

With the fall of Richmond, Lee's forces had no choice. They had to run—south and west, towards Roanoke, and then south into North Carolina—or they had to surrender. Grant was behind them, coming from Richmond and Petersburg. Sheridan was there in the west, ready to meet whatever Lee could throw against him and determined to close the path of escape.

They had spent much of the night in conference with Sheridan and his forward scouts. The land ahead was rolling hills, cut by Sailor's Creek, a small waterway that fed into the Appomattox River. There were marshy bottomlands to the southwest. Merritt's light infantry, supported by Charlie's cavalry, was assigned to stop any attempt to slip through the shallow, marshy section of the creek. It would be hard going.

The men took up their positions at dawn. Waiting was one of those things all soldiers learned how to do. Charlie stayed on the heights above the expected battleground, waiting and watching. That was all they could do. Charlie saw some movement along the front line. Dewees was letting the men of Company D move forward too soon.

"Duncan! Get down there and get Dewees and his men back in line. Now!"

Duncan took off at a hard gallop.

"Richard, did we not tell that young idiot that holding the line was all important?"

"Yes, we did. What does the fool think he is doing?"

"Hell, if I knew, I would do something about it. Byrnes warned me we would have trouble with him being over-eager. You want to go down there and give him hell, or shall I?"

"I suppose I could do it. I have not really yelled at anyone today."

"Then go do it. But get back in a hurry. You still have to manage coordination with the artillery, and the scouts tell me Gordon's cavalry is coming our way with a bunch of supply wagons. I will need you here when he arrives."

Richard tossed a crisp salute. "Yes, Sir."

Charlie watched as Richard rode down to Company D's position. He could see his second standing in his stirrups, shouting at Dewees. The first man who broke formation without advance notification might find himself taking fire from the Federal artillery behind them.

As Richard started back, Charlie could see a cloud of dust in the distance and hints of movement. Lee had split his forces into three columns, and his army was on its way. They were about to face the southern column, which was comprised of one quarter of all of the remaining Southern forces in Virginia.

~

Gordon's cavalry came on, desperate. They were hungry; they were clothed in rags. They were short of ammunition. The wagons bogged down in the marshy terrain. Gordon's troops fought like devils. It was exactly what Charlie had expected—and feared.

Dewees was a fool. He let his men go too soon and they took at least two rounds from Federal artillery before he realized what both Charlie and Richard had told him: follow the plan. That was the rule. Follow the plan.

Elizabeth, who normally was reasonably calm in battle, started cursing like a sailor when she realized she was treating wounds inflicted by their own forces.

The General pulled Swallow's A Company and Braddock's H Company from the reserve lines and sent them down to relieve Dewees. Andrews and M'Cabe, Companies C and E, were assigned to Merritt's right flank. With controlled artillery support and a sound infantry brigade at their core, the Federal Army slowly moved in on the smaller Confederate force. It was a rout. Sheridan's forces, a total of approximately eighteen thousand mixed infantry, cavalry, and heavy artillery, had faced some thirteen thousand five hundred of Lee's remaining troops.

By the end of the day, Sheridan's forces had captured seven thousand seven hundred men, most of whom had sustained some sort of injury. Eight Confederate generals, including Robert E. Lee's oldest son, George Washington Custis Lee, were captured. There was a total of about two thousand injuries in the Union forces and less than two hundred deaths. The Southern force had been devastated. Later, Richard was told that Lee, seeing men fleeing along the roads, asked, "My God, has the army dissolved?"

Charlie considered himself fortunate. He had only three letters to write home to parents, wives, and families announcing the death of a loved one.

∼

He walked through the field hospital that Elizabeth and Samuelson had set up on the heights above Sailor's Creek. He stopped and talked to a number of men, encouraging them, congratulating them on their accomplishments. Finally, he just stood and waited as Elizabeth finished treating the last—and least seriously hurt—of the wounded.

She stood there in the makeshift surgery tent, bloodied to the elbows, her field uniform covered with a piece of bloodstained canvas pinned on as an apron. For a few moments, the only people in the tent were Elizabeth and Charlie. Silently, he went to her, put his arms around her, and let her lean on his shoulder.

Finally, she gathered herself, only to let go with a tirade of magnificent proportions. "God damn it, Charlie! What the bloody hell happened? I had to dig our own canister shot out of those boys."

"I am so sorry, Elizabeth. Dewees broke formation early; it put the men in the path of the first rounds while the artillery was getting its range."

"So what about you, Charlie? You put a green commander in the vanguard. How stupid was that?"

"I put Company D in the vanguard because they won the right at the Gymkhana and I could not go back on my word to them. Dewees has been in service since the beginning; I thought he would have better sense."

"Well, see to it that he somehow manages to follow orders in the future, or he is going to get more men killed. We were damned lucky as it was. I have a couple of critical cases, but only three deaths so far. You tell that little idiot from me that he is responsible for the loss of a total of seventeen arms, nine legs, and God know how many horses."

"I will. I will also see to it that he personally manages the disposal of the limbs." Charlie took a deep breath. He had more bad news to deliver. "You realize that we are now in the midst of a running battle?"

"Yes, I assume we are going to chase them down. Samuelson and I are as ready as we can be."

"Thank you, Elizabeth. I will send Dewees to you shortly. You have my permission to flay him as much as you like."

He turned to leave. As he reached the tent flap, Elizabeth called out, "Charlie, take care of yourself. You have four people who really need you to go home when this is over."

He nodded and walked out.

Charlie sent Duncan to fetch Dewees. As he waited in his tent, he started a letter home. Before he had gotten past the first couple of lines, the Captain knocked.

"Enter."

Dewees came in and stood at ramrod attention. His commander said nothing to relieve his tension.

"So, what the hell do you have to say for yourself?"

"Sir, I allowed my eagerness to get the better of me, Sir."

The General stood up and moved to stand directly in front of the man. Less than two inches separated their noses. In an icy tone, he began. "You let your stupidity get the better of you. You disobeyed a direct order—issued three times, no less. I could have your ass before a firing squad this evening for that alone. But no, that was not enough. You knew we had artillery that needed to get a range on their shot. But you let our men ride into their field of fire." By now, Charlie was spraying spit with each word. "You have one third of your company down with injuries on the first day of what we know will be a hard running battle. There are twenty-six severed limbs and nine dead horses that need to be disposed of properly. Because you 'let your eagerness get the better of you.'" Charlie's voice had been rising with each word. He was now yelling outright, something he almost never did. "You will personally see to it! And tomorrow morning, you will report to me in person before a single man of your company takes a step! Dismissed!"

Dewees scurried from the tent on his way to do the onerous duty

Charlie had assigned him, and then to talk to his men about being too eager.

Jocko and Richard entered together. Charlie sighed and put aside his barely begun letter home.

"Yes, Gentlemen?"

Richard spoke first. "How shall I order the men, Charlie? Do we march tomorrow?"

"I do not have Sheridan's orders yet, but I suspect we do. This has all the earmarks of a running battle."

"All right. I will order fast rations, have them get what sleep they can, and be ready to move at dawn."

Charlie nodded, tired and distracted with thoughts of what the next few days might bring. It was only going to get worse. Richard hurried out to see to the men.

Jocko spoke up. "A courier just arrived from Sheridan's command. He requests your presence in a half hour. I grabbed some bread and ham for you, and have a fresh horse ready."

Charlie sighed, slumped in his chair, and closed his eyes. He had gotten less than two hours of sleep the night before; it looked as though tonight would be no better. "If you have a fresh horse, I assume that Jack is still lame."

"Yes, I am afraid so. He is doing better, but I would not ask him to carry you yet."

"Well, give him a carrot and a scratch for me. I will be back whenever I can get back. Is Duncan ready to ride with me?"

"Waiting outside the tent. Charlie, do you need…"

"I need this war to be over. I need to be home. I need some sleep. But you cannot give me any of those things, old friend. Keep the lamp burning; I am going to need some rest before we march tomorrow."

∼

Friday, April 7, 1865

Charlie rose before dawn, having gotten to bed sometime around midnight. He knew that the day would be hard. Sheridan had ordered the two cavalry forces—his and Custer's—to ride south and west, circumventing the main body of Lee's forces, to take and hold the rail line from Roanoke to Appomattox. There was one objective —to prevent Lee from receiving his supplies and thereby stop him from getting to North Carolina.

Richard and Charlie met over the early morning coffee pot. It was so early that the only light was from the low burning fires and a few torches. False dawn had yet to light the sky.

"So, Charlie, where do we go today?"

"We ride at dawn for the western part of Appomattox County— some place called Appomattox Station. We are back on railroad detail —and damn it, this time that glory hound Custer is in command."

"Custer? My God, Charlie—that man is plain dangerous."

"I know. I spent a good bit of last night listening to him complain about how his boys missed out on the action since he simply flanked Ewell's forces while we got to face Gordon head on."

Richard thought for a moment. "You know, Charlie, I have always wondered about something."

"Yes?"

"You have more experience than he does and to be honest, more success in the field. Yet he has climbed the ladder more quickly than you. Why did you avoid the politics?"

Charlie took a long drink from his coffee mug, regarding his old friend and wondering if Richard had started to become suspicious about Charlie's secret. "I am just a soldier, up from the ranks. You know as well as I do just how nasty the politics are, Richard, so I just did my job, kept my head down, and stayed out of the games that McClellan and Custer and those fellows play. Taking care of my men is enough for me."

Richard slapped Charlie on the shoulder. "And you do a damned fine job. I have learned more from you than from any other officer in the Army, I believe. Now, what is on for today?"

"We need to move quickly. Assign one of the companies to stay behind to escort the supplies and wounded; they must follow us as quickly as they can. Oh, hell. Since most of the wounded are Dewees', assign him. Have Raiford be temporarily assigned to Company A. He does not deserve to lose his position as color bearer just because Dewees was an ass."

"Good idea. And Swallow at least knows what he is doing."

"We move at dawn. Let us get to it."

They rode hard for most of the day. It would not have taken so long, but for two distinct challenges. The first was the need to move around the main body of Lee's forces and get ahead of them. Lee's infantry and artillery slowed the progress of his forces of around thirty thousand men, but they still covered a good bit of territory. The second was a more difficult problem. Men were deserting from the Confederate forces by the score—they simply left their companies and started walking home. Charlie and his men kept running into bunches of these dispirited souls on the back roads they were traveling. The first few times, things were tense. But Charlie and his men quickly realized the deserters presented no real threat.

The third bunch of ragged men they came across was trying to roast a couple of skinny rabbits they had caught. Charlie looked at these half starved, exhausted souls and immediately ordered Duncan to find them a ham and some bread.

They rode on, and by around three o'clock, reached a little train station in the middle of nowhere.

Charlie met with Custer while the men set up a makeshift overnight camp.

"Well, Redmond. If we are fortunate, we will see some action tomorrow."

"General, if we are fortunate, we will manage a surrender tomorrow. The less bloodshed, the better."

"Oh, Redmond, where is your sporting sense? Oh, yes, some men might get hurt, but that is part of the risk of war. You might say, the price of glory."

"General Custer, you and I have a different perception of the glory, as you call it, of battle. Particularly battle against men I have known for twenty years, whom I fought beside in Mexico, and who I now see as tired, dispirited, and hungry. General, they are already defeated. We now have only to complete the inevitable with as much dignity and honor as possible."

"Well, Sir, I can see your point of view. I still want to write my name on at least one more battle in this conflict. Therefore, tomorrow, my brigade will take the lead. We will set the forward scouts, with the objective of taking, and if necessary destroying, any supply trains intended to relieve the rebels. You will serve as our reserves, and as defense against any effort by Lee's vanguard from the east."

"Yes, Sir. My men will provide as much support as you require. Sergeant Nailer, who you have already met, will serve as my personal courier."

The two men examined the maps and scouting reports and determined details of deployment for the following day. Charlie then returned to camp, decidedly disturbed at Custer's attitude, but grateful that he might actually be able to get some sleep that night.

The 13th established camp in a protected site halfway between the isolated train station and the nearby town of Appomattox Courthouse. It had an area, sheltered from northern winds by a low rise of hills, which was ideal for Elizabeth's medical staff, and was on high ground that could be easily defended from raiders. Around sundown, Elizabeth, escorted by Company D, arrived at the camp.

The more severely wounded had been transferred to the main hospital facilities within Grant's army; only the walking wounded traveled with the contingent. Charlie rode to meet them.

"Well, Dewees, how was the trip here?"

"Uneventful, Sir. We received orders from General Merritt to let the rebel deserters go their way, though we passed several groups of them."

"And the injured? Did they make the trip well?"

"You will have to ask Dr. Walker, Sir. I have not checked on them recently."

"Then you shall come with me and do so now, Sir. Your first duty as an officer is to tend to the care of your men."

Dewees hung his head. "Yes, Sir." Clearly, the qualities of leadership he had learned from Montgomery were not up to the standards of this career officer. He wondered what else he had done wrong.

That evening, Charlie and Richard met to go over the plans for the next day. They split the force, putting Richard and half the men facing back to the east to guard against any surprise by Lee's vanguard. The other half were ranged to the west, to support Custer in the event he had problems with the escorts for the expected supply trains.

Having briefed each company commander on his duties for the following day, Charlie finally managed to get to bed at a reasonable hour. He literally dropped into bed like a sack of flour and fell into a deep sleep. The past few days had taken their toll. Rebecca's letter, started two days earlier, would just have to wait another day.

Saturday, April 8, 1865

The ground was soft; it had rained the night before. Charlie's mount, one of the reserve horses, was not as sure footed as Jack. Before the sun was high, Charlie thought his tailbone was going to crack.

It was quiet for much of the morning. They rode circuits up and down the rail line, looking for any sign of a train, not expecting anything as Custer's men were ahead of them further down the line.

Just before lunchtime, a messenger came riding in from Custer's command post. "Move up, we have a major problem."

Charlie instructed Duncan, to signal the men to move forward at all speed. As they rode, Charlie asked the courier what the problem was.

"They have guns, Sir. No infantry that we can see, but howitzers to guard the train. They have General Custer's men pinned down."

Charlie rode up to where Custer and his officers were huddled behind a rise, discussing the problem. It was artillery against cavalry —a situation that no one had ever faced before.

Charlie rode up to the group of officers milling around Custer. "The 13th reporting, Sir."

Custer looked almost gleeful. He had a battle on his hands. "How many men do you have riding with you, General?"

"I have about five hundred mounted, Sir. The other half of the regiment is providing protection against an attack from the main body of Lee's forces."

Custer stroked his little goatee. "That should be enough. This is what I want, Redmond. I will use the main body of my troops to hold their attention. I want your men to flank them and press them up against the rail lines. If you can get behind them before they can turn the guns, it should be fairly simple. We have word that General Walker is commanding. He does not have a history of being able to respond rapidly."

"How many guns do they have? How quickly can they reload?" If the guns were too hot, they would have to let them cool for a few minutes before they could reload. "And has the wet ground slowed them down any?"

Richard mumbled behind him, "Too many, too quickly, and not enough."

Custer's aide piped up. "They have about sixty howitzers, and reloads are fairly slow, as they've been pounding away at us for almost an hour. The mud has slowed them, but not as much as we had hoped."

Charlie slipped up to the top of the hill to survey the situation. A supply train was stopped on the tracks, with light artillery on either side serving as escort. To the far right, there was a line of trees, with about five hundred feet of clear pasture on a slight uphill slope. Charlie looked very carefully. If he could get behind the trees without being detected, he had a chance of coming up behind the artillery. On the other hand, if his troopers were detected too early, and one or more of the guns could be turned, there would be a bloodbath. Fortunately, since half the guns were deployed on the other side of the train, it might not be too difficult if Custer could keep the gunners occupied while they got in position.

He returned to the cluster of officers. "Yes, Sir. Give us about a half an hour to get into position."

The conference with his company officers was tense and terse. Each trooper dismounted and carefully wrapped his horse's hooves to help keep them silent. The men slipped behind the tree line, a few at a time.

It looked good. But as they broke from the woods to charge the Confederates' flank, the end gunner swung his howitzer around and let loose with a round of deadly canister shot. Even though the shot was undirected, the effect was devastating, spraying a rain of Minié balls into Charlie's charging troops.

The blast kicked up a fountain of dirt, mixing fragments of the canister casing, the balls inside the casing, and a cloud of rock pieces and dirt up into the faces of the charging men.

Charlie saw Raiford and the flag go down. Young Lieutenant

Swallow snatched the banner up, and the men charged forward. An instant later, Charlie's horse stumbled and fell, a ball embedded in his chest. He grabbed a stray horse, not knowing if the rider had fallen to the shot or if he had just been unseated when the horse shied from the flying debris. At that moment, it did not matter.

Charlie's men charged on. Another gunner started to swing around and train his muzzle on the charging 13th. Then, finally, Charlie heard Custer's men sound the charge. Cavalry came crashing into the jaws of the artillery barrage from two sides. From the calm that had reigned no more than five minutes earlier, the world had become total mayhem.

As the 13th closed on the artillery emplacement, many of the men jumped from their horses to engage the rebel gunners hand to hand. Horses milled, men fought with saber and sidearm. Charlie, followed closely by Duncan, rode into the midst of the turmoil. With sword in hand, Charlie started to cut a path to the command position, close to the train's engine. He thought all of the guns were incapacitated, for, having fired their loaded round, the gunners would not be able to reload once they were engaged in hand to hand combat.

He was wrong.

One gunnery team still had a loaded howitzer. The charge hit to Charlie's right, a shattering blast. Men from both sides went down. Charlie felt fire and flame tear through his right arm, his leg, and his hand. The horse fell, dead in his tracks. The sense of falling was the last thing Charlie felt. In that instant, knowing he was dying, he cried out, "Rebecca!"

Duncan heard Charlie cry out. The Sergeant had taken a ball in his arm, his horse had fallen, but he was still on his feet.

"General? General Charlie! Oh, my God!"

Jocko had stayed with the support staff. He was coordinating the movement of reserve horses and the medical support team. Jack was almost healed, so Jocko decided give him a light workout. He had just finished when Jack bolted.

Jocko hung on. No horse was going to get the better of him, even General Charlie's damned pig-headed stallion. Ten minutes of hard galloping later, Jocko had passed Custer's emplacement and been dragged through a small stand of trees. The scene in front of him horrified him.

There was Duncan, on his knees, blood pouring down one arm, trying to staunch the flow of blood from what looked like Charlie's entire right side. The General was soaked in blood and a small pool was gathering under him. His face was sheet white, and he was clearly unconscious.

Jocko pulled his coat and shirt off, ripping them to use them as bandages. He pulled Duncan up by the collar of his coat. "Go. Take Jack. Get Dr. Walker and a crew here immediately."

Duncan nodded, unable to speak for crying and leapt on the waiting horse.

Very gently, Jocko checked Charlie's wounds. They were bad, very bad. His shoulder was ripped up, half his hand had been torn off, and several chunks were gone from his buttock. The worst was a gaping wound, almost as wide as Jocko's hand, in the heavy muscles of his thigh. Most of the blood was from the hand and the thigh wound. Jocko packed his shirt in the thigh and used the sleeve of his jacket to tie it off, trying to slow the flow of blood. He removed his belt and tied off Charlie's wrist with a makeshift tourniquet. The shoulder would just have to wait. It was seeping, but not gushing. Then he waited.

The makeshift camp was roaring with activity. Before leaving, Dr Walker had issued orders that made a lot of the men feel like she was

a fully commissioned officer. The orders were simple. Get a tent raised for General Redmond and make sure it was outfitted with a warm bed, a stove, and lanterns. And not a word of his injuries was to leave the camp—especially not to Rebecca—until Elizabeth gave approval.

The men did her bidding without question. They knew General Redmond was hurt, they just did not know how badly. They watched as their commander was brought back into camp on a stretcher. Jocko and Samuelson carefully carried the litter, with Whitman and Dr Walker half walking, half running ahead of them into his tent.

Somber looks were traded as the men silently wondered when Dr. Walker would come to tell them that General Redmond had succumbed to his injuries.

Inside the tent, Elizabeth tossed her cloak off and quickly began washing her hands. "All right. Jocko, post a guard on this tent. No one, and I mean no one gets in here until after I have treated him."

"Right away, Doctor." With a grimly determined look, Jocko left the tent.

Elizabeth dried her hands and nodded to Whitman and Samuelson, "Get him out of that uniform. And prepare him for surgery."

She looked down at her friend, more dead than alive, and for the first time in a very long time, Dr. Elizabeth Walker felt sick. She found an apron in the pile of supplies and draped it over her neck as Whitman cut Charlie out of the tattered remnants of his uniform and Samuelson prepared all the equipment the doctor would need.

Elizabeth leaned over, taking a wet cloth to remove the blood spatter from Charlie's face. "Listen to me, you stubborn bastard. Charlie Redmond is not a quitter. You have never run from anything in all the years I have known you. You need not start now. I do not want to have to go face Rebecca with the news you have died."

She looked at the wounds as best she could without removing the packing that was keeping Charlie from bleeding to death. She had just started removing the bandages against his hip and leg when Jocko came back into the tent.

"Dr. Walker, I am afraid you are needed."

"I am needed here."

"Ma'am, there is a soldier with a serious wound…"

"How bad?" Charlie would want and expect her to tend to his troops before taking care of him.

"Bad, Ma'am."

She blew a disgusted breath and looked to Samuelson. "Repack that, I will be back as soon as I can. Go ahead and treat the hand as best as you can, and the shoulder as well."

Samuelson nodded. "Yes, Doctor."

An hour later Elizabeth returned to the tent. Charlie's shoulder and hand had been treated and re-bandaged. She lifted his hand and examined the bandages. "How many fingers?"

"He lost the third and fourth finger, Doctor. They were completely blown off. Fortunately, it is a relatively clean wound."

Placing his hand at his side, she examined the shoulder. "And this?"

"More severe, but we managed to clean and repair it. The General may lose some use of the arm, but at least it is still attached."

Elizabeth nodded and prepared to deal with the leg. "Which is more than we can probably hope for here."

As she removed the bandages, Charlie moaned. "Liz…a…beth…"

"I am here, Charlie."

"Bad?"

"Yes, Charlie, it is bad. I think we are going to have to take your leg."

"No."

"Charlie, there may be no option."

"No."

"I do not think I can save your leg. If I do not take it, you will die."

Charlie nodded slowly. "Then...so...be...it." He drew a deep breath and was once again unconscious.

Elizabeth looked to the faces in the room. "Come on. We have to try and save this leg."

CHAPTER 33

Elizabeth, Samuelson, and Whitman stayed in Charlie's tent, working long hours to try and save his mangled leg. Elizabeth sent Jocko to try and get some sleep; someone would have to sit with Charlie through the night and watch for any hemorrhaging or fever. Jocko was the obvious choice. Instead, the man had taken up a position in front of the tent, waiting and keeping others away. Richard was ducking back and forth between the command tent and Charlie's tent. He had received orders to march to Appomattox Courthouse in the morning to join Sheridan in an attempt to keep Lee contained.

The effort that had cost Charlie so dearly had done much to help the cause. They had captured three supply trains carrying the critical supplies Grant believed would have enabled Lee to reach North Carolina and avoid surrendering. It was little comfort to Richard and the men of the 13th Pennsylvania.

Finally, Elizabeth and Samuelson emerged. Whitman stayed to

watch over the patient for a while until he could be relieved. Richard looked at Elizabeth carefully. She was drawn and gray-skinned from exhaustion. Charlie's blood was splattered all over her apron and dress. "Darling, how are you? And how is he?"

"I am all right. But I have my doubts that Charlie will survive the night. A third of his posterior right hip and buttock is missing. He lost more blood than any one man should. We have done everything we can. The rest is up to God and our friend."

"Dear God, Elizabeth, how can I tell Rebecca?"

She sighed and shook her head. "I do not know. If it comes to it, I think I should be the one to travel to Culpeper and tell her. However, I want to wait until it is absolutely necessary. You never know, Richard. Charlie is a fighter, he may survive."

Jocko, who had been listening to this conversation, broke in. "How dare you write him off? He will live. He has to. That baby girl back in Culpeper needs him. Miss Rebecca needs him. You have to pull him through."

"Jocko, I have done everything for him medically that I can. His wounds are severe, he lost a lot of blood and, by all rights, I should have amputated that leg, but he did not want that. Believe me, I do not want to lose our friend any more than you do, but we have to be prepared for the possibility."

"If he does die, I will deal with it when it happens. Until then, I will be doing everything I can to get him back to his lady and their babies." Jocko turned and slipped into the tent to sit vigil with his oldest friend.

Richard looked at his retreating back. "If I had not received orders to stand at Appomattox Courthouse tomorrow morning, I think I might join him."

"We will all be taking our turns with him, Richard. The best thing you can do for him is to do your duty and hopefully bring a quick end to this horror. I need to get cleaned up. Having Charlie's blood all over my hands is making me ill."

"Of course, Elizabeth. I am sorry. I have been keeping you.

Come, Jamison has been keeping water hot for you, and some hot food and coffee as well."

~

Jocko sat quietly beside Charlie's cot, checking the bandages every few minutes and softly sponging his friend's forehead with a cool cloth. When not tending to Charlie's body, Jocko had been reading Rebecca's letters to him, hoping that somehow her words, even in his voice, would tend to his spirit. It was very late; the camp was still except for the calls of the sentries as they made their rounds.

Charlie stirred, fretful in his pain and fever. He opened his eyes, expecting to see St. Peter. Instead, he saw Jocko's concerned features.

"J..jocko?" Charlie could hardly speak he was so drained.

"Right here, Charlie boy. Looking out for ya like always. Glad to see you have decided to join us again."

Charlie lay there, gathering his strength for a few moments before replying. "Not for long, I fear." He dampened his lips. "Jocko. Favor?"

"Anything for you, you know that. But you are going to be fine. Oh, Miss Rebecca will skin me alive if I go back without ya."

A look of such intense longing crossed Charlie's features that Jocko nearly cried out for him. "Sword. Watch. Take them home. Take care of them for me." He caught his breath. "Tell her... love her."

"Stop talking like that, Charlie. You have to go home. Miss Rebecca needs you. And what of little Em and your two boys? They need their Papa. Come on, Charlie, think of your family. They love you and need you."

"Love them. Take care..." Charlie slipped back into unconsciousness.

Jocko looked at his friend, tears in his eyes. He took Charlie's good hand in his, and bowed his head. He then did something he had not done since he was a lad in his mother's house. "Hail Mary, full of grace..."

~

Sunday, April 9, 1865

At dawn, Richard led the 13th Pennsylvania into the line alongside the rest of Sheridan's cavalry, to the right of Custer's forces, which were at the center. John Broun Gordan's infantry and FitzHugh Lee's cavalry faced them through the early mist. The Confederates advanced, and Sheridan's troops fell back slowly, opening a gap in the middle of their line. There, standing ready to meet the Confederate advance was Grant's infantry. They had covered the ninety-five miles from Petersburg in three days.

The Confederates withdrew. There were about seven hundred casualties on the field, approximately evenly divided between Union and Confederate forces. Most were injured, not dead. That afternoon, Grant and Lee met and terms of surrender were negotiated. The order was given, "Stack arms." The war in Virginia was over.

Stillness fell over the battlefield as twenty eight thousand Confederate soldiers surrendered and began the long process of signing their paroles. The Union artillery began a long, somber salute to their vanquished enemy—a two hundred-gun salute that thundered in the stillness. There was no celebration, no wild exuberance, just a quiet, thankful peace.

The men of the 13th played their role, and then hurried back to their encampment to sit vigil for their fallen leader.

~

Whitman slipped into Charlie's tent. Jocko had been up for almost two days, first preparing for battle and then sitting at Charlie's side. He would not allow anyone else to tend his fallen commander.

"Jocko, you need to get some rest. If you fall down, we will be hard pressed to take care of him. Let me watch him for a while. Get some food and at least a nap."

Jocko looked around the tent, spying a spot in the corner where he could toss a bedroll. "All right then, a little food could not hurt. I will not be long. Then I can bunk down in that corner for a bit."

"Watch yourself out there. Dr. Walker and Samuelson are up to their elbows in injuries. There was another battle this morning."

"And how did it go? How many more will there be?"

"I believe it is over. Did you hear the guns rumbling? It was not a barrage—it was a salute. The Virginians are stacking arms."

Relief washed over Jocko like a raging river. "Oh, thank the Lord!" He leaned over and whispered, "You hear that, Charlie boy. It is over, time to go home to Miss Rebecca and the children."

Charlie stirred, restless and very feverish. Whitman checked the bandages. While there was no serious bleeding, there was a small but ominous yellow stain. "Jocko? When you have eaten, stop by the hospital tent and ask Dr. Walker to look in over here as soon as she can."

"I can fetch her now." With that Jocko was out of the tent and in search of the good doctor.

Jocko found Elizabeth in the makeshift surgery. She was covered in blood, having just finished amputating a man's shattered leg. She looked exhausted; and there were more men waiting. "Excuse me, Dr. Walker."

"Yes, Jocko."

"Mr. Whitman just looked in on Gen'l Charlie. He said you need to check in on him as soon as you can."

Elizabeth nodded, looking around at the wounded men. "All right, as soon as I am finished here, Jocko. I promise."

Jocko was less than thrilled with her response, but knew she had a duty to tend to all of the men in the regiment, not just Charlie. The problem was, he did not particularly care for all of the men of the regiment, but Charlie was his boss, his friend. Disheartened, he wandered off to the enlisted men's mess tent.

Once inside he found himself looking into the eyes of two-dozen worried men. A corporal found the courage to step forward. "How is the General?"

Jocko lifted his chin. "Boys, I will be honest. 'Tis not a pretty sight. But our Gen'l Charlie is a fighter. And we all know he has more to fight for than most men."

"I heard he lost his arm," a voice in the back offered quietly.

"Nay, he still has both arms. He took a bad hit to his shoulder, but Doctor Walker stitched him back together. He did lose part of his hand, though. Blown right away. Our General is a tough'un. If any man of you had taken those wounds, you would be dead now. He is still with us."

One of the cooks stepped forward with a small covered pot. "Sergeant Jackson, here is the broth you asked me to prepare. If there is anything any of us can do for the General, you will let us know?"

"Of course. We get some of this good beef broth in him and start building him back up, he will be right as rain soon enough. So keep the broth coming, please. Oh, and some scalded milk, if you can find it."

"We will find it. If the General needs it, we will find it."

Jocko slapped the man on the shoulder. "Good man. I will be sure to tell the General of your contribution."

Jocko walked out of the mess tent with a sandwich in one hand, and the pot of broth in the other. He stopped by his own tent and grabbed his bedroll, which he slung over his back. Walking back to Charlie's tent to resume his vigil, he again turned to the God he had not talked to in years. *Please, God. I have never asked you for anything for me, but let Charlie live. Please.*

~

It was several hours before Elizabeth managed to clear the most urgent cases and join Whitman and Jocko in Charlie's tent. Jocko was passed out in the corner. Whitman was hovering over the injured man, his coat off, his shirt sleeves rolled up, alternately sponging his forehead and neck with cool water and plying fluids into him, a spoonful at a time.

Elizabeth placed a light finger in Charlie's neck to feel for the swallowing reflex. "Is he taking it?"

"He is. He is even lucid occasionally, although only for a moment or two. But the fever is rising, and I have not been able to do anything to stop it. And I do not like the way one of his bandages looks, but I waited until you got here to take a look at the wound."

"Then let us see to it." She sighed and pulled a campstool up next to Charlie's cot. She had barely any energy left, and she did not want to waste what she did have in standing unnecessarily.

Whitman peeled back the bandage over Charlie thigh and buttock. The wound was ghastly. The injury itself was terrible. Charlie's flank looked like a piece of chopped meat. But infection had set in. It was swollen, an angry red with pockets of pus. The smell was revolting.

Elizabeth swallowed hard against the stench, fighting furiously to keep from losing the contents of her stomach. "Oh, Lord. Get me a surgical tray. I am going to have to remove more of this infected area." She licked her lips and made a decision. "And prepare the amputation equipment. If I cannot get this cleaned up properly, we are going to take this leg."

Jocko had awakened while they were looking at Charlie's injuries. "Dr. Walker, you cannot take his leg. That would be worse than death for him. I have heard that warm salt water will clean up infections. If we could get some, I could keep washing it."

"Jocko, I do not want to take this leg. But would you see our friend dead if we can do something to prevent it? Of course we will do everything we can first. While I tend to removing more of this infection, you go find your warm salt bath. But I am telling you now that if it does not work, I am taking this leg. I cannot let him die if there is another option."

"Yes, Ma'am. 'Tis just that Charlie is so...he needs...Oh, hell, you know what I mean." Jocko realized what he had just said to Dr. Walker and flushed with embarrassment. "Pardon my language, Ma'am. I will go get some boiled water and salt."

"It is all right, Jocko, I understand. This is difficult on all of us. We will see our friend through."

Whitman returned with a complete surgical tray just as Jocko was leaving. Jocko looked at Whitman fiercely. "Do not let her take that leg if it can be prevented. He would kill himself, I think, if he lost it."

Monday, April 10, 1865

Elizabeth had trimmed away the dead flesh and drained the pockets of infection. This time, instead of trying to sew the wound closed, she left it open, to drain, and so that it could be washed down regularly with the salt and boiled water Jocko had made. She also made a tonic of feverwort, chamomile, and willow bark to try and control the fever. But still the fever slowly climbed higher.

They stripped him naked and washed his whole body down in cool water, but the fever slowly gained ground. Charlie was unconscious and at times delirious. They were terrified that in his thrashing, he would tear open his stitches. The only thing that Jocko and Whitman had to help them was the fact that he was so weak from blood loss. They could restrain him easily.

They continued to work on the infections. The thigh wound began to heal, slowly losing the angry swelling. The gashes in his buttocks and shoulder were not so cooperative.

Jocko looked at Whitman that night and laughed—a totally humorless laugh. "Well, at least she cannot amputate his arse."

Tuesday, April 11, 1865

The word had moved across the country like wildfire. Lee had surrendered. Tarent kept Rebecca advised of all the rumors that were filtering back from the front. There were rumors of heavy fighting prior to the surrender, and Sheridan's name was attached to all of those rumors but no details were available. Rebecca had received Charlie's last letter, written six days ago on the eve of what was clearly a four-day running battle. After that, she had heard nothing. Finally, she could not stand it. She asked Tarent to hitch Shannon to her little basket trap and, with Em beside her, drove into town.

She arrived at Major Byrnes' office and stalked in, brushing past his junior officers and ignoring all of their efforts to be polite to their General's wife and daughter. Most of the men in the office knew that Charlie was injured; but orders had come down—very specific orders. Mrs. Redmond was not to be told anything without Dr. Walker or Colonel Polk's permission.

"Major, is there any news of my husband today?"

Byrnes had been dreading this moment. He was perfectly aware the General's life hung in the balance, but he had orders not to tell her and he would obey those orders. "Ma'am, I am unable to tell you anything. I have been informed that the whereabouts of the General is a matter of some sensitivity. You must know that even though the Army of Virginia has surrendered, we are still in a state of war; and some things remain too sensitive to allow either dispatch or telegram communications."

Rebecca took a deep breath, picked Emily up from the floor, and sat her squarely in the center of the Major's desk. "Tell her that. Tell her that the whereabouts of her Papa are too sensitive for us to know." She lifted a brow in challenge. "Go ahead. Tell her you do not know anything of her Papa, for whom she has cried for nearly every day of the last two months."

Byrnes looked at the child sitting on his desk, looking at him with guileless blue eyes. Em smiled shyly at the officer. "Want Papa, pwease?"

"I am sorry, little one, I honestly do not know exactly where your Papa is. But I will send a telegram to headquarters to find out."

"Major," Rebecca lifted Em into her arms, "I do not need to know all the details. I just need to know if my husband is alive or not. I have a dreadful feeling that he may not be. Please prove me wrong."

"Ma'am, I can say with some surety that when I received this morning's dispatches from the 13th, your husband was alive. Beyond that, I do not know."

Rebecca fought tears: some borne of fear, others from relief. At least Charlie was alive. "Thank you, Major. Thank you very much. When you get more information, I would be grateful."

"Ma'am, I swear, when I have information I can share with you, I will personally ride out to deliver it."

Thursday, April 13, 1865

All day Wednesday, Charlie held his own—neither better nor worse. On Thursday, as time, infection, and fever took their toll, Charlie slowly faded. He was delirious all of the time, but too weak to do more than twitch and mumble. The infection in his side was tenacious. The wound continued to seep. While Jocko's saltwater baths had helped the shoulder, they had not been sufficient to overcome the larger infection in his buttock.

Finally, Elizabeth realized that it was time to send for Rebecca. She owed Rebecca the right to say goodbye to her husband if it was at all possible.

"We need to send for Rebecca. She should be here when..." She just shook her head, unwilling to admit she believed Charlie was going to die and that she had failed him not only as a friend, but also as a doctor.

Richard moved to her side. "Are you sure? I can send one of our couriers."

"No." Whitman had been sitting quietly on the other side of

Charlie's bed, patiently bathing the vicious wound with salt water. "She deserves to have a friend at her side when she makes this trip. I will go."

Elizabeth smiled at him. "I think that is a very kind gesture. You should prepare to leave as soon as possible."

"I will leave at first light. Colonel, can you provide me with a courier's pass?"

"Of course, I will issue one right away. I will also send a letter stating you are on a mission of mercy and should be allowed to pass without delay."

"Thank you, Sir. I wish I did not have to make this trip, but I will make it as gentle on Rebecca as possible."

Friday, April 14, 1865

Whitman left at first light, riding one of the Army's best courier horses. It was a long ride, about one hundred and thirty miles. He changed horses every hour and made excellent time, arriving in Culpeper late in the afternoon.

His first stop was Major Byrnes' office, in part to remove some of the dust of the road, and in part to gain some support in this most difficult task. He carried special orders from General Grant, who had ordered a car be added to the dispatch train to carry Rebecca southward to Appomattox.

Somewhat less filthy, but still exhausted after a long, hard ride, Whitman rode the last mile to the house. His heart was filled with compassion for the young woman he was going to see. She had seen too much grief in her life.

Beulah opened the door to find Mr. Whitman holding his hat in his hands.

"Oh Lord, 'tis General Charlie. He is dead." She waited patiently for him to answer, but tears were forming in her eyes even then.

"No, Beulah, General Charlie is not dead. But we fear he may be dying. I have come to take Mrs. Redmond to him. Is she here?"

"Of course, Sir. Come in, I will fetch her."

Whitman stepped inside and waited. Within a minute, Rebecca came down the hall, stopping about half way to him. "He is dead."

"No, Miss Rebecca, he is not dead; but he is in a very bad way. General Grant is sending a train for you in the morning. I thought you would need a friend at hand. So, since I am the one least able to care for him, I came to get you. Jocko is by his side, and Elizabeth and Samuelson are doing everything they can."

The dam broke and Rebecca collapsed where she stood, tears streaming, and gasping for air as she sobbed. She had felt for days that something was wrong, but no one would tell her anything. "I knew it. I knew it."

"Miss Rebecca, please, calm yourself. General Charlie needs you. He is strong; he is getting the best care possible. But the injuries are very serious. He needs your strength—now and in the future."

She felt his arms go around her as he knelt down. "They should have told me."

"Elizabeth was hoping to be able to send good news. At least, she has managed, so far, to save his leg."

"How bad is it? What happened to him?"

"He was hit with a blast of canister shot. His right side is badly ripped up. He has serious wounds to his shoulder, right buttock and thigh, as well as having lost two fingers off his right hand. The wound in his buttock is badly infected. The injuries are so severe that he may never regain full mobility." Whitman felt that Rebecca deserved the most clinically precise description possible. That would get the shock over more quickly and prepare her for the sight of her husband when they arrived. If he did not survive until they got back, it would give her a framework to understand why.

"When did it happen?"

"At Appomattox Station, the day before the surrender."

"He has survived this long?"

"Yes, Ma'am. Duncan saw him go down and got to him quickly. I understand that Jack went a little crazy and dragged Jocko to them as well. Between the two of them, they kept the General from bleeding to death. Your husband is a stubborn man, Mrs. Redmond. He promised you he would come back, and he is trying his best to do just that."

"Then there is hope." With Whitman's assistance, they stood. "Thank you for coming. Please have Beulah give you a room so that you may clean up, and then have Lizbet prepare you a hot meal. I will start gathering my things and try to explain this to Emily."

"Thank you, Ma'am, but I can stay in town with the garrison if that would be easier for you."

"No, not at all. We have more than enough room for a dear friend such as yourself."

"Then I will attend to my own needs. Reg and Beulah will take care of me, and I will be ready for you tomorrow at dawn. The train is due at the station at seven."

Rebecca nodded and turned on her heel. She knew where she would probably find Em. Standing outside Charlie's office door, she took a deep breath and gathered herself together. She was surpisred to discover that Em was happily in the nursery with her brothers and Tess. Opening the door, she found Tess and Em playing by the fire. The little girl was putting together a wooden puzzle Jeremiah had carved for her with the knife Duncan had given him. She looked over to see Charlie and Andrew sleeping quite peacefully in their respective bassinets.

"Tess, I need to speak with Emily. Could you leave us for a few minutes?"

"Yes, Ma'am. I will be in the kitchen with Sarah if you need me, Ma'am." Tess could see that Rebecca had been crying. She knew that Sarah and Beulah were her best sources of information.

Rebecca sat down in front of the fire with her daughter and opened her arms. Emily giggled and crawled right into her lap. "Hello, my little darling."

"'Lo, Mama. See Jermia toy!"

"I see, sweetheart. It was very nice of him to make you that toy. I know it is one of your favorites."

Em looked at Rebecca and could see the tear tracks on her face. "Mama sad?"

"No, my little darling. Mama is not sad. Mama is happy. I have found out news of your Papa."

"Papa. Papa! Papa come home?"

"Yes, Papa will be coming home. But Papa is far from home, and Mama must go get him and bring him home."

Emily's face grew its familiar thundercloud. "Mama go away? No. Mama, no go. Papa come home."

"Emily, Mama has to go get Papa. He is a long way from home. You do not want him to get lost do you?"

Emily assumed a look of long-suffering patience. Obviously, she had to explain this very evident fact to the silly grownup Mama. "Papa grownup. Papa smart. Come home witout Mama."

"Yes, Em, Papa is very smart, but Papa has been hurt. So Mama has to go get him to make him feel better."

"Papa has booboo? Oh. Mama go fix booboo?"

Rebecca smiled. "Yes, Mama has to go fix Papa's booboo. Then Mama will bring Papa home."

"Papa home good!" Em looked at Rebecca suspiciously.

"I do not know, my little darling, but I promise you this, it will be just as quickly as we can. We want to be home with you and your brothers. Now I have a favor to ask of my very big girl."

"Yes, Mama?"

"I need you to help Tess care for your brothers while I am gone. You need to be the lady of the house. Can you do that?"

"Yes, Mama. Em big girl. Em two."

"Yes, I know. So you promise to be a good girl and help while Mama is gone?"

Em stood up in front of Rebecca and nodded solemnly. "Em good. Em promise."

~

Rebecca sat by the fire in their room, holding the Bible that she and Charlie had read from when he had first arrived. She was exhausted and yet far too nervous to sleep. She wanted morning to come so that she could be on her way.

She looked over to the big bed, wishing Charlie were there that very moment so she could crawl into the safety that was their love and sleep the night through. She slipped from the chair; kneeling near the window she looked at the clear sky and the bright moon, and she laced her hands together.

"Dear God, please, please allow my Charlie to live. You, more than anyone, know what a kind, good person you have created. We need her here with us. Please, do not take her from those of us who love her so deeply. Amen."

She waited there for a moment, continuing to look out the window. Just as she was getting up, a falling star streaked across the sky as if it was an answer from the Almighty Himself.

~

Saturday, April 15, 1865

Mr. Whitman was up and ready at first light, just as he had promised. Rebecca was also ready, with a small handbag her only luggage.

"Mrs. Redmond, do you have all you need?"

"Everything except my husband, Mr. Whitman. Let us go."

"After you, Ma'am. Major Byrnes has sent a trap for us. It is already outside."

Rebecca led the way; a trooper took her bag and then helped her in. Mr. Whitman took a seat next to her, and she reached over and took his hand. "Thank you for being with me."

"Jocko wanted to come, but he could not bring himself to leave his "Gen'l Charlie." And Richard would have come himself, but

Sheridan has him running like a rat in a trap. I was the obvious choice, since Elizabeth cannot leave him."

"I really do appreciate it. It is nice to have a friend close at times like these."

"I am honored, Ma'am. And I felt strongly that you should have a friend. General Grant was kind enough to offer his own train, as he is in Washington now and occupied with settling the surrender."

"I am grateful this is over. I just hope I can have Charlie home again. I hope we are not too late."

"I have to tell you, Ma'am, having seen him the day he was injured; I am amazed at his strength. He lost so much blood, I was sure he would not survive the night."

Rebecca closed her eyes against the image of wounds she could only imagine. "Charlie is very strong and determined. If he has survived this long, I believe there is a good chance he will recover."

"Under normal circumstances, I would agree, Miss Rebecca. But there is a terrible infection we have not been able to control. That, the fever from it, and the loss of blood, taken together are making it very hard for him."

Rebecca chewed her lip then turned to face her friend. "Mr. Whitman, I know that Elizabeth is a fine doctor and she is doing everything she thinks will help. But has she tried using honey?"

"Honey? No, I believe they have been using salt water washes."

"Honey is very effective in fighting infections. My mother absolutely refused to use anything else. On the farm we used it on everything from people to horses. However, it is considered folk medicine. I do not know if Elizabeth will be willing to try it."

"Miss Rebecca, the General is dear to each of you, in your own way. If you have something that will help, I am sure she will try it. She has already tried everything she knows."

~

The rest of the trip was reasonably uneventful. General Grant had obtained priority clearance for their train. With that, they managed an average of thirty miles an hour, excellent time by any standards.

They arrived at Appomattox Station at about noon. Rebecca looked around at the land that was freshly torn and ravaged by the battle seven days earlier. She looked to Whitman as they dismounted from the train onto the shell pocked station platform. "Was this the place?"

"Yes."

"How many died here?"

"I honestly do not know. The battle stretched out along about seven miles of track, with both Charlie's and General Custer's forces. I know Dr. Walker and General Custer's surgeon both had their hands full."

"A waste. A dreadful waste. Come, Mr. Whitman, help me find my husband."

Whitman looked down the road to the east and saw a wagon approaching. Squinting in the bright light, he saw a figure he thought was Polk at the reins. "It seems that Colonel Polk has sent a wagon, Ma'am."

"So it does." Rebecca walked toward the wagon. When it stopped, Richard jumped down, and immediately he and Rebecca shared a hug.

"Richard, is Charlie…"

"No. He is still alive."

"Thank God."

"Let me take you to him. But, Rebecca, you need to be prepared. He has been horribly injured."

"I know. Mr. Whitman described the extent of his injuries for me. I do not care about that, Richard. I only want to be with him."

"You may have to convince him of that. He has been delirious, but all he talks about, I am told, is how he is not…not the husband you deserve. I do not know if that is the result of this injury, or if it is the fever talking."

"It does not matter. We can help him overcome this."

"Rebecca, you need to understand. These are truly ugly injuries. Elizabeth wanted to amputate the leg at the hip."

She took a deep breath and nodded. "I understand. It does not matter, Richard. Now please take me to my husband."

They rode down the road in silence, each consumed with their own thoughts. As they approached the camp, they came upon a scene of turmoil.

Richard stood on the running board, yelling for order. Finally, he understood. "The President has been shot. Lincoln is dead."

Rebecca's head dropped. Her chin to her chest, she said a quick prayer and took a deep calming breath before starting to climb out of the wagon.

Jocko had been waiting for her. He sprang to her side and lifted her down, ready to escort her to Charlie. Lincoln and politics could wait. "Thank God, you are here."

At the back of the wagon, Walt Whitman quietly began to cry.

"If I could have come last night, I would have. Where is he?"

"I will take you to him, but before you go in, Dr. Walker says you need to get cleaned up."

"All right. Anything."

Jocko lead her to the Officers' Mess, where he had partitioned off an area and had warm, boiled water and soap waiting for her. "Get washed, and put on one of the aprons I have here for you. Then I will take you to his tent. We set up a separate tent for him, rather than the usual surgery. It is clean and private. I have had a cot put in it for you, as well."

"Thank you, Jocko. I will only be a moment."

As she washed up, Jocko called to her, "Sergeant Jamison wants to know if you want something to eat? Or some tea before you go over?"

"Could you have it taken to his tent? I really just want to be with Charlie. Everything else can wait."

"Yes, certainly. I will tell him to have a tray sent over."

"Thank you." Rebecca quickly scrubbed her arms and face, using the damp cloth to remove or dampen down any dirt that might be clinging to her clothing and then she slipped the apron over her head, tying it off before returning to Jocko. "Shall we?"

"If you wish. Are you sure you are ready?"

"I am more than ready, Jocko, and if I am not taken to my husband soon, I will tear this camp apart tent by tent until I find him."

"Yes, Ma'am." Jocko offered her his arm and escorted her to the large tent set off from the rest of the camp, shaded by old oak trees, and currently guarded by Duncan, even though his arm was neatly bandaged and in a sling.

Rebecca stopped and touched the young man. "Duncan, are you hurt very badly?"

"M-mi-miss Rebecca. Umm. No, Ma'am. Just a sc-scr-scratch. Ma'am. I am sorry. I t-tried."

"Tried?"

Duncan bowed his head. "Yes, M-ma-ma'am. I tried, but there was so m-much b-bl-blood. And I c-co-could n-not..."

"Duncan," she ran her hand over his good arm, "I am sure you did everything properly, and that I have you to thank for the fact that my husband is alive."

He hung his head even lower. "No, M-ma-ma'am. It was Jocko and Jack, n-no-not m-me."

"I do not believe that, and I do not want you to believe that, either. I am sure when he is able, the General will thank you himself."

"He c-ca-called your name, you know."

"No, I did not know. Thank you for telling me. Thank you for being there to hear it."

"It was the last th-th-thing I heard h-him say." Duncan looked up at her, tears running down his cheeks. "I w-wi-wish it had b-been me."

Rebecca moved forward and wrapped her arm around his shoulders. "You should not speak like that, Duncan. I do not like it, and the General certainly would not like it. You did what you had to do, and I am convinced you saved my husband's life. For that I am grateful to you, always. Now stop saying these things and be glad you are both alive." She gave him a hug and pulled back with a smile. "That is an order by proxy. When the General is capable, I will have him reaffirm it."

Duncan managed a watery smile and pulled himself to attention. With a left handed salute, he responded, "Yes, M-ma-ma'am, Mrs. G-general, M-ma'am."

Rebecca patted his cheek. "Good boy, Duncan." She turned and opened the tent flap. As she stepped inside, she got her first good look at Charlie. Without taking another step, she turned to the side of the tent and promptly vomited.

CHAPTER 34

Saturday, April 15, 1865

Elizabeth looked up and glared at Rebecca. She was working on a particularly nasty and sensitive part of Charlie's wound, trying to save a vital tendon from being destroyed by the invasive infection. "If you must do that, at least take it outside."

Rebecca gasped and gratefully took a cup of water Jocko thrust into her hand. She rinsed her mouth, spitting into a bucket near the door. "I am sorry." She wanted to cry, but she knew now was not the time; now was the time to be strong. She took a tentative step toward Charlie. "How is he?"

Elizabeth continued to focus on the wound she was cleaning. "To be honest, I am not sure why he is still alive, but he is, and as long as he continues to fight, we have a chance to save him. I just have not yet found the source of the continued infection. So I keep looking." She glanced up for a moment, and then barked an order. "Jocko, get someone to clean that mess up, please."

Rebecca took another step forward. Elizabeth's appearance frightened her almost as much as Charlie's. Charlie's wounds and injuries were physical; Elizabeth's were clearly emotional. "Can... can...I hold his hand?"

Elizabeth sighed deeply. "Rebecca, if there is anything you can do to give him strength, please do. I am sorry I snapped at you. It is just that I am so tired and have tried so hard. I swear I do not know what else to do. I just cannot seem to beat this infection."

Rebecca found a crate and sat down on Charlie's other side. She took his hand. With her other hand, she gently ran her fingers through his hair. "I am here, my love." She leaned over and gently kissed his fevered brow. Then she looked at Elizabeth. "If it is not too presumptuous of me, I would like to make a suggestion."

"I will take any suggestion you have. Jocko came up with washing the wounds with boiled brine. It has helped some."

"I know it may not make much sense, but when I was growing up, my mother always used honey to draw out infections. I never knew her to use anything else."

Elizabeth frowned and looked at Charlie's wound. Somehow she knew there still had to be something from the shell left in the wound that was causing this continued infection. But finding some small shard in that mess of chopped meat was almost impossible. Anything that would tend to draw it out would help. "Would you alternate it with the brine washes?"

"Yes, honey applied to warm soaked cloths, left just long enough to draw the infection to the top, then cleansed with the salt solution or possibly alcohol."

"Or perhaps a hot honey compress? Left on for say half an hour at a time? Then cleaned with a warm brine wash to flush out anything the honey drew? We would need heat to melt the honey, I would think."

"Yes, that is how it is done, for the most part. My mother used this cure on every living thing on our farm at one time or another."

Jocko spoke up. "Yes, damn me, me mother used honey for every scratch and scrape we had as children. Seemed to work too. I am just sorry I di' not remember it."

Elizabeth looked directly into Rebecca's eyes. "Do you think you could stand to help with it? Charlie is in a pretty bad way, and these are ugly wounds. The stench of the infection is nauseating. It would be very hard, and I do not want to ask you to do anything you do not feel comfortable with."

"I will do whatever you or Charlie need. I did not come here to say goodbye. I came here to take him home."

"Good. Come over and sit beside me. I will show you how to clean and dress each of his wounds."

Rebecca nodded, then pushed up the sleeves of her dress as she moved next to Elizabeth. She took a deep breath, clenched her jaw, and vowed not to vomit again. She also commanded herself not to cry at the sight of Charlie's wounds. Mrs. Redmond was resolute. She was going to save her husband's life.

Elizabeth was working on Charlie's hip and thigh. From halfway between his knee and hip up almost to his waist, his right side was raw. He was missing a chunk about the size of Rebecca's hand of the heavy muscle in his thigh. At least the lower part of the wound was clean and showing signs of beginning to heal. A large chunk of his buttock was also gone, but this site was angry, inflamed and infected. There were several pocket of pus; the wound was oozing and stank of infection. Elizabeth carefully opened the pockets of pus with the tip of a small scalpel, drained the infection, and rinsed the area with warm brine. "When I finish, you can make a honey compress for it, if you would."

"Of course." She looked to Jocko. "Can you please go find some honey? I believe Charlie may have had some in his personal things. It will be in a black clay jar. Lizbet sent it with him, along with a few other comforts from home."

"Yes, Ma'am. I know what you are speaking of. But, I think that we have some in the mess. I can save your special honey for his tea when he can have some. I will be right back with it, and with more boiling water."

"Thank you." Rebecca then set to finding clean cloths that could be used to make the warm honey poultice. She glanced back to watch Elizabeth open yet another pocket of infection which ran red and yellow with pus. She saw Elizabeth clench her jaw as she took a small cloth and dabbed out the mess that was so significant it was running freely onto the sheets.

She found a package of boiled lint in the surgical tray. Sure that she would have what she needed, she turned back to Elizabeth. "Let me finish. You look exhausted."

"Thank you. I appreciate it. You need to learn how to do this if you are to care for him."

"Just tell me what to do." She took the seat Elizabeth vacated and picked up the scalpel. "I am ready."

"Look for the places that look shiny and rounded. The shine is from the flesh being drawn tight from the infection underneath. Make a small incision, perhaps a finger's width long, and let it drain. If you can, press on either side of the lump to push out any additional pus." Elizabeth looked at Rebecca, who had paled noticeably. "It does not hurt as much as you might think, and it feels much better afterwards. The pressure and heat of the infection is terribly painful."

Rebecca nodded, wondering briefly if she could actually do this. Then she remembered she had helped her father do similar things to injured horses, and if she could do it for an animal, she could certainly do it for someone she loved. She steadied her hand and made the first cut, being very careful to do exactly what Elizabeth had told her. "Like this?"

"Good, but you need to cut a little deeper—you will actually feel your knife break through to the infection. It is considerably less dense than the muscle tissue."

"All right." She tried again, making the cut a little deeper and a little longer. When she did, the cyst broke open covering her fingers in sticky yellow fluid.

"That is exactly right. You go ahead, I will just watch to make sure you get everything."

Carefully, Rebecca dabbed at the wound, cleaning it out and applying pressure to force out more of the infection. Very soon she was so involved in her job that everything else, including the foul smell, seemed to fade from her consciousness.

Jocko returned more quickly than she expected, or perhaps time had passed more quickly than she noticed.

"I have plenty of good, fresh honey, Miss Rebecca. No sugar crystals in it at all, and it has been strained to get any comb out. And I brought a small pot of boiled water, too, to make the compresses. My mother used to pour about a cup of honey into about two cups of hot water, then soak the lint in it to make a compress. Do you want me to prepare it?"

"Yes please." She answered without looking up from the next area that she was working on. As she made another cut, she felt the blade catch on something. "Elizabeth, I think there is something here. Can you give me more light?"

The Doctor reached into her surgical kit and pulled out a small mirror, which she used to focus a beam of light on the small incision that Rebecca had made. Tersely, she commanded, "Expand the incision." She pulled a pair of forceps out and used them to spread the incision. There was a small sliver of something the color of the red clay mud; it was almost the color of the flesh around it. With a pair of tweezers, she carefully pulled it out of the flesh in which it was embedded. It was a long sliver of half rotten wood.

"Oh, God. How could I have missed this?"

"Elizabeth, look at it. It is the same color as everything else. I would not have seen it. I only found it because the scalpel touched it while I was cutting."

"So do you think that each one of these pockets of infection may be hiding a bit of debris?"

"Me? You are the doctor."

Elizabeth smiled, possibly for the first time in over a week. "Right now, I am feeling more like the fumbling fool than the doctor. Let us finish cleaning up his wounds, get him a bit more stabilized, then do some serious probing."

"All right. Whatever you think it best."

Rebecca sat next to the bed, holding Charlie's good hand and praying. She placed a cool cloth on his forehead, hoping to help bring down the fever that still gripped his body. She, Elizabeth, and Jocko had spent two and a half hours flushing the wound and taking turns pulling out small pieces of wood that had embedded themselves deeply into his flesh.

She leaned over and kissed his cheek. "I love you, Charlie. You need to get better and come home. Your daughter misses you, and there are two baby boys who want to meet their Papa. Please, Charlie."

A soft moan came from the recumbent form, and Charlie's good hand twitched, as if reaching for something.

Lost in the haze of delirium, Charlie thought he could hear Rebecca's voice calling to him. In his mind's eye, he could see her, standing by the pond where they had shared so many tender moments, beckoning to him. He reached out to her, trying to reach her, trying but failing.

"I am here, darling." Rebecca's voice was hopeful as she leaned closer to his cheek, giving it a kiss. "I am right here."

Charlie's eyelids fluttered open. He looked at her, blank and unrecognizing for a moment, then murmured, "'Becca?"

"Yes, my love." She kissed his cheek again and brushed her fingers through his hair.

"Dream of you. Always you." He smiled and relaxed some.

"And I of you. We are together now, Charlie, and I will not leave here without you."

He tossed his head and shifted in the bed, trying to get a little more comfortable. "Hurts. So much. Please make it stop."

"I know it hurts my love, we are doing everything we can. We are going to make you better. I promise."

He stirred again, clenching her hand convulsively. She almost cried when she felt how weak his grip was. "Say goodbye for me."

"No one to say goodbye to, my love. You are going to be just fine, and I am going to take you home to our farm and our babies."

"Home? Home. 'Becca. Sweet 'Becca. Miss you so." He smiled and closed his eyes.

Rebecca leaned over, allowing tears to fall for the first time, as she realized that he did not understand she was there with him. "It is all right, Charlie. I am not leaving. I will be right here with you, until I can take you home. Rest now my darling. Just rest."

"Rest. Yes. Rest." He turned his head into the hand stroking his hair, closed his eyes, and lay still. The only sound in the room was the slight rumble of his breathing and the soft sound of Rebecca crying.

Dusk had dimmed the light in the tent to soft shadows when Elizabeth came in, followed by a trooper carrying a tray with two steaming bowls and a pot of tea.

"I thought you might need some food, dear. You have had a long day. I know I am starving. How is Charlie doing?"

"He was talking a while ago. I thought he was talking to me, and then I realized that he did not know who he was talking to." She reached for the bowl. "Thank you." She took a bite and watched as Elizabeth settled down with her. "Is it true? Is President Lincoln dead?"

"Evidently, yes. The telegram said that he was shot in the head last night by some actor while he was at the theater and died today."

"How horrible. It would seem his dream was prophetic after all. I feel terribly sorry for Mrs. Lincoln."

"I feel more concerned for us, dear. Already, there is a great deal of anger at the South for his death."

"I am sure. What do they know about the man who shot him?"

"Evidently it was one of the Booth boys. John Wilkes, I believe. Ironic, since his father was on stage at that theater not four months ago."

"Oh, Lord, it was his father Charlie and I saw while we were in Washington. We attended a performance at Ford's Theater."

"Well, of the children, Wilkes was the least talented. I always thought he was trying to outdo his brother Edwin—and usually failed. Perhaps this is his way of being famous. Pretty poor solution, in my opinion."

"Did they catch him? Do you know?"

"I believe they are still looking for him. Personally, I hope they catch him and he burns in hell. They will surely execute him for what he has done."

"I do not doubt that. Hopefully, that will be the last of the killing from this mess." Rebecca looked to Charlie and replaced the cloth on his forehead. "It has cost us all too much."

Elizabeth finished the last bit of stew in her bowl. "Well, this is just the beginning. What will it take to put this land back to work? To repair the damage? I have seen fields that were so soaked with blood and torn up with canister shot, I doubt anything will ever be grown there again."

"To be honest, Elizabeth, I have little care about that. The South brought these problems on itself. I just want to make Charlie better and take him home. I have little sympathy for these fools who did not know when all was lost, who did not have the brains God gave a nanny goat, to know when to stop. They should have stopped months ago and because they did not, look at what they did to Charlie."

Elizabeth was a bit startled. She had seen Rebecca angry, offended, annoyed, lost, depressed, and downright ready to kill Mrs. Williams. She had never seen this deep, despairing bitterness before. "My dear, it has been a long and very difficult day. You have a long, hard road ahead of you nursing Charlie back to health. Can I give you something to help you sleep? Jocko and Samuelson will take turns watching over Charlie tonight."

"No. No, I want to be able to come if he needs me." She gestured to the other side of the tent, where a blanket had been strung. "Jocko has provided me with a place to sleep when I get tired, but I do not want to leave Charlie."

"I did not mean for you to leave him, dear. I just thought you would need some sleep sometime, and the men will be happy to watch and call you if he wakes."

Rebecca looked at Charlie, whose face twitched with pain. "He does not know I am here. I want him to know I am here."

Elizabeth's heart almost broke at how forlorn Rebecca looked as she said those words. "My dear, he is delirious. Now that we have dug out all the debris from his wounds, he should start to improve. At some level, I think he does know you are here. He is trying more, trying to cooperate, to stay still when we work on him. His hand must hurt as much or more than his leg, but he held it still while you worked on it today. He has been trying to pull it away from me."

Rebecca nodded and could no longer be strong. The tears began to fall.

～

Sunday, April 16, 1865

After letting her cry herself out, Elizabeth convinced Rebecca that Charlie would probably sleep through the night. Reluctantly, she accepted a mild sedative from the concerned physician, and settled onto the cot Jocko had made up for her.

She slept late the next morning after a restless night broken by the need to get up repeatedly and check on Charlie. Jocko, having taken over from Samuelson sometime in the middle of the night, let her sleep.

The first thing she heard that morning was Charlie's voice, talking to Jocko.

"Jocko?"

"Yes, Charlie. I am here."

"'Becca?"

"She is here as well, Charlie."

"Dream. 'Becca"

"Dreamed, Charlie?"

"Dream. 'Becca."

Slowly, she stepped out from behind the blanket and approached his bed. "It was not a dream, my love." She took his hand and smiled at him.

Charlie looked up at her smiling face, floating above him and nearly passed out. "'Becca?"

"Yes, my dear. I came as soon as I could." She ran her fingers over his forehead and through his hair, relieved beyond measure that his fever seemed to be going down.

Charlie closed his eyes and just savored her touch for a moment. Then his eyes popped open. "Hurts. Am I dead?"

"You have been wounded, but it is nothing we cannot deal with. All that matters is that you are alive." She smiled and kissed his cheek. "And the war is over, Charlie. When you are well, we can go home."

A look of bewilderment came over his face. "War?"

"Yes, Charlie, it is over. Lee surrendered."

"Good. War is bad. Very bad." Charlie closed his eyes and rolled his head on the pillow, groaning softly. "Hurt."

"I know, darling, but it is over now. All we have to worry about is making you well enough to go home. You have a little girl who is desperate to have her Papa home, and you have two fine healthy sons waiting for you."

"'Becca? Em? Sons?" Charlie tossed his head. "Dreams. All dreams." He tried to shift his body and groaned. "Make it stop hurting."

"We are trying, dear." All Rebecca could think of to do was to talk with him, to try and bring him up out of his delirium. "Charlie, our daughter Em is growing like a weed. She talks of you constantly, and she is waiting for us to come home. She misses her Papa."

Charlie's brow wrinkled in concentration. "Em daughter. Sons?"

"Beautiful and healthy, waiting for you to come home so they can be properly christened." She watched the strain in Charlie's face as he tried to understand what she was saying. "Rest, dear heart. We can talk later."

He closed his eyes for a few minutes, and then opened them to look directly into Rebecca's eyes. "How bad?"

"You are going to be fine, my love. We will get you through."

His hand closed around her wrist. "Tell me."

She took her seat next to him. "It is bad, Charlie. You have lost a lot of mass in your thigh and buttock. You were wounded in the shoulder, and you lost two fingers on your right hand. You have been fighting infection for ten days. But it does not matter. What matters is that you are alive."

Charlie laid there, eyes closed, trying to absorb the implications of her stark statement through the haze. A few fingers he could live without, but what about the shoulder, and his leg? Finally, bleakly, he asked, "Will I walk?"

"Yes. Yes, you will be able to walk. Elizabeth did everything she could, Charlie. You asked her not to take your leg and she did not, though she thought she might have to. You will be able to get up and about again."

"Crippled?"

She sighed. "Charlie, it does depend on your definition of cripple. Will you be able to run your circuit at the farm? No, probably not. Will you be able to run the farm? Yes. Will you be able to be a father to the children? Yes, without question."

Charlie was quiet for a long time. Finally, he spoke again. "Thought I died. Guess not. Dead is not supposed to hurt." He closed his eyes and slept.

~

Monday, April 24, 1865

Elizabeth had slipped a small amount of laudanum into Rebecca's tea that morning, hoping the exhausted woman would go to sleep. Over the last few days, Rebecca had sat, quietly bathing Charlie's wounds with alternating washes of warm honey and salt water every hour, and soothing his fevered forehead with cool water in the interim. The doctor was concerned at her friend's refusal to leave Charlie and finally decided to take matters into her own hands. She slipped into the tent in the early afternoon to find Charlie's fever down for the first time in days.

She sat down on her stool and took Charlie's injured hand into her own to check on the condition of the bandages.

Charlie groaned and his eyelids fluttered open. He laid there, a grimace on his face, watching Elizabeth for some sign of his condition.

"Welcome back, dear friend. I am not going to bother to ask how you feel. I am sure I know." She smiled at him and then went back to inspecting the bandage, quite pleased to see that the wound had stopped seeping and the bandage was still clean.

Charlie, his throat dry and raw from days of fever and slow force-feeding, croaked, "Hurts. How bad?"

"It is not pretty, Charlie. I will not lie to you. You have been severely injured, but we did manage to save your leg."

Charlie groaned involuntarily as Elizabeth adjusted the splints and bandages on his hand. "Fingers?"

"You lost two fingers on your right hand and I suspect there will be limited use of the ones that remain, but you also managed to keep your hand. How much do you remember?"

"Most of it. Shoulder, leg, hand. All bad?"

"Charlie, the wounds are substantial, but you are alive, and after time to recover, I believe you will find you are still going to live a long, happy life. Granted you will have limitations, but nothing you cannot overcome."

"Still ride?"

"I think so. You may have to have a special saddle made to accommodate your leg for a while. You are going to find your knee is somewhat stiff. With proper care, I do not foresee any severe problems."

"Walk? Dance? Run?"

She chuckled. "Yes, you will walk. I am sure you and Rebecca will find a way to dance; I have no doubt about that. As for running, I doubt you will ever run again, Charlie."

Charlie lay there and thought about that for a bit. Then gathered himself through the pain and asked one more question. "Scars. How bad?"

Elizabeth chewed her lip for a moment, then decided the truth was the best, "The scars are going to be severe."

Charlie closed his eyes. Something went out of him in that moment. "Hurts. Bad. Real bad."

"I know." She scratched her neck. "Would you like something for the pain? I can place you on a schedule that will keep you unaware of the pain, until your body has had time to heal a little more."

The idea of being disconnected from the world was very appealing. What would Rebecca think of a scarred, disabled, fraudulent man? It was bad enough that they would have to maintain the fiction of man and woman, but now, how repulsive would Charlie's scarred and mutilated body be to her? "Yes. Out. No pain, please." *No thoughts, either.*

"All right." She patted his arm. "I will prepare the medication and be right back." She left the tent to fetch her bag and the supplies she would need to take care of her friend's pain.

Charlie lay in his bed and carefully examined each area of pain in his body. His shoulder felt like a falling tree had crushed it. His flank felt like it had been flayed by a butcher, chopped for sausage, and cooked over a hot fire. He knew that he was missing fingers on his right hand, but he could feel them all; and they all felt as if someone had attached red-hot daggers to each one. He could not imagine what he must look like. But whatever it was, he knew it was ugly. No longer would he be Rebecca's "Greek Goddess." Rebecca had said that the beauty of Charlie's body took her breath away. Any beauty Charlie may have had was gone, torn away in a blast of hot metal and rock. *Now,* Charlie's little voice taunted, *your body will do what it should have done in the first place—repulse her.*

When Elizabeth returned, Charlie eagerly swallowed the slightly bitter brew she offered him. Oblivion was welcome for many reasons.

Rebecca sat holding Charlie's hand, wishing he would come to and not too happy that he was being kept sedated. Elizabeth entered the tent with a pot of tea in one hand and a small kettle of soup in the other.

"Elizabeth, I really would prefer if we could let him come out of sedation. He seems half dead like this."

"I do understand, dear, but he was in so much pain. Having that much muscle exposed is agony, and the hand is not much better. Also, if we are to get him home, the only way to do it is to sedate him. Heavily."

Rebecca sighed, nodding and wiping away tears at the same time. "When do you think I will be able to take him home?"

"Well, now that his fever has broken, I do not see any reason to delay. General Grant has offered his train car to carry him. That will make it easier. And I think you would be much happier to have him at home than here."

"Of course I would. I hope being home will help him get better quickly, too. Em will be so excited to have him home. It is going to be difficult to make her understand that time with Papa will be limited at first."

"You realize he will have to be unconscious for literally the entire trip? And that Em may be very frightened when her papa is as incapacitated as her mama was?"

"I know, but Charlie is going to get better. Constance never had that chance."

Elizabeth thought for a moment. She had seen serious depression set in after major injuries before, and was concerned that Charlie might be inclined toward it. "Rebecca, there is something else you may have to deal with."

"Yes?"

"It is not uncommon for men who have been very badly injured to become terribly melancholy. They may feel their injuries make them somehow less than they were. I have seen them literally turn their faces to the wall. I pray that Charlie will not go that way, but I wanted to warn you."

"I think, unfortunately, it would be very easy for Charlie to do that, but I will do everything in my power to keep it from happening. I only hope I am enough."

"Then I will see if I can arrange for the train car for tomorrow."

Tuesday, April 25, 1865

The next morning was hellish. Elizabeth and Samuelson needed to stay with the regiment; there were too many injured men to care for to allow them to leave with Charlie. Whitman, as a civilian volunteer, chose to go with the General and his wife; however, he was in deep mourning over Lincoln's death and the frightening rumors that were circulating as a result of that terrible act. Duncan, because he was already on injury leave, and Jocko, whose duty was to stay with his General, managed the logistical details.

Everything that could be draped with mourning banners showed black. Every man in the regiment wore a black armband. Even the train car had black bunting draped on its handrails. The entire army had gone into mourning for Lincoln.

Elizabeth had prepared Charlie as well as she could. He was carefully strapped to his cot, and heavily sedated. The men of the regiment had taken turns hand carrying his stretcher to keep from jostling the injured man.

The doctor had less success in preparing Rebecca. She was shaken at how pale Charlie was in the light of day, and how thin he had become in the days since his injury. His good hand, once wiry and strong, lay on the gray blanket looking almost skeletal and nearly transparent.

"Elizabeth, do you think it is safe to take him home? I am not sure he is strong enough; maybe we should wait another day or so."

The Doctor looked at her patient critically, and then turned to Rebecca. "I honestly think he will be better off in a real bed, in a proper room, and with good food and tender care than he will here in a tent with a dirt floor, in an Army camp that is rapidly becoming a refugee center. Take him home, Rebecca. He needs to be there, and so do you."

Rebecca nodded, and then embraced her friend. "Thank you for everything. I know he would not be alive now if it were not for you. Promise me you will come as soon as you can."

"Absolutely—the very first minute I can get away from here, I will. And I believe you and I have a wedding to plan. I am just sorry Richard could not be here to see you off."

"Give him my love and thank him, as well." With a deep sigh she turned, and allowed Jocko to help her aboard the train.

Duncan was sitting at the far end of the car, beside the bed they had set up for Charlie, already positioned to watch over the heavily drugged man. The sling he wore to cradle his injured arm made things awkward, but he had braced himself to keep Charlie stable while the train jerked as it started. Whitman was sitting at the table in the middle of the car, with a pencil in hand and a notebook open before him, mumbling, "My Captain, my Captain" to himself.

Jocko settled Rebecca in a soft chair, kneeling in front of it. "Miss Rebecca, I want to say that I know things are not going to be easy with getting Gen'l Charlie back up on his feet, but I promise you, I will do whatever may be required to see to it."

"Thank you, Jocko. I know I can count on you. Charlie and I need our friends close to us right now."

"I wired ahead to Major Byrnes to have transport waiting for us when we get in. And I warned him of how badly injured the General is. He has a team of men who have volunteered to carry him home, and a carriage will be waiting for you. I think carrying him by hand will be less stressful for him than bouncing around in the back of a wagon."

Rebecca glanced at her husband, who was indeed sleeping soundly. "He inspires great loyalty."

"He does indeed. There are many men in this and his previous regiments who are alive because of what he does. He takes care of his men first, and we will take care of him."

Rebecca stood, patting Jocko's shoulder as she did. Taking a moment to get the movement of the train, she walked to Charlie and took Duncan's place at her husband's side. She took his good hand and leaned over, placing a kiss on his forehead. "We will be home soon, darling."

A particularly hard lurch tossed the car a bit to the side, and Charlie groaned in pain, even through the laudanum-induced stupor.

Rebecca stood and covered his chest gently with her own body, to give him a feeling of being protected. "It is all right, my love, you are going to be fine." She placed a kiss on his cheek, allowing her lips to linger for a moment.

The trip continued, a hell for Rebecca, with each hard lurch or stop bringing a groan of pain from Charlie. Yet the drugs kept him too sedated to talk, or to even acknowledge her presence. By the time they reached Culpeper, six hours later, Rebecca was emotionally and physically exhausted. Shortly before they arrived, Whitman gave Charlie another dose of laudanum to ease the painful transition from the train to Redmond Stables and his own bed.

Charlie's men carried his litter home in a relay over the course of the three miles from the station to the house. They knew the slow, steady pace of walking would be less traumatic for him than being moved in a wagon. Arriving at the house, Rebecca allowed the men in the last relay to carry Charlie up the stairs to their room.

As soon as they had been seen coming, the house was alive with people. They immediately overwhelmed Rebecca. She ordered the troopers upstairs and sent Jocko and Whitman to settle Charlie into bed; they were the only ones she could trust.

As she watched them take him upstairs, she was immediately besieged by the staff and Emily.

"Mama!"

Rebecca smiled through her own exhaustion and knelt down to greet her daughter. "Hello, my little darling."

"Mama home." Em wrapped her arms around Rebecca's neck, gracing her with a kiss to the cheek."

"Yes. Mama is home. Home to stay."

"Papa?" Em looked expectantly behind Rebecca and then around the room. "Papa?"

"Papa is upstairs."

"Papa!" She turned and started the effort of getting up the steps when Rebecca caught her and sat on the step with her. She pulled Em into her lap and then looked to Beulah, Tess, Lizbet, Ginny, and Reg who were all waiting expectantly for information. When the train had arrived draped in black, a rider had rushed to the house and told everyone that Miss Rebecca was back, but that the General must be dead.

"Emily, your Papa is very sick."

"No."

"Em, I am sorry, but Papa is very sick."

At that moment, Em burst out crying. "Papa!"

"No, no, Papa is going to be fine, but he needs time to get well."

"Mama sick. Mama go away. Papa sick. Papa go away."

The look on the little girl's face was tearing Rebecca up. She wanted to take Em up and prove to her that Charlie would be all right, but at the moment she was not entirely sure of that herself.

"Papa will be fine, but he needs to rest. I promise, I will take you to see him as soon as I can." Tears filled Rebecca's eyes, partly from fear and partly from exhaustion. She was simply too tired to think clearly. "Em, Mama needs to change. Go with Tess, and we will go see Papa later when he has had a chance to rest."

Em looked into her Mama's face and knew it would be best if she did what she was asked. She sensed now might not be the time to have a fit. "Yes, Mama."

Rebecca kissed her daughter and handed her off to Tess. "How are the boys?"

"Fine, Miss Rebecca." Ginny stepped forward. "They are just fine. Sleeping."

"Thank goodness for that." She addressed all of them. "I need to go see to the General. I will be down later to tell you everything."

She stood and headed up the steps, with her staff watching every tired step. They were worried about their mistress. She looked as though she had been through hell. It was obvious that she had not slept properly and that she had not been eating, and had not had a proper bath in a very long time. Lizbet looked to her family, then back up the steps. "Miss Rebecca, please wait. Let me come help you." And with that the young woman was up the steps right behind Rebecca.

Wednesday, April 26, 1865

Very slowly, Charlie woke. His head felt like it had been stuffed with cotton batting, every part of his body ached, and it felt as if the devil himself was roasting his entire right side. It seemed to him that the field hospital had become far more comfortable than he remembered from the past. Slowly, he opened his eyes and looked around. He realized he was lying in his own bed, on the side that Rebecca usually slept on. "My God, I cannot be home. This must be a dream. A horrible dream." He spoke aloud, trying to break out of this terrible dream.

Jocko spoke from the chair he was sitting in by the window on the far side of the bed. "It is no dream, Gen'l C. You are home." The man rose and came toward the bed. "You were wounded. Do you remember?"

"I remember being blown off my horse. Duncan was there. Then you and Jack were there. I thought I was going to die."

"You did not die, Gen'l. Dr. Walker did her best."

"I remember asking her to not take the leg."

Charlie lifted his bandaged hand. Agony tore through his shoulder from moving the arm. From the shape of the bandage, it was clear that part of the hand was missing. "Are you sure I am not dead, and this is just my punishment?"

Jocko looked at his old friend with a mixture of sorrow and pity. "Charlie," he snorted, "you are stuck with us for a while longer. I expect God decided to put you through Purgatory beforehand so you can go straight up when you do finally die." He cleared his throat, becoming more serious. "Charlie, you have been very badly wounded. Half your hand was blown away. Your whole right side is a mess. You are missing a lot of muscle tissue, but you have no broken bones other than your hand, and eventually, you will heal. You have to keep that in mind in the coming weeks."

"What do you mean?" Charlie tried to move his right leg. The pain was so intense he had to stifle a scream. And he failed to move the leg. When he could talk again, he panted, "Jesus, Jocko. Will I walk?"

"Maybe with a cane."

Charlie closed his eyes. It was bad enough that he could not offer Rebecca a real life with a real man. Now she had a maimed cripple on her hands. In a flat voice, he asked, "How did I get home?"

"We brought you home in General Grant's train."

Charlie thought for a long time. While he lay there, Jocko carefully checked the bandages. There was no sign of seepage, so he left them.

"Where is Miss Rebecca?"

"Downstairs with the children, I believe."

"Where is she sleeping?"

"She used the davenport last night, so as not to disturb or hurt you."

"Jocko. Do me a favor?"

"Anything, Gen'l C."

"Set up a cot down in my office. I need to give Miss Rebecca her bed and a place to sleep in comfort. Do what you need to do to move me down there today."

"Charlie, do you think that is a good idea? Miss Rebecca is —"

Charlie snapped. "Jocko, do not question me. Just get me moved as quickly as you can. And do not tell Miss Rebecca until it is done."

After putting Em down for her nap, with a promise they would see Papa when she woke, Rebecca went to check on Charlie. When she stepped into the room, she was shocked to find the bed empty and Lizbet changing the sheets.

"Where is General Charlie?"

"General Charlie asked Mister Jocko to move him to his office downstairs."

"What?"

"I do not know more than that, Miss Rebecca. They moved him, and then Mister Jocko told me to remake your bed with fresh linens."

Rebecca left the room. She was furious and upset, a very bad combination when it came to Rebecca Redmond; Jocko was about to get it with both barrels. "Jocko!" she yelled, as she descended the stairs.

Jocko was on his way upstairs from the office when he heard Miss Rebecca bellow. He hurried up the last steps to the main floor and found her standing, hands on her hips, in the middle of the hall, looking very angry. "Yes, Ma'am?"

"Would you care to tell me why you moved Charlie to his office?"

"Because, Ma'am, he ordered me to. Said the bed was too soft, and that you needed a place to sleep in comfort."

"And you did not think to check with me first?" Rebecca was shaking now, partly from anger and partly from frustration. "How in the name of God am I supposed to care for him if he is down there?"

"Ma'am, he specifically asked that either Mr. Whitman or I take care of his wounds. He said he dinna want you to be dirtying your hands with his blood."

Rebecca stood shocked. She did not know how to respond to that. She had been taking care of Charlie for days already. "I need to talk to him."

"Yes, Ma'am, I believe you do. I do not know what is wrong, but something is."

Rebecca marched down the stairs and knocked on the office door. "Charlie? It is Rebecca," she said needlessly. "May I come in?"

Silence met her knock.

She knocked again. "Charlie, please. Please let me come in. I need to see you. I need to talk to you."

More silence.

She took a deep breath and opened the door. Going inside, she closed it gently behind her. "Charlie?"

He lay on his cot, face turned toward the windows looking out on the back yard, down toward the pond.

He turned his head and looked at her as she entered. Very quietly, he said, "Hello, Rebecca."

She smiled and moved to the cot, kneeling down and placing her hand on his back. "Hello, darling. Please tell me why you had Jocko move you down here."

"You need your bed, and with me in this condition, it cannot be easy or pleasant for you to share it with me. The bed was too soft, and the things I need to take care of me are here in the winter kitchen. I thought being closer would be good. Easier. Simpler."

"I see. All right, I can accept that, but I had hoped to have you closer to the children. Em is begging to see you, and you have yet to meet the boys."

Em. Em, who thought her Papa was the best man in the world. He could not let Em see him like this. "Rebecca, I do not have the energy to see Em. I do not want her seeing me like this. Ever."

"Charlie. Charlie, sweetheart. Em has missed you; she has cried for you nearly every day. She will not care about all of this. All she will care about is that her Papa has come home. Charlie, this child has already lost two parents; do not take a third from her."

Charlie steeled his jaw. "Rebecca, look at me. What kind of a parent can I be right now? I am barely human."

"Charlie, yes, right now you need to rest and heal, but in time you are going to be fine and..."

"Jesus Christ, Rebecca. Look at me. Look at me! I have always been a shadow of a man, a bad imitation. Now I am only pieces! I cannot walk. My hand is gone. I will be nothing but a mass of scars when I heal. I can only be a burden, so leave me. Create a life for yourself, for the children. They do not need to have a sad half-man, who cannot even go to the bathroom alone, for a father. Leave me."

"Charlie...please...do not say..."

"Rebecca—go. Go! Please, just go."

Rebecca stood, feeling tears forming in her eyes. She backed up from Charlie. "I love you. Nothing that has happened will change that." Tears slipped down her cheeks as she turned and left the room.

Jocko had followed Rebecca down the stairs and stood in the shadows, wanting to help, feeling like a wretch for listening in, and lost as to what to do to help his friend and the magnificent lady who loved his General.

FRIDAY, MAY 5, 1865

Almost a week and a half had passed since Rebecca had brought Charlie home. After that horrible first day, he had stayed in his office, refusing admittance to anyone except Jocko or Whitman. Eventually, even Whitman was barred when the man took him to task for excluding Rebecca from his sick room.

Elizabeth arrived late in the afternoon, having come by carriage from the now dissolved field hospital in Appomattox. Samuelson was with her. So was Black Jack. Richard and one company from the 13th had accompanied her, as protection on the road was vital now that the country was swarming with men who had signed their oaths and were trying to get home. The rest of the 13th was on its way by troop train to Bucks County, Pennsylvania or Columbus, Ohio to muster out of the Army and return to civilian life. The men accompanying Richard had no homes to return to; they thought that Culpeper was as good a place as any to build new lives. Arriving in Culpeper, they parted company, with the men reporting to Byrnes for lodging in town, and Richard, Samuelson and Elizabeth turning south and west towards Redmond Stables.

Beulah and Reg were at the door to greet the little party. Richard wanted to drive around to the stables to put the horses away, but Reg quietly shook his head and hurried off to tend the horses. Rebecca, hearing the commotion, came from the nursery where she had been tending a disconsolate little girl. She was so relieved to see the little group, she literally flew down the stairs into Elizabeth's arms. "Oh, God, I am so glad to see you, I cannot even begin to tell you."

Elizabeth gently hugged the woman she had come to regard as a sister. "What is it, Rebecca?"

"It is Charlie. He is...is..." She dissolved into tears, unable to express the pain and frustration that had settled firmly in her soul and darkly over her heart.

Elizabeth looked at Richard over the head of the sobbing woman in her arms, a dark frown of concern on her features. Gently, Richard lifted Rebecca into his arms and half carried the woman into the back parlor. Elizabeth signaled to Beulah to bring tea, and sent Samuelson off to find Jocko or Whitman and find out what was really going on.

Richard settled Rebecca into a comfortable chair and offered his handkerchief. "Now, dear lady, tell us what is going on with that reprobate."

"He has turned away from me. He will not see me. He will not see Em. He has yet to see the boys. Em is beside herself, crying for him at every turn. Nothing satisfies her. She stands at his office door, which he has locked, and begs him to open the door. The only one he will let into the room is Jocko, and even then it is only for food. I am completely lost. I just do not know what to do."

Elizabeth looked at Richard, her heart falling in her chest. She had feared this kind of reaction from Charlie. It happened too often with physically robust and very active men when they discovered that they would never again be able to do the things they were accustomed to. In Charlie's case, because his charade was so dependent on his physicality, the impact could only be devastating. "I had hoped that he would be stronger than this, but it is not unknown, dear. Injuries as extensive as Charlie has suffered leave their mark on the soul as well as on the body. I will do what I can, though. Shall I go and see to him now?"

"Please. Perhaps you can get through to him. I do not think he understands that we still love him and need him."

Elizabeth raised her eyebrow. "No, I suppose that stubborn fool does not realize that at all. He never did understand that there are many of us who love him."

"Please go talk to him. Maybe he will listen to you."

Elizabeth left the parlor, to find Jocko waiting in the hall for her. "So, Jocko, just how bad is it?"

"Well, let me tell you, that stubborn ass is barely eating now. All he does is lie in that bed and stare out the window. He will not even talk about Rebecca or the children. I have even taken the precaution of removing all his firearms from the room."

"Is he up and about? He should be walking at least a few steps by now."

"He refuses except to rise and lock the door."

Elizabeth rolled her eyes and clenched her teeth. "Damn him. He is giving up."

Jocko looked at the ground, refusing to meet her eyes. "I fear so. Please try, Doctor."

"Of course." She patted his shoulder and turned for Charlie's office.

Elizabeth and Jocko proceeded down the stairs. There, they found little Emily crouched by the door, holding her puppy, Papa, to her chest and crying softly. The sight of the little girl waiting at her father's door nearly destroyed Elizabeth. Gently she went to Em and lifted her in her arms. "Shush, little one. We are going to see if we cannot make your Papa right again." She turned to Jocko. "The key, if you please," knowing perfectly well that he had to have one. Silently, he handed it over to her and relieved her of the bundle of quietly weeping child and long-suffering puppy.

Elizabeth waited until Jocko was well out of view with Em before she unlocked the door and entered the room. She saw him there, his back to her, as Jocko said, staring out the window. "Hello, Charlie."

He did not move or acknowledge her entry. She could tell from the tension in his body that he knew she was there; he just refused to respond.

"Are you proud of yourself, General Redmond?"

He did not respond.

"You are tearing up your home and your family. Rebecca is nearly hysterical with worry about you, and do not tell me you cannot hear little Emily crying for you outside this door."

Elizabeth's words pierced Charlie's soul. It was terrible to listen to your own death being mourned before you were gone. If he could just end it quickly, it would be over and they could start building a new life. There was that new man that Jocko said Rebecca had hired to help work with the horses. A fine looking man, from what Charlie could tell, who was obviously good with the animals and whom Charlie could see made Rebecca smile.

"You are a fool, do you know that? All your life you have hoped to find this—a wife and a family—and now you have both. Why are you trying to destroy it, Charlie? And you may as well answer me. I am not leaving until you do."

Charlie rolled over onto his back, wincing when the bandages rubbed against his tender, just healing flesh, and glared at Elizabeth. "Look at me, Elizabeth and tell me honestly. Will I ever be whole again? Will I ever be able to hold my children in this arm?" He lifted his right arm as far as he could, which was scant inches above the bed. "Will I teach my sons to run and ride with this leg?" He snorted. "And my beloved. What will she see when she looks at my body? Will she see the "Greek Goddess" she once called me, or will she see a cripple, riddled with terrible, ugly scars, who can no longer stand to be touched because of the pain? Leave me, Elizabeth. The Charlie you knew died at Appomattox Station."

"You...you..." Elizabeth tried to control her anger, then decided against it. "Damn you, Charlie Redmond! Do you have any idea how many people worked to save your life? Do you have any idea that when you were wounded, your men mourned more for you than for President Lincoln when he was killed? Damn it, Charlie, men who were free to leave when the truce was signed, stayed in camp until the day you were sent home. And what about me? I worked so hard to save your life! I should have taken your leg. It caused us days of trouble, but we were tireless in your care so you would not lose it. Damn you! Damn you taking your life for granted when so many men and boys lost theirs..." She was shaking so hard now it was all she could do to resist the urge to slap him.

Charlie looked at her coldly. "You should have let me die." He turned back away from her, to resume his vigil through the window. Here was his dream; he wanted it to be the last thing he ever saw, since he could not bear to look into Rebecca's eyes and know how terribly he had failed her.

"How dare you! I am a doctor, and my first oath is to save lives. You may take it for granted Charlie, and you may not care now, but there are people who love you and who want you around. You can believe whatever you like, but do not dare to ever tell me that I should have let you die!"

Jocko, having turned Em over to her mother and given the puppy into Colonel Richard's care, quietly returned to the room. He heard the last words and knew that Charlie would not respond. Silently, he took Elizabeth's arm and escorted her from the room, closing the door behind them.

Charlie lay silently looking out the window, unseeing, blinded by the tears that filled his eyes and soaked his pillow.

Monday, May 8, 1865

Rebecca found that having Richard and Elizabeth around did help ease the stress, if not the pain, of the situation with Charlie. The unexpected return of her cousin, Albert, from the war had eased the difficulties of trying to run the stables with just Tarent and MacFarlane's help. She had heard he was dead, though there had never been a confirmation of his demise. He was cut from the same cloth as her father, and was more comfortable with horses than people.

That left her heartache and the children for Rebecca to manage —more than enough for one woman to deal with at any time. It was a beautiful day, clear with bright sunshine. Rebecca thought that spending some time in the sun, with the babies and the puppy might help ease Em's melancholy. So Sarah prepared a picnic lunch and the whole family, including Richard, Elizabeth, and Albert, adjourned to the little patio by the pond for lunch.

Em sat on the ground with Albert and played with some stick figures he had fashioned for her. Richard was holding his namesake and making truly silly noises, which almost made Rebecca's frustration and the pain melt away as she watched him. She held little Charlie close to her and looked up to the windows of Charlie's office. "I am at my wits' end, Elizabeth. I am so tired."

"I know, dear. So am I. Somehow, something has to get through to him. But I swear, I have no idea as to what." Elizabeth thought for a moment. "So, tell me about your handsome cousin."

Rebecca smiled at Albert, who was trying so hard to make Em laugh. "He is my father's sister's eldest son. Of her three boys, he is the only one to return from the war, and like me, he has no family left. So he came here. I loved Albert like a brother when I was a child, and I am glad to have him here."

"He has brought some cheer into this house. I am glad you have help."

Rebecca nodded, shifting little Charlie when he started fussing. "I hope someday Charlie will want to meet the entire family."

Albert interrupted their conversation. "Excuse me, Doctor Walker, but about that black stallion you brought in with you? He really needs to be exercised, but no one seems to be able to saddle him. I wonder if you would mind if I gave it a try?"

Elizabeth and Richard both chuckled. Richard responded. "Young man, that horse has never been ridden by anyone but General Redmond and, on very rare occasions, Sergeant Jackson. If you are brave enough to step into the stall or the ring with him, please feel free. Just be warned. Jack has a temper all his own."

Em heard the name of her Papa's horse. If Jack was at the house, then so was Papa. Excitement lit her face. "Jack, Jack, Jack," she chanted.

Albert looked surprised. This was the most animated he had seen his little cousin since he had arrived. "Do you want to go with me to see Jack, Em?"

She nodded emphatically and climbed to her feet. "Jack, Papa 'orsey."

Rebecca could not help it. Em was so determined and so charming about it and she was so relieved that Em finally was showing interest in something—anything—that she laughed out loud.

Albert hefted the child in his arms. He had shed his coat in the warm weather and stood in just his shirtsleeves, holding the little girl who was holding onto his neck tightly. "Then let us go see a 'orsey."

Charlie lay in his cot, watching the scene play out before him. His wife, his children, his friends, and this strange, handsome man in the place where he wanted to be with all his heart and knew he could never be again. His heart lay shattered in the remains of his mangled flesh, rotting on the field at Appomattox Station. The man was tall, dark haired, well built, with a flashing smile and an easy grace. Em clearly trusted and loved him. He could make Rebecca smile. Maybe this was the man that Rebecca should have been with. Charlie wished with all his heart that Jocko had left him at least a pistol.

He watched as the man lifted Em in his arms and walked toward the stables. They entered, and a few minutes later, emerged with Jack on a lunge lead. The three of them entered the small paddock, with Jack following the man like a well-trained nag. Where was Charlie's fierce warhorse?

With Em perched on his shoulders, the man put Jack through his ground paces. One of the grooms brought Jack's saddle and bridle, taking Em from the man's arms for a few moments while the man tacked Jack up. Then, with Jack standing quietly for him, the man swung up into the saddle, took Em from the groom and set her in front of him, and trotted Jack out of the paddock.

Charlie could not stand it anymore. He struggled to pull himself up from the bed and worked his way around the room, looking for something, anything that he could use to end his life. There was nothing left for him. He cleared the old desk, searching in the drawers for a knife, a rope, anything. Finally, in his weakened state, he fell into the old leather chair by the fireplace. There he sat and sobbed out his rage, his frustration, and all the pain in his soul.

Seeing Jack just made Em more determined. She thought very carefully in her two-year-old mind about why her Papa did not want to see her. That afternoon, when she should have been taking her nap, the little girl thought long and hard. Finally, it occurred to her that the only reason why Papa would not see her was because she had been a bad girl. She knew she had not been the brave girl she promised she would be when Papa was gone, and that she had tried Mama 'Becca's patience more than once. And she had wailed and cried when they had put Mama in the box and taken her to the church and put her into the ground. She had not been the brave, good girl Papa wanted her to be. Maybe Papa would stop punishing her if she promised to be good again.

Very quietly, Em got out of her bed and calling Puppy Papa to her side, crept down the stairs to the hall. She looked around, wanting to be very sure that none of the grownups caught her out of bed when she was supposed to be napping. When the hall was empty, she slipped to the back stairs and down them. There she and Puppy Papa turned toward the door to Papa's office and she gathered all of her two-year-old courage. She just had to get her Papa to see her. She missed him so much, and she was so sorry she had been bad.

She moved down the hall, stumbling once on her sleeping gown, and stubbing her hand. She looked at it and she wanted to cry, but if she cried she would be bad and Papa would not see her. She shook her hand and went to the door, giving it a tap with her hand. "Papa, Em good. Pwease, Papa."

She waited, and when there was no answer, she tried again, even though the tears were starting. "Papa, Em be good."

Charlie sat in his chair, lost in his own pain and bleak, hopeless rage. He heard his daughter's voice, but thought it was a delusion, brought to him by his own mind to torment him. After all, he had seen her laughing and playing with the big, dark haired man just a few hours before.

"Papa, I be good. Pwomise. Pwease!" She leaned against the door, her body shuddering with the tears she was so desperate to hold in so she would not be bad for her Papa. "Papa! Em love Papa!"

Charlie was in hell. *Oh, Em. I love you. That is why I have to let you go. I am broken, little one, and no good for you anymore. Please, you and your mama need someone who is not like me. You need a real father, not a broken old woman whose whole life is a lie. Please, baby, forget me. Please.* But he could not make himself go to the door, because he knew if he saw her, his resolve would break. He knew if he saw his little daughter in so much pain, he would break, and take her in his good arm and try to make her feel better. And he just could not do that to her—or to himself.

Emily slumped against the door, then slid down it, sobbing, trying not to make any noise. Her puppy tried to ease her pain by licking her tears away, but she lashed out and slapped her away, causing the pup to yelp and stagger back, her tail tucked between her legs. Em had never hit her before. But Puppy Papa would not leave her little girl. "Stop! Papa mad at Em. Papa not love Em."

Charlie could not stand it. He tried to rise from the chair, but the combination of his injuries and the lack of food conspired to make it impossible. He collapsed back into his chair. Reaching for the door again, he passed out.

Jocko came down the stairs. It was time to try to get the General to eat something again. There he found the little girl, slumped on the floor sobbing. The puppy was hiding under the stairs, whimpering. Jocko rushed to the child and picked her up. "Ah, little lass, come here. Tell Uncle Jocko."

"Em bad. Papa not love Em. Pwease." She grabbed his shirt and looked directly into his eyes. "Tell Papa Em good."

"Oh, lass, Em is very good." *Your papa is being a total ass, and I am about ready to tell him so.* "Papa is sick, honey. And he does not want you to get what he has." *A terminal case of stupidity, I would say.* "Let me take you upstairs. It is time to get ready for supper."

"Papa sick? Papa die? No pwease, Papa not die. Em love Papa. Pwease." She broke down and sobbed now; all her little two-year-old reserve was gone with the thoughts that Papa would die. They would put him in a box, too.

"No, little one, your Papa is not going to die. I promise." *Not unless I kill him personally.* "You let Uncle Jocko take you upstairs to Tess and I promise, you will see your Papa within the next few days."

Em sniffed and laid her head on Jocko's shoulder. Her little body was still shaking, and she just let him carry her away from Papa's door.

Jocko walked up the stairs, carrying the exhausted child gently. As he got to the top of the first flight of stairs and was starting up the stairs to the second floor, he heard a crash coming from the back parlor. He turned back down the stairs to check. "Hush, little one," he admonished as Em stirred on his shoulder, curiosity almost overcoming her sorrow. "We need to check on your Mama for a minute."

Rebecca stood in the middle of the parlor looking at her bleeding hand and the broken glass in the window. Before she knew it, the door was opening, Richard, followed by Elizabeth, and Jocko, carrying Em, entered the room. "What!" she yelled, still shaking from her own anger and frustration. "I am at the end! I cannot take any more! I have done all I can!"

Elizabeth looked at the bleeding hand. "Rebecca, what have you done?"

Richard reached for his handkerchief and immediately moved toward Rebecca to staunch the blood.

Em looked at her Mama, standing there bleeding and yelling, and she immediately started to wail.

Jocko just stood there, stock still, holding the wailing child, his face slowly turning a fascinating shade of red.

Rebecca looked to Em. "Please stop that incessant crying! It is not doing anyone any good!" She pulled back the moment Richard tried to touch her. "No, I do not want any help! Just leave me alone. I should have known this would end in disaster! I have taken in every waif, orphan, and refugee that has come my way. I put my love and trust in Charlie, and he has turned me out. I am finished. I cannot take any more!"

Em looked at Mama with terrified eyes. Yes, she knew her Mama wished she would not cry so much, but she never yelled. And all that blood. Em put her fist in her mouth and tried to stop her own tears. She was terrified.

Elizabeth looked at Rebecca. Rebecca was hysterical, that was obvious. She stepped toward her friend, intending to take her and help her get some control.

"Stop! Just stop!" Rebecca backed away. It was clear that she was not aware of how badly she was cut; the blood was dripping down her hand, leaving drops on the carpet. "He does not care. It does not matter to him that he is destroying this family. Why should it matter to me now?"

Elizabeth stepped forward and slapped Rebecca full in the face. "Stop it. Just stop it, Rebecca. You are terrifying Em."

Rebecca blinked, stunned. She looked to her daughter who was curled tight into Jocko's arms, trying not to cry and failing. "I am sorry, my little darling. Mama is sorry." Tears slipped from her eyes now, and she just sat down on the closest chair. "I am so sorry."

Jocko's jaw was set. He stepped up to Rebecca and thrust Em into her arms. "Take care of your daughter. She needs you more than you can know. I will be back in a bit." Turning, he stomped out of the room.

Rebecca held Em close and rocked her. "Mama is sorry, Em, so sorry. I did not mean to yell." She was about to bring her other hand over to comfort her daughter when she saw the blood. She presented it to Elizabeth. "Could you...please? I am sorry, Elizabeth. I do not know what came over me." She glanced to Richard. "I apologize to you as well."

Silently, Elizabeth checked Rebecca's hand for glass shards and then used Richard's handkerchief as a makeshift bandage.

Richard looked at the woman, pressed to her limits and beyond, and spoke quietly. "It is all right, Rebecca. I am surprised you have lasted this long. If it were me, I would have been beating the door down. All we can do now is pray that Charlie comes to his senses soon."

"I have been praying every day since I brought him home." She looked to Em who was finally calming and kissed her baby on the head. "I love you, my little darling."

Jocko stormed down the stairs. He had endured enough, and the lady of this house most certainly had. He was nearly at a run by the time he reached Charlie's door, and the momentum was more than enough for him to kick the door in.

Bursting into the room, he saw Charlie sitting in the chair, eyes glazed over, staring into space.

"Well, you have finally done it, you damn fool!"

Charlie just looked at him, lost and confused.

"Go ahead and sit there like an idiot. Go ahead and feel sorry for yourself. I am done feeling sorry for you! I have just seen your beautiful, strong wife lose her senses. Dr. Walker is up there right now probably putting stitches in her hand, because she put it through a pane of glass. It is her and your little ones that I will spend my time feeling sorry for now."

Charlie shook himself. "Rebecca? Stitches?"

"Yes, stitches in her hand. She cut her hand, because the burden you have placed on her shoulders with your stubbornness has finally gotten to her. Not to mention that I found your little girl outside your door today, promising to be good and begging me to make you love her again."

Charlie closed his eyes. In a calm, patient tone, as if explaining to a child, he started. "Look at me, Jocko. I was never the man that Rebecca and Em need. And now, I am not even a whole human being. All I can do is be a burden for them. So they will feel pain now, and I am sorry, but then I will be gone and they can have a real life. They have all the money they need. Maybe that dark haired gentleman that Rebecca seems to like and Em loves to play with will care for them."

Jocko could not help it; he started laughing. "You are an ass. Do you know who that young man is?"

"No. I assume he is some Southern soldier returning home after the war. He seems to have come courting Rebecca." Charlie started to say something else, but just could not get it out of his mouth. He was going to say "I wish him well," but the truth was that he wished the man to hell. Rebecca was the only love Charlie would ever have, and he no longer deserved her, if he ever had.

"That is her cousin, you mule-headed son of a bitch. Her aunt's eldest boy. Rebecca is all the family he has left, so he came here. I hate to tell you this, Charlie boy, but the only person Rebecca wants in her life in that way is you."

Charlie half rose out of his chair. He glared at Jocko. "You fool. How can you say that? You have seen what my body has become. How could anyone ever want to touch someone who looks like me? Let alone a gentle, sensitive lady like Rebecca. Jesus Christ, Jocko. Before Rebecca, the only ones who would touch me were whores, paid to be discreet and responsive. She wanted me, not this mangled excuse for a body. What am I supposed to do? Limp up to her and make love? I cannot even make it to the door right now, let alone up the stairs. And when I do, and I see revulsion and pity on her face, what then? What of my children, who will only know a Papa who limps around, cannot teach them to ride, to hunt, to shoot—to be men and women of pride? What pride can a cripple teach them? How am I supposed to run this farm—from a chair? Jocko, I have nothing left to give them. Let me go."

"You do not remember, do you? You do not remember Rebecca being at your side in camp, do you? She performed surgery on you, Charlie, when Elizabeth was far too exhausted to do it properly any longer. That lady took those instruments in hand and took care of your wounds. She knows what you look like, Charlie, and she has not shied away from it yet. As for your children, Christ! Em only wants her Papa; she could not care less about your wounds. Your boys will grow up with it. It will be normal for them, as normal as you will allow it to be. Dr. Walker believes you will ride again, if you get off your lazy, feeling-sorry-for-yourself arse, and do what you are supposed to do to get better. There is nothing we can do to help you if you will not help yourself first."

Charlie only caught the first part of Jocko's speech. He was stunned. "She was there? I thought I was dreaming? She was the one who... Oh, God. I have been such a fool. How did she get there?

What happened? You have to tell me, Jocko. How bad a mess have I made of things?"

Jocko's brow lifted slowly over his eye, creeping up his forehead, and he put his fists on his hips. "Oh, so that is how it is? I see. Yes, she was there. Elizabeth sent for her when we thought you were going to die, but she came, resolute that you would not die. She even came up with the treatment for the infection that nearly cost you that leg you were so worried about. She stayed by your side until Elizabeth put a sedative in her tea to make her sleep. She never turned away from you. Then she brought you home and wanted to help you get better, and you turned her out, Charlie boy. You drove her away." He sighed, putting his hands to his sides. "All you have to do is ask to see her and she will be here. Yes, Charlie, you have bloody well made a mess of things, and you are damn lucky you have a forgiving woman in Rebecca, 'cause if it were me, right now, I would let you rot." More softly, he added, "Charlie, she only wants you."

He looked down at himself, dressed in a dirty nightshirt, shoeless, and probably smelling a bit ripe since he had refused Jocko's assistance in bathing. "Jocko, can you help me get cleaned up a bit?" He looked pitiful, lost and confused, and very ashamed, but somehow more himself than he had been in days.

"It would be my pleasure. It is good to have my friend back. I did not much care for the fool who had taken his place."

Charlie was shaky, but game. "Neither did I."

Getting Charlie cleaned up was more of a project than either man expected. By the time they were through, he was shaved, smelled good, and was dressed in a loose pair of trousers, a shirt and his robe and slippers. He was also exhausted. But he was also determined to begin the process of making amends with his wife and daughter.

"Jocko, how am I going to get up the stairs? I can barely stand for a minute, let alone walk."

"Wait just a moment." Jocko stepped out of the office and across the hall to the kitchen, where he found, as he expected, Reg chatting with Sarah as they washed the supper dishes. "Reg, come with me for a moment." The two men essentially picked Charlie up in a sling made of their arms and carried him up the stairs to the door of the back parlor. "Well, Charlie boy, from here you are on your own."

Reg laid his hand on Charlie's arm. "Wait a moment, Sir." He scooted to the large umbrella stand by the front door and pulled out an old cane, left by some absentminded visitor years before. "This may help."

The two men stepped back from Charlie and watched as he cautiously knocked on the parlor door.

Rebecca looked up from little Charlie's slumbering face. She was cradling one son, while the other slept nearby and Em slept on the couch. After her outburst and when Elizabeth finished with her hand, she had felt an overwhelming desire to be close to her children. "Come in."

Charlie opened the door and then switched the cane to his good hand. Slowly, he shuffled into the parlor, and then just stood there, looking at his family. He looked into Rebecca's eyes, trying to find words. "I am so, so sorry."

She stood, being very careful of her son, and walked to him. She was not sure what to say to him; a wrong word might set him off again. "I love you."

"I love you. I just did not know...I think we need to talk." He stopped, unable to continue in the face of his own overwhelming stupidity. "May I sit down?"

"Of course." She smiled and moved so he could get to the closest chair. "I am sorry, too."

Charlie gingerly settled himself in the chair. "I dreamed you were there."

"It was not a dream. I was there." She sat down in the chair across from him, taking the time to place little Charlie in his cradle. "I came as soon as Elizabeth sent for me."

"Jocko said you did surgery on me."

"Well, I doubt Elizabeth would consider it surgery, but I did tend to your wounds, helping to get rid of some of the infection."

"So you have seen how bad it is?"

"Yes." She nodded, never taking her eyes from his. She did not want him to think she was repulsed by him. "I have."

"And you do not find it repellant?"

"No." She moved from her chair and settled at his feet, gently resting her hand on his good leg. "I love you. What matters to me is that you are alive, that the war is over, and you are home."

"I cannot be what I was."

"Which was? Do you mean to tell me that you can no longer love the children or me? That we can no longer have long talks and plan our future? Do you think so little of me that you think I base my love of you on the fact that you could run the circuit of my farm? I always wondered what sane person would want to do that anyhow." She gave a smile, trying to make him understand what was truly important to her.

He bowed his head. "I have hurt you and Em very badly."

"Charlie, it is nothing that cannot be fixed. We have just been so worried about you. Em only wants her Papa. She thinks you do not love her anymore." Tears filled Rebecca's eyes. "She is just a little girl, she does not understand."

Very tentatively, Charlie reached his hand out to touch Rebecca's shining hair. The soft texture between his fingers nearly broke his control. "I think, perhaps, you do not either."

"I want to, darling, but you have to be willing to talk to me. I cannot understand anything if you stay locked away in your office."

Charlie took a deep breath. "Rebecca, I know I may not deserve it, but I want to come home - really come home. If you will have me and all of my melancholia and my overblown sense of honor."

"You are home. You always have been. You just needed to find it for yourself. I do not know what brought you from the office, but I thank God it happened. I love you, Charlie, and the children and I need you here with us."

"Well, beloved, you should be very nice to Jocko, who went out of his way to tell me exactly how big a horse's ass I have been."

"Then I will see to it he is properly rewarded. I know you have a long way to go, Charlie, and I want you to know I am prepared to walk that road with you."

He lifted the hand that was resting on his knee and raised it to his lips. Very softly and very reverently, he kissed her hand. "I love you, Rebecca. And I have found that I need your love and happiness more than anything in the world. For a while, I was willing to die in the hopes you would find someone to be happy with - I thought I thought that your cousin was courting you. Jocko made me realize that it takes a lot more courage to be willing to live so that you will be happy."

"That is exactly what it will take to make me happy. Do you know if you had died, there would never have been another for me? In you, I have found my life and my love. You arc all I want."

Charlie reached out to her and cupped her cheek in his good hand. "And you are all I ever dreamed of and more. I do love you, darling. I never wanted to hurt you. Can you forgive me?"

"Of course. I am just happy to have you back. Now, if you are up to it?" She glanced to Em, who was sucking on her thumb as she slept on the couch.

"Oh, Lord. Poor Em. Rebecca, how much have I hurt her? I heard her crying outside the door, and I tried to get to her, but I just could not. I did not have the strength."

"I think all will be forgiven if you will see her now."

"Can you wake her for me? I would love to hold her, but I, um, well, just getting here pretty much took everything I have."

Rebecca smiled and moved to the couch, where she gently ran her fingers through Em's hair. "Wake up, my little darling, there is someone here to see you."

Charlie sat in his chair, smiling gently at his daughter. "Em? Come sit on Papa's lap—but be gentle, please."

Em lifted her head and a smile broke across her face. "Papa!" She climbed down from the couch and, with help from Rebecca and another warning to be careful of Papa, she was where she most wanted to be, in her Papa's arms. "Papa." She cuddled into him. Her weight on his injuries was excruciatingly painful, but he bore it with good cheer. Em's well-being was far more important.

"Hey there, little one. How is my good girl?"

She did not respond. She just cuddled into his lap and kept saying "Papa," over and over again.

"I have missed you, imp. I hear tell you have been a very, very good girl."

Em nodded. Very carefully, she leaned up and kissed his cheek. "Love Papa."

Charlie hugged the little girl very close with his good arm. "I love you very much, Em. And I promise, you can come into my office whenever you want from now on."

"Papa see Chawy, see Andy?"

"Your brothers have been asleep, but I expect that Mama will introduce me soon. I wanted to see you, first."

"Em happy you home."

"I am very happy to be home. I got lost for a while, but Uncle Jocko and Mama helped me find my way."

"You in you office. Em knew."

Charlie looked at Rebecca, and they both tried very hard to not laugh out loud. "Yes, Em. Papa was in his office."

"I know." She huffed and cuddled back into his arms. "Papa no work, no more."

Charlie laughed. "Em, Papa has to work. But I promise, Papa will only work as much as he has to, and you can visit me whenever you want." He turned to Rebecca, "That is true for you, too, dear."

Rebecca nodded and placed her hand on his knee. "I am glad. Will you please move back into our room as well?"

"If you want me, I would very much like to. I have missed you more than I can ever tell you."

"I want you to, very much. As long as being in bed with me does not cause you pain. You said the bed upstairs was too soft."

Charlie looked down and tightened his lips. "That was not the problem, dear."

"No? What was it?"

He looked directly into her eyes. "I was afraid. Afraid you would find me...repugnant."

"I understand. You needed time." She looked at Charlie's bandaged hand. "I wish I had understood it earlier. I was expecting too much too soon."

"No, dear. You were not expecting too much. You were expecting your husband to come back to you. The problem was that I left your husband on that field, and had to find him again." Charlie was trying to be discreet, with Em drowsing on his lap.

"Have you found him?"

"I think I have. He is somewhat shaky and a bit scared, but he is back."

"Good." She was about to say something else when Andrew began wailing. She closed her eyes against the sound and smiled. "That is our boy." She moved and picked him up. "Come, Andrew, let me introduce you to your Papa."

Charlie nudged Em, who was half asleep on his lap. "Em, little one, can you make room for your brother? I cannot hold him in my right arm yet."

Em opened sleepy eyes, looking to her brother. "Papa hold Andy." She climbed down from his lap, but stayed near his legs. She watched as the baby was placed in Charlie's arm. "Andy cwies." She sighed. "Lots."

Charlie found himself looking into a pair of blue eyes, crinkled with sleep and irritation. Here was your basic baby, red faced, with good lungs, based on the amount of sound coming out of his mouth right now, and a cap of fine reddish blond hair. Charlie looked up at Rebecca. "Constance's?"

"Yes."

"Hello, Andrew Richard Redmond. I am your Papa. It is a pleasure to meet you, young sir."

The baby looked to the sound of Charlie's voice, stopped crying, and proceeded to yawn.

Charlie laughed and handed his younger son back to Rebecca. "He is beautiful, love. And his hair is like yours."

After placing Andrew in his bed, Rebecca moved to the other cradle and picked up their eldest son. "And this," she presented him, "is Charles Huger Redmond the Second."

Charlie Two was a solid little boy with a shock of black hair standing up from his head like a bantam rooster's, and bright blue eyes that regarded his father very solemnly. "Hello, son. I do hope you do not turn out to be as stubborn as your father." Charlie looked up at Rebecca and smiled. "We celebrated his arrival with a small found feast—roast goat. I do hope it was not predictive of his personality."

"No, he is very sweet. A good little boy who does not fuss and entertains himself most of the time."

"Well, dear wife, I would say that you have built us a lovely family while I was gone."

Tess came and bundled the children away to bed. Em was a little reluctant to go, but Charlie promised her that he would be in the bedroom upstairs in the morning, and she could come and visit him as soon as she woke up.

Charlie and Rebecca talked late into the night. Charlie laid all of his fears and uncertainties before Rebecca, trying to make her understand why he had thought she would be better off without him, and ending up by convincing himself even more of what a fool he had been.

Rebecca palmed Charlie's cheek. "You are exhausted, my love. We need to sleep."

"I am tired, dear, but I fear that I will have to forego sleeping with you for one more night. I just do not think I can get up the stairs."

"Oh, I think I can find a way for us to be together. I cannot go another night without being near you."

Charlie caught his breath. She had been rather distant physically throughout the evening. Patting his knee and leaning her head against his good thigh was the limit of her contact. He found that as the night progressed, he longed for her touch. No, he was not in any shape to make love, but he needed to feel her arms around him again and he ached for just a touch from her lips. "I would love to be with you, dear. So whatever you devise, I will be happy."

"Then I shall be right back." She left the parlor, returning a few minutes later with a pile of bedding that was bigger than she was. After a few minutes, there was a bed placed on the floor near the fireplace. She turned and held out a nightshirt. "Would you like me to help you get dressed for bed?"

"I have no other options, dear. I just cannot do it myself yet. The arm and hand will not cooperate." He saw the slightly dashed look on her face and added, "But even if I could do it, I would love your assistance."

She nodded and approached him slowly. "Tell me if I hurt you." Carefully she unbelted his robe and helped him slip out of it. Then the clothes began to come off. She was very careful about Charlie's right side. "Are you all right?"

Charlie was breathing a little hard. Moving that right arm was painful, and anything that nudged the raw bones of his hand was also difficult. She had not yet gotten to the most serious wounds. "I am as right as I get nowadays, dear. You are far gentler than Jocko."

"I would hope so," she chuckled and began rolling the sleep shirt.

"Do you have any suggestion for what you think might be the best way to do this? To be honest Charlie, it would be easier for you to sleep nude, but it is difficult to say who might walk in here."

"If you get it on the right arm first, then over my head, I can work my left arm into it. Then all you have to do is get my trousers off."

"All right." She helped pull the shirt over his head, slowly and carefully. "Now just hold it up while I take off your trousers." She worked the buttons and the hook free. "I am sure this is going to be painful, but I will do it as quickly as possible."

He held his breath while she carefully eased his trousers over the bandages on his hip and thigh. She looked at them carefully for a moment, and seeing no signs of seepage, patted him on his calf. He looked down at her and smiled. "Painless, dear."

"Good." She very gently touched Charlie's right leg. "These do not bother or concern me, Charlie. You are still the most beautiful thing I have ever seen."

He looked at her, seeing the truth in her eyes. He could only smile and shake his head. "You, my beloved, are terribly biased. I hope you stay that way."

"There is nothing biased about how I feel about you." She helped him pull the sleep shirt down. "Now, can we get you to the bed?"

He grinned at his lovely wife. "I certainly think you are the most stunning, beautiful, feisty thing I have ever set eyes on. And yes, I think if you give me a hand, I can lower myself down there."

Rebecca held his left hand firmly as Charlie moved from the couch to the bedding on the floor.

With a shaky moment or two, he managed to get down onto the bed without doing major damage. She carefully arranged herself so that the injuries were properly supported and then sank into the soft padding. Extending his left hand to Rebecca, he shyly asked, "May I offer you a shoulder?"

"Absolutely, just let me get changed."

He laid back and watched Rebecca as she started to remove her dress. Watching Rebecca emerge from the whalebone and skirts of her clothing to display her slender, elegant body was always a delight for him.

She settled her nightgown over her head and gently climbed into bed. "I would like to be close to you, but I do not want to hurt you."

"Rebecca, I have missed you for so long, having you not come over here hurts far more than anything your touch may do to me. I am starting to heal; it is not as bad as it was."

She sighed and placed her head on his shoulder, then gently draped her arm over his waist. "Is this all right?"

Charlie smiled. He was home. "It is perfect, darling. There is just one thing missing."

"Yes?"

Charlie turned her head and gently laid his lips on Rebecca's forehead. "Just one thing. Your lips on mine."

EPILOGUE

Thursday, June 1, 1865
Culpeper County, Virginia

Dear Major Swallow,

I write to you as one of my first activities after regaining use of what is left of my hand. I have also written to your brother to extend my personal condolences on the loss of your young cousin, Joshua. His death is mourned and honored. He fell in a good cause, as I believe our ability to keep those supplies captured at Appomattox Station from General Lee's forces was the most telling action that led to the final surrender.

Indeed, as my last official act as an officer in the United States Army, I am writing to the family of each man who fell that day, for in my opinion, to ride into the face of those howitzers was truly an act of immense courage. I know that Colonel Polk long since prepared the official notifications, but as their commanding officer, I feel an obligation to honor the valiant fallen. We all knew that day just how important it was to keep those supplies from getting through; though I would have taken a different approach from General Custer's, we had a job to do, we did it, and the result was, as we both know, the cessation of the war in Virginia. I thank God every day for the end of this most painful disruption of our national family. Trooper Raiford fell still holding the flag; your cousin and then Trooper Franklin followed him, so that the Colors of the 13th Pennsylvania never flagged on that day.

I mourn, too, the loss of Captains Hoffstader and Avery and many of their men. Companies I and B took a major blow in that last charge under General Sheridan at Appomattox Courthouse. Thank God that General Grant's infantry was there to support us, for I believe the Southerners were desperate and would have been truly formidable had we not had that support. Dewees fell, too, that day, successfully rescuing a pocket of his men who had been entrapped by enemy forces. He gave the ultimate gift—his life for his men's.

I have not had word of all the others who were injured but I understand most recovered from their wounds. I would be most grateful if you would advise me of the status of your men in Pennsylvania. I am asking Captain Braddock to keep me advised of the condition of the Ohioans who mustered out under his charge.

Several of our men have chosen to settle here in Culpeper and build new lives. In particular, Tarent and MacFarlane are working the stables here for me, and Jocko has chosen to remain as well. It surprised me that young Duncan Nailer stayed on, but then, he and Mrs. Carter seem to be exploring their common friendship through young Jeremiah. I would not be surprised to see them marry sometime in the future.

Richard Polk has taken over from Major Byrnes as the Military/Civilian liaison in the area. I would not be surprised if he resigned his commission and took up civilian politics in this community. As one would expect of Colonel Polk, he has managed to charm the ladies and make the gentlemen his cronies. We do expect him to be somewhat tamed in the coming months, as he and Dr. Walker will wed next month. I do not expect the good Doctor will allow our friend much latitude in his personal dealings in the future.

I hope this letter has found you in good health and happily reunited with your family, and look forward to receiving word from you on the progress of our men as they return to civilian life.
Cordially,
Chas. Redmond
Brig. General, U.S. Army (Ret.)

Charlie looked at the letter he had written, one of almost a hundred sending condolences and inquiring after the health and status of his men who had been killed or injured in the last days of the war. He sat back and considered the events of the past month, since he had truly begun his journey to recovery.

The last part of May had been an interesting time on the farm. Many of the families who had been taken in had found their way to other things. Charlie and Rebecca had purchased another two dozen horses. This had resulted in Tarent and MacFarlane hiring on another three hands to help take care of the rapidly growing herd.

Richard and Elizabeth set a date for their wedding. Rebecca considered it to be one of the things that inspired Charlie to work harder to get better. He was getting stronger every day and took getting out of the house very seriously. He had managed to avoid his own wedding plans, and, now that more plans were in the offing, was once again purposely making himself scarce. Wedding plans were a little more than the General could handle.

There had also been an incident that helped Charlie and Albert get to know each other better. Shannon, in a fit of pregnant pique, bit Jack on the neck, removing a chunk of flesh about the size of a ten dollar gold piece. Charlie's arm was still not serviceable enough to do the hard work, but he calmed Jack while Albert did the work of patching the horse up. It gave the two a chance to get to know each other, and it gave Charlie a chance to thank Albert for taking care of the farm and Rebecca while he was unable to do so.

Jocko had managed to start formally courting Mrs. White, and

Duncan had done the same with Jeremiah's mother, Samantha Carter. Rebecca wondered if she would ever see her husband in the house again if they all decided to get married.

Culpeper was slowly starting to recover from the horrors to which it had been subjected, and people were starting to settle into the community once again. A few new buildings were being constructed, including the new schoolhouse. Someone had suggested Richard would make a fine marshal once his retirement was ratified, and he had been heard to be considering it, but he would have to see what the future Mrs. Polk would have to say about it.

Charlie and Richard had discussed the idea of building a clinic for Elizabeth as a wedding gift, but they were hopeless at keeping the secret and she soon found out. A short time later she hired a young man who had recently returned home to draw up the plans.

He had begun correspondence with Mr. Cooke about the possibility of opening a bank in Culpeper. The need for investment capital was great, and Charlie felt he would soon see progress in that direction.

Evenings were spent with their friends and with their children. Em was learning her alphabet, making both her mama and papa very proud. Little Charlie was starting to push himself up and hold his head up for longer amounts of time. Andy had a minor bout of colic, which kept Rebecca and Charlie up for three days straight, but they were more than happy to be tending to the youngest of their brood.

Bedtime had found Charlie and Rebecca settling into a new ritual. Rebecca first washed Charlie's wounds with warm water, then applied a lotion Elizabeth had given them. She said it would help Charlie's scars fade; and while they would never be completely gone, would help to reduce them. Charlie loved the extra attention, and his fears that Rebecca would be repulsed by his injuries began to fade along with the scars.

Of course, Rebecca knew he was simply being spoiled rotten and she would still be applying lotion long after there was no further need, but she really did not mind. All that mattered to her was that Charlie was there with her.

Charlie smiled. It was good to be getting back into a routine, good to be able to walk upstairs under his own power. With daily exercise, he was beginning to regain use of his right arm, and to regain some strength in his right leg. The extensive loss of muscle tissue meant he would never be totally normal; but he kept working and exercising, trying to build up some flexibility and strength in the ravaged tissue. His right hand still ached, and Elizabeth warned him that he would probably feel the ghosts of those missing fingers for the rest of his life, but he could hold a pen, a knife, and a fork now, so he was spared the indignity of having to have his food cut up for him like a child.

The back door to his office banged open. Em had learned several new things, one of which was that Charlie's office was always available to her when her father was in it.

"Papa, look. Fishy in rock. Why, Papa?" Tess trailed behind her impetuous charge.

Charlie looked at the rock clutched in his daughter's rather grubby hand. "It is called a fossil, Em. When this fishy died a long, long time ago, the body lay on the sand at the bottom of the pond. More sand covered it up and over time, the sand turned into rock." Charlie and Tess exchanged sympathetic looks, and then Charlie motioned for the nanny to leave; he would look after his daughter for a while.

Em looked at the piece of sandstone and thought for a minute. "Why, Papa?"

Charlie rolled his eyes. "Why" had remained Em's favorite word, and at times he was hard pressed to come up with an answer he thought she might be able to understand. Finally, he had an idea. "Come with me, little one."

They walked down to the pond, where Charlie picked up a

handful of wet, clay-riddled sand. "See, Em. It is loose sand, right?" She nodded as he pressed it into a compact ball. "Now, when I press on it, it gets harder." She nodded again. "When things press on it for a long time—a very long time—it will get even harder." He took the wet clay ball and walked with the child to the stone barn. "So, we will find a big rock and press it even more, then let it dry out. Then you can see it get even harder." Em watched, fascinated, as Charlie found a couple of stones and made a makeshift brick mold. "Now, we will come back in a couple of days and see what happens."

Charlie felt very proud of himself. He had started his daughter on the path of experimentation. Then it started again.

"Papa? Why are rocks hard?"

Charlie's shoulders slumped. Then he had an inspiration. It was almost lunchtime. "Let us go ask your Mama."

Rebecca stood at the window of the back parlor and watched her oldest child and husband make their way up the lawn. Em was grubby, as she often was lately. That child could, and would, get into anything and everything. Keeping her filthy fingers out of her mouth was a major challenge. Charlie walked along steadily, leaning on one crutch to support his weight. Soon, she thought, he would graduate to a cane for good.

The child was cautious not to knock her father's crutch away— that had happened once, and the results had been very messy all around. Charlie had been in agony, Em had been frightened that she had hurt her Papa, and Puppy Papa, who followed Em everywhere, had cowered under the davenport for most of the day.

Rebecca went downstairs to meet them by the winter kitchen. While most of the food was now being prepared in the summer kitchen to minimize the heat in the main house, a small fire was kept going here to keep the water tank warm. "My stars, you two are both a mess. Come in here and get cleaned up." She led them into the mudroom off to the side of the kitchen and worked away at the more muddy sections of Em's robust little body—hands, arms, face, and feet. "Keeping you in shoes is impossible, little one. What did you do with them this time?"

"Papa's office," the child mumbled as her face was briskly wiped down with a warm washcloth.

"Charlie Redmond. I swear you encourage her to go barefoot."

Charlie looked not at all abashed. "Well, dear, I would have liked to when I was her age, so what is the harm?"

"Charlie, no proper lady goes barefoot, even if she is just two."

"Two and four mons, Mama." Em had continued her efforts in learning to count. She counted everything she could, including her own age. Every morning, she asked Tess to tell her how old she was—in months. If she could have gotten away with it, she would have asked how old she was in days. She understood days. Months were just lots of days to her.

"Then at nearly three, you should most definitely be wearing shoes."

Em looked to Charlie and then to Rebecca. "Yes, Mama."

Rebecca took Em's rock and placed it off to the side while she washed her hands.

"Mama, that Em's rock!" the child protested, reaching for it.

"Yes, and you can have it back after lunch, but for now you are clean and I would like you to stay that way while we eat."

"Yes, Mama."

Rebecca lifted the child from the sink and turned to Charlie, whose hands were also filthy. "You too, General Redmond. Time to clean up for lunch."

"Yes, Mama." He grinned, moving to the sink, where he got snapped on the good side of his bottom with a towel.

Em had been taken away for her nap right after lunch. Charlie and Rebecca were enjoying coffee in the dining room when Reg showed Richard and Elizabeth in. Richard looked exhausted and Elizabeth had an arm full of cloth swatches. Charlie rolled his eyes and wondered how quickly he could find an excuse for the men to vacate the room.

They joined Charlie and Rebecca at the table, and immediately the ladies began talking fabric choices for Elizabeth's wedding dress. Richard poured a cup of coffee and then pulled something from his pocket and laid it on the table near Charlie. "Young Jeremiah asked me to give this to you. Seems the boy has found a natural talent for working with leather, and he said he heard you and Duncan talking about your desire to have one."

Charlie picked up what turned out to be a glove crafted from soft black leather. It was made for his right hand, to help cover the scars. He looked at it and smiled before slipping it on. "It is a perfect fit. How did he do it?"

"He used a pair of your cavalry gloves as a pattern, and with a little guidance from Elizabeth about your injury, he fashioned it."

"That was very nice of him. I will have to thank him for that and offer him the position of chief glove maker."

Richard looked over to Elizabeth and Rebecca, who were in serious wedding mode. "I just keep telling myself it will be over in two weeks."

"It is the best thing you will ever do." Charlie smiled. "Next to becoming a father."

Richard smiled. "You know, I never thought about me being a father, but watching you with little Em and now with the two babies, I think I just might enjoy it. I even enjoyed taking care of Em while you two were in Washington."

"So, have you two decided if we are to do the military routine for the wedding?"

"Yes, particularly since she has some retired general coming down to give her away. It is a shame her parents moved back to England. I think they would love to see their daughter wed."

"They would. However, I believe the general who has consented to give her away is an old friend of her father's." Charlie sighed. "I will have to figure out how to make my dress uniform look at least presentable on this new body of mine." He sipped his coffee and then said slyly, "You know, Elizabeth told me her family never expected her to marry once she went to medical school. They told her that no man in his right mind would want to marry a woman with a career."

Richard laughed. "And who said I was in my right mind? I served as your executive officer for how many years?"

Charlie raised an eyebrow. "And that was a symptom of your basic insanity? I would say your willingness to participate in all of this wedding planning is far more indicative of your mental health, or lack of it."

Both men looked over at the ladies, who were discussing the difference between three different lace swatches. For the life of them, neither Charlie nor Richard could see any difference at all between them.

"Shall we go out on the porch for a smoke and escape this hotbed of feminine plotting and planning?"

"Certainly. I always like getting my hands on your cigars. Where does your tobacconist get them from, Charlie?"

"A tobacconist in Washington brings them in from Cuba for me. All you have to do is be willing to pay the price for them—and know who to ask."

The two men adjourned to the back porch, enjoying the soft breeze from the mountains in the early summer heat.

For a few minutes, the men just smoked quietly, each enjoying the mild weather. Then Charlie asked, "So, are you going to run for office when you retire?"

"I have been thinking seriously about it. It would mean I would have to spend some time in Richmond, but I know you and Rebecca will make sure Elizabeth does not fade away for lack of company."

"We will certainly look after her when you are gone—as much as she will let us. How goes the house?"

"It will be finished before the wedding, or so I am told. I do hope so; it will be nice to carry my lady across the threshold. Though I doubt she will allow me to do as dramatic a version of it as you did, my friend. My Elizabeth is far more pragmatic than romantic, I fear."

"Well, it will not be the same anyway, since your wedding feast is here, not at your new house."

"She got a telegram from Phil Sheridan the other day, saying he was coming down for the wedding and bringing something for her with him. Do you know anything about it?"

Charlie grinned. "I have an idea, but I think I would rather let General Sheridan confirm it rather than raise any expectations."

"Speaking of expectations, how goes the bank idea?"

"Cooke and I have been corresponding. Since I have at least a reasonable percentage of capital to invest personally, I am cautiously optimistic that we will have a bank here before the end of the year."

At that moment, Rebecca's head emerged through the rear doors. "Charlie, Richard, could you come in and look at this for a moment. Elizabeth and I cannot decide between the eggshell or the off-white linen."

Both men groaned and dutifully entered the parlor to look at two pieces of linen that looked to be virtually identical.

Friday, June 16, 1865

Sheridan's train arrived on time, a novel experience given the continued disruption as Virginia attempted to transition from wartime to peacetime business. Richard met him and escorted him to the waiting carriage.

"So, Polk, ready to commit yourself?"

"Yes, Sir. I told you I wanted to marry her and I have kept my part of the bargain."

"So you did, Sir, so you did. I must confess, as witness to the event, it was the oddest proposal I have ever seen a man make. But I am honored to be here."

They rode in silence for a while, Sheridan happily chewing on his cigar and enjoying the fact that the land once again looked tended. Charlie's influence was bringing Culpeper back from the devastation of the war more quickly than he had expected.

"Oh, by the way, Polk, is Dr. Walker at the house? I have a little something for her she may enjoy receiving—totally separate from the wedding, of course."

"Yes, Sir. I believe you will see her at supper."

"Good, good. And is there a gentlemen's event this evening?"

"Well, nothing like what we did for Redmond, but yes, I believe some of the local men have plans for us tonight. Redmond's batman, Jackson, has opened an inn on the south side of town. I believe we are expected to join them this evening."

"Well, good. I can use a glass or two of Jocko's rum punch."

Supper that night was quietly celebratory. The plans for tomorrow's wedding were all laid; guests had arrived and been appropriately housed, Sarah was looking pleased with the plans for the meal, and all seemed to be in order.

As supper was ending, Sheridan looked at Elizabeth, his old friend, and grinned. "It will be very strange to call you Doctor Polk after so long, my dear."

"Well, you do not have to. I am planning to retain my own name, thank you."

Sheridan's eyebrows rose at that announcement. It was unheard of. But then, many of the things Elizabeth Walker did were unheard of. "So, Polk, how do you feel about this... break from tradition?"

"I expected it, actually. Elizabeth is now and always has been one of the most stubborn women I know. Fortunately, I like stubborn women."

A laugh went around the table, with Polk blushing and Elizabeth looking mildly offended.

Charlie cleared his throat and, looking around the table, announced, "Well, ladies and gentlemen, it appears we are finished with dinner. I believe, gentlemen, it is time for us to leave the fairer sex to their evening."

"One moment, Redmond." Sheridan stood at his place at the table. "I have a small item for Dr. Walker." He reached into his breast pocket and withdrew an official looking document and a slim, elegant box. He unfolded the paper and read.

Award of the Medal of Honor for Meritorious Service.

Whereas it appears from official reports that Dr. Elizabeth Walker, a doctor of medicine, has rendered valuable service to the Government, and her efforts have been earnest and beneficial in a variety of ways, and that she was assigned to duty and served as an assistant surgeon attached to the 49th Ohio Cavalry and then as surgeon to the 13th Pennsylvania Cavalry, upon the recommendation of Major Generals Sheridan and Sherman, and faithfully served as contract surgeon in the service of the United States, and has devoted herself with much patriotic zeal to the sick and wounded soldiers, both in the field and hospitals, to the detriment of her own health; and

Whereas by reason of her not being a commissioned officer in the military service, a brevet or honorary rank cannot, under existing laws, be conferred upon her; and

Whereas in the opinion of the President an honorable recognition of her services and sufferings should be made:

It is ordered, that a testimonial thereof shall be hereby made and given to the said Dr. Elizabeth Walker, and that the Medal of Honor for Meritorious Services be given her.

Given under my hand in the city of Washington, D.C., this eleventh day of June, A.D. 1865.

Andrew Johnson

President, United States of America

Sheridan folded the document, and opened the case. In it was the medal, struck of solid gold, and suspended from gold pin with a fine blue satin ribbon. "May I, Doctor Walker?"

Elizabeth was torn between blushing and beaming. "By all means, General Sheridan." She stood as he pinned the medal to her dress and then he softly kissed her on the cheek. She sat and stroked the medal, looking rather stunned.

Charlie stood. "To my friend, my physician, and my savior, for without her, I would not be here today to make this toast and see her wed on the morrow. Many more men than I can count also owe her their lives. I give you Doctor Elizabeth Walker."

The rest of the people at the table stood and joined Charlie. "Dr. Walker!"

The gentlemen had gone off to their own celebration and the ladies adjourned to the rear parlor for their own festivities where they were joined by Mrs. Carter, Mrs. Cooper, and Mrs. White. The men would be more in number, but Rebecca was sure the ladies would have just as good a time.

Sarah had laid out a very nice table of refreshments. Rebecca was peering into the bowl of punch, which had been set in the center of the table. Elizabeth joined her, looking in after her to see what was so fascinating. "What are you doing?"

"I think it is missing something."

Elizabeth ladled up a small cup and tasted it. "No, I think it is lovely, very fruity and refreshing."

"Trust me," Rebecca grinned and moved to a cabinet where she retrieved a bottle of Charlie's best rum. "It is missing something."

Elizabeth's eyebrows rose. "I take it you want me to go to my own wedding with a hangover?"

"Well, my dear, you can drink slowly. However, if you should be in need, Sarah has a remedy that will take care of you." And with that, she poured the bottle into the punch. "I simply do not see why the men should have all the fun."

Elizabeth looked at her friend with wide eyes. She knew what

Sarah used as a remedy for the hangover. It worked, but just trying to get it down one's throat was, in her opinion, probably worse than the hangover itself. "Oh, well, what the devil. Let us emulate our masculine partners on this one night. And Rebecca Redmond - if I am miserable tomorrow and need Sarah's cure, you have to drink one with me."

Rebecca ladled out two cups and handed one to the doctor. "It is best enjoyed with a friend." She took a healthy drink of hers and coughed just a bit. "Very smooth," she choked, hoping her eyes would not tear up.

Elizabeth, having been involved in drinking contests with the gentlemen when out in the field, had the good sense to sip hers. "I think I will wait until the rest of our guests arrive before I indulge to the point of senselessness."

A moment later the parlor doors opened and the rest of the ladies entered, escorted by Reg, who was trying desperately to be polite but make a quick retreat from this den of ladies. Ladies of any color in a bunch made Reg nervous.

Rebecca was kind enough to warn the ladies of the punch and told them she would be happy to provide other resources if they desired. She was not surprised when her offer was declined, and each lady pulled a cup from the bowl.

Mrs. Cooper lifted her cup to her friends. "It is a party. Let us celebrate."

Charlie quietly closed the door and headed up the stairs, using his left hand on the banister to steady himself. He was by no means completely drunk, but he was nicely tight and, for the first time in a very long time, the pain in his body was all but forgotten.

He took the steps slowly, carefully, then at the top he walked down the hall to their bedroom. He noticed the light was on and filtering under the door. Quietly he pushed the door open and immediately noticed something was not quite right. Just inside the door, at his feet, was the top of Rebecca's dress. A foot or so past that was her skirt. He grinned like an idiot and began following the trail of clothing, which consisted of the layers required to make his wife's dress look so full. A trail of discarded fabric could only mean one thing.

He stopped when he finally saw her, sitting up on the settee near the fireplace. She was naked from the waist up, clad only in her pantalets. She had one shoe on and one bare foot, the other shoe and stocking had somehow managed to find their way to the center of the bed.

Quietly, he divested himself of his coat, tie, vest, and boots. Clad only in his shirt, breeches, and socks, he padded over to the settee and stroked Rebecca's hair. "Rebecca, dear," he whispered.

"Hmm..." She opened rather bleary eyes, and then she smiled. "Charlie, you are home."

"Good evening, darling. Um. Did you...wear yourself out this evening?"

"Huh? Oh no, the ladies and I had a delig...deligh...a good time."

The unmistakable aroma of rum hit Charlie straight in the face. Since he had been drinking brandy that night, the difference in aromas was unmistakable. "Um, Rebecca, darling, have you been indulging in the rum?"

"Not just me." She giggled. "I think Mr. Cooper is in for quite the surprise tonight." She began giggling harder to the extent that she fell over on the couch, continuing to laugh.

He suddenly had a vivid image spring into his head, of five very outspoken women sitting around the parlor, with every inhibition they owned erased by the power of his Demerarra rum. It was a frightening image. "Darling, you need to get to bed. Let me help you finish undressing."

"Ooo, Charlie, are you going to undress me and take me to bed?" She opened one eye and graced him with an almost predatory look.

He knew that look. He had first seen it on the last night they had spent at the Willard. He checked in with his body and decided that yes, perhaps he was finally ready for the...exertion that satisfying that look required. In a low, slightly husky voice, he responded. "That, my dear, is exactly what I am going to do."

"Oh good." She sat up and pulled Charlie to her. "I love you, I have missed making love with you." She gave him a kiss he would have felt to his boots had he still been wearing them. As it was, his toes were very warm.

~

Saturday, June 17, 1865

The ladies spent the night at Redmond Stables. The plan was to prepare as much as possible, then withdraw to Mrs. Cooper's for final touches. However, the effects of the previous evening were having a definite impact on the speed with which the ladies started their day.

Elizabeth staggered down to the kitchen, looking for Sarah and her magical hangover cure. The cook had taken time from her labors out in the summer kitchen to come in to the main house to prepare breakfast for the family. "Lord a mercy, Miss Elizabeth. What happened to you?"

Rebecca appeared at that moment, using the doorjamb to support her rather shaky frame.

Elizabeth very slowly turned her head to the blonde. "She happened to me."

Rebecca shaded her eyes against the morning glare as Charlie breezed in from the mudroom and opened the shades. "Good morning, ladies. It is a beautiful day. In fact, I would say a perfect day for a wedding." He smiled benignly, knowing full well that Rebecca had a head that could define the term "morning after." He suspected Elizabeth and the other ladies were in no better shape. "Sarah, I think a pair of poached eggs on toast would be just the thing today—light enough to save plenty of room for your lovely dinner, but enough to stick to your ribs and stay with you. Why, let us make your morning simple. The same thing for Miss Elizabeth and Miss Rebecca."

Rebecca groaned and let her head drop to the table. "You are an evil man, Charles Huger Redmond."

"But, darling, last night you told me how wonderful you thought I was."

She raised her head and gave him an insincere smile. "Anything said in the heat of passion cannot be held against me."

Charlie leered. "My dear, I would happily hold anything against you that you wish." He took pity on the two sad figures in front of him. "But for right now, Sarah, I think you need to mix up a major batch of your hangover cure. These two definitely need some, and I suspect there are three more candidates for your remedy. Oh, and while you are at it, please bottle up a dose. Colonel Polk is not at his best this morning either."

"Did you get my groom drunk, Charlie?" Elizabeth managed to ask from between her hands, which were currently holding up her head.

"No more than my wife got you drunk, Elizabeth. And to be absolutely precise, I believe it was the drinking contest between your husband-to-be and Jocko that was the final straw for our rather bilious friend."

"Oh, he should know better than that." She grinned, somehow happy in the knowledge Richard was no better off than she was.

Sarah set two glasses filled with a thick black fluid in front of the two sufferers. "Drink up, ladies. It will cure what ails you."

Rebecca paled a little when the odor hit her nose. She looked to Charlie, "Darling, would it be easier just to kill me?"

"I had to drink that stuff before I married you, dear. Turnabout is fair play."

Rebecca nodded and picked up the cup. Closing her eyes she said a quick prayer, then downed it. Making a face reminiscent of Em when she had to take medicine, she slammed the glass down. "Oh, please do not ever let me do that again."

"Shall I lock up the rum, dear?"

The day remained clear, and by three in the afternoon, the ladies were all prepared for the great event. Elizabeth was lovely in ecru silk and ivory lace. Rebecca's lavender and dove gray was sedate and understated. They were ready. Earlier that day, the gentleman who would give Elizabeth away had joined them. He was an old friend of Elizabeth's father, and Charlie's, as well as having been an advocate for Elizabeth when she first entered service with the Army before the war began. Knowing that he would be recognized, with his close clipped beard, gray hair, and sad eyes, General Robert E. Lee donned his Confederate dress uniform for perhaps the last time. They were ready.

Charlie managed to get Richard put back together, and both men had put on their dress uniforms in good form. Charlie had discarded his crutch a week before and was almost dapper with his new Malacca cane as the two men took their place before the altar. Reverend Williams signaled for the processional to start, and everyone in the church turned to await the arrival of the bride. Mrs. Williams played the first chords, and Elizabeth and her party stepped into the doorway.

Then suddenly the music stopped as the organist fainted dead away. Seeing her reaction, the entire crowd turned to see what had caused Mrs. Williams to stop playing. A few rushed to her side, fanning her and looking hastily in their reticules for some smelling salts. The rest of the congregation looked more closely at Elizabeth and the man who was her escort. Without a word, the assembled crowd stood in respect for the General. Mrs. Cooper smacked the now revived Mrs. Williams on the shoulder, and the music began again.

Elizabeth walked in stately grace up the aisle to the eagerly waiting Richard. She took her place beside him, and her escort glanced over at Charlie. "Redmond." He nodded a graceful greeting.

"General Lee, Sir." Charlie smiled, and both men, along with the rest of the congregation turned to witness the marriage.

The guests assembled in the hall and reception room at the house. A gentle buzz went around the room as they waited for the wedding party to arrive. Finally, Charlie's largest carriage appeared. The best man and matron of honor dismounted first, followed by General Lee, representing Elizabeth's family, and then the groom and his lovely bride. The five of them entered the house amid much laughter and applause. Richard and Elizabeth were occupied for quite a while, greeting all of their guests; Charlie took the opportunity to retreat to a quiet corner, a comfortable chair, and a nearly private chat among the attending generals.

Lee looked Charlie up and down. "Glad to see you are up and about, Charlie. I doubt you remember the last time you saw me. I came to see how you were doing when I heard you were wounded at Appomattox Station. Elizabeth let me in, but would not let me try to wake you."

Rebecca took the time to go and check on the children. The boys were sleeping, having just been fed and bathed, but Emily was sitting in her own little chair in her Sunday best waiting patiently for her Mama. "Em go pawty?"

"Certainly, my darling girl. Come along, we can show Aunt Elizabeth what she can anticipate."

Mother and child slipped back downstairs, where Em immediately located her father. "Papa!" was a well enough known cry to clear a path for the very active child to make a beeline for her father. Charlie caught her and lifted her up in his arms. "General Lee, may I present my daughter, Emily."

Lee smiled and offered his hand. "Miss Emily, how are you today?"

"Vewy well, tank you. How you?"

Charlie beamed. His little girl was becoming quite the little lady of the house. His smile faded a bit when he saw Mrs. Williams standing not too far off, obviously waiting for an introduction. Charlie sighed.

"General, may I please introduce one of the leading ladies of the community, Mrs. Williams?"

The General turned to the lady Charlie indicated. General Sheridan nodded to the woman coldly as Lee looked at his old students with a twinkle in his eye. "Ah, yes, the wife of the minister, I believe. Madam, perhaps you need to get your organ repaired. Sheridan, do we know anyone who repairs organs? I would be happy to send someone to you." Lee turned back to Charlie and Emily. "Redmond, she is a lovely child. Somehow I always knew you would settle down."

"Thank you. She is the apple of her Papa's eye," Charlie said with the pride that only a father could have.

"A fine child. I am glad to see her Papa survived to see her grow into womanhood." The older man paused, and then went on, addressing both Charlie and Sheridan. "I understand we faced one another head on in those last few days. I commend you both. It was an excellent tactic."

Charlie could only nod politely. "I am just grateful it is over, and I pray my sons never have to face the same challenges. I hope we have learned from our mistakes."

The party progressed with few social gaffes and much joy. General Lee excused himself early. He had a train to catch to take him on to Lynchburg and the position that waited for him at Washington College. It was also a very good excuse to escape from Mrs. Williams, who had shadowed the man for most of the evening, proving she could be as obsequious with her social superiors as she was contentious with those she thought beneath her.

The last toast was drunk, the last dance ended, and more food consumed than was probably good for folks. Elizabeth and Richard departed in a lovely little basket trap amid flying flowers and rice, laughter ringing though the air. Very shortly after the bride and groom left, the last of the guests followed them down the road.

Rebecca stood there watching everyone leave with her arm wrapped securely around Charlie's waist. She looked up and smiled. "A lovely beginning, do you not think so, love?"

He looked down at the blonde head resting on his shoulder and smiled. Standing together in the silence of the evening, he could almost hear her heart speaking to his. "Yes, my dear, a lovely beginning."

The End
(Story continues in the novel "Paths of Peace")

Thank you for taking the time to read **Words Heard in Silence**. If you enjoyed it, please consider telling your friends or posting a short review. Word of mouth is an author's best friend and much appreciated.

Thank you,
T. Novan & Taylor Rickard

OTHER FICTION BY T. NOVAN & TAYLOR RICKARD

Redmond Civil War Romance Series

- Words Heard in Silence
- Paths of Peace
- Enemies In The Gates
- Honor They Father

Other Fiction by T. Novan

- Madam President (with Advocate)
- First Lady (with Advocate)
- The Claiming of Ford

ABOUT AUSXIP PUBLISHING

www.ausxippublishing.com

AUSXIP Publishing publishes quality fiction and non-fiction with strong female characters that inspire, strengthen and enrich the soul. Stories that build up, create a sense of achievement and most importantly to entertain.

AUSXIP Publishing Newsletter
https://newsletter.ausxippublishing.com

AUSXIP Publishing Store:
https://store.ausxippublishing.com

Facebook:
https://facebook.com/ausxippublishing

Twitter:
https://twitter.com/ausxippublish